WORDSWORTH
OF WORLD LITE

General Editor: Tom Griffith

THE LIFE AND VOYAGES OF
CHRISTOPHER COLUMBUS

THE LIFE AND VOYAGES OF

CHRISTOPHER COLUMBUS

Washington Irving

❖

with an introduction
by Hugh Griffith

WORDSWORTH CLASSICS
OF WORLD LITERATURE

In loving memory of
MICHAEL TRAYLER
the founder of Wordsworth Editions

I

Customers interested in other titles from
Wordsworth Editions can visit our website at
www.wordsworth-editions.com

For our latest list and a full mail order service contact
Bibliophile Books, 5 Thomas Road, London E14 7BN
Tel: +44 0207 515 9222
Fax: +44 0207 538 4115
e-mail: orders@bibliophilebooks.com

This edition published 2008 by Wordsworth Editions Limited
8B East Street, Ware, Hertfordshire SG12 9HJ

ISBN 978 1 84022 069 8

Typeset in Great Britain by Roperford Editorial
Printed and bound by Clays Ltd, St Ives plc

CONTENTS

ILLUSTRATIONS

INTRODUCTION

The name of Columbus is so well-known that we can easily forget it was a literary invention, for the use of scholars and educated officials. To Italians he is Cristoforo Colombo, just as he was when he grew up in his home city of Genoa. The Spanish, who first mocked his pretensions, then employed and finally revered him, knew him as Cristóbal Colón. But it is the Latin form of his name that has stuck most firmly, at least in the Anglo-Saxon world. Columbus discovered America. That much we know, or think we know.

But what does this mean? To those of us who live in northern latitudes, 'America' inevitably calls up a picture of the vast expanses now filled by Canada and the United States. Yet Columbus never so much as caught sight of the northern continent. He first sighted land in the Bahamas, but turned south from there and made his base on the island he named La Española ('Little Spain'), now divided between Haiti and the Dominican Republic. A year later he spent much time sailing along the coast of Cuba, thinking it must be part of the mainland of Asia. On his fourth and final voyage he touched the coast of Honduras in Central America and from there sailed south and east along the coast as far as Panama. Yet even then he was still looking for the strait that he believed would take him through to India.

It would generally be agreed that to discover something means recognising what it is, at least to some extent, and giving some kind of account of it. Picking up a piece of rock that contains iron ore is not discovering iron, if you have no idea that the iron is in there. We know Columbus reached Central America, having sailed further west than any European had done before him. But if he believed it was an island, that hardly amounts to discovering America. The discoverer of a new land needs not only to be in a place for the first time, he should also be able to give it a context and relate it to what is already known. It is for this reason alone that it makes sense to say of a European that he 'discovered' America even though there were people living there at the time. They were there first, it is true, but they lacked any knowledge of other lands and seas on the globe. It therefore remained for others to locate the places in which they lived and fit them into a geographical picture.

The achievement of Columbus

On his third voyage, which took place in 1498, Columbus sailed much further south than he had previously done. The reason was gold. An opinion commonly held at the time was that the same products were to be found at the same latitude on the earth's surface. Since the Portuguese had recently found gold in west Africa, there ought to be gold in the New World on the same latitude; and this would mean going southwards as far as 10° N, much closer to the equator than Cuba and La Española (Hispaniola, as we northerners call it). So having dispatched three vessels by the more regular route to Hispaniola, with supplies for the new colony there, Columbus took three more ships down as far as the Cape Verde Islands and began the crossing from there. Sailing west, they were becalmed in the doldrums and languished there for more than a week, stifled by the heat and sickened by the smell of the food rotting down below.

On 31 July Columbus saw an island with three hills and named it Trinidad, in honour of the Holy Trinity. This became his temporary base for exploring the region. In the Gulf of Paria, which separates Trinidad from the mainland (now Venezuela), he was astonished by the force of the currents. Even more astonishing was the underlying explanation for it. The currents, he discovered, were caused by a huge volume of fresh water flowing into the Gulf. A flow of those proportions could only come from a great river – the kind of river that no island could produce. His reasoning was entirely correct: he was close to one of the outlets of the Orinoco, which begins in the northern range of the Andes. Thus he wrote in his journal for 13 August, 'I believe that this is a very large continent which until now has remained unknown.'

On reaching Hispaniola he sent a letter to his patrons Ferdinand and Isabella, the 'Catholic monarchs' of Aragón and Castile, in which he amplified this claim. He reported finding 'an enormous land, to be found in the south, of which until the present time nothing has been known'.

It was soon settled beyond any doubt that there was a continent where Columbus had said, and that it was new in the context of European exploration. But there have always been plenty of people prepared to dispute that Columbus should have the credit for discovering it. If names count for anything, it is they who have won the day. We may talk of the 'pre-Columbian' civilisations of the Aztecs, Maya and Incas, but for all other purposes we use the title of America, keeping alive the name of the Florentine explorer Amerigo Vespucci.

Vespucci first saw the mainland of South America in 1499, a year after Columbus, when another Spanish expedition was sent out to explore this southern continent more extensively. Vespucci, a pilot on that voyage, wrote a report of it – giving as his date the previous year, to make it appear that he had been there before Columbus. He describes a long passage north-westwards along the coast of what is now Brazil. After transferring his services to the king of Portugal, Vespucci then made a further voyage in 1501–02, during which (if his report is true) he sailed down most of the coast of South America. (On the strength of a letter supposed to be from Vespucci and published in 1504, it was believed for over 400 years that he had made two other voyages, making four in all; during the first of these, in the year 1497, he had 'discovered' the coasts of Honduras, Mexico and Florida. The letter was exposed in 1926 as a forgery.)

Vespucci may not have sailed as far south as he would have us believe. But there can be no doubt that he was in a much stronger position than Columbus when it came to making statements about the extent of the new continent. It may be right to grant priority to Columbus – if we can accept that he correctly identified what he had found. But it was Vespucci who did more than anyone to make the discovery known and to demonstrate the existence of a New World to the inhabitants of the Old.

A way to Asia

There were at least two sorts of people fascinated by cosmology and geography in the second half of the 15th century. Those of a bookish and mathematical bent wanted to create a model of the world that would be comprehensible and consistent with the known facts. This model might or might not agree with the theories and hints derived from the ancient Greeks, whose ideas were granted the utmost respect. Second, there were practical seafarers and their masters. Their interest in the truth was no less strong, but its aims were slightly different. What drove them was a desire to make new paths over the sea. Whatever the east could supply had until now made its way, both by land and up the Persian Gulf, to the eastern shores of the Mediterranean. But Arabs and Venetians controlled the trading posts, forcing the price of all goods higher with tolls and taxes. For the final consumer of spices, dyes and silk, the cost was prohibitive. The countries of Europe, especially those to the west and the north, would be well served if a way could be found to bypass the shearing shed of the Levant and trade directly with Asia.

Genoese sailors in the 14th century had braved the terrors of the Atlantic, reaching as far south as the Canaries and the west coast of Africa. These first little colonies were soon dislodged by the Portuguese. Columbus himself, who had married a Portuguese wife and settled in Lisbon, travelled to those regions on various occasions in the 1470s and 1480s. But still no one knew how far Africa projected southwards, or whether it was possible to sail round the bottom of it and reach Asia that way. The answer became clear as soon as Vasco da Gama returned from his momentous voyage in 1499: access to India and all the east was indeed possible.

Not that this was known to Columbus, or anyone else, in 1484 when he first applied to the king of Portugal to mount an expedition going west into the Atlantic. Whether Asia could be reached by sailing in that direction, as Columbus believed, was the cosmological question of all cosmological questions. The fact that the earth was a sphere had been known since the time of Ptolemy in the 2nd century AD; and his *Geography* had included the information that the known world consisted of one land mass stretching continuously from the western end of Europe to the eastern end of Asia. An ocean, it was said, lay between them. A ship sailing west from Portugal or Spain ought therefore, if it went on sailing for long enough, to find Asia. But this was speculation. No one knew anything about that ocean. Besides, if the world was as large as had been calculated – and the ancient calculations of the earth's circumference at the equator were remarkably accurate – then the ocean lying between Asia and Europe must take up nearly half of the surface of the globe. No ship could possibly sail such a distance without putting in for supplies.

Columbus disagreed. To him it seemed that such a journey must be possible. He sustained himself with two arguments. One was that the usual estimate of the size of the globe was wrong. The world was smaller than everyone thought and therefore the distance across the ocean would be shorter. The second was that Marco Polo's account of his travels, dating from the 13th century, suggested that Asia extended further to the east than appeared from Ptolemy's reckoning. Furthermore, Polo had reported that the island of Cipangu stood a full 1500 miles out to sea, eastwards from China, and there were more than a thousand other islands off the coast of Asia. On the location of Cipangu (Japan) Polo was wildly misleading, and as for the dimensions of the globe Columbus was wrong and everyone else was right. He therefore had no sound reasons for thinking, when he found islands in the Caribbean Sea, that they must be close to the coast of Asia. But if his theoretical knowledge was shaky, so was that of his opponents.

A new world

Various beliefs in the existence of other lands or another continent had been wafting around in the intellectual air for a very long time. When Ptolemy wrote that there was one continuous land mass containing both Europe and Asia, he meant only the known world. He also said that there were unknown lands to the south. Christian doctrine was hostile to this idea, on the grounds that the apostles must have preached Christ's word to the entire world. If there was any unknown land it would have to be uninhabited. But that did not stop people wondering. Some cartographers, even without knowing its shape or anything else about it, included a southern continent on their maps.

Possible locations for such a land were discussed by Pierre d'Ailly in his *Imago Mundi*, a book that Columbus owned and knew almost by heart – though his interest was primarily in d'Ailly's theory that the distance across the ocean to Asia might be quite short. Ancient myths could also be thrown into the melting-pot, telling of islands far out in the Atlantic. According to Greek tradition, the Hesperides ('nymphs of evening') lived on an island far out west beyond the ocean. Plato recounted a story of the lost island of Atlantis, swallowed up in an earthquake thousand of years before his time. If these were fantasy, perhaps there was some truth in one of the others: the Isle of Brasil, the lost island of Antilia, or the land of the Amazons.

Perhaps the most extraordinary thing is the speed with which a fog of guesswork was transformed into a clear picture of what had been discovered and the space it occupied on the map. When Columbus returned from his first voyage in 1493, there were some who accepted his claim that he had wintered on an island in Asiatic waters and had even sailed along the coast of China. Most scholars, however, remained sceptical. They were not prepared to believe that the world really was so much smaller than their calculations told them. One of these was Peter Martyr (Pietro Martire di Anghiera), an Italian humanist at the court of Fernando and Isabel, who concluded straight away that Columbus had discovered lands that were previously unknown. He employed the description 'antipodes' – the standard term then in use for any hypothetical land on the opposite side of the world from the land mass of Europe and Asia. He also called these discoveries a 'new world'.

In 1493 this was still a matter for scholarly debate. Yet within 10 years Columbus had found a continental river in Venezuela and Vespucci had sailed down the coast of Brazil. Not only that, but the Portuguese had also discovered Brazil by mistake with their second expedition to India. Experimenting with a dog-leg approach to rounding Africa in order to avoid the problem of contrary winds, Pedro Alvares Cabral took his ships far out into the Atlantic using the trade winds and stayed on this south-westerly course until they hit South America. In 1507, only a year after the death of Columbus, Martin Waldseemüller wrote an introduction to a new edition of Ptolemy's *Geography*. This was accompanied by a map, which included the new islands in the Caribbean and a very creditable attempt at representing South America. Central America and even part of the southeast coast of North America were depicted. To the west of these lay another great stretch of ocean separating the new discoveries from Asia.

It was Columbus who had made possible this revolution of understanding. Yet when it came he was unwilling to accept it. Even after finding the new continent, he was still determined to accommodate it within a scheme where the world was small and Asia was not so far away. It was the route to Asia that he had counted on to bring him glory, riches and titles to pass down to his descendants. He had not looked for an unknown and undeveloped continent, and he was not excited by the thought that he might have found one.

Columbus: in search of an assessment

As he waited, year after year, for royal advisers to consider his case and committees to meet and decide on it, Columbus must often have felt that his dream would come to nothing. A more balanced and pragmatic individual would have accepted early on that he stood no chance of overcoming the scepticism and inertia of the officials whose help was essential. Kings and queens, however interested in commerce and exploration, had competing claims on their attention. There was always the next war to be thinking about, the next pope or the next marriage. To keep pressing his case in the face of repeated rejection, Columbus had to be convinced that he was right. It was not enough to be courageous, eloquent and persistent – a strong dose of obstinacy was also required, to the point where a theory became an obsession.

Columbus grew up as the son of a weaver and never had a thorough formal education. He had a good command of Latin and other languages, read widely and wrote voluminously. But his learning was typical of the autodidact – selective, and often lacking in a proper appreciation of the due weight to be placed on different kinds of evidence. It could hardly have been otherwise. Highly respected scholars of impeccable judgement have no need to leave home to risk death on the ocean. Columbus, however, had a powerful incentive – desire for glory. Coming from quite lowly origins, he had ambitions of ennoblement for himself and his family. During all his negotiations with the Spanish monarchs, one demand was constant and non-negotiable: he was to be Admiral, Viceroy and Governor of all lands discovered. These titles were to be his for life and were to descend to his successors in perpetuity.

Perpetuity, of course, can turn out to be rather shorter than expected. Columbus was given his titles, and they did pass to his successors. But the trading privileges granted to him were quickly reduced or withdrawn, and after his death the extensive powers inherited by his son Diego on the island of Hispaniola were soon whittled down by the Spanish throne and eventually annulled. The insistence on visible honours and special grants was entirely understandable, even admirable. Columbus was risking his life, and any success in the enterprise would be solely due to his knowledge and skill. His ambition, however, inevitably aroused hostility. The powers he sought were exceptional, particularly when demanded by a foreigner. And Columbus had a tendency to distort the truth in a variety of ways. Often he was led to magnify his exploits in order to vindicate his original claims, even when these had been exaggerated.

That Columbus made enemies, therefore, is not surprising. To him, it seemed that all was delay, prevarication and frustration of his intentions. To many in the Spanish court, it seemed that he was an upstart whose pretensions were insufferable. That his first voyage should have ended in triumph gave them all the more reason to hope that disaster would follow. The sad tale of the colony on Hispaniola was a measure of the failure on all sides – Columbus insisting on his rights as governor even as chaos spread, his enemies forming schemes to multiply the grievances against him and bring him home in disgrace. Given the nature of the man the outcome was perhaps inevitable. Columbus had never trained himself in the arts of flattery or diplomacy. He was not adept at organising matters with a view to ensuring general satisfaction. In addition, he was not helped by the fact that many of the early colonists were dragooned and threatened to make them go: a good number were criminals who were offered Hispaniola as an alternative to prison.

It might be thought pre-emptive to make any assessment here of the character of Columbus. It is surely in Irving's biography of the man that his nature should be revealed, not in the introduction. Yet something needs to be added to the picture. When Irving wrote his book, the customary style for biography was more reverential than it is today. The life of a great man was something to be held up as a model not just of achievement but of behaviour. It was almost axiomatic that noble thoughts and deeds must spring from a mind that was entirely innocent of vainglory or dishonesty. The fashion was set by Southey's *Life of Nelson* and it lasted for the rest of the nineteenth century. Thus Irving's Columbus is not only a hero, the embodiment of courage and endurance, he is almost saintlike in his magnanimity in the face of unjust persecution. Without wishing to knock Columbus off a pedestal which he richly deserves, we may remind ourselves that a hero does not have to possess all the good qualities under the sun. A daring explorer and a navigator of genius may not be the perfect choice for the founder and governor of a new colony.

Irving had gone to Spain in 1826, invited (at his own prompting) to come under the umbrella of the U.S. Legation in Madrid. The project suggested to him by Alexander Hill Everett, the U.S. Minister, was to translate into English a newly published collection of material relating to the Spanish conquests. It consisted of original sources, almost all in manuscript, culled with painstaking scholarship over a period of 30 years from all over Spain, and Irving was quick to see that this put him in the perfect position to write a fully documented biography of Columbus. He was by then America's most famous writer, but increasingly prone to fits of anxiety about his own talent and how he should be using it. Before the biography was published, he confessed to feeling uneasy about its reception: 'How it will please the public I cannot anticipate. I have lost confidence in the favourable disposition of my countrymen and look forward to cold scrutiny and stern criticism, as this is a line of writing in which I have not hitherto ascertained my own powers.'

He need not have worried. When it appeared in 1828, *The Life and Voyages of Christopher Columbus* was an instant success. Irving was proposed for membership of Spain's Real Academia de la Historia by Martín Fernández de Navarrete, the eminent historian whose *Collección de viages y descubrimientos* had been Irving's starting point. We may find an excess of reverence in the assessment of its subject, but it can hardly be denied that Irving has performed his task with scrupulous care. The citation of sources is a model of historical method and Irving has resisted the temptation to wander from the facts and indulge in imaginings of his own. Both as a study of Columbus and a precise narrative of the first steps in Spanish colonisation, the book continues to command respect.

The life of Washington Irving

Diedrich Knickerbocker and Geoffrey Crayon, Rip Van Winkle and Ichabod Crane – these are names that still mean something to many Americans, but in other parts of the world where English is spoken and read they are most likely to be greeted with a puzzled frown. If there is a sense of vague familiarity, it is mixed with fear that someone might ask for precise details of who they are or where to find them. Once upon a time, the name of Washington Irving might have brought enlightenment. No longer. Literary fashions change, and a reputation that shone brilliantly in one century remained steadfastly dim all through the next. So what became of Washington Irving and who was he in the first place?

Irving was born in 1783, the youngest of eleven children. His father William was a Scottish Presbyterian who had emigrated to America and made a success of himself in New York as a hardware merchant and auctioneer. Two of the sons took a degree from Columbia College, but once he had left school Washington largely looked after his own education. He read widely but haphazardly and spent long hours exploring every hidden alley and remote corner of New York (a city whose population then numbered around 80,000). 'I knew every spot where a murder or robbery had been committed, or a ghost seen', he later wrote. Further afield, he explored the banks of the Hudson, talking to the inhabitants of the Dutch villages and noting their habits. There were some thoughts of studying law, and he even became an enthusiastic disciple of his last teacher, Josiah Ogden Hoffman. It was not the law, however, that was the real attraction. Far more appealing was the company of Hoffman's two young daughters and the pleasure to be had from joining in their family excursions.

During the summer of 1803 the Hoffmans took Irving with them on a trip by boat and oxcart into Canada. Irving kept the girls amused, played the flute, recited Shakespeare and filled notebooks with what he had seen. His eye was drawn to the comical or sentimental side of human affairs, and the more picturesque sights of the countryside.

He was, in fact, turning into a writer. The previous year he had already begun turning out articles in the form of letters addressed to the *Morning Chronicle*, a new magazine edited by his brother Peter. They poked good-natured fun at the style of manners, dress and marriage in New York, as well as the pestilential habits of actors, managers, theatregoers and critics. These juvenile essays, under the pseudonym of Jonathan Oldstyle, Gent., were the forerunners of Irving's contributions to a similar venture called *Salmagundi*, which ran for just a year from January 1807 to January 1808. This was a periodical produced by Irving and two other members of a literary club called the 'nine worthies'. Like the *Chronicle*, it was a mixture of whimsy and gentle satire. The title page carried the following declaration: 'In hoc est hoax, cum quiz et jokesez. Et smokem, toastem, roastem folksez, Fee, faw fum.' And the material it was printed on (or so they said) was 'hot-pressed vellum paper, as that is held in highest estimation for buckling up young ladies' hair'.

Two-hundred-year-old humour, especially of the more topical kind, easily wilts under stern scrutiny. But there is no denying the high spirits and sheer geniality of this stuff. Irving and his companions had a genuine gift for entertaining, at least in New York, 'where the people – heaven help them – are the most irregular, crazy-headed, quick-silver, eccentric, whim-whamsical set of mortals that were ever jumbled together'. It was all frivolous and irreverent, but utterly free of malice.

It was time for Irving to produce something on his own, and he did, though this was partly by accident. *A History of New York*, his first great success, started out as a joint venture with his brother Peter, but when his co-author was called away to manage the European arm of the family business Washington was left to write the whole thing himself. Even then his own name achieved little prominence at first, since the idea was to pretend that the author was a hare-brained eccentric by the name of Diedrich

Knickerbocker, who had disappeared leaving only the manuscript of the book behind him. It had the appearance of a guide to the early Dutch founders of New York; but much of it was invention, and the factual parts were presented with such an air of mock gravity that the effect was ludicrous. Wouter Van Twiller (a real historical figure) was described in the following terms:

> So invincible was his gravity that he was never known to laugh or even to smile through the whole course of a long and prosperous life. Nay, if a joke were uttered in his presence, that set light-minded hearers in a roar, it was observed to throw him into a state of perplexity.

As more details are filled in of Van Twiller's physical characteristics, the absurdity is allowed to grow more extravagant:

> He was exactly five feet six inches in height, and six feet five inches in circumference. His head was a perfect sphere, and of such stupendous dimensions, that dame Nature, with all her sex's ingenuity, would have been puzzled to construct a neck capable of supporting it; wherefore she wisely declined the attempt, and settled it firmly on the top of his backbone, just between the shoulders.

Not all Americans of Dutch descent were amused to have their ancestors made ridiculous, but the rest of the world was happy enough, including some big literary hitters on the other side of the Atlantic. Byron, Coleridge and Scott all recorded their keen enjoyment, and in later years Dickens wore out his copy with re-reading.

While still engaged in this carefree burlesque of a book, Irving was struck by tragedy. Matilda Hoffman, aged only 17 but already his intended bride, died in April 1809. Whether this was the reason, or whether he was bewildered at having suddenly become the first writer in his newly independent nation to be acknowledged in Europe as a real talent, Irving lost direction. For several years he drifted between one activity and another, until in 1815 he made a conscious effort to make a new start. He sailed to England and spent the next 17 years away from his home country. At first his writing was impelled more by a resolution to avoid being idle than any positive inspiration. Now in his mid-thirties, he feared that his mind had lost 'much of its cheerfulness and some of its activity'. But in 1819 he sent home a packet which was soon printed in New York as the first number of *The Sketch Book of Geoffrey Crayon, Gent*. This contained five sketches, of which the fifth was 'Rip Van Winkle'.

Six more numbers appeared at irregular intervals over the next year and a half, meeting with warm praise from readers both in America and England. Most of the sketches were on English themes; there was some storytelling, but most of the essays were of a moralising or reflective nature. They included titles such as 'The Country Church', 'Rural Funerals' and 'The Christmas Dinner'. Irving had borrowed mood and atmosphere from, among other sources, Goldsmith's *The Deserted Village*, Thomson's *The Seasons* and George Crabbe's dark-hued pictures of rustic life. However, for one story, 'The Legend of Sleepy Hollow', he returned to the banks of the Hudson River, whose first Dutch settlers had supplied him with the material for his first triumph. The little village of Sleepy Hollow became famous as the setting for a gothic horror – Ichabod Crane riding to his death pursued by the Headless Horseman – and its sleepiness was never the same again.

Irving was beginning to collect legends and tales from a variety of European countries. Headless horsemen were a staple feature of German stories, and now he broadened his reach to include Italian, Spanish and French sources. *Tales of a Traveller*, from 1824, was a mixture of some of these, but it was poorly received. Irving was dismissed as unoriginal and timorous. This was the start of another phase of depression when he believed his talent had dribbled away to nothing. The truth was that he had never been able to strike enough of a spark to kindle a real fire of his own; now, confronting this unwelcome truth, he began to wonder if he was really a biographer. And so, in 1826, he embarked on his Spanish adventure.

Two years of disciplined toil on Columbus did indeed produce a biography of acknowledged brilliance, but perhaps more important was the awakening of a desire to go further back into the past. In the picturesque setting of the Alhambra palace in Granada Irving recaptured his touch with an artful blend of chivalry and pathos. He began with *The Conquest of Granada*, 'something of an experiment', as he described it, using old histories 'embellished, as I am able, by the imagination, and adapted to the romantic taste of the day'. The result was halfway between a history and a romance.

This was followed by *The Alhambra*, a personal memoir of his stay in the crumbling and neglected Moorish palace. For relaxation, he loved to sit at his window, watching the movements in the town down below, listening to the sounds that drifted up from the distant houses of its inhabitants. Immersed in the delights of a picturesque present, he gave himself up to dreams of the past. The romantic spirit of Walter Scott became sensualised in the languorous heat of the south.

Columbus and the two books he wrote in Granada re-established Irving's position as America's most important writer. In 1832, the same year that *The Alhambra* was published, he returned to America for the first time in 17 years. Before leaving England he had accepted an honorary doctorate from Oxford. Back home, the city of New York received him as guest of honour at an official dinner of welcome. He turned down an offer of nomination to Congress, and later on the chance to stand as mayor of New York. New places, new ways of life could still stir him to action. He travelled out west to get a sense of life on the frontier and learn about the fur trade; those days under the open skies and nights by the campfire were recorded in *A Tour of the Prairies*. But sober respectability kept creeping up on him, to the point where in 1842 he was appointed U.S. minister to Madrid, an office he fulfilled with his usual suave affability for four years.

Biography made up the bulk of his last works. *Oliver Goldsmith*, published in 1849, was described by Irving as 'a tribute of gratitude to the memory of an author whose writings were the delight of my childhood, and have been a source of enjoyment to me throughout life'. There was a natural sympathy based on similarity of outlook and character. Irving praised Goldsmith for his 'whimsical, yet amiable views of human life and nature; the unforced humor, blending so happily with good feeling and good sense, and singularly dashed at times with a pleasing melancholy' – but he might just as well have been talking about himself.

With *Mahomet and His Successors* Irving paid the last instalment of the debt he felt he owed to the Islamic past. He had always possessed the gift of sifting his sources so as to extract only the most compelling or attractive elements. Sadly, this gift had deserted him when he came to his last project, a vast and laborious *Life of George Washington*. Irving was over 70 when the first volume came out in 1855, and there were four more massive and over-reverent volumes to come. The task was completed in 1859; in November of that year Washington Irving died and was buried in the cemetery of Sleepy Hollow.

Irving's later reputation

Irving's life and character present no great mysteries. He was genial, well-liked and open in his dealings. Other people interested him; he enjoyed meeting new faces and learning (or simply hazarding a guess) about the quirks and oddities of their owners. As for his writing, to judge from his own account its aims were admirable and uncomplicated:

> If I can by a lucky chance, in these days of evil, rub out one wrinkle from the brow of care, or beguile the heavy heart of one moment of sadness, if I can, now and then, penetrate the gathering film of misanthropy, prompt a benevolent view of human nature, and make my reader more in good humor with his fellow-beings and himself, surely, surely, I shall not then have written entirely in vain.

Admirable, perhaps, but is that enough? Might he not have aspired higher? Ought he not to have been scorched by some inner fire of rage or passion? Were his musings not too tentative, too sentimental, too careful to avoid giving any offence? Would his style not have been improved by a little more tartness, a little less charm?

Later generations certainly thought so. Irving's stock had started falling by the time the Civil War was over, and with each succeeding decade it sank lower. By the time Twain came along, Americans knew they preferred something rowdier, more rumbustious. Cussedness of temper now had the edge over politeness. The realism of the newer writers – Twain, Harte, Bierce, London – made Irving's manner look antiquated and artificial. Many of them had been out west. They had something new to tell about the rough-and-ready lives of the American frontier, and they told it with directness and vitality. This was like a gust of fresh air; in comparison, the old-style virtues of the eastern literary establishment seemed stuffy and genteel. There was a further advantage. The American west was beyond the reach of the great giants of European literature, and likely to remain so. In this territory

American writers were unassailably supreme. No longer need they feel that their best efforts looked scraggy and stunted up against the examples of the past; they could stop behaving like children anxious for the approval of their European parents.

This was bad enough for Irving, but worse was to come in the shape of the modernists. What hope of resurrection could there be for Irving once the grandest eminences of literature had agreed that profound truths can only emerge from darkness, horror, alienation and despair? What chance for the merely droll and whimsical when readers had been trained to expect shock, provocation and dissent? Irving's pictures were too full of light and sunshine; if there were faults in his characters they were generally harmless enough or (more likely) positively ridiculous. He had not the forensic coolness to dissect (or even detect) the self-deceiving distortion of motive, nor the temperament to be very interested. And he was much too polite to trawl through the waste-bins of human nature just to see what foul secrets might be hidden there.

If any more sticks were needed to beat Irving with, there were his politics – no great cause for shame, certainly, but hardly revolutionary enough to satisfy most twentieth-century critics. What had Irving ever written about the working man? How had his elegance and polish helped to advance the great cause of democratic equality that all literature with any claim to relevance must be striving to promote? All things considered, Irving was too comfortable a read. He shook no preconceptions, undermined no beliefs.

Today, perhaps we are in a better position to allow him a fighting chance. It is easier now to see that realism and modernism were themselves also products of their time, each one helping to define the period of its existence just as the cult of sensibility had helped to define the period when Irving was writing. Once it becomes a part of history, no literary movement has a prior claim on our attention simply for having superseded an earlier one. 'B comes after A' means something different from 'B is better than A'. And while the realists and the moderns felt hugely superior to Washington Irving because, of course, they knew so much better, it now seems plain that they knew rather less than they thought they did. It is easy enough to laugh at an earlier generation for being so silly; not so easy to avoid looking silly oneself when the wheel has turned a little more.

Washington Irving was not Mark Twain, of that we may be sure. Nor was he Herman Melville or Scott Fitzgerald or William Faulkner. But to accuse him of lacking their qualities is hardly intelligent criticism. In deciding whether Washington Irving still deserves a place on our shelf, only one question is worth considering, and this is the most obvious one. Are we interested in what he had to say? No further justification is needed.

HUGH GRIFFITH

SUGGESTIONS FOR FURTHER READING

Felipe Fernandez-Armesto, *Columbus* (Oxford University Press), Oxford 1991

Samuel Eliot Morison, *Admiral of the Ocean Sea: A Life of Christopher Columbus* (Little, Brown), Boston 1942

Samuel Eliot Morison, *The European Discovery of America: The Southern Voyages A.D. 1492–1616* (Oxford University Press), New York 1974

Hugh Thomas, *Rivers of Gold: The Rise of the Spanish Empire* (Weidenfeld & Nicolson), London 2003

Claude G. Bowers, *The Spanish Adventures of Washington Irving* (Houghton Mifflin), Boston 1940

William L. Hedges, *Washington Irving* (Johns Hopkins Press), Baltimore 1965

James W. Tuttleton (ed.) *Washington Irving: The Critical Reaction* (AMS Press), New York 1993

THE LIFE AND VOYAGES OF
CHRISTOPHER COLUMBUS

Portrait of Columbus

BOOK I

Whether in old times, beyond the reach of history or tradition, and in some remote period of civilization, when, as some imagine, the arts may have flourished to a degree unknown to those whom we term the ancients, there existed an intercourse between the opposite shores of the Atlantic; whether the Egyptian legend, narrated by Plato, respecting the island of Atalantis was indeed no fable, but the obscure tradition of some vast country, engulfed by one of those mighty convulsions of our globe which have left traces of the ocean on the summits of lofty mountains, must ever remain matters of vague and visionary speculation. As far as authenticated history extends, nothing was known of *terra firma*, and the islands of the western hemisphere, until their discovery towards the close of the fifteenth century. A wandering bark may occasionally have lost sight of the landmarks of the old continents, and been driven by tempests across the wilderness of waters long before the invention of the compass, but never returned to reveal the secrets of the ocean. And though, from time to time, some document has floated to the shores of the Old World, giving to its wondering inhabitants evidences of land far beyond their watery horizon, yet no one ventured to spread a sail and seek that land enveloped in mystery and peril. Or if the legends of the Scandinavian voyagers be correct, and their mysterious Vinland was the coast of Labrador, or the shore of Newfoundland, they had but transient glimpses of the New World, leading to no certain or permanent knowledge, and in a little time lost again to mankind. Certain it is that at the beginning of the fifteenth century, when the most intelligent minds were seeking in every direction for the scattered lights of geographical knowledge, a profound ignorance prevailed among the learned as to the western regions of the Atlantic; its vast waters were regarded with awe and wonder, seeming to bound the world as with a chaos, into which conjecture could not penetrate and enterprise feared to adventure. We need no greater proofs of this than the description given of the Atlantic by Xerif al Edrisi, surnamed the Nubian, an eminent Arabian writer, whose countrymen were the boldest navigators of the middle ages, and possessed all that was then known of geography.

'The ocean,' he observes, 'encircles the ultimate bounds of the inhabited earth, and all beyond it is unknown. No one has been able to verify anything concerning it, on account of its difficult and perilous navigation, its great obscurity, its profound depth, and frequent tempests, through fear of its mighty fishes and its haughty winds; yet there are many islands in it, some peopled, others uninhabited. There is no mariner who dares to enter into its deep waters; or if any have done so, they have merely kept along its coasts, fearful of departing from them. The waves of this ocean, although they roll as high as mountains, yet maintain themselves without breaking; for if they broke, it would be impossible for ship to plough them.' *

It is the object of the following work to relate the deeds and fortunes of the mariner who first had the judgment to divine, and the intrepidity to brave, the mysteries of this perilous deep; and who, by his hardy genius, his inflexible constancy, and his heroic courage, brought the ends of the earth into communication with each other. The narrative of his troubled life is the link which connects the history of the Old World with that of the New.

* *Description of Spain*, by Xerif al Edrisi: Conde's Spanish translation, Madrid, 1799.

CHAPTER I

Christopher Columbus, or Colombo, as the name is written in Italian,* was born in the city of Genoa, about the year 1435. He was the son of Dominico Colombo, a wool-comber, and Susannah Fontanarossa, his wife, and it would seem that his ancestors had followed the same handicraft for several generations in Genoa. Attempts have been made to prove him of illustrious descent, and several noble houses have laid claim to him since his name has become so renowned as to confer rather than receive distinction. It is possible some of them may be in the right, for the feuds in Italy in those ages had broken down and scattered many of the noblest families, and while some branches remained in the lordly heritage of castles and domains, others were confounded with the humblest population of the cities. The fact, however, is not material to his fame; and it is a higher proof of merit to be the object of contention among various noble families than to be able to substantiate the most illustrious lineage. His son Fernando had a true feeling on the subject. 'I am of opinion,' says he, 'that I should derive less dignity from any nobility of ancestry than from being the son of such a father.'

Columbus was the oldest of four children; having two brothers, Bartholomew and Giacomo, or James (written Diego in Spanish), and one sister, of whom nothing is known but that she was married to a person in obscure life called Giacomo Bavarello. At a very early age Columbus evinced a decided inclination for the sea; his education, therefore, was mainly directed to fit him for maritime life,

---

* Columbus Latinized his name in his letters, according to the usage of his time, when Latin was the language of learned correspondence. In subsequent life, when in Spain, he recurred to what was supposed to be the original Roman name of the family, Colonus, which he abbreviated to Colon, to adapt it to the Castilian tongue. Hence he is known in Spanish history as Christoval Colon. In the present work the name will be written Columbus, being the one by which he is most known throughout the world.

Genoa

but was as general as the narrow means of his father would permit. Besides the ordinary branches of reading, writing, grammar, and arithmetic, he was instructed in the Latin tongue, and made some proficiency in drawing and design. For a short time, also, he was sent to the University of Pavia, where he studied geometry, geography, astronomy, and navigation. He then returned to Genoa, where, according to a contemporary historian, he assisted his father in his trade of wool-combing.[*] This assertion is indignantly contradicted by his son Fernando, though there is nothing in it improbable, and he gives us no information of his father's occupation to supply its place. He could not, however, have remained long in this employment, as, according to his own account, he entered upon a nautical life when but fourteen years of age.[†]

In tracing the early history of a man like Columbus, whose actions have had a vast effect on human affairs, it is interesting to notice how much has been owing to external influences, how much to an inborn propensity of the genius. In the latter part of his life, when, impressed with the sublime events brought about through his agency, Columbus looked back upon his career with a solemn and superstitious feeling, he attributed his early and irresistible inclination for the sea, and his passion for geographical studies, to an impulse from the Deity preparing him for the high decrees he was chosen to accomplish.[‡]

The nautical propensity, however, evinced by Columbus in early life is common to boys of enterprising spirit and lively imagination brought up in maritime cities, to whom the sea is the highroad to adventure and the region of romance. Genoa, too, walled in and straitened on the land side by rugged mountains, yielded but little scope for enterprise on shore; while an opulent and widely extended commerce, visiting every country, and a roving marine battling in every sea, naturally led forth her children upon the waves as their propitious element. Many, too, were induced to emigrate by the violent factions which raged within the bosom of the city, and often dyed its streets with blood. A

---

[*] Agostino Giustiniani, *Ann. de Genova.* His assertion has been echoed by other historians – namely, Anton Gallo *de Navigationi Colombi*, etc., Muratori, tom. 23; Barta Senaraga *de Rebus Genuensibus*, Muratori, tom. 24.

[†] *Hist. del Almirante*, cap. 4.

[‡] *Letter to the Castilian sovereigns*, 1501.

historian of Genoa laments this proneness of its youth to wander. They go, said he, with the intention of returning when they shall have acquired the means of living comfortably and honourably in their native place; but we know, from long experience, that of twenty who thus depart scarce two return, either dying abroad or taking to themselves foreign wives, or being loath to expose themselves to the tempest of civil discords which distract the republic.*

The strong passion for geographical knowledge, also, felt by Columbus in early life, and which inspired his after career, was incident to the age in which he lived. Geographical discovery was the brilliant path of light which was for ever to distinguish the fifteenth century. During a long night of monkish bigotry and false learning, geography, with the other sciences, had been lost to the European nations. Fortunately it had not been lost to mankind; it had taken refuge in the bosom of Africa. While the pedantic schoolmen of the cloisters were wasting time and talent, and confounding erudition by idle reveries and sophistical dialectics, the Arabian sages, assembled at Senaar, were taking the measurement of a degree of latitude, and calculating the circumference of the earth, on the vast plains of Mesopotamia.

True knowledge, thus happily preserved, was now making its way back to Europe. The revival of science accompanied the revival of letters. Among the various authors which the awakening zeal for ancient literature had once more brought into notice were Pliny, Pomponius Mela, and Strabo. From these was regained a fund of geographical knowledge which had long faded from the public mind. Curiosity was aroused to pursue this forgotten path thus suddenly reopened. A translation of the work of Ptolemy had been made into Latin, at the commencement of the century, by Emanuel Chrysoleras, a noble and learned Greek, and had thus been rendered more familiar to the Italian students. Another translation had followed, by James Angel de Scarpiaria, of which fair and beautiful copies became common in the Italian libraries.†️ The writings also began to be sought after of Averroes, Alfraganus, and other Arabian sages, who had kept the sacred fire of science alive during the interval of European darkness.

* Foglieta, *Istoria de Genova*, lib. ii.
† Andres, *Hist. B. Let.*, lib. iii. cap. 2.

The knowledge thus reviving was limited and imperfect; yet, like the return of morning light, it seemed to call a new creation into existence, and broke, with all the charm of wonder, upon imaginative minds. They were surprised at their own ignorance of the world around them. Every step was discovery, for every region beyond their native country was in a manner *terra incognita*.

Such was the state of information and feeling with respect to this interesting science in the early part of the fifteenth century. An interest still more intense was awakened by the discoveries which began to be made along the Atlantic coasts of Africa, and must have been particularly felt among a maritime and commercial people like the Genoese. To these circumstances may we ascribe the enthusiastic devotion which Columbus imbibed in his childhood for cosmographical studies, and which influenced all his after fortunes.

The short time passed by him at the University of Pavia was barely sufficient to give him the rudiments of the necessary sciences. The familiar acquaintance with them which he evinced in after life must have been the result of diligent self-schooling in casual hours of study amid the cares and vicissitudes of a rugged and wandering life. He was one of those men of strong natural genius who, from having to contend at their very outset with privations and impediments, acquire an intrepidity in encountering and a facility in vanquishing difficulties throughout their career. Such men learn to effect great purposes with small means, supplying this deficiency by the resources of their own energy and invention. This, from his earliest commencement, throughout the whole of his life, was one of the remarkable features in the history of Columbus. In every undertaking the scantiness and apparent insufficiency of his means enhance the grandeur of his achievements.

Columbus, as has been observed, commenced his nautical career when about fourteen years of age. His first voyages were made with a distant relative named Colombo, a hardy veteran of the seas, who had risen to some distinction by his bravery, and is occasionally mentioned in old chronicles – sometimes as commanding a squadron of his own, sometimes as an admiral in the Genoese service. He appears to have been bold and adventurous, ready to fight in any cause, and to seek quarrel wherever it might lawfully be found.

The seafaring life of the Mediterranean in those days was hazardous and daring. A commercial expedition resembled a warlike cruise, and the maritime merchant had often to fight his way from port to port. Piracy was almost legalized. The frequent feuds between the Italian states; the cruisings of the Catalonians; the armadas fitted out by private noblemen, who exercised a kind of sovereignty in their own domains, and kept petty armies and navies in their pay; the roving ships and squadrons of private adventurers, a kind of naval Condottieri, sometimes employed by hostile governments, sometimes scouring the seas in search of lawless booty – these, with the holy wars waged against the Mohammedan powers, rendered the narrow seas, to which navigation was principally confined, scenes of hardy encounters and trying reverses.

Such was the rugged school in which Columbus was reared, and it would have been deeply interesting to have marked the early development of his genius amidst its stern adversities. All this instructive era of his history, however, is covered with darkness. His son Fernando, who could have best elucidated it, has left it in obscurity, or has now and then perplexed us with cross lights; perhaps unwilling, from a principle of mistaken pride, to reveal the indigence and obscurity from which his father so gloriously emerged.

The first voyage in which we have any account of his being engaged was a naval expedition, fitted out in Genoa in 1459 by John of Anjou, Duke of Calabria, to make a descent upon Naples, in the hope of recovering that kingdom for his father, King Reinier, or Renato, otherwise called René, Count of Provence. The republic of Genoa aided him with ships and money. The brilliant nature of the enterprise attracted the attention of daring and restless spirits. The chivalrous nobleman, the soldier of fortune, the hardy corsair, the desperate adventurer, the mercenary partisan, all hastened to enlist under the banner of Anjou. The veteran Colombo took a part in this expedition, either with galleys of his own or as a commander of the Genoese squadron, and with him embarked his youthful relative, the future discoverer.

The struggle of John of Anjou for the crown of Naples lasted about four years, with varied fortune, but was finally unsuccessful. The naval part of the expedition in which Columbus was engaged signalized itself by acts of intrepidity; and at one time, when the duke was reduced to take refuge in the island of Ischia, a handful of galleys scoured and controlled the Bay of Naples.[*]

In the course of this gallant but ill-fated enterprise, Columbus was detached on a perilous cruise, to cut out a galley from the harbour of Tunis. This is incidentally mentioned by himself in a letter written many years afterwards. 'It happened to me,' he says, 'that King Reinier (whom God has taken to himself) sent me to Tunis to capture the galley *Fernandina*, and when I arrived off the island of St Pedro in Sardinia, I was informed that there were two ships and a carrack with the galley; by which intelligence my crew were so troubled that they determined to proceed no further, but to return to Marseilles for another vessel and more people. As I could not by any means compel them, I assented apparently to their wishes, altering the point of the compass and spreading all sail. It was then evening, and next morning we were within the Cape of Carthagena, while all were firmly of opinion that they were sailing towards Marseilles.'[†]

We have no further record of this bold cruise into the harbour of Tunis; but in the foregoing particulars we behold early indications of that resolute and persevering spirit which insured him success in

[*] Colenuccio, *Istoria de Nap.*, lib. vii. cap. 17.
[†] Letter of Columbus to the Catholic sovereigns, vide *Hist. del Almirante*, cap. 4.

his more important undertakings. His expedient to beguile a discontented crew into a continuation of the enterprise by deceiving
them with respect to the ship's course, will be found in unison
with a stratagem of altering the reckoning to which he had
recourse in his first voyage of discovery.

During an interval of many years we have but one or two
shadowy traces of Columbus. He is supposed to have been principally engaged on the Mediterranean and up the Levant – sometimes in commercial voyages, sometimes in the warlike contests
between the Italian states, sometimes in pious and predatory
expeditions against the Infidels. Historians have made him in 1474
captain of several Genoese ships in the service of Louis XI of
France, and endangering the peace between that country and
Spain by running down and capturing Spanish vessels at sea, on his
own responsibility, as a reprisal for an irruption of the Spaniards
into Roussillon.* Again, in 1475, he is represented as brushing with
his Genoese squadron in ruffling bravado by a Venetian fleet
stationed off the island of Cyprus, shouting, 'Viva San Georgio!'
the old war-cry of Genoa, thus endeavouring to pique the jealous
pride of the Venetians and provoke a combat, though the rival
republics were at peace at the time.

These transactions, however, have been erroneously attributed
to Columbus. They were the deeds, or misdeeds, either of his
relative the old Genoese admiral, or of a nephew of the same, of
kindred spirit, called Colombo the Younger, to distinguish him
from his uncle. They both appear to have been fond of rough
encounters, and not very scrupulous as to the mode of bringing
them about. Fernando Columbus describes this Colombo the
Younger as a famous corsair, so terrible for his deeds against the
Infidels that the Moorish mothers used to frighten their unruly
children with his name. Columbus sailed with him occasionally, as
he had done with his uncle, and, according to Fernando's account,
commanded a vessel in his squadron on an eventful occasion.

Colombo the Younger, having heard that four Venetian galleys, richly laden, were on their return voyage from Flanders, lay in
wait for them on the Portuguese coast, between Lisbon and
Cape St Vincent. A desperate engagement took place; the vessels
grappled each other, and the crews fought hand to hand and from

---

* Chaufepie, *Suppl. to Bayle*, vol. ii., article 'Columbus'.

ship to ship. The battle lasted from morning until evening, with great carnage on both sides. The vessel commanded by Columbus was engaged with a huge Venetian galley. They threw hand-grenades and other fiery missiles, and the galley was wrapped in flames. The vessels were fastened together by chains and grappling irons, and could not be separated; both were involved in one conflagration, and soon became a mere blazing mass. The crews threw themselves into the sea; Columbus seized an oar, which was floating within reach, and being an expert swimmer attained the shore, though full two leagues distant. It pleased God, says his son Fernando, to give him strength, that he might preserve him for greater things. After recovering from his exhaustion he repaired to Lisbon, where he found many of his Genoese countrymen, and was induced to take up his residence.*

Such is the account given by Fernando of his father's first arrival in Portugal, and it has been currently adopted by modern historians; but on examining various histories of the times, the battle here described appears to have happened several years after the date of the arrival of Columbus in that country. That he was engaged in the contest is not improbable, but he had previously resided for some time in Portugal. In fact, on referring to the history of that kingdom, we shall find, in the great maritime enterprises in which it was at that time engaged, ample attractions for a person of his inclinations and pursuits; and we shall be led to conclude that his first visit to Lisbon was not the fortuitous result of a desperate adventure, but was undertaken in a spirit of liberal curiosity, and in the pursuit of honourable fortune.

* *Hist. del Almirante*, cap. 5.

CHAPTER 3

The career of modern discovery had commenced shortly before the time of Columbus, and at the period of which we are treating was prosecuted with great activity by Portugal. Some have attributed its origin to a romantic incident in the fourteenth century. An Englishman, of the name of Macham, flying to France with a lady of whom he was enamoured, was driven far out of sight of land by stress of weather, and after wandering about the high seas, arrived at an unknown and uninhabited island, covered with beautiful forests, which was afterwards called Madeira. Others have treated this account as a fable, and have pronounced the Canaries to be the first-fruits of modern discovery. This famous group, the Fortunate Islands of the ancients, in which they placed their garden of the Hesperides, and whence Ptolemy commenced to count the longitude, had been long lost to the world. There are vague accounts, it is true, of their having received casual visits, at wide intervals, during the obscure ages, from the wandering bark of some Arabian, Norman, or Genoese adventurer; but all this was involved in uncertainty, and led to no beneficial result. It was not until the fourteenth century that they were effectually rediscovered and restored to mankind. From that time they were occasionally visited by the hardy navigators of various countries. The greatest benefit produced by their discovery was, that the frequent expeditions made to them emboldened mariners to venture far upon the Atlantic, and familiarized them, in some degree, to its dangers.

The grand impulse to discovery was not given by chance, but was the deeply meditated effort of one master-mind. This was Prince Henry of Portugal, son of John the First, surnamed the Avenger, and Philippa of Lancaster, sister of Henry the Fourth of England. The character of this illustrious man, from whose enterprises the genius of Columbus took excitement, deserves particular mention.

Having accompanied his father into Africa, in an expedition against the Moors, at Ceuta he received much information concerning the coast of Guinea, and other regions in the interior hitherto unknown to Europeans, and conceived an idea that important discoveries were to be made by navigating along the western coast of Africa. On returning to Portugal, this idea became his ruling thought. Withdrawing from the tumult of a court to a country retreat in the Algarves, near Sagres, in the neighbourhood of Cape St Vincent, and in full view of the ocean, he drew around him men eminent in science, and prosecuted the study of those branches of knowledge connected with the maritime arts. He was an able mathematician, and made himself master of all the astronomy known to the Arabians of Spain.

On studying the works of the ancients, he found what he considered abundant proofs that Africa was circumnavigable. Eudoxus of Cyzicus was said to have sailed from the Red Sea into the ocean, and to have continued on to Gibraltar; and Hanno the Carthaginian, sailing from Gibraltar with a fleet of sixty ships, and following the African coast, was said to have reached the shores of Arabia. It is true these voyages had been discredited by several ancient writers; and the possibility of circumnavigating Africa, after being for a long time admitted by geographers, was denied by Hipparchus, who considered each sea shut up and land-bound in its peculiar basin; and that Africa was a continent continuing onward to the south pole, and surrounding the Indian sea, so as to join Asia beyond the Ganges. This opinion had been adopted by Ptolemy, whose works, in the time of Prince Henry, were the highest authority in geography. The prince, however, clung to the ancient belief that Africa was circumnavigable, and found his opinion sanctioned by various learned men of more modern date. To settle this question, and achieve the circumnavigation of Africa, was an object worthy the ambition of a prince, and his mind was fired with the idea of the vast benefits that would arise to his country should it be accomplished by Portuguese enterprise.

The Italians, or Lombards, as they were called in the north of Europe, had long monopolized the trade of Asia. They had formed commercial establishments at Constantinople and in the Black Sea, where they received the rich produce of the Spice

Islands, lying near the equator, and the silks, the gums, the perfumes, the precious stones, and other luxurious commodities of Egypt and southern Asia, and distributed them over the whole of Europe. The republics of Venice and Genoa rose to opulence and power in consequence of this trade. They had factories in the most remote parts, even in the frozen regions of Muscovy and Norway. Their merchants emulated the magnificence of princes. All Europe was tributary to their commerce. Yet this trade had to pass through various intermediate hands, subject to the delays and charges of internal navigation, and the tedious and uncertain journeys of the caravan. For a long time, the merchandise of India was conveyed by the Gulf of Persia, the Euphrates, the Indus, and the Oxus, to the Caspian and the Mediterranean seas; thence to take a new destination for the various marts of Europe. After the Soldan of Egypt had conquered the Arabs, and restored trade to its ancient channel, it was still attended with great cost and delay. Its precious commodities had to be conveyed by the Red Sea, thence on the backs of camels to the banks of the Nile, whence they were transported to Egypt to meet the Italian merchants. Thus, while the opulent traffic of the East was engrossed by these adventurous monopolists, the price of every article was enhanced by the great expense of transportation.

It was the grand idea of Prince Henry, by circumnavigating Africa to open a direct and easy route to the source of this commerce, to turn it in a golden tide upon his country. He was, however, before the age in thought, and had to counteract ignorance and prejudice, and to endure the delays to which vivid and penetrating minds are subjected from the tardy co-operations of the dull and the doubtful. The navigation of the Atlantic was yet in its infancy. Mariners looked with distrust upon a boisterous expanse which appeared to have no opposite shore, and feared to venture out of sight of the landmarks. Every bold headland and farstretching promontory was a wall to bar their progress. They crept timorously along the Barbary shores, and thought they had accomplished a wonderful expedition when they had ventured a few degrees beyond the Straits of Gibraltar. Cape Non was long the limit of their daring; they hesitated to double its rocky point, beaten by winds and waves, and threatening to thrust them forth upon the raging deep.

Independent of these vague fears, they had others, sanctioned by philosophy itself. They still thought that the earth, at the equator, was girdled by a torrid zone, over which the sun held his vertical and fiery course, separating the hemispheres by a region of impassive heat. They fancied Cape Bojador the utmost boundary of secure enterprise, and had a superstitious belief that whoever doubled it would never return.* They looked with dismay upon the rapid currents of its neighbourhood, and the furious surf which beats upon its arid coast. They imagined that beyond it lay the frightful region of the torrid zone, scorched by a blazing sun – a region of fire, where the very waves, which beat upon the shores, boiled under the intolerable fervour of the heavens.

To dispel these errors, and to give a scope to navigation equal to the grandeur of his designs, Prince Henry established a naval college and erected an observatory at Sagres; and he invited thither the most eminent professors of the nautical faculties, appointing as president James of Mallorca, a man learned in navigation and skilful in making charts and instruments.

The effects of this establishment were soon apparent. All that was known relative to geography and navigation was gathered together and reduced to system. A vast improvement took place in maps. The compass was also brought into more general use, especially among the Portuguese, rendering the mariner more bold and venturous, by enabling him to navigate in the most gloomy day and in the darkest night. Encouraged by these advantages, and stimulated by the munificence of Prince Henry, the Portuguese marine became signalized for the hardihood of its enterprises and the extent of its discoveries. Cape Bojador was doubled; the region of the tropics penetrated, and divested of its fancied terrors; the greatest part of the African coast, from Cape Blanco to Cape de Verde, explored; and the Cape de Verde and Azore Islands, which lay three hundred leagues distant from the continent, were rescued from the oblivious empire of the ocean.

To secure the quiet prosecution and full enjoyment of his discoveries, Henry obtained the protection of a papal bull, granting to the crown of Portugal sovereign authority over all the lands it might discover in the Atlantic, to India inclusive, with plenary

* Mariana, *Hist. Esp.*, lib. ii. cap. 22.

indulgence to all who should die in these expeditions; at the same time menacing with the terrors of the church all who should interfere in these Christian conquests.*

Henry died on the 13th of November 1473, without accomplishing the great object of his ambition. It was not until many years afterwards that Vasco da Gama, pursuing with a Portuguese fleet the track he had pointed out, realized his anticipations by doubling the Cape of Good Hope, sailing along the southern coast of India, and thus opening a highway for commerce to the opulent regions of the East. Henry, however, lived long enough to reap some of the richest rewards of a great and good mind. He beheld, through his means, his native country in a grand and active career of prosperity. The discoveries of the Portuguese were the wonder and admiration of the fifteenth century, and Portugal, from being one of the least among nations, suddenly rose to be one of the most important.

All this was effected, not by arms, but by arts; not by the stratagems of a cabinet, but by the wisdom of a college. It was the great achievement of a prince, who has well been described 'full of thoughts of lofty enterprise and acts of generous spirit'; one who bore for his device the magnanimous motto, 'The talent to do good', the only talent worthy the ambition of princes.†

Henry, at his death, left it in charge to his country to prosecute the route to India. He had formed companies and associations, by which commercial zeal was enlisted in the cause, and it was made a matter of interest and competition to enterprising individuals.‡ From time to time Lisbon was thrown into a tumult of excitement by the launching forth of some new expedition, or the return of a squadron with accounts of new tracts explored and new kingdoms visited. Everything was confident promise and sanguine anticipation. The miserable hordes of the African coast were magnified into powerful nations, and the voyagers continually heard of opulent countries further on. It was as yet the twilight of geographical knowledge; imagination went hand in hand with discovery, and as the latter groped its slow and cautious way, the former peopled all beyond with wonders. The fame of the Portuguese discoveries,

---

* Vasconcelos. *Hist. de Juan II.*

† Joam de Barros, *Asia*, decad. i.

‡ Lafitau, *Conquêtes des Portugais*, tom. i. lib. i.

and of the expeditions continually setting out, drew the attention of the world. Strangers from all parts – the learned, the curious, and the adventurous – resorted to Lisbon to inquire into the particulars or to participate in the advantages of these enterprises. Among these was Christopher Columbus, whether thrown there, as has been asserted, by the fortuitous result of a desperate adventure, or drawn thither by liberal curiosity and the pursuit of honourable fortune.*

* Herrera, decad. i. lib. i.

CHAPTER 4

Columbus arrived at Lisbon about the year 1470. He was at that time in the full vigour of manhood, and of an engaging presence. Minute descriptions are given of his person by his son Fernando, by Las Casas, and others of his contemporaries.* According to these accounts he was tall, well-formed, muscular, and of an elevated and dignified demeanour. His visage was long, and neither full nor meagre; his complexion fair and freckled, and inclined to ruddy; his nose aquiline; his cheek bones were rather high; his eyes light gray, and apt to enkindle; his whole countenance had an air of authority. His hair, in his youthful days, was of a light colour; but care and trouble, according to Las Casas, soon turned it gray, and at thirty years of age it was quite white. He was moderate and simple in diet and apparel, eloquent in discourse, engaging and affable with strangers, and his amiableness and suavity in domestic life strongly attached his household to his person. His temper was naturally irritable;† but he subdued it by the magnanimity of his spirit, comporting himself with a courteous and gently gravity, and never indulging in any intemperance of language. Throughout his life he was noted for strict attention to the offices of religion, observing rigorously the fasts and ceremonies of the church; nor did his piety consist in mere forms, but partook of that lofty and solemn enthusiasm with which his whole character was strongly tinctured.

While at Lisbon, he was accustomed to attend religious service at the chapel of the convent of All Saints. In this convent were certain ladies of rank, either resident as boarders or in some religious capacity. With one of these Columbus became acquainted. She was Doña Felipa, daughter of Bartolomeo Moñis de Perestrello, an Italian cavalier, lately deceased, who had been

* *Hist. del Almirante*, cap. 3; Las Casas, *Hist. Ind.*, lib. i. cap. 2, MS.
† Illescas, *Hist. Pontifical.*, lib. vi.

Lisbon in the Fifteenth Century

one of the most distinguished navigators under Prince Henry, and had colonized and governed the island of Porto Santo. The acquaintance soon ripened into attachment, and ended in marriage. It appears to have been a match of mere affection, as the lady was destitute of fortune.

The newly-married couple resided with the mother of the bride. The latter, perceiving the interest which Columbus took in all matters concerning the sea, related to him all she knew of the voyages and expeditions of her late husband, and brought him all his papers, charts, journals, and memorandums.[*] In this way he became acquainted with the routes of the Portuguese, their plans and conceptions; and having, by his marriage and residence, become naturalized in Portugal, he sailed occasionally in the expeditions to the coast of Guinea. When on shore he supported his family by making maps and charts. His narrow circumstances obliged him to observe a strict economy; yet we are told that he appropriated a part of his scanty means to the succour of his aged father at Genoa,[†] and to the education of his younger brothers.[‡]

The construction of a correct map or chart in those days required a degree of knowledge and experience sufficient to entitle the possessor to distinction. Geography was but just emerging from the darkness which had enveloped it for ages. Ptolemy was still a standard authority. The maps of the fifteenth century display a mixture of truth and error, in which facts handed down from antiquity, and others revealed by recent discoveries, are confused with popular fables and extravagant conjectures. At such a period, when the passion for maritime discovery was seeking every aid to facilitate its enterprises, the knowledge and skill of an able cosmographer like Columbus would be properly appreciated, and the superior correctness of his maps and charts would give him notoriety among men of science.[§] We accordingly find him, at an early period of his residence in Lisbon, in correspondence with Paulo

[*] Oviedo, *Cronica de las Indias*, lib. ii. cap 2.

[†] Ibid.

[‡] Muñoz, *Hist. del N. Mundo*, lib. ii.

[§] The importance which began to be attached to cosmographical knowledge is evident from the distinction which Mauro, an Italian friar, obtained from having projected an universal map, esteemed the most accurate of the time. A *facsimile* of this map, upon the same scale as the original, is now deposited in the British Museum, and it has been published, with a geographical commentary, by the

Toscanelli of Florence, one of the most scientific men of the day, whose communications had great influence in inspiriting him to his subsequent undertakings.

While his geographical labours thus elevated him to a communion with the learned, they were peculiarly calculated to foster a train of thoughts favourable to nautical enterprise. From constantly comparing maps and charts, and noting the progress and direction of discovery, he was led to perceive how much of the world remained unknown, and to meditate on the means of exploring it. His domestic concerns, and the connections he had formed by marriage, were all in unison with this vein of speculation. He resided for some time at the recently-discovered island of Porto Santo, where his wife had inherited some property; and during his residence there she bore him a son, whom he named Diego. This residence brought him, as it were, on the very frontier of discovery. His wife's sister was married to Pedro Correo, a navigator of note, who had at one time been governor of Porto Santo. Being frequently together in the familiar intercourse of domestic life, their conversation naturally turned upon the discoveries prosecuting in their vicinity along the African coasts, upon the long-sought-for route to India, and upon the possibility of some unknown lands existing in the west.

In their island residence too they must have been frequently visited by the voyagers going to and from Guinea. Living thus, surrounded by the stir and bustle of discovery, communing with persons who had risen by it to fortune and honour, and voyaging in the very tracks of its recent triumphs, the ardent mind of Columbus kindled up to enthusiasm in the cause. It was a period of general excitement to all who were connected with maritime life, or who resided in the vicinity of the ocean. The recent discoveries had inflamed their imaginations, and had filled them with visions of other islands, of greater wealth and beauty, yet to be discovered in

learned Zurla. The Venetians struck a medal in honour of him, on which they denominated him *Cosmographus incomparabilis* (Colline del Bussol. *Naut.* p. 2, c. 5). Yet Ramusio, who had seen this map in the monastery of San Michele de Murano, considers it merely an improved copy of a map brought from Cathay by Marco Polo (Ramusio, t. ii. p. 17, Ed. Venet. 1606). We are told that Americus Vespucius paid one hundred and thirty ducats (equivalent to five hundred and fifty-five dollars in our time) for a map of sea and land, made at Mallorca, in 1439, by Gabriel de Valseca (Barros, D. l. i. c. 15; Derroto por Tofino, Introd. p. 25).

the boundless wastes of the Atlantic. The opinions and fancies of
the ancients on the subject were again put in circulation. The story
of Antilla, a great island in the ocean, discovered by the Carthag-
inians, was frequently cited, and Plato's imaginary Atlantis once
more found firm believers. Many thought that the Canaries and
Azores were but wrecks which had survived its submersion, and
that other and larger fragments of that drowned land might yet exist
in remoter parts of the Atlantic.

One of the strongest symptoms of the excited state of the
popular mind at this eventful era was the prevalence of rumours
respecting unknown islands casually seen in the ocean. Many of
these were mere fables, fabricated to feed the predominant humour of the public; many had their origin in the heated imaginations
of voyagers, beholding islands in those summer clouds which lie
along the horizon, and often beguile the sailor with the idea of
distant lands.

On such airy basis, most probably, was founded the story told
to Columbus by one Antonio Leone, an inhabitant of Madeira,
who affirmed that sailing thence westward one hundred leagues
he had seen three islands at a distance. But the tales of the kind
most positively advanced and zealously maintained were those
related by the people of the Canaries, who were long under a
singular optical delusion. They imagined that, from time to time,
they beheld a vast island to the westward, with lofty mountains
and deep valleys. Nor was it seen in cloudy and dubious weather,
but in those clear days common to tropical climates, and with all
the distinctness with which distant objects may be discerned in
their pure, transparent atmosphere. The island, it is true, was only
seen at intervals; while at other times, and in the clearest weather,
not a vestige of it was to be descried. When it did appear,
however, it was always in the same place and under the same
form. So persuaded were the inhabitants of the Canaries of its
reality that application was made to the King of Portugal for
permission to discover and take possession of it; and it actually
became the object of several expeditions. The island, however,
was never to be found, though it still continued occasionally to
cheat the eye.

There were all kinds of wild and fantastic notions concerning
this imaginary land. Some supposed it to be the Antilla mentioned

by Aristotle; others, the Island of Seven Cities, so called from an ancient legend of seven bishops, who, with a multitude of followers, fled from Spain at the time of its conquest by the Moors, and, guided by Heaven to some unknown island in the ocean, founded on it seven splendid cities; while some considered it another legendary island, on which it was said a Scottish priest of the name of St Brandan had landed in the sixth century. This last legend passed into current belief. The fancied island was called by the name of St Brandan, or St Borondon, and long continued to be actually laid down in maps far to the west of the Canaries. The same was done with the fabulous island of Antilla; and these erroneous maps and phantom islands have given rise at various times to assertions that the New World had been known prior to the period of its generally reputed discovery.

Columbus, however, considers all these appearances of land as mere illusions. He supposes that they may have been caused by rocks lying in the ocean, which, seen at a distance, under certain atmospherical influences, may have assumed the appearance of islands; or that they may have been floating islands, such as are mentioned by Pliny, and Seneca, and others, formed of twisted roots, or of a light and porous stone, and covered with trees, and which may have been driven about the ocean by the winds.

The islands of St Brandan, of Antilla, and of the Seven Cities, have long since proved to be fabulous tales or atmospherical delusions. Yet the rumours concerning them derive interest, from showing the state of public thought with respect to the Atlantic while its western regions were yet unknown. They were all noted down with curious care by Columbus, and may have had some influence over his imagination. Still, though of a visionary spirit, his penetrating genius sought in deeper sources for the aliment of his meditations. Aroused by the impulse of passing events, he turned anew, says his son Fernando, to study the geographical authors which he had read before, and to consider the astronomical reasons which might corroborate the theory gradually forming in his mind. He made himself acquainted with all that had been written by the ancients or discovered by the moderns relative to geography. His own voyages enabled him to correct many of their errors and appreciate many of their theories. His genius having thus taken its decided bent, it is interesting to notice from what a mass of acknowledged facts, rational hypotheses, fanciful narrations, and popular rumours, his grand project of discovery was wrought out by the strong workings of his vigorous mind.

CHAPTER 5

It has been attempted in the preceding chapters to show how Columbus was gradually kindled up to his grand design by the spirit and events of the times in which he lived. His son Fernando, however, undertakes to furnish the precise data on which his father's plan of discovery was founded.* 'He does this,' he observes, 'to show from what slender argument so great a scheme was fabricated and brought to light, and for the purpose of satisfying those who may desire to know distinctly the circumstances and motives which led his father to undertake this enterprise.'

As this statement was formed from notes and documents found among his father's papers, it is too curious and interesting not to deserve particular mention. In this memorandum he arranged the foundation of his father's theory under three heads: 1. The nature of things. 2. The authority of learned writers. 3. The reports of navigators.

Under the first head, he set down as a fundamental principle that the earth was a terraqueous sphere or globe, which might be travelled round from east to west, and that men stood foot to foot when on opposite points. The circumference from east to west, at the equator, Columbus divided, according to Ptolemy, into twenty-four hours of fifteen degrees each, making three hundred and sixty degrees. Of these he imagined, comparing the globe of Ptolemy with the earlier map of Marinus of Tyre, that fifteen hours had been known to the ancients, extending from the Straits of Gibraltar, or rather from the Canary Islands, to the city of Thinae in Asia, a place set down as at the eastern limits of the known world. The Portuguese had advanced the western frontier one hour more by the discovery of the Azores and Cape de Verde Islands. There remained, then, according to the estimation of Columbus, eight hours, or one-third of the circumference of the

* *Hist. del Almirante*, cap. 6, 7, 8.

earth, unknown and unexplored. This space might, in a great measure, be filled up by the eastern regions of Asia, which might extend so far as nearly to surround the globe, and to approach the western shores of Europe and Africa. The tract of ocean intervening between these countries, he observes, would be less than might at first be supposed, if the opinion of Alfraganus, the Arabian, were admitted, who, by diminishing the size of the degrees, gave to the earth a smaller circumference than did other cosmographers – a theory to which Columbus seems at times to have given faith. Granting these premises, it was manifest that, by pursuing a direct course from east to west, a navigator would arrive at the extremity of Asia, and discover any intervening land.

Under the second head are named the authors whose writings had weight in convincing him that the intervening ocean could be but of moderate expanse, and easy to be traversed. Among these, he cites the opinion of Aristotle, Seneca, and Pliny, that one might pass from Cadiz to the Indies in a few days; of Strabo also, who observes that the ocean surrounds the earth, bathing on the east the shores of India, on the west, the coasts of Spain and Mauritania; so that it is easy to navigate from one to the other on the same parallel.*

In corroboration of the idea that Asia, or, as he always terms it, India, stretched far to the east, so as to occupy the greater part of the unexplored space, the narratives are cited of Marco Polo and John Mandeville. These travellers had visited, in the thirteenth and fourteenth centuries, the remote parts of Asia, far beyond the regions laid down by Ptolemy; and their accounts of the extent of that continent to the eastward had a great effect in convincing Columbus that a voyage to the west, of no long duration, would bring him to its shores, or to the extensive and wealthy islands which lie adjacent. The information concerning Marco Polo is probably derived from Paulo Toscanelli, a celebrated doctor of Florence, already mentioned, with whom Columbus corresponded in 1474, and who transmitted to him a copy of a letter which he had previously written to Fernando Martinez, a learned canon of Lisbon. This letter maintains the facility of arriving at India by a western course, asserting the distance to be but four thousand miles, in a direct line from Lisbon to the province of Mangi, near

* Strab. *Cos.*, lib. i. ii.

Cathay, since determined to be the northern coast of China. Of this country he gives a magnificent description, drawn from the work of Marco Polo. He adds that in the route lay the islands of Antilla and Cipango, distant from each other only two hundred and twenty-five leagues, abounding in riches, and offering convenient places for ships to touch at and obtain supplies on the voyage.

Under the third head are enumerated various indications of land in the west, which had floated to the shores of the known world. It is curious to observe how, when once the mind of Columbus had become heated in the inquiry, it attracted to it every corroborating circumstance, however vague and trivial. He appears to have been particularly attentive to the gleams of information derived from veteran mariners who had been employed in the recent voyages to the African coasts; and also from the inhabitants of lately discovered islands, placed, in a manner, on the frontier posts of geographical knowledge. All these are carefully noted down among his memorandums, to be collocated with the facts and opinions already stored up in his mind.

Such, for instance, is the circumstance related to him by Martin Vicenti, a pilot in the service of the King of Portugal, that, after sailing four hundred and fifty leagues to the west of Cape St Vincent, he had taken from the water a piece of carved wood, which evidently had not been laboured with an iron instrument. As the winds had drifted it from the west, it might have come from some unknown land in that direction.

Pedro Correo, brother-in-law of Columbus, is likewise cited, as having seen, on the island of Porto Santo, a similar piece of wood, which had drifted from the same quarter. He had heard also from the King of Portugal that reeds of an immense size had floated to some of those islands from the west, in the description of which Columbus thought he recognized the immense reeds said by Ptolemy to grow in India.

Information is likewise noted, given him by the inhabitants of the Azores, of trunks of huge pine trees, of a kind that did not grow upon any of the islands, wafted to their shores by the westerly winds; but especially of the bodies of two dead men, cast upon the island of Flores, whose features differed from those of any known race of people.

To these is added the report of a mariner of the port of St Mary, who asserted that, in the course of a voyage to Ireland, he had seen land to the west, which the ship's company took for some extreme part of Tartary. Other stories of a similar kind are noted, as well as rumours concerning the fancied islands of St Brandan, and of the Seven Cities, to which, as has already been observed, Columbus gave but little faith.

Such is an abstract of the grounds on which, according to Fernando, his father proceeded from one position to another, until he came to the conclusion that there was undiscovered land in the western part of the ocean; that it was attainable; that it was fertile; and finally, that it was inhabited.

It is evident that several of the facts herein enumerated must have become known to Columbus after he had formed his opinion, and merely served to strengthen it; still, everything that throws any light upon the process of thought which led to so great an event is of the highest interest; and the chain of deductions here furnished, though not perhaps the most logical in its concatenation, yet, being extracted from the papers of Columbus himself, remains one of the most interesting documents in the history of the human mind.

On considering this statement attentively, it is apparent that the grand argument which induced Columbus to his enterprise was that placed under the first head, namely, that the most eastern part of Asia known to the ancients could not be separated from the Azores by more than a third of the circumference of the globe; that the intervening space must, in a great measure, be filled up by the unknown residue of Asia; and that, if the circumference of the world was, as he believed, less than was generally supposed, the Asiatic shores could easily be attained by a moderate voyage to the west.

It is singular how much the success of this great undertaking depended upon two happy errors, the imaginary extent of Asia to the east, and the supposed smallness of the earth – both errors of the most learned and profound philosophers, but without which Columbus would hardly have ventured upon his enterprise. As to the idea of finding land by sailing directly to the west, it is at present so familiar to our minds as in some measure to diminish the merits of the first conception and the hardihood of the first

attempt: but in those days, as has well been observed, the circumference of the earth was yet unknown; no one could tell whether
the ocean were not of immense extent, impossible to be traversed;
nor were the laws of specific gravity and of central gravitation
ascertained, by which, granting the rotundity of the earth, the
possibility of making the tour of it would be manifest.* The practicability, therefore, of finding land by sailing to the west was one
of those mysteries of nature which are considered incredible whilst
matters of mere speculation, but the simplest things imaginable
when they have once been ascertained.

When Columbus had formed his theory, it became fixed in his
mind with singular firmness, and influenced his entire character
and conduct. He never spoke in doubt or hesitation, but with as
much certainty as if his eyes had beheld the promised land. No trial
or disappointment could divert him from the steady pursuit of his
object. A deep religious sentiment mingled with his meditations,
and gave them at times a tinge of superstition, but it was of a
sublime and lofty kind: he looked upon himself as standing in the
hand of Heaven, chosen from among men for the accomplishment
of its high purpose; he read, as he supposed, his contemplated
discovery foretold in Holy Writ, and shadowed forth darkly in the
mystic revelations of the prophets. The ends of the earth were to
be brought together, and all nations and tongues and languages
united under the banners of the Redeemer. This was to be the
triumphant consummation of his enterprise, bringing the remote
and unknown regions of the earth into communion with Christian
Europe, carrying the light of the true faith into benighted and
pagan lands, and gathering their countless nations under the holy
dominion of the church.

The enthusiastic nature of his conceptions gave an elevation to
his spirit and a dignity and loftiness to his whole demeanour. He
conferred with sovereigns almost with a feeling of equality. His
views were princely and unbounded; his proposed discovery was
of empires; his conditions were proportionally magnificent; nor
would he ever, even after long delays, repeated disappointments,
and under the pressure of actual penury, abate what appeared to be
extravagant demands for a mere possible discovery.

* Malte-Brun, *Géographie Universelle*, tom. xiv. Note sur le Découverte de
l'Amérique.

Those who could not conceive how an ardent and comprehensive genius could arrive, by presumptive evidence, at so firm a conviction, sought for other modes of accounting for it. When the glorious result had established the correctness of the opinion of Columbus, attempts were made to prove that he had obtained previous information of the lands which he pretended to discover. Among these was an idle tale of a tempest-tossed pilot, said to have died in his house, bequeathing him written accounts of an unknown land in the west, upon which he had been driven by adverse winds. This story, according to Fernando Columbus, had no other foundation than one of the popular tales about the shadowy island of St Brandan, which a Portuguese captain, returning from Guinea, fancied he had beheld beyond Madeira. It circulated for a time in idle rumour, altered and shaped to suit their purposes by such as sought to tarnish the glory of Columbus. At length it found its way into print, and has been echoed by various historians, varying with every narration, and full of contradictions and improbabilities.

An assertion has also been made that Columbus was preceded in his discoveries by Martin Behem, a contemporary cosmographer, who, it was said, had landed accidentally on the coast of South America, in the course of an African expedition; and that it was with the assistance of a map, or globe, projected by Behem, on which was laid down the newly-discovered country, that Columbus made his voyage. This rumour originated in an absurd misconstruction of a Latin manuscript, and was unsupported by any documents; yet it has had its circulation, and has even been revived not many years since with more zeal than discretion, but is now completely refuted and put to rest. The land visited by Behem was the coast of Africa beyond the equator. The globe he projected was finished in 1492, while Columbus was absent on his first voyage: it contains no trace of the New World, and thus furnishes conclusive proof that its existence was yet unknown to Behem.

There is a certain meddlesome spirit which, in the garb of learned research, goes prying about the traces of history, casting down its monuments, and marring and mutilating its fairest trophies. Care should be taken to vindicate great names from such pernicious erudition. It defeats one of the most salutary purposes of history, that of furnishing examples of what human genius and laudable enterprise may accomplish. For this purpose some pains have been taken in the preceding chapters to trace the rise and progress of this grand idea in the mind of Columbus, to show that it was the conception of his genius, quickened by the impulse of the age, and aided by those scattered gleams of knowledge which fell ineffectually upon ordinary minds.

CHAPTER 6

It is impossible to determine the precise time when Columbus first conceived the design of seeking a western route to India. It is certain, however, that he meditated it as early as the year 1474, though as yet it lay crude and unmatured in his mind. This fact, which is of some importance, is sufficiently established by the correspondence already mentioned with the learned Toscanelli of Florence, which took place in the summer of that year. The letter of Toscanelli is in reply to one from Columbus, and applauds the design which he had expressed of making a voyage to the west. To demonstrate more clearly the facility of arriving at India in that direction, he sent him a map, projected partly according to Ptolemy, and partly according to the descriptions of Marco Polo, the Venetian. The eastern coast of Asia was depicted in front of the western coasts of Africa and Europe, with a moderate space of ocean between them, in which were placed at convenient distances Cipango, Antilla, and the other islands.* Columbus was greatly animated by the letter and chart of Toscanelli, who was considered one of the ablest cosmographers of the day. He appears to have procured the work of Marco Polo, which had been translated into various languages, and existed in manuscript in most libraries. This author gives marvellous accounts of the riches of the realms of Cathay and Mangi, or Mangu, since ascertained to be Northern and Southern China, on the coast of which, according to the map of Toscanelli, a voyager sailing directly west would be sure to arrive. He describes in unmeasured terms the power and grandeur of the sovereign of these countries, the Great Khan of Tartary, and the splendour and magnitude of his capitals

* This map, by which Columbus sailed on his first voyage of discovery, Las Casas (lib. i. cap. 12) says he had in his possession at the time of writing his history. It is greatly to be regretted that so interesting a document should be lost. It may yet exist among the chaotic lumber of the Spanish archives. Few documents of mere curiosity would be more precious.

of Cambalu and Quinsai, and the wonders of the island of Cipango or Zipangi, supposed to be Japan. This island he places opposite Cathay, five hundred leagues in the ocean. He represents it as abounding in gold, precious stones, and other choice objects of commerce, with a monarch whose palace was roofed with plates of gold instead of lead. The narrations of this traveller were by many considered fabulous, but though full of what appear to be splendid exaggerations, they have since been found substantially correct. They are thus particularly noted, from the influence they had over the imagination of Columbus. The work of Marco Polo is a key to many parts of his history. In his applications to the various courts, he represented the countries he expected to discover as those regions of inexhaustible wealth which the Venetian had described. The territories of the Grand Khan were the objects of inquiry in all his voyages, and in his cruisings among the Antilles he was continually flattering himself with the hopes of arriving at the opulent island of Cipango and the coasts of Mangi and Cathay.

While the design of attempting the discovery in the west was maturing in the mind of Columbus, he made a voyage to the north of Europe. Of this we have no other memorial than the following passage, extracted by his son from one of his letters: − 'In the year 1477, in February, I navigated one hundred leagues beyond Thule, the southern part of which is seventy-three degrees distant from the equator, and not sixty-three, as some pretend; neither is it situated within the line which includes the west of Ptolemy, but is much more westerly. The English, principally those of Bristol, go with their merchandise to this island, which is as large as England. When I was there the sea was not frozen, and the tides were so great as to rise and fall twenty-six fathom.'*

The island thus mentioned is generally supposed to have been Iceland, which is far to the west of the Ultima Thule of the ancients, as laid down in the map of Ptolemy.

Several more years elapsed without any decided efforts on the part of Columbus to carry his design into execution. He was too poor to fit out the armament necessary for so important an exped-ition. Indeed it was an enterprise only to be undertaken in the employ of some sovereign state, which could assume dominion

* *Hist. del Almirante*, cap. 4.

over the territories he might discover, and reward him with dignities and privileges commensurate to his services. It is asserted that he at one time endeavoured to engage his native country, Genoa, in the undertaking, but without success. No record remains of such an attempt, though it is generally believed, and has strong probability in its favour. His residence in Portugal placed him at hand to solicit the patronage of that power; but Alphonso, who was then on the throne, was too much engrossed in the latter part of his reign with a war with Spain, for the succession of the Princess Juana to the crown of Castile, to engage in peaceful enterprises of an expensive nature. The public mind, also, was not prepared for so perilous an undertaking. Notwithstanding the many recent voyages to the coast of Africa and the adjacent islands, and the introduction of the compass into more general use, navigation was still shackled with impediments, and the mariner rarely ventured far out of sight of land.

Discovery advanced slowly along the coasts of Africa, and the mariners feared to cruise far into the southern hemisphere, with the stars of which they were totally unacquainted. To such men the project of a voyage directly westward into the midst of that boundless waste, to seek some visionary land, appeared as extravagant as it would be at the present day to launch forth in a balloon into the regions of space in quest of some distant star.

The time, however, was at hand that was to extend the sphere of navigation. The era was propitious to the quick advancement of knowledge. The recent invention of the art of printing enabled men to communicate rapidly and extensively their ideas and discoveries. It drew forth learning from libraries and convents, and brought it familiarly to the reading desk of the student. Volumes of information, which before had existed only in costly manuscripts, carefully treasured up, and kept out of the reach of the indigent scholar and obscure artist, were now in every hand. There was, henceforth, to be no retrogression in knowledge, nor any pause in its career. Every step in advance was immediately and simultaneously and widely promulgated, recorded in a thousand forms, and fixed for ever. There could never again be a dark age; nations might shut their eyes to the light, and sit in wilful darkness, but they could not trample it out; it would still shine on, dispensed to happier parts of the world by the diffusive powers of the press.

At this juncture, in 1481, a monarch ascended the throne of Portugal of different ambition from Alphonso. John II, then in the twenty-fifth year of his age, had imbibed the passion for discovery from his grand-uncle, Prince Henry, and with his reign all its activity revived. His first care was to build a fort at St George de la Miña, on the coast of Guinea, to protect the trade carried on in that neighbourhood for gold-dust, ivory, and slaves.

The African discoveries had conferred great glory upon Portugal, but as yet they had been expensive rather than profitable. The accomplishment of the route to India, however, it was expected, would repay all cost and toil, and open a source of incalculable wealth to the nation. The project of Prince Henry, which had now been tardily prosecuted for half a century, had excited a curiosity about the remote parts of Asia, and revived all the accounts, true and fabulous, of travellers.

Besides the work of Marco Polo, already mentioned, there was the narrative of Rabbi Benjamin ben Jonah, of Tudela, a Spanish Jew, who set out from Saragossa in 1173 to visit the scattered remnants of the Hebrew tribes. Wandering with unwearied zeal on this pious errand, over most parts of the known world, he penetrated China, and passed thence to the southern islands of Asia.* There were also the narratives of Carpini and Ascelin, two friars, despatched, the one in 1246, the other in 1247, by Pope Innocent IV, as apostolic ambassadors, for the purpose of converting the Grand Khan of Tartary; and the journal of William Rubruquis (or Ruysbroek), a celebrated Cordelier, sent on a similar errand in 1253, by Louis IX of France, then on his unfortunate crusade into Palestine. These pious but chimerical missions had proved abortive; but the narratives of them being revived in the fifteenth century, served to inflame the public curiosity respecting the remote parts of Asia.

In these narratives we first find mention made of the renowned Prester John, a Christian king, said to hold sway in a remote part of the East, who was long an object of curiosity and research, but whose kingdom seemed to shift its situation in the tale of every traveller, and to vanish from the search as effectually as the

---

* Bergeron, *Voyages en Asie*, tom. i. The work of Benjamin of Tudela, originally written in Hebrew, was so much in repute that the translation went through sixteen editions. Andres, *Hist. B. Let.*, ii. cap. 6.

unsubstantial island of St Brandan. All the speculations concerning this potentate and his Oriental realm were again put in circulation. It was fancied that traces of his empire were discovered in the interior of Africa, to the east of Benin, where there was a powerful prince, who used a cross among the insignia of royalty. John II partook largely of the popular excitement produced by these narrations. In the early part of his reign he actually sent missions in quest of Prester John, to visit whose dominions became the romantic desire of many a religious enthusiast. The magnificent idea he had formed of the remote parts of the East made him extremely anxious that the splendid project of Prince Henry should be realized, and the Portuguese flag penetrate to the Indian seas. Impatient of the slowness with which his discoveries advanced along the coast of Africa, and of the impediments which every cape and promontory presented to nautical enterprise, he called in the aid of science to devise some means by which greater scope and certainty might be given to navigation. His two physicians, Roderigo and Joseph, the latter a Jew, the most able astronomers and cosmographers of his kingdom, together with the celebrated Martin Behem, entered into a learned consultation on the subject. The result of their conferences and labours was the application of the astrolabe to navigation, enabling the seaman, by the altitude of the sun, to ascertain his distance from the equator.* This instrument has since been improved and modified into the modern quadrant, of which, even at its first introduction, it possessed all the essential advantages.

It is impossible to describe the effect produced upon navigation by this invention. It cast it loose at once from its long bondage to the land, and set it free to rove the deep. The mariner now, instead of coasting the shores like the ancient navigators, and, if driven from the land, groping his way back in doubt and apprehension by the uncertain guidance of the stars, might adventure boldly into unknown seas, confident of being able to trace his course by means of the compass and the astrolabe.

It was shortly after this event, which had prepared guides for discovery across the trackless ocean, that Columbus made the first attempt, of which we have any clear and indisputable record, to procure royal patronage for his enterprise. The court of Portugal

* Barros, decad. i. lib. iv. cap. 2; Maffei, lib. vi. pp. 6 and 7.

had shown extraordinary liberality in rewarding nautical discovery. Most of those who had succeeded in her service had been appointed to the government of the islands and countries they had discovered, although many of them were foreigners by birth. Encouraged by this liberality, and by the anxiety evinced by King John II to accomplish a passage by sea to India, Columbus obtained an audience of that monarch, and proposed, in case the king would furnish him with ships and men, to undertake a shorter and more direct route than that along the coast of Africa. His plan was to strike directly to the west, across the Atlantic. He then unfolded his hypothesis with respect to the extent of Asia, describing also the immense riches of the island of Cipango, the first land at which he expected to arrive. Of this audience we have two accounts, written in somewhat of an opposite spirit – one by his son Fernando, the other by Joam de Barros, the Portuguese historiographer. It is curious to notice the different views taken of the same transaction by the enthusiastic son, and by the cool, perhaps prejudiced, historian.

The king, according to Fernando, listened to his father with great attention, but was discouraged from engaging in any new scheme of the kind by the cost and trouble already sustained in exploring the route by the African coast, which as yet remained unaccomplished. His father, however, supported his proposition by such excellent reasons, that the king was induced to give his consent. The only difficulty that remained was the terms; for Columbus, being a man of lofty and noble sentiments, demanded high and honourable titles and rewards, to the end, says Fernando, that he might leave behind him a name and family worthy of his deeds and merits.*

Barros, on the other hand, attributes the seeming acquiescence of the king merely to the importunities of Columbus. He considered him, says the historian, a vainglorious man, fond of displaying his abilities, and given to fantastic fancies, such as that respecting the island of Cipango.† But, in fact, this idea of Columbus being vain, was taken up by the Portuguese writers in after years; and as to the island of Cipango, it was far from being considered chimerical by the king, who, as has been shown by his mission in

---

* *Hist del Almirante*, cap. 10.

† Barros, *Asia*, decad. i. lib. iii. cap. 2.

search of Prester John, was a ready believer in these travellers' tales concerning the East. The reasoning of Columbus must have produced an effect on the mind of the monarch, since it is certain that he referred the proposition to a learned junto, charged with all matters relating to maritime discovery.

This junto was composed of two able cosmographers, masters Roderigo and Joseph, and the king's confessor, Diego Ortiz de Cazadilla, Bishop of Ceuta, a man greatly reputed for his learning, a Castilian by birth, and generally called Cazadilla, from the name of his native place. This scientific body treated the project as extravagant and visionary.

Still the king does not appear to have been satisfied. According to his historian Vasconcelos,* he convoked his council, composed of prelates and persons of the greatest learning in the kingdom, and asked their advice, whether to adopt this new route of discovery, or to pursue that which they had already opened.

It may not be deemed superfluous to notice briefly the discussion of the council on this great question. Vasconcelos reports a speech of the Bishop of Ceuta, in which he not only objected to the proposed enterprise, as destitute of reason, but even discountenanced any further prosecution of the African discoveries. 'They tended,' he said, 'to distract the attention, drain the resources, and divide the power of the nation, already too much weakened by recent war and pestilence. While their forces were thus scattered abroad on remote and unprofitable expeditions, they exposed themselves to attack from their active enemy, the King of Castile. The greatness of monarchs,' he continued, 'did not arise so much from the extent of their dominions, as from the wisdom and ability with which they governed. In the Portuguese nation it would be madness to launch into enterprises without first considering them in connection with its means. The king had already sufficient undertakings in hand of certain advantage, without engaging in others of a wild, chimerical nature. If he wished employment for the active valour of the nation, the war in which he was engaged against the Moors of Barbary was sufficient, wherein his triumphs were of solid advantage, tending to cripple and enfeeble those neighbouring foes who had proved themselves so dangerous when possessed of power.'

* Vasconcelos, *Vida del Rey Don Juan.*

This cool and cautious speech of the Bishop of Ceuta, directed against enterprises which were the glory of the Portuguese, touched the national pride of Don Pedro de Meneses, Count of Villa Real, and drew from him a lofty and patriotic reply. It has been said by an historian that this reply was in support of the proposition of Columbus; but that does not clearly appear. He may have treated the proposal with respect, but his eloquence was employed for those enterprises in which the Portuguese were already engaged.

'Portugal,' he observed, 'was not in its infancy, nor were its princes so poor as to lack means to engage in discoveries. Even granting that those proposed by Columbus were conjectural, why should they abandon those commenced by their late Prince Henry, on such solid foundations, and prosecuted with such happy prospects? Crowns,' he observed, 'enriched themselves by commerce, fortified themselves by alliance, and acquired empires by conquest. The views of a nation could not always be the same; they extended with its opulence and prosperity. Portugal was at peace with all the princes of Europe. It had nothing to fear from engaging in an extensive enterprise. It would be the greatest glory for Portuguese valour to penetrate into the secrets and horrors of the ocean sea, so formidable to the other nations of the world. Thus occupied, it would escape the idleness engendered in a long interval of peace – idleness, that source of vice, that silent file, which, little by little, wore away the strength and valour of a nation. It was an affront,' he added, 'to the Portuguese name to menace it with imaginary perils, when it had proved itself so intrepid in encountering those which were most certain and tremendous. Great souls were formed for great enterprises. He wondered much that a prelate so religious as the Bishop of Ceuta should oppose this undertaking, the ultimate object of which was to augment the Catholic faith, and spread it from pole to pole, reflecting glory on the Portuguese nation, and yielding empire and lasting fame to its princes.' He concluded by declaring that, 'although a soldier, he dared to prognosticate, with a voice and spirit as if from heaven, to whatever prince should achieve this enterprise, more happy success and durable renown than had ever been obtained by sovereign the most valorous and fortunate.' *

---

* Vasconcelos, lib. iv; La Clede, *Hist. Portugal*, lib. xiii. tom. iii.

The warm and generous eloquence of the count overpowered the cold-spirited reasonings of the bishop as far as the project of circumnavigating Africa was concerned, which was prosecuted with new ardour and triumphant success. The proposition of Columbus, however, was generally condemned by the council.

Seeing that King John still manifested an inclination for the enterprise, it was suggested to him by the Bishop of Ceuta that Columbus might be kept in suspense while a vessel, secretly despatched in the direction he should point out, might ascertain whether there were any foundation for his theory. By this means all its advantages might be secured without committing the dignity of the crown by formal negotiations about what might prove a mere chimera. King John, in an evil hour, had the weakness to permit a stratagem so inconsistent with his usual justice and magnanimity. Columbus was required to furnish, for the consideration of the council, a detailed plan of his proposed voyage, with the charts and documents according to which he intended to shape his course. These being procured, a caravel was despatched with the ostensible design of carrying provisions to the Cape de Verde islands, but with private instructions to pursue the designated route. Departing from those islands, the caravel stood westward for several days, until the weather became stormy, when the pilots, seeing nothing but an immeasurable waste of wild tumbling waves still extending before them, lost all courage, and put back, ridiculing the project of Columbus as extravagant and irrational.[*]

This unworthy attempt to defraud him of his enterprise roused the indignation of Columbus, and he declined all offers of King John to renew the negotiation. The death of his wife, which had occurred some time previously, had dissolved the domestic tie which bound him to Portugal. He determined therefore to abandon a country where he had been treated with so little faith, and to look elsewhere for patronage. Before his departure he engaged his brother Bartholomew to carry proposals to the King of England, though he does not appear to have entertained great hope from that quarter, England by no means possessing at the time the spirit of nautical enterprise which has since distinguished her. The great reliance of Columbus was on his own personal exertions.

[*] *Hist. del Almirante*, cap. 8; Herrera, decad. i. lib. i. cap. 7.

It was towards the end of 1484 that he left Lisbon, taking with him his son Diego. His departure had to be conducted with secrecy, lest, as some assert, it should be prevented by King John; but lest, as others surmise, it should be prevented by his creditors.* Like many other great projectors, while engaged upon schemes of vast benefit to mankind, he had suffered his own affairs to go to ruin, and was reduced to struggle hard with poverty; nor is it one of the least interesting circumstances in his eventful life that he had, in a manner, to beg his way from court to court to offer to princes the discovery of a world.

* This surmise is founded on a letter from King John to Columbus, written some years afterwards, inviting him to return to Portugal, and insuring him against arrest on account of any process, civil or criminal, which might be pending against him. See Navarrete, *Colec.*, tom. ii. doc. 3.

BOOK 2

CHAPTER I

1485

The immediate movements of Columbus on leaving Portugal are involved in uncertainty. It is said that about this time he made a proposition of his enterprise in person, as he had formerly done by letter, to the government of Genoa. The republic, however, was in a languishing decline, and embarrassed by a foreign war. Caffa, her great deposit in the Crimea, had fallen into the hands of the Turks, and her flag was on the point of being driven from the Archipelago. Her spirit was broken with her fortunes, for with nations, as with individuals, enterprise is the child of prosperity, and is apt to languish in evil days, when there is most need of its exertion. Thus Genoa, disheartened by her reverses, shut her ears to the proposition of Columbus, which might have elevated her to tenfold splendour, and perpetuated within her grasp the golden wand of commerce. While at Genoa, Columbus is said to have made arrangements, out of his scanty means, for the comfort of his aged father. It is also affirmed that about this time he carried his proposal to Venice, where it was declined on account of the critical state of national affairs. This, however, is merely traditional, and unsupported by documentary evidence. The first firm and indisputable trace we have of Columbus after leaving Portugal is in the south of Spain, in 1485, where we find him seeking his fortune among the Spanish nobles, several of whom had vast possessions, and exercised almost independent sovereignty in their domains.

Foremost among these were the Dukes of Medina Sidonia and Medina Celi, who had estates like principalities lying along the sea-coast, with ports and shipping and hosts of retainers at their command. They served the crown in its Moorish wars more as allied princes than as vassals, bringing armies into the field led by themselves, or by captains of their own appointment. Their domestic establishments were on almost a regal scale; their palaces were filled with persons of merit, and young cavaliers of noble birth, to be reared under their auspices in the exercise of arts and arms.

Columbus had many interviews with the Duke of Medina Sidonia, who was tempted for a time by the splendid prospects held out; but their very splendour threw a colouring of improbability over the enterprise, and he finally rejected it as the dream of an Italian visionary.

The Duke of Medina Celi was likewise favourable at the outset. He entertained Columbus for some time in his house, and was actually on the point of granting him three or four caravels which lay ready for sea in his harbour of Port St Mary, opposite Cadiz, when he suddenly changed his mind, deterred by the consideration that the enterprise, if successful, would involve discoveries too important to be grasped by any but a sovereign power, and that the Spanish government might be displeased at his undertaking it on his own account. Finding, however, that Columbus intended to make his next application to the King of France, and loath that an enterprise of such importance should be lost to Spain, the duke wrote to Queen Isabella, recommending it strongly to her attention. The queen made a favourable reply, and requested that Columbus might be sent to her. He accordingly set out for the Spanish court, then at Cordova, bearing a letter to the queen from the duke, soliciting that, in case the expedition should be carried into effect, he might have a share in it, and the fitting out of the armament from his port of St Mary, as a recompense for having waived the enterprise in favour of the crown.[*]

The time when Columbus thus sought his fortunes at the court of Spain coincided with one of the most brilliant periods of the

[*] Letter of the Duke of Medina Celi to the Grand Cardinal. Navarrete, *Colec.*, vol. ii. p. 20.

N.B. In the previous editions of this work the first trace we have of Columbus in Spain is at the gate of the convent of La Rabida, in Andalusia. Subsequent investigations have induced me to conform to the opinion of the indefatigable and accurate Navarrete, given in his third volume of documents, that the first trace of Columbus in Spain was his application to the Dukes of Medina Sidonia and Medina Celi, and that his visit to the convent of La Rabida was some few years subsequent.

Spanish monarchy. The union of the kingdoms of Aragon and Castile by the marriage of Ferdinand and Isabella had consolidated the Christian power in the Peninsula, and put an end to those internal feuds which had so long distracted the country and insured the domination of the Moslems. The whole force of united Spain was now exerted in the chivalrous enterprise of the Moorish conquest. The Moors, who had once spread over the whole country like an inundation, were now pent up within the mountain boundaries of the kingdom of Granada. The victorious armies of Ferdinand and Isabella were continually advancing, and pressing this fierce people within narrower limits. Under these sovereigns the various petty kingdoms of Spain began to feel and act as one nation, and to rise to eminence in arts as well as arms. Ferdinand and Isabella, it has been remarked, lived together not like man and wife, whose estates are common, under the orders of the husband, but like two monarchs strictly allied.* They had separate claims to sovereignty, in virtue of their respective kingdoms; they had separate councils, and were often distant from each other in different parts of their empire, each exercising the royal authority. Yet they were so happily united by common views, common interests, and a great deference for each other, that this double administration never prevented a unity of purpose and of action. All acts of sovereignty were executed in both their names, all public writings were subscribed with both their signatures, their likenesses were stamped together on the public coin, and the royal seal displayed the united arms of Castile and Aragon.

Ferdinand was of the middle stature, well proportioned, and hardy and active from athletic exercise. His carriage was free, erect, and majestic. He had a clear serene forehead, which appeared more lofty from his head being partly bald. His eyebrows were large and parted, and, like his hair, of a bright chestnut; his eyes were clear and animated; his complexion was somewhat ruddy, and scorched by the toils of war; his mouth moderate, well formed, and gracious in its expression; his teeth white, though small and irregular; his voice sharp; his speech quick and fluent. His genius was clear and comprehensive, his judgment grave and certain. He was simple in dress and diet, equable in his temper, devout in his religion, and so indefatigable in business that it was

---

* Voltaire, *Essai sur les Mœurs*, etc.

said he seemed to repose himself by working. He was a great observer and judge of men, and unparalleled in the science of the cabinet. Such is the picture given of him by the Spanish historians of his time. It has been added, however, that he had more of bigotry than religion; that his ambition was craving rather than magnanimous; that he made war less like a paladin than a prince, less for glory than for mere dominion; and that his policy was cold, selfish, and artful. He was called the wise and prudent in Spain; in Italy, the pious; in France and England, the ambitious and per-fidious.* He certainly was one of the most subtle statesmen, but one of the most thorough egotists, that ever sat upon a throne.

While giving his picture, it may not be deemed impertinent to sketch the fortunes of a monarch whose policy had such an effect upon the history of Columbus and the destinies of the New World. Success attended all his measures. Though a younger son, he had ascended the throne of Aragon by inheritance, Castile he obtained by marriage, Granada and Naples by conquest, and he seized upon Navarre as appertaining to anyone who could take possession of it, when Pope Julius II excommunicated its sovereigns, Juan and Catalina, and gave their throne to the first occupant.† He sent his forces into Africa, and subjugated, or reduced to vassalage, Tunis, Tripoli, Algiers, and most of the Barbary powers. A new world was also given to him, without cost, by the discoveries of Columbus, for the expense of the enterprise was borne exclusively by his consort Isabella. He had three objects at heart from the commence-ment of his reign, which he pursued with bigoted and persecuting zeal – the conquest of the Moors, the expulsion of the Jews, and the establishment of the Inquisition in his dominions. He accomplished them all, and was rewarded by Pope Innocent VIII with the appellation of Most Catholic Majesty – a title which his successors have tenaciously retained.

Contemporary writers have been enthusiastic in their descrip-tions of Isabella, but time has sanctioned their eulogies. She is one of the purest and most beautiful characters in the pages of history. She was well formed, of the middle size, with great dignity and gracefulness of deportment, and a mingled gravity and sweetness of

* Voltaire, *Essai sur les Mœurs*, ch. 14.
† Pedro Salar di Mendoza, *Monarq. de Esp.*, lib. iii. cap. 5 (Madrid, 1770, tom. i. p. 402); Gonzalo de Illescas, *Hist. Pontif.*, lib. vi. cap. 23, § 3.

demeanour. Her complexion was fair; her hair auburn, inclining
to red; her eyes were of a clear blue, with a benign expression; and
there was a singular modesty in her countenance, gracing, as it did,
a wonderful firmness of purpose and earnestness of spirit. Though
strongly attached to her husband, and studious of his fame, yet she
always maintained her distinct rights as an allied prince. She
exceeded him in beauty, in personal dignity, in acuteness of
genius, and in grandeur of soul.* Combining the active and
resolute qualities of man with the softer charities of woman, she
mingled in the warlike councils of her husband, engaged personally in his enterprises,† and in some instances surpassed him in the
firmness and intrepidity of her measures; while, being inspired
with a truer idea of glory, she infused a more lofty and generous
temper into his subtle and calculating policy.

It is in the civil history of their reign, however, that the character
of Isabella shines most illustrious. Her fostering and maternal care
was continually directed to reform the laws and heal the ills
engendered by a long course of internal wars. She loved her
people, and while diligently seeking their good, she mitigated, as
much as possible, the harsh measures of her husband, directed to
the same end, but inflamed by a mistaken zeal. Thus, though
almost bigoted in her piety, and perhaps too much under the
influence of ghostly advisers, still she was hostile to every measure
calculated to advance religion at the expense of humanity. She
strenuously opposed the expulsion of the Jews and the establishment of the Inquisition, though, unfortunately for Spain, her
repugnance was slowly vanquished by her confessors. She was
always an advocate for clemency to the Moors, although she was
the soul of the war against Granada. She considered that war
essential to protect the Christian faith, and to relieve her subjects
from fierce and formidable enemies. While all her public thoughts
and acts were princely and august, her private habits were simple,
frugal, and unostentatious. In the intervals of state business she
assembled round her the ablest men in literature and science, and
directed herself by their counsels in promoting letters and arts.

* Garibay, *Hist. de España*, tom ii. lib. xviii. cap. 1.

† Several suits of armour *cap-à-pie*, worn by Isabella, and still preserved in the
royal arsenal at Madrid, show that she was exposed to personal danger in her
campaigns.

Through her patronage, Salamanca rose to that height which it assumed among the learned institutions of the age. She promoted the distribution of honours and rewards for the promulgation of knowledge. She fostered the art of printing recently invented, and encouraged the establishment of presses in every part of the kingdom; books were admitted free of all duty, and more, we are told, were printed in Spain, at that early period of the art, than in the present literary age.[*]

It is wonderful how much the destinies of countries depend at times upon the virtues of individuals, and how it is given to great spirits, by combining, exciting, and directing the latent powers of a nation, to stamp it, as it were, with their own greatness. Such beings realize the idea of guardian angels, appointed by Heaven to watch over the destinies of empires. Such had been Prince Henry for the kingdom of Portugal; and such was now for Spain the illustrious Isabella.

[*] *Elogio de la Reina Catholica*, por Diego Clemencin. Madrid, 1821.

When Columbus arrived at Cordova, he was given in charge to Alonzo de Quintanilla, Comptroller of the Treasury of Castile, but was disappointed in his expectation of receiving immediate audience from the queen. He found the city in all the bustle of military preparation. It was a critical juncture of the war. The rival kings of Granada, Muley Boabdil the uncle, and Mohammed Boabdil the nephew, had just formed a coalition, and their league called for prompt and vigorous measures.

All the chivalry of Spain had been summoned to the field. The streets of Cordova echoed to the tramp of steed and sound of trumpet, as day by day the nobles arrived with their retainers, vying with each other in the number of their troops and the splendour of their appointments. The court was like a military camp. The king and queen were surrounded by the flower of Spanish chivalry − by those veteran cavaliers who had distinguished themselves in so many hardy conflicts with the Moors, and by the prelates and friars who mingled in martial council, and took deep interest and agency in this war of the faith.

This was an unpropitious moment to urge a suit like that of Columbus. In fact, the sovereigns had not a moment of leisure throughout this eventful year. Early in the spring the king marched off to lay siege to the Moorish city of Loxa; and though the queen remained at Cordova, she was continually employed in forwarding troops and supplies to the army, and at the same time attending to the multiplied exigencies of civil government. On the 12th of June she repaired to the camp, then engaged in the siege of Moclin, and both sovereigns remained for some time in the Vega of Granada, prosecuting the war with unremitting vigour. They had barely returned to Cordova to celebrate their victories by public rejoicings, when they were obliged to set out for Gallicia, to suppress a rebellion of the Count of Lemos. Thence they repaired to Salamanca for the winter.

During the summer and autumn of this year, Columbus remained at Cordova, a guest in the house of Alonzo de Quintanilla, who proved a warm advocate of his theory. Through his means he became acquainted with Antonio Geraldini, the Pope's nuncio, and his brother, Alexander Geraldini, preceptor to the younger children of Ferdinand and Isabella; both valuable friends about court. Wherever he obtained a candid hearing from intelligent auditors, the dignity of his manners, his earnest sincerity, the elevation of his views, and the practical shrewdness of his demonstrations, commanded respect even where they failed to produce conviction.

While thus lingering in idle suspense in Cordova, he became attached to a lady of the city, Beatrix Enriquez by name, of a noble family, though in reduced circumstances. Their connection was not sanctioned by marriage, yet he cherished sentiments of respect and tenderness for her to his dying day. She was the mother of his second son, Fernando, born in the following year (1487), whom he always treated on terms of perfect equality with his legitimate son Diego, and who after his death became his historian.

In the winter Columbus followed the court to Salamanca. Here his zealous friend Alonzo de Quintanilla exerted his influence to obtain for him the countenance of the celebrated Pedro Gonzalez de Mendoza, Archbishop of Toledo and Grand Cardinal of Spain. This was the most important personage about the court, and was facetiously called by Peter Martyr the 'third king of Spain'. The king and queen had him always by their side, in peace and war. He accompanied them in their campaigns, and they never took any measures of consequence without consulting him. He was a man of sound judgment and quick intellect, eloquent in conversation, and able in the despatch of business. His appearance was lofty and venerable; he was simple yet curiously nice in his apparel, and of gracious and gentle deportment. Though an elegant scholar, yet, like many learned men of his day, he was but little skilled in cosmography. When the theory of Columbus was first mentioned to him, it struck him as involving heterodox opinions, incompatible with the form of the earth as described in the sacred Scriptures. Further explanations had their force with a man of his quick apprehension and sound sense. He perceived at any rate there could be nothing irreligious in attempting to extend the bounds of human knowledge and to ascertain the works of creation. His scruples once removed, he permitted Columbus to be introduced to him, and gave him a courteous reception. The latter knew the importance of his auditor, and that a conference with the grand cardinal was almost equivalent to a communication with the throne. He exerted himself to the utmost, therefore, to explain and demonstrate his proposition. The clear-headed cardinal listened with profound attention. He was pleased with the noble and earnest manner of Columbus, which showed him to be no common schemer. He felt the grandeur and at the same time the simplicity of his theory, and the force of many of the arguments by which it was supported. He determined that it was a matter highly worthy of the consideration of the sovereigns, and through his representations Columbus at length obtained admission to the royal presence.[*]

We have but scanty particulars of this audience, nor can we ascertain whether Queen Isabella was present on the occasion. The contrary seems to be most probably the case. Columbus appeared in the royal presence with modesty yet self-possession, neither dazzled nor daunted by the splendour of the court or the awful majesty of the throne. He unfolded his plan with eloquence and zeal, for he felt himself, as he afterwards declared, kindled as with a fire from on high, and considered himself the agent chosen by Heaven to accomplish its grand designs.[†]

Ferdinand was too keen a judge of men not to appreciate the character of Columbus. He perceived that, however soaring might be his imagination, and vast and visionary his views, his scheme had scientific and practical foundation. His ambition was excited by the possibility of discoveries far more important than those which had shed such glory upon Portugal; and perhaps it was not the least recommendation of the enterprise to this subtle and grasping monarch, that, if successful, it would enable him to forestall that rival nation in the fruits of their long and arduous struggle, and by opening a direct course to India across the ocean, to bear off from them the monopoly of Oriental commerce.

[*] Oviedo, lib. ii. cap 4; Salazar, *Cron. G. Cardinal.*, lib. i. cap. 62.
[†] Letter to the sovereigns in 1501.

Still, as usual, Ferdinand was cool and wary, and would not trust his own judgment in a matter that involved so many principles and science. He determined to take the opinion of the most learned men in the kingdom, and to be guided by their decision. Fernando de Talavera, prior of the monastery of Prado and confessor of the queen, one of the most erudite men of Spain, and high in the royal confidence, was commanded to assemble the most learned astronomers and cosmographers for the purpose of holding a conference with Columbus, and examining him as to the grounds on which he founded his proposition. After they had informed themselves fully on the subject, they were to consult together, and make a report to the sovereign of their collective opinion.*

* *Hist. del Almirante*, cap. 11.

CHAPTER 3
1486

The interesting conference relative to the proposition of Columbus took place in Salamanca, the great seat of learning in Spain. It was held in the Dominican convent of St Stephen, in which he was lodged and entertained with great hospitality during the course of the examination.*

Religion and science were at that time, and more especially in that country, closely associated. The treasures of learning were immured in monasteries, and the professors' chairs were exclusively filled from the cloister. The domination of the clergy extended over the state as well as the church, and posts of honour and influence at court, with the exception of hereditary nobles, were almost entirely confined to ecclesiastics. It was even common to find cardinals and bishops in helm and corselet at the head of armies; for the crosier had been occasionally thrown by for the lance during the holy war against the Moors. The era was distinguished for the revival of learning, but still more for the prevalence of religious zeal, and Spain surpassed all other countries of Christendom in the fervour of her devotion. The Inquisition had just been established in that kingdom, and every opinion that savoured of heresy made its owner obnoxious to odium and persecution.

Such was the period when a council of clerical sages was convened in the collegiate convent of St Stephen to investigate the new theory of Columbus. It was composed of professors of astronomy, geography, mathematics, and other branches of science, together with various dignitaries of the church, and learned friars. Before this erudite assembly Columbus presented himself to propound and defend his conclusions. He had been scoffed at as a visionary by the vulgar and the ignorant; but he was

* *Hist. de Chiapa*, por Remesal, lib. ii cap. 27.

convinced that he only required a body of enlightened men to listen dispassionately to his reasonings to ensure triumphant conviction.

The greater part of this learned junto, it is very probable, came prepossessed against him, as men in place and dignity are apt to be against poor applicants. There is always a proneness to consider a man under examination as a kind of delinquent or impostor, whose faults and errors are to be detected and exposed. Columbus, too, appeared in a most unfavourable light before a scholastic body: an obscure navigator, a member of no learned institution, destitute of all the trappings and circumstances which sometimes gives oracular authority to dullness, and depending upon the mere force of natural genius. Some of the junto entertained the popular notion that he was an adventurer, or at best a visionary; and others had that morbid impatience of any innovation upon established doctrine which is apt to grow upon dull and pedantic men in cloistered life.

What a striking spectacle must the hall of the old convent have presented at this memorable conference – a simple mariner, standing forth in the midst of an imposing array of professors, friars, and dignitaries of the church; maintaining his theory with natural eloquence, and, as it were, pleading the cause of the New World. We are told that when he began to state the grounds of his belief, the friars of St Stephen alone paid attention to him,* that convent being more learned in the sciences than the rest of the university. The others appear to have intrenched themselves behind one dogged position – that after so many profound philosophers and cosmographers had been studying the form of the world, and so many able navigators had been sailing about it for several thousand years, it was great presumption in an ordinary man to suppose that there remained such a vast discovery for him to make.

Several of the objections proposed by this learned body have been handed down to us, and have provoked many a sneer at the expense of the University of Salamanca; but they are proofs, not so much of the peculiar deficiency of that institution, as of the imperfect state of science at the time, and the manner in which knowledge, though rapidly extending, was still impeded in its progress by monastic bigotry. All subjects were still contemplated through the obscure medium of those ages, when the lights of antiquity were trampled

* Remesal, *Hist. de Chiapa*, lib. xi. cap. 7.

out and faith was left to fill the place of inquiry. Bewildered in a maze of religious controversy, mankind had retraced their steps and receded from the boundary line of ancient knowledge. Thus, at the very threshold of the discussion, instead of geographical objections, Columbus was assailed with citations from the Bible and the Testament – the book of Genesis, the Psalms of David, the prophets, the epistles, and the gospels. To these were added the expositions of various saints and reverend commentators – St Chrysostom and St Augustine, St Jerome and St Gregory, St Basil and St Ambrose, and Lactantius Firmianus, a redoubted champion of the faith. Doctrinal points were mixed up with philosophical discussions, and a mathematical demonstration was allowed no weight if it appeared to clash with a text of Scripture or a commentary of one of the fathers. Thus the possibility of antipodes in the southern hemisphere, an opinion so generally maintained by the wisest of the ancients as to be pronounced by Pliny the great contest between the learned and the ignorant, became a stumbling-block with some of the sages of Salamanca. Several of them stoutly contradicted this fundamental position of Columbus, supporting themselves by quotations from Lactantius and St Augustine, who were considered in those days as almost evangelical authority. But though these writers were men of consummate erudition, and two of the greatest luminaries of what has been called the golden age of ecclesiastical learning, yet their writings were calculated to perpetuate darkness in respect to the sciences.

The passage cited from Lactantius to confute Columbus is in a strain of gross ridicule, unworthy of so grave a theologian. 'Is there any one so foolish,' he asks, 'as to believe that there are antipodes with their feet opposite to ours – people who walk with their heels upward and their heads hanging down; that there is a part of the world in which all things are topsy-turvy – where the trees grow with their branches downward, and where it rains, hails, and snows upward? The idea of the roundness of the earth,' he adds, 'was the cause of inventing this fable of the antipodes, with their heels in the air; for these philosophers having once erred, go on in their absurdities, defending one with another.'

Objections of a graver nature were advanced on the authority of St Augustine. He pronounces the doctrine of antipodes to be incompatible with the historical foundations of our faith; since to assert that there were inhabited lands on the opposite side of the globe would be to maintain that there were nations not descended from Adam, it being impossible for them to have passed the intervening ocean. This would be therefore to discredit the Bible, which expressly declares that all men are descended from one common parent.

Such were the unlooked-for prejudices which Columbus had to encounter at the very outset of his conference, and which certainly savour more of the convent than the university. To his simplest proposition, the spherical form of the earth, were opposed figurative texts of Scripture. They observed that in the Psalms the heavens are said to be extended like a hide* – that is, according to commentators, the curtain or covering of a tent, which, among the ancient pastoral nations, was formed of the hides of animals – and that St Paul, in his Epistle to the Hebrews, compares the heavens to a tabernacle, or tent, extended over the earth, which they thence inferred must be flat.

Columbus, who was a devoutly religious man, found that he was in danger of being convicted, not merely of error, but of heterodoxy. Others more versed in science admitted the globular form of the earth, and the possibility of an opposite and habitable hemisphere; but they brought up the chimera of the ancients, and maintained that it would be impossible to arrive there, in consequence of the insupportable heat of the torrid zone. Even granting this could be passed, they observed that the circumference of the earth must be so great as to require at least three years to the voyage, and those who should undertake it must perish of hunger and thirst, from the impossibility of carrying provisions for so long a period. He was told, on the authority of Epicurus, that, admitting the earth to be spherical, it was only inhabitable in the northern hemisphere, and in that section only was canopied by the heavens; that the opposite half was a chaos, a gulf, or a mere waste of water. Not the least absurd objection advanced was that should a ship even succeed in reaching, in this way, the extremity of India, she could never get back again; for the rotundity of the globe would present a kind of mountain, up which it would be impossible for her to sail with the most favourable wind.†

* 'Extendens coelum sicut pellem' (Ps. ciii). In the English translation it is Ps. civ. 3.
† *Hist. del Almirante*, cap. 11.

Such are specimens of the errors and prejudices, the mingled
ignorance and erudition and the pedantic bigotry, with which
Columbus had to contend throughout the examination of his
theory. Can we wonder at the difficulties and delays which he
experienced at courts, when such vague and crude notions were
entertained by the learned men of a university? We must not
suppose, however, because the objections here cited are all which
remain on record, that they are all which were advanced; these
only have been perpetuated on account of their superior absurdity.
They were probably advanced by but few, and those persons
immersed in theological studies, in cloistered retirement, where
the erroneous opinions derived from books had little opportunity
of being corrected by the experience of the day.

There were no doubt objections advanced more cogent in their
nature and more worthy of that distinguished university. It is but
justice to add, also, that the replies of Columbus had great weight
with many of his learned examiners. In answer to the Scriptural
objections, he submitted that the inspired writers were not speaking technically as cosmographers, but figuratively, in language
addressed to all comprehensions. The commentaries of the fathers
he treated with deference as pious homilies, but not as philosophical propositions which it was necessary either to admit or
refute. The objections drawn from ancient philosophers he met
boldly and ably upon equal terms, for he was deeply studied on all
points of cosmography. He showed that the most illustrious of
those sages believed both hemispheres to be inhabitable, though
they imagined that the torrid zone precluded communication; and
he obviated conclusively that difficulty, for he had voyaged to St
George la Miña in Guinea, almost under the equinoctial line, and
had found that region not merely traversable, but abounding in
population, in fruits, and pasturage.

When Columbus took his stand before this learned body, he had
appeared the plain and simple navigator, somewhat daunted, perhaps, by the greatness of his task and the august nature of his
auditory. But he had a degree of religious feeling which gave him a
confidence in the execution of what he conceived his great errand,
and he was of an ardent temperament that became heated in action
by its own generous fires. Las Casas, and others of his contemporaries, have spoken of his commanding person, his elevated

demeanour, his air of authority, his kindling eye, and the persuasive intonations of his voice. How must they have given majesty and force to his words as, casting aside his maps and charts, and discarding for a time his practical and scientific lore, his visionary spirit took fire at the doctrinal objections of his opponents, and he met them upon their own ground, pouring forth those magnificent texts of Scripture and those mysterious predictions of the prophets which, in his enthusiastic moments, he considered as types and annunciations of the sublime discovery which he proposed!

Among the number who were convinced by the reasoning and warmed by the eloquence of Columbus was Diego de Deza, a worthy and learned friar of the order of St Dominic, at that time professor of theology in the convent of St Stephen, but who became afterwards Archbishop of Seville, the second ecclesiastical dignitary of Spain. This able and erudite divine was a man whose mind was above the narrow bigotry of bookish lore – one who could appreciate the value of wisdom even when uttered by unlearned lips. He was not a mere passive auditor; he took a generous interest in the cause, and by seconding Columbus with all his powers, calmed the blind zeal of his more bigoted brethren, so as to obtain for him a dispassionate if not an unprejudiced hearing. By their united efforts, it is said, they brought over the most learned men of the schools.* One great difficulty was to reconcile the plan of Columbus with the cosmography of Ptolemy, to which all scholars yielded implicit faith. How would the most enlightened of those sages have been astonished had anyone apprised them that the man, Copernicus, was then in existence, whose solar system should reverse the grand theory of Ptolemy, which stationed the earth in the centre of the universe!

Notwithstanding every exertion, however, there was a preponderating mass of inert bigotry and learned pride in this erudite body which refused to yield to the demonstrations of an obscure foreigner, without fortune or connections or any academic honours. 'It was requisite,' says Las Casas, 'before Columbus could make his solutions and reasonings understood, that he should remove from his auditors those erroneous principles on which their objections were founded – a task always more difficult than that of teaching the doctrine.' Occasional conferences took place,

* Remesal, *Hist. de Chiapa*, lib. xi. cap. 7.

but without producing any decision. The ignorant, or what is worse, the prejudiced, remained obstinate in their opposition, with the dogged perseverance of dull men; the more liberal and intelligent felt little interest in discussions wearisome in themselves and foreign to their ordinary pursuits; even those who listened with approbation to the plan regarded it only as a delightful vision, full of probability and promise, but one which never could be realized. Fernando de Talavera, to whom the matter was especially intrusted, had too little esteem for it, and was too much occupied with the stir and bustle of public concerns, to press it to a conclusion; and thus the inquiry experienced continual procrastination and neglect.

The Castilian court departed from Salamanca early in the spring of 1487, and repaired to Cordova, to prepare for the memorable campaign against Malaga. Fernando de Talavera, now Bishop of Avila, accompanied the queen as her confessor, and as one of her spiritual counsellors in the concerns of the war. The consultations of the board at Salamanca were interrupted by this event before that learned body could come to a decision; and for a long time Columbus was kept in suspense, vainly awaiting the report that was to decide the fate of his application.

It has generally been supposed that the several years which he wasted in irksome solicitation were spent in the drowsy and monotonous attendance of antechambers; but it appears, on the contrary, that they were often passed amidst scenes of peril and adventure, and that, in following up his suit, he was led into some of the most striking situations of this wild, rugged, and mountainous war. Several times he was summoned to attend conferences in the vicinity of the sovereigns, when besieging cities in the very heart of the Moorish dominions; but the tempest of warlike affairs, which hurried the court from place to place, and gave it all the bustle and confusion of a camp, prevented those conferences from taking place, and swept away all concerns that were not immediately connected with the war. Whenever the court had an interval of leisure and repose, there would again be manifested a disposition to consider his proposal; but the hurry and tempest would again return, and the question be again swept away.

The spring campaign of 1487, which took place shortly after the conference at Salamanca, was full of incident and peril. King Ferdinand had nearly been surprised and cut off by the old Moorish monarch before Velez Malaga, and the queen and all the court at Cordova were for a time in an agony of terror and suspense until assured of his safety.

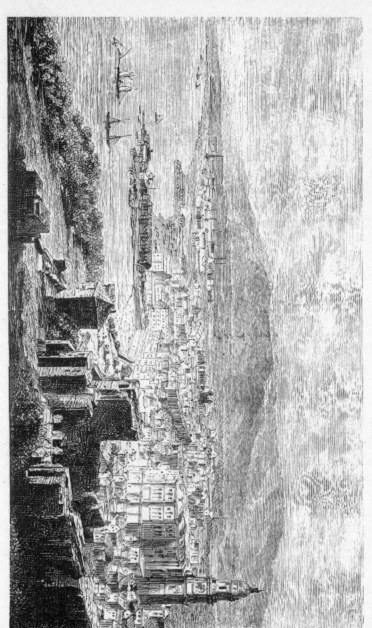

Malaga

When the sovereigns were subsequently encamped before the city of Malaga, pressing its memorable siege, Columbus was summoned to the court. He found it drawn up in its silken pavilions on a rising ground commanding the fertile valley of Malaga. The encampments of the warlike nobility of Spain extended in a semicircle on each side, to the shores of the sea, strongly fortified, glittering with the martial pomp of that chivalrous age and nation, and closely investing that important city.

The siege was protracted for several months, but the vigorous defence of the Moors, their numerous stratagems and fierce and frequent sallies, allowed but little leisure in the camp. In the course of this siege the application of Columbus to the sovereigns was nearly brought to a violent close, a fanatic Moor having attempted to assassinate Ferdinand and Isabella. Mistaking one of the gorgeous pavilions of the nobility for the royal tent, he attacked Don Alvaro de Portugal and Doña Beatrix de Bobadilla, Marchioness of Moya, instead of the king and queen. After wounding Don Alvaro dangerously, he was foiled in a blow aimed at the marchioness, and immediately cut to pieces by the attendants.[*] The lady here mentioned was of extraordinary merit and force of character. She eventually took a great interest in the suit of Columbus, and had much influence in recommending it to the queen, with whom she was a particular favourite.[†]

Malaga surrendered on the 18th of August 1487. There appears to have been no time during its stormy siege to attend to the question of Columbus, though Fernando de Talavera, the Bishop of Avila, was present, as appears by his entering the captured city in solemn and religious triumph. The campaign being ended, the court returned to Cordova, but was almost immediately driven from that city by the pestilence.

For upwards of a year the court was in a state of continual migration – part of the time in Saragossa, part of the time invading the Moorish territories by the way of Murcia, and part of the time in Valladolid and Medina del Campo. Columbus attended it in some of its movements, but it was vain to seek a quiet and attentive hearing from a court surrounded by the din of arms and continually on the march. Wearied and discouraged by these

[*] Pulgar, *Cronica*, cap. 87. P. Martyr.
[†] *Retrato del Buen Vassallo*, lib. ii. cap. 16.

delays, he began to think of applying elsewhere for patronage, and appears to have commenced negotiations with King John II for a return to Portugal. He wrote to that monarch on the subject, and received a letter in reply dated 20th March 1488, inviting him to return to his court, and assuring him of protection from any suits of either a civil or criminal nature that might be pending against him. He received also a letter from Henry VII of England, inviting him to that country, and holding out promises of encouragement.

There must have been strong hopes, authorized about this time by the conduct of the Spanish sovereigns, to induce Columbus to neglect these invitations; and we find ground for such a supposition in a memorandum of a sum of money paid to him by the treasurer Gonzalez, to enable him to comply with a summons to attend the Castilian court. By the date of this memorandum the payment must have been made immediately after Columbus had received the letter of the King of Portugal. It would seem to have been the aim of King Ferdinand to prevent his carrying his proposition to another and a rival monarch, and to keep the matter in suspense until he should have leisure to examine it, and if advisable, to carry it into operation.

In the spring of 1489 the long-adjourned investigation appeared to be on the eve of taking place. Columbus was summoned to attend a conference of learned men, to be held in the city of Seville. A royal order was issued for lodgings to be provided for him there, and the magistrates of all cities and towns through which he might pass on his way were commanded to furnish accommodations gratis for himself and his attendants. A provision of the kind was necessary in those days, when even the present wretched establishments, called posadas, for the reception of travellers, were scarcely known.

The city of Seville complied with the royal command; but as usual the appointed conference was postponed, being interrupted by the opening of a campaign, 'in which,' says an old chronicler of the place, 'the same Columbus was found fighting, giving proofs of the distinguished valour which accompanied his wisdom and his lofty desires.' *

The campaign in which Columbus is here said to have borne so honourable a part was one of the most glorious of the war of

* Diego Ortiz de Zuñiga, *Ann. de Sevilla*, lib. xii., anno 1489, p. 404.

Granada. Queen Isabella attended with all her court, including as usual a stately train of prelates and friars, among whom is particularly mentioned the procrastinating arbiter of the pretensions of Columbus, Fernando de Talavera. Much of the success of the campaign is ascribed to the presence and counsel of Isabella. The city of Baza, which was closely besieged, and had resisted valiantly for upwards of six months, surrendered soon after her arrival; and on the 22nd of December, Columbus beheld Muley Boabdil, the elder of the two rival kings of Granada, surrender in person all his remaining possessions, and his right to the crown, to the Spanish sovereigns.

During this siege a circumstance took place which appears to have made a deep impression on the devout and enthusiastic spirit of Columbus. Two reverend friars arrived one day at the Spanish camp, and requested admission to the sovereigns on business of great moment. They were two of the brethren of the convent established at the Holy Sepulchre at Jerusalem. They brought a message from the Grand Soldan of Egypt, threatening to put to death all the Christians in his dominions, to lay waste their convents and churches, and to destroy the sepulchre, if the sovereigns did not desist from the war against Granada. The menace had no effect in altering the purpose of the sovereigns; but Isabella granted a yearly and perpetual sum of one thousand ducats in gold[*] for the support of the monks who had charge of the sepulchre, and sent a veil, embroidered with her own hands, to be hung up at its shrine.[†]

The representations of these friars of the sufferings and indignities to which Christians were subjected in the Holy Land, together with the arrogant threat of the Soldan, roused the pious indignation of the Spanish cavaliers, and many burned with ardent zeal once more to revive the contests of the faith on the sacred plains of Palestine. It was probably from conversation with these friars, and from the pious and chivalrous zeal thus awakened in the warrior throng around him, that Columbus first conceived an enthusiastic idea, or rather made a kind of mental vow, which remained more or less present to his mind until the very day of his death. He determined that should his projected enterprise be successful, he

---

[*] Or 1,423 dollars, equivalent to 4,269 dollars in our time.
[†] Garibay, *Compend. Hist.*, lib. xviii. cap. 36.

would devote the profits arising from his anticipated discoveries
to a crusade for the rescue of the Holy Sepulchre from the power
of the Infidels.

If the bustle and turmoil of this campaign prevented the intended conference, the concerns of Columbus fared no better
during the subsequent rejoicings. Ferdinand and Isabella entered
Seville in February 1490 with great pomp and triumph. There
were then preparations made for the marriage of their eldest
daughter, the Princess Isabella, with the Prince Don Alonzo,
heir-apparent of Portugal. The nuptials were celebrated in the
month of April with extraordinary splendour. Throughout the
whole winter and spring the court was in a continual tumult of
parade and pleasure, and nothing was to be seen at Seville but
feasts, tournaments, and torch-light processions. What chance
had Columbus of being heard amid these alternate uproars of
war and festivity?

During this long course of solicitation he supported himself in
part by making maps and charts, and was occasionally assisted by
the purse of the worthy friar Diego de Deza. It is due to the
sovereigns to say, also, that whenever he was summoned to follow
the movements of the court, or to attend any appointed consultation, he was attached to the royal suite, and lodgings were
provided for him and sums issued to defray his expenses. Memorandums of several of these sums still exist in the book of accounts
of the royal treasurer, Francisco Gonzalez of Seville, which has
lately been found in the archives of Simancas; and it is from
these minutes that we have been enabled, in some degree, to
follow the movements of Columbus during his attendance upon
this rambling and warlike court.

During all this time he was exposed to continual scoffs and
indignities, being ridiculed by the light and ignorant as a mere
dreamer, and stigmatized by the illiberal as an adventurer. The
very children, it is said, pointed to their foreheads as he passed,
being taught to regard him as a kind of madman.

The summer of 1490 passed away, but still Columbus was
kept in tantalizing and tormenting suspense. The subsequent
winter was not more propitious. He was lingering at Cordova
in a state of irritating anxiety, when he learned that the sovereigns were preparing to depart on a campaign in the Vega of

Granada, with a determination never to raise their camp from before that city until their victorious banners should float upon its towers.

Columbus was aware that when once the campaign was opened and the sovereigns were in the field, it would be in vain to expect any attention to his suit. He was wearied, if not incensed, at the repeated postponements he had experienced, by which several years had been consumed. He now pressed for a decisive reply with an earnestness that would not admit of evasion. Fernando de Talavera, therefore, was called upon by the sovereigns to hold a definitive conference with the scientific men to whom the project had been referred, and to make a report of their decision. The bishop tardily complied, and at length reported to their majesties, as the general opinion of the junto, that the proposed scheme was vain and impossible, and that it did not become such great princes to engage in an enterprise of the kind on such weak grounds as had been advanced.[*]

Notwithstanding this unfavourable report, the sovereigns were unwilling to close the door upon a project which might be productive of such important advantages. Many of the learned members of the junto also were in its favour, particularly Fray Diego de Deza, tutor to Prince Juan, who from his situation and clerical character had access to the royal ear, and exerted himself strenuously in counteracting the decision of the board. A degree of consideration, also, had gradually grown up at court for the enterprise, and many men distinguished for rank and merit had become its advocates. Fernando de Talavera, therefore, was commanded to inform Columbus, who was still at Cordova, that the great cares and expenses of the wars rendered it impossible for the sovereigns to engage in any new enterprise; but that when the war was concluded they would have both time and inclination to treat with him about what he proposed.[†]

This was but a starved reply to receive after so many days of weary attendance, anxious expectation, and deferred hope. Columbus was unwilling to receive it at second hand, and repaired to the court at Seville to learn his fate from the lips of the sovereigns. Their reply was virtually the same, declining to engage in the enterprise for the

[*] *Hist. del Almirante*, cap. 2.
[†] *Hist. del Almirante*, cap. 2.

present, but holding out hopes of patronage when relieved from the cares and expenses of the war.

Columbus looked upon this indefinite postponement as a mere courtly mode of evading his importunity, and supposed that the favourable dispositions of the sovereigns had been counteracted by the objections of the ignorant and bigoted. Renouncing all further confidence, therefore, in vague promises, which had so often led to disappointment, and giving up all hopes of countenance from the throne, he turned his back upon Seville, indignant at the thoughts of having been beguiled out of so many precious years of waning existence.

CHAPTER 5

About half a league from the little sea-port of Palos de Moguer, in Andalusia, there stood, and continues to stand at the present day, an ancient convent of Franciscan friars, dedicated to Santa Maria de Rabida. One day a stranger on foot, in humble guise, but of a distinguished air, accompanied by a small boy, stopped at the gate of the convent, and asked of the porter a little bread and water for his child. While receiving this humble refreshment, the prior of the convent, Juan Perez de Marchena, happening to pass by, was struck with the appearance of the stranger, and observing from his air and accent that he was a foreigner, entered into conversation with him, and soon learned the particulars of his story. That stranger was Columbus.* He was on his way to the neighbouring town of Huelva, to seek his brother-in-law, who had married a sister of his deceased wife.†

The prior was a man of extensive information. His attention had been turned in some measure to geographical and nautical science, probably from his vicinity to Palos, the inhabitants of which were among the most enterprising navigators of Spain, and made frequent voyages to the recently discovered islands and countries on the African coast. He was greatly interested by the conversation of Columbus, and struck with the grandeur of his views. It was a remarkable occurrence in the monotonous life of the cloister, to have a man of such singular character, intent on so extraordinary an enterprise, applying for bread and water at the gate of his convent.

* 'Lo dicho Almirante Colon veniendo á la Rabida, que es un monastério de frailes en esta villa, el cual demandó á la porteria que le diesen para aquel niñico, que era niño, pan i agua que bebiese.' The testimony of Garcia Fernandez exists in manuscript among the multifarious writings of the Pleito or lawsuit, which are preserved at Seville. I have made use of an authenticated extract, copied for the late historian, Juan Baut. Muñoz.

† Probably Pedro Correo, already mentioned, from whom he had received information of signs of land in the west, observed near Puerto Santo.

When he found, however, that the voyager was on the point of abandoning Spain to seek patronage in the court of France, and that so important an enterprise was about to be lost for ever to the country, the patriotism of the good friar took the alarm. He detained Columbus as his guest, and diffident of his own judgment, sent for a scientific friend to converse with him. That friend was Garcia Fernandez, a physician, resident in Palos, the same who furnishes this interesting testimony. Fernandez was equally struck with the appearance and conversation of the stranger. Several conferences took place at the convent, at which several of the veteran mariners of Palos were present. Among these was Martin Alonzo Pinzon, the head of a family of wealthy and experienced navigators of the place, celebrated for their adventurous expeditions. Facts were related by some of these navigators in support of the theory of Columbus. In a word, his project was treated with a deference in the quiet cloisters of La Rabida, and among the seafaring men of Palos, which had been sought in vain among the sages and philosophers of the court. Martin Alonzo Pinzon, especially, was so convinced of its feasibility that he offered to engage in it with purse and person, and to bear the expenses of Columbus in a renewed application to the court.

Friar Juan Perez was confirmed in his faith by the concurrence of those learned and practical councillors. He had once been confessor to the queen, and knew that she was always accessible to persons of his sacred calling. He proposed to write to her immediately on the subject, and entreated Columbus to delay his journey until an answer could be received. The latter was easily persuaded, for he felt as if, in leaving Spain, he was again abandoning his home. He was also reluctant to renew, in another court, the vexations and disappointments experienced in Spain and Portugal.

The little council at the convent of La Rabida now cast round their eyes for an ambassador to depart upon this momentous mission. They chose one Sebastian Rodriguez, a pilot of Lepe, one of the most shrewd and important personages in this maritime neighbourhood. The queen was at this time at Santa Fé, the military city which had been built in the Vega before Granada, after the conflagration of the royal camp. The honest pilot acquitted himself faithfully, expeditiously, and successfully, in his embassy. He found access to the benignant princess, and delivered the epistle of the friar. Isabella had always been favourably disposed to the proposition of Columbus. She wrote in reply to Juan Perez, thanking him for his timely services, and requesting that he would repair immediately to the court, leaving Christopher Columbus in confident hope until he should hear further from her. This royal letter was brought back by the pilot at the end of fourteen days, and spread great joy in the little junto at the convent. No sooner did the warm-hearted friar receive it, than he saddled his mule, and departed privately, before midnight, for the court. He journeyed through the conquered countries of the Moors, and rode into the newly erected city of Santa Fé, where the sovereigns were superintending the close investment of the capital of Granada.

The sacred office of Juan Perez gained him a ready entrance in a court distinguished for religious zeal; and, once admitted to the presence of the queen, his former relation, as father confessor, gave him great freedom of counsel. He pleaded the cause of Columbus with characteristic enthusiasm, speaking, from actual knowledge, of his honourable motives, his professional knowledge and experience, and his perfect capacity to fulfil the undertaking. He represented the solid principles upon which the enterprise was founded, the advantage that must attend its success, and the glory it must shed upon the Spanish crown. It is probable that Isabella had never heard the proposition urged with such honest zeal and impressive eloquence. Being naturally more sanguine and susceptible than the king, and more open to warm and generous impulses, she was moved by the representations of Juan Perez, which were warmly seconded by her favourite, the Marchioness of Moya, who entered into the affair with a woman's disinterested enthusiasm.* The queen requested that Columbus might be again sent to her, and, with the kind considerateness which characterized her, bethinking herself of his poverty and his humble plight, ordered that twenty thousand maravedies† in florins should be forwarded to him, to bear his travelling expenses, to provide him with a mule for his journey, and to furnish him with decent raiment, that he might make a respectable appearance at the court.

The worthy friar lost no time in communicating the result of his mission; he transmitted the money and a letter, by the hands of an

---

* *Retrato del Buen Vassallo*, lib. ii. cap. 16.

† Or 72 dollars, and equivalent to 216 dollars of the present day.

inhabitant of Palos, to the physician Garcia Fernandez, who delivered them to Columbus. The latter complied with the instructions
conveyed in the epistle. He exchanged his threadbare garb for one
more suited to the sphere of a court, and, purchasing a mule, set out
once more, reanimated by hopes, for the camp before Granada.*

* Most of the particulars of this visit of Columbus to the convent of La Rabida are
from the testimony rendered by Garcia Fernandez in the lawsuit between Diego,
the son of Columbus, and the crown.

CHAPTER 6

1492

When Columbus arrived at the court he experienced a favourable reception, and was given in hospitable charge to his steady friend Alonzo de Quintanilla, the accountant-general. The moment, however, was too eventful for his business to receive immediate attention. He arrived in time to witness the memorable surrender of Granada to the Spanish arms. He beheld Boabdil, the last of the Moorish kings, sally forth from the Alhambra, and yield up the keys of that favourite seat of Moorish power; while the king and queen, with all the chivalry and rank and magnificence of Spain, moved forward in proud and solemn procession to receive this token of submission. It was one of the most brilliant triumphs in Spanish history. After near eight hundred years of painful struggle, the Crescent was completely cast down, the Cross exalted in its place, and the standard of Spain was seen floating on the highest tower of the Alhambra. The whole court and army were abandoned to jubilee. The air resounded with shouts of joy, with songs of triumph, and hymns of thanksgiving. On every side were beheld military rejoicings and religious oblations, for it was considered a triumph, not merely of arms, but of Christianity. The king and queen moved in the midst, in more than common magnificence, while every eye regarded them as more than mortal – as if sent by Heaven for the salvation and building up of Spain.[*] The court was thronged by the most illustrious of that warlike country and stirring era – by the flower of its nobility, by the most dignified of its prelacy, by bards and minstrels, and all the retinue of a romantic and picturesque age. There was nothing but the glittering of arms, the rustling of robes, the sound of music and festivity.

Do we want a picture of our navigator during this brilliant and triumphant scene? It is furnished by a Spanish writer: 'A man

[*] Mariana, *Hist. de España*, lib. xxv. cap. 18.

obscure and but little known followed at this time the court. Confounded in the crowd of importunate applicants, feeding his imagination in the corners of antechambers with the pompous project of discovering a world, melancholy and dejected in the midst of the general rejoicing, he beheld with indifference, and almost with contempt, the conclusion of a conquest which swelled all bosoms with jubilee, and seemed to have reached the utmost bounds of desire. That man was Christopher Columbus.'*

The moment had now arrived, however, when the monarchs stood pledged to attend to his proposals. The war with the Moors was at an end. Spain was delivered from its intruders, and its sovereigns might securely turn their views to foreign enterprise. They kept their word with Columbus. Persons of confidence were appointed to negotiate with him, among whom was Fernando de Talavera, who, by the recent conquest, had risen to be Archbishop of Granada. At the very outset of their negotiation, however, unexpected difficulties arose. So fully imbued was Columbus with the grandeur of his enterprise, that he would listen to none but princely conditions. His principal stipulation was that he should be invested with the titles and privileges of admiral and viceroy over the countries he should discover, with one-tenth of all gains, either by trade or conquest. The courtiers who treated with him were indignant at such a demand. Their pride was shocked to see one whom they had considered as a needy adventurer aspiring to rank and dignities superior to their own. One observed with a sneer that it was a shrewd arrangement which he proposed, whereby he was secure, at all events, of the honour of a command, and had nothing to lose in case of failure. To this Columbus promptly replied by offering to furnish one-eighth of the cost, on condition of enjoying an eighth of the profits. To do this, he no doubt calculated on the proffered assistance of Martin Alonzo Pinzon, the wealthy navigator of Palos.

His terms, however, were pronounced inadmissible. Fernando de Talavera had always considered Columbus a dreaming speculator, or a needy applicant for bread; but to see this man, who had for years been an indigent and threadbare solicitor in his antechamber, assuming so lofty a tone, and claiming an office that approached to the awful dignity of the throne, excited the

* Clemencin, *Elogio de la Reina Catholica*, p. 20.

astonishment as well as the indignation of the prelate. He represented to Isabella that it would be degrading to the dignity of so illustrious a crown to lavish such distinguished honours upon a nameless stranger. Such terms, he observed, even in case of success, would be exorbitant; but in case of failure, would be cited with ridicule, as evidence of the gross credulity of the Spanish monarchs.

Isabella was always attentive to the opinions of her ghostly advisers, and the archbishop, being her confessor, had peculiar influence. His suggestions checked her dawning favour. She thought the proposed advantages might be purchased at too great a price. More moderate conditions were offered to Columbus, and such as appeared highly honourable and advantageous. It was all in vain; he would not cede one point of his demands, and the nogotiation was broken off.

It is impossible not to admire the great constancy of purpose and loftiness of spirit displayed by Columbus ever since he had conceived the sublime idea of his discovery. More than eighteen years had elapsed since his correspondence with Paulo Toscanelli of Florence, wherein he had announced his design. The greatest part of that time had been consumed in applications at various courts. During that period, what poverty, neglect, ridicule, contumely, and disappointment had he not suffered! Nothing, however, could shake his perseverance, nor make him descend to terms which he considered beneath the dignity of his enterprise. In all his negotiations he forgot his present obscurity, he forgot his present indigence; his ardent imagination realized the magnitude of his contemplated discoveries, and he felt himself negotiating about empire.

Though so large a portion of his life had worn away in fruitless solicitings, though there was no certainty that the same weary career was not to be entered upon at any other court, yet so indignant was he at the repeated disappointments he had experienced in Spain, that he determined to abandon it for ever rather than compromise his demands. Taking leave of his friends, therefore, he mounted his mule, and sallied forth from Santa Fé in the beginning of February 1492, on his way to Cordova, whence he intended to depart immediately for France.

When the few friends who were zealous believers in the theory of Columbus saw him really on the point of abandoning the country, they were filled with distress, considering his departure an irreparable loss to the nation. Among the number was Luis de St Angel, receiver of the ecclesiastical revenues in Aragon. Determined if possible to avert the evil, he obtained an immediate audience of the queen, accompanied by Alonzo de Quintanilla. The exigency of the moment gave him courage and eloquence. He did not confine himself to entreaties, but almost mingled reproaches, expressing astonishment that a queen who had evinced the spirit to undertake so many great and perilous enterprises, should hesitate at one where the loss could be so trifling, while the gain might be incalculable. He reminded her how much might be done for the glory of God, the exaltation of the church, and the extension of her own power and dominion. What cause of regret to herself, of triumph to her enemies, of sorrow to her friends, should this enterprise, thus rejected by her, be accomplished by some other power! He reminded her what fame and dominion other princes had acquired by their discoveries; here was an opportunity to surpass them all. He entreated her majesty not to be misled by the assertions of learned men, that the project was the dream of a visionary. He vindicated the judgment of Columbus, and the soundness and practicability of his plans. Neither would even his failure reflect disgrace upon the crown. It was worth the trouble and expense to clear up even a doubt upon a matter of such importance; for it belonged to enlightened and magnanimous princes to investigate questions of the kind, and to explore the wonders and secrets of the universe. He stated the liberal offer of Columbus to bear an eighth of the expense, and informed her that all the requisites for this great enterprise consisted but of two vessels, and about three thousand crowns.

These and many more arguments were urged with that persuasive power which honest zeal imparts; and it is said the Marchioness of Moya, who was present, exerted her eloquence to persuade the queen. The generous spirit of Isabella was enkindled. It seemed as if, for the first time, the subject broke upon her mind in its real grandeur, and she declared her resolution to undertake the enterprise.

There was still a moment's hesitation. The king looked coldly on the affair, and the royal finances were absolutely drained by the war. Some time must be given to replenish them. How could she draw on an exhausted treasury for a measure to which the king was adverse? St Angel watched this suspense with trembling anxiety. The next moment reassured him. With an enthusiasm worthy of herself and of the cause, Isabella exclaimed, 'I undertake the enterprise for my own crown of Castile, and will pledge my jewels to raise the necessary funds.' This was the proudest moment in the life of Isabella; it stamped her renown for ever as the patroness of the discovery of the New World.

St Angel, eager to secure this noble impulse, assured her majesty that there would be no need of pledging her jewels, as he was ready to advance the necessary funds. His offer was gladly accepted. The funds really came from the coffers of Aragon; seventeen thousand florins were advanced by the accountant of St Angel out of the treasury of King Ferdinand. That prudent monarch, however, took care to have his kingdom indemnified some few years afterwards; for in remuneration of this loan, a part of the first gold brought by Columbus from the New World was employed in gilding the vaults and ceilings of the royal saloon in the grand palace of Saragoza, in Aragon, anciently the Aljaferia, or abode of the Moorish kings.[*]

Columbus had pursued his lonely journey across the Vega and reached the bridge of Pinos, about two leagues from Granada, at the foot of the mountain of Elvira – a pass famous in the Moorish wars for many a desperate encounter between the Christians and Infidels. Here he was overtaken by a courier from the queen, spurring in all speed, who summoned him to return to Santa Fé. He hesitated for a moment, being loath to subject himself again to the delays and equivocations of the court. When informed, however, of the sudden zeal for the enterprise excited in the mind of the queen, and the positive promise she had given to undertake it, he no longer felt a doubt, but, turning the reins of his mule, hastened back with joyful alacrity to Santa Fé, confiding in the noble probity of that princess.

[*] Argensola, *Annales de Aragon*, lib. i. cap. 10.

On arriving at Santa Fé, Columbus had an immediate audience of the queen, and the benignity with which she received him atoned for all past neglect. Through deference to the zeal she thus suddenly displayed, the king yielded his tardy concurrence; but Isabella was the soul of this grand enterprise. She was prompted by lofty and generous enthusiasm, while the king proved cold and calculating in this as in all his other undertakings.

A perfect understanding being thus effected with the sovereigns, articles of agreement were ordered to be drawn out by Juan de Coloma, the royal secretary. They were to the following effect: —

1. That Columbus should have, for himself during his life, and his heirs and successors for ever, the office of admiral in all the lands and continents which he might discover or acquire in the ocean, with similar honours and prerogatives to those enjoyed by the high-admiral of Castile in his district.

2. That he should be viceroy and governor-general over all the said lands and continents; with the privilege of nominating three candidates for the government of each island or province, one of whom should be selected by the sovereigns.

3. That he should be entitled to reserve for himself one-tenth of all pearls, precious stones, gold, silver, spices, and all other articles and merchandises, in whatever manner found, bought, bartered, or gained within this admiralty, the costs being first deducted.

4. That he, or his lieutenant, should be the sole judge in all causes and disputes arising out of traffic between those countries and Spain, provided the high-admiral of Castile had similar jurisdiction in his district.

5. That he might then, and at all after times, contribute an eighth part of the expense in fitting out vessels to sail on this enterprise, and receive an eighth part of the profits.

The last stipulation, which admits Columbus to bear an eighth of the enterprise, was made in consequence of his indignant proffer, on being reproached with demanding ample emoluments while incurring no portion of the charge. He fulfilled this engagement, through the assistance of the Pinzons of Palos, and added a third vessel to the armament. Thus one-eighth of the expense attendant on this grand expedition, undertaken by a powerful nation, was actually borne by the individual who conceived it, and who likewise risked his life on its success.

The capitulations were signed by Ferdinand and Isabella, at the city of Santa Fé, in the Vega or plain of Granada, on the 17th of April, 1492. A letter of privilege, or commission to Columbus, of similar purport, was drawn out in form, and issued by the sovereigns in the city of Granada, on the thirtieth of the same month. In this, the dignities and prerogatives of viceroy and governor were made hereditary in his family; and he and his heirs were authorized to prefix the title of Don to their names – a distinction accorded in those days only to persons of rank and estate, though it has since lost all value from being universally used in Spain.

All the royal documents issued on this occasion bore equally the signatures of Ferdinand and Isabella, but her separate crown of Castile defrayed all the expense; and during her life few persons except Castilians were permitted to establish themselves in the new territories.*

The port of Palos de Moguer was fixed upon as the place where the armament was to be fitted out, Columbus calculating, no doubt, on the co-operation of Martin Alonzo Pinzon, resident there, and on the assistance of his zealous friend the prior of the convent of La Rabida. Before going into the business details of this great enterprise, it is due to the character of the illustrious man who conceived and conducted it most especially to notice the elevated even though visionary spirit by which he was actuated. One of his principal objects was undoubtedly the propagation of the Christian faith. He expected to arrive at the extremity of Asia, and to open a direct and easy communication with the vast and magnificent empire of the Grand Khan. The conversion of that heathen potentate had, in former times, been a favourite aim of

* Charlevoix, *Hist. St Domingo*, lib. i. p. 79.

various pontiffs and pious sovereigns, and various missions had
been sent to the remote regions of the East for that purpose.
Columbus now considered himself about to effect this great
work – to spread the light of revelation to the very ends of the
earth, and thus to be the instrument of accomplishing one of the
sublime predictions of Holy Writ. Ferdinand listened with com-
placency to these enthusiastic anticipations. With him, however,
religion was subservient to interest; and he had found, in the
recent conquest of Granada, that extending the sway of the church
might be made a laudable means of extending his own dominions.
According to the doctrines of the day, every nation that refused to
acknowledge the truths of Christianity was fair spoil for a Christian
invader; and it is probable that Ferdinand was more stimulated by
the accounts given of the wealth of Mangi, Cathay, and other
provinces belonging to the Grand Khan, than by any anxiety for
the conversion of him and his semi-barbarous subjects.

Isabella had nobler inducements; she was filled with a pious zeal
at the idea of effecting such a great work of salvation. From
different motives, therefore, both of the sovereigns accorded with
the views of Columbus in this particular, and when he afterwards
departed on his voyage, letters were actually given him for the
Grand Khan of Tartary.

The ardent enthusiasm of Columbus did not stop here. Anticipating boundless wealth from his discoveries, he suggested that
the treasures thus acquired should be consecrated to the pious
purpose of rescuing the Holy Sepulchre of Jerusalem from the
power of the Infidels. The sovereigns smiled at this sally of
the imagination, but expressed themselves well pleased with it,
and assured him that even without the funds he anticipated,
they should be well disposed to that holy undertaking.* What
the king and queen, however, may have considered a mere sally
of momentary excitement, was a deep and cherished design
of Columbus. It is a curious and characteristic fact, which has
never been particularly noticed, that the recovery of the Holy
Sepulchre was one of the great objects of his ambition, meditated
throughout the remainder of his life, and solemnly provided for

---

* 'Protestè a vuestras Altezas que toda la ganancia desta mi empresa se gastase en la
conquista de Jerusalem, y vuestras Altezas e rieron, y dijeron que les placia, y que
sin este tenian aquella gana.' – *Primer Viage de Colon*, Navarrete, tom. i. p. 117.

in his will. In fact, he subsequently considered it the main work for which he was chosen by Heaven as an agent, and that his great discovery was but a preparatory dispensation of Providence to furnish means for its accomplishment.

A home-felt mark of favour, characteristic of the kind and considerate heart of Isabella, was accorded to Columbus before his departure from the court. An albala or letter-patent was issued by the queen on the 8th of May, appointing his son Diego page to Prince Juan, the heir-apparent, with an allowance for his support – an honour granted only to the sons of persons of distinguished rank.*

Thus gratified in his dearest wishes, after a course of delays and disappointments sufficient to have reduced any ordinary man to despair, Columbus took leave of the court on the 12th of May, and set out joyfully for Palos. Let those who are disposed to faint under difficulties in the prosecution of any great and worthy undertaking remember that eighteen years elapsed after the time that Columbus conceived his enterprise before he was enabled to carry it into effect; that the greater part of that time was passed in almost hopeless solicitation, amidst poverty, neglect, and taunting ridicule; that the prime of his life had wasted away in the struggle; and that when his perseverance was finally crowned with success, he was about his fifty-sixth year. His example should encourage the enterprising never to despair.

* Navarrete, *Colec. de Viages*, tom. ii. doc. 11.

CHAPTER 8

On arriving at Palos, Columbus repaired immediately to the neighbouring convent of La Rabida, where he was received with open arms by the worthy prior, Fray Juan Perez, and again became his guest.* The port of Palos, for some misdemeanour, had been condemned by the royal council to serve the crown for one year with two armed caravels; and these were destined to form part of the armament of Columbus, who was furnished with the necessary papers and vouchers to enforce obedience in all matters necessary for his expedition.

On the following morning, the 23rd of May, Columbus, accompanied by Fray Juan Perez, whose character and station gave him great importance in the neighbourhood, proceeded to the church of St George, in Palos, where the alcalde, the regidors, and many of the inhabitants of the place had been notified to attend. Here, in presence of them all, in the porch of the church, a royal order was read by a notary public, commanding the authorities of Palos to have two caravels ready for sea within ten days after this notice, and to place them and their crews at the disposal of Columbus. The latter was likewise empowered to procure and fit out a third vessel. The crews of all three were to receive the ordinary wages of seamen employed in armed vessels, and to be paid four months in advance. They were to sail in such direction as Columbus, under the royal authority, should command, and were to obey him in all things, with merely one stipulation, that neither he nor they were to go to St George la Miña, on the coast of Guinea, nor any other of the lately discovered possessions of Portugal. A certificate of their good conduct, signed by Columbus, was to be the discharge of their obligation to the crown.†

* Oviedo, *Cronica de las Indias*, lib. ii. cap. 5.
† Navarrete, *Colec. de Viages*, tom. ii. doc. 6.

Orders were likewise read, addressed to the public authorities, and the people of all ranks and conditions, in the maritime borders of Andalusia, commanding them to furnish supplies and assistance of all kinds, at reasonable prices, for the fitting out of the vessels; and penalties were denounced on such as should cause any impediment. No duties were to be exacted for any articles furnished to the vessels; and all criminal processes against the person or property of any individual engaged in the expedition were to be suspended during his absence, and for two months after his return.[*]

With these orders the authorities promised implicit compliance, but when the nature of the intended expedition came to be known, astonishment and dismay fell upon the little community. The ships and crews demanded for such a desperate service were regarded in the light of sacrifices. The owners of vessels refused to furnish them; the boldest seamen shrank from such a wild and chimerical cruise into the wilderness of the ocean. All kinds of frightful tales and fables were conjured up concerning the unknown regions of the deep; and nothing can be a stronger evidence of the boldness of this undertaking, than the extreme dread of it in a community composed of some of the most adventurous navigators of the age.

Weeks elapsed without a vessel being procured, or anything else being done in fulfilment of the royal orders. Further mandates were therefore issued by the sovereigns, ordering the magistrates of the coast of Andalusia to press into the service any vessels they might think proper, belonging to Spanish subjects, and to oblige the masters and crews to sail with Columbus in whatever direction he should be sent by royal command. Juan de Peñalosa, an officer of the royal household, was sent to see that this order was properly complied with, receiving two hundred maravedies a day as long as he was occupied in the business, which sum, together with other penalties expressed in the mandate, was to be exacted from such as should be disobedient and delinquent. This letter was acted upon by Columbus in Palos and the neighbouring town of Moguer, but apparently with as little success as the preceding. The communities of those places were thrown into complete confusion, tumults took place, but nothing of consequence was effected. At length Martin Alonzo Pinzon stepped forward, with his brother Vicente Yañez Pinzon, both navigators of great courage and ability, owners of

[*] Navarrete, *Colec. de Viages*, tom. ii. doc. 8, 9.

vessels, and having seamen in their employ. They were related, also, to many of the seafaring inhabitants of Palos and Moguer, and had great influence throughout the neighbourhood. They engaged to sail on the expedition, and furnished one of the vessels required. Others, with their owners and crews, were pressed into the service by the magistrates, under the arbitrary mandate of the sovereigns; and it is a striking instance of the despotic authority exercised over commerce in those times, that respectable individuals should thus be compelled to engage, with persons and ships, in what appeared to them a mad and desperate enterprise.

During the equipment of the vessels, troubles and difficulties arose among the seamen who had been compelled to embark. These were fomented and kept up by Gomez Rascon and Christoval Quintero, owners of the *Pinta*, one of the ships pressed into the service. All kinds of obstacles were thrown in the way by these people and their friends to retard or defeat the voyage. The caulkers employed upon the vessels did their work in a careless and imperfect manner, and on being commanded to do it over again, absconded.* Some of the seamen who had enlisted willingly repented of their hardihood, or were dissuaded by their relatives, and sought to retract; others deserted and concealed themselves. Everything had to be effected by the most harsh and arbitrary measures, and in defiance of popular prejudice and opposition.

The influence and example of the Pinzons had a great effect in allaying this opposition, and inducing many of their friends and relatives to embark. It is supposed that they had furnished Columbus with funds to pay the eighth part of the expense which he was bound to advance. It is also said that Martin Alonzo Pinzon was to divide with him his share of the profits. As no immediate profit, however, resulted from this expedition, no claim of the kind was ever brought forward. It is certain, however, that the assistance of the Pinzons was all-important, if not indispensable, in fitting out and launching the expedition.†

After the great difficulties made by various courts in patronizing this enterprise, it is surprising how inconsiderable an armament

---

* Las Casas, *Hist. Ind.* lib. i. cap. 77, MS.

† These facts concerning the Pinzons are mostly taken from the testimony given, many years afterwards, in a suit between Don Diego, the son of Columbus, and the crown.

was required. It is evident that Columbus had reduced his requisitions to the narrowest limits, lest any great expense should cause impediment. Three small vessels were apparently all that he had requested. Two of them were light barks, called caravels, not superior to river and coasting craft of more modern days. Representations of this class of vessels exist in old prints and paintings. They are delineated as open, and without deck in the centre, but built up high at the prow and stern, with forecastles and cabins for the accommodation of the crew. Peter Martyr, the learned contemporary of Columbus, says that only one of the three vessels was decked. The smallness of the vessels was considered an advantage by Columbus, in a voyage of discovery, enabling him to run close to the shores, and to enter shallow rivers and harbours. In his third voyage, when coasting the Gulf of Paria, he complained of the size of his ship, being nearly a hundred tons burden. But that such long and perilous expeditions into unknown seas should be undertaken in vessels without decks, and that they should live through the violent tempests by which they were frequently assailed, remain among the singular circumstances of these daring voyages.

At length, by the beginning of August, every difficulty was vanquished and the vessels were ready for sea. The largest, which had been prepared expressly for the voyage, and was decked, was called the *Santa Maria*; on board of this ship Columbus hoisted his flag. The second, called the *Pinta*, was commanded by Martin Alonzo Pinzon, accompanied by his brother Francisco Martin as pilot. The third, called the *Niña*, had lateen sails, and was commanded by the third of the brothers, Vicente Yañez Pinzon. There were three other pilots, Sancho Ruiz, Pedro Alonzo Niño, and Bartolomeo Roldan. Rodrigo Sanchez of Segovia was inspector-general of the armament, and Diego de Arana, a native of Cordova, chief alguazil. Rodrigo de Escobedo went as royal notary, an officer always sent in the armaments of the crown, to take official notes of all transactions. There were also a physician and a surgeon, together with various private adventurers, several servants, and ninety mariners, making in all one hundred and twenty persons.[*]

The squadron being ready to put to sea, Columbus, impressed with the solemnity of his undertaking, confessed himself to the friar Juan Perez, and partook of the sacrament of the communion. His

[*] Charlevoix, *Hist. St Domingo*, lib. i.; Muñoz, *Hist. Nuevo Mundo*, lib. ii.

example was followed by his officers and crew, and they entered
upon their enterprise full of awe, and with the most devout and
affecting ceremonials, committing themselves to the especial guidance and protection of Heaven. A deep gloom was spread over the
whole community of Palos at their departure, for almost everyone
had some relative or friend on board of the squadron. The spirits of
the seamen, already depressed by their own fears, were still more
cast down at the affliction of those they left behind, who took leave
of them with tears and lamentations and dismal forebodings, as of
men they were never to behold again.

BOOK 3

CHAPTER I

1492

When Columbus set sail on this memorable voyage, he commenced a regular journal, intended for the inspection of the Spanish sovereigns. Like all his other transactions, it evinces how deeply he was impressed with the grandeur and solemnity of his enterprise. He proposed to keep it, as he afterwards observed, in the manner of the Commentaries of Caesar. It opened with a stately prologue, wherein, in the following words, were set forth the motives and views which led to his expedition:

In nomine D. N. Jesu Christi. Whereas most Christian, most high, most excellent, and most powerful princes, King and Queen of the Spains, and of the islands of the sea, our sovereigns, in the present year of 1492, after your highnesses had put an end to the war with the Moors who ruled in Europe, and had concluded that warfare in the great city of Granada, where, on the second of January, of this present year, I saw the royal banners of your highnesses placed by force of arms on the towers of the Alhambra, which is the fortress of that city, and beheld the Moorish king sally forth from the gates of the city, and kiss the royal hands of your highnesses and of my lord the prince; and immediately in that same month, in consequence of the information which I had given to your highnesses of the lands of India, and of a prince who is called the Grand Khan, which is to say in our language, king of kings; how that many times he and his predecessors had sent to Rome to entreat for doctors of our holy faith, to instruct him in the same; and that the Holy Father had never provided him with them, and thus so many people were lost, believing in idolatries, and imbibing doctrines of perdition; therefore your highnesses, as Catholic

Christians and princes, lovers and promoters of the holy Christian
faith, and enemies of the sect of Mahomet, and of all idolatries and
heresies, determined to send me, Christopher Columbus, to the said
parts of India, to see the said princes, and the people and lands, and
discover the nature and disposition of them all, and the means to be
taken for the conversion of them to our holy faith; and ordered that I
should not go by land to the east, by which it is the custom to go, but
by a voyage to the west, by which course, unto the present time, we
do not know for certain that anyone hath passed. Your highnesses,
therefore, after having expelled all the Jews from your kingdoms and
territories, commanded me, in the same month of January, to proceed
with a sufficient armament to the said parts of India; and for this
purpose bestowed great favours upon me, ennobling me, that thenceforward I might style myself Don, appointing me high admiral of the
Ocean sea, and perpetual viceroy and governor of all the islands and
continents I should discover and gain, and which henceforward may
be discovered and gained in the Ocean sea; and that my eldest son
should succeed me, and so on from generation to generation for ever.
I departed, therefore, from the city of Granada on Saturday, the 12th
of May, of the same year 1492, to Palos, a sea-port, where I armed
three ships, well calculated for such service, and sailed from that port
well furnished with provisions and with many seamen, on Friday, the
3rd of August, of the same year, half an hour before sunrise, and took
the route for the Canary Islands of your highnesses, to steer my course
thence, and navigate until I should arrive at the Indies, and deliver the
embassy of your highnesses to those princes, and accomplish that
which you had commanded. For this purpose I intend to write during
this voyage, very punctually from day to day, all that I may do, and
see, and experience, as will hereafter be seen. Also, my sovereign
princes, beside describing each night all that has occurred in the day,
and in the day the navigation of the night, I propose to make a chart,
in which I will set down the waters and lands of the Ocean sea in their
proper situations under their bearings; and further, to compose a
book, and illustrate the whole in picture by latitude from the equinoctial, and longitude from the west; and, upon the whole, it will be
essential that I should forget sleep, and attend closely to the navigation
to accomplish these things, which will be a great labour.*

* Navarrete, *Colec. de Viages*, tom. i. p. 1.

Thus are formally and expressly stated by Columbus the objects of this extraordinary voyage. The material facts still extant of his journal will be found incorporated in the present work.[*]

It was on Friday, the 3rd of August 1492, early in the morning, that Columbus set sail from the bar of Saltes, a small island formed by the arms of the Odiel, in front of the town of Huelva, steering in a south-westerly direction for the Canary Islands, whence it was his intention to strike due west. As a guide by which to sail, he had prepared a map or chart, improved upon that sent him by Paulo Toscanelli. Neither of these now exists, but the globe or planisphere finished by Martin Behem in this year of the admiral's first voyage is still extant, and furnishes an idea of what the chart of Columbus must have been. It exhibits the coasts of Europe and Africa from the south of Ireland to the end of Guinea; and opposite to them, on the other side of the Atlantic, the extremity of Asia, or, as it was termed, India. Between them is placed the island of Cipango, or Japan, which, according to Marco Polo, lay fifteen hundred miles distant from the Asiatic coast. In his computations Columbus advanced this island about a thousand leagues too much to the east, supposing it to be about the situation of Florida;[†] and at this island he hoped first to arrive.

The exultation of Columbus at finding himself, after so many years of baffled hope, fairly launched on his grand enterprise, was checked by his want of confidence in the resolution and perseverance of his crews. As long as he remained within reach of Europe, there was no security that, in a moment of repentance and alarm, they might not renounce the prosecution of the voyage,

---

[*] An abstract of this journal, made by Las Casas, has recently been discovered, and is published in the first volume of the collection of Señor Navarrete. Many passages of this abstract had been previously inserted by Las Casas in his *History of the Indies*, and the same journal had been copiously used by Fernando Columbus in the history of his father. In the present account of this voyage, the author has made use of the journal contained in the work of Señor Navarrete, the manuscript history of Las Casas, the *History of the Indies* by Herrera, the *Life of the Admiral* by his son, the *Chronicle of the Indies* by Oviedo, the manuscript history of Ferdinand and Isabella by Andres Bernaldes, curate of Los Palacios, and the *Letters and Decades of the Ocean Sea* by Peter Martyr, all of whom, with the exception of Herrera, were contemporaries and acquaintances of Columbus. These are the principal authorities which have been consulted, though scattered lights have occasionally been obtained from other sources.

[†] Malte-Brun, *Géograph. Universelle*, tom. ii. p. 283.

and insist on a return. Symptoms soon appeared to warrant his apprehensions. On the third day the *Pinta* made signal of distress; her rudder was discovered to be broken and unhung. This Columbus surmised to be done through the contrivance of the owners of the caravel, Gomez Rascon and Christoval Quintero, to disable their vessel, and cause her to be left behind. As has already been observed, they had been pressed into the service greatly against their will, and their caravel seized upon for the expedition, in conformity to the royal orders.

Columbus was much disturbed at this occurrence. It gave him a foretaste of further difficulties to be apprehended from crews partly enlisted on compulsion, and all full of doubt and foreboding. Trivial obstacles might, in the present critical state of his voyage, spread panic and mutiny through his ships, and entirely defeat the expedition.

The wind was blowing strongly at the time, so that he could not render assistance without endangering his own vessel. Fortunately Martin Alonzo Pinzon commanded the *Pinta*, and being an adroit and able seaman, succeeded in securing the rudder with cords, so as to bring the vessel into management. This, however, was but a temporary and inadequate expedient; the fastenings gave way again on the following day, and the other ships were obliged to shorten sail until the rudder could be secured.

This damaged state of the *Pinta*, as well as her being in a leaky condition, determined the admiral to touch at the Canary Islands, and seek a vessel to replace her. He considered himself not far from those islands, though a different opinion was entertained by the pilots of the squadron. The event proved his superiority in taking observations and keeping reckonings, for they came in sight of the Canaries on the morning of the 9th.

They were detained upwards of three weeks among these islands, seeking in vain another vessel. They were obliged, therefore, to make a new rudder for the *Pinta*, and repair her for the voyage. The lateen sails of the *Niña* were also altered into square sails, that she might work more steadily and securely, and be able to keep company with the other vessels.

While sailing among these islands, the crew were terrified at beholding the lofty peak of Teneriffe sending forth volumes of flame and smoke, being ready to take alarm at any extraordinary

Peak of Teneriffe

phenomenon, and to construe it into a disastrous portent. Columbus took great pains to dispel their apprehensions, explaining the
natural causes of those volcanic fires, and verifying his explanations
by citing Mount Etna and other well-known volcanoes.

While taking in wood and water and provisions in the island of
Gomera, a vessel arrived from Ferro, which reported that three
Portuguese caravels had been seen hovering off that island, with
the intention, it was said, of capturing Columbus. The admiral
suspected some hostile stratagem on the part of the King of
Portugal, in revenge for his having embarked in the service of
Spain. He therefore lost no time in putting to sea, anxious to get
far from those islands, and out of the track of navigation, trembling
lest something might occur to defeat his expedition, commenced
under such inauspicious circumstances.

CHAPTER 2

1492

Early in the morning of the 6th of September, Columbus set sail from the island of Gomera, and now might be said first to strike into the region of discovery, taking leave of these frontier islands of the Old World, and steering westward for the unknown parts of the Atlantic. For three days, however, a profound calm kept the vessels loitering with flagging sails within a short distance of the land. This was a tantalizing delay to Columbus, who was impatient to find himself far out of sight of either land or sail, which, in the pure atmospheres of these latitudes, may be descried at an immense distance. On the following Sunday, the 9th of September, at daybreak, he beheld Ferro, the last of the Canary Islands, about nine leagues distant. This was the island whence the Portuguese caravels had been seen; he was therefore in the very neighbourhood of danger. Fortunately a breeze sprang up with the sun, their sails were once more filled, and in the course of the day the heights of Ferro gradually faded from the horizon.

On losing sight of this last trace of land, the hearts of the crews failed them. They seemed literally to have taken leave of the world. Behind them was everything dear to the heart of man – country, family, friends, life itself; before them everything was chaos, mystery, and peril. In the perturbation of the moment they despaired of ever more seeing their homes. Many of the rugged seamen shed tears, and some broke into loud lamentations. The admiral tried in every way to soothe their distress, and to inspire them with his own glorious anticipations. He described to them the magnificent countries to which he was about to conduct them – the islands of the Indian seas, teeming with gold and precious stones; the regions of Mangi and Cathay, with their cities of unrivalled wealth and splendour. He promised them land and riches, and everything that could arouse their cupidity or inflame their imaginations. Nor were these promises made for purposes of mere deception; he certainly believed that he should realize them all.

He now issued orders to the commanders of the other vessels, that, in the event of separation by any accident, they should continue directly westward; but that, after sailing seven hundred leagues, they should lay by from midnight until daylight, as at about that distance he confidently expected to find land. In the meantime, as he thought it possible he might not discover land within the distance thus assigned, and as he foresaw that the vague terrors already awakened among the seamen would increase with the space which intervened between them and their homes, he commenced a stratagem which he continued throughout the voyage. He kept two reckonings – one correct, in which the true way of the ship was noted, and which was retained in secret for his own government; in the other, which was open to general inspection, a number of leagues was daily subtracted from the sailing of the ship, so that the crews were kept in ignorance of the real distance they had advanced.*

On the 11th of September, when about one hundred and fifty leagues west of Ferro, they fell in with part of a mast, which from its size appeared to have belonged to a vessel of about a hundred and twenty tons burden, and which had evidently been a long time in the water. The crews, tremblingly alive to everything that could excite their hopes or fears, looked with rueful eye upon this wreck of some unfortunate voyager drifting ominously at the entrance of those unknown seas.

On the 13th of September, in the evening, being about two hundred leagues from the island of Ferro, Columbus for the first time noticed the variation of the needle – a phenomenon which had never before been remarked. He perceived about nightfall that the needle, instead of pointing to the north star, varied about half a point, or between five and six degrees, to the north-west, and still more on the following morning. Struck with this circumstance, he

---

* It has been erroneously stated that Columbus kept two journals. It was merely in the reckoning, or log-book, that he deceived the crew. His journal was entirely private, and intended for his own use and the perusal of the sovereigns. In a letter written from Granada, in 1503, to Pope Alexander VII, he says that he had kept an account of his voyages, in the style of the *Commentaries* of Caesar, which he intended to submit to his holiness.

observed it attentively for three days, and found that the variation increased as he advanced. He at first made no mention of this phenomenon, knowing how ready his people were to take alarm; but it soon attracted the attention of the pilots, and filled them with consternation. It seemed as if the very laws of nature were changing as they advanced, and that they were entering another world, subject to unknown influences.* They apprehended that the compass was about to lose its mysterious virtues; and without this guide, what was to become of them in a vast and trackless ocean?

Columbus tasked his science and ingenuity for reasons with which to allay their terror. He observed that the direction of the needle was not to the polar star, but to some fixed and invisible point. The variation, therefore, was not caused by any fallacy in the compass, but by the movement of the north star itself, which, like the other heavenly bodies, had its changes and revolutions, and every day described a circle round the pole. The high opinion which the pilots entertained of Columbus as a profound astronomer gave weight to this theory, and their alarm subsided. As yet the solar system of Copernicus was unknown; the explanation of Columbus, therefore, was highly plausible and ingenious, and it shows the vivacity of his mind, ever ready to meet the emergency of the moment. The theory may at first have been advanced merely to satisfy the minds of others, but Columbus appears subsequently to have remained satisfied with it himself. The phenomenon has now become familiar to us, but we still continue ignorant of its cause. It is one of those mysteries of nature, open to daily observation and experiment, and apparently simple from their familiarity, but which on investigation make the human mind conscious of its limits, baffling the experience of the practical and humbling the pride of science.

* Las Casas, *Hist. Ind.*, lib. i. cap. 6.

CHAPTER 3

1492

On the 14th of September, the voyagers were rejoiced by the sight of what they considered harbingers of land. A heron and a tropical bird called the *rabo de junco*,[*] neither of which is supposed to venture far to sea, hovered about the ships. On the following night they were struck with awe at beholding a meteor, or, as Columbus calls it in his journal, a great flame of fire, which seemed to fall from the sky into the sea, about four or five leagues distant. These meteors, common in warm climates, and especially under the tropics, are always seen in the serene azure sky of those latitudes, falling as it were from the heavens, but never beneath a cloud. In the transparent atmosphere of one of those beautiful nights, where every star shines with the purest lustre, they often leave a luminous train behind them which lasts for twelve or fifteen seconds, and may well be compared to a flame.

The wind had hitherto been favourable, with occasional though transient clouds and showers. They had made great progress each day, though Columbus, according to his secret plan, contrived to suppress several leagues in the daily reckoning left open to the crew.

They had now arrived within the influence of the trade-wind, which, following the sun, blows steadily from east to west between the tropics, and sweeps over a few adjoining degrees of ocean. With this propitious breeze directly aft, they were wafted gently but speedily over a tranquil sea, so that for many days they did not shift a sail. Columbus perpetually recurs to the bland and temperate serenity of the weather, which in this tract of the ocean is soft and refreshing without being cool. In his artless and expressive language, he compares the pure and balmy mornings to those of April in Andalusia, and observes that they wanted but the song of the nightingale to complete the illusion. 'He had reason to say so,'

[*] The water-wagtail.

observes the venerable Las Casas; 'for it is marvellous the suavity which we experience when half way towards these Indias; and the more the ships approach the lands, so much more do they perceive the temperance and softness of the air, the clearness of the sky, and the amenity and fragrance sent forth from the groves and forests – much more certainly than in April in Andalusia.'[*]

They now began to see large patches of herbs and weeds drifting from the west, and increasing in quantity as they advanced. Some of these weeds were such as grow about rocks, others such as are produced in rivers; some were yellow and withered, others so green as to have apparently been recently washed from land. On one of these patches was a live crab, which Columbus carefully preserved. They saw also a white tropical bird, of a kind which never sleeps upon the sea. Tunny-fish also played about the ships, one of which was killed by the crew of the *Niña*. Columbus now called to mind the account given by Aristotle of certain ships of Cadiz, which, coasting the shores outside of the Straits of Gibraltar, were driven westward by an impetuous east wind, until they reached a part of the ocean covered with vast fields of weeds, resembling sunken islands, among which they beheld many tunny-fish. He supposed himself arrived in this weedy sea, as it had been called, from which the ancient mariners had turned back in dismay, but which he regarded with animated hope, as indicating the vicinity of land. Not that he had yet any idea of reaching the object of his search, the eastern end of Asia; for, according to his computation, he had come but three hundred and sixty leagues[†] since leaving the Canary Islands, and he placed the mainland of India much further on.

On the 18th of September the same weather continued: a soft steady breeze from the east filled every sail, while, to use the words of Columbus, the sea was as calm as the Guadalquivir at Seville. He fancied that the water of the sea grew fresher as he advanced, and noticed this as a proof of the superior sweetness and purity of the air.[‡]

The crews were all in high spirits; each ship strove to get in the advance, and every seaman was eagerly on the look-out, for the

[*] Las Casas, *Hist. Ind.*, lib. i. cap. 36, MS.
[†] Of twenty to the degree of latitude, the unit of distance throughout this work.
[‡] Las Casas, *Hist. Ind.*, lib. i. cap. 36.

sovereigns had promised a pension of ten thousand maravedies to him who should first discover land. Martin Alonzo Pinzon crowded all canvas, and, as the *Pinta* was a fast sailer, he generally kept the lead. In the afternoon he hailed the admiral and informed him that from the flight of a great number of birds, and from the appearance of the northern horizon, he thought there was land in that direction.

There was in fact a cloudiness in the north, such as often hangs over land; and at sunset it assumed such shapes and masses that many fancied they beheld islands. There was a universal wish, therefore, to steer for that quarter. Columbus, however, was persuaded that they were mere illusions. Everyone who has made a sea voyage must have witnessed the deceptions caused by clouds resting upon the horizon, especially about sunset and sunrise, which the eye, assisted by the imagination and desire, easily converts into the wished-for land. This is particularly the case within the tropics, where the clouds at sunset assume the most singular appearances.

On the following day there were drizzling showers, unaccompanied by wind, which Columbus considered favourable signs. Two boobies also flew on board the ships – birds which, he observed, seldom fly twenty leagues from land. He sounded, therefore, with a line of two hundred fathoms, but found no bottom. He supposed he might be passing between islands, lying to the north and south, but was unwilling to waste the present favouring breeze by going in search of them; besides, he had confidently affirmed that land was to be found by keeping steadfastly to the west; his whole expedition had been founded on such a presumption. He should, therefore, risk all credit and authority with his people were he to appear to doubt and waver, and to go groping blindly from point to point of the compass. He resolved, therefore, to keep one bold course always westward, until he should reach the coast of India; and afterwards, if advisable, to seek these islands on his return.[*]

Notwithstanding his precaution to keep the people ignorant of the distance they had sailed, they were now growing extremely uneasy at the length of the voyage. They had advanced much further west than ever man had sailed before; and though already

[*] *Hist. del Almirante*, cap. 20; Extracts from Journal of Columb., Navarrete, tom. i. p.16.

beyond the reach of succour, still they continued daily leaving vast tracts of ocean behind them, and pressing onward and onward into that apparently boundless abyss. It is true they had been flattered by various indications of land, and still others were occurring, but all mocked them with vain hopes: after being hailed with a transient joy, they passed away, one after another, and the same interminable expanse of sea and sky continued to extend before them. Even the bland and gentle breeze, uniformly aft, was now conjured by their ingenious fears into a cause of alarm; for they began to imagine that the wind in these seas might always prevail from the east, and if so, would never permit their return to Spain.

Columbus endeavoured to dispel these gloomy presages, some-times by argument and expostulation, sometimes by awakening fresh hopes and pointing out new signs of land. On the 20th of September the wind veered, with light breezes from the south-west. These, though adverse to their progress, had a cheering effect upon the people, as they proved that the wind did not always prevail from the east.* Several birds also visited the ships; three, of a small kind, which keep about groves and orchards, came singing in the morning, and flew away again in the evening. Their song cheered the hearts of the dismayed mariners, who hailed it as the voice of land. The larger fowl, they observed, were strong of wing, and might venture far to sea; but such small birds were too feeble to fly far, and their singing showed that they were not exhausted by their flight.

On the following day there was either a profound calm, or light winds from the south-west. The sea, as far as the eye could reach, was covered with weeds; a phenomenon often observed in this part of the ocean, which has sometimes the appearance of a vast inundated meadow. This has been attributed to immense quantities of submarine plants, which grow at the bottom of the sea until ripe, when they are detached by the motion of the waves and currents, and rise to the surface.† These fields of weeds were at first regarded with great satisfaction; but at length they became, in many places, so dense and matted as in some degree to impede the sailing of the

---

* 'Mucho me fue necessario este viento contrario, porque mi gente andaban muy estimulados, que pensaban que no ventaban estos mares vientos para volver á España.' – *Primer Viage de Colon*, Navarrete, tom. i. p. 12.

† Humboldt, *Personal Narrative*, book i. cap. 1.

ships, which must have been under very little headway. The crews now called to mind some tale about the frozen ocean, where ships were said to be sometimes fixed immovable. They endeavoured, therefore, to avoid, as much as possible, these floating masses, lest some disaster of the kind might happen to themselves.[*] Others considered these weeds as proof that the sea was growing shallower, and began to talk of lurking rocks and shoals and treacherous quicksands, and of the danger of running aground, as it were, in the midst of the ocean, where their vessels might rot and fall to pieces, far out of the track of human aid, and without any shore where the crews might take refuge. They had evidently some confused notion of the ancient story of the sunken island of Atalantis, and feared that they were arriving at that part of the ocean where navigation was said to be obstructed by drowned lands and the ruins of an engulfed country.

To dispel these fears, the admiral had frequent recourse to the lead; but though he sounded with a deep-sea line, he still found no bottom. The minds of the crews, however, had gradually become diseased. They were full of vague terrors and superstitious fancies; they construed everything into a cause of alarm, and harassed their commander by incessant murmurs.

For three days there was a continuance of light summer airs from the southward and westward, and the sea was as smooth as a mirror. A whale was seen heaving up its huge form at a distance, which Columbus immediately pointed out as a favourable indication, affirming that these fish were generally in the neighbourhood of land. The crews, however, became uneasy at the calmness of the weather. They observed that the contrary winds which they experienced were transient and unsteady, and so light as not to ruffle the surface of the sea, which maintained a sluggish calm like a lake of dead water. Everything differed, they said, in these strange regions from the world to which they had been accustomed. The only winds which prevailed with any constancy and force were from the east, and they had not power to disturb the torpid stillness of the ocean; there was a risk, therefore, either of perishing amidst stagnant and shoreless waters, or of being prevented by contrary winds from ever returning to their native country.

[*] *Hist. del Almirante*, cap. 18.

Columbus continued with admirable patience to reason with these fancies, observing that the calmness of the sea must undoubtedly be caused by the vicinity of land in the quarter whence the wind blew, which, therefore, had not space sufficient to act upon the surface and heave up large waves. Terror, however, multiplies and varies the forms of ideal danger a thousand times faster than the most active wisdom can dispel them. The more Columbus argued, the more boisterous became the murmurs of his crew, until, on Sunday, the 25th of September, there came on a heavy swell of the sea, unaccompanied by wind. This phenomenon often occurs on the broad ocean, being either the expiring undulations of some past gale, or the movement given to the sea by some distant current of wind; it was, nevertheless, regarded with astonishment by the mariners, and dispelled the imaginary terrors occasioned by the calm.

Columbus, who as usual considered himself under the immediate eye and guardianship of Heaven in this solemn enterprise, intimates in his journal that this swelling of the sea seemed providentially ordered to allay the rising clamours of his crew, comparing it to that which so miraculously aided Moses when conducting the children of Israel out of the captivity of Egypt.*

---

* 'Como la mar estuviese mansa y llana murmuraba la gente diciendo que, pues por alli no habia mar grande que nunca ventaria para volver á España; pero despues alzóse mucho la mar y sin viento, que los asombraba; por lo cual dice aqui el Almirante; *asi que muy necesario me fué la mar alta, que no parecio, salvo el tiempo de los Judios cuando salieron de Egipto contra Moyses que los sacaba de captiverio.*' – Journal of Columb., Navarrete, tom. i. p. 12.

The situation of Columbus was daily becoming more and more critical. In proportion as he approached the regions where he expected to find land, the impatience of his crews augmented. The favourable signs which increased his confidence were derided by them as delusive, and there was danger of their rebelling, and obliging him to turn back, when on the point of realizing the object of all his labours. They beheld themselves with dismay still wafted onward, over the boundless wastes of what appeared to them a mere watery desert surrounding the habitable world. What was to become of them should their provisions fail? Their ships were too weak and defective even for the great voyage they had already made; but if they were still to press forward, adding at every moment to the immense expanse behind them, how should they ever be able to return, having no intervening port where they might victual and refit?

In this way they fed each other's discontents, gathering together in little knots, and fomenting a spirit of mutinous opposition. And when we consider the natural fire of the Spanish temperament and its impatience of control, and that a great part of these men were sailing on compulsion, we cannot wonder that there was imminent danger of their breaking forth into open rebellion and compelling Columbus to turn back. In their secret conferences they exclaimed against him as a desperado, bent, in a mad fantasy, upon doing something extravagant to render himself notorious. What were their sufferings and dangers to one evidently content to sacrifice his own life for the chance of distinction? What obligations bound them to continue on with him, or when were the terms of their agreement to be considered as fulfilled? They had already penetrated unknown seas, untraversed by a sail, far beyond where man had ever before ventured. They had done enough to

gain themselves a character for courage and hardihood in undertaking such an enterprise and persisting in it so far. How much
further were they to go in quest of a merely conjectured land?
Were they to sail on until they perished, or until all return became impossible? In such case they would be the authors of their
own destruction.

On the other hand, should they consult their safety and turn
back before too late, who would blame them? Any complaints
made by Columbus would be of no weight. He was a foreigner,
without friends or influence; his schemes had been condemned by
the learned and discountenanced by people of all ranks. He had no
party to uphold him, and a host of opponents whose pride of
opinion would be gratified by his failure. Or, as an effectual means
of preventing his complaints, they might throw him into the sea,
and give out that he had fallen overboard while busy with his
instruments contemplating the stars; a report which no one would
have either the inclination or the means to controvert.[*]

Columbus was not ignorant of the mutinous disposition of his
crew, but he still maintained a serene and steady countenance,
soothing some with gentle words, endeavouring to stimulate the
pride or avarice of others, and openly menacing the refractory
with signal punishment should they do anything to impede the
voyage.

On the 25th of September the wind again became favourable,
and they were able to resume their course directly to the west. The
airs being light and the sea calm, the vessels sailed near to each
other, and Columbus had much conversation with Martin Alonzo
Pinzon on the subject of a chart, which the former had sent three
days before on board of the *Pinta*. Pinzon thought that, according
to the indications of the map, they ought to be in the neighbourhood of Cipango and the other islands which the admiral had
therein delineated. Columbus partly entertained the same idea, but
thought it possible that the ships might have been borne out of
their track by the prevalent currents, or that they had not come so
far as the pilots had reckoned. He desired that the chart might be
returned, and Pinzon, tying it to the end of a cord, flung it on
board to him. While Columbus, his pilot, and several of his
experienced mariners were studying the map, and endeavouring

[*] *Hist. del Almirante*, cap. 19; Herrera, *Hist. Ind.*, decad. i. lib. i. cap. 10.

to make out from it their actual position, they heard a shout from the *Pinta*, and looking up, beheld Martin Alonzo Pinzon mounted on the stern of his vessel, crying, 'Land! land! señor; I claim my reward!' He pointed at the same time to the south-west, where there was indeed an appearance of land at about twenty-five leagues' distance. Upon this Columbus threw himself on his knees and returned thanks to God, and Martin Alonzo repeated the *Gloria in excelsis*, in which he was joined by his own crew and that of the admiral.*

The seamen now mounted to the mast-head or climbed about the rigging, straining their eyes in the direction pointed out. The conviction became so general of land in that quarter, and the joy of the people so ungovernable, that Columbus found it necessary to vary from his usual course, and stand all night to the south-west. The morning light, however, put an end to all their hopes as to a dream. The fancied land proved to be nothing but an evening cloud, and had vanished in the night. With dejected hearts they once more resumed their western course, from which Columbus would never have varied, but in compliance with their clamorous wishes.

For several days they continued on with the same propitious breeze, tranquil sea, and mild, delightful weather. The water was so calm that the sailors amused themselves with swimming about the vessel. Dolphins began to abound, and flying-fish, darting into the air, fell upon the decks. The continued signs of land diverted the attention of the crews, and insensibly beguiled them onward.

On the 1st of October, according to the reckoning of the pilot of the admiral's ship, they had come five hundred and eighty leagues west since leaving the Canary Islands. The reckoning which Columbus showed the crew was five hundred and eighty-four, but the reckoning which he kept privately was seven hundred and seven.† On the following day the weeds floated from east to west, and on the third day no birds were to be seen.

The crews now began to fear that they had passed between islands, from one to the other of which the birds had been flying. Columbus had also some doubts of the kind, but refused to alter his westward course. The people again uttered murmurs and

* Journal of Columb., *Primer Viage*, Navarrete, tom. i.
† Navarrete, tom. i. p. 16.

menaces; but on the following day they were visited by such flights of birds, and the various indications of land became so numerous, that from a state of despondency they passed to one of confident expectation.

Eager to obtain the promised pension, the seamen were continually giving the cry of land on the least appearance of the kind. To put a stop to these false alarms, which produced continual disappointments, Columbus declared that should anyone give such notice, and land not be discovered within three days afterwards, he should thenceforth forfeit all claim to the reward.

On the evening of the 6th of October, Martin Alonzo Pinzon began to lose confidence in their present course, and proposed that they should stand more to the southward. Columbus, however, still persisted in steering directly west.* Observing this difference of opinion in a person so important in his squadron as Pinzon, and fearing that chance or design might scatter the ships, he ordered that, should either of the caravels be separated from him, it should stand to the west, and endeavour as soon as possible to join company again. He directed also that the vessels should keep near to him at sunrise and sunset, as at these times the state of the atmosphere is most favourable to the discovery of distant land.

On the morning of the 7th of October, at sunrise, several of the admiral's crew thought they beheld land in the west, but so indistinctly that no one ventured to proclaim it, lest he should be mistaken, and forfeit all chance of the reward. The *Niña*, however, being a good sailer, pressed forward to ascertain the fact. In a little while a flag was hoisted at her mast-head, and a gun discharged, being the preconcerted signals for land. New joy was awakened throughout the little squadron, and every eye was turned to the west. As they advanced, however, their cloud-built hopes faded away, and before evening the fancied land had again melted into air.†

The crews now sank into a degree of dejection proportioned to their recent excitement, but new circumstances occurred to arouse them. Columbus, having observed great flights of small field-birds going toward the south-west, concluded they must be secure of some neighbouring land, where they would find food and a

* Journ. of Columbus, Navarrete, tom. i. p. 17.
† *Hist. del Almirante*, cap. 20; Journ. of Columbus, Navarrete, tom. i.

resting-place. He knew the importance which the Portuguese voyagers attached to the flight of birds, by following which they had discovered most of their islands. He had now come seven hundred and fifty leagues, the distance at which he had computed to find the island of Cipango. As there was no appearance of it, he might have missed it through some mistake in the latitude. He determined therefore, on the evening of the 7th of October, to alter his course to the west-south-west, the direction in which the birds generally flew, and continue that direction for at least two days. After all, it was no great deviation from his main course, and would meet the wishes of the Pinzons, as well as be inspiriting to his followers generally.

For three days they stood in this direction, and the further they went the more frequent and encouraging were the signs of land. Flights of small birds of various colours, some of them such as sing in the fields, came flying about the ships, and then continued toward the south-west, and others were heard also flying by in the night. Tunny-fish played about the smooth sea, and a heron, a pelican, and a duck were seen, all bound in the same direction. The herbage which floated by was fresh and green, as if recently from land, and the air, Columbus observes, was sweet and fragrant as April breezes in Seville.

All these, however, were regarded by the crews as so many delusions beguiling them on to destruction; and when, on the evening of the third day, they beheld the sun go down upon a shoreless horizon, they broke forth into turbulent clamour. They exclaimed against this obstinacy in tempting fate by continuing on into a boundless sea. They insisted upon turning home, and abandoning the voyage as hopeless. Columbus endeavoured to pacify them by gentle words and promises of large rewards; but finding that they only increased in clamour, he assumed a decided tone. He told them it was useless to murmur. The expedition had been sent by the sovereigns to seek the Indies, and, happen what might, he was determined to persevere until, by the blessing of God, he should accomplish the enterprise.[*]

[*] *Hist. del Almirante*, cap. 20; Las Casas, lib. i.; Journal of Columb., Navarrete, *Colec.* tom. i. p. 19.

It has been asserted by various historians that Columbus, a day or two previous to coming in sight of the New World, capitulated with his mutinous crew,

Columbus was now at open defiance with his crew, and his situation became desperate. Fortunately the manifestations of the vicinity of land were such on the following day as no longer to admit a doubt. Besides a quantity of fresh weeds, such as grow in rivers, they saw a green fish of a kind which keeps about rocks; then a branch of thorn with berries on it, and recently separated from the tree, floated by them; then they picked up a reed, a small board, and, above all, a staff artificially carved. All gloom and mutiny now gave way to sanguine expectation, and throughout the day each one was eagerly on the watch, in hopes of being the first to discover the long-sought-for land.

In the evening, when, according to invariable custom on board of the admiral's ship, the mariners had sung the *Salve Regina*, or vesper hymn to the Virgin, he made an impressive address to his

---

promising, if he did not discover land within three days, to abandon the voyage. There is no authority for such an assertion, either in the history of his son Fernando or that of the Bishop Las Casas, each of whom had the admiral's papers before him. There is no mention of such a circumstance in the extracts made from the journal by Las Casas, which have recently been brought to light; nor is it asserted by either Peter Martyr or the curate of Los Palacios, both contemporaries and acquaintances of Columbus, and who could scarcely have failed to mention so striking a fact, if true. It rests merely upon the authority of Oviedo, who is of inferior credit to either of the authors above cited, and was grossly misled as to many of the particulars of this voyage by a pilot of the name of Hernan Perez Matheo, who was hostile to Columbus. In the manuscript process of the memorable lawsuit between Don Diego, son of the admiral, and the fiscal of the crown, is the evidence of one Pedro de Bilbao, who testifies that he heard many times that some of the pilots and mariners wished to turn back, but that the admiral promised them presents, and entreated them to wait two or three days, before which time he should discover land. ('Pedro de Bilbao oyo muchas veces que algunos pilotos y marineros querian volverse sino fuera por el Almirante que les prometio donos, les rogó esperasen dos o tres dias i que antes del termino descubriera tierra.') This, if true, implies no capitulation to relinquish the enterprise.

On the other hand, it was asserted by some of the witnesses in the above-mentioned suit that Columbus, after having proceeded some few hundred leagues without finding land, lost confidence and wished to turn back, but was persuaded and even piqued to continue by the Pinzons. This assertion carries falsehood on its very face. It is in total contradiction to that persevering constancy and undaunted resolution displayed by Columbus, not merely in the present voyage, but from first to last of his difficult and dangerous career. This testimony was given by some of the mutinous men, anxious to exaggerate the merits of the Pinzons, and to depreciate that of Columbus. Fortunately the extracts from the journal of the latter, written from day to day with guileless simplicity and all the air of truth, disprove these fables, and show that on the very day previous to his discovery he expressed a peremptory determination to persevere in defiance of all dangers and difficulties.

crew. He pointed out the goodness of God in thus conducting them by soft and favouring breezes across a tranquil ocean, cheering their hopes continually with fresh signs, increasing as their fears augmented, and thus leading and guiding them to a promised land. He now reminded them of the orders he had given on leaving the Canaries, that, after sailing westward seven hundred leagues, they should not make sail after midnight. Present appearances authorized such a precaution. He thought it probable they would make land that very night. He ordered, therefore, a vigilant look-out to be kept from the forecastle, promising to whomsoever should make the discovery a doublet of velvet, in addition to the pension to be given by the sovereigns.[*]

The breeze had been fresh all day, with more sea than usual, and they had made great progress. At sunset they had stood again to the west, and were ploughing the waves at a rapid rate, the *Pinta* keeping the lead from her superior sailing. The greatest animation prevailed throughout the ships; not an eye was closed that night. As the evening darkened, Columbus took his station on the top of the castle or cabin on the high poop of his vessel, ranging his eye along the dusky horizon, and maintaining an intense and unremitting watch. About ten o'clock he thought he beheld a light glimmering at a great distance. Fearing his eager hopes might deceive him, he called to Pedro Gutierrez, gentleman of the king's bed-chamber, and inquired whether he saw such a light; the latter replied in the affirmative. Doubtful whether it might not yet be some delusion of the fancy, Columbus called Rodrigo Sanchez of Segovia, and made the same inquiry. By the time the latter had ascended the round-house, the light had disappeared. They saw it once or twice afterwards in sudden and passing gleams, as if it were a torch in the bark of a fisherman, rising and sinking with the waves, or in the hand of some person on shore, borne up and down as he walked from house to house. So transient and uncertain were these gleams that few attached any importance to them; Columbus, however, considered them as certain signs of land, and, moreover, that the land was inhabited.

They continued their course until two in the morning, when a gun from the *Pinta* gave the joyful signal of land. It was first descried by a mariner named Rodrigo de Triana; but the reward

[*] *Hist. del Almirante*, cap. 21.

was afterwards adjudged to the admiral, for having previously perceived the light. The land was now clearly seen about two leagues distant, whereupon they took in sail, and laid-to, waiting impatiently for the dawn.

The thoughts and feelings of Columbus in this little space of time must have been tumultuous and intense. At length, in spite of every difficulty and danger, he had accomplished his object. The great mystery of the ocean was revealed; his theory, which had been the scoff of sages, was triumphantly established; he had secured to himself a glory durable as the world itself.

It is difficult to conceive the feelings of such a man at such a moment, or the conjectures which must have thronged upon his mind as to the land before him covered with darkness. That it was fruitful was evident from the vegetables which floated from its shores. He thought, too, that he perceived the fragrance of aromatic groves. The moving light he had beheld proved it the residence of man. But what were its inhabitants? Were they like those of the other parts of the globe, or were they some strange and monstrous race, such as the imagination was prone in those times to give to all remote and unknown regions? Had he come upon some wild island far in the Indian Sea, or was this the famed Cipango itself, the object of his golden fancies? A thousand speculations of the kind must have swarmed upon him, as, with his anxious crews, he waited for the night to pass away, wondering whether the morning light would reveal a savage wilderness, or dawn upon spicy groves, and glittering fanes, and gilded cities, and all the splendour of Oriental civilization.

BOOK 4

CHAPTER I

It was on Friday morning, the 12th of October, that Columbus
first beheld the New World. As the day dawned he saw before
him a level island, several leagues in extent, and covered with
trees like a continual orchard. Though apparently uncultivated, it
was populous, for the inhabitants were seen issuing from all parts
of the woods and running to the shore. They were perfectly
naked, and, as they stood gazing at the ships, appeared by their
attitudes and gestures to be lost in astonishment. Columbus made
signal for the ships to cast anchor, and the boats to be manned and
armed. He entered his own boat, richly attired in scarlet, and
holding the royal standard; whilst Martin Alonzo Pinzon, and
Vincent Yañez, his brother, put off in company in their boats,
each with a banner of the enterprise emblazoned with a green
cross, having on either side the letters F and Y, the initials of the
Castilian monarchs Fernando and Ysabel, surmounted by crowns.

As he approached the shore, Columbus, who was disposed for all
kinds of agreeable impressions, was delighted with the purity and
suavity of the atmosphere, the crystal transparency of the sea, and
the extraordinary beauty of the vegetation. He beheld, also, fruits
of an unknown kind upon the trees which overhung the shores.
On landing he threw himself on his knees, kissed the earth, and
returned thanks to God with tears of joy. His example was
followed by the rest, whose hearts indeed overflowed with the
same feelings of gratitude. Columbus then rising drew his sword,
displayed the royal standard, and assembling round him the two
captains, with Rodrigo de Escobedo, notary of the armament,
Rodrigo Sanchez, and the rest who had landed, he took solemn
possession in the name of the Castilian sovereigns, giving the

island the name of San Salvador. Having complied with the requisite forms and ceremonies, he called upon all present to take the oath of obedience to him, as admiral and viceroy, representing the persons of the sovereigns.[*]

The feelings of the crew now burst forth in the most extravagant transports. They had recently considered themselves devoted men, hurrying forward to destruction; they now looked upon themselves as favourites of fortune, and gave themselves up to the most unbounded joy. They thronged around the admiral with overflowing zeal, some embracing him, others kissing his hands. Those who had been most mutinous and turbulent during the voyage were now most devoted and enthusiastic. Some begged favours of him, as if he had already wealth and honours in his gift. Many abject spirits, who had outraged him by their insolence, now crouched at his feet, begging pardon for all the trouble they had caused him, and promising the blindest obedience for the future.[†]

The natives of the island, when, at the dawn of day, they had beheld the ships hovering on their coast, had supposed them monsters which had issued from the deep during the night. They had crowded to the beach, and watched their movements with awful anxiety. Their veering about, apparently without effort, and the shifting and furling of their sails, resembling huge wings, filled them with astonishment. When they beheld their boats approach the shore, and a number of strange beings clad in glittering steel, or raiment of various colours, landing upon the beach, they fled in affright to the woods. Finding, however, that there was no attempt to pursue or molest them, they gradually recovered from their terror, and approached the Spaniards with great awe, frequently prostrating themselves on the earth, and making signs of adoration. During the ceremonies of taking possession, they remained gazing in timid admiration of the complexion, the beards, the shining armour, and splendid dress of the Spaniards. The admiral partic-

---

[*] In the *Tablas Chronologicas* of Padre Claudio Clemente is conserved a form of prayer, said to have been used by Columbus on this occasion, and which, by order of the Castilian sovereigns, was afterwards used by Balboa, Cortez, and Pizarro in their discoveries. 'Domine Deus aeterne et omnipotens, sacro tuo verbo cœlum, et terrum, et mare creâsti; benedicatur et glorificetur nomen tuum, laudetur tua majestas, quæ dignita est per humilem servum tuum, ut ejus sacrum nomen agnoscatur, et prædicetur in hac altera mundi parte.' – *Tab. Chron. de los Descub.*, decad. i. Valencia, 1689.

[†] Oviedo, lib. i. cap. 6; Las Casas, *Hist. Ind.*, lib. i. cap. 40.

ularly attracted their attention, from his commanding height, his air of authority, his dress of scarlet, and the deference which was paid him by his companions – all which pointed him out to be the commander.* When they had still further recovered from their fears, they approached the Spaniards, touched their beards, and examined their hands and faces, admiring their whiteness. Columbus was pleased with their gentleness and confiding simplicity, and suffered their scrutiny with perfect acquiescence, winning them by his benignity. They now supposed that the ships had sailed out of the crystal firmament which bounded their horizon, or had descended from above on their ample wings, and that these marvellous beings were inhabitants of the skies.†

The natives of the island were no less objects of curiosity to the Spaniards, differing, as they did, from any race of men they had ever seen. Their appearance gave no promise of either wealth or civilization, for they were entirely naked, and painted with a variety of colours. With some it was confined merely to a part of the face, the nose, or around the eyes; with others it extended to the whole body, and gave them a wild and fantastic appearance. Their complexion was of a tawny or copper hue, and they were entirely destitute of beards. Their hair was not crisped, like the recently-discovered tribes of the African coast, under the same latitude, but straight and coarse, partly cut short above the ears, but some locks were left long behind and falling upon their shoulders. Their features, though obscured and disfigured by paint, were agreeable; they had lofty foreheads and remarkably fine eyes. They were of moderate stature and well shaped. Most of them appeared to be under thirty years of age. There was but one female with them, quite young, naked like her companions, and beautifully formed.

As Columbus supposed himself to have landed on an island at the extremity of India, he called the natives by the general appellation of Indians, which was universally adopted before the true nature of his discovery was known, and has since been extended to all the aboriginals of the New World.

* Las Casas, *Hist. Ind.*, lib. i. cap. 40.

† The idea that the white men came from heaven was universally entertained by the inhabitants of the New World. When, in the course of subsequent voyages, the Spaniards conversed with the cacique Nicaragua, he inquired how they came down from the skies, whether flying, or whether they descended on clouds. Herrera, decad. iii. lib. iv. cap. 5.

The islanders were friendly and gentle. Their only arms were lances, hardened at the end by fire, or pointed with a flint or the teeth or bone of a fish. There was no iron to be seen; nor did they appear acquainted with its properties, for when a drawn sword was presented to them they unguardedly took it by the edge.

Columbus distributed among them coloured caps, glass beads, hawks' bells, and other trifles, such as the Portuguese were accustomed to trade with among the nations of the Gold Coast of Africa. They received them eagerly, hung the beads round their necks, and were wonderfully pleased with their finery, and with the sound of the bells. The Spaniards remained all day on shore, refreshing themselves after their anxious voyage amidst the beautiful groves of the island, and returned on board late in the evening, delighted with all they had seen.

On the following morning, at break of day, the shore was thronged with the natives. Some swam off to the ships; others came in light barks which they called canoes, formed of a single tree, hollowed, and capable of holding from one man to the number of forty or fifty. These they managed dexterously with paddles, and, if overturned, swam about in the water with perfect unconcern, as if in their natural element, righting their canoes with great facility, and baling them with calabashes.*

They were eager to procure more toys and trinkets, not, apparently, from any idea of their intrinsic value, but because everything from the hands of the strangers possessed a supernatural virtue in their eyes, as having been brought from heaven; they even picked up fragments of glass and earthenware as valuable prizes. They had but few objects to offer in return, except parrots, of which great numbers were domesticated among them, and cotton yarn, of which they had abundance, and would exchange large balls of five and twenty pounds weight for the merest trifle. They brought also cakes of a kind of bread called cassava, which constituted a principal part of their food, and was afterwards an important article of provisions with the Spaniards. It was formed from a great root called yuca, which they cultivated in fields. This they cut into small morsels, which they grated or scraped, and strained in a press,

---

* The calabashes of the Indians, which served the purposes of glass and earthenware, supplying them with all sorts of domestic utensils, were produced on stately trees of the size of elms.

making a broad thin cake, which was afterwards dried hard, and would keep for a long time, being steeped in water when eaten. It was insipid, but nourishing, though the water strained from it in the preparation was a deadly poison. There was another kind of yuca destitute of this poisonous quality, which was eaten in the root, either boiled or roasted.*

The avarice of the discoverers was quickly excited by the sight of small ornaments of gold, worn by some of the natives in their noses. These the latter gladly exchanged for glass beads and hawks' bells; and both parties exulted in the bargain, no doubt admiring each other's simplicity. As gold, however, was an object of royal monopoly in all enterprises of discovery, Columbus forbade any traffic in it without his express sanction; and he put the same prohibition on the traffic for cotton, reserving to the crown all trade for it, wherever it should be found in any quantity.

He inquired of the natives where this gold was procured. They answered him by signs, pointing to the south, where, he understood them, dwelt a king of such wealth that he was served in vessels of wrought gold. He understood, also, that there was land to the south, the south-west, and the north-west; and that the people from the last-mentioned quarter frequently proceeded to the south-west in quest of gold and precious stones, making in their way descents upon the islands, and carrying off the inhabitants. Several of the natives showed him scars of wounds received in battles with these invaders. It is evident that a great part of this fancied intelligence was self-delusion on the part of Columbus; for he was under a spell of the imagination, which gave its own shapes and colours to every object. He was persuaded that he had arrived among the islands described by Marco Polo as lying opposite Cathay, in the Chinese Sea, and he construed everything to accord with the account given of those opulent regions. Thus the enemies which the natives spoke of as coming from the north-west he concluded to be the people of the mainland of Asia, the subjects of the Great Khan of Tartary, who were represented by the Venetian traveller as accustomed to make war upon the islands, and to enslave their inhabitants. The country to the south, abounding in gold, could be no other than the famous island of Cipango; and the king who was served out of vessels of gold must be the monarch

* Acosta, *Hist. Ind.*, lib. iv. cap. 17.

whose magnificent city and gorgeous palace, covered with plates of gold, had been extolled in such splendid terms by Marco Polo.

The island where Columbus had thus, for the first time, set his foot upon the New World, was called by the natives Guanahanè. It still retains the name of San Salvador, which he gave to it, though called by the English, Cat Island. The light which he had seen the evening previous to his making land may have been on Watling's Island, which lies a few leagues to the east. San Salvador is one of the great cluster of the Lucayos, or Bahama Islands, which stretch south-east and north-west, from the coast of Florida to Hispaniola, covering the northern coast of Cuba.

On the morning of the 14th of October, the admiral set off at daybreak with the boats of the ships to reconnoitre the island, directing his course to the north-east. The coast was surrounded by a reef of rocks, within which there was depth of water and sufficient harbour to receive all the ships in Christendom. The entrance was very narrow; within there were several sand-banks, but the water was as still as in a pool.[*]

The island appeared throughout to be well wooded, with streams of water, and a large lake in the centre. As the boats proceeded they passed two or three villages, the inhabitants of which, men as well as women, ran to the shores, throwing themselves on the ground, lifting up their hands and eyes, either giving thanks to Heaven, or worshipping the Spaniards as supernatural beings. They ran along parallel to the boats, calling after the Spaniards, and inviting them by signs to land, offering them various fruits and vessels of water. Finding, however, that the boats continued on their course, many threw themselves into the sea and swam after them, and others followed in canoes. The admiral received them all with kindness, giving them glass beads and other trifles, which were received with transport as celestial presents; for the invariable idea of the savages was that the white men had come from the skies.

In this way they pursued their course, until they came to a small peninsula, which with two or three day's labour might be separated from the mainland and surrounded with water, and was therefore specified by Columbus as an excellent situation for a fortress. On this were six Indian cabins, surrounded by groves and gardens as beautiful as those of Castile. The sailors being wearied

---

[*] *Primer Viage de Colon*, Navarrete, tom. i.

with rowing, and the island not appearing to the admiral of sufficient importance to induce colonization, he returned to the ships, taking seven of the natives with him, that they might acquire the Spanish language and serve as interpreters.

Having taken in a supply of wood and water, they left the island of San Salvador the same evening, the admiral being impatient to arrive at the wealthy country to the south, which he flattered himself would prove the famous island of Cipango.

On leaving San Salvador, Columbus was at a loss which way to direct his course. A great number of islands, green and level and fertile, invited him in different directions. The Indians on board of his vessel intimated by signs that they were innumerable, well peopled, and at war with one another. They mentioned the names of above a hundred. Columbus now had no longer a doubt that he was among the islands described by Marco Polo as studding the vast sea of Chin, or China, and lying at a great distance from the mainland. These, according to the Venetian, amounted to between seven and eight thousand, and abounded with drugs and spices and odoriferous trees, together with gold and silver and many other precious objects of commerce.[*]

Animated by the idea of exploring this opulent archipelago, he selected the largest island in sight for his next visit. It appeared to be about five leagues' distance; and he understood from his Indians that the natives were richer than those of San Salvador, wearing bracelets and anklets and other ornaments of massive gold.

The night coming on, Columbus ordered that the ships should lie-to, as the navigation was difficult and dangerous among these unknown islands, and he feared to venture upon a strange coast in the dark. In the morning they again made sail, but meeting with counter-currents it was not until sunset that they anchored at the island. The next morning (16th) they went on shore, and Columbus took solemn possession, giving the island the name of Santa Maria de la Concepcion. The same scene occurred with the inhabitants as with those of San Salvador. They manifested the same astonishment and awe, the same gentleness and simplicity, and the same nakedness and absence of all wealth. Columbus looked in vain for bracelets and anklets of gold, or for any other

[*] Marco Polo, book iii. chap. 4: English translation by W. Marsden.

precious articles; they had been either fictions of his Indian guides, or his own misinterpretations.

Returning on board, he prepared to make sail, when one of the Indians of San Salvador, who was on board of the *Niña*, plunged into the sea, and swam to a large canoe filled with natives. The boat of the caravel put off in pursuit, but the Indians managed their light bark with too much velocity to be overtaken, and, reaching the island, fled to the woods. The sailors took the canoe as a prize, and returned on board the caravel. Shortly afterwards a small canoe approached one of the ships from a different part of the island, with a single Indian on board, who came to offer a ball of cotton in exchange for hawks' bells. As he paused when close to the vessel, and feared to enter, several sailors threw themselves into the sea and took him prisoner.

Columbus having seen all that passed from his station on the high poop of the vessel, ordered the captive to be brought to him. He came trembling with fear, and humbly offered his ball of cotton as a gift. The admiral received him with the utmost benignity, and declining his offering, put a coloured cap upon his head, strings of green beads around his arms, and hawks' bells in his ears; then ordering him and his ball of cotton to be replaced in the canoe, dismissed him, astonished and overjoyed. He ordered that the canoe also which had been seized, and was fastened to the *Niña*, should be cast loose, to be regained by its proprietors. When the Indian reached the shore his countrymen thronged round him, examining and admiring his finery, and listening to his account of the kind treatment he experienced.

Such were the gentle and sage precautions continually taken by Columbus to impress the natives favourably. Another instance of the kind occurred after leaving the island of Conception, when the caravels stood for the larger island several leagues to the west. Midway between the two islands they overtook a single Indian in a canoe. He had a mere morsel of cassava bread and a calabash of water for sea stores, and a little red paint, like dragon's blood, for personal decoration when he should land. A string of glass beads, such as had been given to the natives of San Salvador, showed that he had come thence, and was probably passing from island to island to give notice of the ships. Columbus admired the hardihood of this simple navigator, making such an extensive voyage in so frail a bark. As the island was still distant, he ordered that both the Indian and his canoe should be taken on board, where he treated him with the greatest kindness, giving him bread and honey to eat, and wine to drink. The weather being very calm, they did not reach the island until too dark to anchor, through fear of cutting their cables with rocks. The sea about these islands was so transparent that in the day-time they could see the bottom and choose their ground, and so deep that at two gun-shot distance there was no anchorage. Hoisting out the canoe of their Indian voyager, therefore, and restoring to him all his effects, they sent him joyfully ashore to prepare the natives for their arrival, while the ships lay-to until morning.

This kindness had the desired effect. The natives surrounded the ships in their canoes during the night, bringing fruits and roots, and the pure water of their springs. Columbus distributed trifling presents among them, and to those who came on board he gave sugar and honey.

Landing the next morning, he gave to this island the name of Fernandina, in honour of the king; it is the same at present called Exuma. The inhabitants were similar in every respect to those of the preceding islands, excepting that they appeared more ingenious and intelligent. Some of the women wore mantles and aprons of cotton, but for the most part they were entirely naked. Their habitations were constructed in the form of a pavilion, or high circular tent, of branches of trees, of reeds, and palm-leaves. They were kept very clean and neat, and sheltered under spreading trees. For beds they had nets of cotton extended from two posts, which they called *hamacs*, a name since in universal use among seamen.

In endeavouring to circumnavigate the island, Columbus found, within two leagues of the north-west cape, a noble harbour, sufficient to hold a hundred ships, with two entrances formed by an island which lay in the mouth of it. Here, while the men landed with the casks in search of water, he reposed under the shade of the groves, which, he says, were more beautiful than any he had ever beheld; 'the country was as fresh and green as in the month of May in Andalusia; the trees, the fruits, the herbs, the flowers, the very stones, for the most part, as different from those of Spain as night from day.' * The inhabitants gave the same proofs as the other

* *Primer Viage de Colon*, Navarrete, lib. i.

islanders of being totally unaccustomed to the sight of civilized man. They regarded the Spaniards with awe and admiration, approached them with propitiatory offerings of whatever their poverty, or rather their simple and natural mode of life, afforded – the fruits of their fields and groves, the cotton, which was their article of greatest value, and their domesticated parrots. They took those who were in search of water to the coolest springs, the sweetest and freshest runs, filling their casks, and rolling them to the boats; thus seeking in every way to gratify their celestial visitors.

However pleasing this state of primeval poverty might be to the imagination of a poet, it was a source of continual disappointment to the Spaniards, whose avarice had been whetted to the quick by scanty specimens of gold, and by the information of golden islands continually given by the Indians.

Leaving Fernandina on the 19th of October, they steered to the south-east in quest of an island called Saometo, where Columbus understood, from the signs of the guides, there was a mine of gold, and a king, the sovereign of all the surrounding islands, who dwelt in a large city, and possessed great treasures, wearing rich clothing and jewels of gold. They found the island, but neither the monarch nor the mine: either Columbus had misunderstood the natives, or they, measuring things by their own poverty, had exaggerated the paltry state and trivial ornaments of some savage chieftain. Delightful as the other islands had appeared, Columbus declared that this surpassed them all. Like those, it was covered with trees and shrubs and herbs of unknown kind. The climate had the same soft temperature; the air was delicate and balmy; the land was higher, with a fine verdant hill; the coast of a fine sand, gently laved by transparent billows.

At the south-west end of the island he found fine lakes of fresh water, overhung with groves, and surrounded by banks covered with herbage. Here he ordered all the casks of the ships to be filled. 'Here are large lakes,' says he in his journal, 'and the groves about them are marvellous, and here and in all the island everything is green, as in April in Andalusia. The singing of the birds is such that it seems as if one would never desire to depart hence. There are flocks of parrots which obscure the sun, and other birds, large and small, of so many kinds, all different from ours, that it is wonderful; and beside, there are trees of a thousand species, each having its particular fruit, and all of marvellous flavour, so that I am in the greatest trouble in the world not to know them, for I am very certain that they are each of great value. I shall bring home some of them as specimens, and also some of the herbs.' To this beautiful island he gave the name of his royal patroness, Isabella; it is the same at present called Isla Larga and Exumeta. Columbus was intent on discovering the drugs and spices of the East, and on approaching this island had fancied he perceived in the air the spicy odours said to be wafted from the islands of the Indian seas. 'As I arrived at this cape,' says he, 'there came thence a fragrance so good and soft of the flowers or trees of the land, that it was the sweetest thing in the world. I believe there are here many herbs and trees which would be of great price in Spain for tinctures, medicines, and spices; but I know nothing of them, which gives me great concern.'*

The fish which abounded in these seas partook of the novelty which characterized most of the objects in this new world. They rivalled the birds in tropical brilliancy of colour, the scales of some of them glancing back the rays of light like precious stones. As they sported about the ships they flashed gleams of gold and silver through the clear waves; and the dolphins, taken out of their element, delighted the eye with the changes of colour ascribed in fable to the chameleon.

No animals were seen in these islands, excepting a species of dog which never barked, a kind of coney or rabbit called 'utia' by the natives, together with numerous lizards and guanas. The last were regarded with disgust and horror by the Spaniards, supposing them to be fierce and noxious serpents; but they were afterwards found to be perfectly harmless, and their flesh to be esteemed a great delicacy by the Indians.

For several days Columbus hovered about this island, seeking in vain to find its imaginary monarch, or to establish a communication with him, until at length he reluctantly became convinced of his error. No sooner, however, did one delusion fade away than another succeeded. In reply to the continual inquiries made by the Spaniards after the source whence they procured their gold, the natives uniformly pointed to the south. Columbus now began to hear of an island in that direction, called Cuba; but all that he

* *Primer Viage de Colon*, Navarrete, cap. 1.

could collect concerning it by the signs of the natives was coloured by his imagination. He understood it to be of great extent, abounding in gold, and pearls, and spices, and carrying on an extensive commerce in those precious articles, and that large merchant ships came to trade with its inhabitants.

Comparing these misinterpreted accounts with the coast of Asia, as laid down on his map, after the descriptions of Marco Polo, he concluded that this island must be Cipango, and the merchant ships mentioned must be those of the Grand Khan, who maintained an extensive commerce in these seas. He formed his plan accordingly, determining to sail immediately for this island, and make himself acquainted with its ports, cities, and productions, for the purpose of establishing relations of traffic. He would then seek another great island called Bohio, of which the natives gave likewise marvellous accounts. His sojourn in those islands would depend upon the quantity of gold, spices, precious stones, and other objects of Oriental trade, which he should find there. After this he would proceed to the mainland of India, which must be within ten days' sail, seek the city Quinsai, which, according to Marco Polo, was one of the most magnificent capitals in the world; he would there deliver in person the letters of the Castilian sovereigns to the Grand Khan; and, when he received his reply, return triumphantly to Spain with this document, to prove that he had accomplished the great object of his voyage.* Such was the splendid scheme with which Columbus fed his imagination when about to leave the Bahamas in quest of the island of Cuba.

* Journal of Columbus, Navarrete, tom. i.

CHAPTER 3

1492

For several days the departure of Columbus was delayed by contrary winds and calms, attended by heavy showers, which last had prevailed, more or less, since his arrival among the islands. It was the season of the autumnal rains, which in those torrid climates succeed the parching heats of summer, commencing about the decrease of the August moon, and lasting until the month of November.

At length, at midnight, October 24th, he set sail from the island of Isabella, but was nearly becalmed until mid-day. A gentle wind then sprang up, and, as he observes, began to blow most amorously. Every sail was spread, and he stood towards the west-south-west, the direction in which he was told the land of Cuba lay from Isabella. After three days' navigation, in the course of which he touched at a group of seven or eight small islands, which he called Islas de Areña, supposed to be the present Mucaras Islands, and having crossed the Bahama bank and channel, he arrived, on the morning of the 28th October, in sight of Cuba. The part which he first discovered is supposed to be the coast to the west of Nuevitas del Principe.

As he approached this noble island he was struck with its magnitude and the grandeur of its features: its high and airy mountains, which reminded him of those of Sicily; its fertile valleys and long sweeping plains watered by noble rivers; its stately forests; its bold promontories and stretching headlands, which melted away into the remotest distance. He anchored in a beautiful river, of transparent clearness, free from rocks and shoals, its banks overhung with trees. Here, landing and taking possession of the island, he gave it the name of Juana, in honour of Prince Juan, and to the river the name of San Salvador.

On the arrival of the ships, two canoes put off from the shore, but fled on seeing the boat approach to sound the river for anchorage. The admiral visited two cabins abandoned by their inhabitants. They contained but a few nets made of the fibres of the palm-tree, hooks and harpoons of bone, and some other fishing implements, and one of the kind of dogs he had met with on the smaller islands, which never bark. He ordered that nothing should be taken away or deranged.

Returning to his boat, he proceeded for some distance up the river, more and more enchanted with the beauty of the country. The banks were covered with high and wide-spreading trees; some bearing fruits, others flowers, while in some both fruit and flower were mingled, bespeaking a perpetual round of fertility. Among them were many palms, but different from those of Spain and Africa: with the great leaves of these the natives thatched their cabins.

The continued eulogies made by Columbus on the beauty of the country were warranted by the kind of scenery he was beholding. There is a wonderful splendour, variety, and luxuriance in the vegetation of those quick and ardent climates. The verdure of the groves and the colours of the flowers and blossoms derive a vividness from the transparent purity of the air and the deep serenity of the azure heavens. The forests, too, are full of life, swarming with birds of brilliant plumage. Painted varieties of parrots and woodpeckers create a glitter amidst the verdure of the grove, and humming-birds rove from flower to flower, resembling, as has well been said, animated particles of a rain-bow. The scarlet flamingoes, too, seen sometimes through an opening of a forest in a distant savanna, have the appearance of soldiers drawn up in battalion, with an advance scout on the alert to give notice of approaching danger. Nor is the least beautiful part of animated nature the various tribes of insects peopling every plant, and displaying brilliant coats of mail, which sparkle like precious gems.*

Such is the splendour of animal and vegetable creation in these tropical climates, where an ardent sun imparts its own lustre to every object, and quickens nature into exuberant fecundity. The

* The ladies of Havanna, on gala occasions, wear in their hair numbers of those insects, which have a brilliancy equal to rubies, sapphires, or diamonds.

birds, in general, are not remarkable for their notes, for it has been observed that in the feathered race sweetness of song rarely accompanies brilliancy of plumage. Columbus remarks, however, that there were various kinds which sang sweetly among the trees, and he frequently deceived himself in fancying that he heard the voice of the nightingale, a bird unknown in these countries. He was, in fact, in a mood to see everything through a favouring medium. His heart was full to overflowing, for he was enjoying the fulfilment of his hopes, and the hard-earned but glorious reward of his toils and perils. Everything round him was beheld with the enamoured and exulting eye of a discoverer, where triumph mingles with admiration; and it is difficult to conceive the rapturous state of his feelings while thus exploring the charms of a virgin world won by his enterprise and valour.

From his continual remarks on the beauty of scenery, and from his evident delight in rural sounds and objects, he appears to have been extremely open to those happy influences exercised over some spirits by the graces and wonders of nature. He gives utterance to these feelings with characteristic enthusiasm, and at the same time with the artlessness and simplicity of diction of a child. When speaking of some lovely scene among the groves, or along the flowery shores of these favoured islands, he says, 'One could live there for ever.' Cuba broke upon him like an elysium. 'It is the most beautiful island,' he says, 'that the eyes ever beheld; full of excellent ports and profound rivers.' The climate was more temperate here than in the other islands, the nights being neither hot nor cold, while the birds and crickets sang all night long. Indeed there is a beauty in a tropical night in the depth of the dark blue sky, the lambent purity of the stars, and the resplendent clearness of the moon, that spreads over the rich landscape and the balmy groves a charm more captivating than the splendour of the day.

In the sweet smell of the woods, and the odour of the flowers, Columbus fancied he perceived the fragrance of Oriental species; and along the shores he found shells of the kind of oyster which produces pearls. From the grass growing to the very edge of the water, he inferred the peacefulness of the ocean which bathes these islands, never lashing the shores with angry surges. Ever since his arrival among these Antilles, he had experienced nothing but soft and gentle weather, and he concluded that a perpetual serenity reigned over these happy seas. He was little suspicious of the occasional bursts of fury to which they are liable. Charlevoix, speaking from actual observation, remarks: 'The sea of those islands is commonly more tranquil than ours; but, like certain people who are excited with difficulty, and whose transports of passion are as violent as they are rare, so when the sea becomes irritated, it is terrible. It breaks all bounds, overflows the country, sweeps away all things that oppose it, and leaves frightful ravages behind, to mark the extent of its inundations. It is after these tempests, known by the name of hurricanes, that the shores are covered with marine shells which greatly surpass in lustre and beauty those of the European seas.'* It is a singular fact, however, that the hurricanes which almost annually devastate the Bahamas, and other islands in the immediate vicinity of Cuba, have been seldom known to extend their influence to this favoured land. It would seem as if the very elements were charmed into gentleness as they approached it.

In a kind of riot of the imagination, Columbus finds at every step something to corroborate the information he had received, or fancied he had received, from the natives. He had conclusive proofs, as he thought, that Cuba possessed mines of gold and groves of spices, and that its shores abounded with pearls. He no longer doubted that it was the island of Cipango, and, weighing anchor, coasted along westward, in which direction, according to the signs of his interpreters, the magnificent city of its king was situated. In the course of his voyage, he landed occasionally, and visited several villages, particularly one on the banks of a large river, to which he gave the name of Rio de los Mares.† The houses were neatly built of branches of palm-trees in the shape of pavil-ions; not laid out in regular streets, but scattered here and there among the groves, and under the shade of broad spreading trees, like tents in a camp; as is still the case in many of the Spanish settlements, and in the villages in the interior of Cuba. The inhabitants fled to the mountains or hid themselves in the woods. Columbus carefully noted the architecture and furniture of their dwellings. The houses were better built than those he had hitherto seen, and were kept extremely clean. He found in them rude

* Charlevoix, *Hist. St Domingo*, lib. i. p. 20. Paris, 1730.
† Now called Savannah la Mer.

statues and wooden masks, carved with considerable ingenuity. All these were indications of more art and civilization than he had observed in the smaller islands, and he supposed they would go on increasing as he approached *terra firma*. Finding in all the cabins implements for fishing, he concluded that these coasts were inhabited merely by fishermen, who carried their fish to the cities in the interior. He thought also he had found the skulls of cows, which proved that there were cattle in the island; though these are supposed to have been skulls of the manati or sea-calf found on this coast.

After standing to the north-west for some distance, Columbus came in sight of a great headland, to which, from the groves with which it was covered, he gave the name of the Cape of Palms, and which forms the eastern entrance to what is now known as Laguna de Moron. Here three Indians, natives of the island of Guanahanè, who were on board of the *Pinta*, informed the commander, Martin Alonzo Pinzon, that behind the cape there was a river, whence it was but four days' journey to Cubanacan, a place abounding in gold. By this they designated a province situated in the centre of Cuba; *nacan*, in their language, signifying the midst. Pinzon, however, had studied intently the map of Toscanelli, and had imbibed from Columbus all his ideas respecting the coast of Asia. He concluded, therefore, that the Indians were talking of Cublai Khan, the Tartar sovereign, and of certain parts of his dominions described by Marco Polo.[*] He understood from them that Cuba was not an island, but *terra firma,* extending a vast distance to the north, and that the king who reigned in this vicinity was at war with the Great Khan.

This tissue of errors and misconceptions he immediately communicated to Columbus. It put an end to the delusion in which the admiral had hitherto indulged, that this was the island of Cipango; but it substituted another no less agreeable. He concluded that he must have reached the mainland of Asia, or, as he termed it, India; and if so, he could not be at any great distance from Mangi and Cathay, the ultimate destination of his voyage. The prince in question, who reigned over this neighbouring country, must be some Oriental potentate of consequence. He resolved, therefore, to seek the river beyond the Cape of Palms, and despatch a present

[*] Las Casas, lib. i. cap. 44, MS.

to the monarch, with one of the letters of recommendation from the Castilian sovereigns; and after visiting his dominions, he would proceed to the capital of Cathay, the residence of the Grand Khan.

Every attempt to reach the river in question, however, proved ineffectual. Cape stretched beyond cape; there was no good anchorage; the wind became contrary; and the appearance of the heavens threatening rough weather, he put back to the Rio de los Mares.

On the 1st of November, at sunrise, he sent the boats on shore to visit several houses; but the inhabitants fled to the woods. He supposed that they must mistake his armament for one of the scouring expeditions sent by the Grand Khan to make prisoners and slaves. He sent the boat on shore again in the afternoon, with an Indian interpreter, who was instructed to assure the people of the peaceable and beneficent intentions of the Spaniards, and that they had no connection with the Grand Khan. After the Indian had proclaimed this from the boat to the savages upon the beach – part of it, no doubt, to their great perplexity – he threw himself into the water and swam to shore. He was well received by the natives, and succeeded so effectually in calming their fears, that before evening there were more than sixteen canoes about the ships, bringing cotton yarn and other simple articles of traffic. Columbus forbade all trading for anything but gold, that the natives might be tempted to produce the real riches of their country. They had none to offer; all were destitute of ornaments of the precious metals excepting one, who wore in his nose a piece of wrought silver. Columbus understood this man to say that the king lived about the distance of four days' journey in the interior; that many messengers had been despatched to give him tidings of the arrival of the strangers upon the coast; and that in less than three days' time messengers might be expected from him in return, and many merchants from the interior to trade with the ships. It is curious to observe how ingeniously the imagination of Columbus deceived him at every step, and how he wove everything into an uniform web of false conclusions. Poring over the map of Toscanelli, referring to the reckonings of his voyage, and musing on the misinterpreted words of the Indians, he imagined that he must be on the borders of Cathay, and about one hundred leagues from the capital of the Grand Khan. Anxious to arrive there, and to delay as little as possible in the territories of an inferior prince, he determined not to await the arrival of messengers and merchants, but to despatch two envoys to seek the neighbouring monarch at his residence.

For this mission he chose two Spaniards, Rodrigo de Jerez and Luis de Torres – the latter a converted Jew, who knew Hebrew and Chaldaic, and even something of Arabic, one or other of which Columbus supposed might be known to this Oriental prince. Two Indians were sent with them as guides, one a native of Guanahanè, and the other an inhabitant of the hamlet on the bank of the river. The ambassadors were furnished with strings of beads and other trinkets for travelling expenses. Instructions were given them to inform the king that Columbus had been sent by the Castilian sovereigns, a bearer of letters and a present, which he was to deliver personally, for the purpose of establishing an amicable intercourse between the powers. They were likewise to inform themselves accurately about the situation and distances of certain provinces, ports, and rivers, which the admiral specified by name from the descriptions which he had of the coast of Asia. They were, moreover, provided with specimens of spices and drugs, for the purpose of ascertaining whether any articles of the kind abounded in the country. With these provisions and instructions the ambassadors departed, six days being allowed them to go and return. Many at the present day will smile at this embassy to a naked savage chieftain in the interior of Cuba, in mistake for an Asiatic monarch; but such was the singular nature of this voyage, a continual series of golden dreams, and all interpreted by the deluding volume of Marco Polo.

CHAPTER 4

While awaiting the return of his ambassadors, the admiral ordered the ships to be careened and repaired, and employed himself in collecting information concerning the country. On the day after their departure he ascended the river in boats for the distance of two leagues, until he came to fresh water. Here landing, he climbed a hill to obtain a view of the interior. His view, however, was shut in by thick and lofty forests of wild but beautiful luxuriance. Among the trees were some which he considered linaloes; many were odoriferous, and he doubted not possessed valuable aromatic qualities. There was a general eagerness among the voyagers to find the precious articles of commerce which grow in the favoured climes of the East, and their imaginations were continually deceived by their hopes.

For two or three days the admiral was excited by reports of cinnamon-trees, and nutmegs, and rhubarb; but on examination they all proved fallacious. He showed the natives specimens of those and various other spices and drugs, and understood from them that those articles abounded to the south-east. He showed them gold and pearls also, and several old Indians spoke of a country where the natives wore ornaments of them round their necks, arms, and ankles. They repeatedly mentioned the word Bohio, which Columbus supposed to be the name of the place in question, and that it was some rich district or island. They mingled, however, great extravagances with their imperfect accounts, describing nations at a distance who had but one eye, others who had the heads of dogs, and who were cannibals, cutting the throats of their prisoners and sucking their blood.*

All these reports of gold and pearls and spices, many of which were probably fabrications to please the admiral, tended to keep up the persuasion that he was among the valuable coasts and islands of

* *Primer Viage de Colon*, Navarrete, lxxi. p. 48.

the East. On making a fire to heat the tar for careening the ships, the seamen found that the wood they burned sent forth a powerful odour, and on examining it declared that it was mastic. The wood abounded in the neighbouring forests, insomuch that Columbus flattered himself a thousand quintals of this precious gum might be collected every year, and a more abundant supply procured than that furnished by Scio and other islands of the Archipelago. In the course of their researches in the vegetable kingdom, in quest of the luxuries of commerce, they met with the potato, a humble root, little valued at the time, but a more precious acquisition to man than all the spices of the East.

On the 6th of November, the two ambassadors returned, and everyone crowded to hear tidings of the interior of the country, and of the prince to whose capital they had been sent. After penetrating twelve leagues, they had come to a village of fifty houses, built similarly to those of the coast, but larger, the whole village containing at least a thousand inhabitants. The natives received them with great solemnity, conducted them to the best house, and placed them in what appeared to be intended for chairs of state, being wrought out of single pieces of wood into the forms of quadrupeds. They then offered them fruits and vegetables. Having complied with the laws of savage courtesy and hospitality, they seated themselves on the ground around their visitors, and waited to hear what they had to communicate.

The Israelite, Luis de Torres, found his Hebrew, Chaldaic, and Arabic of no avail, and the Lucayan interpreter had to be the orator. He made a regular speech, after the Indian manner, in which he extolled the power, the wealth, and munificence of the white men. When he had finished, the Indians crowded round these wonderful beings, whom, as usual, they considered more than human. Some touched them, examining their skin and raiment, others kissed their hands and feet in token of submission or adoration. In a little while the men withdrew, and were succeeded by the women, and the same ceremonies were repeated. Some of the women had a slight covering of netted cotton round the middle, but in general both sexes were entirely naked. There seemed to be ranks and orders of society among them, and a chieftain of some authority, whereas among all the natives they had previously met with a complete equality seemed to prevail.

There was no appearance of gold or other precious articles; and when they showed specimens of cinnamon, pepper, and other spices, the inhabitants told them they were not to be found in that neighbourhood, but far off to the south-west.

The envoys determined, therefore, to return to the ships. The natives would fain have induced them to remain for several days; but seeing them bent on departing, a great number were anxious to accompany them, imagining they were about to return to the skies. They took with them, however, only one of the principal men with his son, who were attended by a domestic.

On their way back, they for the first time witnessed the use of a weed which the ingenious caprice of man has since converted into a universal luxury, in defiance of the opposition of the senses. They beheld several of the natives going about with firebrands in their hands, and certain dried herbs which they rolled up in a leaf, and lighting one end, put the other in their mouths, and continued exhaling and puffing out the smoke. A roll of this kind they called tobacco, a name since transferred to the plant of which the rolls were made. The Spaniards, although prepared to meet with wonders, were struck with astonishment at this singular and apparently nauseous indulgence.*

On their return to the ships, they gave favourable accounts of the beauty and fertility of the country. They had met with many hamlets of four or five houses, well peopled, embowered among trees laden with unknown fruits of tempting hue and delightful flavour. Around them were fields cultivated with the agi or sweet pepper, potatoes, maize or Indian corn, a species of lupine or pulse, and yuca, whereof they made their cassava bread. These, with the fruits of the groves, formed their principal food. There were vast quantities of cotton, some just sown, some in full growth. There was great store of it also in their houses, some wrought into yarn or into nets, of which they made their hammocks. They had seen

---

* *Primer Viage de Colon*, Navarrete, tom. i. p. 51. 'Hallaron por el camino mucha gente que atravesaban a sus pueblos mugeres y hombres: siempre los hombres con un tison en las manos y ciertos yerbas para tomar sus sahumerios, que son unas yerbas secas metidas en una cierta hoja seca tambien à manera de mosquete hecho de papel de los que hacon los muchachos la Pascua del Espiritu Santo, y encondido por una parte de el, por la otra chupan ó sorban ó reciben con el resuello por adentro aquel humo; con el qual se adormecen las carnes y cuasi emborracho, y asi diz que no sienten el caasancio. Estos mosquetos, ó como los llamáremas, llamen ellos tabacos.' – Las Casas, *Hist. Gen. Ind.*, lib. i. cap. 46.

many birds of rare plumage but unknown species, many ducks, several small partridges; and they heard the song of a bird which they had mistaken for the nightingale. All that they had seen, however, betokened a primitive and simple state of society. The wonder with which they had been regarded showed clearly that the people were strangers to civilized man; nor could they hear of any inland city superior to the one they had visited.

The report of the envoys put an end to many splendid fancies of Columbus about the barbaric prince and his capital. He was cruising, however, in a region of enchantment, in which pleasing chimeras started up at every step, exercising by turns a power over his imagination. During the absence of the emissaries, the Indians had informed him, by signs, of a place to the eastward where the people collected gold along the river banks by torchlight, and afterwards wrought it into bars with hammers. In speaking of this place, they again used the words Babeque and Bohio, which he, as usual, supposed to be the proper names of islands or countries. The true meaning of these words has been variously explained. It is said that they were applied by the Indians to the coast of *terra firma*, called also by them Caritaba.* It is also said that Bohio means a house, and was often used by the Indians to signify the populousness of an island. Hence it was frequently applied to Hispaniola, as well as the more general name of Hayti, which means high land, and occasionally Quisqueya (that is, the whole), on account of its extent.

The misapprehension of these and other words was a source of perpetual error to Columbus. Sometimes he supposed Babeque and Bohio to signify the same island, sometimes to be different places or islands; and Quisqueya he supposed to mean Quisai or Quinsai (that is, the celestial city), mentioned by Marco Polo.

His great object was to arrive at some opulent and civilized country of the East with which he might establish commercial relations, and whence he might carry home a quantity of Oriental merchandise as a rich trophy of his discovery. The season was advancing; the cool nights gave hints of approaching winter; he resolved therefore not to proceed further to the north, nor to linger about uncivilized places, which at present he had not the means of colonizing, but to return to the east-south-east, in quest

* Muñoz, *Hist. N. Mundo*, cap. 3.

of Babeque, which he trusted might prove some rich and civilized island on the coast of Asia.

Before leaving the river, to which he had given the name of Rio de Mares, he took several of the natives to carry with him to Spain, for the purpose of teaching them the language, that in future voyages they might serve as interpreters. He took them of both sexes, having learned from the Portuguese discoverers that the men were always more contented on the voyage, and serviceable on their return, when accompanied by females. With the religious feeling of the day, he anticipated great triumphs to the faith and glory to the crown, from the conversion of these savage nations through the means of the natives thus instructed. He imagined that the Indians had no system of religion, but a disposition to receive its impressions, as they regarded with great reverence and attention the religious ceremonies of the Spaniards, soon repeating by rote any prayer taught them, and making the sign of the cross with the most edifying devotion. They had an idea of a future state, but limited and confused. 'They confess the soul to be immortal,' says Peter Martyr; 'and having put off the bodily clothing, they imagine it goes forth to the woods and the mountains, and that it liveth there perpetually in caves. Nor do they exempt it from eating and drinking, but that it should be fed there. The answering voices heard from caves and hollows, which the Latines call echoes, they suppose to be the souls of the departed wandering through those places.'*

From the natural tendency to devotion which Columbus thought he discovered among them, from their gentle natures and their ignorance of all warlike arts, he pronounces it an easy matter to make them devout members of the church and loyal subjects of the crown. He concludes his speculations upon the advantages to be derived from the colonization of these parts by anticipating a great trade for gold, which must abound in the interior; for pearls and precious stones, of which, though he had seen none, he had received frequent accounts; for gums and spices, of which he thought he had found indubitable traces; and for the cotton, which grew wild in vast quantities. Many of these articles, he observes, would probably find a nearer market than Spain in the ports and cities of the Great Khan, at which he had no doubt of soon arriving.†

* P. Martyr, decad. viii. cap. 9: M. Lock's translation, 1612.
† *Primer Viage de Colon*, Navarrete, tom. i.

On the 12th of November, Columbus turned his course to the east-south-east, to follow back the direction of the coast. This may be considered another critical change in his voyage, which had a great effect upon his subsequent discoveries. He had proceeded far within what is called the old channel, between Cuba and the Bahamas. In two or three days more he would have discovered his mistake in supposing Cuba a part of *terra firma*, an error in which he continued to the day of his death. He might have had intimation also of the vicinity of the continent, and have stood for the coast of Florida, or have been carried thither by the Gulf Stream; or, continuing along Cuba, where it bends to the south-west, might have struck over to the opposite coast of Yucatan, and have realized his most sanguine anticipations in becoming the discoverer of Mexico. It was sufficient glory for Columbus, how-ever, to have discovered a new world. Its more golden regions were reserved to give splendour to succeeding enterprises.

He now ran along the coast for two or three days without stopping to explore it, as no populous towns or cities were to be seen. Passing by a great cape, to which he gave the name of Cape Cuba, he struck eastward in search of Babeque; but on the 14th a head wind and boisterous sea obliged him to put back and anchor in a deep and secure harbour, to which he gave the name of Puerto del Principe. Here he erected a cross on a neighbouring height in token of possession. A few days were passed in exploring with his boats an archipelago of small but beautiful islands in the vicinity, since known as El Jardin del Rey, or the king's garden. The gulf studded with these islands he named the sea of Nuestra Señora. In modern days it has been a lurking-place for pirates, who have found secure shelter and concealment among the channels and solitary harbours of this archipelago. These islands were covered with noble trees, among which the Spaniards thought they discovered mastic and aloes.

On the 19th Columbus again put to sea, and for two days made ineffectual attempts, against head winds, to reach an island directly east, about sixty miles distant, which he supposed to be Babeque. The wind continuing obstinately adverse, and the sea rough, he put his ship about towards evening of the 20th, making signals for the other vessels to follow him. His signals were unattended to by the *Pinta*, which was considerably to the eastward. Columbus repeated the signals, but they were still unattended to. Night coming on, he shortened sail and hoisted signal-lights to the masthead, thinking Pinzon would yet join him, which he could easily do, having the wind astern; but when the morning dawned the *Pinta* was no longer to be seen.*

Columbus was disquieted by this circumstance. Pinzon was a veteran navigator, accustomed to hold a high rank among his nautical associates. The squadron had, in a great measure, been manned and fitted out through his influence and exertions. He could ill brook subordination therefore to Columbus, whom he perhaps did not consider his superior in skill and knowledge, and who had been benefited by his purse. Several misunderstandings and disputes had accordingly occurred between them in the course of the voyage; and when Columbus saw Pinzon thus parting company without any appointed rendezvous, he suspected either that he intended to take upon himself a separate command and prosecute the enterprise in his own name, or hasten back to Spain and bear off the glory of the discovery. To attempt to seek him, however, was fruitless: he was far out of sight; his vessel was a superior sailer; and it was impossible to say what course he had steered. Columbus stood back, therefore, for Cuba, to finish the exploring of its coast; but he no longer possessed his usual serenity of mind and unity of purpose, and was embarrassed in the prosecution of his discoveries by doubts of the designs of Pinzon.

On the 24th of November he regained Point Cuba, and anchored in a fine harbour formed by the mouth of a river, to which he gave the name of St Catherine. It was bordered by rich meadows. The neighbouring mountains were well wooded, having pines tall

* Las Casas, *Hist. Ind.*, tom. i. cap. 27; *Hist. del Almirante*, cap. 29; Journal of Columbus, Navarrete, tom. i.

enough to make masts for the finest ships, and noble oaks. In the bed of the river were found stones veined with gold.

Columbus continued for several days coasting the residue of Cuba, extolling the magnificence, freshness, and verdure of the scenery, the purity of the rivers, and the number and commodiousness of the harbours. Speaking in his letters to the sovereigns of one place, to which he gave the name of Puerto Santo, he says, in his artless but enthusiastic language: 'The amenity of this river, and the clearness of the water, through which the sand at the bottom may be seen; the multitude of palm-trees of various forms, the highest and most beautiful that I have met with, and an infinity of other great and green trees; the birds in rich plumage, and the verdure of the fields, render this country, most serene princes, of such marvellous beauty that it surpasses all others in charms and graces, as the day doth the night in lustre. For which reason I often say to my people that, much as I endeavour to give a complete account of it to your majesties, my tongue cannot express the whole truth, nor my pen describe it; and I have been so overwhelmed at the sight of so much beauty, that I have not known how to relate it.'*

The transparency of the water, which Columbus attributed to the purity of the rivers, is the property of the ocean in these latitudes. So clear is the sea in the neighbourhood of some of these islands, that in still weather the bottom may be seen as in a crystal fountain; and the inhabitants dive down four or five fathoms in search of conchs and other shell-fish, which are visible from the surface. The delicate air and pure waters of these islands are among their greatest charms.

As a proof of the gigantic vegetation, Columbus mentions the enormous size of the canoes formed from single trunks of trees. One that he saw was capable of containing one hundred and fifty persons. Among other articles found in the Indian dwellings was a cake of wax, which he took to present to the Castilian sovereigns. 'For where there is wax,' said he, 'there must be a thousand other good things.'† It is since supposed to have been brought from Yucatan, as the inhabitants of Cuba were not accustomed to gather wax.‡

* *Hist. del Almirante*, cap. 29.
† Journal of Columbus, Navarrete, tom. i.
‡ Herrera, *Hist. Ind.*, decad. i.

On the 5th of December he reached the eastern end of Cuba, which he supposed to be the eastern extremity of Asia; he gave it, therefore, the name of Alpha and Omega, the beginning and the end. He was now greatly perplexed what course to take. If he kept along the coast, as it bent to the south-west, it might bring him to the more civilized and opulent parts of India; but if he took this course, he must abandon all hope of finding the island of Babeque, which the Indians now said lay to the north-east, and of which they still continued to give the most marvellous accounts. It was a state of embarrassment characteristic of this extraordinary voyage, to have a new and unknown world thus spread out to the choice of the explorer, where wonders and beauties invited him on every side, but where, whichever way he turned, he might leave the true region of profit and delight behind.

CHAPTER 6

1492

While Columbus was steering at large beyond the eastern extremity of Cuba, undetermined what course to take, he descried
land to the south-east, gradually increasing upon the view, its high
mountains towering above the clear horizon, and giving evidence of an island of great extent. The Indians, on beholding it,
exclaimed 'Bohio', the name by which Columbus understood
them to designate some country which abounded in gold. When
they saw him standing in that direction, they showed great signs of
terror, imploring him not to visit it, assuring him by signs that the
inhabitants were fierce and cruel, that they had but one eye, and
were cannibals. The wind being unfavourable, and the nights long,
during which they did not dare to make sail in these unknown
seas, they were a great part of two days working up to the island.

In the transparent atmosphere of the tropics objects are descried
at a great distance, and the purity of the air and serenity of the
deep blue sky give a magical effect to the scenery. Under these
advantages the beautiful island of Hayti revealed itself to the eye as
they approached. Its mountains were higher and more rocky than
those of the other islands; but the rocks rose from among rich
forests. The mountains swept down into luxuriant plains and green
savannas; while the appearance of cultivated fields, of numerous
fires at night and columns of smoke by day, showed it to be
populous. It rose before them in all the splendour of tropical
vegetation, one of the most beautiful islands of the world, and
doomed to be one of the most unfortunate.

In the evening of the 6th of December, Columbus entered a
harbour at the western end of the island, to which he gave the
name of St Nicholas, by which it is called at the present day. The
harbour was spacious and deep, surrounded with large trees, many
of them loaded with fruit; while a beautiful plain extended in front

of the port, traversed by a fine stream of water. From the number of canoes seen in various parts, there were evidently large villages in the neighbourhood; but the natives had fled with terror at sight of the ships.

Leaving the harbour of St Nicholas on the 7th, they coasted along the northern side of the island. It was lofty and mountainous, but with green savannas and long sweeping plains. At one place they caught a view up a rich and smiling valley that ran far into the interior, between two mountains, and appeared to be in a high state of cultivation.

For several days they were detained in a harbour which they called Port Concepcion;* a small river emptied into it, after winding through a delightful country. The coast abounded with fish, some of which even leapt into their boats. They cast their nets, therefore, and caught great quantities, and among them several kinds similar to those of Spain – the first fish they had met with resembling those of their own country. The notes of the bird which they mistook for the nightingale, and of several others to which they were accustomed, reminded them strongly of the groves of their distant Andalusia. They fancied the features of the surrounding country resembled those of the more beautiful provinces of Spain, and, in consequence, the admiral named the island Hispaniola.

Desirous of establishing some intercourse with the natives, who had abandoned the coast on his arrival, he despatched six men, well armed, into the interior. They found several cultivated fields and traces of roads, and places where fires had been made; but the inhabitants had fled with terror to the mountains.

Though the whole country was solitary and deserted, Columbus consoled himself with the idea that there must be populous towns in the interior, where the people had taken refuge; and that the fires he had beheld had been signal-fires, like those lighted up on the mountains of Spain, in the times of Moorish war, to give the alarm when there was any invasion of the sea-board.

* Now known by the name of the Bay of Moustique.

Note: the author has received very obliging and interesting letters, dated in 1847, from T. S. Heneken, Esq., many years a resident of St Domingo, giving names, localities, and other particulars connected with the transactions of Columbus in that island. These will be thankfully made use of, and duly cited, in the course of the work.

On the 12th of December, Columbus, with great solemnity, erected a cross on a commanding eminence at the entrance of the harbour, in sign of having taken possession. As three sailors were rambling about the vicinity they beheld a large number of the natives, who immediately took flight; but the sailors pursued them, and captured a young female, whom they brought to the ships. She was perfectly naked, a bad omen as to the civilization of the island; but an ornament of gold in the nose gave hope of the precious metal. The admiral soon soothed her terror by his kindness, and by presents of beads, brass rings, hawks' bells, and other trinkets, and, having had her clothed, sent her on shore, accompanied by several of the crew and three of the Indian in terpreters. So well pleased was she with her finery, and with the kind treatment she had experienced, that she would gladly have remained with the Indian women whom she found on board. The party sent with her returned on board late in the night without venturing to her village, which was far inland. Confident of the favourable impression which the report given by the woman must produce, the admiral, on the following day, despatched nine stout-hearted, well-armed men to seek the village, accompanied by a native of Cuba as an interpreter. They found it about four and a half leagues to the south-east, in a fine valley, on the banks of a beautiful river.* It contained one thousand houses; but the inhab-itants fled as they approached. The interpreter overtook them, and assured them of the goodness of these strangers, who had descended from the skies, and went about the world making precious and beautiful presents. Thus assured, the natives ventured back to the number of two thousand. They approached the Spaniards with slow and trembling steps, often pausing and putting their hands upon their heads, in token of profound reverence and submission. They were a well-formed race, fairer and handsomer than the natives of the other islands.† While the Spaniards were conversing with them by means of their interpreter, another multitude approached, headed by the husband of the female captive. They brought her in triumph on their shoulders, and the

* This village was formerly known by the name of Gros Morne, situated on the banks of the river of 'Trois Rivières', which empties itself half a mile west of Port de Paix. Navarrete, tom. i.

† Las Casas, lib. i. cap. 53, MS.

husband was profuse in his gratitude for the kindness with which she had been treated, and the magnificent presents which had been bestowed upon her.

The Indians now conducted the Spaniards to their houses, and set before them cassava bread, fish, roots, and fruits of various kinds. They brought also great numbers of domesticated parrots, and, indeed, offered freely whatever they possessed. The great river flowing through this valley was bordered with noble forests, among which were palms, bananas, and many trees covered with fruit and flowers. The air was mild as in April; the birds sang all day long, and some were even heard in the night. The Spaniards had not learned as yet to account for the difference of seasons in this opposite part of the globe; they were astonished to hear the voice of this supposed nightingale singing in the midst of December, and considered it a proof that there was no winter in this happy climate. They returned to the ships enraptured with the beauty of the country, surpassing, as they said, even the luxuriant plains of Cordova. All that they complained of was, that they saw no signs of riches among the natives. And here it is impossible to refrain from dwelling on the picture given by the first discoverers of the state of manners in this eventful island before the arrival of the white men. According to their accounts, the people of Hayti existed in that state of primitive and savage simplicity which some philosophers have fondly pictured as the most enviable on earth, surrounded by natural blessings, without even a knowledge of artificial wants. The fertile earth produced the chief part of their food almost without culture; their rivers and sea-coast abounded with fish; and they caught the utia, the guana, and a variety of birds. This, to beings of their frugal and temperate habits, was great abundance, and what nature furnished thus spontaneously, they willingly shared with all the world. Hospitality, we are told, was with them a law of nature universally observed; there was no need of being known to receive its succours; every house was as open to the stranger as his own.* Columbus, too, in a letter to Luis de St Angel, observes: 'True it is that after they felt confidence, and lost their fear of us, they were so liberal with what they possessed, that it would not be believed by those who had not seen it. If anything was asked of them, they never said no, but rather gave it

* Charlevoix, *Hist. St Domingo*, lib. i.

cheerfully, and showed as much amity as if they gave their very hearts; and whether the thing were of value, or of little price, they were content with whatever was given in return . . . In all these islands it appears to me that the men are all content with one wife, but they give twenty to their chieftain or king. The women seem to work more than the men; and I have not been able to understand whether they possess individual property, but rather think that whatever one has all the rest share, especially in all articles of provisions.'*

One of the most pleasing descriptions of the inhabitants of this island is given by old Peter Martyr, who gathered it, as he says, from the conversations of the admiral himself. 'It is certain,' says he, 'that the land among these people is as common as the sun and water; and that 'mine and thine', the seeds of all mischief, have no place with them. They are content with so little, that in so large a country they have rather superfluity than scarceness; so that they seemed to live in the golden world, without toil, living in open gardens, not intrenched with dikes, divided with hedges, or defended with walls. They deal truly one with another, without laws, without books, and without judges. They take him for an evil and mischievous man who taketh pleasure in doing hurt to another; and albeit they delight not in superfluities, yet they make provision for the increase of such roots whereof they make their bread, contented with such simple diet, whereby health is preserved and disease avoided.'†

Much of this picture may be overcoloured by the imagination, but it is generally confirmed by contemporary historians. They all concur in representing the life of these islanders as approaching to the golden state of poetical felicity; living under the absolute but patriarchal and easy rule of their caciques, free from pride, with few wants, an abundant country, a happily-tempered climate, and a natural disposition to careless and indolent enjoyment.

---

* Letter of Columbus to Luis de St Angel, Navarrete, tom. i. p. 167.
† Peter Martyr, decad. i. lib. iii.: transl. of Richard Eden, 1555.

CHAPTER 7

1492

When the weather became favourable, Columbus made another attempt, on the 14th of December, to find the island of Babeque, but was again baffled by adverse winds. In the course of this attempt, he visited an island lying opposite to the harbour of Concepcion, to which, from its abounding in turtle, he gave the name of Tortugas.* The natives had fled to the rocks and forests, and alarm fires blazed along the heights. The country was so beautiful that he gave to one of the valleys the name of Valle de Paraiso, or the Vale of Paradise, and called a fine stream the Guadalquivir, after that renowned river which flows through some of the fairest provinces of Spain.†

Setting sail on the 16th of December at midnight, Columbus steered again for Hispaniola. When half-way across the gulf which separates the islands, he perceived a canoe navigated by a single Indian, and, as on a former occasion, was astonished at his hardihood in venturing so far from land in so frail a bark, and at his adroitness in keeping it above water, as the wind was fresh and there was some sea running. He ordered both him and his canoe to be taken on board; and having anchored near a village on the coast of Hispaniola, at present known as Puerto de Paz, he sent him on shore well regaled and enriched with various presents.

In the early intercourse with these people kindness never seems to have failed in its effect. The favourable accounts given by this Indian, and by those with whom the Spaniards had communicated in their previous landings, dispelled the fears of the islanders. A friendly intercourse soon took place, and the ships were visited by a cacique of the neighbourhood. From this chieftain and his counsellors Columbus had further information of the island of

---

* This island in after-times became the headquarters of the famous buccaneers.

† Journal of Columbus, Navarrete, *Colec.*, tom. i. p. 91.

Babeque, which was described as lying at no great distance. No mention is afterwards made of this island, nor does it appear that he made any further attempt to seek it. No such island exists in the ancient charts, and it is probable that this was one of the numerous misinterpretations of Indian words which led the first discoverers into so many fruitless researches. The people of Hispaniola appeared handsomer to Columbus than any he had yet met with, and of a gentle and peaceable disposition. Some of them had ornaments of gold, which they readily gave away or exchanged for any trifle. The country was finely diversified with lofty mountains and green valleys, which stretched away inland as far as the eye could reach. The mountains were of such easy ascent that the highest of them might be ploughed with oxen, and the luxuriant growth of the forests manifested the fertility of the soil. The valleys were watered by numerous clear and beautiful streams. They appeared to be cultivated in many places, and to be fitted for grain, for orchards, and pasturage.

While detained at this harbour by contrary winds, Columbus was visited by a young cacique, who came borne by four men on a sort of litter, and attended by two hundred of his subjects. The admiral being at dinner when he arrived, the young chieftain ordered his followers to remain without, and entering the cabin took his seat beside Columbus, not permitting him to rise or use any ceremony. Only two old men entered with him, who appeared to be his counsellors, and who seated themselves at his feet. If anything were given him to eat or drink, he merely tasted it, and sent it to his followers, maintaining an air of great gravity and dignity. He spoke but little, his two counsellors watching his lips and catching and communicating his ideas. After dinner he presented the admiral with a belt curiously wrought, and two pieces of gold. Columbus gave him a piece of cloth, several amber beads, coloured shoes, and a flask of orange-flower water. He showed him a Spanish coin, on which were the likenesses of the king and queen, and endeavoured to explain to him the power and grandeur of those sovereigns. He displayed also the royal banners and the standard of the cross. But it was all in vain to attempt to convey any clear idea by these symbols. The cacique could not be made to believe that there was a region on the earth which produced these wonderful people and wonderful things. He joined in the common idea that the Spaniards were more than mortal, and that the country and sovereigns they talked of must exist somewhere in the skies.

In the evening the cacique was sent on shore in the boat with great ceremony, and a salute fired in honour of him. He departed in the state in which he had come, carried on a litter, accompanied by a great concourse of his subjects. Not far behind him was his son, borne and escorted in like manner, and his brother on foot, supported by two attendants. The presents which he had received from the admiral were carried triumphantly before him.

They procured but little gold in this place, though whatever ornaments the natives possessed they readily gave away. The region of promise lay still further on, and one of the old counsellors of the cacique told Columbus that he would soon arrive at islands rich in the precious ore. Before leaving this place, the admiral caused a large cross to be erected in the centre of the village; and from the readiness with which the Indians assisted, and their implicit imitation of the Spaniards in their acts of devotion, he inferred that it would be an easy matter to convert them all to Christianity.

On the 19th of December they made sail before daylight, but with an unfavourable wind; and on the evening of the 20th they anchored in a fine harbour, to which Columbus gave the name of St Thomas, supposed to be what at present is called the Bay of Acùl. It was surrounded by a beautiful and well-peopled country. The inhabitants came off, some in canoes, some swimming, bringing fruits of various unknown kinds, of great fragrance and flavour. These they gave freely with whatever else they possessed, especially their golden ornaments, which they saw were particularly coveted by the strangers. There was a remarkable frankness and generosity about these people. They had no idea of traffic, but gave away everything with spontaneous liberality. Columbus would not permit his people, however, to take advantage of this free disposition, but ordered that something should always be given in exchange. Several of the neighbouring caciques visited the ships, bringing presents, and inviting the Spaniards to their villages, where, on going to land, they were most hospitably entertained.

On the 22nd of December a large canoe filled with natives came on a mission from a grand cacique named Guacanagari, who commanded all that part of the island. A principal servant of the chieftain came in the canoe, bringing the admiral a present of a broad belt, wrought ingeniously with coloured beads and bones, and a wooden mask, the eyes, nose, and tongue of which were of gold. He delivered also a message from the cacique, begging that the ships might come opposite to his residence, which was on a part of the coast a little further to the eastward. The wind preventing an immediate compliance with this invitation, the admiral sent the notary of the squadron, with several of the crew, to visit the cacique. He resided in a town, situated on a river, at what they called Punta Santa, at present Grande Rivière. It was the largest and best built town they had yet seen. The cacique received them in a kind of public square, which had been swept and prepared for the occasion, and treated them with great honour, giving to each a dress of cotton. The inhabitants crowded round them, bringing provisions and refreshments of various kinds. The seamen were received into their houses as distinguished guests. They gave them garments of cotton, and whatever else appeared to have value in their eyes, asking nothing in return; but if anything were given, appearing to treasure it up as a sacred relic.

The cacique would have detained them all night, but their orders obliged them to return. On parting with them, he gave them presents of parrots and pieces of gold for the admiral; and they were attended to their boats by a crowd of the natives, carrying the presents for them, and vying with each other in rendering them service.

During their absence the admiral had been visited by a great number of canoes and several inferior caciques. All assured him that the island abounded with wealth. They talked especially of Cibao, a region in the interior, further to the east, the cacique of which, as far as they could be understood, had banners of wrought gold. Columbus, deceiving himself as usual, fancied that this name Cibao must be a corruption of Cipango, and that this chieftain with golden banners must be identical with the magnificent prince of that island mentioned by Marco Polo.[*]

---

[*] Journal of Columbus, Navarrete, *Colec.*, tom. i.; *Hist. del Almirante*, cap. 32; Herrera, decad. i. lib. i. cap. 15, 16.

CHAPTER 8

1492

On the morning of the 24th of December, Columbus set sail from
Port St Thomas before sunrise, and steered to the eastward, with
an intention of anchoring at the harbour of the cacique Guacanagari. The wind was from the land, but so light as scarcely to fill
the sails, and the ships made but little progress. At eleven o'clock at
night, being Christmas eve, they were within a league or a league
and a half of the residence of the cacique; and Columbus, who had
hitherto kept watch, finding the sea calm and smooth, and the ship
almost motionless, retired to rest, not having slept the preceding
night. He was, in general, extremely wakeful on his coasting
voyages, passing whole nights upon deck in all weathers; never
trusting to the watchfulness of others where there was any difficulty or danger to be provided against. In the present instance he
felt perfectly secure; not merely on account of the profound calm,
but because the boats on the preceding day, in their visit to the
cacique, had reconnoitred the coast, and had reported that there
were neither rocks nor shoals in their course.

No sooner had he retired than the steersman gave the helm in
charge to one of the ship-boys, and went to sleep. This was in
direct violation of an invariable order of the admiral, that the helm
should never be intrusted to the boys. The rest of the mariners
who had the watch took like advantage of the absence of Columbus, and in a little while the whole crew was buried in sleep. In
the meantime the treacherous currents, which run swiftly along
this coast, carried the vessel quietly, but with force, upon a sand-
bank. The heedless boy had not noticed the breakers, although
they made a roaring that might have been heard a league. No
sooner, however, did he feel the rudder strike, and hear the tumult
of the rushing sea, than he began to cry for aid. Columbus, whose
careful thoughts never permitted him to sleep profoundly, was the

first on deck. The master of the ship, whose duty it was to have been on watch, next made his appearance, followed by others of the crew, half awake. The admiral ordered them to take the boat and carry out an anchor astern, to warp the vessel off. The master and the sailors sprang into the boat; but, confused as men are apt to be when suddenly awakened by an alarm, instead of obeying the commands of Columbus, they rowed off to the other caravel, about half a league to windward.

In the meantime, the master had reached the caravel, and made known the perilous state in which he had left the vessel. He was reproached with his pusillanimous desertion. The commander of the caravel manned his boat and hastened to the relief of the admiral, followed by the recreant master covered with shame and confusion.

It was too late to save the ship, the current having set her more upon the bank. The admiral, seeing that his boat had deserted him, that the ship had swung across the stream, and that the water was continually gaining upon her, ordered the mast to be cut away, in the hope of lightening her sufficiently to float her off. Every effort was in vain. The keel was firmly bedded in the sand, the shock had opened several seams, while the swell of the breakers, striking her broadside, left her each moment more and more aground, until she fell over on one side. Fortunately the weather continued calm, otherwise the ship must have gone to pieces, and the whole crew might have perished amidst the currents and breakers.

The admiral and her men took refuge on board the caravel. Diego de Arana, chief judge of the armament, and Pedro Gutierrez, the king's butler, were immediately sent on shore as envoys to the cacique Guacanagari, to inform him of the intended visit of the admiral, and of his disastrous shipwreck. In the meantime, as a light wind had sprung up from shore, and the admiral was ignorant of his situation, and of the rocks and banks that might be lurking around him, he lay-to until daylight.

The habitation of the cacique was about a league and a half from the wreck. When he heard of the misfortune of his guest, he manifested the utmost affliction, and even shed tears. He immediately sent all his people, with all the canoes, large and small, that could be mustered; and so active were they in their assistance, that in a little while the vessel was unloaded. The cacique himself, and his brothers and relatives, rendered all the aid in their power, both on sea and land; keeping vigilant guard that everything should be conducted with order, and the property secured from injury or theft. From time to time he sent some one of his family, or some principal person of his attendants, to console and cheer the admiral, assuring him that everything he possessed should be at his disposal.

Never, in a civilized country, were the vaunted rites of hospitality more scrupulously observed than by this uncultivated savage. All the effects landed from the ship were deposited near his dwelling; and an armed guard surrounded them all night, until houses could be prepared in which to store them. There seemed, however, even among the common people, no disposition to take advantage of the misfortune of the stranger. Although they beheld what must in their eyes have been inestimable treasures, cast, as it were, upon their shores, and open to depredation, yet there was not the least attempt to pilfer, nor in transporting the effects from the ship had they appropriated the most trifling article. On the contrary, a general sympathy was visible in their countenances and actions, and to have witnessed their concern one would have supposed the misfortune to have happened to themselves.*

'So loving, so tractable, so peaceable are these people,' says Columbus in his journal, 'that I swear to your majesties there is not in the world a better nation, nor a better land. They love their neighbours as themselves, and their discourse is ever sweet and gentle, and accompanied with a smile; and though it is true that they are naked, yet their manners are decorous and praiseworthy.'

* *Hist. del Almirante*, cap. 32; Las Casas, lib. i. cap. 9.

CHAPTER 9

1492

On the 26th of December, Guacanagari came on board of the caravel *Niña* to visit the admiral, and observing him to be very much dejected, was moved to tears. He repeated the message which he had sent, entreating Columbus not to be cast down by his misfortune, and offering everything he possessed that might render him aid or consolation. He had already given three houses to shelter the Spaniards, and to receive the effects landed from the wreck, and he offered to furnish more if necessary.

While they were conversing, a canoe arrived from another part of the island, bringing pieces of gold to be exchanged for hawks' bells. There was nothing upon which the natives set so much value as upon these toys. The Indians were extravagantly fond of the dance, which they performed to the cadence of certain songs, accompanied by the sound of a kind of drum, made from the trunk of a tree, and the rattling of hollow bits of wood: but when they hung the hawks' bells about their persons, and heard the clear musical sound responding to the movements of the dance, nothing could exceed their wild delight.

The sailors who came from the shore informed the admiral that considerable quantities of gold had been brought to barter, and large pieces were eagerly given for the merest trifle. This information had a cheering effect upon Columbus. The attentive cacique, perceiving the lighting up of his countenance, asked what the sailors had communicated. When he learned its purport, and found that the admiral was extremely desirous of procuring gold, he assured him by signs that there was a place not far off, among the mountains, where it abounded to such a degree as to be held in little value, and promised to procure him thence as much as he desired. The place to which he alluded, and which he called Cibao, was in fact a mountainous region afterwards found to contain valuable mines; but Columbus still confounded the name with that of Cipango.*

Guacanagari dined on board of the caravel with the admiral, after which he invited him to visit his residence. Here he had prepared a collation as choice and abundant as his simple means afforded, consisting of utias, or coneys, fish, roots, and various fruits. He did everything in his power to honour his guest and cheer him under his misfortune, showing a warmth of sympathy yet delicacy of attention which could not have been expected from his savage state. Indeed, there was a degree of innate dignity and refinement displayed in his manners that often surprised the Spaniards. He was remarkably nice and decorous in his mode of eating, which was slow and with moderation, washing his hands when he had finished, and rubbing them with sweet and odoriferous herbs, which Columbus supposed was done to preserve their delicacy and softness. He was served with great deference by his subjects, and conducted himself towards them with a gracious and prince-like majesty. His whole deportment, in the enthusiastic eyes of Columbus, betokened the inborn grace and dignity of lofty lineage.[†]

In fact, the sovereignty among the people of this island was hereditary, and they had a simple but sagacious mode of maintaining, in some degree, the verity of descent. On the death of a cacique without children, his authority passed to those of his sisters in preference to those of his brothers, being considered most likely to be of his blood; for they observed that a brother's reputed children may by accident have no consanguinity with their uncle, but those of his sister must certainly be the children of their mother. The form of government was completely despotic – the caciques had entire control over the lives, the property, and even the religion of their subjects. They had few laws, and ruled according to their judgment and their will; but they ruled mildly, and were implicitly and cheerfully obeyed. Throughout the course of the disastrous history of these islanders, after their discovery by the Europeans, there are continual proofs of their affectionate and devoted fidelity to their caciques.

After the collation, Guacanagari conducted Columbus to the beautiful groves which surrounded his residence. They were

* *Primer Viage de Colon*, Navarrete, tom. i. p. 114.

† Las Casas, lib. i. cap. 70, MS.; *Primer Viage de Colon*, Navarrete, tom. i. p. 114.

attended by upwards of a thousand of the natives, all perfectly naked, who performed several national games and dances which Guacanagari had ordered to amuse the melancholy of his guest.

When the Indians had finished their games, Columbus gave them an entertainment in return, calculated at the same time to impress them with a formidable idea of the military power of the Spaniards. He sent on board the caravel for a Moorish bow and a quiver of arrows, and a Castilian who had served in the wars of Granada, and was skilful in the use of them. When the cacique beheld the accuracy with which this man used his weapons, he was greatly surprised, being himself of an unwarlike character and little accustomed to the use of arms. He told the admiral that the Caribs, who often made descents upon his territory and carried off his subjects, were likewise armed with bows and arrows. Columbus assured him of the protection of the Castilian monarchs, who would destroy the Caribs; for he let him know that he had weapons far more tremendous, against which there was no defence. In proof of this, he ordered a Lombard or heavy cannon, and an arquebuse, to be discharged.

On hearing the report the Indians fell to the ground as though they had been struck by a thunderbolt; and when they saw the effect of the ball, rending and shivering the trees like a stroke of lightning, they were filled with dismay. Being told, however, that the Spaniards would defend them with these arms against their dreaded enemies the Caribs, their alarm was changed into exultation, considering themselves under the protection of the sons of heaven, who had come from the skies armed with thunder and lightning.

The cacique now presented Columbus with a mask carved of wood, with the eyes, ears, and various other parts of gold. He hung plates of the same metal round his neck, and placed a kind of golden coronet upon his head. He dispensed presents also among the followers of the admiral, acquitting himself in all things with a munificence that would have done honour to an accomplished prince in civilized life.

Whatever trifles Columbus gave in return were regarded with reverence as celestial gifts. The Indians, in admiring the articles of European manufacture, continually repeated the word *turey*, which in their language signifies heaven. They pretended to distinguish the different qualities of gold by the smell. In the same way, when any article of tin, of silver, or other white metal was given them to which they were unaccustomed, they smelt it and declared it 'turey' (of excellent quality), giving in exchange pieces of the finest gold. Everything, in fact, from the hands of the Spaniards, even a rusty piece of iron, an end of a strap, or a head of a nail, had an occult and supernatural value, and smelt of turey. Hawks' bells, however, were sought by them with a mania only equalled by that of the Spaniards for gold. They could not contain their ecstasies at the sound, dancing and playing a thousand antics. On one occasion an Indian gave half a handful of gold dust in exchange for one of these toys, and no sooner was he in possession of it than he bounded away to the woods, looking often behind him, fearing the Spaniards might repent of having parted so cheaply with such an inestimable jewel! [*]

The extreme kindness of the cacique, the gentleness of his people, the quantities of gold which were daily brought to be exchanged for the veriest trifles, and the information continually received of sources of wealth in the interior of this island, all contributed to console the admiral for his misfortune.

The shipwrecked crew also became fascinated with their easy and idle mode of life. Exempted by their simplicity from the cares and toils which civilized man inflicts upon himself by his many artificial wants, the existence of these islanders seemed to the Spaniards like a pleasant dream. They disquieted themselves about nothing. A few fields, cultivated almost without labour, furnished the roots and vegetables which formed a great part of their diet. Their rivers and coast abounded with fish; their trees were laden with fruits of golden or blushing hue, and heightened by a tropical sun to delicious flavour and fragrance. Softened by the indulgence of nature, and by a voluptuous climate, a great part of their day was passed in indolent repose, and in the evenings they danced in their fragrant groves to their national songs, or to the sound of their silvan drums.

Such was the indolent and holiday life of these simple people, which, if it had not the great scope of enjoyment nor the high seasoned poignancy of pleasure which attend civilization, was certainly destitute of most of its artificial miseries. The venerable

[*] Las Casas, lib. i. cap. 70, MS.

Las Casas, speaking of their perfect nakedness, observes: 'It seemed almost as if they were existing in the state of primeval innocence of our first parents, before their fall brought sin into the world.' He might have added that they seemed exempt likewise from the penalty inflicted on the children of Adam, that they should eat their bread by the sweat of their brow.

When the Spanish mariners looked back upon their own toil-some and painful life, and reflected on the cares and hardships that must still be their lot if they returned to Europe, it is no wonder that they regarded with a wistful eye the easy and idle existence of these Indians. Wherever they went they met with caressing hospitality. The men were simple, frank, and cordial; the women loving and compliant, and prompt to form those connections which anchor the most wandering heart. They saw gold glittering around them, to be had without labour, and every enjoyment to be procured without cost. Captivated by these advantages, many of the seamen represented to the admiral the difficulties and sufferings they must encounter on a return voyage, where so many would be crowded in a small caravel, and entreated permission to remain in the island.*

* *Primer Viage de Colon*, Navarrete, tom. i. p. 116.

The solicitude expressed by many of his people to be left behind, added to the friendly and pacific character of the natives, now suggested to Columbus the idea of forming the germ of a future colony. The wreck of the caravel would afford materials to construct a fortress, which might be defended by her guns and supplied with her ammunition; and he could spare provisions enough to maintain a small garrison for a year. The people who thus remained on the island could explore it, and make themselves acquainted with its mines and other sources of wealth; they might at the same time procure by traffic a large quantity of gold from the natives; they could learn their language, and accustom themselves to their habits and manners, so as to be of great use in future intercourse. In the meantime the admiral could return to Spain, report the success of his enterprise, and bring out reinforcements.

No sooner did this idea break upon the mind of Columbus than he set about accomplishing it with his accustomed promptness and celerity. The wreck was broken up and brought piece-meal to shore, and a site chosen and preparations made for the erection of a tower. When Guacanagari was informed of the intention of the admiral to leave a part of his men for the defence of the island from the Caribs, while he returned to his country for more, he was greatly overjoyed. His subjects manifested equal delight at the idea of retaining these wonderful people among them, and at the prospect of the future arrival of the admiral with ships freighted with hawks' bells and other precious articles. They eagerly lent their assistance in building the fortress, little dreaming that they were assisting to place on their necks the galling yoke of perpetual and toilsome slavery.

The preparations for the fortress were scarcely commenced, when certain Indians, arriving at the harbour, brought a report that a great vessel, like those of the admiral, had anchored in the river at the eastern end of the island. These tidings for a time dispelled a thousand uneasy conjectures which had harassed the mind of Columbus, for of course this vessel could be no other than the *Pinta*. He immediately procured a canoe from Guacanagari, with several Indians to navigate it, and despatched a Spaniard with a letter to Pinzon, couched in amicable terms, making no complaints of his desertion, but urging him to join company immediately.

After three days' absence the canoe returned. The Spaniard reported that he had pursued the coast for twenty leagues, but had neither seen nor heard anything of the *Pinta;* he considered the report, therefore, as incorrect. Other rumours, however, were immediately afterwards circulated at the harbour of this large vessel to the eastward; but, on investigation, they appeared to Columbus to be equally undeserving of credit. He relapsed, therefore, into his doubts and anxieties in respect to Pinzon. Since the shipwreck of his vessel, the desertion of that commander had become a matter of still more serious moment, and had obliged him to alter all his plans. Should the *Pinta* be lost, as was very possible in a voyage of such extent, and exposed to so many uncommon perils, there would then be but one ship surviving of the three which had set sail from Palos, and that one an indifferent sailer. On the precarious return of that crazy bark across an immense expanse of ocean would depend the ultimate success of the expedition. Should that one likewise perish, every record of this great discovery would be swallowed up with it; the name of Columbus would only be remembered as that of a mad adventurer, who, despising the opinions of the learned and the counsels of the wise, had departed into the wilds of the ocean, never to return; the obscurity of his fate, and its imagined horrors, might deter all future enterprise, and thus the New World might remain, as heretofore, unknown to civilized man. These considerations determined Columbus to abandon all further prosecution of his voyage; to leave unexplored the magnificent regions which were inviting him on every hand; to give up all hope for the present of finding his way to the dominions of the Grand Khan; and to lose no time in returning to Spain and reporting his discovery.

While the fortress was building, he continued to receive every day new proofs of the amity and kindness of Guacanagari. Whenever he went on shore to superintend the works, he was entertained in the most hospitable manner by that chieftain. He had the largest house in the place prepared for his reception, strewed or carpeted with palm-leaves, and furnished with low stools of a black and shining wood that looked like jet. When he received the admiral, it was always in a style of princely generosity, hanging around his neck some jewel of gold, or making him some present of similar value.

On one occasion he came to meet him on his landing, attended by five tributary caciques, each carrying a coronet of gold. They conducted him with great deference to the house already mentioned, where, seating him in one of the chairs, Guacanagari took off his own coronet of gold and placed it upon his head. Columbus, in return, took from his neck a collar of fine-coloured beads, which he put round that of the cacique. He invested him with his own mantle of fine cloth, gave him a pair of coloured boots, and put on his finger a large silver ring, upon which metal the Indians set a great value, it not being found in their island.

The cacique exerted himself to the utmost to procure a great quantity of gold for the admiral before his departure for Spain. The supplies thus furnished, and the vague accounts collected through the medium of signs and imperfect interpretations, gave Columbus magnificent ideas of the wealth in the interior of this island. The names of caciques, mountains, and provinces were confused together in his imagination, and supposed to mean various places where great treasure was to be found; above all, the name of Cibao continually occurred, the golden region among the mountains, whence the natives procured most of the ore for their ornaments. In the pimento or red pepper which abounded in the island, he fancied he found a trace of Oriental spices, and he thought he had met with specimens of rhubarb.

Passing, with his usual excitability, from a state of doubt and anxiety to one of sanguine anticipation, he now considered his shipwreck as a providential event mysteriously ordained by heaven to work out the success of his enterprise. Without this seeming disaster, he should never have remained to find out the secret wealth of the island, but should merely have touched at various parts of the coast and passed on. As a proof that the particular hand of Providence was exerted in it, he cites the circumstance of his having been wrecked in a perfect calm, without wind or wave, and the desertion of the pilot and mariners when sent to carry out an anchor astern; for, had they performed his orders, the vessel would have been hauled off, they would have pursued their voyage, and the treasures of the island would have remained a secret. But now he looked forward to glorious fruits to be reaped from this seeming evil. 'For he hoped,' he said, 'that when he returned from Spain, he should find a ton of gold collected in traffic by those whom he had left behind, and mines and spices discovered in such quantities that the sovereigns, before three years, would be able to undertake a crusade for the deliverance of the Holy Sepulchre;' the grand object to which he had proposed that they should dedicate the fruits of this enterprise.

Such was the visionary yet generous enthusiasm of Columbus the moment that prospects of vast wealth broke upon his mind. What in some spirits would have awakened a grasping and sordid avidity to accumulate, immediately filled his imagination with plans of magnificent expenditure. But how vain are our attempts to interpret the inscrutable decrees of Providence! The shipwreck, which Columbus considered an act of divine favour to reveal to him the secrets of the land, shackled and limited all his after discoveries. It linked his fortunes for the remainder of his life to this island, which was doomed to be to him a source of cares and troubles, to involve him in a thousand perplexities, and to becloud his declining years with humiliation and disappointment.

So great was the activity of the Spaniards in the construction of their fortress, and so ample the assistance rendered by the natives, that in ten days it was sufficiently complete for service. A large vault had been made, over which was erected a strong wooden tower, and the whole was surrounded by a wide ditch. It was stored with all the ammunition saved from the wreck, or that could be spared from the caravel; and the guns being mounted, the whole had a formidable aspect, sufficient to overawe and repulse this naked and unwarlike people. Indeed, Columbus was of opinion that but little force was necessary to subjugate the whole island. He considered a fortress and the restrictions of a garrison more requisite to keep the Spaniards themselves in order and prevent their wandering about and committing acts of licentiousness among the natives.

The fortress being finished, he gave it, as well as the adjacent village and the harbour, the name of La Navidad, or the Nativity, in memorial of their having escaped from the shipwreck on Christmas day. Many volunteered to remain on the island, from whom he selected thirty-nine of the most able and exemplary, and among them a physician, ship-carpenter, caulker, cooper, tailor, and gunner, all expert at their several callings. The command was given to Diego de Arana, a native of Cordova, and notary and alguazil to the armament, who was to retain all the powers vested in him by the Catholic sovereigns. In case of his death, Pedro Gutierrez was to command, and, he dying, Rodrigo de Escobedo. The boat of the wreck was left with them, to be used in fishing, a variety of seeds to sow, and a large quantity of articles for traffic, that they might procure as much gold as possible against the admiral's return.[*]

As the time drew nigh for his departure, Columbus assembled those who were to remain in the island, and made them an earnest

---

[*] *Primer Viage de Colon*, Navarrete, tom. i; *Hist. del Almirante*, cap. 33.

address, charging them, in the name of the sovereigns, to be obedient to the officer left in command; to maintain the utmost respect and reverence for the cacique Guacanagari and his chieftains, recollecting how deeply they were indebted to his goodness, and how important a continuance of it was to their welfare; to be circumspect in their intercourse with the natives, avoiding disputes, and treating them always with gentleness and justice; and, above all, being discreet in their conduct towards the Indian women, misconduct in this respect being the frequent source of troubles and disasters in the intercourse with savage nations. He warned them, moreover, not to scatter themselves asunder, but to keep together for mutual safety; and not to stray beyond the friendly territory of Guacanagari. He enjoined it upon Arana and the others in command to acquire a knowledge of the productions and mines of the island, to procure gold and spices, and to seek along the coast a better situation for a settlement, the present harbour being inconvenient and dangerous, from the rocks and shoals which beset its entrance.

On the 2nd of January 1493, Columbus landed to take a farewell of the generous cacique and his chieftains, intending the next day to set sail. He gave them a parting feast at the house devoted to his use, and commended to their kindness the men who were to remain, especially Diego de Arana, Pedro Gutierrez, and Rodrigo de Escobedo, his lieutenants, assuring the cacique that when he returned from Castile he would bring abundance of jewels more precious than any he or his people had yet seen. The worthy Guacanagari showed great concern at the idea of his departure, and assured him that, as to those who remained, he should furnish them with provisions, and render them every service in his power.

Once more, to impress the Indians with an idea of the warlike prowess of the white men, Columbus caused the crews to perform skirmishes and mock-fights with swords, bucklers, lances, crossbows, arquebuses, and cannon. The Indians were astonished at the keenness of the swords, and at the deadly power of the crossbows and arquebuses; but they were struck with awe when the heavy Lombards were discharged from the fortress, wrapping it in wreaths of smoke, shaking the forests with their report, and shivering the trees with the balls of stone used in artillery in those times. As these tremendous powers, however, were all to be

Cape Haytien at the present time

employed for their protection, they rejoiced while they trembled, since no Carib would now dare to invade their island.[*]

The festivities of the day being over, Columbus embraced the cacique and his principal chieftains, and took a final leave of them. Guacanagari shed tears, for while he had been awed by the dignified demeanour of the admiral, and the idea of his super-human nature, he had been completely won by the benignity of his manners. Indeed, the parting scene was sorrowful on all sides. The arrival of the ships had been an event of wonder and excite-ment to the islanders, who had as yet known nothing but the good qualities of their guests, and had been enriched by their celestial gifts; while the rude seamen had been flattered by the blind deference paid them, and captivated by the kindness and unlimited indulgence with which they had been treated.

The sorest parting was between the Spaniards who embarked and those who remained behind, from the strong sympathy caused by companionship in perils and adventures. The little garrison, however, evinced a stout heart, looking forward to the return of the admiral from Spain with large reinforcements, when they promised to give him a good account of all things in the island. The caravel was detained a day longer by the absence of some of the Indians whom they were to take to Spain. At length the signal-gun was fired. The crew gave a parting cheer to the handful of comrades thus left in the wilderness of an unknown world, who echoed their cheering as they gazed wistfully after them from the beach, but who were destined never to welcome their return.

*Note about the localities in the preceding chapter,
extracted from the letter of T. S. Heneken, Esq.*

Guacanagari's capital town was called Guarico. From the best information I can gather, it was situated a short distance from the beach, where the village of Petit Anse now stands, which is about two miles south-east of Cape Haytien.

Oviedo says that Columbus took in water for his homeward voyage from a small stream to the north-west of the anchorage; and presuming him to have been at anchor off Petit Anse, this

* *Primer Viage de Colon*, Navarrete, tom. i. p. 121.

stream presents itself falling from the Picolet Mountain, crossing the present town of Cape Haytien, and emptying into the bay near the Arsenal.

The stream which supplied Columbus with water was dammed up at the foot of the mountain by the French when in possession of the country, and its water now feeds a number of public fountains.

Punta Santa could be no other than the present Point Picolet.

Beating up from St Nicholas Mole along an almost precipitous and iron-bound coast, a prospect of unrivalled splendour breaks upon the view on turning this point; the spacious bay, the extensive plains, and the distant cordilleras of the Cibao Mountains, impose upon the mind an impression of vastness, fertility, and beauty.

The fort of La Navidad must have been erected near Haut du Cap, as it could be approached in boats by rowing up the river, and there is no other river in the vicinity that admits a passage for boats.

The locality of the town of Guacanagari has always been known by the name of Guarico. The French first settled at Petit Anse; subsequently they removed to the opposite side of the bay and founded the town of Cape François, now Cape Haytien ; but the old Indian name Guarico continues in use among all the Spanish inhabitants of the vicinity.

BOOK 5

CHAPTER I

1493

It was on the 4th of January that Columbus set sail from La Navidad on his return to Spain. The wind being light, it was necessary to tow the caravel out of the harbour and clear of the reefs. They then stood eastward, towards a lofty promontory destitute of trees, but covered with grass, and shaped like a tent, having at a distance the appearance of a towering island, being connected with Hispaniola by a low neck of land. To this promontory Columbus gave the name of Monte Christi, by which it is still known. The country in the immediate neighbourhood was level, but farther inland rose a high range of mountains, well wooded, with broad, fruitful valleys between them, watered by abundant streams. The wind being contrary, they were detained for two days in a large bay to the west of the promontory. On the 6th, they again made sail with a land breeze, and, weathering the cape, advanced ten leagues, when the wind again turned to blow freshly from the east. At this time a sailor, stationed at the masthead to look out for rocks, cried out that he beheld the *Pinta* at a distance. The certainty of the fact gladdened the heart of the admiral, and had an animating effect throughout the ship; for it was a joyful event to the mariners once more to meet with their comrades, and to have a companion bark in their voyage through these lonely seas.

The *Pinta* came sweeping towards them, directly before the wind. The admiral was desirous of having a conversation with Martin Alonzo Pinzon; and seeing that all attempt was fruitless from the obstinacy of the adverse wind, and that there was no safe anchorage in the neighbourhood, he put back to the bay a little west of Monte

Christi, whither he was followed by the *Pinta*. On their first interview, Pinzon endeavoured to excuse his desertion, alleging that he had been compelled to part company by stress of weather, and had ever since been seeking to rejoin the admiral. Columbus listened passively but dubiously to his apologies, and the suspicions he had conceived appeared to be warranted by subsequent information. He was told that Pinzon had been excited by accounts given him by one of the Indians on board of his vessel of a region to the eastward abounding in gold. Taking advantage, therefore, of the superior sailing of his vessel, he had worked to windward, when the other ships had been obliged to put back, and had sought to be the first to discover and enjoy this golden region. After separating from his companions, he had been entangled for several days among a cluster of small islands, supposed to have been the Caicos, but had at length been guided by the Indians to Hispaniola. Here he remained three weeks, trading with the natives, in the river already mentioned, and collected a considerable quantity of gold, one half of which he retained as captain, the rest he divided among his men to secure their fidelity and secrecy.

Such were the particulars privately related to Columbus, who, however, repressed his indignation at this flagrant breach of duty, being unwilling to disturb the remainder of his voyage with any altercations with Pinzon, who had a powerful party of relatives and townsmen in the armament. To such a degree, however, was his confidence in his confederates impaired, that he determined to return forthwith to Spain, though, under other circumstances, he would have been tempted to explore the coast in hopes of freighting his ships with treasure.[*]

The boats were accordingly despatched to a large river in the neighbourhood, to procure a supply of wood and water for the voyage. This river, called by the natives the Yaqui, flows from the mountains of the interior and throws itself into the bay, receiving in its course the contributions of various minor streams. Many particles of gold were perceived among the sands at its mouth, and others were found adhering to the hoops of the water casks.[†]

---

[*] *Hist. del Almirante*, cap. 34.

[†] Las Casas suggests that these may have been particles of marcasite, which abounds in this river and in the other streams which fall from the mountains of Cibao.— Las Casas, *Hist. Ind.*, lib. i. cap. 76.

Columbus gave it, therefore, the name of Rio del Oro, or the Golden River: it is at present called the Santiago.

In this neighbourhood were turtles of great size. Columbus also mentions in his journal that he saw three mermaids, which elevated themselves above the surface of the sea, and he observes that he had before seen such on the coasts of Africa. He adds that they were by no means the beautiful beings they had been represented, although they possessed some traces of the human countenance. It is supposed that these must have been manati or sea-calves, seen indistinctly and at a distance; and that the imagination of Columbus, disposed to give a wonderful character to everything in this New World, had identified these misshapen animals with the sirens of ancient story.

On the evening of the 9th January they again made sail, and on the following day arrived at the river where Pinzon had been trading, to which Columbus gave the name of Rio de Gracia; but it took the appellation of its original discoverer, and long continued to be known as the river of Martin Alonzo.* The natives of this place complained that Pinzon, on his previous visit, had violently carried off four men and two girls. The admiral, finding they were retained on board of the *Pinta* to be carried to Spain and sold as slaves, ordered them to be immediately restored to their homes, with many presents, and well clothed, to atone for the wrong they had experienced. This restitution was made with great unwillingness and many high words on the part of Pinzon.

The wind being favourable – for in these regions the trade-wind is often alternated during autumn and winter by north-westerly breezes – they continued coasting the island until they came to a high and beautiful headland, to which they gave the name of Capo del Enamorado, or the Lovers' Cape, but which at present is known as Cape Cabron. A little beyond this, they anchored in a bay, or rather gulf, three leagues in breadth, and extending so far inland that Columbus at first supposed it an arm of the sea, separating Hispaniola from some other land. On landing they found the natives quite different from the gentle and pacific people hitherto met with on this island. They were of a ferocious aspect, and hideously painted. Their hair was long, tied behind, and

* It is now called Porto Caballo, but the surrounding plain is called the Savanna of Martin Alonzo. – T. S. HENEKEN.

decorated with the feathers of parrots and other birds of gaudy plumage. Some were armed with war-clubs; others had bows of the length of those used by the English archers, with arrows of slender reeds pointed with hard wood, or tipped with bone or the tooth of a fish. Their swords were of palm wood, as hard and heavy as iron; not sharp, but broad, nearly of the thickness of two fingers, and capable, with one blow, of cleaving through a helmet to the very brains.* Though thus prepared for combat, they made no attempt to molest the Spaniards; on the contrary, they sold them two of their bows and several of their arrows, and one of them was prevailed upon to go on board of the admiral's ship.

Columbus was persuaded, from the ferocious looks and hardy undaunted manner of this wild warrior, that he and his companions were of the nation of Caribs, so much dreaded throughout these seas, and that the gulf in which he was anchored must be a strait separating their island from Hispaniola. On inquiring of the Indian, however, he still pointed to the east, as the quarter where lay the Caribbean Islands. He spoke also of an island, called Mantinino, which Columbus fancied him to say was peopled merely by women, who received the Caribs among them once a year, for the sake of continuing the population of their island. All the male progeny resulting from such visits were delivered to the fathers, the female remained with the mothers.

This Amazonian island is repeatedly mentioned in the course of the voyages of Columbus, and is another of his self-delusions, to be explained by the work of Marco Polo. That traveller described two islands near the coast of Asia, one inhabited solely by women, the other by men, between which a similar intercourse subsisted;† and Columbus, supposing himself in that vicinity, easily interpreted the signs of the Indians to coincide with the descriptions of the Venetian.

Having regaled the warrior, and made him various presents, the admiral sent him on shore, in hopes, through his mediation, of opening a trade for gold with his companions. As the boat approached the land, upwards of fifty savages, armed with bows and arrows, war-clubs, and javelins, were seen lurking among the trees. On a word from the Indian who was in the boat, they

* Las Casas, *Hist. Ind.*, lib. i. cap. 77, MS.
† Marco Polo, book iii. chap. 34: Eng. edit. of Marsden.

laid by their arms and came forth to meet the Spaniards. The latter, according to directions from the admiral, endeavoured to purchase several of their weapons, to take as curiosities to Spain. They parted with two of their bows; but, suddenly conceiving some distrust, or thinking to overpower this handful of strangers, they rushed to the place where they had left their weapons, snatched them up, and returned with cords, as if to bind the Spaniards. The latter immediately attacked them, wounded two, put the rest to flight, and would have pursued them, but were restrained by the pilot who commanded the boat. This was the first contest with the Indians, and the first time that native blood was shed by the white men in the New World. Columbus was grieved to see all his exertions to maintain an amicable intercourse vain: he consoled himself with the idea, however, that if these were Caribs, or frontier Indians of warlike character, they would be inspired with a dread of the force of weapons of the white men, and be deterred from molesting the little garrison of Fort Nativity. The fact was that these were of a bold and hardy race, inhabiting a mountainous district called Ciguay, extending five-and-twenty leagues along the coast and several leagues into the interior. They differed in language, look, and manners from the other natives of the island, and had the rude but independent and vigorous character of mountaineers.

Their frank and bold spirit was evinced on the day after the skirmish, when a multitude appearing on the beach, the admiral sent a large party, well armed, on shore in the boat. The natives approached as freely and confidently as if nothing had happened; neither did they betray, throughout their subsequent intercourse, any signs of lurking fear or enmity. The cacique who ruled over the neighbouring country was on the shore. He sent to the boat a string of beads formed of small stones, or rather of the hard part of shells, which the Spaniards understood to be a token and assurance of amity; but they were not yet aware of the full meaning of this symbol, the wampum belt, the pledge of peace, held sacred among the Indians. The chieftain followed shortly after, and entering the boat with only three attendants, was conveyed on board of the caravel.

This frank and confiding conduct, so indicative of a brave and generous nature, was properly appreciated by Columbus. He received the cacique cordially, set before him a collation such as the caravel afforded, particularly biscuits and honey, which were great dainties with the Indians, and after showing him the wonders of the vessel, and making him and his attendants many presents, sent them to land highly gratified. The residence of the cacique was at such a distance that he could not repeat his visit, but, as a token of high regard, he sent to the admiral his coronet of gold. In speaking of these incidents, the historians of Columbus have made no mention of the name of this mountain chief. He was doubtless the same who, a few years afterwards, appears in the history of the island under the name of Mayonabex, cacique of the Ciguayans, and will be found acquitting himself with valour, frankness, and magnanimity under the most trying circumstances.

Columbus remained a day or two longer in the bay, during which time the most friendly intercourse prevailed with the natives, who brought cotton and various fruits and vegetables, but still maintained their warrior character, being always armed with bows and arrows. Four young Indians gave such interesting accounts of the islands situated to the east, that Columbus determined to touch there on his way to Spain, and prevailed on them to accompany him as guides. Taking advantage of a favourable wind, therefore, he sailed before daylight on the 16th of January from this bay, to which, in consequence of the skirmish with the natives, he gave the name of Golfo de las Flechas, or the Gulf of Arrows, but which is now known by the name of the Gulf of Samana.

On leaving the bay, Columbus at first steered to the north-east, in which direction the young Indians assured him he would find the island of the Caribs, and that of Mantinino, the abode of the Amazons, it being his desire to take several of the natives of each, to present to the Spanish sovereigns. After sailing about sixteen leagues, however, his Indian guides changed their opinion, and pointed to the south-east. This would have brought him to Porto Rico, which, in fact, was known among the Indians as the island of Carib. The admiral immediately shifted sail and stood in this direction. He had not proceeded two leagues, however, when a most favourable breeze sprang up for the voyage to Spain. He observed a gloom gathering on the countenances of the sailors as they diverged from the homeward route. Reflecting upon the little hold he had upon the feelings and affections of these men, the insubordinate spirit they had repeatedly evinced, the uncertainty of the good faith of Pinzon, and the leaky condition of his ships, he was suddenly brought to a pause. As long as he protracted his return, the whole fate of his discovery was at the mercy of a thousand contingencies, and an adverse accident might bury himself, his crazy barks, and all the records of his voyage for ever in the ocean. Repressing, therefore, the strong inclination to seek further discoveries, and determined to place what he had already made beyond the reach of accident, he once more shifted sail, to the great joy of his crews, and resumed his course for Spain.*

* Journ. of Columb., Navarrete, tom. i.; Las Casas, *Hist. Ind.*, lib. i. cap 77; *Hist. del Almirante*, cap. 34, 35.

CHAPTER 2

1493

The trade-winds, which had been so propitious to Columbus on his outward voyage, were equally adverse to him on his return. The favourable breeze soon died away, and throughout the remainder of January there was a prevalence of light winds from the eastward, which prevented any great progress. He was frequently detained also by the bad sailing of the *Pinta,* the foremast of which was so defective that it could carry but little sail. The weather continued mild and pleasant, and the sea so calm that the Indians whom they were taking to Spain would frequently plunge into the water and swim about the ships. They saw many tunny-fish, one of which they killed, as likewise a large shark. These gave them a temporary supply of provisions, of which they soon began to stand in need, their sea stock being reduced to bread and wine and Agi peppers, which last they had learned from the Indians to use as an important article of food.

In the early part of February, having run to about the thirty-eighth degree of north latitude, and got out of the tract swept by the trade-winds, they had more favourable breezes, and were enabled to steer direct for Spain. From the frequent changes of their course, the pilots became perplexed in their reckonings, differing widely among themselves, and still more widely from the truth. Columbus, besides keeping a careful reckoning, was a vigilant observer of those indications furnished by the sea, the air, and the sky; the fate of himself and his ships, in the unknown regions which he traversed, often depended upon these observations; and the sagacity at which he arrived, in deciphering the signs of the elements, was looked upon by the common seamen as something almost supernatural. In the present instance he noticed where the great bands of floating weeds commenced, and where they finished; and in emerging from among them, concluded himself to be in about the same degree of longitude as when he encountered them on his outward voyage – that is to say, about two hundred and sixty leagues west of Ferro. On the 10th of February, Vicente Yañez Pinzon, and the pilots Ruiz and Bartolomeo Roldan, who were on board of the admiral's ship, examined the charts and compared their reckonings to determine their situation, but could not come to any agreement. They all supposed themselves at least one hundred and fifty leagues nearer Spain than what Columbus believed to be the true reckoning, and in the latitude of Madeira, whereas he knew them to be nearly in a direction for the Azores. He suffered them, however, to remain in their error, and even added to their perplexity, that they might retain but a confused idea of the voyage, and he alone possess a clear knowledge of the route to the newly-discovered countries.[*]

On the 12th of February, as they were flattering themselves with soon coming in sight of land, the wind came on to blow violently, with a heavy sea. They still kept their course to the east, but with great labour and peril. On the following day, after sunset, the wind and swell increased; there were three flashes of lightning in the north-north-east, considered by Columbus as signals of an approaching tempest. It soon burst upon them with frightful violence. Their small and crazy vessels, open and without decks, were little fitted for the wild storms of the Atlantic; all night they were obliged to scud under bare poles. As the morning dawned of the 14th, there was a transient pause, and they made a little sail; but the wind rose again from the south with redoubled vehemence, raging throughout the day, and increasing in fury in the night; while the vessels laboured terribly in a cross sea, the broken waves of which threatened at each moment to overwhelm them or dash them to pieces. For three hours they lay-to, with just sail enough to keep them above the waves; but the tempest still augmenting, they were obliged again to scud before the wind. The *Pinta* was soon lost sight of in the darkness of the night. The admiral kept as much as possible to the north-east, to approach the coast of Spain, and made signal-lights at the mast-head for the *Pinta* to do the same, and to keep in company. The latter, however, from the weakness of her foremast, could not hold the wind, and was obliged to scud before it, directly north. For some time she replied to the signals of

[*] Las Casas, *Hist. Ind.*, lib. i. cap. 70.

the admiral; but her lights gleamed more and more distant, until they ceased entirely, and nothing more was seen of her.

Columbus continued to scud all night, full of forebodings of the fate of his own vessel and of fears for the safety of that of Pinzon. As the day dawned, the sea presented a frightful waste of wild broken waves lashed into fury by the gale. He looked round anxiously for the *Pinta*, but she was nowhere to be seen. He now made a little sail to keep his vessel ahead of the sea, lest its huge waves should break over her. As the sun rose, the wind and the waves rose with it, and throughout a dreary day the helpless bark was driven along by the fury of the tempest.

Seeing all human skill baffled and confounded, Columbus endeavoured to propitiate Heaven by solemn vows and acts of penance. By his orders a number of beans, equal to the number of persons on board, were put into a cap, on one of which was cut the sign of the cross. Each of the crew made a vow that should he draw forth the marked bean he would make a pilgrimage to the shrine of Santa Maria de Guadalupe, bearing a wax taper of five pounds weight. The admiral was the first to put in his hand, and the lot fell upon him. From that moment he considered himself a pilgrim, bound to perform the vow. Another lot was cast in the same way for a pilgrimage to the chapel of our Lady of Loretto, which fell upon a seaman named Pedro de Villa; and the admiral engaged to bear the expenses of his journey. A third lot was also cast for a pilgrimage to Santa Clara de Moguer, to perform a solemn mass, and to watch all night in the chapel; and this likewise fell upon Columbus.

The tempest still raging with unabated violence, the admiral and all the mariners made a vow that, if spared, wherever they first landed they would go in procession, barefooted and in their shirts, to offer up prayers and thanksgivings in some church dedicated to the Holy Virgin. Besides these general acts of propitiation, each one made his private vow, binding himself to some pilgrimage, or vigil, or other rite of penitence and thanksgiving at his favourite shrine. The heavens, however, seemed deaf to their vows; the storm grew still more wild and frightful, and each man gave himself up for lost. The danger of the ship was augmented by the want of ballast, the consumption of the water and provisions having lightened her so much that she rolled and tossed about at the mercy of the waves. To remedy this, and to render her more steady, the admiral ordered that all the empty casks should be filled with sea-water, which in some measure gave relief.

During this long and awful conflict of the elements the mind of Columbus was a prey to the most distressing anxiety. He feared that the *Pinta* had foundered in the storm. In such case the whole history of his discovery, the secret of the New World, depended upon his own feeble bark, and one surge of the ocean might bury it for ever in oblivion. The tumult of his thoughts may be judged from his own letter to the sovereigns. 'I could have supported this evil fortune with less grief,' said he, 'had my person alone been in jeopardy, since I am a debtor for my life to the supreme Creator, and have at other times been within a step of death. But it was a cause of infinite sorrow and trouble to think that after having been illuminated from on high with faith and certainty to undertake this enterprise, after having victoriously achieved it, and when on the point of convincing my opponents, and securing to your high-nesses great glory and vast increase of dominions, it should please the divine Majesty to defeat all by my death. It would have been more supportable, also, had I not been accompanied by others who had been drawn on by my persuasions, and who, in their distress, cursed not only the hour of their coming, but the fear inspired by my words which prevented their turning back, as they had at various times determined. Above all, my grief was doubled when I thought of my two sons, whom I had left at school in Cordova, destitute, in a strange land, without any testimony of the services rendered by their father, which, if known, might have inclined your highnesses to befriend them. And although, on the one hand, I was comforted by faith that the Deity would not permit a work of such great exaltation to his Church, wrought through so many troubles and contradictions, to remain imperfect; yet, on the other hand, I reflected on my sins, as a punishment for which he might intend that I should be deprived of the glory which would redound to me in this world.' *

In the midst of these gloomy apprehensions an expedient suggested itself, by which, though he and his ships should perish, the glory of his achievement might survive to his name, and its advantages be secured to his sovereigns. He wrote on parchment

* *Hist. del Almirante*, cap. 36.

a brief account of his voyage and discovery, and of his having taken possession of the newly-found lands in the name of their Catholic majesties. This he sealed and directed to the king and queen; superscribing a promise of a thousand ducats to whomsoever should deliver the packet unopened. He then wrapped it in a waxed cloth, which he placed in the centre of a cake of wax, and enclosing the whole in a large barrel, threw it into the sea, giving his men to suppose he was performing some religious vow. Lest this memorial should never reach the land, he enclosed a copy in a similar manner, and placed it upon the poop, so that, should the caravel be swallowed up by the waves, the barrel might float off and survive.

These precautions in some measure mitigated his anxiety; and he was still more relieved when, after heavy showers, there appeared at sunset a streak of clear sky in the west, giving hopes that the wind was about to shift to that quarter. These hopes were confirmed; a favourable breeze succeeded, but the sea still ran so high and tumultuously that little sail could be carried during the night.

On the morning of the 15th, at daybreak, the cry of land was given by Rui Garcia, a mariner in the main-top. The transports of the crew, at once more gaining sight of the Old World, were almost equal to those experienced on first beholding the New. The land bore east-north-east, directly over the prow of the caravel; and the usual diversity of opinion concerning it arose among the pilots. One thought it the island of Madeira; another the rock of Cintra, near Lisbon; the most part, deceived by their ardent wishes, placed it near Spain. Columbus, however, from his private reckonings and observations, concluded it to be one of the Azores. A nearer approach proved it to be an island. It was but five leagues distant, and the voyagers were congratulating themselves upon the assurance of speedily being in port, when the wind veered again to the east-north-east, blowing directly from the land, while a heavy sea kept rolling from the west.

For two days they hovered in sight of the island, vainly striving to reach it, or to arrive at another island of which they caught glimpses occasionally through the mist and rack of the tempest. On the evening of the 17th they approached so near the first island as to cast anchor; but parting their cable, had to put to sea again, where they remained beating about until the following morning, when they anchored under shelter of its northern side. For several days Columbus had been in such a state of agitation and anxiety as scarcely to take food or repose. Although suffering greatly from a gouty affection to which he was subject, yet he had maintained his watchful post on deck, exposed to wintry cold, to the pelting of the storm, and the drenching surges of the sea. It was not until the night of the 17th that he got a little sleep, more from the exhaustion of nature than from any tranquillity of mind. Such were the difficulties and perils which attended his return to Europe. Had one-tenth part of them beset this outward voyage, his timid and factious crew would have risen in arms against the enterprise, and he never would have discovered the New World.

CHAPTER 3

1493

On sending the boat to land, Columbus ascertained the island to be St Mary's, the most southern of the Azores, and a possession of the crown of Portugal. The inhabitants, when they beheld the light caravel riding at anchor, were astonished that it had been able to live through the gale which had raged for fifteen days with unexampled fury; but when they heard from the boat's crew that this tempest-tossed vessel brought tidings of a strange country beyond the ocean, they were filled with wonder and curiosity. To the inquiries about a place where the caravel might anchor securely, they replied by pointing out a harbour in the vicinity, but prevailed on three of the mariners to remain on shore and gratify them with further particulars of this unparalleled voyage.

In the evening, three men of the island hailed the caravel, and a boat being sent for them, they brought on board fowls, bread, and various refreshments from Juan de Castañeda, governor of the island, who claimed an acquaintance with Columbus, and sent him many compliments and congratulations. He apologized for not coming in person, owing to the lateness of the hour and the distance of his residence, but promised to visit the caravel the next morning, bringing further refreshments, and the three men, whom he still kept with him to satisfy his extreme curiosity respecting the voyage. As there were no houses on the neighbouring shore, the messengers remained on board all night.

On the following morning Columbus reminded his people of their vow to perform a pious procession at the first place where they should land. On the neighbouring shore, at no great distance from the sea, was a small hermitage or chapel dedicated to the Virgin, and he made immediate arrangements for the performance of the rite. The three messengers, on returning to the village, sent a priest to perform mass, and one-half of the crew landing, walked in procession, barefooted and in their shirts, to the chapel, while the admiral awaited their return, to perform the same ceremony with the remainder.

An ungenerous reception, however, awaited the poor tempest-tossed mariners on their first return to the abode of civilized men, far different from the sympathy and hospitality they had experienced among the savages of the New World. Scarcely had they begun their prayers and thanksgivings when the rabble of the village, horse and foot, headed by the governor, surrounded the hermitage and took them all prisoners.

As an intervening point of land hid the hermitage from the view of the caravel, the admiral remained in ignorance of this transaction. When eleven o'clock arrived without the return of the pilgrims, he began to fear that they were detained by the Portuguese, or that the boat had been shattered upon the surf-beaten rocks which bordered the island. Weighing anchor, therefore, he stood in a direction to command a view of the chapel and the adjacent shore; whence he beheld a number of armed horsemen, who, dismounting, entered the boat and made for the caravel. The admiral's ancient suspicions of Portuguese hostility towards himself and his enterprise were immediately revived; and he ordered his men to arm themselves, but to keep out of sight, ready either to defend the vessel or surprise the boat. The latter, however, approached in a pacific manner. The governor of the island was on board, and coming within hail, demanded assurance of personal safety in case he should enter the caravel. This the admiral readily gave, but the Portuguese still continued at a wary distance. The indignation of Columbus now broke forth. He reproached the governor with his perfidy, and with the wrong he did, not merely to the Spanish monarchs, but to his own sovereign, by such a dishonourable outrage. He informed him of his own rank and dignity; displayed his letters patent, sealed with the royal seal of Castile; and threatened him with the vengeance of his government. Castañeda replied in a vein of contempt and defiance, declaring that all he had done was in conformity to the commands of the king his sovereign.

After an unprofitable altercation, the boat returned to shore, leaving Columbus much perplexed by this unexpected hostility, and fearful that a war might have broken out between Spain and

Portugal during his absence. The next day the weather became so tempestuous that they were driven from their anchorage, and obliged to stand to sea toward the island of St Michael. For two days the ship continued beating about in great peril, half of her crew being detained on shore, and the greater part of those on board being landsmen and Indians, almost equally useless in difficult navigation. Fortunately, although the waves ran high, there were none of those cross seas which had recently prevailed, otherwise, being so feebly manned, the caravel could scarcely have lived through the storm.

On the evening of the 22nd, the weather having moderated, Columbus returned to his anchorage at St Mary's. Shortly after his arrival a boat came off, bringing two priests and a notary. After a cautious parley and an assurance of safety they came on board, and requested a sight of the papers of Columbus, on the part of Castañeda, assuring him that it was the disposition of the governor to render him every service in his power, provided he really sailed in service of the Spanish sovereigns. Columbus supposed it a manoeuvre of Castañeda to cover a retreat from the hostile position he had assumed. Restraining his indignation, however, and expressing his thanks for the friendly disposition of the governor, he showed his letters of commission, which satisfied the priests and the notary. On the following morning the boat and mariners were liberated. The latter, during their detention, had collected information from the inhabitants which elucidated the conduct of Castañeda.

The King of Portugal, jealous lest the expedition of Columbus might interfere with his own discoveries, had sent orders to his commanders of islands and distant ports to seize and detain him wherever he should be met with.[*] In compliance with these orders, Castañeda had, in the first instance, hoped to surprise Columbus in the chapel; and, failing in that attempt, had intended to get him in his power by stratagem, but was deterred by finding him on his guard. Such was the first reception of the admiral on his return to the Old World; an earnest of the crosses and troubles with which he was to be requited throughout life, for one of the greatest benefits that ever man conferred upon his fellow-beings.

---

[*] *Hist. del Almirante*, cap. 39; Las Casas, *Hist. Ind.*, lib. i. cap. 72.

Columbus remained two days longer at the island of St Mary's, endeavouring to take in wood and ballast, but was prevented by the heavy surf which broke upon the shore. The wind veering to the south, and being dangerous for vessels at anchor off the island, but favourable for the voyage to Spain, he set sail on the 24th of February, and had pleasant weather until the 27th, when, being within one hundred and twenty-five leagues of Cape St Vincent, he again encountered contrary gales and a boisterous sea. His fortitude was scarcely proof against these perils and delays, which appeared to increase the nearer he approached his home, and he could not help uttering a complaint at thus being repulsed, as it were, 'from the very door of the house'. He contrasted the rude storms which raged about the coasts of the Old World with the genial airs, the tranquil seas, and balmy weather which he supposed perpetually to prevail about the countries he had discovered. 'Well,' says he, 'may the sacred theologians and sage philosophers declare that the terrestrial paradise is in the uttermost extremity of the East, for it is the most temperate of regions.'

After experiencing several days of stormy and adverse weather, about midnight on Saturday, the 2nd of March, the caravel was struck by a squall of wind, which rent all her sails, and, continuing to blow with resistless violence, obliged her to scud under bare poles, threatening her each moment with destruction. In this hour of darkness and peril the crew again called upon the aid of Heaven. A lot was cast for the performance of a barefooted pilgrimage to the shrine of Santa Maria de la Cueva, in Huelva; and, as usual, the lot fell upon Columbus. There was something singular in the recurrence of this circumstance. Las Casas devoutly considers it as an intimation from the Deity to the admiral that these storms were all on his account, to humble his pride, and prevent his arrogating to himself the glory of a discovery which was the work of God, and for which he had merely been chosen as an instrument.[*]

Various signs appeared of the vicinity of land, which they supposed must be the coast of Portugal. The tempest, however, increased to such a degree that they doubted whether any of them would survive to reach a port. The whole crew made a vow, in case their lives were spared, to fast upon bread and water the following Saturday. The turbulence of the elements was still greater in the course of the following night. The sea was broken, wild, and mountainous; at one moment the light caravel was tossed high in the air, and the next moment seemed sinking in a yawning abyss. The rain at times fell in torrents, and the lightning flashed and thunder pealed from various parts of the heavens.

In the first watch of this fearful night the seamen gave the usually welcome cry of land, but it now only increased the general alarm. They knew not where they were, nor where to look for a harbour; they dreaded being driven on shore or dashed upon rocks; and thus the very land they had so earnestly desired was a terror to them. Taking in sail, therefore, they kept to sea as much as possible, and waited anxiously for the morning light.

At daybreak, on the 4th of March, they found themselves off the rock of Cintra, at the mouth of the Tagus. Though entertaining a strong distrust of the goodwill of Portugal, the still-prevailing tempest left Columbus no alternative but to run in for shelter. He accordingly anchored, about three o'clock, opposite to Rastello, to the great joy of the crew, who returned thanks to God for their escape from so many perils.

The inhabitants came off from various parts of the shore, congratulating them upon what they considered a miraculous preservation. They had been watching the vessel the whole morning with great anxiety, and putting up prayers for her safety. The oldest mariners of the place assured Columbus they had never known so tempestuous a winter; many vessels had remained for months in port weatherbound, and there had been numerous shipwrecks.

Immediately on his arrival, Columbus despatched a courier to the King and Queen of Spain with tidings of his discovery. He wrote also to the King of Portugal, then at Valparaiso, requesting permission to go with his vessel to Lisbon; for a report had gone

[*] Las Casas, *Hist. Ind.*, lib. i. cap. 73.

abroad that his caravel was laden with gold, and he felt insecure in the mouth of the Tagus, in the neighbourhood of a place like Rastello, scantily peopled by needy and adventurous inhabitants. To prevent any misunderstanding as to the nature of his voyage, he assured the king that he had not been on the coast of Guinea, nor to any other of the Portuguese colonies, but had come from Cipango and the extremity of India, which he had discovered by sailing to the west.

On the following day, Don Alonzo de Acuña, the captain of a large Portuguese man-of-war stationed at Rastello, summoned Columbus on board his ship, to give an account of himself and his vessel. The latter asserted his rights and dignities as admiral of the Castilian sovereigns, and refused to leave his vessel or to send anyone in his place. No sooner, however, did the commander learn his rank, and the extraordinary nature of his voyage, than he came to the caravel with great sound of drums, fifes, and trumpets, manifesting the courtesy of a brave and generous spirit, and making the fullest offer of his services.

When the tidings reached Lisbon of this wonderful bark, anchored in the Tagus, freighted with the people and productions of a newly-discovered world, the effect may be more easily conceived than described. Lisbon, for nearly a century, had derived its chief glory from its maritime discoveries; but here was an achievement that eclipsed them all. Curiosity could scarcely have been more excited had the vessel come freighted with the wonders of another planet. For several days the Tagus presented a gay and moving picture, covered with barges and boats of every kind swarming round the caravel. From morning till night the vessel was thronged with visitors, among whom were cavaliers of high distinction and various officers of the crown. All hung with rapt attention upon the accounts given by Columbus and his crew of the events of their voyage, and of the New World they had discovered, and gazed with insatiable curiosity upon the specimens of unknown plants and animals, but, above all, upon the Indians, so different from any race of men hitherto known. Some were filled with generous enthusiasm at the idea of a discovery so sublime and so beneficial to mankind; the avarice of others was inflamed by the description of wild, unappropriated regions teeming with gold, with pearls, and spices; while others repined at the

incredulity of the king and his councillors, by which so immense
an acquisition had been for ever lost to Portugal.

On the 8th of March, a cavalier, called Don Martin de Noroña,
came with a letter from King John, congratulating Columbus on
his arrival, and inviting him to the court, which was then at
Valparaiso, about nine leagues from Lisbon. The king, with his
usual magnificence, issued orders at the same time that everything
which the admiral required for himself, his crew, or his vessel
should be furnished promptly and abundantly, without cost.

Columbus would gladly have declined the royal invitation,
feeling distrust of the good faith of the king; but tempestuous
weather had placed him in his power, and he thought it prudent to
avoid all appearance of suspicion. He set forth, therefore, that very
evening for Valparaiso, accompanied by his pilot. The first night
he slept at Sacamben, where preparations had been made for his
honourable entertainment. The weather being rainy, he did not
reach Valparaiso until the following night. On approaching the
royal residence, the principal cavaliers of the king's household
came forth to meet him, and attended him with great ceremony to
the palace. His reception by the monarch was worthy of an
enlightened prince. He ordered him to seat himself in his presence,
an honour only granted to persons of royal dignity; and after many
congratulations on the result of his enterprise, assured him that
everything in his kingdom that could be of service to his sovereigns or himself was at his command.

A long conversation ensued, in which Columbus gave an account
of his voyage and of the countries he had discovered. The king
listened with much seeming pleasure, but with secret grief and
mortification, reflecting that this splendid enterprise had once
been offered to himself, and had been rejected. A casual observation showed what was passing in his thoughts. He expressed a
doubt whether the discovery did not really appertain to the crown
of Portugal, according to the capitulations of the treaty of 1479
with the Castilian sovereigns. Columbus replied that he had never
seen those capitulations, nor knew anything of their nature; his
orders had been not to go to La Miña nor the coast of Guinea,
which orders he had carefully observed. The king made a gracious
reply, expressing himself satisfied that he had acted correctly, and
persuaded that these matters would be readily adjusted between

the two powers without the need of umpires. On dismissing Columbus for the night, he gave him in charge as guest to the Prior of Crato, the principal personage present, by whom he was honourably and hospitably entertained.

On the following day the king made many minute inquiries as to the soil, productions, and people of the newly-discovered countries, and the route taken in the voyage; to all which Columbus gave the fullest replies, endeavouring to show in the clearest manner that these were regions heretofore undiscovered and unappropriated by any Christian power. Still the king was uneasy lest this vast and undefined discovery should in some way interfere with his own newly-acquired territories. He doubted whether Columbus had not found a short way to those very countries which were the object of his own expeditions, and which were comprehended in the papal bull granting to the crown of Portugal all the lands which it should discover from Cape Non to the Indies.

On suggesting these doubts to his councillors, they eagerly confirmed them. Some of these were the very persons who had once derided this enterprise, and scoffed at Columbus as a dreamer. To them its success was a source of confusion, and the return of Columbus, covered with glory, a deep humiliation. Incapable of conceiving the high and generous thoughts which elevated him at that moment above all mean considerations, they attributed to all his actions the most petty and ignoble motives. His rational exultation was construed into an insulting triumph, and they accused him of assuming a boastful and vainglorious tone when talking with the king of his discovery, as if he would revenge himself upon the monarch for having rejected his propositions.* With the greatest eagerness, therefore, they sought to foster the doubts which had sprung up in the royal mind. Some who had seen the natives brought in the caravel declared that their colour, hair, and manners agreed with the descriptions of the people of that part of India which lay within the route of the Portuguese

---

* Vasconcelos, *Vida de D. Juan II*, lib. vi. The Portuguese historians in general charge Columbus with having conducted himself loftily, and talking in vaunting terms of his discoveries, in his conversations with the king. It is evident their information must have been derived from prejudiced courtiers. Faria y Souza, in his *Europa Portuguesa* (Parte iii. cap. 4), goes so far as to say that Columbus entered into the port of Rastello merely to make Portugal sensible, by the sight of the trophies of his discovery, how much she had lost by not accepting his propositions.

discoveries, and which had been included in the papal bull. Others observed that there was but little distance between the Terceira Islands and those which Columbus had discovered, and that the latter, therefore, clearly appertained to Portugal. Seeing the king much perturbed in spirit, some even went so far as to propose, as a means of impeding the prosecution of these enterprises, that Columbus should be assassinated, declaring that he deserved death for attempting to deceive and embroil the two nations by his pretended discoveries. It was suggested that his assassination might easily be accomplished without incurring any odium: advantage might be taken of his lofty deportment to pique his pride, provoke him into an altercation, and then despatch him as if in casual and honourable encounter.

It is difficult to believe that such wicked and dastardly counsel could have been proposed to a monarch so upright as John II; but the fact is asserted by various historians, Portuguese as well as Spanish,* and it accords with the perfidious advice formerly given to the monarch in respect to Columbus. There is a spurious loyalty about courts which is often prone to prove its zeal by its baseness; and it is the weakness of kings to tolerate the grossest faults when they appear to arise from personal devotion.

Happily, the king had too much magnanimity to adopt the iniquitous measure proposed. He did justice to the great merit of Columbus, and honoured him as a distinguished benefactor of mankind; and he felt it his duty, as a generous prince, to protect all strangers driven by adverse fortune to his ports. Others of his council suggested a more bold and martial line of policy. They advised that Columbus should be permitted to return to Spain; but that, before he could fit out a second expedition, a powerful armament should be despatched, under the guidance of two Portuguese mariners who had sailed with the admiral, to take possession of the newly-discovered country – possession being, after all, the best title, and an appeal to arms the clearest mode of settling so doubtful a question.

This counsel, in which there was a mixture of courage and craft, was more relished by the king, and he resolved privately but promptly to put it in execution, fixing upon Don Francisco de

* Vasconcelos, *Vida del Rei Don Juan II*, lib. vi.; Garcia de Resende, *Vida do Dom Joam II*; Las Casas, *Hist. Ind.*, lib. i. cap. 74, MS.

Almeida, one of the most distinguished captains of the age, to command the expedition.[*]

In the meantime, Columbus, after being treated with distinguished attention, was escorted back to his ship by Don Martin de Noroña and a numerous train of cavaliers of the court, a mule being provided for himself, and another for his pilot, to whom the king made a present of twenty espadinas or ducats of gold.[†] On his way, Columbus stopped at the monastery of San Antonio, at Villa Franca, to visit the queen, who had expressed an earnest wish to see this extraordinary and enterprising man, whose achievement was the theme of every tongue. He found her attended by a few of her favourite ladies, and experienced the most flattering reception. Her majesty made him relate the principal events of his voyage, and describe the countries he had found, and she and her ladies hung with eager curiosity upon his narration. That night he slept at Llandra; and being on the point of departing in the morning, a servant of the king arrived to attend him to the frontier, if he preferred to return to Spain by land, and to provide horses, lodgings, and everything he might stand in need of at the royal expense. The weather, however, having moderated, he preferred returning in his caravel. Putting to sea, therefore, on the 13th of March, he arrived safely at the bar of Saltes on sunrise on the 15th, and at mid-day entered the harbour of Palos, whence he had sailed on the 3rd of August in the preceding year, having taken not quite seven months and a half to accomplish this most momentous of all maritime enterprises.[‡]

---

[*] Vasconcelos, lib. vi.

[†] Twenty-eight dollars in gold of the present day, and equivalent to seventy-four dollars, considering the depreciation of the precious metals.

[‡] Works generally consulted in this chapter – Las Casas, *Hist. Ind.*, lib. i. cap. 17; *Hist. del Almirante*, cap. 39, 40, 41; Journal of Columb., Navarrete, tom. i.

CHAPTER 5

1493

The triumphant return of Columbus was a prodigious event in the history of the little port of Palos, where everybody was more or less interested in the fate of his expedition. The most important and wealthy sea-captains of the place had engaged in it, and scarcely a family but had some relative or friend among the navigators. The departure of the ships upon what appeared a chimerical and desperate cruise had spread gloom and dismay over the place, and the storms which had raged throughout the winter had heightened the public despondency. Many lamented their friends as lost, while imagination lent mysterious horrors to their fate, picturing them as driven about over wild and desert wastes of water without a shore, or as perishing amidst rocks and quicksands and whirlpools, or a prey to those monsters of the deep with which credulity peopled every distant and unfrequented sea. There was something more awful in such a mysterious fate than in death itself under any defined and ordinary form.*

Great was the agitation of the inhabitants, therefore, when they beheld one of the ships standing up the river; but when they learned that she returned in triumph from the discovery of a world, the whole community broke forth into transports of joy. The bells were rung, the shops shut, all business was suspended; for a time there was nothing but hurry and tumult. Some were anxious to know the fate of a relative, others of a friend, and all to learn the particulars of so wonderful a voyage. When Columbus

---

* In the maps and charts of those times, and even in those of a much later date, the variety of formidable and hideous monsters depicted in all remote parts of the ocean evince the terrors and dangers with which the imagination clothed it. The same may also be said of distant and unknown lands: the remote parts of Asia and Africa have monsters depicted in them which it would be difficult to trace to any originals in natural history.

landed, the multitude thronged to see and welcome him, and a grand procession was formed to the principal church to return thanks to God for so signal a discovery made by the people of that place – forgetting, in their exultation, the thousand difficulties they had thrown in the way of the enterprise. Wherever Columbus passed he was hailed with shouts and acclamations. What a contrast to his departure a few months before, followed by murmurs and execrations; or, rather, what a contrast to his first arrival at Palos, a poor pedestrian, craving bread and water for his child at the gate of a convent!

Understanding that the court was at Barcelona, he felt disposed to proceed thither immediately in his caravel. Reflecting, however, on the dangers and disasters he had already experienced on the seas, he resolved to proceed by land. He despatched a letter to the king and queen, informing them of his arrival; and soon after departed for Seville to await their orders, taking with him six of the natives whom he had brought from the New World. One had died at sea, and three were left ill at Palos.

It is a singular coincidence, which appears to be well authenticated, that on the very evening of the arrival of Columbus at Palos, and while the peals of triumph were still ringing from its towers, the *Pinta*, commanded by Martin Alonzo Pinzon, likewise entered the river. After her separation from the admiral in the storm, she had been driven before the gale into the Bay of Biscay, and had made the port of Bayonne. Doubting whether Columbus had survived the tempest, Pinzon had immediately written to the sovereigns, giving information of the discovery he had made, and had requested permission to come to court and communicate the particulars in person. As soon as the weather permitted, he had again set sail, anticipating a triumphant reception in his native port of Palos. When, on entering the harbour, he beheld the vessel of the admiral riding at anchor, and learned the enthusiasm with which he had been received, the heart of Pinzon died within him. It is said that he feared to meet Columbus in this hour of his triumph, lest he should put him under arrest for his desertion on the coast of Cuba; but he was a man of too much resolution to indulge in such a fear. It is more probable that a consciousness of his misconduct made him unwilling to appear before the public in the midst of their enthusiasm for Columbus; and perhaps he sickened at the honours heaped upon a man whose superiority he had been so unwilling to acknowledge. Getting into his boat, therefore, he landed privately, and kept out of sight until he heard of the admiral's departure. He then returned to his home, broken in health and deeply dejected, considering all the honours and eulogiums heaped upon Columbus as so many reproaches on himself. The reply of the sovereigns to his letter at length arrived. It was of a reproachful tenor, and forbade his appearance at court. This letter completed his humiliation; the anguish of his feelings gave virulence to his bodily malady, and in a few days he died, a victim to deep chagrin.*

Let no one, however, indulge in harsh censures over the grave of Pinzon. His merits and services are entitled to the highest praise; his errors should be regarded with indulgence. He was one of the foremost in Spain to appreciate the project of Columbus, animating him by his concurrence, and aiding him with his purse when poor and unknown at Palos. He afterwards enabled him to procure and fit out ships when even the mandates of the sovereigns were ineffectual; and finally embarked in the expedition with his brothers and his friends, staking life, property, everything upon the event. He thus entitled himself to participate largely in the glory of this immortal enterprise; but unfortunately, forgetting for a moment the grandeur of the cause, and the implicit obedience due to his commander, he yielded to the incitements of self-interest, and committed that act of insubordination which has cast a shade upon his name. In extenuation of his fault, however, may be alleged his habits of command, which rendered him impatient of control, his consciousness of having rendered great services to the expedition, and of possessing property in the ships. That he was a man of great professional merit is admitted by all his contemporaries. That he naturally possessed generous sentiments and an honourable ambition is evident from the poignancy with which he felt the disgrace drawn on him by his misconduct. A mean man would not have fallen a victim to self-upbraiding for having been convicted of a mean action. His story shows how one lapse from duty may counterbalance the merits of a thousand services;

* Muñoz, *Hist. N. Mundo*, lib. iv. § 14; Charlevoix, *Hist. St Domin.*, lib. ii.

how one moment of weakness may mar the beauty of a whole life of virtue; and how important it is for a man, under all circumstances, to be true, not merely to others, but to himself. *

* After a lapse of years the descendants of the Pinzons made strenuous representations to the crown of the merits and services of their family, endeavouring to prove, among other things, that but for the aid and encouragement of Martin Alonzo and his brothers, Columbus would never have made his discovery. Some of the testimony rendered on this and another occasion was rather extravagant and absurd. The Emperor Charles V, however, taking into consideration the real services of the brothers in the first voyage, and the subsequent expeditions and discoveries of that able and intrepid navigator Vicente Yañez Pinzon, granted to the family the well-merited rank and privileges of *Hidalguia*, a degree of nobility which constituted them noble hidalgos, with the right of prefixing the title of Don to their names. A coat-of-arms was also given them, emblematical of their services as discoverers. These privileges and arms are carefully preserved by the family at the present day.

The Pinzons at present reside principally in the little city of Moguer, about a league from Palos, and possess vineyards and estates about the neighbourhood. They are in easy if not affluent circumstances, and inhabit the best houses in Moguer. Here they have continued, from generation to generation, since the time of the discovery, filling places of public trust and dignity, enjoying the good opinion and good-will of their fellow-citizens, and flourishing in nearly the same state in which they were found by Columbus on his first visit to Palos. It is rare, indeed, to find a family in this fluctuating world so little changed by the revolutions of nearly three centuries and a half

Whatever Palos may have been in the time of Columbus, it is now a paltry village of about four hundred inhabitants, who subsist chiefly by labouring in the fields and vineyards. The Convent of La Rabida still exists, but is inhabited merely by two friars, with a novitiate and a lay brother. It is situated on a hill, surrounded by a scattered forest of pine trees, and overlooks the low, sandy country of the sea-coast, and the windings of the river by which Columbus sallied forth upon the ocean.

CHAPTER 6

The letter of Columbus to the Spanish monarchs had produced the greatest sensation at court. The event he announced was considered the most extraordinary of their prosperous reign, and following so close upon the conquest of Granada, was pronounced a signal mark of divine favour for that triumph achieved in the cause of the true faith. The sovereigns themselves were for a time dazzled by this sudden and easy acquisition of a new empire of indefinite extent and apparently boundless wealth, and their first idea was to secure it beyond the reach of dispute. Shortly after his arrival in Seville, Columbus received a letter from them expressing their great delight, and requesting him to repair immediately to court, to concert plans for a second and more extensive expedition. As the summer, the time favourable for a voyage, was approaching, they desired him to make any arrangements at Seville or elsewhere that might hasten the expedition, and to inform them, by the return of the courier, what was to be done on their part. This letter was addressed to him by the title of 'Don Christopher Columbus, our admiral of the Ocean sea, and viceroy and governor of the islands discovered in the Indies.' At the same time he was promised still further rewards. Columbus lost no time in complying with the commands of the sovereigns. He sent a memorandum of the ships, men, and munitions requisite, and having made such dispositions at Seville as circumstances permitted, set out for Barcelona, taking with him the six Indians and the various curiosities and productions brought from the New World.

The fame of his discovery had resounded throughout the nation, and as his route lay through several of the finest and most populous provinces of Spain, his journey appeared like the progress of a sovereign. Wherever he passed the country poured forth its inhabitants, who lined the road and thronged the villages. The streets, windows, and balconies of the towns were filled with eager spectators, who rent the air with acclamations. His journey was continually impeded by the multitude pressing to gain a sight of him and of the Indians, who were regarded with as much astonishment as if they had been natives of another planet. It was impossible to satisfy the craving curiosity which assailed him and his attendants at every stage with innumerable questions. Popular rumour, as usual, had exaggerated the truth, and had filled the newly-found country with all kinds of wonders.

About the middle of April Columbus arrived at Barcelona, where every preparation had been made to give him a solemn and magnificent reception. The beauty and serenity of the weather in that genial season and favoured climate contributed to give splendour to this memorable ceremony. As he drew near the place, many of the youthful courtiers and hidalgos, together with a vast concourse of the populace, came forth to meet and welcome him. His entrance into this noble city has been compared to one of those triumphs which the Romans were accustomed to decree to conquerors. First were paraded the Indians, painted according to their savage fashion, and decorated with their national ornaments of gold. After these were borne various kinds of live parrots, together with stuffed birds and animals of unknown species, and rare plants supposed to be of precious qualities; while great care was taken to make a conspicuous display of Indian coronets, bracelets, and other decorations of gold, which might give an idea of the wealth of the newly-discovered regions. After this followed Columbus on horseback, surrounded by a brilliant cavalcade of Spanish chivalry. The streets were almost impassable from the countless multitude, the windows and balconies were crowded with the fair, the very roofs were covered with spectators. It seemed as if the public eye could not be sated with gazing on these trophies of an unknown world, or on the remarkable man by whom it had been discovered. There was a sublimity in this event that mingled a solemn feeling with the public joy. It was looked upon as a vast and signal dispensation of Providence in reward for the piety of the monarchs; and the majestic and venerable appearance of the discoverer, so different from the youth and buoyancy generally expected from roving enterprise, seemed in harmony with the grandeur and dignity of his achievement.

To receive him with suitable pomp and distinction, the sovereigns had ordered their throne to be placed in public under a rich canopy of brocade of gold, in a vast and splendid saloon. Here the king and queen awaited his arrival, seated in state, with the Prince Juan beside them, and attended by the dignitaries of their court and the principal nobility of Castile, Valencia, Catalonia, and Aragon, all impatient to behold the man who had conferred so incalculable a benefit upon the nation. At length Columbus entered the hall, surrounded by a brilliant crowd of cavaliers, among whom, says Las Casas, he was conspicuous for his stately and commanding person, which, with his countenance, rendered venerable by his gray hairs, gave him the august appearance of a senator of Rome. A modest smile lighted up his features, showing that he enjoyed the state and glory in which he came.[*] And certainly nothing could be more deeply moving to a mind inflamed by noble ambition, and conscious of having greatly deserved, than these testimonials of the admiration and gratitude of a nation, or rather of a world. As Columbus approached, the sovereigns rose, as if receiving a person of the highest rank. Bending his knees, he offered to kiss their hands; but there was some hesitation on their part to permit this act of homage. Raising him in the most gracious manner, they ordered him to seat himself in their presence, a rare honour in this proud and punctilious court.[†]

At their request he now gave an account of the most striking events of his voyage, and a description of the islands discovered. He displayed specimens of unknown birds and other animals; of rare plants of medicinal and aromatic virtues; of native gold in dust, in crude masses, or laboured into barbaric ornaments; and, above all, the natives of these countries, who were objects of intense and inexhaustible interest. All these he pronounced mere harbingers of greater discoveries yet to be made, which would add realms of incalculable wealth to the dominions of their majesties, and whole nations of proselytes to the true faith.

When he had finished, the sovereigns sank on their knees, and raising their clasped hands to heaven, their eyes filled with tears of joy and gratitude, poured forth thanks and praises to God for so great a providence. All present followed their example; a deep

[*] Las Casas, *Hist. Ind.*, lib. i. cap. 78, MS.
[†] Las Casas, *Hist. Ind.*, lib i. cap. 78; *Hist. del Almirante*, cap. 81.

Columbus giving an account of his voyage to
Ferdinand and Isabella

and solemn enthusiasm pervaded that splendid assembly, and prevented all common acclamations of triumph. The anthem *Te Deum Laudamus*, chanted by the choir of the royal chapel, with the accompaniment of instruments, rose in full body of sacred harmony, bearing up, as it were, the feelings and thoughts of the auditors to heaven; 'so that,' says the venerable Las Casas, 'it seemed as if in that hour they communicated with celestial delights.' Such was the solemn and pious manner in which the brilliant court of Spain celebrated this sublime event, offering up a grateful tribute of melody and praise, and giving glory to God for the discovery of another world.

When Columbus retired from the royal presence, he was attended to his residence by all the court, and followed by the shouting populace. For many days he was the object of universal curiosity, and wherever he appeared, was surrounded by an admiring multitude.

While his mind was teeming with glorious anticipations, his pious scheme for the deliverance of the Holy Sepulchre was not forgotten. It has been shown that he suggested it to the Spanish sovereigns at the time of first making his propositions, holding it forth as the great object to be effected by the profits of his discoveries. Flushed with the idea of the vast wealth now to accrue to himself, he made a vow to furnish within seven years an army, consisting of four thousand horse and fifty thousand foot, for the rescue of the Holy Sepulchre, and a similar force within the five following years. This vow was recorded in one of his letters to the sovereigns, to which he refers, but which is no longer extant; nor is it certain whether it was made at the end of his first voyage, or at a subsequent date, when the magnitude and wealthy result of his discoveries became more fully manifest. He often alludes to it vaguely in his writings, and he refers to it expressly in a letter to Pope Alexander VI, written in 1502, in which he accounts also for its non-fulfilment. It is essential to a full comprehension of the character and motives of Columbus that this visionary project should be borne in recollection. It will be found to have entwined itself in his mind with his enterprise of discovery, and that a holy crusade was to be the consummation of those divine purposes for which he considered himself selected by Heaven as an agent. It shows how much his mind was elevated above selfish and mercenary views – how it was filled with those devout and heroic schemes which in the time of the crusades had inflamed the thoughts and directed the enterprises of the bravest warriors and most illustrious princes.

The joy occasioned by the great discovery of Columbus was not confined to Spain. The tidings were spread far and wide by the communications of ambassadors, the correspondence of the learned, the negotiations of merchants, and the reports of travellers, and the whole civilized world was filled with wonder and delight. How gratifying would it have been had the press at that time, as at present, poured forth its daily tide of speculation on every passing occurrence! With what eagerness should we seek to know the first ideas and emotions of the public on an event so unlooked-for and sublime! Even the first announcements of it by contemporary writers, though brief and incidental, derive interest from being written at the time, and from showing the casual way in which such great tidings were conveyed about the world. Allegretto Allegretti, in his annals of Sienna for 1493, mentions it as just made known there by the letters of their merchants who were in Spain, and by the mouths of various travellers.* The news was brought to Genoa by the return of her ambassadors, Francisco Marchesi and Giovanni Antonio Grimaldi, and was recorded among the triumphant events of the year;† for the republic, though she may have slighted the opportunity of making herself mistress of the discovery, has ever since been tenacious of the glory of having given birth to the discoverer. The tidings were soon carried to England, which as yet was but a maritime power of inferior importance. They caused, however, much wonder in London, and great talk and admiration in the court of Henry VII, where the discovery was pronounced 'a thing more divine than human'. We have this on the authority of Sebastian Cabot himself, the future discoverer of the northern continent of America, who was in London

---

* *Diarii Senesi* de Alleg. Allegretti; Muratori, *Ital. Script.*, tom. xxiii.
† Foglieta, *Istoria de Genova*, lib. ii.

at the time, and was inspired by the event with a generous spirit of emulation.[*]

Every member of civilized society, in fact, rejoiced in the occurrence, as one in which he was more or less interested. To some it opened a new and unbounded field of inquiry; to others, of enterprise; and every one awaited with intense eagerness the further development of this unknown world, still covered with mystery, the partial glimpses of which were so full of wonder. We have a brief testimony of the emotions of the learned in a letter written at the time by Peter Martyr to his friend Pomponius Laetus. 'You tell me, my amiable Pomponius,' he writes, 'that you leaped for joy, and that your delight was mingled with tears, when you read my epistle, certifying to you the hitherto hidden world of the antipodes. You have felt and acted as became a man eminent for learning; for I can conceive no aliment more delicious than such tidings to a cultivated and ingenuous mind. I feel a wonderful exultation of spirits when I converse with intelligent men who have returned from these regions. It is like an accession of wealth to a miser. Our minds, soiled and debased by the common concerns of life and the vices of society, become elevated and ameliorated by contemplating such glorious events.'[†]

Notwithstanding this universal enthusiasm, however, no one was aware of the real importance of the discovery. No one had an idea that this was a totally distinct portion of the globe, separated by oceans from the ancient world. The opinion of Columbus was universally adopted, that Cuba was the end of the Asiatic continent, and that the adjacent islands were in the Indian seas. This agreed with the opinions of the ancients, heretofore cited, about the moderate distance from Spain to the extremity of India, sailing westwardly. The parrots were also thought to resemble those described by Pliny, as abounding in the remote parts of Asia. The lands, therefore, which Columbus had visited were called the West Indies, and as he seemed to have entered upon a vast region of unexplored countries, existing in a state of nature, the whole received the comprehensive appellation of 'The New World'.

During the whole of his sojourn at Barcelona the sovereigns took every occasion to bestow on Columbus personal marks of

[*] Hakluyt, *Collect. Voyages*, vol. iii. p. 7.
[†] *Letters of P. Martyr*, let. 153.

their high consideration. He was admitted at all times to the royal presence, and the queen delighted to converse with him on the subject of his enterprises. The king, too, appeared occasionally on horseback, with Prince Juan on one side, and Columbus on the other. To perpetuate in his family the glory of his achievement, a coat of arms was assigned him, in which the royal arms, the castle and lion, were quartered with his proper bearings, which were a group of islands surrounded by waves. To these arms was afterwards annexed the motto:

> A Castilla y á Leon
> Nuevo mundo dio Colon.
>
> To Castile and Leon
> Columbus gave a new world.

The pension which had been decreed by the sovereigns to him who in the first voyage should discover land was adjudged to Columbus, for having first seen the light on the shore. It is said that the seaman who first descried the land was so incensed at being disappointed of what he conceived his merited reward, that he renounced his country and his faith, and going into Africa turned Mussulman – an anecdote which rests merely on the authority of Oviedo,[*] who is extremely incorrect in his narration of this voyage, and inserts many falsehoods told him by the enemies of the admiral.

It may, at first sight, appear but little accordant with the acknowledged magnanimity of Columbus to have borne away the prize from this poor sailor; but this was a subject in which his whole ambition was involved, and he was doubtless proud of the honour of being personally the discoverer of the land as well as projector of the enterprise.

Next to the countenance shown him by the king and queen may be mentioned that of Pedro Gonzalez de Mendoza, the Grand Cardinal of Spain, and first subject of the realm, a man whose elevated character for piety, learning, and high prince-like qualities, gave signal value to his favours. He invited Columbus to a banquet, where he assigned him the most honourable place at table, and had him served with the ceremonials which in those punctilious times were observed towards sovereigns. At this

---

[*] Oviedo, *Cronica de las Indias*, lib. ii. cap. 2.

repast is said to have occurred the well-known anecdote of the egg. A shallow courtier present, impatient of the honours paid to Columbus, and meanly jealous of him as a foreigner, abruptly asked him whether he thought that, in case he had not discovered the Indies, there were not other men in Spain who would have been capable of the enterprise? To this Columbus made no immediate reply, but, taking an egg, invited the company to make it stand on one end. Everyone attempted it, but in vain; whereupon he struck it upon the table so as to break the end, and left it standing on the broken part – illustrating in this simple manner, that when he had once shown the way to the New World, nothing was easier than to follow it.*

The favour shown Columbus by the sovereigns ensured him for a time the caresses of the nobility, for in court everyone vies with his neighbour in lavishing attentions upon the man 'whom the king delighteth to honour'. Columbus bore all these caresses and distinctions with becoming modesty, though he must have felt a proud satisfaction in the idea that they had been wrested, as it were, from the nation by his courage and perseverance. One can hardly recognize in the individual thus made the companion of princes, and the theme of general wonder and admiration, the same obscure stranger who but a short time before had been a common scoff and jest in this very court, derided by some as an adventurer, and pointed at by others as a madman. Those who had treated him with contumely during his long course of solicitation, now sought to efface the remembrance of it by adulations. Everyone who had given him a little cold countenance, or a few courtly smiles, now arrogated to himself the credit of having been a patron, and of having promoted the discovery of the New World. Scarce a great man about the court but has been enrolled by his historian or biographer among the benefactors of Columbus; though, had one-tenth part of this boasted patronage been really exerted, he would never have had to linger seven years soliciting for an armament of three caravels. Columbus knew well the weakness of the patronage that had been given him. The only friends mentioned by him with gratitude, in his after letters, as

---

* This anecdote rests on the authority of the Italian historian Benzoni (lib. i. p. 12, ed. Venetia, 1572). It has been condemned as trivial, but the simplicity of the reproof constitutes its severity, and was characteristic of the practical sagacity of Columbus. The universal popularity of the anecdote is a proof of its merit.

having been really zealous and effective, were those two worthy friars, Diego de Deza, afterwards Bishop of Palencia and Seville, and Juan Perez, the prior of the convent of La Rabida.

Thus honoured by the sovereigns, courted by the great, idolized by the people, Columbus, for a time, drank the honeyed draught of popularity, before enmity and detraction had time to drug it with bitterness. His discovery burst with such sudden splendour upon the world as to dazzle envy itself, and to call forth the general acclamations of mankind. Well would it be for the honour of human nature could history, like romance, close with the consummation of the hero's wishes; we should then leave Columbus in the full fruition of great and well-merited prosperity. But his history is destined to furnish another proof, if proof be wanting, of the inconstancy of public favour, even when won by distinguished services. No greatness was ever acquired by more incontestable, unalloyed, and exalted benefits rendered to mankind; yet none ever drew on its possessor more unremitting jealousy and defamation, or involved him in more unmerited distress and difficulty. Thus it is with illustrious merit: its very effulgence draws forth the rancorous passions of low and grovelling minds, which too often have a temporary influence in obscuring it to the world, as the sun, emerging with full splendour into the heavens, calls up, by the very fervour of its rays, the rank and noxious vapours which, for a time, becloud its glory.

CHAPTER 8

1493

In the midst of their rejoicings, the Spanish sovereigns lost no time in taking every measure necessary to secure their new acquisitions. Although it was supposed that the countries just discovered were part of the territories of the Great Khan, and of other Oriental princes, considerably advanced in civilization, yet there does not appear to have been the least doubt of the right of their Catholic majesties to take possession of them. During the crusades a doctrine had been established among Christian princes extremely favourable to their ambitious designs. According to this, they had the right to invade, ravage, and seize upon the territories of all infidel nations, under the plea of defeating the enemies of Christ and extending the sway of his church on earth. In conformity to the same doctrine, the Pope, from his supreme authority over all temporal things, was considered as empowered to dispose of all heathen lands to such potentates as would engage to reduce them to the dominion of the church, and to propagate the true faith among their benighted inhabitants. It was in virtue of this power that Pope Martin V and his successors had conceded to the crown of Portugal all the lands it might discover from Cape Bojador to the Indies; and the Catholic sovereigns, in a treaty concluded in 1479 with the Portuguese monarch, had engaged themselves to respect the territorial rights thus acquired. It was to this treaty that John II alluded in his conversation with Columbus, wherein he suggested his title to the newly-discovered countries.

On the first intelligence received from the admiral of his success, therefore, the Spanish sovereigns took the immediate precaution to secure the sanction of the Pope. Alexander VI had recently been elevated to the holy chair – a pontiff whom some historians have stigmatized with every vice and crime that could disgrace humanity, but whom all have represented as eminently able and politic.

He was a native of Valencia, and being born a subject of the
crown of Aragon, it might be inferred, was favourably disposed to
Ferdinand; but in certain questions which had come before him
he had already shown a disposition not the most cordial towards
the Catholic monarch. At all events, Ferdinand was well aware of
his worldly and perfidious character, and endeavoured to manage
him accordingly. He despatched ambassadors, therefore, to the
court of Rome, announcing the new discovery as an extraordinary
triumph of the faith, and setting forth the great glory and gain
which must redound to the church from the dissemination of
Christianity throughout these vast and heathen lands. Care was
also taken to state that the present discovery did not in the least
interfere with the possessions ceded by the holy chair to Portugal,
all which had been sedulously avoided. Ferdinand, who was at
least as politic as he was pious, insinuated a hint at the same time
by which the Pope might perceive that he was determined, at all
events, to maintain his important acquisitions. His ambassadors
were instructed to state that, in the opinion of many learned men,
these newly-discovered lands having been taken possession of by
the Catholic sovereigns, their title to the same did not require the
Papal sanction; still, as pious princes, obedient to the holy chair,
they supplicated his holiness to issue a bull, making a concession
of them, and of such others as might be discovered, to the crown
of Castile.

The tidings of the discovery were received, in fact, with great
astonishment and no less exultation by the court of Rome. The
Spanish sovereigns had already elevated themselves to high consequence in the eyes of the church by their war against the Moors
in Spain, which had been considered in the light of a pious
crusade; and though richly repaid by the acquisition of the kingdom of Granada, it was thought to entitle them to the gratitude of
all Christendom. The present discovery was a still greater achievement: it was the fulfilment of one of the sublime promises to the
church; it was giving to it 'the heathen for an inheritance, and the
uttermost parts of the earth for a possession.' No difficulty, therefore, was made in granting what was considered but a modest
request for so important a service, though it is probable that the
acquiescence of the worldly-minded pontiff was quickened by the
insinuations of the politic monarch.

A bull was accordingly issued, dated May 2, 1493, ceding to the Spanish sovereigns the same rights, privileges, and indulgences in respect to the newly-discovered regions as had been accorded to the Portuguese with regard to their African discoveries, under the same condition of planting and propagating the Catholic faith. To prevent any conflicting claims, however, between the two powers in the wide range of their discoveries, another bull was issued on the following day, containing the famous line of demarcation by which their territories were thought to be clearly and permanently defined. This was an ideal line drawn from the north to the south pole, a hundred leagues to the west of the Azores and the Cape de Verd Islands. All land discovered by the Spanish navigators to the west of this line, and which had not been taken possession of by any Christian power before the preceding Christmas, was to belong to the Spanish crown; all land discovered in the contrary direction was to belong to Portugal. It seems never to have occurred to the pontiff that, by pushing their opposite careers of discovery, they might some day or other come again in collision, and renew the question of territorial right at the antipodes.

In the meantime, without waiting for the sanction of the court of Rome, the utmost exertions were made by the sovereigns to fit out a second expedition. To insure regularity and despatch in the affairs relative to the New World, they were placed under the superintendence of Juan Rodriguez de Fonseca, Archdeacon of Seville, who was successively promoted to the sees of Badajoz, Palencia, and Burgos, and finally appointed Patriarch of the Indies. He was a man of family and influence; his brothers Alonzo and Antonio were seniors, or lords, of Coca and Alaejos, and the latter was Comptroller-general of Castile. Juan Rodriguez de Fonseca is represented by Las Casas as a worldly man, more calculated for temporal than spiritual concerns, and well adapted to the bustling occupation of fitting out and manning armadas. Notwithstanding the high ecclesiastical dignities to which he rose, his worldly employments seem never to have been considered incompatible with his sacred functions. Enjoying the perpetual though unmerited favour of the sovereigns, he maintained the control of Indian affairs for about thirty years. He must undoubtedly have possessed talents for business to insure him such a perpetuity of office; but he was malignant and vindictive,

and in the gratification of his private resentments not only heaped
wrongs and sorrows upon the most illustrious of the early discoverers, but frequently impeded the progress of their enterprises,
to the great detriment of the crown. This he was enabled to do
privately and securely by his official situation. His perfidious
conduct is repeatedly alluded to, but in guarded terms, by contemporary writers of weight and credit, such as the curate of
Los Palacios, and the bishop Las Casas; but they evidently were
fearful of expressing the fulness of their feelings. Subsequent
Spanish historians, always more or less controlled by ecclesiastical
supervision, have likewise dealt too favourably with this base-
minded man. He deserves to be held up as a warning example of
those perfidious beings in office who too often lie like worms at
the root of honourable enterprise, blighting, by their unseen
influence, the fruits of glorious action, and disappointing the
hopes of nations.

To assist Fonseca in his duties, Francisco Pinelo was associated
with him as treasurer, and Juan de Soria as contador or comptroller. Their office, for the transaction of Indian affairs, was fixed
at Seville, extending its vigilance at the same time to the port of
Cadiz, where a custom-house was established for this new branch
of navigation. Such was the germ of the Royal India House, which
afterwards rose to such great power and importance. A correspondent office was ordered to be instituted in Hispaniola, under
the direction of the admiral. These offices were to interchange
registers of the cargoes, crews, and munition of each ship, by
accountants who sailed with it. All persons thus employed were
dependants upon the two comptrollers-general, superior ministers
of the royal revenue, since the crown was to be at all the expenses
of the colony, and to receive all the emoluments.

The most minute and rigorous account was to be exacted of all
expenses and proceeds, and the most vigilant caution observed as
to the persons employed in the concerns of the newly-discovered
lands. No one was permitted to go there either to trade or to form
an establishment without express license from the sovereigns, from
Columbus, or from Fonseca, under the heaviest penalties. The
ignorance of the age as to enlarged principles of commerce, and
the example of the Portuguese in respect to their African possessions, have been cited in excuse of the narrow and jealous spirit

here manifested; but it always more or less influenced the policy of Spain in her colonial regulations.

Another instance of the despotic sway maintained by the crown over commerce is manifested in a royal order that all ships in the ports of Andalusia, with their captains, pilots, and crews, should be held in readiness to serve in this expedition. Columbus and Fonseca were authorized to freight or purchase any of those vessels they might think proper, and to take them by force if refused, even though they had been freighted by other persons, paying what they should conceive a reasonable price. They were furthermore authorized to take the requisite provisions, arms, and ammunition from any place or vessel in which they might be found, paying a fair price to the owners; and they might compel, not merely mariners, but any officer holding any rank or station whatever, whom they should deem necessary to the service, to embark in the fleet on a reasonable pay and salary. The civil authorities, and all persons of rank and standing, were called upon to render all requisite aid in expediting the armament, and warned against creating any impediment, under penalty of privation of office and confiscation of estate.

To provide for the expenses of the expedition, the royal revenue arising from two-thirds of the church tithes was placed at the disposition of Pinelo; and other funds were drawn from a disgraceful source – from the jewels and other valuables, the sequestrated property, of the unfortunate Jews banished from the kingdom according to a bigoted edict of the preceding year. As these resources were still inadequate, Pinelo was authorized to supply the deficiency by a loan. Requisitions were likewise made for provisions of all kinds, as well as for artillery, powder, muskets, lances, corselets, and crossbows. This latter weapon, notwithstanding the introduction of firearms, was still preferred by many to the arquebuse, and considered more formidable and destructive; the other having to be used with a match-lock, and being so heavy as to require an iron rest. The military stores which had accumulated during the war with the Moors of Granada furnished a great part of these supplies. Almost all the preceding orders were issued by the 23rd of May, while Columbus was yet at Barcelona. Rarely has there been witnessed such a scene of activity in the dilatory offices of Spain.

As the conversion of the heathen was professed to be the grand object of these discoveries, twelve zealous and able ecclesiastics were chosen for the purpose to accompany the expedition. Among these was Bernardo Buyl or Boyle, a Benedictine monk of talent and reputed sanctity, but one of those subtle politicians of the cloister who in those days glided into all temporal concerns. He had acquitted himself with success in recent negotiations with France relative to the restitution of Rousillon. Before the sailing of the fleet he was appointed by the Pope his apostolical vicar for the New World, and placed as superior over his ecclesiastical brethren. This pious mission was provided with all things necessary for the dignified performance of its functions, the queen supplying from her own chapel the ornaments and vestments to be used on all solemn occasions. Isabella, from the first, took the most warm and compassionate interest in the welfare of the Indians. Won by the accounts given by Columbus of their gentleness and simplicity, and looking upon them as committed by Heaven to her especial care, her heart was filled with concern at their destitute and ignorant condition. She ordered that great care should be taken of their religious instruction, that they should be treated with the utmost kindness, and enjoined Columbus to inflict signal punishment on all Spaniards who should be guilty of outrage or injustice towards them.

By way, it is said, of offering to Heaven the first-fruits of these pagan nations, the six Indians whom Columbus had brought to Barcelona were baptized with great state and ceremony – the king, the queen, and Prince Juan officiating as sponsors. Great hopes were entertained that, on their return to their native country, they would facilitate the introduction of Christianity among their countrymen. One of them, at the request of Prince Juan, remained in his household, but died not long afterwards: a Spanish historian remarked that, according to what ought to be our pious belief, he was the first of his nation that entered heaven.[*]

Before the departure of Columbus from Barcelona, the provisional agreement made at Santa Fé was confirmed, granting him the titles, emoluments, and prerogatives of admiral, viceroy, and governor of all the countries he had discovered or might discover. He was intrusted also with the royal seal, with authority to use the

[*] Herrera, *Hist. Ind.*, decad. i. lib. ii. cap. 5.

name of their majesties in granting letters patent and commissions within the bounds of his jurisdiction; with the right also, in case of absence, to appoint a person in his place, and to invest him, for the time, with the same powers.

It had been premised in the agreement, that for all vacant offices in the government of the islands and mainland, he should nominate three candidates, out of which number the sovereigns should make a choice; but now, to save time and to show their confidence in Columbus, they empowered him to appoint at once such persons as he thought proper, who were to hold their offices during the royal pleasure. He had likewise the title and command of captain-general of the armament about to sail, with unqualified powers as to the government of the crews, the establishments to be formed in the New World, and the ulterior discoveries to be undertaken.

This was the honeymoon of royal favour, during which Columbus enjoyed the unbounded and well-merited confidence of his sovereigns, before envious minds had dared to insinuate a doubt of his integrity. After receiving every mark of public honour and private regard, he took leave of the sovereigns on the 28th of May. The whole court accompanied him from the palace to his dwelling, and attended also to pay him farewell honours on his departure from Barcelona for Seville.

The anxiety of the Spanish monarchy for the speedy departure of the expedition was heightened by the proceedings of the court of Portugal. John II had unfortunately among his councillors certain politicians of that short-sighted class who mistake craft for wisdom. By adopting their perfidious policy he had lost the New World when it was an object of honourable enterprise: in compliance with their advice he now sought to retrieve it by stratagem. He had accordingly prepared a large armament, the avowed object of which was an expedition to Africa, but its real destination to seize upon the newly-discovered countries. To lull suspicion, Don Ruy de Sande was sent ambassador to the Spanish court, requesting permission to procure certain prohibited articles from Spain for this African voyage. He required, also, that the Spanish sovereigns should forbid their subjects to fish beyond Cape Bojador, until the possessions of the two nations should be properly defined. The discovery of Columbus, the real object of solicitude, was treated as an incidental affair. The manner of his arrival and reception in Portugal was mentioned; the congratulations of King John on the happy result of his voyage; his satisfaction at finding that the admiral had been instructed to steer westward from the Canary Islands; and his hope that the Castilian sovereigns would continue to enjoin a similar track on their navigators – all to the south of those islands being granted by papal bull to the crown of Portugal. He concluded by intimating the entire confidence of King John, that should any of the newly-discovered islands appertain by right to Portugal, the matter would be adjusted in that spirit of amity which existed between the two crowns.

Ferdinand was too wary a politician to be easily deceived. He had received early intelligence of the real designs of King John, and before the arrival of his ambassador had himself despatched Don

Lope de Herrera to the Portuguese court, furnished with double instructions, and with two letters of widely opposite tenor. The first was couched in affectionate terms, acknowledging the hospitality and kindness shown to Columbus, and communicating the nature of his discoveries; requesting at the same time that the Portuguese navigators might be prohibited from visiting those newly-discovered lands, in the same manner that the Spanish sovereigns had prohibited their subjects from interfering with the African possessions of Portugal.

In case, however, the ambassador should find that King John had either sent, or was about to send, vessels to the New World, he was to withhold the amicable letter, and present the other, couched in stern and peremptory terms, and forbidding any enterprise of the kind.[*] A keen diplomatic game ensued between the two sovereigns, perplexing to any spectator not acquainted with the secret of their play. Resende, in his history of King John II, informs us that the Portuguese monarch, by large presents, or rather bribes, held certain of the confidential members of the Castilian cabinet in his interest, who informed him of the most secret councils of their court. The roads were thronged with couriers; scarce was an intention expressed by Ferdinand to his ministers but it was conveyed to his rival monarch. The result was that the Spanish sovereigns seemed as if under the influence of some enchantment. King John anticipated all their movements, and appeared to dive into their very thoughts. Their ambassadors were crossed on the road by Portuguese ambassadors, empowered to settle the very points about which they were going to make remonstrances. Frequently, when Ferdinand proposed a sudden and perplexing question to the envoys at his court, which apparently would require fresh instructions from the sovereigns, he would be astonished by a prompt and positive reply; most of the questions which were likely to occur having, through secret information, been foreseen and provided for. As a surmise of treachery in the cabinet might naturally arise, King John, while he rewarded his agents in secret, endeavoured to divert suspicions from them upon others, making rich presents of jewels to the Duke del Infantado and other Spanish grandees of incorruptible integrity.[†]

[*] Herrera, *Hist. Ind.*, decad. i. lib. ii.; Zurita, *Anales de Aragon*, lib. i. cap. 25.
[†] Resende, *Vida del Rey Dom Joam II*, cap. 157; Faria y Souza, *Europa Portuguesa*, tom. ii. cap. 4. p. 3.

Such is the intriguing diplomatic craft which too often passes for refined policy, and is extolled as the wisdom of the cabinet; but all corrupt and disingenuous measures are unworthy of an enlightened politician and a magnanimous prince. The grand principles of right and wrong operate in the same way between nations as between individuals: fair and open conduct and inviolable faith, however they may appear adverse to present purposes, are the only kind of policy that will insure ultimate and honourable success.

King John, having received intelligence, in the furtive manner that has been mentioned, of the double instructions furnished to Don Lope de Herrera, received him in such a manner as to prevent any resort to his peremptory letter. He had already despatched an extra envoy to the Spanish court to keep it in good humour, and he now appointed Doctor Pero Diaz and Don Ruy de Pena ambassadors to the Spanish sovereigns, to adjust all questions relative to the new discoveries, and promised that no vessel should be permitted to sail on a voyage of discovery within sixty days after their arrival at Barcelona.

These ambassadors were instructed to propose, as a mode of effectually settling all claims, that a line should be drawn from the Canaries due west: all lands and seas north of it to appertain to the Castilian court; all south to the crown of Portugal, excepting any islands already in possession of either power.*

Ferdinand had now the vantage-ground: his object was to gain time for the preparation and departure of Columbus, by entangling King John in long diplomatic negotiations.† In reply to his proposals, he despatched Don Pedro de Ayala and Don Garcia Lopez de Caravajal on a solemn embassy to Portugal, in which there was great outward pomp and parade, and many professions of amity, but the whole purport of which was to propose to submit the territorial questions which had risen between them to arbitration, or to the court of Rome. This stately embassy moved with becoming slowness, but a special envoy was sent in advance to apprise the King of Portugal of its approach, in order to keep him waiting for its communications.

King John understood the whole nature and object of the embassy, and felt that Ferdinand was foiling him. The ambassadors

* Zurita, lib. i. cap. 25; Herrera, decad. i. lib. ii cap. 5.
† Vasconcelos, *Don Juan II*, lib. vi

at length arrived, and delivered their credentials with great form and ceremony. As they retired from his presence, he looked after them contemptuously. 'This embassy from our cousin,' said he, 'wants both head and feet.' He alluded to the character both of the mission and the envoys. Don Garcia de Caravajal was vain and frivolous, and Don Pedro de Ayala was lame of one leg.[*]

In the height of his vexation, King John is even said to have held out some vague show of hostile intentions, taking occasion to let the ambassadors discover him reviewing his cavalry, and dropping ambiguous words in their hearing, which might be construed into something of menacing import.[†] The embassy returned to Castile, leaving him in a state of perplexity and irritation; but whatever might be his chagrin, his discretion prevented him from coming to an open rupture. He had some hopes of interference on the part of the Pope, to whom he had sent an embassy, complaining of the pretended discoveries of the Spaniards as infringing the territories granted to Portugal by papal bull, and earnestly imploring redress. Here, as has been shown, his wary antagonist had been beforehand with him, and he was doomed again to be foiled. The only reply his ambassador received was a reference to the line of partition from pole to pole so sagely devised by his holiness.[‡] Such was this royal game of diplomacy, where the parties were playing for a newly-discovered world. John II was able and intelligent, and had crafty councillors to advise him in all his moves; but whenever deep and subtle policy was required, Ferdinand was master of the game.

[*] Vasconcelos, lib. vi.; Barros, *Asia*, d. i. lib. iii. cap. 2.
[†] Vasconcelos, lib. vi.
[‡] Herrera, decad. i. lib. ii. cap. 5.

CHAPTER 10

1493

Distrustful of some attempt on the part of Portugal to interfere with their discoveries, the Spanish sovereigns, in the course of their negotiations, wrote repeatedly to Columbus, urging him to hasten his departure. His zeal, however, needed no incitement. Immediately on arriving at Seville, in the beginning of June, he proceeded with all diligence to fit out the armament, making use of the powers given him to put in requisition the ships and crews which were in the harbours of Andalusia. He was joined soon after by Fonseca and Soria, who had remained for a time at Barcelona; and with their united exertions, a fleet of seventeen vessels, large and small, was soon in a state of preparation. The best pilots were chosen for the service, and the crews were mustered in presence of Soria, the comptroller. A number of skilful husbandmen, miners, carpenters, and other mechanics, were engaged for the projected colony. Horses, both for military purposes and for stocking the country, cattle, and domestic animals of all kinds, were likewise provided. Grain, seeds of various plants, vines, sugar-canes, grafts, and saplings were embarked; together with a great quantity of merchandise, consisting of trinkets, beads, hawks' bells, looking-glasses, and other showy trifles, calculated for trafficking with the natives. Nor was there wanting an abundant supply of provisions of all sorts, munitions of war, and medicines and refreshments for the sick.

An extraordinary degree of excitement prevailed respecting this expedition. The most extravagant fancies were entertained with respect to the New World. The accounts given by the voyagers who had visited it were full of exaggeration; for in fact they had nothing but vague and confused notions concerning it, like the recollection of a dream, and it has been shown that Columbus himself had beheld everything through the most delusive medium. The vivacity of his descriptions and the sanguine anticipations of his ardent spirit, while they roused the public to a wonderful degree of enthusiasm, prepared the way for bitter disappointment. The cupidity of the avaricious was inflamed with the idea of regions of unappropriated wealth, where the rivers rolled over golden sands, and the mountains teemed with gems and precious metals; where the groves produced spices and perfumes, and the shores of the ocean were sown with pearl. Others had conceived visions of a loftier kind. It was a romantic and stirring age, and the wars with the Moors being over, and hostilities with the French suspended, the bold and restless spirits of the nation, impatient of the monotony of peaceful life, were eager for employment. To these the New World presented a vast field for wild enterprise and extraordinary adventure, so congenial to the Spanish character in that period of its meridian fervour and brilliancy. Many hidalgos of high rank, officers of the royal household, and Andalusian cavaliers, schooled in arms, and inspired with a passion for hardy achievements by the romantic wars of Granada, pressed into the expedition, some in the royal service, others at their own cost. To them it was the commencement of a new series of crusades, surpassing in extent and splendour the chivalrous enterprises to the Holy Land. They pictured to themselves vast and beautiful islands of the ocean to be overrun and subdued; their internal wonders to be explored, and the banner of the Cross to be planted on the walls of the cities they were supposed to contain. Thence they were to make their way to the shores of India, or rather Asia, penetrate into Mangi and Cathay, convert, or, what was the same thing, conquer the Grand Khan, and thus open a glorious career of arms among the splendid countries and semi-barbarous nations of the East. Thus, no one had any definite idea of the object or nature of the service on which he was embarking, or the situation and character of the region to which he was bound. Indeed, during this fever of the imagination, had sober facts and cold realities been presented, they would have been rejected with disdain; for there is nothing of which the public is more impatient than of being disturbed in the indulgence of any of its golden dreams.

Among the noted personages who engaged in the expedition was a young cavalier of the name of Don Alonzo de Ojeda, celebrated for his extraordinary personal endowments and his daring spirit, and who distinguished himself among the early discoverers by many perilous expeditions and singular exploits. He was of a good family, cousin-german to the venerable Father Alonzo de Ojeda, Inquisitor of Spain; had been brought up under the patronage of the Duke of Medina Celi, and had served in the wars against the Moors. He was of small stature but vigorous make, well proportioned, dark complexioned, of handsome, animated countenance, and incredible strength and agility. Expert at all kinds of weapons, accomplished in all manly and warlike exercises, an admirable horseman, and a partisan soldier of the highest order; bold of heart, free of spirit, open of hand; fierce in fight, quick in brawl, but ready to forgive and prone to forget an injury — he was for a long time the idol of the rash and roving youth who engaged in the early expeditions to the New World, and has been made the hero of many wonderful tales. On introducing him to historical notice, Las Casas gives an anecdote of one of his exploits, which would be unworthy of record but that it exhibits the singular character of the man.

Queen Isabella being in the tower of the cathedral of Seville, better known as the Giralda, Ojeda, to entertain her majesty, and to give proofs of his courage and agility, mounted on a great beam which projected in the air twenty feet from the tower, at such an immense height from the ground that the people below looked like dwarfs, and it was enough to make Ojeda himself shudder to look down. Along this beam he walked briskly, and with as much confidence as though he had been pacing his chamber. When arrived at the end, he stood on one leg, lifting the other in the air; then turning nimbly round, he returned in the same way to the tower, unaffected by the giddy height, whence the least false step would have precipitated him and dashed him to pieces. He afterwards stood with one foot on the beam, and placing the other against the wall of the building, threw an orange to the summit of the tower, a proof, says Las Casas, of immense muscular strength. Such was Alonzo de Ojeda, who soon became conspicuous among the followers of Columbus, and was always foremost in every enterprise of an adventurous nature; who courted peril as if for the very love of danger, and seemed to fight more for the pleasure of fighting than for the sake of distinction.[*]

[*] Las Casas, lib. i, MS.; Pizarro, *Varones Illustres*; Herrera, *Hist. Ind.*, decad. i. lib. ii. cap. 5.

The number of persons permitted to embark in the expedition had been limited to one thousand, but such was the urgent application of volunteers to be allowed to enlist without pay that the number had increased to twelve hundred. Many more were refused for want of room in the ships for their accommodation, but some contrived to get admitted by stealth, so that eventually about fifteen hundred set sail in the fleet. As Columbus, in his laudable zeal for the welfare of the enterprise, provided everything that might be necessary in various possible emergencies, the expenses of the outfit exceeded what had been anticipated. This gave rise to occasional demurs on the part of the comptroller, Juan de Soria, who sometimes refused to sign the accounts of the admiral, and in the course of their transactions seemed to have forgotten the deference due both to his character and station. For this he received repeated and severe reprimands from the sovereigns, who emphatically commanded that Columbus should be treated with the greatest respect, and everything done to facilitate his plans and yield him satisfaction. From similar injunctions inserted in the royal letters to Fonseca, the Archdeacon of Seville, it is probable that he also had occasionally indulged in the captious exercise of his official powers. He appears to have demurred to various requisitions of Columbus, particularly one for footmen and other domestics for his immediate service, to form his household and retinue as admiral and viceroy – a demand which was considered superfluous by the prelate, as all who embarked in the expedition were at his command. In reply, the sovereigns ordered that he should be allowed ten *escuderos de à pie*, or footmen, and twenty persons in other domestic capacities; and reminded Fonseca of their charge that, both in the nature and mode of his transactions with the admiral, he should study to give him content; observing that, as the whole armament was intrusted to his command, it was but reasonable that his wishes should be consulted, and no one embarrass him with punctilios and difficulties.*

These trivial differences are worthy of particular notice, from the effect they appear to have had on the mind of Fonseca; for from them we must date the rise of that singular hostility which he ever afterwards manifested towards Columbus, which every year increased in rancour, and which he gratified in the most

* Navarrete, *Colec.*, tom. ii: Documentos, No. 62–66.

invidious manner by secretly multiplying impediments and vexations in his path.

While the expedition was yet lingering in port, intelligence was
received that a Portuguese caravel had set sail from Madeira and
steered for the west. Suspicions were immediately awakened that
she was bound for the lately-discovered lands. Columbus wrote an
account of it to the sovereigns, and proposed to despatch a part of
his fleet in pursuit of her. His proposition was approved, but not
carried into effect. On remonstrances being made to the court of
Lisbon, King John declared that the vessel had sailed without his
permission, and that he would send three caravels to bring her
back. This only served to increase the jealousy of the Spanish
monarchs, who considered the whole a deep-laid stratagem, and
that it was intended the vessels should join their forces, and pursue
their course together to the New World. Columbus was urged,
therefore, to depart without and hour's delay, and instructed to
steer wide of Cape St Vincent, and entirely avoid the Portuguese
coasts and islands, for fear of molestation. If he met with any
vessels in the seas he had explored, he was to seize them, and inflict
rigorous punishment on the crews. Fonseca was also ordered to be
on the alert, and in case any expedition sailed from Portugal to
send double the force after it. These precautions, however, proved
unnecessary. Whether such caravels actually did sail, and whether
they were sent with sinister motives by Portugal, does not appear;
nothing was either seen or heard of them by Columbus in the
course of his voyage.

It may be as well, for the sake of distinctness, to anticipate in this
place the regular course of history, and mention the manner in
which this territorial question was finally settled between the rival
sovereigns. It was impossible for King John to repress his disquiet
at the indefinite enterprises of the Spanish monarchs; he did not
know how far they might extend, and whether they might not
forestall him in all his anticipated discoveries in India. Finding,
however, all attempts fruitless to gain by stratagem and advantage
over his wary and skilful antagonist, and despairing of any further
assistance from the court of Rome, he had recourse, at last, to fair
and amicable negotiations, and found, as is generally the case with
those who turn aside into the inviting but crooked paths of craft,
that had he kept to the line of frank and open policy he would

have saved himself a world of perplexity, and have arrived sooner at his object. He offered to leave to the Spanish sovereigns the free prosecution of their western discovery, and to conform to the plan of partition by a meridian line; but he represented that this line had not been drawn far enough to the west – that while it left the wide ocean free to the range of Spanish enterprise, his navigators could not venture more than a hundred leagues west of his possessions, and had no scope or sea-room for their southern voyages.

After much difficulty and discussion this momentous dispute was adjusted by deputies from the two crowns, who met at Tordesillas, in Old Castile, in the following year, and on the 7th of June 1494 signed a treaty, by which the papal line of partition was moved to three hundred and seventy leagues west of the Cape de Verd Islands. It was agreed that within six months an equal number of caravels and mariners, on the part of the two nations, should rendezvous at the island of the Grand Canary, provided with men learned in astronomy and navigation. They were to proceed thence to the Cape de Verd Islands, and thence westward three hundred and seventy leagues, and determine the proposed line from pole to pole, dividing the ocean between the two nations.[*] Each of the two powers engaged solemnly to observe the bounds thus prescribed, and to prosecute no enterprise beyond its proper limits; though it was agreed that the Spanish navigators might traverse freely the eastern parts of the ocean in prosecuting their rightful voyages. Various circumstances impeded the proposed expedition to determine the line, but the treaty remained in force, and prevented all further discussions.

Thus, says Vasconcelos, this great question, the greatest ever agitated between the two crowns, for it was the partition of a new world, was amicably settled by the prudence and address of two of the most politic monarchs that ever swayed the sceptre. It was arranged to the satisfaction of both parties, each holding himself entitled to the vast countries that might be discovered within his boundary, without any regard to the rights of the native inhabitants.

---

[*] Zurita, *Hist. del Rey Fernand.*, lib. i. cap. 29; Vasconcelos, lib. vi.

BOOK 6

CHAPTER I

1493

The departure of Columbus on his second voyage of discovery presented a brilliant contrast to his gloomy embarkation at Palos. On the 25th of September, at the dawn of day, the bay of Cadiz was whitened by his fleet. There were three large ships of heavy burden* and fourteen caravels, loitering with flapping sails, and awaiting the signal to get under way. The harbour resounded with the well-known note of the sailor, hoisting sail or weighing anchor; a motley crowd were hurrying on board, and taking leave of their friends in the prospect of a prosperous voyage and triumphant return. There was the high-spirited cavalier, bound on romantic enterprise; the hardy navigator, ambitious of acquiring laurels in these unknown seas; the roving adventurer, seeking novelty and excitement; the keen, calculating speculator, eager to profit by the ignorance of savage tribes; and the pale missionary from the cloister, anxious to extend the dominion of the church, or devoutly zealous for the propagation of the faith. All were full of animation and lively hope. Instead of being regarded by the populace as devoted men, bound upon a dark and desperate enterprise, they were contemplated with envy, as favoured mortals, bound to golden regions and happy climes, where nothing but wealth and wonder and delights awaited them. Columbus, conspicuous for his height and his commanding appearance, was attended by his two sons Diego and Fernando, the

---

* Peter Martyr says they were carracks (a large species of merchant-vessel, principally used in coasting trade), of one hundred tons burden, and that two of the caravels were much larger than the rest, and more capable of bearing decks from the size of their masts. – Decad. i. lib. i.

Cadiz

eldest but a stripling, who had come to witness his departure,* both proud of the glory of their father. Wherever he passed, every eye followed him with admiration, and every tongue praised and blessed him. Before sunrise the whole fleet was under way; the weather was serene and propitious; and as the populace watched their parting sails brightening in the morning beams, they looked forward to their joyful return, laden with the treasures of the New World.

According to the instructions of the sovereigns, Columbus steered wide of the coasts of Portugal and of its islands, standing to the south-west of the Canaries, where he arrived on the 1st of October. After touching at the Grand Canary, he anchored on the 5th at Gomera, to take in a supply of wood and water. Here also he purchased calves, goats, and sheep, to stock the island of Hispaniola; and eight hogs, from which, according to Las Casas, the infinite number of swine was propagated with which the Spanish settlements in the New World subsequently abounded. A number of domestic fowls were likewise purchased, which were the origin of the species in the New World; and the same might be said of the seeds of oranges, lemons, bergamots, melons, and various orchard fruits,[†] which were thus first introduced into the islands of the west from the Hesperides or Fortunate Islands of the Old World.[‡]

On the 7th, when about to sail, Columbus gave to the commander of each vessel a sealed letter of instructions, in which was specified his route to the harbour of Nativity, the residence of the cacique Guacanagari. This was only to be opened in case of being separated by accident, as he wished to make a mystery, as long as possible, of the exact route to the newly-discovered country, lest adventurers of other nations, and particularly the Portuguese, should follow in his track, and interfere with his enterprises.[§]

After making sail from Gomera, they were becalmed for a few days among the Canaries, until, on the 13th of October, a fair breeze sprang up from the east, which soon carried them out of

---

* *Hist. del Almirante*, cap. 44.

† Las Casas, *Hist. Ind.*, lib. i. cap. 83.

‡ Humboldt is of opinion that there were wild oranges, small and bitter, as well as wild lemons, in the New World prior to the discovery. Caldcleugh also mentions that the Brazilians consider the small bitter wild orange of native origin. – Humboldt, *Essai Politique sur l'Ile de Cuba*, tom. i. p. 68.

§ Las Casas, ubi sup.

sight of the island of Ferro. Columbus held his course to the south-west, intending to keep considerably more to the southward than in his first voyage, in hopes of falling in with the islands of the Caribs, of which he had received such vague and wonderful accounts from the Indians.* Being in the region of the trade-winds, the breeze continued fair and steady, with a quiet sea and pleasant weather; and by the 24th they had made four hundred and fifty leagues west of Gomera, without seeing any of those fields of sea-weeds encountered within a much less distance on their first voyage. At that time their appearance was important, and almost providential, inspiring continual hope, and enticing them forward in their dubious enterprise. Now they needed no such signals, being full of confidence and lively anticipation; and on seeing a swallow circling about the ships, and being visited occasionally by sudden showers, they began to look out cheerily for land.

Towards the latter part of October they had in the night a gust of heavy rain, accompanied by the severe thunder and lightning of the tropics. It lasted for four hours, and they considered themselves in much peril, until they beheld several of those lambent flames playing about the tops of the masts, and gliding along the rigging, which have always been objects of superstitious fancies among sailors. Fernando Columbus makes remarks on them strongly characteristic of the age in which he lived. 'On the same Saturday, in the night, was seen St Elmo, with seven lighted tapers, at the topmast. There was much rain and great thunder. I mean to say, that those lights were seen which mariners affirm to be the body of St Elmo, on beholding which they chant litanies and orisons, holding it for certain that in the tempest in which he appears no one is in danger. Be that as it may, I leave the matter to them; but if we may believe Pliny, similar lights have sometimes appeared to the Roman mariners during tempests at sea, which they said were Castor and Pollux, of which likewise Seneca makes mention.'[†]

* Letter of Dr Chanca.

[†] *Hist. del Almirante*, cap. 45. A similar mention is made of this nautical super-stition in the voyage of Magellan: 'During these great storms they said that St Elmo appeared at the topmast with a lighted candle, and sometimes with two, upon which the people shed tears of joy, receiving great consolation, and saluted him according to the custom of mariners. He remained visible for a quarter of an hour, and then disappeared, with a great flash of lightning, which blinded the people.' – Herrera, decad. ii. lib. iv. cap. 10.

On the evening of Saturday the 2nd of November Columbus was convinced from the colour of the sea, the nature of the waves, and the variable winds and frequent showers, that they must be near to land. He gave orders, therefore, to take in sail, and to maintain a vigilant watch throughout the night. He had judged with his usual sagacity. In the morning a lofty island was descried to the west, at the sight of which there were shouts of joy throughout the fleet. Columbus gave to the island the name of Dominica, from having discovered it on Sunday. As the ships moved gently onward other islands rose to sight, covered with forests, while flights of parrots and other tropical birds passed from one to the other.

The crews were now assembled on the decks of the several ships to return thanks to God for their prosperous voyage and their happy discovery of land, chanting the *Salve Regina* and other anthems. Such was the solemn manner in which Columbus celebrated all his discoveries, and which, in fact, was generally observed by the Spanish and Portuguese voyagers.

The islands among which Columbus had arrived were a part of that beautiful cluster called by some the Antilles, which sweep almost in a semicircle from the eastern end of Porto Rico to the coast of Paria on the southern continent, forming a kind of barrier between the main ocean and the Caribbean Sea.

During the first day that he entered this archipelago Columbus saw no less than six islands of different magnitude. They were clothed in tropical vegetation, and the breezes from them were sweetened by the fragrance of their forests.

After seeking in vain for good anchorage at Dominica he stood for another of the group, to which he gave the name of his ship, Marigalante. Here he landed, displayed the royal banner, and took possession of the archipelago in the name of his sovereigns. The island appeared to be uninhabited; a rich and dense forest overspread it; some of the trees were in blossom, others laden with unknown fruits, others possessing spicy odours, among which was one with the leaf of the laurel and the fragrance of the clove.

Hence they made sail for an island of larger size, with a remarkable mountain. One peak, which proved afterwards to be the crater of a volcano, rose to a great height, with streams of water gushing from it. As they approached within three leagues they beheld a cataract of such height that, to use the words of the narrator, it seemed to be falling from the sky. As it broke into foam in its descent, many at first believed it to be merely a stratum of white rock.* To this land, which was called by the Indians Turuqueira,† the admiral gave the name of Guadalupe, having promised the monks of Our Lady of Guadalupe, in Estremadura, to call some newly-discovered place after their convent.

---

* Letter of Dr Chanca.

† Letter of Dr Chanca. Peter Martyr calls it Carucueira, or Queraquiera, decad. i. lib. ii.

Landing here on the 4th, they visited a village near the shore, the inhabitants of which fled, some even leaving their children behind in their terror and confusion. These the Spaniards soothed with caresses, binding hawks' bells and other trinkets round their arms. This village, like most of those on the island, consisted of twenty or thirty houses, built round a public place or square. The houses were constructed of trunks of trees interwoven with reeds and branches, and thatched with palm-leaves. They were square, not circular like those of the other islands,* and each had its portico or shelter from the sun. One of the porticoes was decorated with images of serpents tolerably carved in wood. For furniture they had hammocks of cotton net, and utensils formed of calabashes or earthenware, equal to the best of those of Hispaniola. There were large quantities of cotton, some in the wool, some in yarn, and some wrought into cloth of very tolerable texture; and many bows and arrows, the latter tipped with sharp bones. Provisions seemed to abound. There were many domesticated geese like those of Europe, and parrots as large as household fowls, with blue, green, white, and scarlet plumage, being the splendid species called guacamayos. Here also the Spaniards first met with the anana, or pineapple, the flavour and fragrance of which astonished and delighted them. In one of the houses they were surprised to find a pan or other utensil of iron, not having ever met with that metal in the New World. Fernando Colon supposes that it was formed of a certain kind of heavy stone found among those islands, which, when burnt, has the appearance of shining iron; or it might have been some utensil brought by the Indians from Hispaniola. Certain it is that no native iron was ever found among the people of these islands.

In another house was the stern-post of a vessel. How had it reached these shores, which appeared never to have been visited by the ships of civilized man? Was it the wreck of some vessel from the more enlightened countries of Asia, which they supposed to lie somewhere in this direction, or a part of the caravel which Columbus had lost at the island of Hispaniola during his first voyage, or a fragment of some European ship which had drifted across the Atlantic? The latter was most probably the case. The constant current which sets over from the coast of Africa, produced

* *Hist. del Almirante*, cap. 62.

by the steady prevalence of the trade-winds, must occasionally bring wrecks from the Old World to the New; and long before the discovery of Columbus the savages of the islands and the coasts may have gazed with wonder at fragments of European barks which have floated to their shores.

What struck the Spaniards with horror was the sight of human bones, vestiges, as they supposed, of unnatural repasts; and skulls apparently used as vases and other household utensils. These dismal objects convinced them that they were now in the abodes of the cannibals, or Caribs, whose predatory expeditions and ruthless character rendered them the terror of these seas.

The boat having returned on board, Columbus proceeded upwards of two leagues, until he anchored, late in the evening, in a convenient port. The island on this side extended for the distance of five-and-twenty leagues, diversified with lofty mountains and broad plains. Along the coast were small villages and hamlets, the inhabitants of which fled in affright. On the following day the boats landed, and succeeded in taking and bringing off a boy and several women. The information gathered from them confirmed Columbus in his idea that this was one of the islands of the Caribs. He learned that the inhabitants were in league with two neighbouring islands, but made war upon all the rest. They even went on predatory enterprises, in canoes made from the hollowed trunks of trees, to the distance of one hundred and fifty leagues. Their arms were bows and arrows pointed with the bones of fishes, or shells of tortoises, and poisoned with the juice of a certain herb. They made descents upon the islands, ravaged the villages, carried off the youngest and handsomest of the women, whom they retained as servants or companions, and made prisoners of the men, to be killed and eaten.

After hearing such accounts of the natives of this island, Columbus was extremely uneasy at finding, in the evening, that Diego Marque, the captain of one of the caravels, and eight men, were missing. They had landed early in the morning without leave, and straying into the woods had not since been seen or heard of. The night passed away without their return. On the following day parties were sent in various directions in quest of them, each with a trumpeter to sound calls and signals. Guns were fired from the ships, and arquebuses on shore; but all to no purpose, and the

parties returned in the evening, wearied with a fruitless search. In
several hamlets they had met with proofs of the cannibal propensities of the natives. Human limbs were suspended to the beams of
the houses, as if curing for provisions; the head of a young man
recently killed was yet bleeding; some parts of his body were
roasting before the fire, others boiling with the flesh of geese and
parrots.[*]

Several of the natives, in the course of the day, had been seen on
the shore gazing with wonder at the ships; but when the boats
approached, they fled to the woods and mountains. Several women
came off to the Spaniards for refuge, being captives from other
islands. Columbus ordered that they should be decorated with
hawks's bells and strings of beads and bugles, and sent on shore,
in hopes of enticing off some of the men. They soon returned
to the boats stripped of their ornaments, and imploring to be
taken on board the ships. The admiral learned from them that
most of the men of the island were absent, the king having sailed
some time before with ten canoes and three hundred warriors, on
a cruise in quest of prisoners and booty. When the men went
forth on these expeditions the women remained to defend their
shores from invasion. They were expert archers, partaking of the
warrior spirit of their husbands, and almost equalling them in
force and intrepidity.[†]

The continued absence of the wanderers perplexed Columbus
extremely. He was impatient to arrive at Hispaniola, but unwilling
to sail while there was a possibility of their being alive and being
recovered. In this emergency Alonzo de Ojeda, the same young
cavalier whose exploit on the tower of the cathedral at Seville has
been mentioned, volunteered to scour the island with forty men in
quest of them. He departed accordingly, and during his absence
the ships took in wood and water, and part of the crews were
permitted to land, wash their clothes, and recreate themselves.

Ojeda and his followers pushed far into the interior, firing off
arquebuses and sounding trumpets in the valleys and from the
summits of cliffs and precipices, but were only answered by their
own echoes. The tropical luxuriance and density of the forests
rendered them almost impenetrable; and it was necessary to wade a

---

[*] Peter Martyr, Letter 147, to Pomponius Laetus. Idem, decad. i. lib. ii.
 [†] Peter Martyr, decad. iii. lib. ix.

great many rivers, or probably the windings and doublings of the same stream. The island appeared to be naturally fertile in the extreme. The forests abounded with aromatic trees and shrubs, among which Ojeda fancied he perceived the odour of precious gums and spices. There was honey in hollow trees and in the clefts of rocks; abundance of fruit also, for, according to Peter Martyr, the Caribs, in their predatory cruisings, were accustomed to bring home the seeds and roots of all kinds of plants from the distant islands and countries which they overran.

Ojeda returned without any tidings of the stragglers. Several days had now elapsed since their disappearance. They were given up for lost, and the fleet was about sailing, when, to the universal joy, a signal was made by them from the shore. When they came on board, their haggard and exhausted looks bespoke what they had suffered. For several days they had been perplexed in trackless forests, so dense as almost to exclude the light of day. They had clambered rocks, waded rivers, and struggled through briers and thickets. Some who were experienced seamen climbed the trees to get a sight of the stars by which to govern their course, but the spreading branches and thick foliage shut out all view of the heavens. They were harassed with the fear that the admiral, thinking them dead, might set sail and leave them in this wilderness, cut off for ever from their homes and the abodes of civilized man. At length, when almost reduced to despair, they had arrived at the sea-shore, and following it for some time, beheld to their great joy the fleet riding quietly at anchor. They brought with them several Indian women and boys; but in all their wanderings they had not met with any man, the greater part of the warriors, as has been said, being fortunately absent on an expedition.

Notwithstanding the hardships they had endured, and his joy at their return, Columbus put the captain under arrest, and stopped part of the rations of the men, for having strayed away without permission; for in a service of such a critical nature it was necessary to punish every breach of discipline.*

* Dr Chanca's Letter; *Hist. del Almirante*, cap. 46.

CHAPTER 3

1493

Weighing anchor on the 10th of November, Columbus steered toward the north-west, along this beautiful archipelago, giving names to the islands as they rose to view – such as Montserrat, Santa Maria la Redonda, Santa Maria la Antigua, and San Martin. Various other islands, lofty and well wooded, appeared to the north, south-west, and south-east; but he forbore to visit them. The weather proving boisterous, he anchored on the 14th at an island called Ayay by the Indians, but to which he gave the name of Santa Cruz. A boat well manned was sent on shore to get water and procure information. They found a village, deserted by the men, but secured a few women and boys, most of them captives from other islands. They soon had an instance of Carib courage and ferocity. While at the village, they beheld a canoe from a distant part of the island come round a point of land and arrive in view of the ships. The Indians in the canoe, two of whom were females, remained gazing in mute amazement at the ships, and were so entranced that the boat stole close upon them before they perceived it. Seizing their paddles they attempted to escape, but the boat being between them and the land, cut off their retreat. They now caught up their bows and arrows and plied them with amazing vigour and rapidity. The Spaniards covered themselves with their bucklers, but two of them were quickly wounded. The women fought as fiercely as the men, and one of them sent an arrow with such force that it passed through and through a buckler.

The Spaniards now ran their boat against the canoe and over-turned it. Some of the savages got upon sunken rocks, others discharged their arrows while swimming, as dexterously as though they had been upon firm land. It was with the utmost difficulty that they could be overcome and taken. One of them who had been transfixed with a lance died soon after being brought aboard the

ships. One of the women, from the obedience and deference paid
to her, appeared to be their queen. She was accompanied by her
son, a young man strongly made, with a frowning brow and lion's
face. He had been wounded in the conflict. The hair of these
savages was long and coarse, their eyes were encircled with paint,
so as to give them a hideous expression, and bands of cotton were
bound firmly above and below the muscular parts of the arms and
legs, so as to cause them to swell to a disproportioned size – a
custom prevalent among various tribes of the New World. Though
captives in chains, and in the power of their enemies, they still
retained a frowning brow and an air of defiance. Peter Martyr, who
often went to see them in Spain, declares, from his own experience
and that of others who accompanied him, that it was impossible to
look at them without a sensation of horror, so menacing and
terrible was their aspect. The sensation was doubtless caused in a
great measure by the idea of their being cannibals. In this skirmish,
according to the same writer, the Indians used poisoned arrows,
and one of the Spaniards died within a few days of a wound
received from one of the females.*

Pursuing his voyage, Columbus soon came in sight of a great
cluster of islands, some verdant and covered with forests, but the
greater part naked and sterile, rising into craggy mountains, with
rocks of a bright azure colour, and some of a glistering white.
These, with his usual vivacity of imagination, he supposed to
contain mines of rich metals and precious stones. The islands lying
close together, with the sea beating roughly in the narrow channels
which divided them, rendered it dangerous to enter among them
with the large ships. Columbus sent in a small caravel with lateen
sails to reconnoitre, which returned with the report that there were
upwards of fifty islands, apparently inhabited. To the largest of this
group he gave the name of Santa Ursula, and called the others the
Eleven Thousand Virgins.†

Continuing his course, he arrived one evening in sight of a great
island covered with beautiful forests and indented with fine havens.
It was called by the natives Boriquen, but he gave it the name of
San Juan Bautista; it is the same since known by the name of Porto

---

* P. Martyr, decad. i. lib. ii; *Hist. del Almirante*, cap. 47; Las Casas, *Hist. Ind.*, cap. 85,
MS; Letter of Dr Chanca.
† P. Martyr, decad. i. lib. ii; Letter of Dr Chanca.

Rico. This was the native island of most of the captives who had
fled to the ships for refuge from the Caribs. According to their
accounts it was fertile and populous, and under the dominion of a
single cacique. Its inhabitants were not given to rove, and possessed
but few canoes. They were subject to frequent invasions from the
Caribs, who were their implacable enemies. They had become
warriors, therefore, in their own defence, using the bow and arrow
and the war-club; and in their contests with their cannibal foes
they retorted upon them their own atrocities, devouring their
prisoners in revenge.

After running for a whole day along the beautiful coast of this
island, they anchored in a bay at the west end, abounding in fish.
On landing they found an Indian village, constructed as usual
round a common square, like a market-place, with one large and
well-built house. A spacious road led thence to the sea-side,
having fences on each side of interwoven reeds, enclosing fruitful
gardens. At the end of the road was a kind of terrace or look-out,
constructed of reeds, and overhanging the water. The whole place
had an air of neatness and ingenuity, superior to the ordinary
residences of the natives, and appeared to be the abode of some
important chieftain. All, however, was silent and deserted. Not a
human being was to be seen during the time they remained at the
place. The natives had concealed themselves at the sight of the
squadron. After remaining here two days, Columbus made sail and
stood for the island of Hispaniola. Thus ended his cruise among
the Caribbee Islands, the account of whose fierce and savage
people was received with eager curiosity by the learned of Europe,
and considered as settling one dark and doubtful question to the
disadvantage of human nature. Peter Martyr, in his letter to
Pomponius Laetus, announces the fact with fearful solemnity.
'The stories of the Lestrigonians and of Polyphemus, who fed on
human flesh, are no longer doubtful! Attend, but beware lest thy
hair bristle with horror!'

That many of the pictures given us of this extraordinary race
of people have been coloured by the fears of the Indians and
the prejudices of the Spaniards is highly probable. They were
constantly the terror of the former, and the brave and obstinate
opponents of the latter. The evidences adduced of their cannibal
propensities must be received with large allowances for the

careless and inaccurate observations of sea-faring men, and the preconceived belief of the fact which existed in the minds of the Spaniards. It was a custom among the natives of many of the islands, and of other parts of the New World, to preserve the remains of their deceased relatives and friends; sometimes the entire body, sometimes only the head, or some of the limbs, dried at the fire, sometimes the mere bones. These, when found in the dwellings of the natives of Hispaniola, against whom no prejudice of the kind existed, were correctly regarded as relics of the deceased, preserved through affection or reverence; but any remains of the kind found among the Caribs were looked upon with horror as proofs of cannibalism.

The warlike and unyielding character of these people, so different from that of the pusillanimous nations around them, and the wide scope of their enterprises and wanderings, like those of the nomad tribes of the Old World, entitle them to distinguished attention. They were trained to war from their infancy. As soon as they could walk, their intrepid mothers put in their hands the bow and arrow, and prepared them to take an early part in the hardy enterprises of their fathers. Their distant roamings by sea made them observant and intelligent. The natives of the other islands only knew how to divide time by day and night, by the sun and moon; whereas these had acquired some knowledge of the stars, by which to calculate the times and seasons.*

The traditional accounts of their origin, though of course extremely vague, are yet capable of being verified to a great degree by geographical facts, and open one of the rich veins of curious inquiry and speculation which abound in the New World. They are said to have migrated from the remote valleys embosomed in the Appalachian Mountains. The earliest accounts we have of them represent them with weapons in their hands, continually engaged in wars, winning their way and shifting their abode, until, in the course of time, they found themselves at the extremity of Florida. Here, abandoning the northern continent, they passed over to the Lucayos; and thence gradually, in the process of years, from island to island of that vast and verdant chain which links, as it were, the end of Florida to the coast of Paria, on the southern continent. The archipelago, extending from Porto Rico to Tobago, was their

* *Hist. del Almirante*, cap. 62.

stronghold, and the island of Guadeloupe in a manner their citadel. Hence they made their expeditions, and spread the terror of their name through all the surrounding countries. Swarms of them landed upon the southern continent, and overran some parts of *terra firma*. Traces of them have been discovered far in the interior of that vast country through which flows the Oroonoko. The Dutch found colonies of them on the banks of the Ikouteka, which empties itself into the Surinam, along the Esquibi, the Maroni, and other rivers of Guayana, and in the country watered by the windings of the Cayenne; and it would appear that they extended their wanderings to the shores of the southern ocean, where, among the aboriginals of Brazil, were some who called themselves Caribs, distinguished from the surrounding Indians by their superior hardihood, subtlety, and enterprise.*

To trace the footsteps of this roving tribe throughout its wide migrations from the Appalachian Mountains of the northern continent, along the clusters of islands which stud the Gulf of Mexico and the Caribbean Sea, to the shores of Paria, and so across the vast regions of Guayana and Amazonia to the remote coast of Brazil, would be one of the most curious researches in aboriginal history, and throw much light upon the mysterious question of the population of the New World.

---

* Rochefort, *Hist. Nat. des Iles Antilles*: Rotterdam, 1665.

CHAPTER 4

1493

On the 22nd of November the fleet arrived off what was soon ascertained to be the eastern extremity of Hayti, or, as the admiral had named it, Hispaniola. The greatest excitement prevailed throughout the armada at the thoughts of soon arriving at the end of their voyage. Those who had been here in the preceding voyage remembered the pleasant days they had passed among the groves of Hayti, and the rest looked forward with eagerness to scenes painted to them with the captivating illusions of the golden age.

As the fleet swept with easy sail along the green shore, a boat was sent to land to bury a Biscayan sailor who had died of the wound of an arrow received in the late skirmish. Two light caravels hovered near the shore to guard the boat's crew while the funeral ceremony was performed on the beach under the trees. Several natives came off to the ship with a message to the admiral from the cacique of the neighbourhood, inviting him to land, and promising great quantities of gold. Anxious, however, to arrive at La Navidad, Columbus dismissed them with presents, and continued his course. Arriving at the Gulf of Las Flechas, or, as it is now called, the Gulf of Semana, the place where, in his preceding voyage, a skirmish had occurred with the natives, he set on shore one of the young Indians of the place who had accompanied him to Spain and had been converted to Christianity. He dismissed him finely apparelled and loaded with trinkets, anticipating favourable effects from his accounts to his countrymen of the wonders he had seen and the kind treatment he had experienced. The young Indian made many fair promises, but either forgot them all on regaining his liberty and his native mountains, or fell a victim to envy caused by his wealth and finery. Nothing was seen or heard of him more.[*] Only one Indian of those who had been to Spain now remained in the fleet – a young

* Herrera, *Hist. Ind.*, decad. i. lib. ii. cap. 9.

Lucayan, native of the island of Guanahanè, who had been baptized
at Barcelona, and had been named after the admiral's brother, Diego
Colon. He continued always faithful and devoted to the Spaniards.

On the 25th Columbus anchored in the harbour of Monte
Christi, anxious to fix upon a place for a settlement in the
neighbourhood of the stream to which, in his first voyage, he had
given the name of the Rio del Oro, or the Golden River. As several
of the mariners were ranging the coast they found, on the green
and moist banks of a rivulet, the bodies of a man and boy; the
former with a cord of Spanish grass about his neck, and his arms
extended and tied by the wrists to a stake in the form of a cross. The
bodies were in such a state of decay that it was impossible to
ascertain whether they were Indians or Europeans. Sinister doubts,
however, were entertained, which were confirmed on the following day; for, on revisiting the shore, they found, at some distance
from the former, two other bodies, one of which, having a beard,
was evidently the corpse of a white man.

The pleasant anticipations of Columbus on his approach to
La Navidad were now overcast with gloomy forebodings. The
experience recently had of the ferocity of some of the inhabitants
of these islands made him doubtful of the amity of others, and
he began to fear that some misfortune might have befallen Arana
and his garrison.

The frank and fearless manner, however, in which a number of
the natives came off to the ships, and their unembarrassed demeanour, in some measure allayed his suspicions; for it did not
appear probable that they would venture thus confidently among
the white men with the consciousness of having recently shed the
blood of their companions.

On the evening of the 27th he arrived opposite the harbour of La
Navidad, and cast anchor about a league from the land, not daring
to enter in the dark, on account of the dangerous reefs. It was too
late to distinguish objects. Impatient to satisfy his doubts, therefore,
he ordered two cannon to be fired. The report echoed along the
shore, but there was no reply from the fort. Every eye was now
directed to catch the gleam of some signal light, every ear listened to
hear some friendly shout; but there was neither light nor shout, nor
any other signs of life – all was darkness and death-like silence.[*]

[*] Letter of Dr Chanca; Navarrete, *Colec. de Viages*, tom. i.

Several hours were passed in dismal suspense, and everyone longed for the morning light to put an end to his uncertainty. About midnight a canoe approached the fleet. When within a certain distance it paused, and the Indians who were in it, hailing one of the vessels, asked for the admiral. When directed to his ship they drew near, but would not venture on board until they saw Columbus. He showed himself at the side of his vessel, and a light being held up, his countenance and commanding person were not to be mistaken. They now entered the ship without hesitation. One of them was a cousin of the cacique Guacanagari, and brought a present from him of two masks ornamented with gold. Columbus inquired about the Spaniards who had remained on the island. The information which the native gave was somewhat confused, or perhaps was imperfectly understood, as the only Indian interpreter on board was the young Lucayan, Diego Colon, whose native language was different from that of Hayti. He told Columbus that several of the Spaniards had died of sickness, others had fallen in a quarrel among themselves, and others had removed to a different part of the island, where they had taken to themselves Indian wives; that Guacanagari had been assailed by Caonabo, the fierce cacique of the golden mountains of Cibao, who had wounded him in battle and burned his village; and that he remained ill of his wound in a neighbouring hamlet, or he would have hastened in person to welcome the admiral.*

Melancholy as were these tidings, they relieved Columbus from a dark and dismal surmise. Whatever disasters had overwhelmed his garrison, it had not fallen a sacrifice to the perfidy of the natives; his good opinion of the gentleness and kindness of these people had not been misplaced, nor had their cacique forfeited the admiration inspired by his benevolent hospitality. Thus the most corroding care was dismissed from his mind; for, to a generous spirit, there is nothing so disheartening as to discover treachery where it has reposed confidence and friendship. It would seem also that some of the garrison were yet alive, though scattered about the island: they would doubtless soon hear of his arrival, would hasten to rejoin him, well qualified to give information of the interior.

* Dr Chanca's Letter; *Hist. del Almirante*, cap. 48; Herrera, *Hist. Ind.*, decad. i. lib. i. cap. 9.

Satisfied of the friendly disposition of the natives, the cheerfulness of the crews was in a great measure restored. The Indians who had come on board were well entertained, and departed in the night gratified with various presents, promising to return in the morning with the cacique Guacanagari. The mariners now awaited the dawn of day with reassured spirits, expecting that the cordial intercourse and pleasant scenes of the first voyage would be renewed.

The morning dawned and passed away, and the day advanced and began to decline, without the promised visit from the cacique. Some apprehensions were now entertained that the Indians who had visited them the preceding night might be drowned, as they had partaken freely of wine, and their small canoe was easy to be overset. There was a silence and an air of desertion about the whole neighbourhood extremely suspicious. On their preceding visit the harbour had been a scene of continual animation – canoes gliding over the clear waters, Indians in groups on the shores or under the trees, or swimming off to the caravel. Now not a canoe was to be seen, not an Indian hailed them from the land, nor was there any smoke rising from among the groves to give a sign of habitation.

After waiting for a long time in vain, Columbus sent a boat to the shore to reconnoitre. On landing, the crew hastened and sought the fortress. It was a ruin: the palisadoes were beaten down, and the whole presented the appearance of having been sacked, burned, and destroyed. Here and there were broken chests, spoiled provisions, and the ragged remains of European garments. Not an Indian approached them. They caught sight of two or three lurking at a distance among the trees, and apparently watching them; but they vanished into the woods on finding themselves observed. Meeting no one to explain the melancholy scene before them, they returned with dejected hearts to the ships, and related to the admiral what they had seen.

Columbus was greatly troubled in mind at this intelligence, and the fleet having now anchored in the harbour, he went himself to shore on the following morning. Repairing to the ruins of the fortress, he found everything as had been described, and searched in vain for the remains of dead bodies. No traces of the garrison were to be seen, but broken utensils and torn vestments scattered here and there among the grass. There were many surmises and conjectures. If the fortress had been sacked, some of the garrison

might yet survive, and might either have fled from the neighbourhood or been carried into captivity. Cannon and arquebuses were
discharged, in hopes, if any of the survivors were hid among rocks
and thickets, they might hear them and come forth; but no one
made his appearance. A mournful and lifeless silence reigned over
the place. The suspicion of treachery on the part of Guacanagari
was again revived, but Columbus was unwilling to indulge it. On
looking further, the village of that cacique was found a mere heap
of burnt ruins, which showed that he had been involved in the
disaster of the garrison.

Columbus had left orders with Arana and the other officers to
bury all the treasure they might procure, or, in case of sudden
danger, to throw it into the well of the fortress. He ordered
excavations to be made, therefore, among the ruins, and the well
to be cleared out. While this search was making, he proceeded
with the boats to explore the neighbourhood, partly in hopes of
gaining intelligence of any scattered survivors of the garrison, and
partly to look out for a better situation for a fortress. After
proceeding about a league he came to a hamlet, the inhabitants of
which had fled, taking whatever they could with them, and hiding
the rest in the grass. In the houses were European articles, which
evidently had not been procured by barter, such as stockings,
pieces of cloth, an anchor of the caravel which had been wrecked,
and a beautiful Moorish robe, folded in the form in which it had
been brought from Spain.*

Having passed some time in contemplating these scattered documents of a disastrous story, Columbus returned to the ruins of the
fortress. The excavations and search in the well had proved fruitless; no treasure was to be found. Not far from the fort, however,
they had discovered the bodies of eleven men buried in different
places, and which were known by their clothing to be Europeans.
They had evidently been for some time in the ground, the grass
having grown upon their graves.

In the course of the day a number of the Indians made their
appearance, hovering timidly at a distance. Their apprehensions
were gradually dispelled until they became perfectly communic-
ative. Some of them could speak a few words of Spanish, and
knew the names of all the men who had remained with Arana. By

* Letter of Dr Chanca; Cura de los Palacios, cap. 120.

this means, and by the aid of the interpreter, the story of the garrison was in some measure ascertained.

It is curious to note this first footprint of civilization in the New World. Those whom Columbus had left behind, says Oviedo, with the exception of the commander, Don Diego Arana, and one or two others, were but little calculated to follow the precepts of so prudent a person or to discharge the critical duties enjoined upon them. They were principally men of the lowest order, or mariners who knew not how to conduct themselves with restraint or sobriety on shore.* No sooner had the admiral departed than all his counsels and commands died away from their minds. Though a mere handful of men surrounded by savage tribes, and dependent upon their own prudence and good conduct and upon the good-will of the natives for very existence, yet they soon began to indulge in the most wanton abuses. Some were prompted by rapacious avarice, and sought to possess themselves, by all kinds of wrongful means, of the golden ornaments and other valuable property of the natives. Others were grossly sensual, and, not content with two or three wives allowed to each by Guacanagari, seduced the wives and daughters of the Indians.

Fierce brawls ensued among them about their ill-gotten spoils and the favours of the Indian women; and the natives beheld with astonishment the beings whom they had worshipped, as descended from the skies, abandoned to the grossest of earthly passions, and raging against each other with worse than brutal ferocity.

Still these dissensions might not have been very dangerous had they observed one of the injunctions of Columbus, and kept together in the fortress, maintaining military vigilance; but all precaution of the kind was soon forgotten. In vain did Don Diego de Arana interpose his authority; in vain did every inducement present itself which could bind man and man together in a foreign land. All order, all subordination, all unanimity was at an end. Many abandoned the fortress and lived carelessly and at random about the neighbourhood, every one for himself, or associated with some little knot of confederates to injure and despoil the rest. Thus factions broke out among them, until ambition arose to complete the destruction of their mimic empire. Pedro Gutierrez and Rod-rigo de Escobedo, whom Columbus had left as lieutenants to the

* Oviedo, *Hist. Ind.*, lib ii. cap. 12.

commander, to succeed him in case of accident, took advantage of these disorders and aspired to an equal share in the authority, if not to the supreme control.[*] Violent affrays succeeded, in which a Spaniard named Jacomo was killed. Having failed in their object, Gutierrez and Escobedo withdrew from the fortress with nine of their adherents and a number of their women, and turned their thoughts on distant enterprise. Having heard marvellous accounts of the mines of Cibao, and the golden sands of its mountain rivers, they set off for that district, flushed with the thoughts of amassing immense treasure. Thus they disregarded another strong injunction of Columbus, which was to keep within the friendly territories of Guacanagari. The region to which they repaired was in the interior of the island, within the province of Maguana, ruled by the famous Caonabo, called by the Spaniards the Lord of the Golden House. This renowned chieftain was a Carib by birth, and possessed the fierceness and enterprise of his nation. He had come an adventurer to Hispaniola, and by his courage and address and his warlike exploits had made himself the most potent of its caciques. The inhabitants universally stood in awe of him from his Carib origin, and he was the hero of the island when the ships of the white men suddenly appeared upon its shores. The wonderful accounts of their power and prowess had reached him among his mountains, and he had the shrewdness to perceive that his consequence must decline before such formidable intruders. The departure of Columbus gave him hopes that their intrusion would be but temporary. The discords and excesses of those who remained, while they moved his detestation, inspired him with increasing confidence. No sooner did Gutierrez and Escobedo, with their companions, take refuge in his dominions than he put them to death. He then formed a league with the cacique of Marien, whose territories adjoined those of Guacanagari on the west, and concerted a sudden attack upon the fortress. Emerging with his warriors from among the mountains, and traversing great tracts of forest with profound secrecy, he arrived in the vicinity of the village without being discovered. The Spaniards, confiding in the gentle and pacific nature of the Indians, had neglected all military precautions. But ten men remained in the fortress with Arana, and these do not appear to have maintained any guard. The rest were quartered in houses in the neighbourhood. In

---

[*] Oviedo, *Hist. Ind.*, lib ii. cap. 12.

the dead of the night, when all were wrapped in sleep, Caonabo and his warriors burst upon the place with frightful yells, got possession of the fortress before its inmates could put themselves upon their defence, and surrounded and set fire to the houses in which the rest of the white men were sleeping. Eight of the Spaniards fled to the sea-side, pursued by the savages, and rushing into the waves were drowned; the rest were massacred. Guacanagari and his subjects fought faithfully in defence of their guests, but not being of a warlike character were easily routed. The cacique was wounded by the hand of Caonabo, and his village was burned to the ground.*

Such was the history of the first European establishment in the New World. It presents in a diminutive compass an epitome of the gross vices which degrade civilization, and the grand political errors which sometimes subvert the mightiest empires. All law and order being relaxed by corruption and licentiousness, public good was sacrificed to private interest and passion, the community was convulsed by divers factions and dissensions, until the whole was shaken asunder by two aspiring demagogues, ambitious of the command of a petty fortress in a wilderness and the supreme control of eight-and-thirty men.

* Herrera, *Hist. Ind.*, decad. i. lib. ii. cap. 9; Letter of Dr Chanca; Peter Martyr, decad. i. lib. ii.; *Hist. del Almirante*, cap. 49; Cura de los Palacios, cap. 120. MS; Muñoz, *Hist. de Nuevo Mundo*, lib. iv.

The tragical story of the fortress, as gathered from the Indians at the harbour, received confirmation from another quarter. One of the captains, Melchor Maldonado, coasting to the east with his caravel in search of some more favourable situation for a settlement, was boarded by a canoe in which were two Indians. One of them was the brother of Guacanagari, and entreated him, in the name of the cacique, to visit him at the village where he lay ill of his wound. Maldonado immediately went to shore with two or three of his companions. They found Guacanagari confined by lameness to his hammock, surrounded by seven of his wives. The cacique expressed great regret at not being able to visit the admiral. He related various particulars concerning the disasters of the garrison, and the part which he and his subjects had taken in its defence, showing his wounded leg bound up. His story agreed with that already related. After treating the Spaniards with his accustomed hospitality, he presented to each of them at parting a golden ornament.

On the following morning Columbus repaired in person to visit the cacique. To impress him with an idea of his present power and importance, he appeared with a numerous train of officers, all richly dressed or in glittering armour. They found Guacanagari reclining in a hammock of cotton net. He exhibited great emotion on beholding the admiral, and immediately adverted to the death of the Spaniards. As he related the disasters of the garrison he shed many tears, but dwelt particularly on the part he had taken in the defence of his guests, pointing out several of his subjects present who had received wounds in the battle. It was evident from the scars that the wounds had been received from Indian weapons.

Columbus was readily satisfied of the good faith of Guacanagari. When he reflected on the many proofs of an open and generous nature which he had given at the time of his shipwreck, he could not believe him capable of so dark an act of perfidy. An exchange of presents now took place. The cacique gave him eight hundred beads of a certain stone called ciba, which they considered highly precious, and one hundred of gold, a golden coronet, and three small calabashes filled with gold dust; and thought himself outdone in munificence when presented with a number of glass beads, hawks' bells, knives, pins, needles, small mirrors, and ornaments of copper, which metal he seemed to prefer to gold.[*]

Guacanagari's leg had been violently bruised by a stone. At the request of Columbus he permitted it to be examined by a surgeon who was present. On removing the bandage no signs of a wound were to be seen, although he shrunk with pain whenever the limb was handled.[†] As some time had elapsed since the battle, the external bruise might have disappeared, while a tenderness remained in the part. Several present, however, who had not been in the first voyage, and had witnessed nothing of the generous conduct of the cacique, looked upon his lameness as feigned, and the whole story of the battle a fabrication, to conceal his real perfidy. Father Boyle especially, who was of a vindictive spirit, advised the admiral to make an immediate example of the chieftain. Columbus, however, viewed the matter in a different light. Whatever prepossessions he might have were in favour of the cacique; his heart refused to believe in his criminality. Though conscious of innocence, Guacanagari might have feared the suspicions of the white men, and have exaggerated the effects of his wound. But the wounds of his subjects, made by Indian weapons, and the destruction of his village, were strong proofs to Columbus of the truth of his story. To satisfy his more suspicious followers, and to pacify the friar, without gratifying his love for persecution, he observed that true policy dictated amicable conduct towards Guacanagari, at least until his guilt was fully ascertained. They had too great a force at present to apprehend anything from his hostility, but violent measures in this early stage of their intercourse with the natives might spread a general panic, and impede all their operations on the island. Most of his officers concurred in this opinion; so it was determined, notwithstanding the inquisitorial suggestions of the

[*] Letter of Dr Chanca; Navarrete, *Col.*, i.
[†] Cura de los Palacios, cap. 120.

friar, to take the story of the Indians for current truth, and to continue to treat them with friendship.

At the invitation of Columbus, the cacique, though still apparently in pain from his wound,[*] accompanied him to the ships that very evening. He had wondered at the power and grandeur of the white men when they first visited his shores with two small caravels; his wonder was infinitely increased on beholding a fleet riding at anchor in the harbour, and on going on board of the admiral's ship, which was a vessel of heavy burden. Here he beheld the Carib prisoners. So great was the dread of them among the timid inhabitants of Hayti that they contemplated them with fear and shuddering, even though in chains.[†] That the admiral had dared to invade these terrible beings in their very island, and had dragged them, as it were, from their strong-holds, was perhaps one of the greatest proofs to the Indians of the irresistible prowess of the white men.

Columbus took the cacique through the ship. The various works of art, the plants and fruits of the Old World, domestic fowls of different kinds, cattle, sheep, swine, and other animals, brought to stock the island, all were wonders to him; but what most struck him with amazement was the horses. He had never seen any but the most diminutive quadrupeds, and was astonished at their size, their great strength, terrific appearance, yet perfect docility.[‡] He looked upon all these extraordinary objects as so many wonders brought from heaven, which he still believed to be the native home of the white men.

On board of the ship were ten of the women delivered from Carib captivity. They were chiefly natives of the island of Boriquen, or Porto Rico. These soon attracted the notice of the cacique, who is represented to have been of an amorous complexion. He entered into conversation with them, for though the islanders spoke different languages, or rather, as is more probable, different dialects of the same language, they were able, in general, to understand each other. Among these women was one distinguished above her companions by a certain loftiness of air and manner. She had been much noticed and admired by the Spaniards,

---

[*] *Hist. del Almirante*, cap. 89.

[†] Peter Martyr, Letter 153 to Pomponius Laetus.

[‡] *Hist. del Almirante*, ubi sup.; Letter of Dr Chanca.

who had given her the name of Catalina. The cacique spoke to her repeatedly with great gentleness of tone and manner, pity in all probability being mingled with his admiration, for though rescued from the hands of the Caribs, she and her companions were in a manner captives on board of the ship.

A collation was now spread before the chieftain, and Columbus endeavoured in every way to revive their former cordial intercourse. He treated his guest with every manifestation of perfect confidence, and talked of coming to live with him in his present residence, and of building houses in the vicinity. The cacique expressed much satisfaction at the idea, but observed that the situation of the place was unhealthy, which was indeed the case. Notwithstanding every demonstration of friendship, however, the cacique was evidently ill at ease. The charm of mutual confidence was broken. It was evident that the gross licentiousness of the garrison had greatly impaired the veneration of the Indians for their heaven-born visitors. Even the reverence for the symbols of the Christian faith, which Columbus endeavoured to inculcate, was frustrated by the profligacy of its votaries. Though fond of ornaments, it was with the greatest difficulty the cacique could be prevailed upon by the admiral to suspend an image of the Virgin about his neck, when he understood it to be an object of Christian adoration.[*]

The suspicions of the chieftain's guilt gained ground with many of the Spaniards. Father Boyle, in particular, regarded him with an evil eye, and privately advised the admiral, now that he had him on board, to detain him prisoner; but Columbus rejected the counsel of the crafty friar, as contrary to sound policy and honourable faith. It is difficult, however, to conceal lurking ill-will. The cacique, accustomed in his former intercourse with the Spaniards to meet with faces beaming with gratitude and friendship, could not but perceive their altered looks. Notwithstanding the frank and cordial hospitality of the admiral, therefore, he soon begged permission to return to land.[†]

The next morning there was a mysterious movement among the natives on shore. A messenger from the cacique inquired of the admiral how long he intended to remain at the harbour, and

---

[*] *Hist. del Almirante*, cap. 49.
[†] Peter Martyr, decad. i. lib. ii.

was informed that he should sail on the following day. In the evening the brother of Guacanagari came on board, under pretext of bartering a quantity of gold. He was observed to converse in private with the Indian women, and particularly with Catalina, the one whose distinguished appearance had attracted the attention of Guacanagari. After remaining some time on board, he returned to the shore. It would seem, from subsequent events, that the cacique had been touched by the situation of this Indian beauty, or captivated by her charms, and had undertaken to deliver her from bondage.

At midnight, when the crew were buried in their first sleep, Catalina awakened her companions. The ship was anchored full three miles from the shore, and the sea was rough; but they let themselves down from the side of the vessel and swam bravely for the shore. With all their precautions, they were overheard by the watch, and the alarm was given. The boats were hastily manned, and gave chase in the direction of a light blazing on the shore, an evident beacon for the fugitives. Such was the vigour of these sea-nymphs that they reached the land in safety. Four were retaken on the beach, but the heroic Catalina, with the rest of her companions, made good their escape into the forest.

When the day dawned, Columbus sent to Guacanagari to demand the fugitives; or if they were not in his possession, that he would have search made for them. The residence of the cacique, however, was silent and deserted – not an Indian was to be seen. Either conscious of the suspicions of the Spaniards and apprehensive of their hostility, or desirous to enjoy his prize unmolested, the cacique had removed with all his effects, his household, and his followers, and had taken refuge with his island beauty in the interior. This sudden and mysterious desertion gave redoubled force to the doubts heretofore entertained, and Guacanagari was generally stigmatized as a traitor to the white men and the perfidious destroyer of the garrison.[*]

[*] Peter Martyr, decad. i. lib. ii; Letter of Dr Chanca; Cura de los Palacios, cap. 120, MS.

The misfortunes of the Spaniards, both by sea and land, in the vicinity of this harbour, threw a gloom round the neighbourhood. The ruins of the fortress, and the graves of their murdered country-men, were continually before their eyes, and the forests no longer looked beautiful while there was an idea that treachery might be lurking in their shades. The silence and dreariness also, caused by the desertion of the natives, gave a sinister appearance to the place. It began to be considered by the credulous mariners as under some baneful influence or malignant star. These were sufficient objections to discourage the founding of a settlement, but there were others of a more solid nature. The land in the vicinity was low, moist, and unhealthy, and there was no stone for building. Columbus determined, therefore, to abandon the place altogether, and found his projected colony in some more favourable situation. No time was to be lost. The animals on board the ships were suffering from long confinement, and the multitude of persons, unaccustomed to the sea, and pent up in the fleet, languished for the refreshment of the land. The lighter caravels, therefore, scoured the coast in each direction, entering the rivers and harbours in search of an advantageous site. They were instructed also to make inquiries after Guacanagari, of whom Columbus, notwithstanding every suspicious appearance, still retained a favourable opinion. The expeditions returned after ranging a considerable extent of coast without success. There were fine rivers and secure ports, but the coast was low and marshy and deficient in stone. The country was generally deserted, or if any natives were seen they fled immediately to the woods. Melchor Maldonado had proceeded to the eastward until he came to the dominions of a cacique, who at first issued forth at the head of his warriors, with menacing aspect, but was readily conciliated. From him he learned that Guacanagari had retired to the mountains. Another party discovered an Indian concealed near a hamlet, having been disabled by a wound received from a lance when fighting against Caonabo. His account of the destruction of the fortress agreed with that of the Indians at the harbour, and concurred to vindicate the cacique from the charge of treachery. Thus the Spaniards continued uncertain as to the real perpetrators of this dark and dismal tragedy.

Being convinced that there was no place in this part of the island favourable for a settlement, Columbus weighed anchor on the 7th of December, with the intention of seeking the port of La Plata. In consequence of adverse weather, however, he was obliged to put into a harbour about ten leagues east of Monte Christi; and on considering the place, was struck with its advantages.

The harbour was spacious, and commanded by a point of land protected on one side by a natural rampart of rocks, and on another by an impervious forest, presenting a strong position for a fortress. There were two rivers, one large and the other small, watering a green and beautiful plain, and offering advantageous situations for mills. About a bowshot from the sea, on the banks of one of the rivers, was an Indian village. The soil appeared to be fertile, the waters to abound in excellent fish, and the climate to be temperate and genial, for the trees were in leaf, the shrubs in flower, and the birds in song, though it was the middle of December. They had not yet become familiarized with the temperature of this favoured island, where the rigours of winter are unknown, where there is a perpetual succession and even intermixture of fruit and flower, and where smiling verdure reigns throughout the year.

Another grand inducement to form their settlement in this place was the information, received from the Indians of the adjacent village, that the mountains of Cibao, where the gold mines were situated, lay at no great distance, and almost parallel to the harbour. It was determined, therefore, that there could not be a situation more favourable for their colony.

An animated scene now commenced. The troops and various persons belonging to the land-service, and the various labourers and artificers to be employed in building, were disembarked. The provisions, articles of traffic, guns and ammunition for defence, and implements of every kind, were brought to shore, as were also the cattle and livestock, which had suffered excessively from long restraint, especially the horses. There was a general joy at escaping from the irksome confinement of the ships, and once more treading the firm earth and breathing the sweetness of the fields. An encampment was formed on the margin of the plain, around a basin or sheet of water, and in a little while the whole place was in activity. Thus was founded the first Christian city of the New World, to which Columbus gave the name of Isabella, in honour of his royal patroness.

A plan was formed, and streets and squares projected. The greatest diligence was then exerted in erecting a church, a public storehouse, and a residence for the admiral. These were built of stone; the private houses were constructed of wood, plaster, reeds, or such materials as the exigency of the case permitted, and for a short time everyone exerted himself with the utmost zeal.

Maladies, however, soon broke out. Many, unaccustomed to the sea, had suffered greatly from confinement and sea-sickness, and from subsisting for a length of time on salt provisions, much damaged, and mouldy biscuit. They suffered great exposure on the land also, before houses could be built for their reception; for the exhalations of a hot and moist climate and a new, rank soil, the humid vapours from rivers, and the stagnant air of close forests, render the wilderness a place of severe trial to constitutions accustomed to old and highly-cultivated countries. The labour also of building houses, clearing fields, setting out orchards, and planting gardens, having all to be done with great haste, bore hard upon men who, after tossing so long upon the ocean, stood in need of relaxation and repose.

The maladies of the mind mingled with those of the body. Many, as has been shown, had embarked in the expedition with visionary and romantic expectations. Some had anticipated the golden regions of Cipango and Cathay, where they were to amass wealth without toil or trouble; others, a region of Asiatic luxury, abounding with delights; and others a splendid and open career for gallant adventures and chivalrous enterprises. What then was their disappointment to find themselves confined to the margin of an island; surrounded by impracticable forests; doomed to struggle with the rudeness of a wilderness; to toil painfully for mere subsistence, and to attain every comfort by the severest exertion. As to gold, it was brought to them from various quarters, but in small quantities, and it was evidently to be procured only by patient and persevering labour. All these disappointments sank deep into their hearts; their spirits flagged as their golden dreams melted away, and the gloom of despondency aided the ravages of disease.

Columbus himself did not escape the prevalent maladies. The arduous nature of his enterprise, the responsibility under which he found himself, not merely to his followers and his sovereigns, but to the world at large, had kept his mind in continual agitation. The cares of so large a squadron; the incessant vigilance required, not only against the lurking dangers of these unknown seas, but against the passions and follies of his followers; the distress he had suffered from the fate of his murdered garrison, and his uncertainty as to the conduct of the barbarous tribes by which he was surrounded, – all these had harassed his mind and broken his rest while on board the ship. Since landing, new cares and toils had crowded upon him, which, added to the exposures incident to his situation in this new climate, completely overpowered his strength. Still, though confined for several weeks to his bed by severe illness, his energetic mind rose superior to the sufferings of the body, and he continued to give directions about the building of the city, and to super-intend the general concerns of the expedition.[*]

* *Hist. del Almirante*, cap. 50; Herrera, *Hist. Ind.*, decad. i. lib. ii. cap. 10; Peter Martyr, decad. i. lib. ii.; Letter of Dr Chanca, etc.

CHAPTER 7

1493

The ships having discharged their cargoes, it was necessary to send the greater part of them back to Spain. Here new anxieties pressed upon the mind of Columbus. He had hoped to find treasures of gold and precious merchandise accumulated by the men left behind on the first voyage, or at least the sources of wealthy traffic ascertained, by which speedily to freight his vessels. The destruction of the garrison had defeated all those hopes. He was aware of the extravagant expectations entertained by the sovereigns and the nation. What would be their disappointment when the returning ships brought nothing but a tale of disaster! Something must be done before the vessels sailed to keep up the fame of his discoveries and justify his own magnificent representations.

As yet he knew nothing of the interior of the island. If it were really the island of Cipango, it must contain populous cities, existing probably in some more cultivated region beyond the lofty mountains with which it was intersected. All the Indians concurred in mentioning Cibao as the tract of country whence they derived their gold. The very name of its cacique, Caonabo, signifying 'the Lord of the Golden House', seemed to indicate the wealth of his dominions. The tracts where the mines were said to abound lay at a distance of but three or four days' journey, directly in the interior. Columbus determined, therefore, to send an expedition to explore it, previous to the sailing of the ships. If the result should confirm his hopes, he would then be able to send home the fleet with confidence, bearing tidings of the discovery of the golden mountains of Cibao.*

The person he chose for this enterprise was Alonzo de Ojeda, the same cavalier who has been already noticed for his daring spirit and great bodily force and agility. Delighting in all service of a

* Herrera, *Hist. Ind.*, decad. i. lib. ii. cap. 10.

hazardous and adventurous nature, Ojeda was the more stimulated to this expedition from the formidable character of the mountain cacique, Caonabo, whose dominions he was to penetrate. He set out from the harbour early in January 1494, accompanied by a small force of well-armed and determined men, several of them young and spirited cavaliers like himself. He struck directly south-ward into the interior. For the two first days the march was toilsome and difficult, through a country abandoned by its inhab-itants; for terror of the Spaniards extended along the sea-coast. On the second evening they came to a lofty range of mountains, which they ascended by an Indian path winding up a steep and narrow defile, and they slept for the night at the summit. Hence, the next morning, they beheld the sun rise with great glory over a vast and delicious plain, covered with noble forests, studded with villages and hamlets, and enlivened by the shining waters of the Yagui.

Descending into this plain, Ojeda and his companions boldly entered the Indian villages. The inhabitants, far from being hostile, overwhelmed them with hospitality, and, in fact, impeded their journey by their kindness. They had also to ford many rivers in traversing this plain, so that they were five or six days in reaching the chain of mountains which locked up, as it were, the golden region of Cibao. They penetrated into this district without meet-ing with any other obstacles than those presented by the rude nature of the country. Caonabo, so redoubtable for his courage and ferocity, must have been in some distant part of his dominions, for he never appeared to dispute their progress. The natives received them with kindness. They were naked and uncivilized, like the other inhabitants of the island; nor were there any traces of the important cities which their imaginations had once pictured forth. They saw, however, ample signs of natural wealth. The sands of the mountain streams glittered with particles of gold; these the natives would skilfully separate and give to the Spaniards, without expecting a recompense. In some places they picked up large specimens of virgin ore from the beds of the torrents, and stones streaked and richly impregnated with it. Peter Martyr affirms that he saw a mass of rude gold weighing nine ounces, which Ojeda himself had found in one of the brooks.*

* Peter Martyr, decad. i. lib. ii.

All these were considered as mere superficial washings of the soil, betraying the hidden treasures lurking in the deep veins and rocky bosoms of the mountains, and only requiring the hand of labour to bring them to light. As the object of his expedition was merely to ascertain the nature of the country, Ojeda led back his little band to the harbour, full of enthusiastic accounts of the golden promise of these mountains. A young cavalier of the name of Gorvalan, who had been despatched at the same time on a similar expedition, and who had explored a different tract of country, returned with similar reports. These flattering accounts served for a time to reanimate the drooping and desponding colonists, and induced Columbus to believe that it was only necessary to explore the mines of Cibao to open inexhaustible sources of riches. He determined, as soon as his health would permit, to repair in person to the mountains and seek a favourable site for a mining establishment.*

The season was now propitious for the return of the fleet, and Columbus lost no time in despatching twelve of the ships under the command of Antonio de Torres, retaining only five for the service of the colony.

By this opportunity he sent home specimens of the gold found among the mountains and rivers of Cibao, and all such fruits and plants as were curious or appeared to be valuable. He wrote in the most sanguine terms of the expeditions of Ojeda and Gorvalan, the last of whom returned to Spain in the fleet. He repeated his confident anticipations of soon being able to make abundant shipments of gold, of precious drugs and spices, the search for them being delayed for the present by the sickness of himself and people, and the cares and labours required in building the infant city. He described the beauty and fertility of the island; its range of noble mountains; its wide, abundant plains, watered by beautiful rivers; the quick fecundity of the soil, evinced in the luxuriant growth of the sugar-cane, and of various grains and vegetables brought from Europe.

As it would take some time, however, to obtain provisions from their fields and gardens, and the produce of their livestock, adequate to the subsistence of the colony, which consisted of about a thousand souls, and as they could not accustom themselves to the food

* *Hist. del Almirante*, cap. 50.

of the natives, Columbus requested present supplies from Spain. Their provisions were already growing scanty. Much of their wine had been lost, from the badness of the casks; and the colonists, in their infirm state of health, suffered greatly from the want of their accustomed diet. There was an immediate necessity of medicines, clothing, and arms. Horses were required likewise for the public works, and for military service – being found of great effect in awing the natives, who had the utmost dread of those animals. He requested also an additional number of workmen and mechanics, and men skilled in mining and in smelting and purifying ore. He recommended various personages to the notice and favour of the sovereigns, among whom was Pedro Margarite, an Aragonian cavalier of the order of St Jago, who had a wife and children to be provided for, and who, for his good services, Columbus begged might be appointed to a command in the order to which he belonged. In like manner he entreated patronage for Juan Aguado, who was about to return in the fleet, making particular mention of his merits. From both of these men he was destined to experience the most signal ingratitude.

In these ships he sent also the men, women, and children taken in the Caribbee Islands, recommending that they should be carefully instructed in the Spanish language and the Christian faith. From the roving and adventurous nature of these people, and their general acquaintance with the various languages of this great archipelago, he thought that, when the precepts of religion and the usages of civilization had reformed their savage manners and cannibal propensities, they might be rendered eminently serviceable as interpreters, and as means of propagating the doctrines of Christianity.

Among the many sound and salutary suggestions in this letter there is one of a most pernicious tendency, written in that mistaken view of natural rights prevalent at the day, but fruitful of much wrong and misery in the world. Considering that the greater the number of these cannibal pagans transferred to the Catholic soil of Spain the greater would be the number of souls put in the way of salvation, he proposed to establish an exchange of them as slaves, against livestock to be furnished by merchants to the colony. The ships to bring such stock were to land nowhere but at the island of Isabella, where the Carib captives would be ready for delivery. A duty was to be levied on each slave for the benefit of the royal revenue. In this way the colony would be furnished with all kinds of livestock free of expense; the peaceful islanders would be freed from warlike and inhuman neighbours; the royal treasury would be greatly enriched; and a vast number of souls would be snatched from perdition, and carried, as it were, by main force to heaven. Such is the strange sophistry by which upright men may sometimes deceive themselves. Columbus feared the disappointment of the sovereigns in respect to the product of his enterprises, and was anxious to devise some mode of lightening their expenses until he could open some ample source of profit. The conversion of infidels, by fair means or foul, by persuasion or force, was one of the popular tenets of the day; and in recommending the enslaving of the Caribs, Columbus thought that he was obeying the dictates of his conscience, when he was in reality listening to the incitements of his interest. It is but just to add that the sovereigns did not accord with his ideas, but ordered that the Caribs should be converted like the rest of the islanders; a command which emanated from the merciful heart of Isabella, who ever showed herself the benign protectress of the Indians.

The fleet put to sea on the 2nd of February 1494. Though it brought back no wealth to Spain, yet expectation was kept alive by the sanguine letter of Columbus, and the specimens of gold which he transmitted. His favourable accounts were corroborated by letters from Friar Boyle, Doctor Chanca, and other persons of credibility, and by the personal reports of Gorvalan. The sordid calculations of petty spirits were as yet overruled by the enthusiasm of generous minds, captivated by the lofty nature of these enterprises. There was something wonderfully grand in the idea of thus introducing new races of animals and plants, of building cities, extending colonies, and sowing the seeds of civilization and of enlightened empire, in this beautiful but savage world. It struck the minds of learned and classical men with admiration, filling them with pleasant dreams and reveries, and seeming to realize the poetical pictures of the olden time. 'Columbus,' says old Peter Martyr, 'has begun to build a city, as he has lately written to me, and to sow our seeds and propagate our animals. Who of us shall now speak with wonder of Saturn, Ceres, and Triptolemus travelling about the earth to spread new inventions among mankind? Or of the Phoenicians, who built Tyre or Sidon, or of the Tyrians themselves, whose roving desires led them to migrate into foreign lands, to build new cities and establish new communities?'*

Such were the comments of enlightened and benevolent men, who hailed with enthusiasm the discovery of the New World, not for the wealth it would bring to Europe, but for the field it would open for glorious and benevolent enterprise, and the blessings and improvements of civilized life which it would widely dispense through barbarous and uncultivated regions.

Note

Isabella at the present day is quite overgrown with forest, in the midst of which are still to be seen, partly standing, the pillars of the church, some remains of the king's storehouses, and part of the residence of Columbus, all built of hewn stone. The small fortress is also a prominent ruin; and a little north of it is a circular pillar, about ten feet high and as much in diameter, of solid masonry, nearly entire, which appears to have had a wooden gallery or battlement round the top for the convenience of room, and in the centre of which was planted the flagstaff. Having discovered the remains of an iron clamp imbedded in the stone, which served to secure the flagstaff itself, I tore it out, and now consign to you this curious relic of the first foothold of civilization in the New World, after it has been exposed to the elements nearly three hundred and fifty years. – *From the Letter of T. S. Heneken, Esq.*

---

* Letter 153 to Pomponius Laetus.

CHAPTER 8

1494

The embryo city of Isabella was rapidly assuming a form. A dry stone wall surrounded it, to protect it from any sudden attack of the natives, although the most friendly disposition was evinced by the Indians of the vicinity, who brought supplies of their simple articles of food and gave them in exchange for European trifles. On the day of the Epiphany, the 6th of February, the church being sufficiently completed, high mass was celebrated with great pomp and ceremony by Friar Boyle and the twelve ecclesiastics. The affairs of the settlement being thus apparently in a regular train, Columbus, though still confined by indisposition, began to make arrangements for his contemplated expedition to the mountains of Cibao, when an unexpected disturbance in his little community for a time engrossed his attention.

The sailing of the fleet for Spain had been a melancholy sight to many whose terms of enlistment compelled them to remain on the island. Disappointed in their expectations of immediate wealth, disgusted with the labours imposed on them, and appalled by the maladies prevalent throughout the community, they began to look with horror upon the surrounding wilderness, as destined to be the grave of their hopes and of themselves. When the last sail disappeared, they felt as if completely severed from their country; and the tender recollections of home, which had been checked for a time by the novelty and bustle around them, rushed with sudden force upon their minds. To return to Spain became their ruling idea; and the same want of reflection which had hurried them into the enterprise, without inquiring into its real nature, now prompted them to extricate themselves from it by any means, however desperate.

Where popular discontents prevail, there is seldom wanting some daring spirit to give them a dangerous direction. One Bernal

Diaz de Piza, a man of some importance, who had held a civil office about the court, had come out with the expedition as comptroller. He seems to have presumed upon his official powers, and to have had early differences with the admiral. Disgusted with his employment in the colony, he soon made a faction among the discontented, and proposed that they should take advantage of the indisposition of Columbus to seize upon some or all of the five ships in the harbour, and return in them to Spain. It would be easy to justify their clandestine return by preferring a complaint against the admiral, representing the fallacy of his enterprises, and accusing him of gross deceptions and exaggerations in his accounts of the countries he had discovered. It is probable that some of these people really considered him culpable of the charges thus fabricated against him; for, in the disappointment of their avaricious hopes, they overlooked the real value of those fertile islands, which were to enrich nations by the produce of their soil. Every country was sterile and unprofitable in their eyes that did not immediately teem with gold. Though they had continual proofs in the specimens brought by the natives to the settlement, or furnished to Ojeda and Gorvalan, that the rivers and mountains in the interior abounded with ore, yet even these daily proofs were falsified in their eyes. One Fermin Cedo, a wrong-headed and obstinate man, who had come out as assayer and purifier of metals, had imbibed the same prejudice against the expedition with Bernal Diaz. He pertinaciously insisted that there was no gold in the island, or, at least, that it was found in such inconsiderable quantities as not to repay the search. He declared that the large grains of virgin ore brought by the natives had been melted; that they had been the slow accumulation of many years, having remained a long time in the families of the Indians, and handed down from generation to generation – which, in many instances, was probably the case. Other specimens of a large size he pronounced of a very inferior quality, and debased with brass by the natives. The words of this man outweighed the evidence of facts, and many joined him in the belief that the island was really destitute of gold. It was not until some time afterwards that the real character of Fermin Cedo was ascertained, and the discovery made that his ignorance was at least equal to his obstinacy and presumption, qualities apt to enter largely into the compound of a meddlesome and mischievous man. *

Encouraged by such substantial co-operation, a number of turbulent spirits concerted to take immediate possession of the ships and make sail for Europe. The influence of Bernal Diaz de Piza at court would obtain for them a favourable hearing, and they trusted to their unanimous representations to prejudice Columbus in the opinion of the public, ever fickle in its smiles, and most ready to turn suddenly and capriciously from the favourite it has most idolized.

Fortunately this mutiny was discovered before it proceeded to action. Columbus immediately ordered the ringleaders to be arrested. On making investigations, a memorial or information against himself, full of slanders and misrepresentations, was found concealed in the buoy of one of the ships. It was in the handwriting of Bernal Diaz. The admiral conducted himself with great moderation. Out of respect to the rank and station of Diaz, he forbore to inflict any punishment, but confined him on board one of the ships, to be sent to Spain for trial, together with the process or investigation of his offence and the seditious memorial which had been discovered. Several of the inferior mutineers were punished according to the degree of their culpability, but not with the severity which their offence deserved. To guard against any recurrence of a similar attempt, Columbus ordered that all the guns and naval munitions should be taken out of four of the vessels and put into the principal ship, which was given in charge to persons in whom he could place implicit confidence.†

This was the first time Columbus exercised the right of punishing delinquents in his new government, and it immediately awakened the most violent animadversions. His measures, though necessary for the general safety, and characterized by the greatest lenity, were censured as arbitrary and vindictive. Already the disadvantage of being a foreigner among the people he was to govern was clearly manifested. He had national prejudices to encounter, of all others the most general and illiberal. He had no natural friends to rally round him; whereas the mutineers had

* Cura de los Palacios, cap. 120, 122, MS.
† Herrera, *Hist. Ind.*, decad. i. lib. ii. cap. 11; *Hist. del Almirante*, cap. 50.

connections in Spain, friends in the colony, and met with sympathy in every discontented mind. An early hostility was thus engendered against Columbus, which continued to increase throughout his life, and the seeds were sown of a series of factions and mutinies which afterwards distracted the island.

Having at length recovered from his long illness, and the mutiny at the settlement being effectually checked, Columbus prepared for his immediate departure for Cibao. He intrusted the command of the city and the ships during his absence to his brother Don Diego, appointing able persons to counsel and assist him. Don Diego is represented by Las Casas, who knew him personally, as a man of great merit and discretion, of a gentle and pacific disposition, and more characterized by simplicity than shrewdness. He was sober in his attire, wearing almost the dress of an ecclesiastic, and Las Casas thinks he had secret hopes of preferment in the church;* indeed, Columbus intimates as much when he mentions him in his will.

As the admiral intended to build a fortress in the mountains, and to form an establishment for working the mines, he took with him the necessary artificers, workmen, miners, munitions, and implements. He was also about to enter the territories of the redoubtable Caonabo: it was important, therefore, to take with him a force that should not only secure him against any warlike opposition, but should spread through the country a formidable idea of the power of the white men, and deter the Indians from any future violence, either towards communities or wandering individuals. Every healthy person, therefore, who could be spared from the settlement was put in requisition, together with all the cavalry that could be mustered, and every arrangement was made to strike the savages with the display of military splendour.

On the 12th of March, Columbus set out at the head of about four hundred men, well armed and equipped, with shining helmets and corselets, with arquebuses, lances, swords, and cross-bows, and followed by a multitude of the neighbouring Indians. They sallied from the city in martial array, with banners flying and sound

* Las Casas, *Hist. Ind.*, lib. i. cap. 82, MS.

of drum and trumpet. Their march for the first day was across the plain between the sea and the mountains, fording two rivers, and passing through a fair and verdant country. They encamped in the evening, in the midst of pleasant fields, at the foot of a wild and rocky pass of the mountains.

The ascent of this rugged defile presented formidable difficulties to the little army, encumbered as it was with various implements and munitions. There was nothing but an Indian footpath, winding among rocks and precipices, or through brakes and thickets, entangled by the rich vegetation of a tropical forest. A number of high-spirited young cavaliers volunteered to open a route for the army. They had probably learned this kind of service in the Moorish wars, where it was often necessary on a sudden to open roads for the march of troops and the conveyance of artillery across the mountains of Granada. Throwing themselves in advance, with labourers and pioneers, whom they stimulated by their example, as well as by promises of liberal reward, they soon constructed the first road formed in the New World, and which was called El Puerto de los Hidalgos, or the Gentlemen's Pass, in honour of the gallant cavaliers who effected it.*

On the following day, the army toiled up this steep defile, and arrived where the gorge of the mountain opened into the interior. Here a land of promise suddenly burst upon their view. It was the same glorious prospect which had delighted Ojeda and his companions. Below lay a vast and delicious plain, painted and enamelled, as it were, with all the rich variety of tropical vegetation. The magnificent forests presented that mingled beauty and majesty of vegetable forms known only to these generous climates. Palms of prodigious height and spreading mahogany trees towered from amid a wilderness of variegated foliage. Freshness and verdure were maintained by numerous streams, which meandered gleaming through the deep bosom of the woodland; while various villages and hamlets, peeping from among the trees, and the smoke of others rising out of the midst of the forests, gave signs of a numerous population. The luxuriant landscape extended as far as the eye could reach, until it appeared to melt away and mingle with the horizon. The Spaniards gazed with rapture upon this soft

---

* *Hist del Almirante,* cap. 50. Hidalgo, that is, Hijo de algo, literally 'a son of somebody', in contradistinction to an obscure and lowborn man, a son of nobody.

voluptuous country, which seemed to realize their ideas of a terrestrial paradise; and Columbus, struck with its vast extent, gave it the name of the Vega Real, or Royal Plain.*

Having descended the rugged pass, the army issued upon the plain in martial style, with great clangour of warlike instruments. When the Indians beheld this shining band of warriors, glittering in steel, emerging from the mountains with prancing steeds and flaunting banners, and heard, for the first time, their rocks and forests echoing to the din of drum and trumpet, they might well have taken such a wonderful pageant for a supernatural vision.

In this way Columbus disposed of his forces whenever he approached a populous village, placing the cavalry in front, for the horses inspired a mingled terror and admiration among the natives. Las Casas observes that at first they supposed the rider and his horse to be one animal, and nothing could exceed their astonishment at seeing the horsemen dismount – a circumstance which shows that the alleged origin of the ancient fable of the centaurs is at least founded in nature. On the approach of the army, the Indians generally fled with terror and took refuge in their houses. Such was their simplicity that they merely put up a slight barrier of reeds

* Las Casas, *Hist. Ind.*, lib. i. cap. 20, MS.

Extract of a Letter from T. S. Heneken, Esq., dated Santiago (St Domingo), 20th September 1847. – The route over which Columbus traced his course from Isabella to the mountains of Cibao exists in all its primitive rudeness. The Puerto de los Hidalgos is still the narrow rugged footpath, winding among rocks and precipices, leading through the only practicable defile which traverses the Monte Christi range of mountains in this vicinity, at present called the pass of Marney; and it is somewhat surprising that, of this first and remarkable footprint of the white man in the New World, there does not at the present day exist the least tradition of its former name or importance.

The spring of cool and delightful water met with in the gorge, in a deep dark glen overshadowed by palm and mahogany trees, near the outlet where the magnificent Vega breaks upon the view, still continues to quench the thirst of the weary traveller. When I drank from this lonely little fountain, I could hardly realize the fact that Columbus must likewise have partaken of its sparkling waters, when at the height of his glory, surrounded by cavaliers attired in the gorgeous costumes of the age, and warriors recently from the Moorish wars.

Judging by the distance stated to have been travelled over the plain, Columbus must have crossed the Yagui near or at Ponton, which very likely received its name from the rafts or pontoons employed to cross the river. Abundance of reeds grow along its banks, and the remains of an Indian village are still very distinctly to be traced in the vicinity. By this route he avoided two large rivers, the Amina and the Mar, which discharge their waters into the Yagui opposite Esperanza.

The road from Ponton to the river Hanique passes through the defiles of La Cuesta and Nicayagua.

at the portal, and seemed to consider themselves perfectly secure. Columbus, pleased to meet with such artlessness, ordered that these frail barriers should be scrupulously respected, and the inhabitants allowed to remain in their fancied security.* By degrees their fears were allayed through the mediation of interpreters and the distribution of trifling presents. Their kindness and gratitude could not then be exceeded, and the march of the army was continually retarded by the hospitality of the numerous villages through which it passed. Such was the frank communion among these people that the Indians who accompanied the army entered without ceremony into the houses, helping themselves to anything of which they stood in need, without exciting surprise or anger in the inhabitants. The latter offered to do the same with respect to the Spaniards, and seemed astonished when they met a repulse. This, it is probable, was the case merely with respect to articles of food; for we are told that the Indians were not careless in their notions of property, and the crime of theft was one of the few which were punished among them with great severity. Food, however, is generally open to free participation in savage life, and is rarely made an object of barter until habits of trade have been introduced by the white men. The untutored savage, in almost every part of the world, scorns to make a traffic of hospitality.

After a march of five leagues across the plain, they arrived at the banks of a large and beautiful stream, called by the natives Yagui, but to which the admiral gave the name of the River of Reeds. He was not aware that it was the same stream which, after winding through the Vega, falls into the sea near Monte Christi, and which, in his first voyage, he had named the River of Gold. On its green banks the army encamped for the night, animated and delighted with the beautiful scenes through which they had passed. They bathed and sported in the waters of the Yagui, enjoying the amenity of the surrounding landscape and the delightful breezes which prevail in that genial season. 'For though there is but little difference,' observes Las Casas, 'from one month to another in all the year in this island, and in most parts of these Indias, yet in the period from September to May it is like living in paradise.'†

* Las Casas, *Hist. Ind.*, lib. i. cap. 90.
† Las Casas, *Hist. Ind.*, lib. i. cap. 90, MS.

On the following morning they crossed this stream by the aid of canoes and rafts, swimming the horses over. For two days they continued their march through the same kind of rich level country, diversified by noble forests and watered by abundant streams, several of which descended from the mountains of Cibao, and were said to bring down gold dust mingled with their sands. To one of these, the limpid waters of which ran over a bed of smooth round pebbles, Columbus gave the name of Rio Verde, or Green River, from the verdure and freshness of its banks. Its Indian name was Nicayagua, which it still retains.* In the course of this march they passed through numerous villages, where they experienced generally the same reception. The inhabitants fled at their approach, putting up their slight barricadoes of reeds; but, as before, they were easily won to familiarity, and tasked their limited means to entertain the strangers.

Thus penetrating into the midst of this great island, where every scene presented the wild luxuriance of beautiful but uncivilized nature, they arrived on the evening of the second day at a chain of lofty and rugged mountains, forming a kind of barrier to the Vega. These, Columbus was told, were the golden mountains of Cibao, whose region commenced at their rocky summits. The country now beginning to grow rough and difficult, and the people being wayworn, they encamped for the night at the foot of a steep defile which led up into the mountains, and pioneers were sent in advance to open a road for the army. From this place they sent back mules for a supply of bread and wine, their provisions beginning to grow scanty; for they had not as yet accustomed themselves to the food of the natives, which was afterwards found to be of that light digestible kind suitable to the climate.

On the next morning they resumed their march up a narrow and steep glen, winding among craggy rocks, where they were obliged to lead the horses. Arrived at the summit, they once more enjoyed a prospect of the delicious Vega, which here presented a still grander appearance, stretching far and wide on either hand like a vast verdant lake. This noble plain, according to Las Casas, is eighty leagues in length, and from twenty to thirty in breadth, and of incomparable beauty.

---

* The name of Rio Verde was afterwards given to a small stream which crosses the road from Santiago to La Vega, a branch of the river Yuna.

They now entered Cibao, the famous region of gold, which, as
if nature delighted in contrarieties, displayed a miser-like poverty
of exterior in proportion to its hidden treasures. Instead of the soft
luxuriant landscape of the Vega, they beheld chains of rocky
and sterile mountains, scantily clothed with lofty pines. The trees
in the valleys also, instead of possessing the rich tufted foliage
common to other parts of the island, were meagre and dwarfish,
excepting such as grew on the banks of streams. The very name of
the country bespoke the nature of the soil – Cibao, in the language
of the natives, signifying a stone. Still, however, there were deep
glens and shady ravines among the mountains, watered by limpid
rivulets, where the green herbage and strips of woodland were the
more delightful to the eye from the neighbouring sterility. But
what consoled the Spaniards for the asperity of the soil was to
observe among the sands of those crystal streams glittering particles
of gold, which, though scanty in quantity, were regarded as
earnests of the wealth locked up within the mountains.

The natives, having been previously visited by the exploring
party under Ojeda, came forth to meet them with great alacrity,
bringing food, and, above all, grains and particles of gold collected
in the brooks and torrents. From the quantities of gold dust in
every stream, Columbus was convinced there must be several
mines in the vicinity. He had met with specimens of amber and
lapis-lazuli, though in very small quantities, and thought that he
had discovered a mine of copper. He was now about eighteen
leagues from the settlement; the rugged nature of the mountains
made a communication, even from this distance, laborious. He
gave up the idea, therefore, of penetrating further into the country,
and determined to establish a fortified post in this neighbourhood,
with a large number of men, as well to work the mines as to
explore the rest of the province. He accordingly selected a pleasant
situation on an eminence almost entirely surrounded by a small
river called the Yanique, the waters of which were as pure as if
distilled, and the sound of its current musical to the ear. In its bed
were found curious stones of various colours, large masses of
beautiful marble, and pieces of pure jasper. From the foot of the
height extended one of those graceful and verdant plains called
savannas, which was freshened and fertilized by the river.*

* Las Casas, *Hist. Ind.*, lib. i. cap. 90, MS.

On this eminence Columbus ordered a strong fortress of wood to be erected, capable of defence against any attack of the natives, and protected by a deep ditch on the side which the river did not secure. To this fortress he gave the name of St Thomas, intended as a pleasant though pious reproof of the incredulity of Fermin Cedo and his doubting adherents, who obstinately refused to believe that the island produced gold, until they beheld it with their eyes and touched it with their hands.*

The natives, having heard of the arrival of the Spaniards in their vicinity, came flocking from various parts, anxious to obtain European trinkets. The admiral signified to them that anything would be given in exchange for gold. Upon hearing this, some of them ran to a neighbouring river, and gathering and sifting its sands, returned in a little while with considerable quantities of gold dust. One old man brought two pieces of virgin ore, weighing an

---

* Ibid. – *From the Letter of T. S. Heneken, Esq., 1847:* – Traces of the old fortress of St Thomas still exist, though, as has happened to the Puerto de los Hidalgos, all tradition concerning it has long been lost.

Having visited a small Spanish village known by the name of Hanique, situated on the banks of that stream, I heard by accident the name of a farm at no great distance, called La Fortaleza. This excited my curiosity, and I proceeded to the spot, a short distance up the river. Yet nothing could be learned from the inhabitants; it was only by ranging the river's banks, through a dense and luxuriant forest, that I by accident stumbled upon the site of the fortress.

The remarkable turn in the river – the ditch, still very perfect – the entrance and the covert ways on each side for descending to the river, with a fine esplanade of beautiful short grass in front, complete the picture described by Las Casas.

The square occupied by the fort is now completely covered with forest trees, undistinguishable from those of the surrounding country, which corresponds to this day exactly with the description given above, three centuries since, by Columbus, Ojeda, and Juan de Luxan.

The only change to notice is, that the neat little Indian villages, swarming with an innocent and happy population, have totally disappeared; there being at present only a few scattered huts of indigent Spaniards to be met with, buried in the gloom of the mountains.

The traces of those villages are rarely to be discovered at the present day. The situation of one near Ponton was well chosen for defence, being built on a high bank between deep and precipitous ravines. A large square occupied the centre. In the rear of each dwelling were thrown the sweepings of the apartments and the ashes from the fires, which form a line of mounds, mixed up with broken Indian utensils. As it lies in the direct road from Isabella, Cibao, and La Vega, and commands the best fording-place in the neighbourhood for crossing the river Yagui in dry seasons, it must, no doubt, have been a place of considerable resort at the time of the discovery: most likely a pontoon or large canoe was stationed here for the facility of communication between St Thomas and Isabella, whence it derived its name.

ounce, and thought himself richly repaid when he received a hawk's bell. On remarking that the admiral was struck with the size of these specimens, he affected to treat them with contempt as insignificant, intimating by signs that in his country, which lay within half a day's journey, they found pieces of gold as big as an orange. Other Indians brought grains of gold weighing ten and twelve drachms, and declared that in the country whence they got them there were masses of ore as large as the head of a child.* As usual, however, these golden tracts were always in some remote valley, or along some rugged and sequestered stream, and the wealthiest spot was sure to be at the greatest distance; for the land of promise is ever beyond the mountain.

* Peter Martyr, decad. i. lib. iii.

While the admiral remained among the mountains, superintending the building of the fortress, he despatched a young cavalier of
Madrid, named Juan de Luxan, with a small band of armed men, to
range about the country and explore the whole of the province,
which, from the reports of the Indians, appeared to be equal in
extent to the kingdom of Portugal. Luxan returned, after a few
days' absence, with the most satisfactory accounts. He had traversed a great part of Cibao, which he found more capable of
cultivation than had at first been imagined. It was generally mountainous, and the soil covered with large round pebbles of a blue
colour; yet there was good pasturage in many of the valleys. The
mountains, also, being watered by frequent showers, produced
grass of surprisingly quick and luxuriant growth, often reaching to
the saddles of the horses. The forests seemed to Luxan to be full of
valuable spices, he being deceived by the odours emitted by those
aromatic plants and herbs which abound in the woodlands of the
tropics. There were great vines also, climbing to the very summits
of the trees, and bearing clusters of grapes entirely ripe, full of
juice, and of a pleasant flavour. Every valley and glen possessed its
stream, large or small, according to the size of the neighbouring
mountain, and all yielding more or less gold in small particles.
Luxan was supposed likewise to have learned from the Indians
many of the secrets of their mountains – to have been shown the
parts where the greatest quantity of ore was found, and to have
been taken to the richest streams. On all these points, however, he
observed a discreet mystery, communicating the particulars to no
one but the admiral.*

The fortress of St Thomas being nearly completed, Columbus
gave it in command to Pedro Margarite, the same cavalier whom

* Peter Martyr, decad. i. lib. iii.

he had recommended to the favour of the sovereigns, and he left with him a garrison of fifty-six men. He then set out on his return to Isabella. On arriving at the banks of the Rio Verde, or Nicayagua, in the Royal Vega, he found a number of Spaniards on their way to the fortress with supplies. He remained, therefore, a few days in the neighbourhood, searching for the best fording-place of the river, and establishing a route between the fortress and the harbour. During this time he resided in the Indian villages, endeavouring to accustom his people to the food of the natives, as well as to inspire the latter with a mingled feeling of goodwill and reverence for the white men.

From the report of Luxan, Columbus had derived some information concerning the character and customs of the natives, and he acquired still more from his own observations in the course of his sojourn among the tribes of the mountains and the plains. And here a brief notice of a few of the characteristics and customs of these people may be interesting. They are given, not merely as observed by the admiral and his officers during his expedition, but as recorded some time afterwards, in a crude dissertation, by a friar of the name of Roman — a poor hermit, as he styled himself, of the order of the Ieronimites, who was one of the colleagues of Father Boyle, and resided for some time in the Vega as a missionary.

Columbus had already discovered the error of one of his opinions concerning these islanders formed during his first voyage — they were not so entirely pacific nor so ignorant of warlike arts as he had imagined. He had been deceived by the enthusiasm of his own feelings, and by the gentleness of Guacanagari and his subjects. The casual descents of the Caribs had compelled the inhabitants of the sea-shore to acquaint themselves with the use of arms. Some of the mountain tribes near the coast, particularly those on the side which looked towards the Caribbee Islands, were of a more hardy and warlike character than those of the plains. Caonabo also, the Carib chieftain, had introduced something of his own warrior spirit into the centre of the island. Yet, generally speaking, the habits of the people were mild and gentle. If wars sometimes occurred among them, they were of short duration, and unaccompanied by any great effusion of blood, and in general they mingled amicably and hospitably with each other.

Columbus had also at first indulged in the error that the natives of Hayti were destitute of all notions of religion, and he had consequently flattered himself that it would be the easier to introduce into their minds the doctrines of Christianity, not aware that it is more difficult to light up the fire of devotion in the cold heart of an atheist, than to direct the flame to a new object when it is already enkindled. There are few beings, however, so destitute of reflection as not to be impressed with the conviction of an overruling deity. A nation of atheists never existed. It was soon discovered that these islanders had their creed, though of vague and simple nature. They believed in one supreme being, inhabiting the sky, who was immortal, omnipotent, and invisible, to whom they ascribed an origin – who had a mother, but no father.* They never addressed their worship directly to him, but employed inferior deities, called zemes, as messengers and mediators. Each cacique had his tutelar deity of this order, whom he invoked and pretended to consult in all his public undertakings, and who was reverenced by his people. He had a house apart as a temple to this deity, in which was an image of his zemi, carved of wood or stone, or shaped of clay or cotton, and generally of some monstrous and hideous form. Each family and each individual had likewise a particular zemi, or protecting genius, like the lares and penates of the ancients. They were placed in every part of their houses, or carved on their furniture; some had them of a small size, and bound them about their foreheads when they went to battle. They believed their zemes to be transferable, with all their powers, and often stole them from each other. When the Spaniards came among them, they often hid their idols, lest they should be taken away. They believed that these zemes presided over every object in nature, each having a particular charge or government. They influenced the seasons and the elements, causing sterile or abundant years, exciting hurricanes and whirlwinds, and tempests of rain and thunder, or sending sweet and temperate breezes and fruitful showers. They governed the seas and forests, the springs and fountains, like the nereids, the dryads, and satyrs of antiquity. They gave success in hunting and fishing. They guided the waters of the mountains into safe channels, and led them down to

* *Escritura de Fr. Roman; Hist. del Almirante.*

wander through the plains in gentle brooks and peaceful rivers; or, if incensed, they caused them to burst forth into rushing torrents and overwhelming floods, inundating and laying waste the valleys.

The natives had their butios, or priests, who pretended to hold communion with these zemes. They practised rigorous fasts and ablutions, and inhaled the powder or drank the infusion of a certain herb, which produced a temporary intoxication or delirium. In the course of this process they professed to have trances and visions, and that the zemes revealed to them future events, or instructed them in the treatment of maladies. They were, in general, great herbalists, and well acquainted with the medicinal properties of trees and vegetables. They cured diseases through their knowledge of simples, but always with many mysterious rites and ceremonies and supposed charms, chanting and burning a light in the chamber of the patient, and pretending to exorcise the malady, to expel it from the mansion, and to send it to the sea or to the mountain.*

Their bodies were painted or tattooed with figures of the zemes, which were regarded with horror by the Spaniards, as so many representations of the devil; and the butios, esteemed as saints by the natives, were abhorred by the former as necromancers. These butios often assisted the caciques in practising deceptions upon their subjects, speaking oracularly through the zemes by means of hollow tubes, inspiriting the Indians to battle by predicting success, or dealing forth such promises or menaces as might suit the purposes of the chieftain.

There is but one of their solemn religious ceremonies of which any record exists. The cacique proclaimed a day when a kind of festival was to be held in honour of his zemes. His subjects assembled from all parts, and formed a solemn procession, the married men and women decorated with their most precious ornaments, the young females entirely naked. The cacique, or the principal personage, marched at their head, beating a kind of drum. In this way they proceeded to the consecrated house or temple, in which were set up the images of the zemes. Arrived at the door, the cacique seated himself on the outside, continuing to beat his drum while the procession entered, the females carrying baskets of cakes,

* Oviedo, *Cron.*, lib. v. cap. 1.

ornamented with flowers, and singing as they advanced. These offerings were received by the butios with loud cries, or rather howlings. They broke the cakes after they had been offered to the zemes, and distributed the portions to the heads of families, who preserved them carefully throughout the year, as preventive of all adverse accidents. This done, the females danced at a given signal, singing songs in honour of the zemes, or in praise of the heroic actions of their ancient caciques. The whole ceremony finished by invoking the zemes to watch over and protect the nation.[*]

Besides the zemes, each cacique had three idols or talismans, which were mere stones, but which were held in great reverence by themselves and their subjects. One, they supposed, had the power to produce abundant harvests, another to remove all pain from women in travail, and the third to call forth rain or sunshine. Three of these were sent home by Columbus to the sovereigns.[†]

The ideas of the natives with respect to the creation were vague and undefined. They gave their own island of Hayti priority of existence over all others, and believed that the sun and moon originally issued out of a cavern in the island to give light to the world. This cavern still exists about seven or eight leagues from Cape François, now Cape Haytien, and is known by the name of La Voûte à Minguet. It is about one hundred and fifty feet in depth, and near the same in height, but very narrow. It receives no light but from the entrance, and from a round hole in the roof, whence it was said the sun and moon issued forth to take their places in the sky. The vault was so fair and regular that it appeared a work of art rather than of nature. In the time of Charlevoix the figures of various zemes were still to be seen cut in the rocks, and there were the remains of niches, as if to receive statues. This cavern was held in great veneration. It was painted, and adorned with green branches and other simple decorations. There were in it two images or zemes. When there was a want of rain, the natives made pilgrimages and processions to it, with songs and dances, bearing offerings of fruits and flowers.[‡]

They believed that mankind issued from another cavern, the large men from a great aperture, the small men from a little cranny.

[*] Charlevoix, *Hist. St Domingo*, lib. i. p. 56.
[†] *Hist. del Almirante*, cap. 61.
[‡] Charlevoix, *Hist. St Domingo*, lib. i. p 60.

La Voûte à Minguet

They were for a long time destitute of women, but, wandering on one occasion near a small lake, they saw certain animals among the branches of the trees, which proved to be women. On attempting to catch them, however, they were found to be as slippery as eels, so that it was impossible to hold them. At length they employed certain men whose hands were rendered rough by a kind of leprosy. These succeeded in securing four of these slippery females, from whom the world was peopled.

While the men inhabited this cavern, they dared only venture forth at night, for the sight of the sun was fatal to them, turning them into trees and stones. A cacique, named Vagoniona, sent one of his men forth from the cave to fish, who, lingering at his sport until the sun had risen, was turned into a bird of melodious note, the same which Columbus mistook for the nightingale. They added that yearly about the time he had suffered this transformation he came in the night, with a mournful song, bewailing his misfortune, which was the cause why that bird always sang in the night season.*

Like most savage nations, they had a tradition concerning the universal deluge, equally fanciful with most of the preceding; for it is singular how the human mind in its natural state is apt to account by trivial and familiar causes for great events. They said that there once lived in the island a mighty cacique, who slew his only son for conspiring against him. He afterwards collected and picked his bones, and preserved them in a gourd, as was the custom of the natives with the relics of their friends. On a subsequent day the cacique and his wife opened the gourd to contemplate the bones of their son, when, to their astonishment, several fish, great and small, leaped out. Upon this the cacique closed the gourd, and placed it on the top of his house, boasting that he had the sea shut up within it, and could have fish whenever he pleased. Four brothers, however, who had been born at the same birth, and were curious intermeddlers, hearing of this gourd, came during the absence of the cacique to peep into it. In their carelessness they suffered it to fall upon the ground, where it was dashed to pieces; when, lo! to their astonishment and dismay, there issued forth a mighty flood, with dolphins, and sharks, and tumbling porpoises, and great spouting whales; and the water spread until it overflowed

* Fray Roman; *Hist. del Almirante*; P. Martyr, decad. i. lib. ix.

the earth, and formed the ocean, leaving only the tops of the mountains uncovered, which are the present islands.*

They had singular modes of treating the dying and the dead. When the life of a cacique was despaired of, they strangled him out of a principle of respect, rather than suffer him to die like the vulgar. Common people were extended in their hammocks, bread and water placed at their head, and they were then abandoned to die in solitude. Sometimes they were carried to the cacique, and if he permitted them the distinction they were strangled. After death the body of a cacique was opened, dried at a fire, and preserved; of others, the head only was treasured up as a memorial, or occasionally a limb. Sometimes the whole body was interred in a cave, with a calabash of water and a loaf of bread; sometimes it was consumed with fire in the house of the deceased.

They had confused and uncertain notions of the existence of the soul when separated from the body. They believed in the apparitions of the departed at night, or by daylight in solitary places, to lonely individuals, sometimes advancing as if to attack them; but upon the traveller's striking at them they vanished, and he struck merely against trees or rocks. Sometimes they mingled among the living, and were only to be known by having no navels. The Indians, fearful of meeting with these apparitions, disliked to go about alone and in the dark.

They had an idea of a place of reward, to which the spirits of good men repaired after death, where they were reunited to the spirits of those they had most loved during life, and to all their ancestors. Here they enjoyed uninterruptedly and in perfection those pleasures which constituted their felicity on earth. They lived in shady and blooming bowers with beautiful women, and banqueted on delicious fruits. The paradise of these happy spirits was variously placed, almost every tribe assigning some favourite spot in their native province. Many, however, concurred in describing this region as being near a lake in the western part of the island, in the beautiful province of Xuragua. Here there were delightful valleys, covered with a delicate fruit called the mamey, about the size of an apricot. They imagined that the souls of the deceased remained concealed among the airy and inaccessible cliffs of the mountains during the day, but descended at night into these

* *Escritura de Fray Roman, pobre Heremito.*

happy valleys, to regale on this consecrated fruit. The living were sparing, therefore, in eating it, lest the souls of their friends should suffer from want of their favourite nourishment.*

The dances to which the natives seemed so immoderately addicted, and which had been at first considered by the Spaniards mere idle pastimes, were found to be often ceremonials of a serious and mystic character. They form indeed a singular and important feature throughout the customs of the aboriginals of the New World. In these are typified, by signs well understood by the initiated, and as it were by hieroglyphic action, their historical events, their projected enterprises, their hunting, their ambuscades, and their battles, resembling in some respects the Pyrrhic dances of the ancients. Speaking of the prevalence of these dances among the natives of Hayti, Peter Martyr observes that they performed them to the chant of certain metres and ballads, handed down from generation to generation, in which were rehearsed the deeds of their ancestors. 'These rhymes or ballads,' he adds, 'they call areytos; and as our minstrels are accustomed to sing to the harp and lute, so do they in like manner sing these songs, and dance to the same, playing on timbrels made of shells of certain fishes. These timbrels they call maguey. They have also songs and ballads of love, and others of lamentation or mourning; some also to encourage them to the wars; all sung to tunes agreeable to the matter.' It was for these dances, as has been already observed, that they were so eager to procure hawks' bells, suspending them about their persons, and keeping time with their sound to the cadence of the singers. This mode of dancing to a ballad has been compared to the dances of the peasants in Flanders during the summer, and to those prevalent throughout Spain to the sound of the castanets, and the wild popular chants said to be derived from the Moors, but which, in fact, existed before their invasion among the Goths who overran the peninsula.†

The earliest history of almost all nations has generally been preserved by rude heroic rhymes and ballads, and by the lays of the minstrels; and such was the case with the areytos of the Indians. 'When a cacique died,' says Oviedo, 'they sang in dirges

---

* *Hist. del Almirante*, cap. 61; Peter Martyr, decad. i. lib. ix.; Charlevoix, *Hist. St Domingo*, lib. i.

† Mariana, *Hist. Esp.*, lib. v. cap. i.

his life and actions, and all the good that he had done was recollected. Thus they formed the ballads or areytos which constituted their history.'* Some of these ballads were of a sacred character, containing their traditional notions of theology, and the superstitions and fables which comprised their religious creeds. None were permitted to sing these but the sons of caciques, who were instructed in them by their butios. They were chanted before the people on solemn festivals, like those already described, accompanied by the sound of a kind of drum made from a hollow tree.†

Such are a few of the characteristics remaining on record of these simple people, who perished from the face of the earth before their customs and creeds were thought of sufficient importance to be investigated. The present work does not profess to enter into detailed accounts of the countries and people discovered by Columbus, otherwise than as they may be useful for the illustration of his history; and perhaps the foregoing are carried to an unnecessary length, but they may serve to give greater interest to the subsequent transactions of the island.

Many of these particulars, as has been observed, were collected by the admiral and his officers during their excursion among the mountains and their sojourn in the plain. The natives appeared to them a singularly idle and improvident race, indifferent to most of the objects of human anxiety and toil. They were impatient of all kinds of labour, scarcely giving themselves the trouble to cultivate the yuca root, the maize, and the potato, which formed the main article of subsistence. For the rest, their streams abounded with fish; they caught the utia or coney, the guana, and various birds; and they had a perpetual banquet from the fruits spontaneously produced by their groves. Though the air was sometimes cold among the mountains, yet they preferred submitting to a little temporary suffering rather than take the trouble to weave garments from the gossampine cotton which abounded in their forests. Thus they loitered away existence in vacant inactivity under the shade of their trees, or amusing themselves occasionally with various games and dances.

* Oviedo, *Cron. de las Indias*, lib. v. cap. 3.
† Fray Roman; *Hist. del Almirante*, cap. 61; P. Martyr, decad. i. lib. ix.; Herrera, *Hist. Ind.*, decad. i. lib. iii. cap. 4; Oviedo, lib. v. cap. 1.

In fact, they were destitute of powerful motives to toil, being free from most of those wants which doom mankind in civilized life, or in less genial climates, to incessant labour. They had no sterile winter to provide against, particularly in the valleys and the plains, where, according to Peter Martyr, 'the island enjoyed perpetual spring-time, and was blessed with continual summer and harvest. The trees preserved their leaves throughout the year, and the meadows continued always green.' 'There is no province, nor any region,' he again observes, 'which is not remarkable for the majesty of its mountains, the fruitfulness of its vales, the pleasantness of its hills and delightful plains, with abundance of fair rivers running through them. There never was any noisome animal found in it, nor yet any ravening four-footed beast – no lion nor bear, no fierce tigers nor crafty foxes, nor devouring wolves, but all things blessed and fortunate.' *

In the soft region of the Vega the circling seasons brought each its store of fruits, and while some were gathered in full maturity, others were ripening on the boughs, and buds and blossoms gave promise of still future abundance. What need was there of garnering up and anxiously providing for coming days to men who lived in a perpetual harvest? What need, too, of toilfully spinning or labouring at the loom where a genial temperature prevailed throughout the year, and neither nature nor custom prescribed the necessity of clothing?

The hospitality which characterizes men in such a simple and easy mode of existence was evinced towards Columbus and his followers during their sojourn in the Vega. Wherever they went it was a continual scene of festivity and rejoicing. The natives hastened from all parts, bearing presents, and laying the treasures of their groves and streams and mountains at the feet of beings whom they still considered as descended from the skies to bring blessings to their island.

Having accomplished the purposes of his residence in the Vega, Columbus, at the end of a few days, took leave of its hospitable inhabitants, and resumed his march for the harbour, returning with his little army through the lofty and rugged gorge of the mountains called the Pass of the Hidalgos. As we accompany him in imagination over the rocky height, whence the Vega first broke

* Peter Martyr, decad. iii. lib. ix., translated by R. Eden. London 1555.

upon the eye of the Europeans, we cannot help pausing to cast back a look of mingled pity and admiration over this beautiful but devoted region. The dream of natural liberty, of ignorant content and loitering idleness, was as yet unbroken, but the fiat had gone forth. The white man had penetrated into the land. Avarice, and pride, and ambition, and pining care, and sordid labour, and withering poverty, were soon to follow, and the indolent paradise of the Indian was about to disappear for ever.

On the 29th of March Columbus arrived at Isabella, highly satisfied with his expedition into the interior. The appearance of
everything within the vicinity of the harbour was calculated to
increase his anticipations of prosperity. The plants and fruits of the
Old World, which he was endeavouring to introduce into the
island, gave promise of rapid increase. The orchards, fields, and
gardens were in a great state of forwardness. The seeds of various
fruits had produced young plants; the sugar-cane had prospered
exceedingly; a native vine, trimmed and dressed with care, had
yielded grapes of tolerable flavour, and cuttings from European
vines already began to form their clusters. On the 30th of March a
husbandman brought to Columbus ears of wheat which had been
sown in the latter part of January. The smaller kind of garden herbs
came to maturity in sixteen days, and the larger kind, such as
melons, gourds, pompions, and cucumbers, were fit for the table
within a month after the seed had been put into the ground. The
soil, moistened by brooks and rivers and frequent showers, and
stimulated by an ardent sun, possessed those principles of quick
and prodigal fecundity which surprise the stranger accustomed to
less vigorous climates.

The admiral had scarcely returned to Isabella when a messenger
arrived from Pedro Margarite, the commander at Fort St Thomas,
informing him that the Indians of the vicinity had manifested
unfriendly feelings, abandoning their villages, and shunning all
intercourse with the white men, and that Caonabo was assembling
his warriors and preparing to attack the fortress. The fact was that
the moment the admiral had departed the Spaniards, no longer
awed by his presence, had, as usual, listened only to their passions,
and exasperated the natives by wresting from them their gold
and wronging them with respect to their women. Caonabo also

had seen with impatience these detested intruders planting their standard in the very midst of his mountains, and he knew that he had nothing to expect from them but vengeance.

The tidings from Margarite, however, caused but little solicitude in the mind of Columbus. From what he had seen of the Indians in the interior he had no apprehensions from their hostility. He knew their weakness and their awe of white men, and, above all, he confided in their terror of the horses, which they regarded as ferocious beasts of prey, obedient to the Spaniards, but ready to devour their enemies. He contented himself therefore with sending Margarite a reinforcement of twenty men, with a supply of provisions and ammunition, and detaching thirty men to open a road between the fortress and the port.

What gave Columbus real and deep anxiety was the sickness, the discontent, and dejection which continued to increase in the settlement. The same principles of heat and humidity which gave such fecundity to the fields were fatal to the people. The exhalations from undrained marshes and a vast continuity of forest, and the action of a burning sun upon a reeking vegetable soil, produced intermittent fevers, and various other of the maladies so trying to European constitutions in the uncultivated countries of the tropics. Many of the Spaniards suffered also under the torments of a disease hitherto unknown to them, the scourge, as was supposed, of their licentious intercourse with the Indian females, but the origin of which, whether American or European, has been a subject of great dispute. Thus the greater part of the colonists were either confined by positive illness or reduced to great debility. The stock of medicines was soon exhausted; there was a lack of medical aid, and of the watchful attendance which is even more important than medicine to the sick. Everyone who was well was either engrossed by the public labours or by his own wants or cares, having to perform all menial offices for himself, even to the cooking of his provisions. The public works therefore languished, and it was impossible to cultivate the soil in a sufficient degree to produce a supply of the fruits of the earth. Provisions began to fail. Much of the stores brought from Europe had been wasted on board ship or suffered to spoil through carelessness, and much had perished on shore from the warmth and humidity of the climate. It seemed impossible for the colonists to accommodate themselves to

the food of the natives, and their infirm condition required the
aliments to which they had been accustomed. To avert an absolute
famine therefore it was necessary to put the people on a short
allowance even of the damaged and unhealthy provisions which
remained. This immediately caused loud and factious murmurs, in
which many of those in office, who ought to have supported
Columbus in his measures for the common safety, took a leading
part. Among those was Father Boyle, a priest as turbulent as he was
crafty. He had been irritated, it is said, by the rigid impartiality of
Columbus, who, in enforcing his salutary measures, made no
distinction of rank or persons, and put the friar and his household
on a short allowance as well as the rest of the community.

In the midst of this general discontent the bread began to grow
scarce. The stock of flour was exhausted, and there was no mode
of grinding corn but by the tedious and toilsome process of the
hand-mill. It became necessary therefore to erect a mill immediately, and other works were required equally important to the
welfare of the settlement. Many of the workmen, however, were ill,
some feigning greater sickness than they really suffered, for there
was a general disinclination to all kind of labour which was not to
produce immediate wealth. In this emergency Columbus put every
healthy person in requisition, and as the cavaliers and gentlemen of
rank required food as well as the lower orders, they were called
upon to take their share in the common labour. This was considered
a cruel degradation by many youthful hidalgos of high blood and
haughty spirit, and they refused to obey the summons. Columbus,
however, was a strict disciplinarian, and felt the importance of
making his authority respected. He resorted therefore to strong and
compulsory measures, and enforced their obedience. This was
another cause of the deep and lasting hostilities that sprang up
against him. It aroused the immediate indignation of every person
of birth and rank in the colony, and drew upon him the resentment
of several of the proud families of Spain. He was inveighed against as
an arrogant and upstart foreigner, who, inflated with a sudden
acquisition of power, and consulting only his own wealth and
aggrandizement, was trampling upon the rights and dignities of
Spanish gentlemen, and insulting the honour of the nation.

Columbus may have been too strict and indiscriminate in his
regulations. There are cases in which even justice may become

oppressive, and where the severity of the law should be tempered with indulgence. What was mere toilsome labour to a common man became humiliation and disgrace when forced upon a Spanish cavalier. Many of these young men had come out, not in the pursuit of wealth, but with romantic dreams inspired by his own representations, hoping, no doubt, to distinguish themselves by heroic achievements and chivalrous adventure, and to continue in the Indies the career of arms which they had commenced in the recent wars of Granada. Others had been brought up in soft luxurious indulgence, in the midst of opulent families, and were little calculated for the rude perils of the seas, the fatigues of the land, and the hardships, the exposures, and deprivations which attend a new settlement in the wilderness. When they fell ill their case soon became incurable. The ailments of the body were increased by sickness of the heart. They suffered under the irritation of wounded pride and the morbid melancholy of disappointed hope. Their sick-bed was destitute of all the tender care and soothing attention to which they had been accustomed, and they sank into the grave in all the sullenness of despair, cursing the day of their departure from their country.

The venerable Las Casas, and Herrera after him, records with much solemnity a popular belief current in the island at the time of his residence there, and connected with the untimely fate of these cavaliers.

In after years, when the seat of the colony was removed from Isabella on account of its unhealthy situation, the city fell to ruin and was abandoned. Like all decayed and deserted places, it soon became an object of awe and superstition to the common people, and no one ventured to enter its gates. Those who passed near it, or hunted the wild swine which abounded in the neighbourhood, declared they heard appalling voices issue from within its walls by night and day. The labourers became fearful therefore of cultivating the adjacent fields. The story went, adds Las Casas, that two Spaniards happened one day to wander among the ruined edifices of the place. On entering one of the solitary streets they beheld two rows of men, evidently, from their stately demeanour, hidalgos of noble blood and cavaliers of the court. They were richly attired in the old Castilian mode, with rapiers by their sides, and broad travelling hats, such as were worn at the time. The two men were

astonished to behold persons of their rank and appearance apparently inhabiting that desolate place unknown to the people of the
island. They saluted them, and inquired whence they came and
when they had arrived. The cavaliers maintained a gloomy silence,
but courteously returned the salutation by raising their hands to
their sombreros or hats, in taking off which their heads came off
also, and their bodies stood decapitated. The whole phantom
assemblage then vanished. So great was the astonishment and
horror of the beholders that they had nearly fallen dead, and
remained stupified for several days.[*]

The foregoing legend is curious as illustrating the superstitious
character of the age, and especially of the people with whom
Columbus had to act. It shows also the deep and gloomy impression made upon the minds of the common people by the
death of these cavaliers, which operated materially to increase the
unpopularity of Columbus, as it was mischievously represented
that they had been seduced from their homes by his delusive
promises, and sacrificed to his private interests.

---

[*] Las Casas, *Hist. Ind.*, lib. i. cap. 92, MS; Herrera, *Hist. Ind.*, decad. i. lib. ii. cap. 12.

The increasing discontents of the motley population of Isabella, and the rapid consumption of the scanty stores which remained, were causes of great anxiety to Columbus. He was desirous of proceeding on another voyage of discovery, but it was indispensable before sailing to place the affairs of the island in such a state as to secure tranquillity. He determined therefore to send all the men that could be spared from Isabella into the interior, with orders to visit the territories of the different caciques and explore the island. By this means they would be roused and animated; they would become accustomed to the climate and to the diet of the natives; and such a force would be displayed as to overawe the machinations of Caonabo or any other hostile cacique. In pursuance of this plan every healthy person not absolutely necessary to the concerns of the city or the care of the sick was put under arms, and a little army mustered, consisting of two hundred and fifty crossbowmen, one hundred and ten arquebusiers, sixteen horsemen, and twenty officers. The general command of the forces was intrusted to Pedro Margarite, in whom Columbus had great confidence as a noble Catalonian and a knight of the order of Santiago. Alonzo de Ojeda was to conduct the army to the fortress of St Thomas, where he was to succeed Margarite in the command; and the latter was to proceed with the main body of the troops on a military tour, in which he was particularly to explore the province of Cibao, and subsequently the other parts of the island.

Columbus wrote a long and earnest letter of instructions to Margarite, by which to govern himself in a service requiring such great circumspection. He charged him above all things to observe the greatest justice and discretion in respect to the Indians, protecting them from all wrong and insult, and treating them in such a manner as to secure their confidence and friendship. At the same time they were to be made to respect the property of the white men, and all thefts were to be severely punished. Whatever provisions were required from them for the subsistence of the army were to be fairly purchased by persons whom the admiral appointed for that purpose. The purchases were to be made in the presence of the agent of the comptroller. If the Indians refused to sell the necessary provisions, then Margarite was to interfere and compel them to do so, acting, however, with all possible gentleness, and soothing them by kindness and caresses. No traffic was to be allowed between individuals and the natives, it being displeasing to the sovereigns and injurious to the service; and it was always to be kept in mind that their majesties were more desirous of the conversion of the natives than of any riches to be derived from them.

A strict discipline was to be maintained in the army, all breach of orders to be severely punished, the men to be kept together and not suffered to wander from the main body, either singly or in small parties, lest they should be cut off by the natives; for though these people were pusillanimous, there were no people so apt to be perfidious and cruel as cowards.[*]

These judicious instructions, which, if followed, might have preserved an amicable intercourse with the natives, are more especially deserving of notice because Margarite disregarded them all, and by his disobedience brought trouble on the colony, obloquy on the nation, destruction on the Indians, and unmerited censure on Columbus.

In addition to the foregoing orders, there were particular directions for the surprising and securing of the persons of Caonabo and his brothers. The warlike character of that chieftain, his artful policy, extensive power, and implacable hostility, rendered him a dangerous enemy. The measures proposed were not the most open and chivalrous, but Columbus thought himself justified in opposing stratagem to stratagem with a subtle and sanguinary foe.

On the 9th of April Alonzo de Ojeda sallied forth from Isabella at the head of the forces, amounting to nearly four hundred men. On arriving at the Rio del Oro, in the Royal Vega, he learned that three Spaniards coming from the fortress of St Thomas had been

---

[*] Letter of Columbus, Navarrete, *Colec.*, tom. ii., Document No. 72.

robbed of their effects by five Indians, whom a neighbouring cacique had sent to assist them in fording the river; and that the cacique, instead of punishing the thieves, had countenanced them and shared their booty. Ojeda was a quick, impetuous soldier, whose ideas of legislation were all of a military kind. Having caught one of the thieves, he caused his ears to be cut off in the public square of the village; he then seized the cacique, his son, and nephew, and sent them in chains to the admiral, after which he pursued his march to the fortress.

In the meantime the prisoners arrived at Isabella in deep dejection. They were accompanied by a neighbouring cacique, who, relying upon the merit of various acts of kindness which he had shown to the Spaniards, came to plead for their forgiveness. His intercessions appeared to be of no avail. Columbus felt the importance of striking awe into the minds of the natives with respect to the property of the white men. He ordered, therefore, that the prisoners should be taken to the public square with their hands tied behind them, their crime and punishment proclaimed by the crier, and their heads struck off. Nor was this a punishment disproportioned to their own ideas of justice, for we are told that the crime of theft was held in such abhorrence among them that, though not otherwise sanguinary in their laws, they punished it with impalement.* It is not probable, however, that Columbus really meant to carry the sentence into effect. At the place of execution the prayers and tears of the friendly cacique were redoubled, pledging himself that there should be no repetition of the offence. The admiral at length made a merit of yielding to his entreaties, and released the prisoners. Just at this juncture a horseman arrived from the fortress, who, in passing by the village of the captive cacique, had found five Spaniards in the power of the Indians. The sight of his horse had put the multitude to flight, though upwards of four hundred in number. He had pursued the fugitives, wounding several with his lance, and had brought off his countrymen in triumph.

Convinced by this circumstance that nothing was to be apprehended from the hostilities of these timid people as long as his orders were obeyed, and confiding in the distribution he had made of his forces, both for the tranquillity of the colony and

* Oviedo, *Hist. Ind.*, lib. v. cap. 3.

the island, Columbus prepared to depart on the prosecution of his discoveries. To direct the affairs of the island during his absence, he formed a junta, of which his brother Don Diego was president, and Father Boyle, Pedro Fernandez Coronel, Alonzo Sanchez Caravajal, and Juan de Luxan were councillors. He left his two largest ships in the harbour, being of too great a size and draught of water to explore unknown coasts and rivers, and he took with him three caravels, the *Niña* or *Santa Clara*, the *San Juan*, and the *Cordera*.

BOOK 7

CHAPTER I

1494

The expedition of Columbus which we are now about to record may appear of minor importance at the present day, leading as it did to no grand discovery, and merely extending along the coasts of islands with which the reader is sufficiently familiar. Some may feel impatient at the development of opinions and conjectures which have long since been proved to be fallacious, and the detail of exploring enterprises, undertaken in error, and which they know must end in disappointment. But to feel these voyages properly, we must, in a manner, divest ourselves occasionally of the information we possess relative to the countries visited; we must transport ourselves to the time, and identify ourselves with Columbus, thus fearlessly launching into seas where as yet a civilized sail had never been unfurled. We must accompany him, step by step, in his cautious but bold advances along the bays and channels of an unknown coast, ignorant of the dangers which might lurk around, or which might await him in the interminable region of mystery that still kept breaking upon his view. We must, as it were, consult with him as to each new reach of shadowy land and long line of promontory that we see faintly emerging from the ocean and stretching along the distant horizon. We must watch with him each light canoe that comes skimming the billows, to gather from the looks, the ornaments, and the imperfect commun-ications of its wandering crew whether those unknown lands are also savage and uncultivated, whether they are islands in the ocean, untrodden as yet by civilized man, or tracts of the old continent of Asia, and wild frontiers of its populous and splendid empires. We must enter into his very thoughts and fancies, find out the data that assisted his judgment and the hints that excited his conjectures, and for a time clothe the regions through which we are accompanying him with the gorgeous colouring of his own imagination. In this way we may delude ourselves into participation of the delights of exploring unknown and magnificent lands, where new wonders and beauties break upon us at every step, and we may ultimately be able, as it were, from our own familiar acquaintance, to form an opinion of the character of this extraordinary man, and of the nature of his enterprises.

The plan of the present expedition of Columbus was to revisit the coast of Cuba at the point where he had abandoned it on his first voyage, and thence to explore it on the southern side. As has already been observed, he supposed it to be a continent, and the extreme end of Asia; and if so, by following its shores in the proposed direction he must eventually arrive at Cathay and those other rich and commercial though semi-barbarous countries described by Mandeville and Marco Polo.*

He set sail with his little squadron from the harbour of Isabella on the 24th of April, and steered to the westward. After touching at Monte Christi, he anchored on the same day at the disastrous harbour of La Navidad. His object in revisiting this melancholy scene was to obtain an interview with Guacanagari, who, he understood, had returned to his former residence. He could not be persuaded of the perfidy of that cacique, so deep was the impression made upon his heart by past kindness; he trusted, therefore, that a frank explanation would remove all painful doubts, and restore a friendly intercourse, which would be highly advantageous to the Spaniards in their present time of scarcity and suffering. Guacanagari, however, still maintained his equivocal conduct, absconding at the sight of the ships; and though several of his subjects assured Columbus that the cacique would soon make him a visit, he did not think it advisable to delay his voyage on such an uncertainty.

Pursuing his course, impeded occasionally by contrary winds, he arrived on the 29th at the port of St Nicholas, whence he beheld the extreme point of Cuba, to which in his preceding voyage he had given the name of Alpha and Omega, but which was called by the natives Bayatiquiri, and is now known as Point

* Cura de los Palacios, cap. 123, MS.

Maysi. Having crossed the channel, which is about eighteen leagues wide, he sailed along the southern coast of Cuba for the distance of twenty leagues, when he anchored in a harbour, to which, from its size, he gave the name of Puerto Grande, at present called Guantanamo. The entrance was narrow and winding though deep; the harbour expanded within, like a beautiful lake in the bosom of a wild and mountainous country, covered with trees, some of them in blossom, others bearing fruit. Not far from the shore were two cottages built of reeds, and several fires blazing in various parts of the beach gave signs of inhabitants. Columbus landed, therefore, attended by several men well armed, and by the young Indian interpreter, Diego Colon, the native of the island of Guanahanè, who had been baptized in Spain. On arriving at the cottages he found them deserted; the fires also were abandoned, and there was not a human being to be seen. The Indians had all fled to the woods and mountains. The sudden arrival of the ships had spread a panic throughout the neighbourhood, and apparently interrupted the preparations for a rude but plentiful banquet. There were great quantities of fish, utias, and guanas; some suspended to the branches of trees, others roasting on wooden spits before the fires.

The Spaniards, accustomed of late to slender fare, fell without ceremony on this bounteous feast thus spread for them, as it were, in the wilderness. They abstained, however, from the guanas, which they still regarded with disgust as a species of serpent, though they were considered so delicate a food by the savages that, according to Peter Martyr, it was no more lawful for the common people to eat of them than of peacocks and pheasants in Spain.*

After their repast, as the Spaniards were roving about the vicinity, they beheld about seventy of the natives collected on the top of a lofty rock, and looking down upon them with great awe and amazement. On attempting to approach them, they instantly disappeared among the woods and clefts of the mountain. One, however, more bold or more curious than the rest, lingered on the brow of the precipice, gazing with timid wonder at the Spaniards, partly encouraged by their friendly signs, but ready in an instant to bound away after his companions.

* P. Martyr, decad. i. lib. iii.

By order of Columbus, the young Lucayan interpreter advanced and accosted him. The expressions of friendship, in his own language, soon dispelled his apprehensions. He came to meet the interpreter; and being informed by him of the good intentions of the Spaniards, hastened to communicate the intelligence to his comrades. In a little while they were seen descending from their rocks and issuing from their forests, approaching the strangers with great gentleness and veneration. Through the means of the interpreter, Columbus learned that they had been sent to the coast by their cacique to procure fish for a solemn banquet which he was about to give to a neighbouring chieftain, and that they roasted the fish to prevent it from spoiling in the transportation. They seemed to be of the same gentle and pacific character with the natives of Hayti. The ravages that had been made among their provisions by the hungry Spaniards gave them no concern, for they observed that one night's fishing would replace all the loss. Columbus, however, in his usual spirit of justice, ordered that ample compensation should be made them; and shaking hands, they parted mutually well pleased.*

Leaving this harbour on the 1st of May, the admiral continued to the westward, along a mountainous coast adorned by beautiful rivers, and indented by those commodious harbours for which this island is so remarkable. As he advanced, the country grew more fertile and populous. The natives crowded to the shores – man, woman, and child – gazing with astonishment at the ships, which glided gently along at no great distance. They held up fruits and provisions, inviting the Spaniards to land; others came off in canoes, bringing cassava bread, fish, and calabashes of water, not for sale, but as offerings to the strangers, whom, as usual, they considered celestial beings descended from the skies. Columbus distributed the customary presents among them, which were received with transports of joy and gratitude. After continuing some distance along the coast, he came to another gulf or deep bay, narrow at the entrance and expanding within, surrounded by a rich and beautiful country. There were lofty mountains sweeping up from the sea, but the shores were enlivened by numerous villages, and cultivated to such a degree as to resemble gardens and orchards. In this harbour, which it is probable was

* P. Martyr, decad. i. lib. iii.

the same at present called St Jago de Cuba, Columbus anchored and passed a night, overwhelmed, as usual, with the simple hospitality of the natives.*

On inquiring of the people of this coast after gold, they uniformly pointed to the south, and, as far as they could be understood, intimated that it abounded in a great island which lay in that direction. The admiral, in the course of his first voyage, had received information of such an island, which some of his followers had thought might be Babeque, the object of so much anxious search and chimerical expectation. He had felt a strong inclination to diverge from his course and go in quest of it, and this desire increased with every new report. On the following day, therefore (the 3rd of May), after standing westward to a high cape, he turned his prow directly south, and abandoning for a time the coast of Cuba, steered off into the broad sea in quest of this reported island.

* Cura de los Palacios, cap. 124, MS.

CHAPTER 2

1494

Columbus had not sailed many leagues before the blue summits of a vast and lofty island at a great distance began to rise like clouds above the horizon. It was two days and nights, however, before he reached its shores, filled with admiration, as he gradually drew near, at the beauty of its mountains, the majesty of its forests, the fertility of its valleys, and the great number of villages with which the whole face of the country was animated.

On approaching the land, at least seventy canoes, filled with savages gaily painted and decorated with feathers, sallied forth more than a league from the shore. They advanced in warlike array, uttering loud yells and brandishing lances of pointed wood. The mediation of the interpreter, and a few presents to the crew of one of the canoes which ventured nearer than the rest, soothed this angry armada, and the squadron pursued its course unmolested. Columbus anchored in a harbour about the centre of the island, to which, from the great beauty of the surrounding country, he gave the name of Santa Gloria.*

On the following morning he weighed anchor at daybreak, and coasted westward in search of a sheltered harbour where his ship could be careened and caulked, as it leaked considerably. After proceeding a few leagues, he found one apparently suitable for the purpose. On sending a boat to sound the entrance, two large canoes, filled with Indians, issued forth, hurling their lances, but from such distance as to fall short of the Spaniards. Wishing to avoid any act of hostility that might prevent future intercourse, Columbus ordered the boat to return on board, and finding there was sufficient depth of water for his ship, entered and anchored in the harbour. Immediately the whole beach was covered with Indians, painted with a variety of colours, but chiefly black, some

* Cura de los Palacios, cap. 125.

partly clothed with palm-leaves, and all wearing tufts and coronets of feathers. Unlike the hospitable islanders of Cuba and Hayti, they appeared to partake of the warlike character of the Caribs, hurling their javelins at the ships, and making the shores resound with their yells and war-whoops.

The admiral reflected that further forbearance might be mistaken for cowardice. It was necessary to careen his ship, and to send men on shore for a supply of water, but previously it was advisable to strike an awe into the savages, that might prevent any molestation from them. As the caravels could not approach sufficiently near to the beach where the Indians were collected, he despatched the boats well manned and armed. These, rowing close to the shore, let fly a volley of arrows from their crossbows, by which several Indians were wounded, and the rest thrown into confusion. The Spaniards then sprang on shore, and put the whole multitude to flight, giving another discharge with their crossbows, and letting loose upon them a dog, who pursued them with sanguinary fury.* This is the first instance of the use of dogs against the natives, which were afterwards employed with such cruel effect by the Spaniards in their Indian wars. Columbus now landed and took formal possession of the island, to which he gave the name of Santiago; but it has retained its original Indian name of Jamaica. The harbour, from its commodiousness, he called Puerto Bueno: it was in the form of a horse-shoe, and a river entered the sea in its vicinity.†

During the rest of the day the neighbourhood remained silent and deserted. On the following morning, however, before sunrise, six Indians were seen on the shore, making signs of amity. They proved to be envoys sent by the caciques with proffers of peace and friendship. These were cordially returned by the admiral; presents of trinkets were sent to the chieftains; and in a little while the harbour again swarmed with the naked and painted multitude, bringing abundance of provisions, similar in kind but superior in quality to those of the other islands.

During three days that the ships remained in this harbour, the most amicable intercourse was kept up with the natives. They appeared to be more ingenious, as well as more warlike, than their

---

* Cura de los Palacios, cap. 125.

† *Hist. del Almirante*, ubi sup.

neighbours of Cuba and Hayti. Their canoes were better constructed, being ornamented with carving and painting at the bow and stern. Many were of great size, though formed of the trunks of single trees, often from a species of the mahogany. Columbus measured one which was ninety-six feet long and eight broad,* hollowed out of one of those magnificent trees which rise like verdant towers amidst the rich forests of the tropics. Every cacique prided himself on possessing a large canoe of the kind, which he seemed to regard as his ship of state. It is curious to remark the apparently innate difference between these island tribes. The natives of Porto Rico, though surrounded by adjacent islands, and subject to frequent incursions of the Caribs, were of a pacific character, and possessed very few canoes; while Jamaica, separated by distance from intercourse with other islands, protected in the same way from the dangers of invasion, and embosomed, as it were, in a peaceful mediterranean sea, was inhabited by a warlike race, and surpassed all the other islands in its maritime armaments.

His ship being repaired, and a supply of water taken in, Columbus made sail, and continued along the coast to the westward, so close to the shore that the little squadron was continually surrounded by the canoes of the natives, who came off from every bay and river and headland, no longer manifesting hostility, but anxious to exchange anything they possessed for European trifles. After proceeding about twenty-four leagues, they approached the western extremity of the island, where, the coast bending to the south, the wind became unfavourable for their further progress along the shore. Being disappointed in his hopes of finding gold in Jamaica, and the breeze being fair for Cuba, Columbus determined to return thither, and not to leave it until he had explored its coast to a sufficient distance to determine the question whether it were *terra firma* or an island.† To the last place at which he touched in Jamaica he gave the name of the Gulf of Buentiempo (or Fair Weather), on account of the propitious wind which blew for Cuba. Just as he was about to sail, a young Indian came off to the ship, and begged the Spaniards would take him to their country. He was followed by his relatives and friends, who endeavoured by the most affecting supplications to dissuade him from his purpose.

* Cura de los Palacios, cap. 124.
† *Hist. del Almirante*, cap. 54.

For some time he was distracted between concern for the distress of his family and an ardent desire to see the home of these wonderful strangers. Curiosity and the youthful propensity to rove prevailed; he tore himself from the embraces of his friends, and, that he might not behold the tears of his sisters, hid himself in a secret part of the ship. Touched by this scene of natural affection, and pleased with the enterprising and confiding spirit of the youth, Columbus gave orders that he should be treated with special kindness.*

It would have been interesting to have known something more of the fortunes of this curious savage, and of the impressions made upon so lively a mind by a first sight of the wonders of civilization – whether the land of the white men equalled his hopes; whether, as is usual with savages, he pined amidst the splendours of cities for his native forests; and whether he ever returned to the arms of his family. The early Spanish historians seem never to have interested themselves in the feelings or fortunes of these first visitors from the New to the Old World. No further mention is made of this youthful adventurer.

* *Hist. del Almirante*, cap. 54.

CHAPTER 3

1494

Setting sail from the Gulf of Buentiempo, the squadron once more steered for the island of Cuba, and on the 18th of May arrived at a great cape, to which Columbus gave the name of Cabo de la Cruz, which it still retains. Here, landing at a large village, he was well received and entertained by the cacique and his subjects, who had long since heard of him and his ships. In fact, Columbus found, from the report of this chieftain, that the numerous Indians who had visited his ships during his cruise along the northern coast in his first voyage had spread the story far and near of these wonderful visitors who had descended from the sky, and had filled the whole island with rumours and astonishment.[*] The admiral endeavoured to ascertain from this cacique and his people whether Cuba was an island or a continent. They all replied that it was an island, but of infinite extent, for they declared that no one had ever seen the end of it. This reply, while it manifested their ignorance of the nature of a continent, left the question still in doubt and obscurity. The Indian name of this province of Cuba was Macaca.

Resuming his course to the west on the following day, Columbus came to where the coast suddenly swept away to the north-east for many leagues, and then curved around again to the west, forming an immense bay, or rather gulf. Here he was assailed by a violent storm, accompanied by awful thunder and lightning, which in these latitudes seem to rend the very heavens. Fortunately the storm was not of long duration, or his situation would have been perilous in the extreme, for he found the navigation rendered difficult by the numerous keys[†] and sand-banks. These increased as he advanced, until the mariner stationed

[*] Cura de los Palacios, cap. 126.
[†] Keys, from *cayos*, rocks which occasionally form small islands on the coast of America.

at the mast-head beheld the sea, as far as the eye could reach, completely studded with small islands; some were low, naked, and sandy, others covered with verdure, and others tufted with lofty and beautiful forests. They were of various sizes, from one to four leagues, and were generally the more fertile and elevated the nearer they were to Cuba. Finding them to increase in number, so as to render it impossible to give names to each, the admiral gave the whole labyrinth of islands, which in a manner enamelled the face of the ocean with variegated verdure, the name of the Queen's Gardens. He thought at first of leaving this archipelago on his right, and standing further out to sea; but he called to mind that Sir John Mandeville and Marco Polo had mentioned that the coast of Asia was fringed with islands to the amount of several thousands. He persuaded himself that he was among that cluster, and resolved not to lose sight of the mainland, by following which, if it were really Asia, he must soon arrive at the dominions of the Grand Khan.

Entering among these islands, therefore, Columbus soon became entangled in the most perplexed navigation, in which he was exposed to continual perils and difficulties from sand-banks, counter currents, and sunken rocks. The ships were compelled, in a manner, to grope their way, with men stationed at the mast-head, and the lead continually going. Sometimes they were obliged to shift their course within the hour to all points of the compass; sometimes they were straitened in a narrow channel, where it was necessary to lower all sail, and tow the vessels out, lest they should run aground; notwithstanding all which precautions, they frequently touched upon sand-banks, and were extricated with great difficulty. The variableness of the weather added to the embarrassment of the navigation, though after a little while it began to assume some method in its very caprices. In the morning the wind rose in the east with the sun, and following his course through the day, died away at sunset in the west. Heavy clouds gathered with the approach of evening, sending forth sheets of lightning and distant peals of thunder, and menacing a furious tempest; but as the moon rose the whole mass broke away, part melting in a shower, and part dispersing by a breeze which sprang up from the land.

There was much in the character of the surrounding scenery to favour the idea of Columbus that he was in the Asiatic archipelago.

As the ships glided along the smooth and glassy canals which separated these verdant islands, the magnificence of their vegetation, the soft odours wafted from flowers, and blossoms, and aromatic shrubs, and the splendid plumage of the scarlet cranes, or rather flamingoes, which abounded in the meadows, and of other tropical birds which fluttered among the groves, resembled what is described of Oriental climes.

These islands were generally uninhabited. They found a considerable village, however, on one of the largest, where they landed on the 22nd of May. The houses were abandoned by their inhabitants, who appeared to depend principally on the sea for their subsistence. Large quantities of fish were found in their dwellings, and the adjacent shore was covered with the shells of tortoises. There were also domesticated parrots, and scarlet cranes, and a number of dumb dogs, which it was afterwards found they fattened as an article of food. To this island the admiral gave the name of Santa Marta.

In the course of his voyage among these islands, Columbus beheld one day a number of the natives in a canoe on the still surface of one of the channels, occupied in fishing, and was struck with the singular means they employed. They had a small fish, the flat head of which was furnished with numerous suckers, by which it attached itself so firmly to any object as to be torn in pieces rather than abandon its hold. Tying a line of great length to the tail of this fish, the Indians permitted it to swim at large. It generally kept near the surface of the water until it perceived its prey, when, darting down swiftly, it attached itself by the suckers to the throat of a fish or to the under shell of a tortoise; nor did it relinquish its prey until both were drawn up by the fisherman and taken out of the water. In this way the Spaniards witnessed the taking of a tortoise of immense size, and Fernando Columbus affirms that he himself saw a shark caught in the same manner on the coast of Veragua. The fact has been corroborated by the accounts of various navigators, and the same mode of fishing is said to be employed on the eastern coast of Africa, at Mozambique and at Madagascar. 'Thus,' it has been observed, 'savage people, who probably have never held communication with each other, offer the most striking analogies in their modes of exercising empire over animals.'* These fishermen came on board of the ships in a fearless manner. They furnished the

* Humboldt, *Essai Politique sur l'Ile de Cuba*, tom. i. p. 364.

Spaniards with a supply of fish, and would cheerfully have given them everything they possessed. To the admiral's inquiries concerning those parts, they said that the sea was full of islands to the south and to the west, but as to Cuba, it continued running to the westward without any termination.

Having extricated himself from this archipelago, Columbus steered for a mountainous part of the island of Cuba about fourteen leagues distant, where he landed at a large village on the 3rd of June. Here he was received with that kindness and amity which distinguished the inhabitants of Cuba, whom he extolled above all the other islanders for their mild and pacific character. Their very animals, he said, were tamer, as well as larger and better, than those of the other islands. Among the various articles of food which the natives brought with joyful alacrity from all parts were stockdoves of uncommon size and flavour: perceiving something peculiar in their taste, Columbus ordered the crops of several newly killed to be opened, in which were found sweet spices.

While the crews of the boats were procuring water and provisions, Columbus sought to gather information from the venerable cacique and several of the old men of the village. They told him that the name of their province was Ornofay; that further to the westward the sea was again covered with innumerable islands, and had but little depth. As to Cuba, none of them had ever heard that it had an end to the westward; forty moons would not suffice to reach to its extremity; in fact, they considered it interminable. They observed, however, that the admiral would receive more ample information from the inhabitants of Mangon, an adjacent province which lay towards the west. The quick apprehension of Columbus was struck with the sound of this name; it resembled that of Mangi, the richest province of the Grand Khan, bordering on the ocean. He made further inquiries concerning the region of Mangon, and understood the Indians to say that it was inhabited by people who had tails like animals, and wore garments to conceal them. He recollected that Sir John Mandeville, in his account of the remote parts of the East, had recorded a story of the same kind as current among certain naked tribes of Asia, and told by them in ridicule of the garments of their civilized neighbours, which they could only conceive useful as concealing some bodily defect.* He became, therefore, more confident than ever that, by keeping along the coast to the westward, he should eventually arrive at the civilized realms of Asia. He flattered himself with the hopes of finding this region of Mangon to be the rich province of Mangi, and its people with tails and garments the long-robed inhabitants of the empire of Tartary.

* Cura de los Palacios, cap. 127.

CHAPTER 4

1494

Animated by one of the pleasing illusions of his ardent imagination, Columbus pursued his voyage, with a prosperous breeze, along the supposed continent of Asia. He was now opposite that part of the southern side of Cuba where, for nearly thirty-five leagues, the navigation is unembarrassed by banks and islands. To his left was the broad and open sea, the dark-blue colour of which gave token of ample depth; to his right extended the richly-wooded province of Ornofay, gradually sweeping up into a range of interior mountains, the verdant coast watered by innumerable streams and studded with Indian villages. The appearance of the ships spread wonder and joy along the sea-coast. The natives hailed with acclamations the arrival of these wonderful beings whose fame had circulated more or less throughout the island, and who brought with them the blessings of heaven. They came off swimming, or in their canoes, to offer the fruits and productions of the land, and regarded the white men almost with adoration. After the usual evening shower, when the breeze blew from the shore and brought off the sweetness of the land, it bore with it also the distant songs of the natives and the sound of their rude music, as they were probably celebrating, with their national chants and dances, the arrival of the white men. So delightful were these spicy odours and cheerful sounds to Columbus, who was at present open to all pleasurable influences, that he declared the night passed away as a single hour.*

It is impossible to resist noticing the striking contrasts which are sometimes presented by the lapse of time. The coast here described, so populous and animated, rejoicing in the visit of the discoverers, is the same that extends westward of the city of Trinidad, along the gulf of Xagua. All is now silent and deserted: civilization, which

* Cura de los Palacios.

has covered some parts of Cuba with glittering cities, has rendered this a solitude. The whole race of Indians has long since passed away, pining and perishing beneath the domination of the strangers whom they welcomed so joyfully to their shores. Before me lies the account of a night recently passed on this very coast by a celebrated traveller; but with what different feelings from those of Columbus! 'I passed,' says he, 'a great part of the night upon the deck. What deserted coasts! not a light to announce the cabin of a fisherman. From Batabano to Trinidad, a distance of fifty leagues, there does not exist a village. Yet in the time of Columbus this land was inhabited even along the margin of the sea. When pits are digged in the soil, or the torrents plough open the surface of the earth, there are often found hatchets of stone and vessels of copper, relics of the ancient inhabitants of the island.'*

For the greater part of two days the ships swept along this open part of the coast, traversing the wide Gulf of Xagua. At length they came to where the sea became suddenly as white as milk and perfectly turbid, as though flour had been mingled with it. This is caused by fine sand, or calcareous particles, raised from the bottom at certain depths by the agitation of the waves and currents. It spread great alarm through the ships, which was heightened by their soon finding themselves surrounded by banks and keys and in shallow water. The further they proceeded the more perilous became their situation. They were in a narrow channel, where they had no room to turn and to beat out; where there was no hold for their anchors, and where they were violently tossed about by the winds, and in danger of being stranded. At length they came to a small island, where they found tolerable anchorage. Here they remained for the night in great anxiety. Many were for abandoning all further prosecution of the enterprise, thinking that they might esteem themselves fortunate should they be able to return from whence they came. Columbus, however, could not consent to relinquish his voyage, now that he thought himself in the route for a brilliant discovery. The next morning he despatched the smallest caravel to explore this new labyrinth of islands, and to penetrate to the mainland in quest of fresh water, of which the ships were in great need. The caravel returned with a report that the canals and keys of this group were as numerous and intricate as

* Humboldt, *Essai Pol. sur Cuba*, tom. ii. p. 25.

those of the Gardens of the Queen; that the mainland was bordered by deep marshes and a muddy coast, where the mangrove-
trees grew within the water and so close together that they formed,
as it were, an impenetrable wall; that within, the land appeared
fertile and mountainous, and columns of smoke, rising from
various parts, gave signs of numerous inhabitants.* Under the
guidance of this caravel, Columbus now ventured to penetrate this
little archipelago, working his way with great caution, toil, and
peril among the narrow channels which separated the sand-banks
and islands, and frequently getting aground. At length he reached a
low point of Cuba, to which he gave the name of Point Serafin,
within which the coast swept off to the east, forming so deep a bay
that he could not see the land at the bottom. To the north,
however, there were mountains afar off, and the intermediate
space was clear and open, the islands in sight lying to the south and
west – a description which agrees with that of the great Bay of
Batabano. Columbus now steered for these mountains, with a fair
wind and three fathoms of water, and on the following day
anchored on the coast near a beautiful grove of palm-trees.

Here a party was sent on shore for wood and water, and they
found two living springs in the midst of the grove. While they
were employed in cutting wood and filling their water-casks, an
archer strayed into the forest with his cross-bow in search of game,
but soon returned, flying with great terror, and calling loudly upon
his companions for aid. He declared that he had not proceeded far
when he suddenly espied through an opening glade a man in a
long white dress, so like a friar of the order of St Mary of Mercy
that at first sight he took him for the chaplain of the admiral. Two
others followed, in white tunics reaching to their knees; and the
three were of as fair complexions as Europeans. Behind these
appeared many more to the number of thirty, armed with clubs
and lances. They made no signs of hostility, but remained quiet,
the man in the long white dress alone advancing to accost him; but
he was so alarmed at their number that he had fled instantly to seek
the aid of his companions. The latter, however, were so daunted
by the reported number of armed natives that they had not
courage to seek them nor to wait their coming, but hurried with
all speed to the ships.

* Cura de los Palacios, cap. 128.

When Columbus heard this story he was greatly rejoiced, for he concluded that these must be the clothed inhabitants of Mangon of whom he had recently heard, and that he had at length arrived at the confines of a civilized country, if not within the very borders of the rich province of Mangi. On the following day he despatched a party of armed men in quest of these people clad in white, with orders to penetrate, if necessary, forty miles into the interior, until they met with some of the inhabitants; for he thought the populous and cultivated parts might be distant from the sea, and that there might be towns and cities beyond the woods and mountains of the coast. The party penetrated through a belt of thick forests which girdled the shore, and then entered upon a great plain or savanna, covered with rank grass and herbage as tall as ripe corn, and destitute of any road or footpath. Here they were so entangled and fettered, as it were, by matted grass and creeping vegetation that it was with the utmost difficulty they could penetrate the distance of a mile, when they had to abandon the attempt, and return weary and exhausted to the ships.

Another party was sent on the succeeding day to penetrate in a different direction. They had not proceeded far from the coast when they beheld the footprints of some large animal with claws, which some supposed the tracks of a lion, others of a griffon,[*] but which were probably made by the alligators which abound in that vicinity. Dismayed at the sight, they hastened back towards the sea-side. In their way they passed through a forest, with lawns and meadows opening in various parts of it, in which were flocks of cranes twice the size of those of Europe. Many of the trees and shrubs sent forth those aromatic odours which were continually deceiving them with the hope of finding Oriental spices. They saw also abundance of grape-vines, that beautiful feature in the vegetation of the New World. Many of these crept to the summits of the highest trees, overwhelming them with foliage, twisting themselves from branch to branch, and bearing

---

[*] Cardinal Pedro de Aliaco, a favourite author with Columbus, speaks repeatedly in his *Imago Mundi* of the existence of griffons in India; and Glanville, whose work, *De Proprietatibus Rerum*, was familiar to Columbus, describes them as having the body and claws of a lion and the head and wings of an eagle, and as infesting the mountains which abounded with gold and precious stones, so as to render the access to them extremely perilous (*De Proprietat. Rerum*, lib. xviii. cap. 150).

ponderous clusters of juicy grapes. The party returned to the ships equally unsuccessful with their predecessors, and pronounced the country wild and impenetrable, though exceedingly fertile. As a proof of its abundance, they brought great clusters of the wild grapes, which Columbus afterwards transmitted to the sovereigns, together with a specimen of the water of the white sea through which he had passed.

As no tribe of Indians was ever discovered in Cuba wearing clothing, it is probable that the story of the men in white originated in some error of the archer, who, full of the idea of the mysterious inhabitants of Mangon, may have been startled in the course of his lonely wandering in the forest by one of those flocks of cranes which it seems abounded in the neighbourhood. These birds, like the flamingoes, feed in company, with one stationed at a distance as sentinel. When seen through the openings of the woodlands, standing in rows along a smooth savanna or in a glassy pool of water, their height and erectness give them at the first glance the semblance of human figures. Whether the story originated in error or in falsehood, it made a deep impression on the mind of Columbus, who was predisposed to be deceived and to believe everything that favoured the illusion of his being in the vicinity of a civilized country.

After he had explored the deep bay to the east, and ascertained that it was not an arm of the sea, he continued westward, and, proceeding about nine leagues, came to an inhabited shore, where he had communications with several of the natives. They were naked as usual, but that he attributed to their being mere fishermen inhabiting a savage coast; he presumed the civilized regions to lie in the interior. As his Lucayan interpreter did not understand the language, or rather dialect, of this part of Cuba, all the information which he could obtain from the natives was necessarily received through the erroneous medium of signs and gesticulations. Deluded by his own favourite hypothesis, he understood from them that among certain mountains which he saw far off to the west there was a powerful king who reigned in great state over many populous provinces; that he wore a white garment which swept the ground; that he was called a saint;* that he never spoke, but

---

* 'Que le llamaban santo e que traia tunica blanca que le arastra por sel suela.' – Cura de los Palacios, cap. 128.

communicated his orders to his subjects by signs, which were
implicitly obeyed.* In all this we see the busy imagination of the
admiral interpreting everything into unison with his preconceived
ideas. Las Casas assures us that there was no cacique ever known in
the island who wore garments or answered in other respects to this
description. This king, with a saintly title, was probably nothing
more than a reflected image haunting the mind of Columbus of
that mysterious potentate, Prester John, who had long figured in
the narrations of all Eastern travellers, sometimes as a monarch,
sometimes as a priest, the situation of whose empire and court was
always a matter of doubt and contradiction, and had recently
become again an object of curious inquiry.

The information derived from these people concerning the coast
to the westward was entirely vague. They said that it continued for
at least twenty days' journey, but whether it terminated there they
did not know. They appeared but little informed of anything out
of their immediate neighbourhood. Taking an Indian from this
place as a guide, Columbus steered for the distant mountains said
to be inhabited by this cacique in white raiment, hoping they
might prove the confines of a more civilized country. He had not
gone far before he was involved in the usual perplexities of keys,
shelves, and sand-banks. The vessels frequently stirred up the sand
and slime from the bottom of the sea; at other times they were
almost embedded in narrow channels, where there was no room to
tack, and it was necessary to haul them forward by means of the
capstan, to their great injury. At one time they came to where the
sea was almost covered with tortoises; at another time flights of
cormorants and wood-pigeons darkened the sun, and one day the
whole air was filled with clouds of gaudy butterflies, until dispelled
by the evening shower.

When they approached the mountainous regions, they found
the coast bordered by drowned lands or morasses, and beset by
such thick forests that it was impossible to penetrate to the
interior. They were several days seeking fresh water, of which
they were in great want. At length they found a spring in a grove
of palm-trees; and near it shells of the pearl oyster, from which
Columbus thought there might be a valuable pearl-fishery in the
neighbourhood.

* Herrera, *Hist. Ind.*, dec. i. lib. ii. cap. 14.

While thus cut off from all intercourse with the interior by a belt of swamp and forests, the country appeared to be well peopled. Columns of smoke ascended from various parts, which grew more frequent as the vessels advanced, until they rose from every rock and woody height. The Spaniards were at a loss to determine whether these arose from villages and towns, or whether from signal-fires, to give notice of the approach of the ships and to alarm the country, such as were usual on European sea-shores when an enemy was descried hovering in the vicinity.

For several days Columbus continued exploring this perplexed and lonely coast, whose intricate channels are seldom visited, even at the present day, excepting by the solitary and lurking bark of the smuggler. As he proceeded, however, he found that the coast took a general bend to the south-west. This accorded precisely with the descriptions given by Marco Polo of the remote coast of Asia. He now became fully assured that he was on that part of the Asiatic continent which is beyond the boundaries of the Old World as laid down by Ptolemy. Let him but continue his course, he thought, and he must surely arrive at the point where this range of coast terminated in the Aurea Chersonesus of the ancients.*

The ardent imagination of Columbus was always sallying in the advance, and suggesting some splendid track of enterprise. Combining his present conjectures as to his situation with the imperfect lights of geography, he conceived a triumphant route for his return to Spain. Doubling the Aurea Chersonesus, he should emerge into the seas frequented by the ancients, and bordered by the luxurious nations of the East. Stretching across the Gulf of the Ganges, he might pass by Taprobana, and, continuing on to the Straits of Babelmandel, arrive on the shores of the Red Sea. Thence he might make his way by land to Jerusalem, take shipping at Joppa, and traverse the Mediterranean to Spain. Or should the route from Ethiopia to Jerusalem be deemed too perilous from savage and warlike tribes, or should he not choose to separate from his vessels, he might sail round the whole coast of Africa, pass triumphantly by the Portuguese in their midway groping along the shores of Guinea, and after having thus circumnavigated the globe, furl his adventurous sails at the Pillars of Hercules, the *ne plus ultra* of the ancient world! Such was the soaring meditation of

---

* The present peninsula of Malacca.

Columbus, as recorded by one of his intimate associates.* Nor is
there anything surprising in his ignorance of the real magnitude
of our globe. The mechanical admeasurement of a known part of
its circle has rendered its circumference a familiar fact in our day;
but in his time it still remained a problem with the most profound
philosophers.

* Cura de los Palacios, cap. 123, MS.

The opinion of Columbus, that he was coasting the continent of
Asia, and approaching the confines of Eastern civilization, was
shared by all his fellow-voyagers, among whom were several able
and experienced navigators. They were far, however, from sharing
his enthusiasm; they were to derive no glory from the success of
the enterprise, and they shrank from its increasing difficulties and
perils. The ships were strained and crazed by the various injuries
they had received in running frequently aground. Their cables and
rigging were worn, their provisions were growing scanty, a great
part of the biscuit was spoiled by the sea-water which oozed in
through innumerable leaks. The crews were worn out by incessant
labour, and disheartened at the appearance of the sea before them,
which continued to exhibit a mere wilderness of islands. They
remonstrated, therefore, against persisting any longer in this voyage.
They had already followed the coast far enough to satisfy their
minds that it was a continent; and though they doubted not that
civilized regions lay in the route they were pursuing, yet their
provisions might be exhausted, and their vessels disabled, before
they could arrive at them.

Columbus, as his imagination cooled, was himself aware of the
inadequacy of his vessels to the contemplated voyage, but felt it of
importance to his fame and to the popularity of his enterprises to
furnish satisfactory proof that the land he had discovered was a
continent. He therefore persisted four days longer in exploring
the coast as it bent to the south-west, until every one declared
there could no longer be a doubt on the subject, for it was
impossible so vast a continuity of land should belong to a mere
island. The admiral was determined, however, that the fact
should not rest on its own assertions merely, having had recent
proofs of a disposition to gainsay his statements and depreciate his

discoveries. He sent round, therefore, a public notary, Fernand Perez de Luna, to each of the vessels, accompanied by four witnesses, who demanded formally of every person on board, from the captain to the ship-boy, whether he had any doubt that the land before him was a continent, the beginning and end of the Indies, by which anyone might return overland to Spain, and by pursuing the coast of which they could soon arrive among civilized people. If anyone entertained a doubt, he was called upon to express it, that it might be removed. On board of the vessels, as has been observed, were several experienced navigators and men well versed in the geographical knowledge of the times. They examined their maps and charts, and the reckonings and journals of the voyage, and after deliberating maturely, declared, under oath, that they had no doubt upon the subject. They grounded their belief principally upon their having coasted for three hundred and thirty-five leagues,* an extent unheard of as appertaining to an island, while the land continued to stretch forward interminably, bending towards the south, conformably to the description of the remote coasts of India.

Lest they should subsequently, out of malice or caprice, contradict the opinion thus solemnly avowed, it was proclaimed by the notary that whoever should offend in such manner, if an officer, should pay a penalty of ten thousand maravedies; if a ship-boy, or person of like rank, he should receive a hundred lashes, and have his tongue cut out. A formal statement was afterwards drawn up by the notary, including the depositions and names of every individual, which document still exists.† This singular process took place near that deep bay called by some the Bay of Philipina, by others of Cortes. At this very time, as has been remarked, a ship-boy from the mast-head might have overlooked the group of islands to the south and beheld the open sea beyond.‡ Two or three days' further sail would have carried Columbus round the extremity of Cuba, would have dispelled his illusion, and might have given an entirely different course to

---

* This calculation evidently includes all the courses of the ships, in their various tacks along the coast. Columbus could hardly have made such an error as to have given this extent to the southern side of the island, even including the inflections of the coast.

† Navarrete, *Colec.*, tom. ii.

‡ Muñoz, *Hist. N. Mundo.* lib. v. p. 217.

his subsequent discoveries. In his present conviction he lived and died, believing, to his last hour, that Cuba was the extremity of the Asiatic continent.

Relinquishing all further investigation of the coast, he stood to the south-east on the 13th of June, and soon came in sight of a large island with mountains rising majestically among this labyrinth of little keys. To this he gave the name of Evangelista. It is at present known as the Island of Pines, and is celebrated for its excellent mahogany.

Here he anchored and took in a supply of wood and water. He then stood to the south, along the shores of the island, hoping by turning its southern extremity to find an open route eastward for Hispaniola, and intending, on his way, to run along the southern side of Jamaica. He had not proceeded far before he came to what he supposed to be a channel, opening to the southeast between Evangelista and some opposite island. After entering for some distance, however, he found himself enclosed in a deep bay, being the Lagoon of Siguanca, which penetrates far into the island.

Observing dismay painted on the faces of his crew at finding themselves thus land-locked and almost destitute of provisions, Columbus cheered them with encouraging words, and resolved to extricate himself from this perplexing maze by retracing his course along Cuba. Leaving the lagoon, therefore, he returned to his last anchoring-place, and set sail thence on the 25th of June, navigating back through the groups of islands between Evangelista and Cuba, and across a tract of the white sea which had so much appalled his people. Here he experienced a repetition of the anxieties, perils, and toils which had beset him in his advance along the coast. The crews were alarmed by the frequent changes in the colour of the water – sometimes green, sometimes almost black, at other times as white as milk; at one time they fancied themselves surrounded by rocks, at another the sea appeared to be a vast sand-bank. On the 30th of June the admiral's ship ran aground with such violence as to sustain great injury. Every effort to extricate her by sending out anchors astern was ineffectual, and it was necessary to drag her over the shoal by the prow. At length they emerged from the clusters of islands called the Jardins and Jardinelles, and came to the open part of the coast of Cuba. Here they once more sailed along the beautiful and fertile province of Ornofay, and were again delighted with fragrant and honeyed airs wafted from the land. Among the mingled odours, the admiral fancied he could perceive that of storax proceeding from the smoke of fires blazing on the shores.*

Here Columbus sought some convenient harbour where he might procure wood and water, and allow his crews to enjoy repose and the recreations of the land, for they were exceedingly enfeebled and emaciated by the toils and privations of the voyage. For nearly two months they had been struggling with perpetual difficulties and dangers, and suffering from a scarcity of provisions. Among these uninhabited keys and drowned shores, their supplies from the natives had been precarious and at wide intervals; nor could the fresh provisions thus furnished last above a day, from the heat and humidity of the climate. It was the same case with any fish they might chance to catch, so that they had to depend almost entirely upon their daily allowance of ships' provisions, which was reduced to a pound of mouldy bread and a small portion of wine. With joy, therefore, they anchored on the 7th of July in the mouth of a fine river, in this genial and abundant region. The cacique of the neighbourhood, who reigned over an extensive territory, received the admiral with demonstrations of mingled joy and reverence, and his subjects came laden with whatever their country afforded – utias, birds of various kinds, particularly large pigeons, cassava bread, and fruits of a rich and aromatic flavour.

It was a custom with Columbus in all remarkable places which he visited to erect crosses in conspicuous situations, to denote the discovery of the country and its subjugation to the true faith. He ordered a large cross of wood, therefore, to be elevated on the bank of this river. This was done on a Sunday morning with great ceremony and the celebration of a solemn mass. When he disembarked for this purpose, he was met upon the shore by the cacique and his principal favourite, a venerable Indian, fourscore years of age, of grave and dignified deportment. The old man brought a string of beads, of a kind to which the Indians attached a mystic value, and a calabash of a delicate kind of fruit; these he presented to the admiral in token of amity. He and the cacique then each took him by the hand, and proceeded with him to the grove,

---

* Humboldt (in his *Essai Polit.*, tom. ii. p. 24) speaks of the fragrance of flowers and honey which exhales from this same coast, and which is perceptible to a considerable distance at sea.

where preparations had been made for the celebration of the mass. A multitude of the natives followed. While mass was performing in this natural temple, the Indians looked on with awe and reverence, perceiving from the tones and gesticulations of the priest, the lighted tapers, the smoking incense, and the devotion of the Spaniards, that it must be a ceremony of a sacred and mysterious nature. When the service was ended, the old man of fourscore, who had contemplated it with profound attention, approached Columbus, and made him an oration in the Indian manner.

'That which thou hast been doing,' said he, 'is well, for it appears to be thy manner of giving thanks to God. I am told that thou hast lately come to these lands with a mighty force, and subdued many countries, spreading great fear among the people; but be not, therefore, vainglorious. Know that, according to our belief, the souls of men have two journeys to perform after they have departed from the body – one to a place dismal and foul, and covered with darkness, prepared for those who have been unjust and cruel to their fellow-men; the other pleasant and full of delight, for such as have promoted peace on earth. If, then, thou art mortal and dost expect to die, and dost believe that each one shall be rewarded according to his deeds, beware that thou wrongfully hurt no man, nor do harm to those who have done no harm to thee.'* The admiral, to whom this speech was explained by his Lucayan interpreter, Diego Colon, was greatly moved by the simple eloquence of this untutored savage. He told him, in reply, that he rejoiced to hear his doctrine respecting the future state of the soul, having supposed that no belief of the kind existed among the inhabitants of these countries; that he had been sent among them by his sovereigns to teach them the true religion, to protect them from harm and injury, and especially to subdue and punish their enemies and persecutors, the cannibals; that, therefore, all innocent and peaceable men might look up to him with confidence as an assured friend and protector.

The old man was overjoyed at these words, but was equally astonished to learn that the admiral, whom he considered so great and powerful, was yet but a subject. His wonder increased when the interpreter told him of the riches and splendour and power of

* Herrera, decad i. lib. xi. cap. 14; *Hist. del Almirante*, cap. 57; Peter Martyr, decad. i. lib. iii.; Cura de los Palacios, cap. 130.

the Spanish monarchs, and of the wonderful things he had beheld on his visit to Spain. Finding himself listened to with eager curiosity by the multitude, the interpreter went on to describe the objects which had most struck his mind in the country of the white men. The splendid cities, the vast churches, the troops of horsemen, the great animals of various kinds, the pompous festivals and tournaments of the court, the glittering armies, and, above all, the bull-fights. The Indians all listened in mute amazement, but the old man was particularly excited. He was of a curious and wandering disposition, and had been a great voyager, having, according to his account, visited Jamaica and Hispaniola, and the remote parts of Cuba.* A sudden desire now seized him to behold the glorious country thus described, and, old as he was, he offered to embark with the admiral. His wife and children, however, beset him with such lamentations and remonstrances that he was obliged to abandon the intention, though he did it with great reluctance, asking repeatedly if the land they spoke of were not heaven, for it seemed to him impossible that earth could produce such wonderful beings.†

* *Hist. del Almirante*, cap. 57.
† Peter Martyr, decad. i. lib iii.

Columbus remained for several days at anchor in the river, to which, from the mass performed on its banks, he gave the name of Rio de la Misa. At length, on the 16th of July, he took leave of the friendly cacique and his ancient counsellor, who beheld his departure with sorrowful countenances. He took a young Indian with him from this place, whom he afterwards sent to the Spanish sovereigns. Leaving to the left the Queen's Gardens, he steered south for the broad open sea and deep blue water, until, having a free navigation, he could stand eastward for Hispaniola. He had scarcely got clear of the islands, however, when he was assailed by furious gusts of wind and rain, which for two days pelted his crazy vessels and harassed his enfeebled crews. At length, as he approached Cape Cruz, a violent squall struck the ships and nearly threw them on their beam-ends. Fortunately they were able to take in sail immediately, and letting go their largest anchors, rode out the transient gale. The admiral's ship was so strained by the injuries received among the islands that she leaked at every seam, and the utmost exertions of the weary crew could not prevent the water from gaining on her. At length they were enabled to reach Cape Cruz, where they anchored on the 18th July, and remained three days, receiving the same hospitable succour from the natives that they had experienced on their former visit. The wind continuing contrary for their return to Hispaniola, Columbus, on the 22nd July, stood across for Jamaica, to complete the circumnavigation of that island. For nearly a month he continued beating to the eastward along its southern coast, experiencing just such variable winds and evening showers as had prevailed along the shores of Cuba. Every evening he was obliged to anchor under the land, often at nearly the same place whence he had sailed in the morning. The natives no longer manifested hostility, but followed the ships in their canoes, bringing supplies of provisions. Columbus was so much delighted with the verdure, freshness, and fertility of this noble land that, had the state of his vessels and crews permitted, he would gladly have remained to explore the interior. He spoke with admiration of its frequent and excellent harbours, but was particularly pleased with a great bay, containing seven islands and surrounded by numerous villages.* Anchoring here one evening, he was visited by a cacique who resided in a large village situated on an eminence of the loftiest and most fertile of the islands. He came attended by a numerous train, bearing refreshments, and manifested great curiosity in his inquiries concerning the Spaniards, their ships, and the regions whence they came. The admiral made his customary reply, setting forth the great power and the benign intentions of the Spanish sovereigns. The Lucayan interpreter again enlarged upon the wonders he had beheld in Spain, the prowess of the Spaniards, the countries they had visited and subjugated, and, above all, their having made descents on the islands of the Caribs, routed their formidable inhabitants, and carried several of them into captivity. To these accounts the cacique and his followers remained listening in profound attention until the night was advanced.

The next morning the ships were under way and standing along the coast with a light wind and easy sail, when they beheld three canoes issuing from among the islands of the bay. They approached in regular order: one, which was very large and handsomely carved and painted, was in the centre, a little in advance of the two others, which appeared to attend and guard it. In this were seated the cacique and his family, consisting of his wife, two daughters, two sons, and five brothers. One of the daughters was eighteen years of age, beautiful in form and countenance; her sister was somewhat younger; both were naked, according to the custom of these islands, but were of modest demeanour. In the prow of the canoe stood the standard-bearer of the cacique, clad in a mantle of variegated feathers, with a tuft of gay plumes on his head, and bearing in his hand a fluttering white banner. Two Indians with caps or helmets of feathers of uniform shape and colour, and their faces painted in a similar manner, beat upon tabors; two others, with hats curiously

* From the description, this must be the great bay east of Portland Point, at the bottom of which is Old Harbour.

wrought of green feathers, held trumpets of a fine black wood, ingeniously carved; there were six others, in large hats of white feathers, who appeared to be guards to the cacique.

Having arrived alongside of the admiral's ship, the cacique entered on board with all his train. He appeared in full regalia. Around his head was a band of small stones of various colours, but principally green, symmetrically arranged, with large white stones at intervals, and connected in front by a large jewel of gold. Two plates of gold were suspended to his ears by rings of very small green stones. To a necklace of white beads, of a kind deemed precious by them, was suspended a large plate, in the form of a fleur-de-lys, of guanin, an inferior species of gold; and a girdle of variegated stones similar to those round his head completed his regal decorations. His wife was adorned in a similar manner, having also a very small apron of cotton, and bands of the same round her arms and legs. The daughters were without ornaments, excepting the eldest and handsomest, who had a girdle of small stones, from which was suspended a tablet the size of an ivy leaf, composed of various coloured stones, embroidered on network of cotton.

When the cacique entered on board the ship he distributed presents of the productions of his island among the officers and men. The admiral was at this time in his cabin engaged in his morning devotions. When he appeared on deck the chieftain hastened to meet him with an animated countenance. 'My friend,' said he, 'I have determined to leave my country and to accompany thee. I have heard from these Indians who are with thee of the irresistible power of thy sovereigns, and of the many nations thou hast subdued in their name. Whoever refuses obedience to thee is sure to suffer. Thou hast destroyed the canoes and dwellings of the Caribs, slaying their warriors, and carrying into captivity their wives and children. All the islands are in dread of thee, for who can withstand thee now that thou knowest the secrets of the land and the weakness of the people? Rather therefore than that thou shouldst take away my dominions, I will embark with all my household in thy ships, and will go to do homage to thy king and queen, and to behold their country, of which thy Indians relate such wonders.' When this speech was explained to Columbus, and he beheld the wife, the sons, and daughters of the cacique, and thought upon the snares to which their ignorance and simplicity would be exposed, he was touched with compassion, and determined not to take them from their native land. He replied to the cacique therefore that he received him under his protection as a vassal of his sovereigns; but having many lands yet to visit before he returned to his country, he would at some future time fulfil his desire. Then taking leave with many expressions of amity, the cacique, with his wife and daughters and all his retinue, re-embarked in the canoes, returning reluctantly to their island, and the ships continued on their course.[*]

[*] Hitherto, in narrating the voyage of Columbus along the coast of Cuba, I have been guided principally by the manuscript history of the curate de los Palacios. His account is the most clear and satisfactory as to names, dates, and routes, and contains many characteristic particulars not inserted in any other history. His sources of information were of the highest kind. Columbus was his guest after his return to Spain in 1496, and left with him manuscripts, journals, and memorandums. From these he made extracts, collating them with the letters of Doctor Chanca and other persons of note who had accompanied the admiral.

I have examined two copies of the MS. of the curate de los Palacios, both in the possession of O. Rich, Esq. One, written in an ancient handwriting, in the early part of the sixteenth century, varies from the other, but only in a few trivial particulars.

On the 19th of August Columbus lost sight of the eastern extremity of Jamaica, to which he gave the name of Cape Farol, at present called Point Morant. Steering eastward, he beheld on the following day that long peninsula of Hispaniola known by the name of Cape Tiburon, but to which he gave the name of Cape San Miguel. He was not aware that it was part of the island of Hayti until, coasting along its southern side, a cacique came off on the 23rd of August, and called him by his title, addressing him with several words of Castilian. The sound of these words spread joy through the ship, and the weary seamen heard with delight that they were on the southern coast of Hispaniola. They had still, however, many toilsome days before them. The weather was boisterous, the wind contrary and capricious, and the ships were separated from each other. About the end of August Columbus anchored at a small island, or rather rock, which rises singly out of the sea opposite to a long cape stretching southward from the centre of the island, to which he gave the name of Cape Beata. The rock at which he anchored had the appearance at a distance of a tall ship under sail, from which circumstance the admiral called it Alto Velo. Several seamen were ordered to climb to the top of the island, which commanded a great extent of ocean, and to look out for the other ships. Nothing of them was to be seen. On their return the sailors killed eight sea-wolves, which were sleeping on the sands. They also knocked down many pigeons and other birds with sticks, and took others with the hand; for in this unfrequented island the animals seemed to have had none of that wildness and timidity produced by the hostility of man.

Being rejoined by the two caravels, he continued along the coast, passing the beautiful country watered by the branches of the Neyva, where a fertile plain, covered with villages and groves, extended

into the interior. After proceeding some distance further to the
east, the admiral learned from the natives who came off to the ships
that several Spaniards from the settlement had penetrated to their
province. From all that he could learn from these people everything
appeared to be going on well in the island. Encouraged by the
tranquillity of the interior, he landed nine men here, with orders to
traverse the island, and give tidings of his safe arrival on the coast.

Continuing to the eastward, he sent a boat on shore for water
near a large village in a plain. The inhabitants issued forth with
bows and arrows to give battle, while others were provided with
cords to bind prisoners. These were the natives of Higuey, the
eastern province of Hispaniola. They were the most warlike
people of the island, having been inured to arms from the frequent
descent of the Caribs. They were said also to make use of poisoned
arrows. In the present instance their hostility was but in appearance. When the crew landed they threw by their weapons, and
brought various articles of food, and asked for the admiral, whose
fame had spread throughout the island, and in whose justice and
magnanimity all appeared to repose confidence. After leaving this
place the weather, which had been so long variable and adverse,
assumed a threatening appearance. A huge fish, as large as a
moderate-sized whale, raised itself out of the water one day,
having a shell on its neck like that of a tortoise, two great fins like
wings, and a tail like that of a tunny-fish. At sight of this fish, and
at the indications of the clouds and sky, Columbus anticipated an
approaching storm, and sought for some secure harbour.* He
found a channel opening between Hispaniola and a small island,
called by the Indians Adamaney, but to which he gave the name of
Saona. Here he took refuge, anchoring beside a key or islet in the
middle of the channel. On the night of his arrival there was an
eclipse of the moon, and taking an observation he found the
difference of longitude between Saona and Cadiz to be five hours
and twenty-three minutes.† This is upwards of eighteen degrees
more than the true longitude – an error which must have resulted
from the incorrectness of his table of eclipses.‡

* Herrera, *Hist. Ind.*, decad. i. lib. ii. cap. 15; *Hist. del Almirante*, cap. 59.
† Herrera, ubi sup.; *Hist. Almirante*, ubi sup.
‡ Five hours, twenty-five minutes, are equal to 80° 40', whereas the true longitude
of Saona is 62° 20' west of Cadiz.

For eight days the admiral's ship remained weather-bound in this channel, during which time he suffered great anxiety for the fate of the other vessels, which remained at sea exposed to the violence of the storm. They escaped, however, uninjured, and once more rejoined him when the weather had moderated.

Leaving the channel of Saona, they reached, on the 24th of September, the eastern extremity of Hispaniola, to which Columbus gave the name of Cape San Rafael, at present known as Cape Engaño. Hence they stood to the south-east, touching at the island of Mona, or, as the Indians called it, Amona, situated between Porto Rico and Hispaniola. It was the intention of Columbus, notwithstanding the condition of the ships, to continue further eastward, and to complete the discovery of the Caribbee Islands; but his physical strength did not correspond to the efforts of his lofty spirit.[*] The extraordinary fatigues both of mind and body during an anxious and harassing voyage of five months had preyed upon his frame. He had shared in all the hardships and privations of the commonest seaman. He had put himself upon the same scanty allowance, and exposed himself to the same buffetings of wind and weather. But he had other cares and trials from which his people were exempt. When the sailor, worn out with the labours of his watch, slept soundly amidst the howling of the storm, the anxious commander maintained his painful vigil through long sleepless nights, amidst the pelting of the tempest and the drenching surges of the sea. The safety of his ships depended upon his watchfulness; but, above all, he felt that a jealous nation and an expecting world were anxiously awaiting the result of his enterprise. During a great part of the present voyage he had been excited by the constant hope of soon arriving at the known parts of India, and by the anticipation of a triumphant return to Spain through the regions of the East, after circumnavigating the globe. When disappointed in these expectations, he was yet stimulated by a conflict with incessant hardships and perils as he made his way back against contrary winds and storms. The moment he was relieved from all solicitude, and beheld himself in a known and tranquil sea, the excitement suddenly ceased, and mind and body sank exhausted by almost superhuman exertions. The very day on which he sailed from Mona he was struck with a sudden malady, which deprived him of

[*] Muñoz, *Hist. N. Mundo*, lib. v. sec. 22.

memory, of sight, and all his faculties. He fell into a deep lethargy, resembling death itself. His crew, alarmed at his profound torpor, feared that death was really at hand. They abandoned therefore all further prosecution of the voyage, and spreading their sails to the east wind so prevalent in those seas, bore Columbus back in a state of complete insensibility to the harbour of Isabella.

BOOK 8

CHAPTER I

1494

The sight of the little squadron of Columbus standing once more into the harbour was hailed with joy by such of the inhabitants of Isabella as remained faithful to him. The long time that had elapsed since his departure on this adventurous voyage, without any tidings arriving from him, had given rise to the most serious apprehensions for his safety, and it began to be feared that he had fallen a victim to his enterprising spirit in some remote part of these unknown seas.

A joyful and heartfelt surprise awaited the admiral on his arrival, in finding at his bedside his brother Bartholomew, the companion of his youth, his confidential coadjutor, and in a manner his second self, from whom he had been separated for several years. It will be recollected that, about the time of the admiral's departure from Portugal, he had commissioned Bartholomew to repair to England, and propose his project of discovery to King Henry VII. Of this application to the English court no precise particulars are known. Fernando Columbus states that his uncle, in the course of his voyage, was captured and plundered by a corsair, and reduced to such poverty that he had for a long time to struggle for a mere subsistence by making sea-charts, so that some years elapsed before he made his application to the English monarch. Las Casas thinks that he did not immediately proceed to England, having found a memorandum, in his handwriting, by which it would appear that he accompanied Bartholomew Diaz, in 1486, in his voyage along the coast of Africa, in the service of the King of Portugal, in the course of which voyage was discovered the Cape of Good Hope.*

---

* The memorandum cited by Las Casas (*Hist. Ind.*, lib. i. cap. 7) is curious, though not conclusive. He says that he found it in an old book belonging to Christopher

It is but justice to the memory of Henry VII to say, that when the proposition was eventually made to him, it met with a more ready attention than from any other sovereign. An agreement was actually made with Bartholomew for the prosecution of the enterprise, and the latter departed for Spain in search of his brother. On

---

Columbus, containing the works of Pedro de Aliaco. It was written in the margin of a treatise on the form of a globe, in the handwriting of Bartholomew Columbus, which was well known to Las Casas, as he had many of his letters in his possession. The memorandum was in a barbarous mixture of Latin and Spanish, and to the following effect:

In the year 1488, in December, arrived at Lisbon Bartholomew Diaz, captain of three caravels, which the King of Portugal sent to discover Guinea, and brought accounts that he had discovered six hundred leagues of territory, four hundred and fifty to the south and one hundred and fifty north, to a cape named by him the Cape of Good Hope; and that by the astrolabe he found the cape 45 degrees beyond the equinoctial line. This cape was 3,100 leagues distant from Lisbon; the which the said captain says he set down, league by league, in a chart of navigation presented by him to the King of Portugal; in all which, adds the writer, I was present (*in quibus omnibus interfui*).

Las Casas expresses a doubt whether Bartholomew wrote this note for himself, or on the part of his brother, but infers that one or both were in this expedition. The inference may be correct with respect to Bartholomew, but Christopher, at the time specified, was at the Spanish court.

Las Casas accounts for a difference in date between the foregoing memorandum and the chronicles of the voyage – the former making the return of Diaz in the year '88, the latter '87. This, he observes, might be because some begin to count the year after Christmas, others at the first of January; and the expedition sailed about the end of August '86, and returned in December '87, after an absence of seventeen months.

Note. – Since publishing the first edition of this work, the author being in Seville, and making researches in the Bibliotheca Columbina, the library given by Fernando Columbus to the cathedral of that city, he came accidentally upon the above-mentioned copy of the work of Pedro Aliaco. He ascertained it to be the same by finding the above-cited memorandum written on the margin, at the eighth chapter of the tract called *Imago Mundi*. It is an old volume in folio, bound in parchment, published soon after the invention of printing, containing a collection in Latin of astronomical and cosmographical tracts of Pedro (or Peter) de Aliaco, Archbishop of Cambray and cardinal, and of his disciple, John Gerson. Pedro de Aliaco was born in 1340, and died, according to some in 1416, according to others in 1425. He was the author of many works, and one of the most learned and scientific men of his day. Las Casas is of opinion that his writings had more effect in stimulating Columbus to his enterprise than those of any other author. 'His work was so familiar to Columbus, that he had filled its whole margin with Latin notes in his handwriting; citing many things which he had read and gathered elsewhere. This book, which was very old,' continues Las Casas, 'I had many times in my hands; and I drew some things from it, written in Latin by the said admiral, Christopher Columbus, to verify certain points appertaining to his history, of which I before was in doubt.' (*Hist. Ind.*, lib. i. cap. 11.)

It was a great satisfaction to the author, therefore, to discover this identical volume, this *Vade Mecum* of Columbus, in a state of good preservation. [It is in

reaching Paris, he first received the joyful intelligence that the discovery was already made; that his brother had returned to Spain in triumph, and was actually at the Spanish court, honoured by the sovereigns, caressed by the nobility, and idolized by the people. The glory of Columbus already shed its rays upon his family, and Bartholomew found himself immediately a person of importance. He was noticed by the French monarch, Charles VIII, who, understanding that he was low in purse, furnished him with one hundred crowns to defray the expenses of his journey to Spain. He reached Seville just as his brother had departed on his second voyage. Bartholomew immediately repaired to the court, then at Valladolid, taking with him his two nephews, Diego and Fernando, who were to serve in the quality of pages to Prince Juan.* He was received with distinguished favour by the sovereigns, who, finding him to be an able and accomplished navigator, gave him the command of three ships freighted with supplies for the colony, and sent him to aid his brother in his enterprises. He had again arrived too late, reaching Isabella just after the departure of the admiral for the coast of Cuba.

The sight of this brother was an inexpressible relief to Columbus, overwhelmed as he was by cares, and surrounded by strangers. His chief dependence for sympathy and assistance had hitherto been on his brother Don Diego; but his mild and peaceable disposition rendered him little capable of managing the concerns of a factious colony. Bartholomew was of a different and more efficient character. He was prompt, active, decided, and of a fearless spirit; whatever he determined, he carried into

---

the cathedral library, E——G, Tab. 178, No. 21.] The notes and citations mentioned by Las Casas are in Latin, with many abbreviations, written in a very small but neat and distinct hand, and run throughout the volume; calling attention to the most striking passages, or to those which bear most upon the theories of Columbus; occasionally containing brief comments, or citing the opinions of other authors, ancient and modern, either in support or contradiction of the text. The memorandum particularly cited by Las Casas, mentioning the voyage of Bartholomew Diaz to the Cape of Good Hope, is to disprove an opinion in the text that the torrid zone was uninhabitable. This volume is a most curious and interesting document, the only one that remains of Columbus prior to his discovery. It illustrates his researches, and in a manner the current of his thoughts, while as yet his great enterprise existed but in idea, and while he was seeking means to convince the world of its practicability. It will be found also to contain the grounds of many of his opinions and speculations on a variety of subjects.

* *Hist. del Almirante*, cap. 60.

instant execution, without regard to difficulty or danger. His person corresponded to his mind – it was tall, muscular, vigorous, and commanding. He had an air of great authority, but somewhat stern, wanting that sweetness and benignity which tempered the authoritative demeanour of the admiral. Indeed, there was a certain asperity in his temper, and a dryness and abruptness in his manners, which made him many enemies; yet, notwithstanding these external defects, he was of a generous disposition, free from all arrogance or malevolence, and as placable as he was brave.

He was a thorough seaman, understanding both the theory and practice of his profession, having been formed, in a great measure, under the eye of the admiral, and being but little inferior to him in science. He was superior to him in the exercise of the pen, according to Las Casas, who had letters and manuscripts of both in his possession. He was acquainted with Latin, but does not appear to have been highly educated; his knowledge, like that of his brother, being chiefly derived from a long course of varied experience and attentive observation. Equally vigorous and penetrating in intellect with the admiral, but less enthusiastic in spirit and soaring in imagination, and with less simplicity of heart, he surpassed him in the subtle and adroit management of business, was more attentive to his interests, and had more of that worldly wisdom which is so important in the ordinary concerns of life. His genius might never have enkindled him to the sublime speculation which ended in the discovery of a world, but his practical sagacity was calculated to turn that discovery to advantage. Such is the description of Bartholomew Columbus, as furnished by the venerable Las Casas from personal observation,[*] and it will be found to accord with his actions throughout the remaining history of the admiral, in the events of which he takes a conspicuous part.

Anxious to relieve himself from the pressure of public business, which weighed heavily upon him during his present malady, Columbus immediately invested his brother Bartholomew with the title and authority of Adelantado, an office equivalent to that of lieutenant-governor. He considered himself entitled to do so from the articles of his arrangement with the sovereigns; but it was looked upon by King Ferdinand as an undue assumption of power, and gave great offence to that jealous monarch, who was exceed-

* Las Casas, *Hist. Ind.*, lib. i. cap. 29.

ingly tenacious of the prerogatives of the crown, and considered dignities of this rank and importance as only to be conferred by royal mandate.* Columbus, however, was not actuated in this appointment by a mere desire to aggrandize his family. He felt the importance of his brother's assistance in the present critical state of the colony, but that this co-operation would be inefficient unless it bore the stamp of high official authority. In fact, during the few months that he had been absent, the whole island had become a scene of discord and violence in consequence of the neglect, or rather the flagrant violation, of those rules which he had prescribed for the maintenance of its tranquillity. A brief retrospect of the recent affairs of the colony is here necessary to explain their present confusion. It will exhibit one of the many instances in which Columbus was doomed to reap the fruits of the evil seed sown by his adversaries.

* Las Casas, *Hist. Ind.*, lib. i. cap. 101.

CHAPTER 2

1494

It will be recollected that, before departing on his voyage, Columbus had given the command of the army to Don Pedro Margarite, with orders to make a military tour of the island, awing the natives by a display of military force, but conciliating their goodwill by equitable and amicable treatment.

The island was, at this time, divided into five domains, each governed by a cacique of absolute and hereditary power, to whom a great number of inferior caciques yielded tributary allegiance. The first or most important domain comprised the middle part of the Royal Vega. It was a rich, lovely country, partly cultivated after the imperfect manner of the natives, partly covered with noble forests, studded with Indian towns, and watered by numerous rivers, many of which, rolling down from the mountains of Cibao on its southern frontier, had gold-dust mingled with their sands. The name of the cacique was Guarionex, whose ancestors had long ruled over the province.

The second, called Marien, was under the sway of Guacanagari, on whose coast Columbus had been wrecked in his first voyage. It was a large and fertile territory, extending along the northern coast from Cape St Nicholas at the western extremity of the island, to the great river Yagui, afterwards called Monte Christi, and including the northern part of the Royal Vega, since called the plain of Cape François, now Cape Haytien.

The third bore the name of Maguana. It extended along the southern coast from the river Ozema to the lakes, and comprised the chief part of the centre of the island lying along the southern face of the mountains of Cibao, the mineral district of Hayti. It was under the dominion of the Carib cacique Caonabo, the most fierce and puissant of the savage chieftains, and the inveterate enemy of the white men.

The fourth took its name from Xaragua, a large lake, and was the most populous and extensive of all. It comprised the whole western coast, including the long promontory of Cape Tiburon, and extended for a considerable distance along the southern side of the island. The inhabitants were finely formed, had a noble air, a more agreeable elocution, and more soft and graceful manners than the natives of the other parts of the island. The sovereign was named Behechio; his sister Anacaona, celebrated throughout the island for her beauty, was the favourite wife of the neighbouring cacique Caonabo.

The fifth domain was Higuey, and occupied the whole eastern part of the island, being bounded on the north by the Bay of Samana and part of the river Yuna, and on the west by the Ozema. The inhabitants were the most active and warlike people of the island, having learned the use of the bow and arrow from the Caribs, who made frequent descents upon their coasts; they were said also to make use of poisoned weapons. Their bravery, however, was but comparative, and was found eventually of little avail against the terror of European arms. They were governed by a cacique named Cotubanama.*

Such were the five territorial divisions of the island at the time of its discovery. The amount of its population has never been clearly ascertained; some have stated it at a million of souls, though this is considered an exaggeration. It must, however, have been very numerous, and sufficient, in case of any general hostility, to endanger the safety of a handful of Europeans. Columbus trusted for safety partly to the awe inspired by the weapons and horses of the Spaniards, and the idea of their superhuman nature, but chiefly to the measures he had taken to conciliate the goodwill of the Indians by gentle and beneficent treatment.

Margarite set forth on his expedition with the greater part of the forces, leaving Alonzo de Ojeda in command of the fortress of St Thomas. Instead, however, of commencing by exploring the rough mountains of Cibao, as he had been commanded, he descended into the fertile region of the Vega. Here he lingered among the populous and hospitable Indian villages, forgetful of the object of his command and of the instructions left him by the admiral. A commander who lapses from duty himself is little

---

* Charlevoix, *Hist. St Domingo*, lib. i. p. 69.

calculated to enforce discipline. The sensual indulgences of Margarite were imitated by his followers, and his army soon became
little better than a crew of riotous marauders. The Indians for a
time supplied them with provisions with their wonted hospitality;
but the scanty stores of those abstemious yet improvident people
were soon exhausted by the Spaniards, one of whom they declared
would consume more in a day than would support an Indian for a
month. If provisions were withheld, or scantily furnished, they
were taken with violence; nor was any compensation given to
the natives, nor means taken to soothe their irritation. The
avidity for gold also led to a thousand acts of injustice and
oppression. But above all, the Spaniards outraged the dearest
feelings of the natives by their licentious conduct with respect to
the women. In fact, instead of guests they soon assumed the tone
of imperious masters; instead of enlightened benefactors, they
became sordid and sensual oppressors.

Tidings of these excesses and of the disgust and impatience they
were awakening among the natives soon reached Don Diego
Columbus. With the concurrence of the council, he wrote to
Margarite reprehending his conduct, and requesting him to proceed on the military tour, according to the commands of the
admiral. The pride of Margarite took fire at this reproof; he
considered, or rather pretended to consider himself independent
in his command, and above all responsibility to the council for his
conduct. Being of an ancient family also, and a favourite of the
king, he affected to look down with contempt upon the newly-
coined nobility of Diego Columbus. His letters, in reply to the
orders of the president and council, were couched in a tone either
of haughty contumely or of military defiance. He continued with
his followers quartered in the Vega, persisting in a course of
outrages and oppressions fatal to the tranquillity of the island.

He was supported in his arrogant defiance of authority by the
cavaliers and adventurers of noble birth who were in the colony,
and who had been deeply wounded in the proud punctilio so
jealously guarded by a Spaniard. They could not forget nor forgive
the stern equity exercised by the admiral in a time of emergency,
in making them submit to the privations and share the labours of
the vulgar. Still less could they brook the authority of his brother
Diego, destitute of his high personal claims to distinction. They

formed, therefore, a kind of aristocratical faction in the colony, affecting to consider Columbus and his family as mere mercenary and upstart foreigners, building up their own fortunes at the expense of the toils and sufferings of the community, and the degradation of Spanish hidalgos and cavaliers.

In addition to these partisans, Margarite had a powerful ally in his fellow-countryman, Friar Boyle, the head of the religious fraternity, one of the members of the council, and apostolical vicar of the New World. It is not easy to ascertain the original cause of the hostility of this holy friar to the admiral, who was never wanting in respect to the clergy. Various altercations, however, had taken place between them. Some say that the friar interfered in respect to the strict measures deemed necessary by the admiral for the security of the colony; others that he resented the fancied indignity offered to himself and his household in putting them on the same short allowance with the common people. He appears, however, to have been generally disappointed and disgusted with the sphere of action afforded by the colony, and to have looked back with regret to the Old World. He had none of that enthusiastic zeal and persevering self-devotion which induced so many of the Spanish missionaries to brave all the hardships and privations of the New World, in the hope of converting its pagan inhabitants.

Encouraged and fortified by such powerful partisans, Margarite really began to consider himself above the temporary authorities of the island. Whenever he came to Isabella, he took no notice of Don Diego Columbus, nor paid any respect to the council, but acted as if he had paramount command. He formed a cabal of most of those who were disaffected to Columbus and discontented with their abode in the colony. Among these the leading agitator was Friar Boyle. It was concerted among them to take possession of the ships which had brought out Don Bartholomew Columbus, and to return in them to Spain. Both Margarite and Boyle possessed the favour of the king, and they deemed it would be an easy matter to justify their abandonment of their military and religious commands by a pretended zeal for the public good, hurrying home to represent the disastrous state of the country through the tyranny and oppression of its rulers. Some have ascribed the abrupt departure of Margarite to his fear of a severe military investigation of his conduct on the return of the admiral; others to his having, in the course of his licentious amours, contracted a malady at that time new and unknown, and which he attributed to the climate and hoped to cure by medical assistance in Spain. Whatever may have been the cause, his measures were taken with great precipitancy, without any consultation of the proper authorities, or any regard to the consequences of his departure. Accompanied by a band of malcontents, he and Friar Boyle took possession of some ships in the harbour, and set sail for Spain – the first general and apostle of the New World thus setting the flagrant example of unauthorized abandonment of their posts.

The departure of Pedro Margarite left the army without a head, and put an end to what little restraint or discipline remained. There is no rabble so licentious as soldiery left to their own direction in a defenceless country. They now roved about in bands, or singly, according to their caprice, scattering themselves among the Indian villages, and indulging in all kinds of excesses, either as prompted by avarice or sensuality. The natives, indignant at having their hospitality thus requited, refused any longer to furnish them with food. In a little while the Spaniards began to experience the pressure of hunger, and seized upon provisions wherever they could be found, accompanying these seizures with acts of wanton violence. At length, by a series of flagrant outrages, the gentle and pacific nature of this people was roused to resentment, and from confiding and hospitable hosts they were converted into vindictive enemies. All the precautions enjoined by Columbus having been neglected, the evils he had apprehended came to pass. Though the Indians, naturally timid, dared not contend with the Spaniards while they kept up any combined and disciplined force, yet they took sanguinary vengeance on them whenever they met with small parties or scattered individuals roving about in quest of food. Encouraged by these petty triumphs, and the impunity which seemed to attend them, their hostilities grew more and more alarming. Guatiguana, cacique of a large town on the banks of the Grand River, in the dominions of Guarionex, sovereign of the Vega, put to death ten Spaniards, who had quartered themselves in his town and outraged the inhabitants by their licentiousness. He followed up this massacre by setting fire to a house in which forty-six Spaniards were lodged.[*] Flushed by this success, he threatened to attack a small fortress called Magdalena, which had recently been

---

[*] Herrera, *Hist. Ind.*, decad. i. lib. ii. cap. 16.

built in his neighbourhood in the Vega, so that the commander, Luis de Arriaga, having but a feeble garrison, was obliged to remain shut up within its walls until relief should arrive from Isabella.

The most formidable enemy of the Spaniards, however, was Caonabo, the Carib cacique of Maguana. With natural talents for war, and intelligence superior to the ordinary range of savage intellect, he had a proud and daring spirit to urge him on, three valiant brothers to assist him, and a numerous tribe at his command.* He had always felt jealous of the intrusion of the white men into the island, but particularly exasperated by the establishment of the fortress of St Thomas, erected in the very centre of his dominions. As long as the army lay within call in the Vega he was deterred from any attack; but when, on the departure of Margarite, it became dismembered and dispersed, the time for striking a signal blow seemed arrived. The fortress remained isolated, with a garrison of only fifty men. By a sudden and secret movement, he might overwhelm it with his forces, and repeat the horrors which he had wreaked upon La Navidad.

The wily cacique, however, had a different kind of enemy to deal with in the commander of St Thomas. Alonzo de Ojeda had been schooled in Moorish warfare. He was versed in all kinds of feints, stratagems, lurking ambuscades, and wild assaults. No man was more fitted, therefore, to cope with Indian warriors. He had a headlong courage, arising partly from the natural heat and violence of his disposition, and, in a great measure, from religious superstition. He had been engaged in wars with Moors and Indians, in public battles and private combats, in fights, feuds, and encounters of all kinds, to which he had been prompted by a rash and fiery spirit and a love of adventure; yet he had never been wounded, nor lost a drop of blood. He began to doubt whether any weapon had power to harm him, and to consider himself under the special protection of the holy Virgin. As a kind of religious talisman, he had a small Flemish painting of the Virgin, given him by his patron, Fonseca, Bishop of Badajoz. This he constantly carried with him, in city, camp, or field, making it the object of his frequent orisons and invocations. In garrison or encampment, it was suspended in his chamber or his tent; in his rough expeditions in the wilderness, he carried it in his knapsack, and whenever

* Herrera, *Hist Ind.*, decad. i. lib. ii. cap. 16.

leisure permitted, would take it out, fix it against a tree, and address his prayers to this military patroness.[*] In a word, he swore by the Virgin, he invoked the Virgin whether in brawl or battle, and under the favour of the Virgin he was ready for any enterprise or adventure. Such was this Alonzo de Ojeda – bigoted in his devotion, reckless in his life, fearless in his spirit, like many of the roving Spanish cavaliers of those days. Though small in size, he was a prodigy of strength and prowess, and the chroniclers of the early discoveries relate marvels of his valour and exploits.

Having reconnoitred the fortress, Caonabo assembled ten thousand warriors, armed with war-clubs, bows and arrows, and lances hardened in the fire; and making his way secretly through the forests, came suddenly in the neighbourhood, expecting to surprise the garrison in a state of careless security. He found Ojeda's forces, however, drawn up warily within his tower, which, being built upon an almost insulated height, with a river nearly surrounding it, and the remaining space traversed by a deep ditch, set at defiance an attack by naked warriors.

Foiled in his attempt, Caonabo now hoped to reduce it by famine. For this purpose, he distributed his warriors through the adjacent forests, and waylaid every pass, so as to intercept any supplies brought by the natives, and to cut off any foraging party from the fortress. This siege or investment lasted for thirty days,[†] and reduced the garrison to great distress. There is a traditional anecdote, which Oviedo relates of Pedro Margarite, the former commander of this fortress, but which may with more probability be ascribed to Alonzo de Ojeda, as having occurred during this siege. At a time when the garrison was sore pressed by famine, an Indian gained access to the fort, bringing a couple of wood-pigeons for the table of the commander. The latter was in an apartment of the tower surrounded by several of his officers. Seeing them regard the birds with the wistful eyes of famishing men, 'It is a pity,' said he, 'that here is not enough to give us all a meal. I cannot consent to feast while the rest of you are starving;' so saying, he turned loose the pigeons from a window of the tower.

During the siege Ojeda displayed the greatest activity of spirit and fertility of resource. He baffled all the arts of the Carib

[*] Herrera, *Hist. Ind.*, decad. i. lib. viii, cap. 4; Pizarro, *Varones Illustres*, cap. 8.
[†] P. Martyr, decad. i. lib. iv.

chieftain, concerting stratagems of various kinds to relieve the garrison and annoy the foe. He sallied forth whenever the enemy appeared in any force, leading the van with that headlong valour for which he was noted, making great slaughter with his single arm, and, as usual, escaping unhurt from amidst showers of darts and arrows.

Caonabo saw many of his bravest warriors slain. His forces were diminishing, for the Indians, unused to any protracted operations of war, grew weary of this siege, and returned daily in numbers to their homes. He gave up all further attempt, therefore, on the fortress, and retired, filled with admiration of the prowess and achievements of Ojeda.*

The restless chieftain was not discouraged by the failure of this enterprise, but meditated schemes of a bolder and more extensive nature. Prowling in secret in the vicinity of Isabella, he noted the enfeebled state of the settlement.† Many of the inhabitants were suffering under various maladies, and most of the men capable of bearing arms were distributed about the country. He now conceived the project of a general league among the caciques, to surprise and overwhelm the settlement, and massacre the Spaniards wherever they could be found. This handful of intruders once exterminated, he trusted the island would be delivered from all further molestation of the kind, little dreaming of the hopeless nature of the contest, and that where the civilized man once plants his foot, the power of the savage is gone for ever.

Reports of the profligate conduct of the Spaniards had spread throughout the island, and inspired hatred and hostility even among tribes who had never beheld them nor suffered from their misdeeds. Caonabo found three of the sovereign caciques inclined to co-operate with him, though impressed with deep awe of the supernatural power of the Spaniards, and of their terrific arms and animals. The league, however, met with unexpected opposition in the fifth cacique, Guacanagari, the sovereign of Marien. His conduct in this time of danger completely manifested the injustice of the suspicions which had been entertained of him by the Spaniards. He refused to join the other caciques with his forces, or to violate those laws of hospitality by which he had considered

* Oviedo, *Cronica de las Indias*, lib. iii. cap 1.
† *Hist. del Almirante*, cap. 60.

himself bound to protect and aid the white men ever since they had been shipwrecked on his coast. He remained quietly in his dominions, entertaining at his own expense a hundred of the suffering soldiery, and supplying all their wants with his accustomed generosity. This conduct drew upon him the odium and hostility of his fellow caciques, particularly of the fierce Carib Caonabo and his brother-in-law Behechio. They made irruptions into his territories, and inflicted on him various injuries and indignities. Behechio killed one of his wives, and Caonabo carried another away captive.[*] Nothing, however, could shake the devotion of Guacanagari to the Spaniards; and as his dominions lay immediately adjacent to the settlement, and those of some of the other caciques were very remote, the want of his co-operation impeded for some time the hostile designs of his confederates.[†]

Such was the critical state to which the affairs of the colony had been reduced, and such the bitter hostility engendered among the people of the island, during the absence of Columbus, and merely in consequence of violating all his regulations. Margarite and Friar Boyle had hastened to Spain to make false representations of the miseries of the island. Had they remained faithfully at their posts, and discharged zealously the trust confided to them, those miseries might have been easily remedied, if not entirely prevented.

[*] *Hist. del Almirante*, cap. 60.
[†] Herrera, *Hist. Ind.*, decad. i. lib. ii. cap. 16.

CHAPTER 4

1494

Immediately after the return of Columbus from Cuba, while he was yet confined to his bed by indisposition, he was gratified by a voluntary visit from Guacanagari, who manifested the greatest concern at his illness, for he appears to have always entertained an affectionate reverence for the admiral. He again spoke with tears of the massacre of Fort Nativity, dwelling on the exertions he had made in defence of the Spaniards. He now informed Columbus of the secret league forming among the caciques; of his opposition to it, and the consequent persecution he had suffered; of the murder of one of his wives and the capture of another. He urged the admiral to be on his guard against the designs of Caonabo, and offered to lead his subjects to the field, to fight by the side of the Spaniards, as well out of friendship for them as in revenge of his own injuries.*

Columbus had always retained a deep sense of the ancient kindness of Guacanagari, and was rejoiced to have all suspicion of his good faith thus effectually dispelled. Their former amicable intercourse was renewed, with this difference, that the man whom Guacanagari had once relieved and succoured as a shipwrecked stranger had suddenly become the arbiter of the fate of himself and all his countrymen.

The manner in which this peaceful island had been exasperated and embroiled by the licentious conduct of the Europeans was a matter of deep concern to Columbus. He saw all his plans of deriving an immediate revenue to the sovereigns completely impeded. To restore the island to tranquillity required skilful management. His forces were but small, and the awe in which the natives had stood of the white men, as supernatural beings, had been in some degree dispelled. He was too ill to take a personal

* Herrera, *Hist. Ind.*, decad. i. lib. ii. cap. 16.

share in any warlike enterprise; his brother Diego was not of a
military character, and Bartholomew was yet a stranger among
the Spaniards, and regarded by the leading men with jealousy.
Still Columbus considered the threatened combination of the
caciques as but imperfectly formed; he trusted to their want of
skill and experience in warfare; and conceived that by prompt
measures, by proceeding in detail, punishing some, conciliating
others, and uniting force, gentleness, and stratagem, he might
succeed in dispelling the threatened storm.

His first care was to send a body of armed men to the relief of
Fort Magdalena, menaced with destruction by Guatiguana, the
cacique of the Grand River, who had massacred the Spaniards
quartered in his town. Having relieved the fortress, the troops
overran the territory of Guatiguana, killing many of his warriors,
and carrying others off captives: the chieftain himself made his
escape.* He was tributary to Guarionex, sovereign cacique of the
Royal Vega. As this Indian prince reigned over a great and
populous extent of country, his friendship was highly important
to the prosperity of the colony, while there was imminent risk of
his hostility, from the unbridled excesses of the Spaniards who
had been quartered in his dominions. Columbus sent for him,
therefore, and explained to him that these excesses had been in
violation of his orders, and contrary to his good intentions
towards the natives, whom it was his wish in every way to please
and benefit. He explained likewise that the expedition against
Guatiguana was an act of mere individual punishment, not of
hostility against the territories of Guarionex. The cacique was
of a quiet and placable disposition, and whatever anger he might
have felt was easily soothed. To link him in some degree to the
Spanish interest, Columbus prevailed on him to give his daughter
in marriage to the Indian interpreter, Diego Colon.† As a stronger
precaution against any hostility on the part of the cacique, and
to insure tranquillity in the important region of the Vega, he
ordered a fortress to be erected in the midst of his territories,
which he named Fort Conception. The easy cacique agreed

* Herrera, decad. i. lib. ii. cap. 16.
† P. Martyr, decad. i. lib. iv. Gio. Battista Spotorno, in his *Memoir of Columbus*,
has been led into an error by the name of this Indian, and observes that Columbus
had a brother named Diego, of whom he seemed to be ashamed, and whom he
married to the daughter of an Indian chief.

without hesitation to a measure fraught with ruin to himself and future slavery to his subjects.

The most formidable enemy remained to be disposed of – Caonabo. His territories lay in the central and mountainous parts of the island, rendered difficult of access by rugged rocks, entangled forests, and frequent rivers. To make war upon this subtle and ferocious chieftain in the depths of his wild woodland territory, and among the fastnesses of his mountains, where, at every step, there would be danger of ambush, would be a work of time, peril, and uncertain issue. In the meanwhile, the settlements would never be secure from his secret and daring enterprises, and the working of the mines would be subject to frequent interruption. While perplexed on this subject, Columbus was relieved by an offer of Alonzo de Ojeda to take the Carib chieftain by stratagem and deliver him alive into his hands. The project was wild, hazardous, and romantic, characteristic of Ojeda, who was fond of distinguishing himself by extravagant exploits and feats of desperate bravery.

Choosing ten bold and hardy followers, well armed and well mounted, and invoking the protection of his patroness the Virgin, whose image as usual he bore with him as a safeguard, Ojeda plunged into the forest, and made his way above sixty leagues into the wild territories of Caonabo, whom he found in one of his most populous towns, the same now called Maguana, near the town of San Juan. Approaching the cacique with great deference as a sovereign prince, he professed to come on a friendly embassy from the admiral, who was Guamiquina, or chief of the Spaniards, and who had sent him an invaluable present.

Caonabo had tried Ojeda in battle; he had witnessed his fiery prowess, and had conceived a warrior's admiration of him. He received him with a degree of chivalrous courtesy, if such a phrase may apply to the savage state and rude hospitality of a wild warrior of the forest. The free, fearless deportment, the great personal strength, and the surprising agility and adroitness of Ojeda in all manly exercises, and in the use of all kinds of weapons, were calculated to delight a savage, and he soon became a great favourite with Caonabo.

Ojeda now used all his influence to prevail upon the cacique to repair to Isabella, for the purpose of making a treaty with

Columbus and becoming the ally and friend of the Spaniards. It is said that he offered him, as a lure, the bell of the chapel of Isabella. This bell was the wonder of the island. When the Indians heard it ringing for mass, and beheld the Spaniards hastening towards the chapel, they imagined that it talked, and that the white men obeyed it. Regarding with superstition all things connected with the Spaniards, they looked upon this bell as something supernatural, and in their usual phrase said it had come from 'turey', or the skies. Caonabo had heard the bell at a distance, in his prowlings about the settlement, and had longed to see it; but when it was proffered to him as a present of peace, he found it impossible to resist the temptation. He agreed, therefore, to set out for Isabella; but when the time came to depart, Ojeda beheld with surprise a powerful force of warriors assembled and ready to march. He asked the meaning of taking such an army on a mere friendly visit. The cacique proudly replied that it did not befit a great prince like himself to go forth scantily attended. Ojeda was little satisfied with this reply. He knew the warlike character of Caonabo and his deep subtlety; he feared some sinister design – a surprise of the fortress of Isabella, or an attempt upon the person of the admiral. He knew also that it was the wish of Columbus either to make peace with the cacique or to get possession of his person without the alternative of open warfare. He had recourse to a stratagem, therefore, which has an air of fable and romance, but which is recorded by all the contemporary historians with trivial variations, and which, Las Casas assures us, was in current circulation in the island when he arrived there, about six years after the event. It accords, too, with the adventurous and extravagant character of the man, and with the wild stratagems and vaunting exploits incident to Indian warfare.

In the course of their march, having halted near the Little Yagui, a considerable branch of the Neyba, Ojeda one day produced a set of manacles of polished steel, so highly burnished that they looked like silver. These he assured Caonabo were royal ornaments which had come from heaven, or the turey of Biscay;* that they were worn by the monarchs of Castile on solemn dances, and other high festivities, and were intended as presents to the cacique. He proposed that Caonabo should go to the river and bathe, after

* The principal iron manufactories of Spain are established in Biscay, where the ore is found in abundance.

which he should be decorated with these ornaments, mounted on
the horse of Ojeda, and should return in the state of a Spanish
monarch, to astonish his subjects. The cacique was dazzled with
the glitter of the manacles, and flattered with the idea of bestriding
one of those tremendous animals so dreaded by his countrymen.
He repaired to the river, and having bathed, was assisted to mount
behind Ojeda, and the shackles were adjusted. Ojeda made several
circuits to gain space, followed by his little band of horsemen, the
Indians shrinking back from the prancing steeds. At length he
made a wide sweep into the forest until the trees concealed him
from the sight of the army. His followers then closed round him,
and drawing their swords, threatened Caonabo with instant death
if he made the least noise or resistance. Binding him with cords to
Ojeda, to prevent his falling or effecting an escape, they put spurs
to their horses, dashed across the river, and made off through the
woods with their prize.*

They had now fifty or sixty leagues of wilderness to traverse on
their way homewards, with here and there large Indian towns.
They had borne off their captive far beyond the pursuit of his
subjects; but the utmost vigilance was requisite to prevent his
escape during this long and toilsome journey, and to avoid exciting the hostilities of any confederate cacique. They had to shun the
populous parts of the country, therefore, or to pass through the
Indian towns at full gallop. They suffered greatly from fatigue,
hunger, and watchfulness, encountering many perils, fording and
swimming the numerous rivers of the plains, toiling through the
deep tangled forests, and clambering over the high and rocky
mountains. They accomplished all in safety, and Ojeda entered
Isabella in triumph from this most daring and characteristic enterprise, with his wild Indian bound behind.

Columbus could not refrain from expressing his great satisfaction
when this dangerous foe was delivered into his hands. The haughty
Carib met him with a lofty and unsubdued air, disdaining to
conciliate him by submission, or to deprecate his vengeance for
the blood of white men which he had shed. He never bowed his

---

* This romantic exploit of Ojeda is recorded at large by Las Casas; by his copyist,
Herrera (decad. i. lib. ii. cap. 16); by Fernando Pizarro in his *Varones Illustres del
Nuevo Mundo*; and by Charlevoix in his *History of St Domingo*. Peter Martyr and
others have given it more concisely, alluding to but not inserting its romantic
details.

spirit to captivity; on the contrary, though completely at the mercy of the Spaniards, he displayed that boasting defiance which is a part of Indian heroism, and which the savage maintains towards his tormentors, even amidst the agonies of the fagot and the stake. He vaunted his achievement in surprising and burning the fortress of Nativity and slaughtering its garrison, and declared that he had secretly reconnoitred Isabella, with an intention of wreaking upon it the same desolation.

Columbus, though struck with the heroism of the chieftain, considered him a dangerous enemy, whom, for the peace of the island, it was advisable to send to Spain. In the meantime he ordered that he should be treated with kindness and respect, and lodged him in a part of his own dwelling, where, however, he kept him a prisoner in chains. This precaution must have been necessary from the insecurity of his prison; for Las Casas observes that the admiral's house not being spacious, nor having many chambers, the passers-by in the street could see the captive chieftain from the portal.[*]

Caonabo always maintained a haughty deportment towards Columbus, while he never evinced the least animosity against Ojeda. He rather admired the latter as a consummate warrior, for having pounced upon him and borne him off in this hawk-like manner from the very midst of his fighting-men.

When Columbus entered the apartment where Caonabo was confined, all present rose, according to custom, and paid him reverence; the cacique alone neither moved nor took any notice of him. On the contrary, when Ojeda entered, though small in person and without external state, Caonabo rose and saluted him with profound respect. On being asked the reason of this, Columbus being Guamiquina, or great chief over all, and Ojeda but one of his subjects, the proud Carib replied that the admiral had never dared to come personally to his house and seize him; it was only through the valour of Ojeda he was his prisoner: to Ojeda, therefore, he owed reverence, not to the admiral.[†]

The captivity of Caonabo was deeply felt by his subjects, for the natives of this island seem generally to have been extremely loyal and strongly attached to their caciques. One of the brothers of

[*] Las Casas, *Hist. Ind.*, lib. i. cap. 102.
[†] Las Casas, ubi sup.

Caonabo, a warrior of great courage and address, and very popular
among the Indians, assembled an army of more than seven thousand men, and led them secretly to the neighbourhood of St
Thomas, where Ojeda was again in command. His intention was
to surprise a number of Spaniards, in hopes of obtaining his
brother in exchange for them. Ojeda, as usual, had notice of the
design, but was not again to be shut up in his fortress. Having been
reinforced by a detachment sent by the Adelantado, he left a
sufficient force in garrison, and with the remainder, and his little
troop of horse, set off boldly to meet the savages. The brother of
Caonabo, when he saw the Spaniards approaching, showed some
military skill, disposing his army in five battalions. The impetuous
attack of Ojeda, however, with his handful of horsemen threw the
Indian warriors into sudden panic. At the furious onset of these
steel-clad beings, wielding their flashing weapons, and bestriding
what appeared to be ferocious beasts of prey, they threw down
their weapons and took to flight. Many were slain, more were
taken prisoners, and among the latter was the brother of Caonabo,
bravely fighting in a righteous yet desperate cause.*

* Oviedo, *Cronica de las Indias*, lib. iii. cap. 1; Charlevoix, *Hist. St Domingo*, lib. ii.
p. 13.

The colony was still suffering greatly from want of provisions. The European stock was nearly exhausted; and such was the idleness and improvidence of the colonists, or the confusion into which they had been thrown by the hostilities of the natives, or such was their exclusive eagerness after the precious metals, that they seem to have neglected the true wealth of the island, its quick and productive soil, and to have been in constant danger of famine though in the midst of fertility.

At length they were relieved by the arrival of four ships, commanded by Antonio Torres, which brought an ample supply of provisions. There were also a physician and an apothecary, whose aid was greatly needed in the sickly state of the colony; but, above all, there were mechanics, millers, fishermen, gardeners, and husbandmen – the true kind of population for a colony.

Torres brought letters from the sovereigns (dated August 16, 1494) of the most gratifying kind, expressing the highest satisfaction at the accounts sent home by the admiral, and acknowledging that everything in the course of his discoveries had turned out as he had predicted. They evinced the liveliest interest in the affairs of the colony, and a desire of receiving frequent intelligence as to his situation, proposing that a caravel should sail each month from Isabella and Spain. They informed him that all differences with Portugal were amicably adjusted, and acquainted him with the conventional agreement with that power relative to a geographical line separating their newly discovered possessions, requesting him to respect this agreement in the course of his discoveries. As in adjusting the arrangement with Portugal, and in drawing the proposed line, it was important to have the best advice, the sovereigns requested Columbus to return and be present at the convention; or, in case that should be inconvenient, to send his brother Bartholomew, or any other person whom he should consider fully competent, furnished with such maps, charts, and designs as might be of service in the negotiation.*

There was another letter, addressed generally to the inhabitants of the colony, and to all who should proceed on voyages of discovery, commanding them to obey Columbus as implicitly as they would the sovereigns themselves, under pain of their high displeasure, and a fine of ten thousand maravedies for each offence.

Such was the well-merited confidence reposed at this moment by the sovereigns in Columbus, but which was soon to be blighted by the insidious reports of worthless men. He was already aware of the complaints and misrepresentations which had been sent home from the colony, and which would be enforced by Margarite and Friar Boyle. He was aware that his standing in Spain was of that uncertain kind which a stranger always possesses in the service of a foreign country, where he has no friends or connections to support him, and where even his very merits increase the eagerness of envy to cast him down. His efforts to promote the working of the mines and to explore the resources of the island had been impeded by the misconduct of Margarite and the disorderly life of the Spaniards in general; yet he apprehended that the very evils which they had produced would be alleged against him, and the want of profitable returns be cited to discredit and embarrass his expeditions.

To counteract any misrepresentations of the kind, Columbus hastened the return of the ships, and would have returned with them, not merely to comply with the wishes of the sovereigns in being present at the settlement of the geographical line, but to vindicate himself and his enterprises from the aspersions of his enemies. The malady, however, which confined him to his bed prevented his departure; and his brother Bartholomew was required to aid, with his practical good sense and his resolute spirit, in regulating the disordered affairs of the island. It was determined, therefore, to send home his brother Diego to attend to the wishes of the sovereigns, and to take care of his interests at court. At the same time he exerted himself to the utmost to send by the ships satisfactory proofs of the value of his discoveries.

* Herrera, decad. i. lib. ii. cap. 17.

He remitted by them all the gold that he could collect, with specimens of other metals, and of various fruits and valuable plants, which he had collected either in Hispaniola or in the course of his voyage. In his eagerness to produce immediate profit, and to indemnify the sovereigns for those expenses which bore hard upon the royal treasury, he sent, likewise, above five hundred Indian prisoners, who, he suggested, might be sold as slaves at Seville.

It is painful to find the brilliant renown of Columbus sullied by so foul a stain. The customs of the times, however, must be pleaded in his apology. The precedent had been given long before, by both Spaniards and Portuguese, in their African discoveries, wherein the traffic in slaves had formed one of the greatest sources of profit. In fact, the practice had been sanctioned by the church itself, and the most learned theologians had pronounced all barbarous and infidel nations who shut their ears to the truths of Christianity fair objects of war and rapine, of captivity and slavery. If Columbus needed any practical illustration of this doctrine, he had it in the conduct of Ferdinand himself, in his late wars with the Moors of Granada, in which he had always been surrounded by a crowd of ghostly advisers, and had professed to do everything for the glory and advancement of the faith. In this holy war, as it was termed, it was a common practice to make inroads into the Moorish territories and carry off *cavalgadas*, not merely of flocks and herds, but of human beings, and those not warriors taken with weapons in their hands, but quiet villagers, labouring peasantry, and helpless women and children. These were carried to the mart at Seville, or to other populous towns, and sold into slavery. The capture of Malaga was a memorable instance where, as a punishment for an obstinate and brave defence, which should have excited admiration rather than revenge, eleven thousand people, of both sexes and of all ranks and ages, many of them highly cultivated and delicately reared, were suddenly torn from their homes, severed from each other, and swept into menial slavery, even though half of their ransoms had been paid. The circumstances are not advanced to vindicate but to palliate the conduct of Columbus. He acted but in conformity to the customs of the times, and was sanctioned by the example of the sovereign under whom he served. Las Casas, the zealous and enthusiastic advocate of the Indians, who suffers no opportunity to escape him of exclaiming in vehement terms against their slavery, speaks with indulgence of Columbus on this head. If those pious and learned men, he observes, whom the sovereigns took for guides and instructors, were so ignorant of the injustice of this practice, it is no wonder that the unlettered admiral should not be conscious of its impropriety.[*]

* Las Casas, *Hist. Ind.*, tom. i. cap. 122, MS.

Notwithstanding the defeat of the Indians by Ojeda, they still retained hostile intentions against the Spaniards. The idea of their cacique being a prisoner and in chains enraged the natives of Maguana, and the general sympathy manifested by other tribes of the island shows how widely that intelligent savage had extended his influence and how greatly he was admired. He had still active and powerful relatives remaining to attempt his rescue or revenge his fall. One of his brothers, Manicaotex by name, a Carib, bold and warlike as himself, succeeded to the sway over his subjects. His favourite wife also, Anacaona, so famous for her charms, had great influence over her brother Behechio, cacique of the populous province of Xaragua. Through these means a violent and general hostility to the Spaniards was excited throughout the island, and the formidable league of the caciques, which Caonabo had in vain attempted to accomplish when at large, was produced by his captivity. Guacanagari, the cacique of Marien, alone remained friendly to the Spaniards, giving them timely information of the gathering storm, and offering to take the field with them as a faithful ally.

The protracted illness of Columbus, the scantiness of his military force, and the wretched state of the colonists in general, reduced by sickness and scarcity to great bodily weakness, had hitherto induced him to try every means of conciliation and stratagem to avert and dissolve the confederacy. He had at length recovered his health, and his followers were in some degree refreshed and invigorated by the supplies brought by the ships. At this time he received intelligence that the allied caciques were actually assembled in great force in the Vega, within two days' march of Isabella, with an intention of making a general assault upon the settlement and overwhelming it by numbers. Columbus resolved to take the field at once, and to carry the war into the territories of the enemy, rather than suffer it to be brought to his own door.

The whole sound and effective force that he could muster, in the present infirm state of the colony, did not exceed two hundred infantry and twenty horse. They were armed with crossbows, swords, lances, and espingardas, or heavy arquebuses, which in those days were used with rests, and sometimes mounted on wheels. With these formidable weapons, a handful of European warriors, cased in steel and covered with bucklers, were able to cope with thousands of naked savages. They had aid of another kind, however, consisting of twenty bloodhounds, animals scarcely less terrible to the Indians than the horses, and infinitely more fatal. They were fearless and ferocious; nothing daunted them, nor, when they had once seized upon their prey, could anything compel them to relinquish their hold. The naked bodies of the Indians offered no defence against their attacks. They sprang on them, dragged them to the earth, and tore them to pieces.

The admiral was accompanied in the expedition by his brother Bartholomew, whose counsel and aid he sought on all occasions, and who had not merely great personal force and undaunted courage, but also a decidedly military turn of mind. Guacanagari also brought his people into the field. Neither he nor his subjects, however, were of a warlike character, or calculated to render much assistance. The chief advantage of his co-operation was, that it completely severed him from the other caciques, and insured the dependence of himself and his subjects upon the Spaniards. In the present infant state of the colony its chief security depended upon jealousies and dissensions sown among the native powers of the island.

On the 27th of March 1495, Columbus issued forth from Isabella with his little army, and advanced by marches of ten leagues a day in quest of the enemy. He ascended again to the mountain pass of the Cavaliers, whence he had first looked down upon the Vega. With what different feelings did he now comtemplate it! The vile passions of the white men had already converted this smiling, beautiful, and once peaceful and hospitable region into a land of wrath and hostility. Wherever the smoke of an Indian town rose from among the trees, it marked a horde of exasperated enemies, and the deep rich forests below him swarmed with lurking warriors.

In the picture which his imagination had drawn of the peaceful and inoffensive nature of this people, he had flattered himself with the idea of ruling over them as a patron and benefactor; but now he found himself compelled to assume the odious character of a conqueror.

The Indians had notice, by their scouts, of his approach, but though they had already had some slight experience of the warfare of the white men, they were confident, from the vast superiority of their numbers, which, it is said, amounted to one hundred thousand men.* This is probably an exaggeration. As Indians never draw out into the open field in order of battle, but lurk among the forests, it is difficult to ascertain their force; and their rapid movements and sudden sallies and retreats from various parts, together with the wild shouts and yells from opposite quarters of the woodlands, are calculated to give an exaggerated idea of their number. The army must, however, have been great, as it consisted of the combined forces of several caciques of this populous island. It was commanded by Manicaotex, the brother of Caonabo. The Indians, who were little skilled in numeration, and incapable of reckoning beyond ten, had a simple mode of ascertaining and describing the force of an enemy, by counting out a grain of maize or Indian corn for every warrior. When, therefore, the spies, who had watched from rocks and thickets the march of Columbus, came back with a mere handful of corn as the amount of his army, the caciques scoffed at the idea of so scanty a number making head against their countless multitude.†

Columbus drew near to the enemy about the place where the town of St Jago has since been built. The Indian army, under Manicaotex, was posted on a plain interspersed with clusters of forest-trees, now known as the Savanna of Matanza. Having ascertained the great force of the enemy, Don Bartholomew advised that their little army should be divided into detachments, and should attack the Indians at the same moment from several quarters. This plan was adopted. The infantry, separating into different bodies, advanced suddenly from various directions, with great din of drums and trumpets, and a destructive discharge of firearms from the covert of the trees. The Indians were thrown

* Las Casas, *Hist. Ind.*, lib. i. cap. 104, MS.
† Las Casas, *Hist. Ind.*, lib. i. cap. 104, MS.

into complete confusion. An army seemed pressing upon them from every quarter, their fellow-warriors to be laid low with thunder and lightning from the forests. While driven together and confounded by these attacks, Alonzo de Ojeda charged their main body impetuously with his troop of cavalry, cutting his way with lance and sabre. The horses bore down the terrified Indians, while their riders dealt their blows on all sides unopposed. The bloodhounds at the same time rushed upon the naked savages, seizing them by the throat, dragging them to the earth, and tearing out their bowels. The Indians, unaccustomed to large and fierce quadrupeds of any kind, were struck with horror when assailed by these ferocious animals. They thought the horses equally fierce and devouring. The contest, if such it might be called, was of short duration.

The Indians fled in every direction with yells and howlings. Some clambered to the top of rocks and precipices, whence they made piteous supplications, and offers of complete submission; many were killed, many made prisoners, and the confederacy was for the time completely broken up and dispersed.

Guacanagari had accompanied the Spaniards into the field, according to his promise, but he was little more than a spectator of this battle, or rather rout. He was not of a martial spirit, and both he and his subjects must have shrunk with awe at this unusual and terrific burst of war, even though on the part of their allies. His participation in the hostilities of the white men was never forgiven by the other caciques, and he returned to his dominions followed by the hatred and execrations of all the islanders.

CHAPTER 7

1494

Columbus followed up his victory by making a military tour through various parts of the island and reducing them to obedience. The natives made occasional attempts at opposition, but were easily checked. Ojeda's troop of cavalry was of great efficacy from the rapidity of its movements, the active intrepidity of its commander, and the terror inspired by the horses. There was no service too wild and hazardous for Ojeda. If any appearance of war arose in a distant part of the country, he would penetrate, with his little squadron of cavalry, through the depths of the forests, and fall like a thunderbolt upon the enemy, disconcerting all their combinations and enforcing implicit submission.

The Royal Vega was soon brought into subjection. Being an immense plain, perfectly level, it was easily overrun by the horsemen, whose appearance overawed the most populous villages. Guarionex, its sovereign cacique, was of a mild and placable character, and though he had been roused to war by the instigation of the neighbouring chieftains, he readily submitted to the domination of the Spaniards. Manicaotex, the brother of Caonabo, was also obliged to sue for peace; and being the prime mover of the confederacy, the other caciques followed his example. Behechio alone, the cacique of Xaragua, and brother-in-law of Caonabo, made no overtures of submission. His territories lay remote from Isabella, at the western extremity of the island, around the deep bay called the Bight of Leogan, and the long peninsula called Cape Tiburon. They were difficult of access, and had not as yet been visited by the white men. He retired into his domains, taking with him his sister, the beautiful Anacaona, wife of Caonabo, whom he cherished with fraternal affection under her misfortunes, who soon acquired almost equal sway over his subjects with himself, and was destined subsequently to make some figure in the events of the island.

Having been forced to take the field by the confederacy of the caciques, Columbus now asserted the right of a conqueror, and considered how he might turn his conquest to most profit. His constant anxiety was to make wealthy returns to Spain, for the purpose of indemnifying the sovereigns for their great expenses; of meeting the public expectations, so extravagantly excited; and, above all, of silencing the calumnies of those who had gone home determined to make the most discouraging representations of his discoveries. He endeavoured, therefore, to raise a large and immediate revenue by imposing heavy tributes on the subjected provinces. In those of the Vega, Cibao, and all the region of the mines, each individual above the age of fourteen years was required to pay, every three months, the measure of a Flemish hawk's bell of gold dust.* The caciques had to pay a much larger amount for their personal tribute. Manicaotex, the brother of Caonabo, was obliged individually to render in, every three months, half a calabash of gold, amounting to one hundred and fifty pesos. In those districts which were distant from the mines, and produced no gold, each individual was required to furnish an arroba (twenty-five pounds) of cotton every three months. Each Indian, on rendering this tribute, received a copper medal as a certificate of payment, which he was to wear suspended round his neck. Those who were found without such documents were liable to arrest and punishment.

The taxes and tributes thus imposed bore hard upon the spirit of the natives, accustomed to be but lightly tasked by their caciques; and the caciques themselves found the exactions intolerably grievous. Guarionex, the sovereign of the Royal Vega, represented to Columbus the difficulty he had in complying with the terms of his tribute. His richly fertile plain yielded no gold; and though the mountains on his borders contained mines, and their brooks and torrents washed down gold dust into the sands of the rivers, yet his subjects were not skilled in the art of collecting it. He proffered, therefore, instead of the tribute required, to cultivate with grain a band of country stretching across the island

* A hawk's bell, according to Las Casas (*Hist. Ind.*, lib. i. cap. 105) contains about three castellanos worth of gold dust, equal to five dollars, and in estimating the superior value of gold in those days, equivalent to fifteen dollars of our time. A quantity of gold worth one hundred and fifty castellanos was equivalent to seven hundred and ninety-eight dollars of the present day.

from sea to sea – enough, says Las Casas, to have furnished all Castile with bread for ten years.*

His offer was rejected. Columbus knew that gold alone would satisfy the avaricious dreams excited in Spain, and insure the popularity and success of his enterprises. Seeing, however, the difficulty that many of the Indians had in furnishing the amount of gold dust required, he lowered the demand to the measure of one-half of a hawk's bell.

To enforce the payment of these tributes, and to maintain the subjection of the island, Columbus put the fortresses already built in a strong state of defence, and erected others. Besides those of Isabella, and St Thomas in the mountains of Cibao, there were now the fortress of Magdalena in the Royal Vega, near the site of the old town of Santiago, on the river Jalaqua, two leagues from the place where the new town was afterwards built; another called Santa Catalina, the site of which is near the Estencia Yaqui; another called Esperanza, on the banks of the river Yaqui, facing the outlet of the mountain pass La Puerta de los Hidalgos, now the pass of Marney; but the most important of those recently erected was Fort Conception, in one of the most fruitful and beautiful parts of the Vega, about fifteen leagues to the east of Esperanza, controlling the extensive and populous domains of Guarionex.†

In this way was the yoke of servitude fixed upon the island and its thraldom effectually insured. Deep despair now fell upon the natives when they found a perpetual task inflicted upon them, enforced at stated and frequently-recurring periods. Weak and indolent by nature, unused to labour of any kind, and brought up in the untasked idleness of their soft climate and their fruitful groves, death itself seemed preferable to a life of toil and anxiety. They saw no end to this harassing evil which had so suddenly fallen upon them, no escape from its all-pervading influence, no prospect of return to that roving independence and ample leisure so dear to the wild inhabitants of the forest. The pleasant life of the island was at an end – the dream in the shade by day; the slumber during the sultry noontide heat by the fountain or the stream, or under the spreading palm-tree; and the song, the dance and the game in the mellow evening, when summoned to their simple

* Las Casas, *Hist. Ind.*. lib. i. cap. 105.
† Las Casas, *Hist. Ind.*, lib. i. cap. 110.

amusements by the rude Indian drum. They were now obliged to grope day by day, with bending body and anxious eye, along the borders of their rivers, sifting the sands for the grains of gold which every day grew more scanty; or to labour in their fields beneath the fervour of a tropical sun, to raise food for their taskmasters, or to produce the vegetable tribute imposed upon them. They sank to sleep weary and exhausted at night, with the certainty that the next day was but to be a repetition of the same toil and suffering. Or if they occasionally indulged in their national dances, the ballads to which they kept time were of a melancholy and plaintive character. They spoke of the times that were past, before the white men had introduced sorrow and slavery and weary labour among them; and they rehearsed pretended prophecies, handed down from their ancestors, foretelling the invasion of the Spaniards – that strangers should come into their island, clothed in apparel, with swords capable of cleaving a man asunder at a blow, under whose yoke their posterity should be subdued. These ballads or areytos they sang with mournful tunes and doleful voices, bewailing the loss of their liberty, and their painful servitude.[*]

They had flattered themselves for a time that the visit of the strangers would be but temporary, and that, spreading their ample sails, their ships would once more bear them back to their home in the sky. In their simplicity they had repeatedly inquired when they intended to return to turey or the heavens. They now beheld them taking root, as it were, in the island. They beheld their vessels lying idle and rotting in the harbour, while the crews, scattered about the country, were building habitations and fortresses, the solid construction of which, unlike their own slight cabins, gave evidence of permanent abode.[†]

Finding how vain was all attempt to deliver themselves by warlike means from these invincible intruders, they now concerted a forlorn and desperate mode of annoyance. They perceived that the settlement suffered greatly from shortness of provisions, and depended in a considerable degree upon the supplies furnished by the natives. The fortresses in the interior also, and the Spaniards quartered in the villages, looked almost entirely to them for subsistence. They agreed among themselves, therefore, not to

[*] Peter Martyr, decad. iii. lib. ix.
[†] Las Casas, *Hist. Ind.*, lib. i. cap. 106.

cultivate the fruits, the roots, and maize, their chief articles of food, and to destroy those already growing; hoping, by producing a famine, to starve the strangers from the island. They little knew, observes Las Casas, one of the characteristics of the Spaniards, who, the more hungry they are, the more inflexible they become, and the more hardened to endure suffering.* They carried their plan generally into effect, abandoning their habitations, laying waste their fields and groves, and retiring to the mountains, where there were roots and herbs and abundance of utias for their subsistence.

This measure did indeed produce much distress among the Spaniards, but they had foreign resources, and were enabled to endure it by husbanding the partial supplies brought by their ships. The most disastrous effects fell upon the natives themselves. The Spaniards stationed in the various fortresses, finding that there was not only no hope of tribute, but a danger of famine from this wanton waste and sudden desertion, pursued the natives to their retreats to compel them to return to labour. The Indians took refuge in the most sterile and dreary heights, flying from one wild retreat to another, the women with their children in their arms or at their backs, and all worn out with fatigue and hunger, and harassed by perpetual alarms. In every noise of the forest or the mountain they fancied they heard the sound of their pursuers; they hid themselves in damp and dismal caverns, or in the rocky banks and margins of the torrents, and not daring to hunt or fish, or even to venture forth in quest of nourishing roots and vegetables, they had to satisfy their raging hunger with unwholesome food. In this way many thousands of them perished miserably through famine, fatigue, terror, and various contagious maladies engendered by their sufferings. All spirit of opposition was at length completely quelled. The surviving Indians returned in despair to their habitations, and submitted humbly to the yoke. So deep an awe did they conceive of their conquerors that it is said a Spaniard might go singly and securely all over the island, and the natives would even transport him from place to place on their shoulders.†

---

* 'No conociendo la propriedad de los Españoles los cuales cuanto mas hambrientos, tanto mayor teson tiennen y mas duros son de sufrir y para sufrir.' – Las Casas, *Hist. Ind.* lib. i, cap. 106.

† Las Casas, *Hist. Ind.*, lib. i. cap. 106; *Hist. del Almirante*, cap. 60.

Before passing on to other events, it may be proper here to notice the fate of Guacanagari, as he makes no further appearance in the course of this history. His friendship for the Spaniards had severed him from his countrymen, but did not exonerate him from the general woes of the island. His territories, like those of the other caciques, were subject to a tribute, which his people, with the common repugnance to labour, found it difficult to pay. Columbus, who knew his worth, and could have protected him, was long absent either in the interior of the island or detained in Europe by his own wrongs. In the interval, the Spaniards forgot the hospitality and services of Guacanagari, and his tribute was harshly exacted. He found himself overwhelmed with opprobrium from his countrymen at large, and assailed by the clamours and lamentations of his suffering subjects. The strangers whom he had succoured in distress, and taken as it were to the bosom of his native island, had become its tyrants and oppressors. Care, and toil, and poverty, and strong-handed violence had spread their curses over the land, and he felt as if he had invoked them on his race. Unable to bear the hostilities of his fellow caciques, the woes of his subjects, and the extortions of his ungrateful allies, he took refuge at last in the mountains, where he died obscurely and in misery.*

An attempt has been made by Oviedo to defame the character of this Indian prince. It is not for Spaniards, however, to excuse their own ingratitude by casting a stigma on his name. He appears to have always manifested towards them that true friendship which shines brightest in the dark days of adversity. He might have played a nobler part, in making a stand, with his brother caciques, to drive these intruders from his native soil; but he appears to have been fascinated by his admiration of the strangers and his personal attachment to Columbus. He was bountiful, hospitable, affectionate, and kind-hearted, competent to rule a gentle and unwarlike people in the happier days of the island, but unfitted, through the softness of his nature, for the stern turmoil which followed the arrival of the white men.

---

* Charlevoix, *Hist. de St Domingo*, lib. ii.

While Columbus was endeavouring to remedy the evils produced by the misconduct of Margarite, that recreant commander and his political coadjutor, Friar Boyle, were busily undermining his reputation in the court of Castile. They accused him of deceiving the sovereigns and the public by extravagant descriptions of the countries he had discovered; they pronounced the island of Hispaniola a source of expense rather than profit; and they drew a dismal picture of the sufferings of the colony, occasioned, as they said, by the oppressions of Columbus and his brothers. They charged them with tasking the community with excessive labour during a time of general sickness and debility; with stopping the rations of individuals on the most trifling pretext, to the great detriment of their health; with wantonly inflicting severe corporal punishments on the common people, and with heaping indignities on Spanish gentlemen of rank. They said nothing, however, of the exigencies which had called for unusual labour; nor of the idleness and profligacy which required coercion and chastisement; nor of the seditious cabals of the Spanish cavaliers, who had been treated with indulgence rather than severity. In addition to these complaints, they represented the state of confusion of the island in consequence of the absence of the admiral, and the uncertainty which prevailed concerning his fate, intimating the probability of his having perished in his foolhardy attempts to explore unknown seas and discover unprofitable lands.

These prejudiced and exaggerated representations derived much weight from the official situations of Margarite and Friar Boyle. They were supported by the testimony of many discontented and factious idlers who had returned with them to Spain. Some of these persons had connections of rank, who were ready to resent, with Spanish haughtiness, what they considered the arrogant assumptions of an ignoble foreigner. Thus the popularity of Columbus received a vital blow, and immediately began to decline. The confidence of the sovereigns also was impaired, and precautions were adopted which savour strongly of the cautious and suspicious policy of Ferdinand.

It was determined to send some person of trust and confidence who should take upon himself the government of the island in case of the continued absence of the admiral, and who, even in the event of his return, should inquire into the alleged evils and abuses, and remedy such as should appear really in existence. The person proposed for this difficult office was Diego Carillo, a commander of a military order; but as he was not immediately prepared to sail with the fleet of caravels about to depart with supplies, the sovereigns wrote to Fonseca, the superintendent of Indian affairs, to send some trusty person with the vessels, to take charge of the provisions with which they were freighted. These he was to distribute among the colonists, under the supervision of the admiral, or, in case of his absence, in the presence of those in authority. He was also to collect information concerning the manner in which the island had been governed, the conduct of persons in office, the causes and authors of existing grievances, and the measures by which they were to be remedied. Having coll-ected such information, he was to return and make report to the sovereigns; but in case he should find the admiral at the island, everything was to remain subject to his control.

There was another measure adopted by the sovereigns about this time, which likewise shows the declining favour of Columbus. On the 10th of April 1495, a proclamation was issued, giving general commission to native-born subjects to settle in the island of Hispaniola, and to go on private voyages of discovery and traffic to the New World. This was granted, subject to certain conditions.

All vessels were to sail exclusively from the port of Cadiz, and under the inspection of officers appointed by the crown. Those who embarked for Hispaniola without pay, and at their own expense, were to have lands assigned to them, and to be pro-visioned for one year, with a right to retain such lands and all houses they might erect upon them. Of all gold which they might collect, they were to retain one-third for themselves and pay two-thirds to the crown. Of all other articles of merchandise, the produce of the island, they were to pay merely one-tenth to the crown. Their purchases were to be made in the presence of officers appointed by the sovereigns, and the royal duties paid into the hands of the king's receiver.

Each ship sailing on private enterprise was to take one or two persons named by the royal officers of Cadiz. One-tenth of the tonnage of the ship was to be at the service of the crown, free of charge. One-tenth of whatever such ships should procure in the newly-discovered countries was to be paid to the crown on their return. These regulations included private ships trading to Hispaniola with provisions.

For every vessel thus fitted out on private adventure, Columbus, in consideration of his privilege of an eighth of tonnage, was to have the right to freight one on his own account.

This general license for voyages of discovery was made in consequence of the earnest applications of Vincent Yañez Pinzon and other able and intrepid navigators, most of whom had sailed with Columbus. They offered to make voyages at their own cost and hazard. The offer was tempting and well-timed. The government was poor, the expeditions of Columbus were expensive, yet their object was too important to be neglected. Here was an opportunity of attaining all the ends proposed, not merely without expense, but with a certainty of gain. The permission, therefore, was granted, without consulting the opinion or the wishes of the admiral. It was loudly complained of by him as an infringement of his privileges, and as disturbing the career of regular and well-organized discovery by the licentious and sometimes predatory enterprises of reckless adventurers. Doubtless, much of the odium that has attached itself to the Spanish discoveries in the New World has arisen from the grasping avidity of private individuals.

Just at this juncture, in the early part of April, while the interests of Columbus were in such a critical situation, the ships commanded by Torres arrived in Spain. They brought intelligence of the safe return of the admiral to Hispaniola, from his voyage along the southern coast of Cuba, with the evidence which he had collected to prove that it was the extremity of the Asiatic continent, and that he had penetrated to the borders of the wealthiest countries of the East. Specimens were likewise brought of the gold, and the various animal and vegetable curiosities, which he had procured in the course of his voyage. No arrival could have been more timely. It at once removed all doubts respecting his safety, and obviated the necessity of part of the precautionary measures then on the point of being taken. The supposed discovery of the rich coast of Asia also threw a temporary splendour about his expedition, and again awakened the gratitude of the sovereigns. The effect was immediately apparent in their measures. Instead of leaving it to the discretion of Juan Rodriguez de Fonseca to appoint whom he pleased to the commission of inquiry about to be sent out, they retracted that power, and nominated Juan Aguado.

He was chosen because, on returning from Hispaniola, he had been strongly recommended to royal favour by Columbus. It was intended, therefore, as a mark of consideration to the latter, to appoint as commissioner a person of whom he had expressed so high an opinion, and who, it was to be presumed, entertained for him a grateful regard.

Fonseca, in virtue of his official station as superintendent of the affairs of the Indies, and probably to gratify his growing animosity for Columbus, had detained a quantity of gold which Don Diego, brother to the admiral, had brought on his own private account. The sovereigns wrote to him repeatedly, ordering him not to demand the gold; or if he had seized it, to return it immediately, with satisfactory explanations, and to write to Columbus in terms calculated to soothe any angry feelings which he might have excited. He was ordered, also, to consult the persons recently arrived from Hispaniola in what manner he could yield satisfaction to the admiral, and to act accordingly. Fonseca thus suffered one of the severest humiliations of an arrogant spirit – that of being obliged to make atonement for its arrogance. It quickened, however, the malice which he had conceived against the admiral and his family. Unfortunately his official situation and the royal confidence which he enjoyed gave him opportunities of gratifying it subsequently in a thousand different ways.

While the sovereigns thus endeavoured to avoid any act which might give umbrage to Columbus, they took certain measures to provide for the tranquillity of the colony. In a letter to the admiral they directed that the number of persons in the settlement should be limited to five hundred, a greater number being considered unnecessary for the service of the island and a burdensome expense to the crown. To prevent further discontents about provisions, they ordered that the rations of individuals should be dealt out in portions every fifteen days; and that all punishment by short allowance, or the stoppage of rations, should be discontinued, as tending to injure the health of the colonists, who required every assistance of nourishing diet to fortify them against the maladies incident to a strange climate.

An able and experienced metallurgist, named Pablo Belvis, was sent out in place of the wrong-headed Fermin Cedo. He was furnished with all the necessary engines and implements for mining, assaying, and purifying the precious metals, and with liberal pay and privileges. Ecclesiastics were also sent to supply the place of Friar Boyle, and of certain of his brethren who desired to leave the island. The instruction and conversion of the natives awakened more and more the solicitude of the queen. In the ships of Torres a large number of Indians arrived, who had been captured in the recent wars with the caciques. Royal orders had been issued that they should be sold as slaves in the markets of Andalusia, as had been the custom with respect to negroes taken on the coast of Africa, and to Moorish prisoners captured in the war with Granada. Isabella, however, had been deeply interested by the accounts given of the gentle and hospitable character of these islanders, and of their great docility. The discovery had been made under her immediate auspices; she looked upon these people as under her peculiar care, and she anticipated with pious enthusiasm the glory of leading them from darkness into the paths of light. Her compassionate spirit revolted at the idea of treating them as slaves, even though sanctioned by the customs of the time. Within five days after the royal order for the sale, a letter was written by the sovereigns to Bishop Fonseca, suspending that order until they could inquire into the cause for which the Indians had been made prisoners, and consult learned and pious theologians whether their sale would be justifiable in the eyes of God.* Much difference of opinion took place among divines on this important question. The queen eventually decided it according to the dictates of her own pure conscience and charitable heart. She ordered that the Indians should be sent back to their native country, and enjoined that the islanders should be conciliated by the gentlest means, instead of

* Letter of the Sovereigns to Fonseca. Navarrete, *Coleccion de los Viages*, i.11, Doc. 92.

being treated with severity. Unfortunately her orders came too late to Hispaniola to have the desired effect. The scenes of warfare and violence, produced by the bad passions of the colonists and the vengeance of the natives, were not to be forgotten, and mutual distrust and rankling animosity had grown up between them, which no after exertions could eradicate.

Juan Aguado set sail from Spain towards the end of August with four caravels, well freighted with supplies of all kinds. Don Diego Columbus returned in this squadron to Hispaniola, and arrived at Isabella in the month of October, while the admiral was absent, occupied in re-establishing the tranquillity of the interior. Aguado, as has already been shown, was under obligations to Columbus, who had distinguished him from among his companions, and had recommended him to the favour of the sovereigns. He was, however, one of those weak men whose heads are turned by the least elevation. Puffed up by a little temporary power, he lost sight not merely of the respect and gratitude due to Columbus, but of the nature and extent of his own commission. Instead of acting as an agent employed to collect information, he assumed a tone of authority, as though the reins of government had been transferred into his hands. He interfered in public affairs, ordered various persons to be arrested, called to account the officers employed by the admiral, and paid no respect to Don Bartholomew Columbus, who remained in command during the absence of his brother. The Adelantado, astonished at this presumption, demanded a sight of the commission under which he acted; but Aguado treated him with great haughtiness, replying that he would show it only to the admiral. On second thoughts, however, lest there should be doubts in the public mind of his right to interfere in the affairs of the colony, he ordered his letter of credence from the sovereigns to be pompously proclaimed by sound of trumpet. It was brief but comprehensive, to the following purport: 'Cavaliers, esquires, and other persons, who by our orders are in the Indies, we send to you Juan Aguado, our groom of the chambers, who will speak to you on our part. We command you to give him faith and credit.'

The report now circulated that the downfall of Columbus and his family was at hand, and that an auditor had arrived empowered to hear and to redress the grievances of the public. This rumour originated with Aguado himself, who threw out menaces of rigid investigations and signal punishments. It was a time of jubilee for offenders. Every culprit started up into an accuser; everyone who by negligence or crime had incurred the wholesome penalties of the laws was loud in his clamours against the oppression of Columbus. There were ills enough in the colony, some incident to its situation, others produced by the misdeeds of the colonists, but all were ascribed to the maladministration of the admiral. He was made responsible alike for the evils produced by others and for his own stern remedies. All the old complaints were reiterated against him and his brothers, and the usual and illiberal cause given for their oppressions – that they were foreigners, who sought merely their own interest and aggrandizement at the expense of the sufferings and the indignities of Spaniards.

Destitute of discrimination to perceive what was true and what false in these complaints, and anxious only to condemn, Aguado saw in everything conclusive testimony of the culpability of Columbus. He intimated, and perhaps thought, that the admiral was keeping at a distance from Isabella through fear of encountering his investigations. In the fulness of his presumption, he even set out with a body of horse to go in quest of him. A vain and weak man in power is prone to employ satellites of his own description. The arrogant and boasting followers of Aguado wherever they went spread rumours among the natives of the might and importance of their chief, and of the punishment he intended to inflict upon Columbus. In a little while the report circulated through the island that a new admiral had arrived to administer the government, and that the former one was to be put to death.

The news of the arrival and of the insolent conduct of Aguado reached Columbus in the interior of the island. He immediately hastened to Isabella to give him a meeting. Aguado, hearing of his approach, also returned there. As everyone knew the lofty spirit of Columbus, his high sense of his services, and his jealous maintenance of his official dignity, a violent explosion was anticipated at the impending interview. Aguado also expected something of the kind, but, secure in his royal letter of credence, he looked forward

with the ignorant audacity of a little mind to the result. The sequel
showed how difficult it is for petty spirits to anticipate the conduct
of a man like Columbus in an extraordinary situation. His natural
heat and impetuosity had been subdued by a life of trials; he had
learned to bring his passions into subjection to his judgment; he
had too true an estimate of his own dignity to enter into a contest
with a shallow boaster like Aguado. Above all, he had a profound
respect for the authority of his sovereigns; for in his enthusiastic
spirit, prone to deep feelings of reverence, his loyalty was inferior
only to his religion. He received Aguado, therefore, with grave
and punctilious courtesy, and retorted upon him his own ostentatious ceremonial, ordering that the letter of credence should
be again proclaimed by sound of trumpet in presence of the
populace. He listened to it with solemn deference, and assured
Aguado of his readiness to acquiesce in whatever might be the
pleasure of his sovereigns.

This unexpected moderation, while it astonished the beholders,
foiled and disappointed Aguado. He had come prepared for a
scene of altercation, and had hoped that Columbus, in the heat and
impatience of the moment, would have said or done something
that might be construed into disrespect for the authority of the
sovereigns. He endeavoured, in fact, some months afterwards, to
procure from the public notaries present a prejudicial statement of
the interview; but the deference of the admiral for the royal letter
of credence had been too marked to be disputed, and all the
testimonials were highly in his favour.[*]

Aguado continued to intermeddle in public affairs; and the
respect and forbearance with which he was uniformly treated by
Columbus, and the mildness of the latter in all his measures to
appease the discontents of the colony, were regarded as proofs of
his loss of moral courage. He was looked upon as a declining man,
and Aguado hailed as the lord of the ascendant. Every dastard spirit
who had any lurking ill-will, any real or imaginary cause of
complaint, now hastened to give it utterance, perceiving that in
gratifying his malice he was promoting his interest, and that in
vilifying the admiral he was gaining the friendship of Aguado.

The poor Indians, too, harassed by the domination of the white
men, rejoiced in the prospect of a change of rulers, vainly hoping

* Herrera, *Hist. Ind.*, decad. i. lib. ii. cap. 18.

that it might produce a mitigation of their sufferings. Many of the
caciques who had promised allegiance to the admiral after their
defeat in the Vega now assembled at the house of Manicaotex, the
brother of Caonabo, near the river Yagui, where they joined in a
formal complaint against Columbus, whom they considered the
cause of all the evils which had sprung from the disobedience and
the vices of his followers.

Aguado now considered the great object of his mission fulfilled.
He had collected information sufficient, as he thought, to insure
the ruin of the admiral and his brothers, and he prepared to return
to Spain. Columbus resolved to do the same. He felt that it was
time to appear at court and dispel the cloud of calumny gathering
against him. He had active enemies, of standing and influence,
who were seeking every occasion to throw discredit upon himself
and his enterprises; and, stranger and foreigner as he was, he had
no active friends at court to oppose their machinations. He feared
that they might eventually produce an effect upon the royal mind
fatal to the progress of discovery. He was anxious to return,
therefore, and explain the real causes of the repeated disappointments with respect to profits anticipated from his enterprises. It is
not one of the least singular traits in this history that, after having
been so many years in persuading mankind that there was a new
world to be discovered, he had almost equal trouble in proving to
them the advantage of its discovery.

When the ships were ready to depart a terrible storm swept the
island. It was one of those awful whirlwinds which occasionally
rage within the tropics, and were called by the Indians 'furicanes'
or 'uricans', a name they still retain with trifling variation. About
mid-day a furious wind sprang up from the east, driving before it
dense volumes of cloud and vapour. Encountering another tempest of wind from the west, it appeared as if a violent conflict
ensued. The clouds were rent by incessant flashes or rather streams
of lightning. At one time they were piled up high in the sky; at
another they swept to the earth, filling the air with a baleful
darkness more dismal than the obscurity of midnight. Wherever
the whirlwind passed whole tracts of forests were shivered and
stripped of their leaves and branches; those of gigantic size which
resisted the blast were torn up by the roots and hurled to a great
distance. Groves were rent from the mountain precipices with vast

masses of earth and rock, tumbling into the valleys with terrific noise, and choking the course of rivers. The fearful sounds in the air and on the earth, the pealing thunder, the vivid lightning, the howling of the wind, the crash of falling trees and rocks, filled everyone with affright, and many thought that the end of the world was at hand. Some fled to caverns for safety; for their frail houses were blown down, and the air was filled with the trunks and branches of trees, and even with fragments of rocks, carried along by the fury of the tempest. When the hurricane reached the harbour, it whirled the ships round as they lay at anchor, snapped their cables, and sank three of them with all who were on board. Others were driven about, dashed against each other, and tossed mere wrecks upon the shore by the swelling surges of the sea, which in some places rolled for three or four miles upon the land. The tempest lasted for three hours. When it had passed away, and the sun again appeared, the Indians regarded each other in mute astonishment and dismay. Never in their memory, nor in the traditions of their ancestors, had their island been visited by such a storm. They believed that the Deity had sent this fearful ruin to punish the cruelties and crimes of the white men, and declared that this people had moved the very air, the water, and the earth to disturb their tranquil life and to desolate their land.*

* Ramusio, tom. iii. p. 7; Peter Martyr, decad. i. lib. iv.

In the recent hurricane the four caravels of Aguado had been destroyed, together with two others which were in the harbour. The only vessel which survived was the *Niña*, and that in a very shattered condition. Columbus gave orders to have her immediately repaired, and another caravel constructed out of the wreck of those which had been destroyed. While waiting until they should be ready for sea, he was cheered by tidings of rich mines in the interior of the island, the discovery of which is attributed to an incident of a somewhat romantic nature.* A young Aragonian, named Miguel Diaz, in the service of the Adelantado, having a quarrel with another Spaniard, fought with him, and wounded him dangerously. Fearful of the consequences, he fled from the settlement, accompanied by five or six comrades, who had either been engaged in the affray or were personally attached to him. Wandering about the island, they came to an Indian village on the southern coast, near the mouth of the river Ozema, where the city of San Domingo is at present situated. They were received with kindness by the natives, and resided for some time among them. The village was governed by a female cacique, who soon conceived a strong attachment for the young Aragonian. Diaz was not insensible to her tenderness; a connection was formed between them, and they lived for some time very happily together.

The recollection of his country and his friends began at length to steal upon the thoughts of the young Spaniard. It was a melancholy lot to be exiled from civilized life and an outcast from among his countrymen. He longed to return to the settlement, but dreaded the punishment that awaited him from the austere justice of the Adelantado. His Indian bride, observing him frequently melancholy and lost in thought, penetrated the cause with the quick

* Oviedo, *Cronica de las Indias*, lib. ii. cap. 13.

intelligence of female affection. Fearful that he would abandon her and return to his countrymen, she endeavoured to devise some means of drawing the Spaniards to that part of the island. Knowing that gold was their sovereign attraction, she informed Diaz of certain rich mines in the neighbourhood, and urged him to persuade his countrymen to abandon the comparatively sterile and unhealthy vicinity of Isabella, and settle upon the fertile banks of the Ozema, promising they should be received with the utmost kindness and hospitality by her nation.

Struck with the suggestion, Diaz made particular inquiries about the mines, and was convinced that they abounded in gold. He noticed the superior fruitfulness and beauty of the country, the excellence of the river, and the security of the harbour at its entrance. He flattered himself that the communication of such valuable intelligence would make his peace at Isabella, and obtain his pardon from the Adelantado. Full of these hopes, he procured guides from among the natives, and taking a temporary leave of his Indian bride, set out with his comrades through the wilderness for the settlement, which was about fifty leagues distant. Arriving there secretly, he learned to his great joy that the man whom he had wounded had recovered. He now presented himself boldly before the Adelantado, relying that his tidings would earn his forgiveness. He was not mistaken. No news could have come more opportunely. The admiral had been anxious to remove the settlement to a more healthy and advantageous situation. He was desirous also of carrying home some conclusive proof of the riches of the island as the most effectual means of silencing the cavils of his enemies. If the representations of Miguel Diaz were correct, here was a means of effecting both these purposes. Measures were immediately taken to ascertain the truth. The Adelantado set forth in person to visit the river Ozema, accompanied by Miguel Diaz, Francisco de Garay, and the Indian guides, and attended by a number of men well armed. They proceeded from Isabella to Magdalena, and thence across the Royal Vega to the fortress of Conception. Continuing on to the south, they came to a range of mountains, which they traversed by a defile two leagues in length, and descended into another beautiful plain, which was called Bonao. Proceeding hence for some distance, they came to a great river called Hayna, running through a fertile country, all the streams of which abounded in gold. On the western bank of this river, and about eight leagues from its mouth, they found gold in greater quantities and in larger particles than had yet been met with in any part of the island, not even excepting the province of Cibao. They made experiments in various places within the compass of six miles, and always with success. The soil seemed to be generally impregnated with that metal, so that a common labourer with little trouble might find the amount of three drachms in the course of a day.[*] In several places they observed deep excavations in the form of pits, which looked as if the mines had been worked in ancient times; a circumstance which caused much speculation among the Spaniards, the natives having no idea of mining, but contenting themselves with the particles found on the surface of the soil or in the beds of the rivers.

The Indians of the neighbourhood received the white men with their promised friendship, and in every respect the representations of Miguel Diaz were fully justified. He was not only pardoned but received into great favour, and was subsequently employed in various capacities in the island, in all which he acquitted himself with great fidelity. He kept his faith with his Indian bride, by whom, according to Oviedo, he had two children. Charlevoix supposes that they were regularly married, as the female cacique appears to have been baptized, being always mentioned by the Christian name of Catalina.[†]

When the Adelantado returned with this favourable report, and with specimens of ore, the anxious heart of the admiral was greatly elated. He gave orders that a fortress should be immediately erected on the banks of the Hayna, in the vicinity of the mines, and that they should be diligently worked. The fancied traces of ancient excavations gave rise to one of his usual veins of golden conjectures. He had already surmised that Hispaniola might be the ancient Ophir. He now flattered himself that he had discovered the identical mines whence King Solomon had procured his gold for the building of the temple of Jerusalem. He supposed that his ships must have sailed by the Gulf of Persia, and round Taprobane to this

---

[*] Herrera, *Hist. Ind.*, decad. i. lib. ii. cap. 18; Peter Martyr, decad. i. lib. iv.

[†] Oviedo, *Cronica de las Ind.*, lib. ii. cap. 13; Charlevoix, *Hist. St Domingo*, lib. ii. p. 146.

island,* which, according to his idea, lay opposite to the extreme end of Asia, for such he firmly believed the island of Cuba.

It is probable that Columbus gave free license to his imagination in these conjectures, which tended to throw a splendour about his enterprises, and to revive the languishing interest of the public. Granting, however, the correctness of his opinion that he was in the vicinity of Asia, an error by no means surprising in the imperfect state of geographical knowledge, all his consequent suppositions were far from extravagant. The ancient Ophir was believed to lie somewhere in the East, but its situation was a matter of controversy among the learned, and remains one of those conjectural questions about which too much has been written for it ever to be satisfactorily decided.

---

* Peter Martyr, decad. i. lib. iv.

BOOK 9

CHAPTER I

1496

The new caravel, the *Santa Cruz*, being finished, and the *Niña* repaired, Columbus made every arrangement for immediate departure, anxious to be freed from the growing arrogance of Aguado, and to relieve the colony from a crew of factious and discontented men. He appointed his brother, Don Bartholomew, to the command of the island, with the title which he had already given him of Adelantado. In case of his death, he was to be succeeded by his brother Don Diego.

On the 10th of March the two caravels set sail for Spain, in one of which Columbus embarked and in the other Aguado. In consequence of the orders of the sovereigns, all those who could be spared from the island, and some who had wives and relatives in Spain whom they wished to visit, returned in these caravels, which were crowded with two hundred and twenty-five passengers – the sick, the idle, the profligate, and the factious. Never did a more miserable and disappointed crew return from a land of promise.

There were thirty Indians also on board of the caravels, among whom were the once redoubtable cacique Caonabo, one of his brothers, and a nephew. The curate of Los Palacios observes that Columbus had promised the cacique and his brother to restore them to their country and their power after he had taken them to visit the King and Queen of Castile.* It is probable that by kind treatment, and by a display of the wonders of Spain and the grandeur and might of its sovereigns, he hoped to conquer their enmity to the Spaniards, and convert them into important instruments towards obtaining a secure and peaceable dominion over

* Cura de los Palacios, cap. 131.

the island. Caonabo, however, was of that proud nature, of wild but vigorous growth, which can never be tamed. He remained a moody and dejected captive. He had too much intelligence not to perceive that his power was for ever blasted; but he retained his haughtiness, even in the midst of his despair.

Being as yet but little experienced in the navigation of these seas, Columbus, instead of working up to the northward, so as to fall in with the tract of westerly winds, took an easterly course on leaving the island. The consequence was that almost the whole of his voyage was a toilsome and tedious struggle against the tradewinds and calms which prevail between the tropics. On the 6th of April he found himself still in the vicinity of the Caribbee Islands, with his crews fatigued and sickly and his provisions rapidly diminishing. He bore away to the southward therefore, to touch at the most important of those islands in search of supplies.

On Saturday, the 9th, he anchored at Marigalante, whence, on the following day, he made sail for Guadalupe. It was contrary to the custom of Columbus to weigh anchor on Sunday when in port; but the people murmured, and observed that when in quest of food it was no time to stand on scruples as to holy days.*

Anchoring off the island of Guadalupe, the boat was sent on shore well armed. Before it could reach the land a large number of females issued from the woods, armed with bows and arrows, and decorated with tufts of feathers, preparing to oppose any descent upon their shores. As the sea was somewhat rough, and a surf broke upon the beach, the boats remained at a distance, and two of the Indians from Hispaniola swam to shore. Having explained to these amazons that the Spaniards only sought provisions, in exchange for which they would give articles of great value, the women referred them to their husbands, who were at the northern end of the island. As the boats proceeded thither, numbers of the natives were seen on the beach, who manifested great ferocity, shouting and yelling and discharging flights of arrows, which, however, fell far short in the water. Seeing the boats approach the land, they hid themselves in the adjacent forest, and rushed forth with hideous cries as the Spaniards were landing. A discharge of firearms drove them to the woods and mountains, and the boats met with no further opposition. Entering the deserted habitations,

* *Hist. del Almirante*, cap. 62.

the Spaniards began to plunder and destroy, contrary to the invariable injunctions of the admiral. Among other articles found in these houses were honey and wax, which Herrera supposes had been brought from Terra Firma, as these roving people collected the productions of distant regions in the course of their expeditions. Fernando Columbus mentions likewise that there were hatchets of iron in their houses. These, however, must have been made of a species of hard and heavy stone, already mentioned, which resembled iron, or they must have been procured from places which the Spaniards had previously visited, as it is fully admitted that no iron was in use among the natives prior to the discovery. The sailors also reported that in one of the houses they found the arm of a man roasting on a spit before a fire; but these facts, so repugnant to humanity, require more solid authority to be credited. The sailors had committed wanton devastations in these dwellings, and may have sought a pretext with which to justify their maraudings to their admiral.

While some of the people were getting wood and water, and making cassava bread, Columbus despatched forty men, well armed, to explore the interior of the island. They returned on the following day with ten women and three boys. The women were of large and powerful form, yet of great agility. They were naked, and wore their long hair flowing loose upon their shoulders; some decorated their heads with plumes of various colours. Among them was the wife of a cacique, a woman of great strength and proud spirit. On the approach of the Spaniards she had fled with an agility which soon left all her pursuers far behind, excepting a native of the Canary Islands remarkable for swiftness of foot. She would have escaped even from him, but perceiving that he was alone and far from his companions, she turned suddenly upon him, seized him with astonishing force, and would have strangled him, had not the Spaniards arrived and taken her, entangled like a hawk with her prey. The warlike spirit of these Carib women, and the circumstances of finding them in armed bands, defending their shores during the absence of their husbands, led Columbus repeatedly into the erroneous idea that certain of these islands were inhabited entirely by women; for which error, as has already been observed, he was prepared by the stories of Marco Polo concerning an island of amazons near the coast of Asia.

Having remained several days at the island, and prepared three weeks' supply of bread, Columbus prepared to make sail. As Guadalupe was the most important of the Caribbee Islands, and in a manner the portal or entrance to all the rest, he wished to secure the friendship of the inhabitants. He dismissed therefore all the prisoners, with many presents, to compensate for the spoil and injury which had been done. The female cacique, however, declined going on shore, preferring to remain and accompany the natives of Hispaniola who were on board, keeping with her also a young daughter. She had conceived a passion for Caonabo, having found out that he was a native of the Caribbee Islands. His character and story, gathered from the other Indians, had won the sympathy and admiration of this intrepid woman.[*]

Leaving Guadalupe on the 20th of April, and keeping in about the twenty-second degree of latitude, the caravels again worked their way against the whole current of the trade-winds, insomuch that on the 20th of May, after a month of great fatigue and toil, they had yet a great part of their voyage to make. The provisions were already so reduced that Columbus had to put everyone on a daily allowance of six ounces of bread and a pint and a half of water. As they advanced the scarcity grew more and more severe, and was rendered more appalling from the uncertainty which prevailed on board the vessels as to their situation. There were several pilots in the caravels, but being chiefly accustomed to the navigation of the Mediterranean or the Atlantic coasts, they were utterly confounded, and lost all reckoning when traversing the broad ocean. Everyone had a separate opinion, and none heeded that of the admiral. By the beginning of June there was an absolute famine on board of the ships. In the extremity of their sufferings, while death stared them in the face, it was proposed by some of the Spaniards, as a desperate alternative, that they should kill and eat their Indian prisoners. Others suggested that they should throw them into the sea, as so many expensive and useless mouths. Nothing but the absolute authority of Columbus prevented this last counsel from being adopted. He represented that the Indians were their fellow-beings, some of them Christians like themselves, and all entitled to similar treatment. He exhorted them to a little patience, assuring them that they would soon make land, for that,

* *Hist. del Almirante*, cap. 63.

according to his reckoning, they were not far from Cape St
Vincent. At this all scoffed, for they believed themselves yet far
from their desired haven, some affirming that they were in the
English Channel, others that they were approaching Galicia. When
Columbus therefore, confident in his opinion, ordered that sail
should be taken in at night, lest they should come upon the land in
the dark, there was a general murmur, the men exclaiming that it
was better to be cast on shore than to starve at sea. The next
morning, however, to their great joy they came in sight of the very
land which Columbus had predicted. From this time he was
regarded by the seamen as deeply versed in the mysteries of the
ocean, and almost oracular in matters of navigation.[*]

On the 11th of June the vessels anchored in the Bay of Cadiz,
after a weary voyage of about three months. In the course of this
voyage the unfortunate Caonabo expired. It is by the mere casual
mention of contemporary writers that we have any notice of this
circumstance, which appears to have been passed over as a matter
of but little moment. He maintained his haughty nature to the last,
for his death is principally ascribed to the morbid melancholy of a
proud but broken spirit.[†] He was an extraordinary character in
savage life. From being a simple Carib warrior, he had risen, by his
enterprise and courage, to be the most powerful cacique and the
dominant spirit of the populous island of Hayti. He was the only
chieftain that appeared to have had sagacity sufficient to foresee the
fatal effects of Spanish ascendency, or military talent to combine
any resistance to its inroads. Had his warriors been of his own
intrepid nature, the war which he raised would have been formidable in the extreme. His fate furnishes, on a narrow scale, a lesson
to human greatness. When the Spaniards first arrived on the coast
of Hayti, their imaginations were inflamed with rumours of a
magnificent prince in the interior, the lord of the Golden House,
the sovereign of the mines of Cibao, who reigned in splendid state
among the mountains; but a short time had elapsed, and this
fancied potentate of the East, stripped of every illusion, was a

[*] *Hist. del Almirante*, cap. 63.

[†] Cura de los Palacios, cap. 131; Peter Martyr, decad. i. lib. iv. Some have
affirmed that Caonabo perished in one of the caravels which foundered in the
harbour of Isabella during the hurricane; but the united testimony of the curate of
Los Palacios, Peter Martyr, and Fernando Columbus, proves that he sailed with
the admiral in his return voyage.

naked and dejected prisoner on the deck of one of their caravels, with none but one of his own wild native heroines to sympathize in his misfortunes. All his importance vanished with his freedom; scarce any mention is made of him during his captivity; and with innate qualities of a high and heroic nature, he perished with the obscurity of one of the vulgar.

Envy and malice had been but too successful in undermining the popularity of Columbus. It is impossible to keep up a state of excitement for any length of time, even by miracles. The world, at first, is prompt and lavish in its admiration, but soon grows cool, distrusts its late enthusiasm, and fancies it has been defrauded of what it bestowed with such prodigality. It is then that the caviller who had been silenced by the general applause puts in his insidious suggestion, detracts from the merit of the declining favourite, and succeeds in rendering him an object of doubt and censure, if not absolute aversion. In three short years the public had become familiar with the stupendous wonder of a newly-discovered world, and was now open to every insinuation derogatory to the fame of the discoverer and the importance of his enterprises.

The circumstances which attended the present arrival of Columbus were little calculated to diminish the growing prejudices of the populace. When the motley crowd of mariners and adventurers who had embarked with such sanguine expectations landed from the vessels in the port of Cadiz, instead of a joyous crew, bounding on shore, flushed with success, and laden with the spoils of the golden Indies, a feeble train of wretched men crawled forth, emaciated by the diseases of the colony and the hardships of the voyage, who carried in their yellow countenances, says an old writer, a mockery of that gold which had been the object of their search, and who had nothing to relate of the New World but tales of sickness, poverty, and disappointment.

Columbus endeavoured, as much as possible, to counteract these unfavourable appearances, and to revive the languishing enthusiasm of the public. He dwelt upon the importance of his recent discoveries along the coast of Cuba, where, as he supposed, he had arrived nearly to the Aurea Chersonesus of the ancients, bordering on some of the richest provinces of Asia. Above all, he boasted of his discovery of the abundant mines on the south side of Hispaniola, which he persuaded himself were those of the ancient Ophir. The public listened to these accounts with sneering incredulity; or if for a moment a little excitement was occasioned, it was quickly destroyed by gloomy pictures drawn by disappointed adventurers.

In the harbour of Cadiz, Columbus found three caravels, commanded by Pedro Alonzo Niño, on the point of sailing with supplies for the colony. Nearly a year had elapsed without any relief of the kind, four caravels which had sailed in the preceding January having been lost on the coast of the Peninsula.[*] Having read the royal letters and despatches of which Niño was the bearer, and being informed of the wishes of the sovereigns, as well as of the state of the public mind, Columbus wrote by this opportunity, urging the Adelantado to endeavour, by every means, to bring the island into a peaceful and productive state, appeasing all discontents and commotions, and seizing and sending to Spain all caciques, or their subjects, who should be concerned in the deaths of any of the colonists. He recommended the most unremitting diligence in exploring and working the mines recently discovered on the river Hayna, and that a place should be chosen in the neighbourhood and a seaport founded. Pedro Alonzo Niño set sail with the three caravels on the 17th of June.

Tidings of the arrival of Columbus having reached the sovereigns, he received a gracious letter from them, dated at Almazen, 12th of July 1496, congratulating him on his safe return, and inviting him to court when he should have recovered from the fatigues of his voyage. The kind terms in which this letter was couched were calculated to reassure the heart of Columbus, who, ever since the mission of the arrogant Aguado, had considered himself out of favour with the sovereigns and fallen into disgrace. As a proof of the dejection of his spirits, we are told that when he made his appearance this time in Spain he was clad in a humble garb resembling in form and colour the habit of a Franciscan monk, simply girded with a cord, and that he had suffered his beard to grow like the brethren of that order.[†] This was probably in fulfilment of some penitential vow made in a moment of danger or despondency – a custom prevalent in those days, and frequently

[*] Muñoz, *Hist. N. Mundo*, lib. vi.
[†] Cura de los Palacios, cap. 131; Oviedo, lib ii. cap. 13.

observed by Columbus. It betokened, however, much humility and depression of spirit, and afforded a striking contrast to his appearance on his former triumphant return. He was doomed, in fact, to yield repeated examples of the reverses to which those are subject who have once launched from the safe shores of obscurity on the fluctuating waves of popular opinion.

However indifferent Columbus might be to his own personal appearance, he was anxious to keep alive the interest in his discoveries, fearing continually that the indifference awakening towards him might impede their accomplishment. On his way to Burgos, therefore, where the sovereigns were expected, he made a studious display of the curiosities and treasures which he had brought from the New World. Among these were collars, bracelets, anklets, and coronets of gold, the spoils of various caciques, and which were considered as trophies won from barbaric princes of the rich coasts of Asia or the islands of the Indian seas. It is a proof of the petty standard by which the sublime discovery of Columbus was already estimated, that he had to resort to this management to dazzle the gross perceptions of the multitude by the mere glare of gold.

He carried with him several Indians also, decorated after their savage fashion, and glittering with golden ornaments, among whom were the brother and nephew of Caonabo, the former about thirty years of age, the latter only ten. They were brought merely to visit the king and queen, that they might be impressed with an idea of the grandeur and power of the Spanish sovereigns, after which they were to be restored in safety to their country. Whenever they passed through any principal place, Columbus put a massive collar and chain of gold upon the brother of Caonabo, as being cacique of the golden country of Cibao. The curate of Los Palacios, who entertained the discoverer and his Indian captives for several days in his house, says that he had this chain of gold in his hands, and that it weighed six hundred castellanos.* The worthy curate likewise makes mention of various Indian masks and images of wood or cotton, wrought with fantastic faces of animals, all of which he supposed were representations of the devil, who, he concludes, must be the object of adoration of these islanders.†

---

* Equivalent to the value of three thousand one hundred and ninety-five dollars of the present time.

† Cura de los Palacios, cap. 131.

The reception of Columbus by the sovereigns was different from what he had anticipated, for he was treated with distinguished favour, nor was any mention made either of the complaints of Margarite and Boyle, or the judicial inquiries conducted by Aguado. However these may have had a transient effect on the minds of the sovereigns, they were too conscious of the great deserts of Columbus, and the extraordinary difficulties of his situation, not to tolerate what they may have considered errors on his part.

Encouraged by the favourable countenance he experienced, and by the interest with which the sovereigns listened to his account of his recent voyage along the coast of Cuba, and the discovery of the mines of Hayna, which he failed not to represent as the Ophir of the ancients, Columbus now proposed a further enterprise, by which he promised to make yet more extensive discoveries, and to annex Terra Firma to their dominions. For this purpose he asked eight ships; two to be despatched to the island of Hispaniola with supplies, the remaining six to be put under his command for a voyage of discovery. The sovereigns readily promised to comply with his request, and were probably sincere in their intentions to do so; but in the performance of their promise Columbus was doomed to meet with intolerable delay, partly in consequence of the operation of public events, partly in consequence of the intrigues of men of office – the two great influences which are continually diverting and defeating the designs of princes.

The resources of Spain were at this moment tasked to the utmost by the ambition of Ferdinand, who lavished all his revenues in warlike expenses and in subsidies. While maintaining a contest of deep and artful policy with France, with the ultimate aim of grasping the sceptre of Naples, he was laying the foundation of a wide and powerful connection by the marriages of the royal children, who were now maturing in years. At this time arose that family alliance which afterwards consolidated such an immense empire under his grandson and successor Charles V.

While a large army was maintained in Italy, under Gonsalvo of Cordova, to assist the King of Naples in recovering his throne, of which he had been suddenly dispossessed by Charles VIII of France, other armies were required on the frontiers of Spain, which were menaced with a French invasion. Squadrons also had

to be employed for the safeguard of the Mediterranean and
Atlantic coasts of the Peninsula; while a magnificent armada of
upwards of a hundred ships, having on board twenty thousand
persons, many of them of the first nobility, was despatched to
convoy the Princess Juana to Flanders, to be married to Philip,
Archduke of Austria, and to bring back his sister Margarita, the
destined bride of Prince Juan.

These widely-extended operations, both of war and amity, put
all the land and naval forces into requisition. They drained the
royal treasury, and engrossed the thoughts of the sovereigns,
obliging them also to journey from place to place in their dominions With such cares of an immediate and homefelt nature
pressing upon their minds, the distant enterprises of Columbus
were easily neglected or postponed. They had hitherto been
sources of expense instead of profit, and there were artful counsellors ever ready to whisper in the royal ear that they were likely
to continue so. What, in the ambitious eyes of Ferdinand, was
the acquisition of a number of wild, uncultivated, and distant
islands, to that of the brilliant domain of Naples; or the intercourse with naked and barbaric princes, to that of an alliance
with the most potent sovereigns of Christendom? Columbus
had the mortification, therefore, to see armies levied and squadrons employed in idle contests about a little point of territory in
Europe, and a vast armada, of upwards of a hundred sail, destined
to the ostentatious service of convoying a royal bride, while
he vainly solicited a few caravels to prosecute his discovery of
a world.

At length, in the autumn, six millions of maravedies were
ordered to be advanced to Columbus for the equipment of his
promised squadron.* Just as the sum was about to be delivered, a
letter was received from Pedro Alonzo Niño, who had arrived at
Cadiz with his three caravels, on his return from the island of
Hispaniola. Instead of proceeding to court in person, or forwarding the despatches of the Adelantado, he had gone to visit his
family at Huelva, taking the despatches with him, and merely
writing in a vaunting style that he had a great amount of gold on
board of his ships.†

---

* Equivalent to 86,956 dollars of the present day.
† Las Casas, *Hist. Ind.*, lib i, cap. 123, MS.

This was triumphant intelligence to Columbus, who immediately concluded that the new mines were in operation, and the treasures of Ophir about to be realized. The letter of Niño, however, was fated to have a most injurious effect on his concerns.

The king at that moment was in immediate want of money to repair the fortress of Salza, in Roussillon, which had been sacked by the French. The six millions of maravedies about to be advanced to Columbus were forthwith appropriated to patch up the shattered castle, and an order was given for the amount to be paid out of the gold brought by Niño. It was not until the end of December, when Niño arrived at court and delivered the despatches of the Adelantado, that his boast of gold was discovered to be a mere figure of speech, and that his caravels were, in fact, freighted with Indian prisoners, from the sale of whom the vaunted gold was to arise.

It is difficult to describe the vexatious effects of this absurd hyperbole. The hopes of Columbus of great and immediate profit from the mines were suddenly cast down, the zeal of his few advocates was cooled, an air of empty exaggeration was given to his enterprises, and his enemies pointed with scorn and ridicule to the wretched cargoes of the caravels as the boasted treasures of the New World. The report brought by Niño and his crew represented the colony as in a disastrous condition, and the despatches of the Adelantado pointed out the importance of immediate supplies; but in proportion as the necessity of the case was urgent, the measure of relief was tardy. All the unfavourable representations hitherto made seemed corroborated, and the invidious cry of 'great cost and little gain' was revived by those politicians of petty sagacity and microscopic eye, who, in all great undertakings, can discern the immediate expense, without having scope of vision to embrace the future profit.

It was not until the following spring of 1497 that the concerns of
Columbus and of the New World began to receive serious attention from the sovereigns. The fleet had returned from Flanders
with the Princess Margarita of Austria. Her nuptials with Prince
Juan, the heir-apparent, had been celebrated at Burgos, the capital
of Old Castile, with extraordinary splendour. All the grandees, the
dignitaries, and chivalry of Spain, together with ambassadors from
the principal potentates of Christendom, were assembled on the
occasion. Burgos was for some time a scene of chivalrous pageant
and courtly revel, and the whole kingdom celebrated with great
rejoicings this powerful alliance, which seemed to insure to the
Spanish sovereigns a continuance of their extraordinary prosperity.

In the midst of these festivities, Isabella, whose maternal heart
had recently been engrossed by the marriages of her children, now
that she was relieved from these concerns of a tender and domestic
nature, entered into the affairs of the New World with a spirit that
showed she was determined to place them upon a substantial
foundation, as well as clearly to define the powers and reward the
services of Columbus. To her protecting zeal all the provisions in
favour of Columbus must be attributed; for the king began to look
coldly on him, and the royal counsellors who had most influence
in the affairs of the Indies were his enemies.

Various royal ordinances dated about this time manifest the
generous and considerate disposition of the queen. The rights,
privileges, and dignities granted to Columbus at Santa Fé were
again confirmed; a tract of land in Hispaniola, fifty leagues in
length and twenty-five in breadth, was offered to him, with the
title of duke or marquess. This, however, Columbus had the
forbearance to decline. He observed that it would only increase
the envy which was already so virulent against him, and would

cause new misrepresentations, as he should be accused of paying more attention to the settlement and improvement of his own possessions than of any other part of the island.*

As the expenses of the expedition had hitherto far exceeded the returns, Columbus had incurred debt rather than reaped profit from the share he had been permitted to take in them. He was relieved, therefore, from his obligation to bear an eighth part of the cost of the past enterprises, excepting the sum which he had advanced towards the first voyage; at the same time, however, he was not to claim any share of what had hitherto been brought from the island. For three ensuing years he was to be allowed an eighth of the gross proceeds of every voyage, and an additional tenth after the costs had been deducted. After the expiration of the three years, the original terms of agreement were to be resumed.

To gratify his honourable ambition also, and to perpetuate in his family the distinction gained by his illustrious deeds, he was allowed the right of establishing a mayorazgo, or perpetual entail of his estates, so that they might always descend with his titles of nobility. This he shortly after exercised in a solemn testament executed at Seville in the early part of 1498, by which he devised his estates to his own male descendants, and on their failure to the male descendants of his brothers, and in default of male heirs to the females of his lineage.

The heir was always to bear the arms of the admiral, to seal with them, to sign with his signature, and in signing never to use any other title than simply 'The Admiral', whatever other titles might be given him by the king, and used by him on other occasions. Such was the noble pride with which he valued this title of his real greatness.

In this testament he made ample provision for his brother, the Adelantado, his son Fernando, and his brother Don Diego, the last of whom, he intimates, had a desire to enter into ecclesiastical life. He ordered that a tenth part of the revenues arising from the mayorazgo should be devoted to pious and charitable purposes, and in relieving all poor persons of his lineage. He made provisions for the giving of marriage-portions to the poor females of his family. He ordered that a married person of his kindred who had been born in his native city of Genoa should be maintained there

* Las Casas, *Hist. Ind.*, lib. i. cap. 123.

in competence and respectability, by way of keeping a domicile for the family there; and he commanded whoever should inherit the mayorazgo always to do everything in his power for the honour, prosperity, and increase of the city of Genoa, provided it should not be contrary to the service of the church and the interests of the Spanish crown. Among various other provisions in this will, he solemnly provides for his favourite scheme, the recovery of the Holy Sepulchre. He orders his son Diego, or whoever else may inherit his estate, to invest from time to time as much money as he can spare in stock in the bank of St George in Genoa, to form a permanent fund, with which he is to stand ready at any time to follow and serve the king in the conquest of Jerusalem. Or should the king not undertake such enterprise, then, when the funds have accumulated to sufficient amount, to set on foot a crusade at his own charge and risk, in hopes that, seeing his determination, the sovereigns may be induced either to adopt the undertaking or to authorize him to pursue it in their name.

Besides this special undertaking for the Catholic faith, he charges his heir, in case there should arise any schism in the church, or any violence menacing its prosperity, to throw himself at the feet of the Pope, and devote his person and property to defend the church from all insult and spoliation. Next to the service of God, he enjoins loyalty to the throne, commanding him at all times to serve the sovereigns and their heirs faithfully and zealously, even to the loss of life and estate. To insure the constant remembrance of this testament, he orders his heir that, before he confesses, he shall give it to his father confessor to read, who is to examine him upon his faithful fulfilment of its conditions.

As Columbus had felt aggrieved by the general license granted in April 1495 to make discoveries in the New World, considering it as interfering with his prerogatives, a royal edict was issued on the 2nd of June 1497, retracting whatever might be prejudicial to his interests, or to the previous grants made him by the crown. 'It was never our intention,' said the sovereigns in their edict, 'in any way to affect the rights of the said Don Christopher Columbus, nor to allow the conventions, privileges, and favours which we have granted him to be encroached upon or violated; but, on the contrary, in consequence of the services which he has rendered us, we intend to confer still further favours on him.' Such, there is every reason to believe, was the sincere intention of the magnanimous Isabella; but the stream of her royal bounty was poisoned or diverted by the base channels through which it flowed.

The favour shown to Columbus was extended likewise to his family. The titles and prerogatives of Adelantado with which he had invested his brother Don Bartholomew had at first awakened the displeasure of the king, who jealously reserved all high dignities of the kind to be granted exclusively by the crown. By a royal letter, the office was now conferred upon Don Bartholomew, as if through spontaneous favour of the sovereigns, no allusion being made to his having previously enjoyed it.

While all these measures were taken for the immediate gratification of Columbus, others were adopted for the interests of the colony. Permission was granted him to take out three hundred and thirty persons in royal pay, of whom forty were to be escuderos or servants, one hundred foot-soldiers, thirty sailors, thirty shipboys, twenty miners, fifty husbandmen, ten gardeners, twenty mechanics of various kinds, and thirty females. He was subsequently permitted to increase the number, if he thought proper, to five hundred; but the additional individuals were to be paid out of the produce and merchandise of the colony. He was likewise authorized to grant lands to all such as were disposed to cultivate vineyards, orchards, sugar plantations, or to form any other rural establishments, on condition that they should reside as householders on the island for four years after such grant, and that all the brazil-wood and precious metals found on their lands should be reserved to the crown.

Nor were the interests of the unhappy natives forgotten by the compassionate heart of Isabella. Notwithstanding the sophisms by which their subjection and servitude were made matters of civil and divine right, and sanctioned by the political prelates of the day, Isabella always consented with the greatest reluctance to the slavery even of those who were taken in open warfare, while her utmost solicitude was exerted to protect the unoffending part of this helpless and devoted race. She ordered that the greatest care should be taken of their religious instruction, and the greatest leniency shown in collecting the tributes imposed upon them, with all possible indulgence to defalcators. In fact, the injunctions given with respect to the treatment both of Indians and Spaniards are the only indications in the royal edicts of any impression having been made by the complaints against Columbus of severity in his government. It was generally recommended by the sovereigns that, whenever the public safety did not require stern measures, there should be manifested a disposition to lenity and easy rule.

When every intention was thus shown on the part of the crown to despatch the expedition to the colony, unexpected difficulties arose on the part of the public. The charm was dispelled which in the preceding voyage had made every adventurer crowd into the service of Columbus. An odium had been industriously thrown upon his enterprises, and his new-found world, instead of a region of wealth and delight, was considered a land of poverty and disaster. There was a difficulty in procuring either ships or men for the voyage. To remedy the first of these deficiencies, one of those arbitrary orders was issued so opposite to our present ideas of commercial policy, empowering the officers of the crown to press into the service whatever ships they might judge suitable for the purposed expedition, together with their masters and pilots, and to fix such price for their remuneration as the officers should deem just and reasonable. To supply the want of voluntary recruits, a measure was adopted, at the suggestion of Columbus,* which shows the desperate alternatives to which he was reduced by the great reaction of public sentiment. This was to commute the sentences of criminals condemned to banishment, to the galleys, or to the mines, into transportation to new settlements, where they were to labour in the public service without pay – those whose sentence was banishment for life, to be transported for ten years; those banished for a specific term, to be transported for half that time. A general pardon was published for all malefactors at large who within a certain time should surrender themselves to the admiral and embark for the colonies – those who had committed offences meriting death, to serve for two years; those whose misdeeds were of a lighter nature, to serve for one year.† Those only were excepted from this indulgence who had committed heresy, treason, coining, murder, and certain other specific crimes. This pernicious measure, calculated to poison the population of an infant community at its very source, was a fruitful cause of trouble

* Las Casas, *Hist. Ind.*, lib. i. cap. 112, MS.
† Muñoz, lib. vi. § 19.

to Columbus, and of misery and detriment to the colony. It has been frequently adopted by various nations, whose superior experience should have taught them better, and has proved the bane of many a rising settlement. It is assuredly as unnatural for a metropolis to cast forth its crimes and vices upon its colonies, as it would be for a parent wilfully to ingraft disease upon his children. In both instances the obligation of nature is vitiated; nor should it be matter of surprise if the seeds of evil thus sown should bring forth bitter retribution.

Notwithstanding all these violent expedients, there was still a ruinous delay in fitting out the expedition. This is partly accounted for by changes which took place in the persons appointed to superintend the affairs of the Indies. These concerns had for a time been consigned to Antonio de Torres, in whose name, conjointly with that of Columbus, many of the official documents had been made out. In consequence of high and unreasonable demands on the part of Torres, he was removed from office, and Juan Rodriguez de Fonseca, Bishop of Badajoz, reinstated. The papers had therefore to be made out anew, and fresh contracts formed. While these concerns were tardily attended to, the queen was suddenly overwhelmed with affliction by the death of her only son Prince Juan, whose nuptials had been celebrated with such splendour in the spring. It was the first of a series of domestic calamities which assailed her affectionate heart, and overwhelmed her with affliction for the remainder of her days. In the midst of her distress, however, she still thought of Columbus. In consequence of his urgent representations of the misery to which the colony must be reduced, two ships were despatched in the beginning of 1498, under the command of Pedro Fernandez Coronal, freighted with supplies. The necessary funds were advanced by the queen herself, out of the moneys intended to form the endowment of her daughter Isabella, then betrothed to Emanuel, King of Portugal. An instance of her kind feeling toward Columbus was also evinced in the time of her affliction: his two sons, Diego and Fernando, had been pages to the deceased prince; the queen now took them, in the same capacity, into her own service.

With all this zealous disposition on the part of the queen, Columbus still met with the most injurious and disheartening delays in preparing the six remaining vessels for his voyage. His

cold-blooded enemy Fonseca, having the superintendence of
Indian affairs, was enabled to impede and retard all his plans. The
various petty officers and agents employed in the concerns of the
armament were many of them minions of the bishop, and knew
that they were gratifying him in annoying Columbus. They
looked upon the latter as a man declining in popularity, who
might be offended with impunity. They scrupled not, therefore,
to throw all kinds of difficulties in his path, and to treat him
occasionally with that arrogance which petty and ignoble men in
place are prone to exercise.

It seems almost incredible at the present day that such important
and glorious enterprises should have been subject to such despicable molestations. Columbus bore them all with silent indignation.
He was a stranger in the land he was benefiting. He felt that the
popular tide was setting against him, and that it was necessary to
tolerate many present grievances for the sake of effecting his great
purposes. So wearied and disheartened, however, did he become
by the impediments artfully thrown in his way, and so disgusted
by the prejudices of the fickle public, that he at one time thought
of abandoning his discoveries altogether. He was chiefly induced
to persevere by his grateful attachment to the queen, and his
desire to achieve something that might cheer and animate her
under her afflictions.*

At length, after all kinds of irritating delays, the six vessels were
fitted for sea, though it was impossible to conquer the popular
repugnance to the service sufficiently to enlist the allotted number
of men. In addition to the persons in employ already enumerated,
a physician, surgeon, and apothecary were sent out for the relief of
the colony, and several priests to replace Friar Boyle and certain of
his discontented brethren, while a number of musicians were
embarked by the admiral to cheer and enliven the colonists.

The insolence which Columbus had suffered from the minions
of Fonseca throughout this long protracted time of preparation
harassed him to the last moment of his sojourn in Spain, and
followed him to the very water's edge. Among the worthless
hirelings who had annoyed him, the most noisy and presuming was
one Ximeno Breviesca, treasurer or accountant of Fonseca. He was
not an old Christian, observes the venerable Las Casas, by which it

* Letter of Columbus to the nurse of Prince Juan.

is to be understood that he was either a Jew or a Moor converted to the Catholic faith. He had an impudent front and an unbridled tongue, and, echoing the sentiments of his patron the bishop, had been loud in his abuse of the admiral and his enterprises. The very day when the squadron was on the point of weighing anchor, Columbus was assailed by the insolence of this Ximeno, either on the shore when about to embark, or on board of his ship where he had just entered. In the hurry of the moment he forgot his usual self-command; his indignation, hitherto repressed, suddenly burst forth. He struck the despicable minion to the ground, and kicked him repeatedly, venting in this unguarded paroxysm the accumulated griefs and vexations which had long rankled in his mind.[*]

Nothing could demonstrate more strongly what Columbus had previously suffered from the machinations of unworthy men than this transport of passion, so unusual in his well-governed temper. He deeply regretted it, and in a letter written some time afterwards to the sovereigns he endeavoured to obviate the injury it might do him in their opinion, through the exaggeration and false colouring of his enemies. His apprehensions were not ill-founded, for Las Casas attributes the humiliating measures shortly after adopted by the sovereigns toward Columbus to the unfavourable impression produced by this affair. It had happened near at home, as it were under the very eye of the sovereigns; it spoke, therefore, more quickly to their feelings than more important allegations from a distance. The personal castigation of a public officer was represented as a flagrant instance of the vindictive temper of Columbus, and a corroboration of the charges of cruelty and oppression sent from the colony. As Ximeno was a creature of the invidious Fonseca, the affair was represented to the sovereigns in the most odious point of view. Thus the generous intentions of princes, and the exalted services of their subjects, are apt to be defeated by the intervention of cold and crafty men in place. By his implacable hostility to Columbus, and the secret obstructions which he threw in the way of the most illustrious of human enterprises, Fonseca has insured perpetuity to his name, coupled with the contempt of every generous mind.

---

[*] Las Casas, *Hist. Ind.*, lib. i. cap. 126, MS.

BOOK 10

CHAPTER I

1498

On the 30th of May 1498, Columbus set sail from the port of San Lucar de Barrameda, with his squadron of six vessels, on his third voyage of discovery. The route he proposed to take was different from that pursued in his former voyages. He intended to depart from the Cape de Verde Islands, sailing to the south-west until he should come under the equinoctial line; then to steer directly westward with the favour of the trade-winds, until he should arrive at land, or find himself in the longitude of Hispaniola. Various considerations induced him to adopt this course. In his preceding voyage, when he coasted the southern side of Cuba, under the belief that it was the continent of Asia, he had observed that it swept off toward the south. From this circumstance, and from information gathered among the natives of the Caribbee Islands, he was induced to believe that a great tract of the mainland lay to the south of the countries he had already discovered. King John II of Portugal appears to have entertained a similar idea, as Herrera records an opinion expressed by that monarch that there was a continent in the southern ocean.[*] If this were the case, it was supposed by Columbus that, in proportion as he approached the equator and extended his discoveries to climates more and more under the torrid influence of the sun, he should find the productions of nature sublimated by its rays to more perfect and precious qualities. He was strengthened in this belief by a letter written to him, at the command of the queen, by one Jayme Ferrer, an eminent and learned lapidary, who, in the course of his trading for precious stones and metals, had been in the Levant and in various

[*] Herrera, *Hist. Ind*, decad. i. lib iii. cap. 9.

parts of the East, had conversed with the merchants of the remote parts of Asia and Africa, and the natives of India, Arabia, and Ethiopia, and was considered deeply versed in geography generally, but especially in the natural histories of those countries whence the valuable merchandise in which he dealt was procured. In this letter Ferrer assured Columbus that, according to his experience, the rarest objects of commerce, such as gold, precious stones, drugs, and spices, were chiefly to be found in the regions about the equinoctial line, where the inhabitants were black or darkly coloured, and that until the admiral should arrive among people of such complexions, he did not think he would find those articles in great abundance.*

Columbus expected to find such people more to the south. He recollected that the natives of Hispaniola had spoken of black men who had once come to their island from the south and south-east, the heads of whose javelins were of a sort of metal which they called guanin. They had given the admiral specimens of this metal, which, on being assayed in Spain, proved to be a mixture of eighteen parts gold, six silver, and eight copper, a proof of valuable mines in the country whence they came. Charlevoix conjectures that these black people may have come from the Canaries, or the western coast of Africa, and been driven by tempest to the shores of Hispaniola.† It is probable, however, that Columbus had been misinformed as to their colour, or had misunderstood his informants. It is difficult to believe that the natives of Africa, or the Canaries, could have performed a voyage of such magnitude in the frail and scantily provided barks they were accustomed to use.

It was to ascertain the truth of all these suppositions, and, if correct, to arrive at the favoured and opulent countries about the equator, inhabited by people of similar complexions with those of the Africans under the line, that Columbus in his present voyage to the New World took a course much farther to the south than that which he had hitherto pursued.

Having heard that a French squadron was cruising off Cape St Vincent, he stood to the south-west after leaving San Lucar, touching at the islands of Porto Santo and Madeira, where he remained a few days, taking in wood and water and other supplies,

* Navarrete, *Colec.*, tom. ii. doc. 68.
† Charlevoix, *Hist. St Domingo*, lib. iii. p. 162.

and then continued his course to the Canary Islands. On the 19th
of June he arrived at Gomara, where there lay at anchor a French
cruiser with two Spanish prizes. On seeing the squadron of Columbus standing into the harbour, the captain of the privateer put to
sea in all haste, followed by his prizes; one of which, in the hurry of
the moment, left part of her crew on shore, making sail with only
four of her armament and six Spanish prisoners. The admiral at first
mistook them for merchant ships alarmed by his warlike appearance. When informed of the truth, however, he sent three of his
vessels in pursuit; but they were too distant to be overtaken. The
six Spaniards, however, on board of one of the prizes, seeing
assistance at hand, rose on their captors, and the admiral's vessel
coming up, the prize was retaken and brought back in triumph to
the port. The admiral relinquished the ship to the captain, and gave
up the prisoners to the governor of the island, to be exchanged for
six Spaniards carried off by the cruiser.[*]

Leaving Gomara on the 21st of June, Columbus divided his
squadron off the island of Ferro: three of his ships he despatched
direct for Hispaniola, to carry supplies to the colony. One of these
ships was commanded by Alonzo Sanchez de Carvajal, native of
Baeza, a man of much worth and integrity; the second by Pedro
de Arana of Cordova, brother of Doña Beatrix Henriquez, the
mother of the admiral's second son Fernando. He was cousin also
of the unfortunate officer who commanded the fortress of La
Navidad at the time of the massacre. The third was commanded
by Juan Antonio Columbus (or Colombo), a Genoese, related to
the admiral, and a man of much judgment and capacity. These
captains were alternately to have the command and bear the
signal light a week at a time. The admiral carefully pointed out
their course. When they came in sight of Hispaniola, they were
to steer for the south side, for the new port and town which he
supposed to be by this time established in the mouth of the
Ozema, according to royal orders sent out by Coronal. With the
three remaining vessels the admiral prosecuted his voyage towards the Cape de Verde Islands. The ship in which he sailed
was decked, the other two were merchant caravels.[†] As he advanced within the tropics, the change of climate and the close

* *Hist. del Almirante*, cap. 65
† Peter Martyr, decad. i. lib. vi.

and sultry weather brought on a severe attack of the gout, followed by a violent fever. Notwithstanding his painful illness, he enjoyed the full possession of his faculties, and continued to keep his reckoning and make his observations with his usual vigilance and minuteness.

On the 27th of June he arrived among the Cape de Verde Islands, which, instead of the freshness and verdure which their name would betoken, presented an aspect of the most cheerless sterility. He remained among these islands but a very few days, being disappointed in his expectation of obtaining goat's flesh for ships' provisions, and cattle for stock for the island of Hispaniola. To procure them would require some delay. In the meantime the health of himself and of his people suffered under the influence of the weather. The atmosphere was loaded with clouds and vapours; neither sun nor star was to be seen. A sultry, depressing temperature prevailed, and the livid looks of the inhabitants bore witness to the insalubrity of the climate.*

Leaving the island of Buena Vista on the 5th of July, Columbus stood to the south-west, intending to continue on until he found himself under the equinoctial line. The currents, however, which ran to the north and north-west among these islands impeded his progress, and kept him for two days in sight of the Island del Fuego. The volcanic summit of this island, which, seen at a distance, resembled a church with a lofty steeple, and which was said at times to emit smoke and flames, was the last point discerned of the Old World.

Continuing to the south-west about one hundred and twenty leagues, he found himself, on the 13th of July, according to his observations, in the fifth degree of north latitude. He had entered that region which extends for eight or ten degrees on each side of the line, and is known among seamen by the name of the calm latitudes. The trade-winds from the south-east and north-east, meeting in the neighbourhood of the equator, neutralize each other, and a steady calmness of the elements is produced. The whole sea is like a mirror, and vessels remain almost motionless, with flapping sails, the crews panting under the heat of a vertical sun unmitigated by any refreshing breeze. Weeks are sometimes employed in crossing this torpid tract of the ocean.

* *Hist. del Almirante*, cap. 65.

The weather for some time past had been cloudy and oppressive, but on the 13th there was a bright and burning sun. The wind suddenly fell, and a dead, sultry calm commenced, which lasted for eight days. The air was like a furnace; the tar melted, the seams of the ships yawned; the salt meat became putrid; the wheat was parched as if with fire; the hoops shrank from the wine and water casks, some of which leaked and others burst; while the heat in the holds of the vessels was so suffocating that no one could remain below a sufficient time to prevent the damage that was taking place. The mariners lost all strength and spirits, and sank under the oppressive heat. It seemed as if the old fable of the torrid zone was about to be realized, and that they were approaching a fiery region where it would be impossible to exist. It is true the heavens were, for a great part of the time, overcast, and there were drizzling showers; but the atmosphere was close and stifling, and there was that combination of heat and moisture which relaxes all the energies of the human frame.

During this time the admiral suffered extremely from the gout, but, as usual, the activity of his mind, heightened by his anxiety, allowed him no indulgence or repose. He was in an unknown part of the ocean, where everything depended upon his vigilance and sagacity, and was continually watching the phenomena of the elements, and looking out for signs of land. Finding the heat so intolerable, he altered his course and steered to the south-west, hoping to find a milder temperature farther on, even under the same parallel. He had observed, in his previous voyages, that after sailing westward a hundred leagues from the Azores, a wonderful change took place in the sea and sky, both becoming serene and bland, and the air temperate and refreshing. He imagined that a peculiar mildness and suavity prevailed over a great tract of ocean extending from north to south, into which the navigator, sailing from east to west, would suddenly enter, as if crossing a line. The event seemed to justify his theory; for after making their way slowly for some time to the westward, through an ordeal of heats and calms, with a murky, stifling atmosphere, the ships all at once emerged into a genial region, a pleasant, cooling breeze played over the surface of the sea and gently filled their sails, the close and drizzling clouds broke away, the sky became serene and clear, and the sun shone forth with all its splendour, but no longer with a burning heat.

Columbus had intended, on reaching this temperate tract, to have stood once more to the south and then westward; but the late parching weather had opened the seams of his ships and caused them to leak excessively, so that it was necessary to seek a harbour as soon as possible, where they might be refitted. Much of the provisions also was spoiled, and the water nearly exhausted. He kept on therefore directly to the west, trusting, from the flights of birds and other favourable indications, he should soon arrive at land. Day after day passed without his expectations being realized. The distresses of his men became continually more urgent; wherefore, supposing himself in the longitude of the Caribbee Islands, he bore away towards the northward in search of them.[*]

On the 31st of July there was not above one cask of water remaining in each ship, when, about mid-day, a mariner at the masthead beheld the summits of three mountains rising above the horizon, and gave the joyful cry of land. As the ships drew nearer, it was seen that these mountains were united at the base. Columbus had determined to give the first land he should behold the name of the Trinity. The appearance of these three mountains united into one struck him as a singular coincidence, and, with a solemn feeling of devotion, he gave the island the name of La Trinidad, which it bears at the present day.[†]

[*] *Hist. del Almirante*, cap. 67.
[†] Ibid.

Shaping his course for the island, Columbus approached its eastern
extremity, to which he gave the name of Punta de la Galera, from
a rock in the sea which resembled a galley under sail. He was
obliged to coast for five leagues along the southern shore before he
could find safe anchorage. On the following day (August 1) he
continued coasting westward, in search of water and a convenient
harbour where the vessels might be careened. He was surprised at
the verdure and fertility of the country, having expected to find it
more parched and sterile as he approached the equator; whereas
he beheld groves of palm-trees and luxuriant forests sweeping
down to the sea-side, with fountains and running streams. The
shores were low and uninhabited; but the country rose in the
interior, was cultivated in many places, and enlivened by hamlets
and scattered habitations. In a word, the softness and purity of the
climate, and the verdure, freshness, and sweetness of the country,
appeared to him to equal the delights of early spring in the beautiful province of Valencia.*

Anchoring at a point to which he gave the name of Punta de la
Playa, he sent the boats on shore for water. They found an
abundant and limpid brook, at which they filled their casks; but
there was no safe harbour for the vessels, nor could they meet with
any of the islanders, though they found prints of footsteps, and
various fishing implements left behind in the hurry of flight. There
were tracks also of animals, which they supposed to be goats, but
which must have been deer, with which, as it was afterwards
ascertained, the island abounded.

While coasting the island, Columbus beheld land to the south,
stretching to the distance of more than twenty leagues. It was that
low tract of coast intersected by the numerous branches of the

* Letter of Columbus to the Sovereigns from Hispaniola, Navarrete, *Colec.*, tom. i.

Orinoco; but the admiral, supposing it to be an island, gave it the name of La Isla Santa, little imagining that he now, for the first time, beheld that continent, that Terra Firma, which had been the object of his earnest search.

On the 2nd of August he continued on to the south-west point of Trinidad, which he called Point Arenal. It stretched towards a corresponding point of Terra Firma, making a narrow pass, with a high rock in the centre, to which he gave the name of El Gallo. Near this pass the ships cast anchor. As they were approaching this place, a large canoe, with five-and-twenty Indians, put off from the shore, but paused on coming within bow-shot, and hailed the ships in a language which no one on board understood. Columbus tried to allure the savages on board by friendly signs, by the display of looking-glasses, basins of polished metal, and various glittering trinkets, but all in vain. They remained gazing in mute wonder for above two hours, with their paddles in their hands, ready to take flight on the least attempt to approach them. They were all young men, well formed, and naked, excepting bands and fillets of cotton about their heads, and coloured cloths of the same about their loins. They were armed with bows and arrows, the latter feathered and tipped with bone, and they had bucklers, an article of armour seen for the first time among the inhabitants of the New World.

Finding all other means to attract them ineffectual, Columbus now tried the power of music. He knew the fondness of the Indians for dances executed to the sound of their rude drums and the chant of their traditional ballads. He ordered something similar to be executed on the deck of his ship, where, while one man sang to the beat of the tabor and the sound of other musical instruments, the ship-boys danced, after the popular Spanish fashion. No sooner, however, did this symphony strike up, than the Indians, mistaking it for a signal of hostilities, put their bucklers on their arms, seized their bows, and let fly a shower of arrows. This rude salutation was immediately answered by the discharge of a couple of crossbows, which put the auditors to flight, and concluded this singular entertainment.

Though thus shy of the admiral's vessel, they approached one of the caravels without hesitation, and, running under the stern, had a parley with the pilot, who gave a cap and mantle to the one who appeared to be the chieftain. He received the presents with great

delight, inviting the pilot by signs to come to land, where he
should be well entertained, and receive great presents in return.
On his appearing to consent, they went to shore to wait for him.
The pilot put off in the boat of the caravel to ask permission of the
admiral; but the Indians, seeing him go on board of the hostile
ship, suspected some treachery, and springing into their canoe,
darted away, nor was anything more seen of them.[*]

The complexion and other physical characteristics of these savages
caused much surprise and speculation in the mind of Columbus.
Supposing himself in the seventh degree of latitude, though actually in the tenth, he expected to find the inhabitants similar to the
natives of Africa under the same parallel, who were black and ill-
shaped, with crisped hair, or rather wool; whereas these were well
formed, had long hair, and were even fairer than those more
distant from the equator. The climate, also, instead of being hotter,
as he approached the equinoctial, appeared more temperate. He
was now in the dog-days, yet the nights and mornings were so
cool that it was necessary to use covering as in winter. This is the
case in many parts of the torrid zone, especially in calm weather,
when there is no wind; for nature, by heavy dews in the long
nights of those latitudes, cools and refreshes the earth after the
great heats of the day. Columbus was at first greatly perplexed by
these contradictions to the course of nature, as observed in the Old
World; they were in opposition also to the expectations he had
founded on the theory of Ferrer the lapidary; but they gradually
contributed to the formation of a theory which was springing up
in his active imagination, and which will be presently shown.

After anchoring at Point Arenal the crews were permitted to
land and refresh themselves. There were no runs of water, but by
sinking pits in the sand they soon obtained sufficient to fill the
casks. The anchorage at this place, however, was extremely
insecure. A rapid current set from the eastward through the strait
formed by the mainland and the island of Trinidad, flowing, as
Columbus observed, night and day, with as much fury as the
Guadalquivir when swollen by floods. In the pass between Point
Arenal and its corresponding point the confined current boiled
and raged to such a degree that he thought it was crossed by a reef

---

[*] *Hist. del Almirante*, cap. 88; P. Martyr, decad. i. lib. vi.; Las Casas, *Hist. Ind.*, lib. i.
cap. 138, MS; Letter of Columbus to the Castilian Sovereigns, Navarrete, *Colec.*,
tom. i.

of rocks and shoals, preventing all entrance, with others extending beyond, over which the waters roared like breakers on a rocky shore. To this pass, from its angry and dangerous appearance, he gave the name of Boca del Sierpe (the Mouth of the Serpent). He thus found himself placed between two difficulties. The continual current from the east seemed to prevent all return, while the rocks which appeared to beset the pass threatened destruction if he should proceed. Being on board his ship, late at night, kept awake by painful illness and an anxious and watchful spirit, he heard a terrible roaring from the south, and beheld the sea heaped up, as it were, into a great ridge or hill the height of the ship, covered with foam, and rolling towards him with a tremendous uproar. As this furious surge approached, rendered more terrible in appearance by the obscurity of night, he trembled for the safety of his vessels. His own ship was suddenly lifted up to such a height that he dreaded lest it should be overturned or cast upon the rocks, while another of the ships was torn violently from her anchorage. The crews were for a time in great consternation, fearing they should be swallowed up; but the mountainous surge passed on, and gradually subsided, after a violent contest with the counter-current of the strait.* This sudden rush of water, it is supposed, was caused by the swelling of one of the rivers which flow into the Gulf of Paria, and which were as yet unknown to Columbus.

Anxious to extricate himself from this dangerous neighbour-hood, he sent the boats on the following morning to sound the depth of water at the Boca del Sierpe, and to ascertain whether it was possible for ships to pass through to the northward. To his great joy, they returned with a report that there were several fathoms of water, and currents and eddies setting both ways, either to enter or return. A favourable breeze prevailing, he immediately made sail, and passing through the formidable strait in safety, found himself in a tranquil expanse beyond.

He was now on the inner side of Trinidad. To his left spread the broad gulf since known by the name of Paria, which he supposed to be the open sea, but was surprised, on tasting it, to find the water fresh. He continued northward, towards a mountain at the north-west point of the island, about fourteen leagues from Point

* Letter of Columbus to the Castilian Sovereigns, Navarrete, *Colec.*, tom. i; Herrera, *Hist. Ind.*, decad. i. lib. iii. cap. 10; *Hist. del Almirante*, cap. 69.

Arenal. Here he beheld two lofty capes opposite each other, one
on the island of Trinidad, the other to the west, on the long
promontory of Paria, which stretches from the mainland and forms
the northern side of the gulf, but which Columbus mistook for an
island, and named Isla de Gracia.

Between these capes there was another pass, which appeared
even more dangerous than the Boca del Sierpe, being beset with
rocks, among which the current forced its way with roaring
turbulence. To this pass Columbus gave the name of Boca del
Dragon. Not choosing to encounter its apparent dangers, he
turned northward on Sunday, the 5th of August, and steered along
the inner side of the supposed island of Gracia, intending to keep
on until he came to the end of it, and then to strike northward into
the free and open ocean, and shape his course for Hispaniola.

It was a fair and beautiful coast, indented with fine harbours
lying close to each other; the country cultivated in many places, in
others covered with fruit trees and stately forests, and watered by
frequent streams. What greatly astonished Columbus was still to
find the water fresh, and that it grew more and more so the further
he proceeded; it being that season of the year when the various
rivers which empty themselves into this gulf are swollen by rains,
and pour forth such quantities of fresh water as to conquer the
saltness of the ocean. He was also surprised at the placidity of the
sea, which appeared as tranquil and safe as one vast harbour, so that
there was no need of seeking a port to anchor in.

As yet he had not been able to hold any communication with
the people of this part of the New World. The shores which he
had visited, though occasionally cultivated, were silent and deserted, and, excepting the fugitive party in the canoe at Point
Arenal, he had seen nothing of the natives. After sailing several
leagues along the coast, he anchored, on Monday, the 6th of
August, at a place where there appeared signs of cultivation, and
sent the boats on shore. They found recent traces of people, but
not an individual was to be seen. The coast was hilly, covered with
beautiful and fruitful groves, and abounding with monkeys. Continuing further westward, to where the country was more level,
Columbus anchored in a river.

Immediately a canoe, with three or four Indians, came off to
the caravel nearest to the shore, the captain of which, pretending a

desire to accompany them to land, sprang into their canoe, over-turned it, and, with the assistance of his seamen, secured the Indians as they were swimming. When brought to the admiral, he gave them beads, hawks' bells, and sugar, and sent them highly gratified on shore, where many of their countrymen were assembled. This kind treatment had the usual effect. Such of the natives as had canoes came off to the ships with the fullest confidence. They were tall of stature, finely formed, and free and graceful in their move-ments. Their hair was long and straight; some wore it cut short, but none of them braided it, as was the custom among the natives of Hispaniola. They were armed with bows, arrows, and targets. The men wore cotton cloths about their heads and loins, beautifully wrought with various colours, so as at a distance to look like silk; but the women were entirely naked. They brought bread, maize, and other eatables, with different kinds of beverage, some white, made from maize, and resembling beer, and others green, of a vinous flavour, and expressed from various fruits. They appeared to judge of everything by the sense of smell, as others examine objects by the sight or touch. When they approached a boat, they smelt to it, and then to the people. In like manner everything that was given them was tried. They set but little value upon beads, but were extravagantly delighted with hawks' bells. Brass was also held in high estimation; they appeared to find something ex-tremely grateful in the smell of it, and called it turey, signifying that it was from the skies.*

From these Indians Columbus understood that the name of their country was Paria, and that farther to the west he would find it more populous. Taking several of them to serve as guides and mediators, he proceeded eight leagues westward to a point which he called Aguja, or the Needle. Here he arrived at three o'clock in the morning. When the day dawned he was delighted with the beauty of the country. It was cultivated in many places, highly populous, and adorned with magnificent vegetation; habitations were interspersed among groves laden with fruits and flowers; grape-vines entwined themselves among the trees, and birds of brilliant plumage fluttered from branch to branch. The air was temperate and bland, and sweetened by the fragrance of flowers and blossoms, and numerous fountains and limpid streams kept

---

* Herrera, *Hist. Ind.*, decad. i. lib. iii. cap. 11.

up a universal verdure and freshness. Columbus was so much charmed with the beauty and amenity of this part of the coast that he gave it the name of the Gardens.

The natives came off in great numbers in canoes, of superior construction to those hitherto seen, being very large and light, with a cabin in the centre for the accommodation of the owner and his family. They invited Columbus, in the name of their king, to come to land. Many of them had collars and burnished plates about their necks of that inferior kind of gold called by the Indians guanin. They said that it came from a high land, which they pointed out, at no great distance to the west; but intimated that it was dangerous to go there, either because the inhabitants were cannibals or the place infested by venomous animals.* But what aroused the attention and awakened the cupidity of the Spaniards was the sight of strings of pearls around the arms of some of the natives. These, they informed Columbus, were procured on the sea-coast, on the northern side of Paria, which he still supposed to be an island; and they showed the mother-of-pearl shells whence they had been taken. Anxious for further information, and to procure specimens of these pearls to send to Spain, he despatched the boats to shore. A multitude of the natives came to the beach to receive them, headed by the chief cacique and his son. They treated the Spaniards with profound reverence, as beings descended from heaven, and conducted them to a spacious house, the residence of the cacique, where they were regaled with bread and various fruits of excellent flavour and the different kinds of beverage already mentioned. While they were in the house, the men remained together at one end of it and the women at the other. After they had finished their collation at the house of the cacique, they were taken to that of his son, where a like repast was set before them. These people were remarkably affable, though, at the same time, they possessed a more intrepid and martial air and spirit than the natives of Cuba and Hispaniola. They were fairer, Columbus observes, than any he had yet seen, though so near to the equinoctial line, where he had expected to find them of the colour of Ethiopians. Many ornaments of gold were seen among them, but all of an inferior quality: one Indian had a piece of the size of an apple. They had various kinds of domesticated parrots –

* Letter of Columbus to the Castilian Sovereigns, Navarrete, *Colec.*, tom. i. p. 252.

one of a light-green colour, with a yellow neck, and the tips of the wings of a bright red; others of the size of domestic fowls, and of a vivid scarlet, excepting some azure feathers in the wings. These they readily gave to the Spaniards; but what the latter most coveted were the pearls, of which they saw many necklaces and bracelets among the Indian women. The latter gladly gave them in exchange for hawks' bells or any article of brass, and several specimens of fine pearls were procured for the admiral to send to the sovereigns.

The kindness and amity of this people were heightened by an intelligent demeanour and a martial frankness. They seemed worthy of the beautiful country they inhabited. It was a cause of great concern both to them and the Spaniards that they could not understand each other's language. They conversed, however, by signs; mutual goodwill made their intercourse easy and pleasant; and at the hour of vespers the Spaniards returned on board of their ships highly gratified with their entertainment.*

* Letter of Columbus; Herrera, *Hist. Ind.*, decad. i. lib. iii. cap. 11; *Hist. del Almirante.* cap 70.

CHAPTER 3

1498

The quantity of fine pearls found among the natives of Paria was sufficient to arouse the sanguine anticipations of Columbus. It appeared to corroborate the theory of Ferrer, the learned jeweller, that as he approached the equator he would find the most rare and precious productions of nature. His active imagination, with its intuitive rapidity, seized upon every circumstance in unison with his wishes, and, combining them, drew thence the most brilliant inferences. He had read in Pliny that pearls are generated from drops of dew which fall into the mouths of oysters: if so, what place could be more propitious to their growth and multiplication than the coast of Paria? The dew in those parts was heavy and abundant, and the oysters were so plentiful that they clustered about the roots and pendent branches of the mangrove-trees which grew within the margin of the tranquil sea. When a branch which had drooped for a time in the water was drawn forth, it was found covered with oysters. Las Casas, noticing this sanguine conclusion of Columbus, observes that the shell-fish here spoken of are not of the kind which produce pearl; for that those, by a natural instinct, as if conscious of their precious charge, hide themselves in the deepest water.[*]

Still imagining the coast of Paria to be an island, and anxious to circumnavigate it, and arrive at the place where these pearls were said by the Indians to abound, Columbus left the Gardens on the 10th of August, and continued coasting westward within the gulf in search of an outlet to the north. He observed portions of Terra Firma appearing towards the bottom of the gulf, which he supposed to be islands, and called them Isabeta and Tramontana, and fancied that the desired outlet to the sea must lie between them. As he advanced, however, he found the water

[*] Las Casas, *Hist. Ind.*, cap. 136.

continually growing shallower and fresher, until he did not dare to venture any further with his ship, which, he observed, was of too great a size for expeditions of this kind, being of a hundred tons burden, and requiring three fathoms of water. He came to anchor, therefore, and sent a light caravel, called the *Correo*, to ascertain whether there was an outlet to the ocean between the supposed islands. The caravel returned on the following day, reporting that at the western end of the gulf there was an opening of two leagues, which led to an inner and circular gulf, surrounded by four openings, apparently smaller gulfs, or rather mouths of rivers, from which flowed the great quantity of fresh water that sweetened the neighbouring sea. In fact, from one of these mouths issued the great river the Cuparipari, or, as it is now called, the Paria. To this inner and circular gulf Columbus gave the name of the Gulf of Pearls, through a mistaken idea that they abounded in its waters, though none, in fact, are found there. He still imagined that the four openings of which the mariners spoke might be intervals between islands, though they affirmed that all the land he saw was connected.* As it was impossible to proceed further westward with his ships, he had no alternative but to retrace his course, and seek an exit to the north by the Boca del Dragon. He would gladly have continued for some time to explore this coast, for he considered himself in one of those opulent regions described as the most favoured upon earth, and which increase in riches towards the equator. Imperious considerations, however, compelled him to shorten his voyage and hasten to St Domingo. The sea-stores of his ships were almost exhausted, and the various supplies for the colony with which they were freighted were in danger of spoiling. He was suffering also extremely in his health. Besides the gout, which had rendered him a cripple for the greater part of the voyage, he was afflicted by a complaint in his eyes, caused by fatigue and over-watching, which almost deprived him of sight. Even the voyage along the coast of Cuba, he observes, in which he was three-and-thirty days almost without sleep, had not so injured his eyes and disordered his frame or caused him so much painful suffering as the present.†

---

* *Hist. del Almirante*, cap. 78.
† Letter of Columbus to the Sovereigns, Navarrete, tom. i. p. 252.

On the 11th of August, therefore, he set sail eastward for the
Boca del Dragon, and was borne along with great velocity by the
current, which, however, prevented him from landing again at
his favourite spot, the Gardens. On Sunday the 13th he anchored
near to the Boca, in a fine harbour, to which he gave the name
of Puerto de Gatos, from a species of monkey called gato paulo
with which the neighbourhood abounded. On the margin of the
sea he perceived many trees which, as he thought, produced the
mirabolane, a fruit only found in the countries of the East. There
were great numbers also of mangroves growing within the water,
with oysters clinging to their branches, their mouths open, as he
supposed, to receive the dew which was afterwards to be transformed to pearls.*

On the following morning, the 14th of August, towards noon,
the ships approached the Boca del Dragon, and prepared to venture
through that formidable pass. The distance from Cape Boto, at the
end of Paria, and Cape Lapa, the extremity of Trinidad, is about five
leagues; but in the interval there are two islands, which Columbus
named Caracol and Delphin. The impetuous body of fresh water
which flows through the gulf, particularly in the rainy months of
July and August, is confined at the narrow outlets between these
islands, where it causes a turbulent sea, foaming and roaring as if
breaking over rocks, and rendering the entrance and exit of the
gulf extremely dangerous. The horrors and perils of such places
are always tenfold to discoverers, who have no chart, nor pilot, nor
advice of previous voyager to guide them. Columbus at first apprehended sunken rocks and shoals; but on attentively considering the
commotion of the strait, he attributed it to the conflict between
the prodigious body of fresh water setting through the gulf and
struggling for an outlet and the tide of salt water struggling to enter.
The ships had scarcely ventured into the fearful channel when the
wind died away, and they were in danger every moment of being
thrown upon the rocks or sands. The current of fresh water,
however, gained the victory, and carried them safely through. The
admiral, when once more in the open sea, congratulated himself
upon his escape from this perilous strait, which, he observes, might
well be called the Mouth of the Dragon.†

* Herrera. *Hist. Ind.*, decad. i. lib. iii. cap. 10.
† Herrera, *Hist. Ind.*, decad. i. lib. iii. cap. 11.

He now stood to the westward, running along the outer coast of Paria, still supposing it an island, and intending to visit the Gulf of Pearls, which he imagined to be at the end of it, opening to the sea. He wished to ascertain whether this great body of fresh water proceeded from rivers, as the crew of the caravel *Correo* had affirmed; for it appeared to him impossible that the streams of mere islands, as he supposed the surrounding lands, could furnish such a prodigious volume of water.

On leaving the Boca del Dragon, he saw to the north-east, many leagues distant, two islands, which he called Assumption and Conception – probably those now known as Tobago and Granada. In his course along the northern coast of Paria he saw several other small islands and many fine harbours, to some of which he gave names; but they have ceased to be known by them. On the 15th he discovered the islands of Margarita and Cubagua, afterwards famous for their pearl-fishery. The island of Margarita, about fifteen leagues in length and six in breadth, was well peopled. The little island of Cubagua, lying between it and the mainland, and only about four leagues from the latter, was dry and sterile, without either wood or fresh water, but possessing a good harbour. On approaching this island, the admiral beheld a number of Indians fishing for pearls, who made for the land. A boat being sent to communicate with them, one of the sailors noticed many strings of pearls round the neck of a female. Having a plate of Valencia ware, a kind of porcelain painted and varnished with gaudy colours, he broke it, and presented the pieces to the Indian woman, who gave him in exchange a considerable number of her pearls. These he carried to the admiral, who immediately sent persons on shore well provided with Valencian plates and hawks' bells, for which in a little time he procured about three pounds weight of pearls, some of which were of a very large size, and were sent by him afterwards to the sovereigns as specimens.*

There was great temptation to visit other spots, which the Indians mentioned as abounding in pearls. The coast of Paria, also, continued extending to the westward as far as the eye could reach, rising into a range of mountains, and provoking examination to ascertain whether, as he began to think, it was

* Charlevoix, *Hist. St Domingo*, lib iii. p. 169.

a part of the Asiatic continent. Columbus was compelled, however, though with the greatest reluctance, to forego this most
interesting investigation.

The malady of his eyes had now grown so virulent that he
could no longer take observations or keep a look-out, but had
to trust to the reports of the pilots and mariners. He bore
away, therefore, for Hispaniola, intending to repose there from
the toils of his voyage and to recruit his health, while he should
send his brother, the Adelantado, to complete the discovery of
this important country. After sailing five days to the north-west,
he made the island of Hispaniola on the 19th of August, fifty
leagues to the westward of the river Ozema, the place of his
destination, and anchored on the following morning under the
little island of Beata.

He was astonished to find himself so mistaken in his calculations, and so far below his destined port; but he attributed it
correctly to the force of the current setting out of the Boca del
Dragon, which, while he had lain-to at nights to avoid running
on rocks and shoals, had borne his ship insensibly to the west.
This current, which sets across the Caribbean Sea, and the
continuation of which now bears the name of the Gulf Stream,
was so rapid that on the 15th, though the wind was but moderate,
the ships had made seventy-five leagues in four-and-twenty
hours. Columbus attributed to the violence of this current the
formation of that pass called the Boca del Dragon, where he
supposed it had forced its way through a narrow isthmus that
formerly connected Trinidad with the extremity of Paria. He
imagined, also, that its constant operation had worn away and
inundated the borders of the mainland, gradually producing
that fringe of islands which stretches from Trinidad to the Lucayos or Bahamas, and which, according to his idea, had originally been part of the solid continent. In corroboration of this
opinion, he notices the form of those islands: narrow from north
to south, and extending in length from east to west, in the
direction of the current.*

The island of Beata, where he had anchored, is about thirty
leagues to the west of the river Ozema, where he expected to find
the new sea-port which his brother had been instructed to

* Letter to the King and Queen, Navarrete, *Colec.*, tom. i.

establish. The strong and steady current from the east, however, and the prevalence of winds from that quarter, might detain him for a long time at the island, and render the remainder of his voyage slow and precarious. He sent a boat on shore, therefore, to procure an Indian messenger to take a letter to his brother, the Adelantado. Six of the natives came off to the ships, one of whom was armed with a Spanish crossbow. The admiral was alarmed at seeing a weapon of the kind in the possession of an Indian. It was not an article of traffic, and he feared could only have fallen into his hands by the death of some Spaniard.* He apprehended that further evils had befallen the settlement during his long absence, and that there had again been troubles with the natives.

Having despatched his messenger, he made sail, and arrived off the mouth of the river on the 30th of August. He was met on the way by a caravel, on board of which was the Adelantado, who, having received his letter, had hastened forth with affectionate ardour to welcome his arrival. The meeting of the brothers was a cause of mutual joy. They were strongly attached to each other; each had had his trials and sufferings during their long separation; and each looked with confidence to the other for comfort and relief. Don Bartholomew appears to have always had great deference for the brilliant genius, the enlarged mind, and the commanding reputation of his brother; while the latter placed great reliance, in times of difficulty, on the worldly knowledge, the indefatigable activity, and the lion-hearted courage of the Adelantado.

Columbus arrived almost the wreck of himself. His voyages were always of a nature to wear out the human frame, having to navigate amidst unknown dangers, and to keep anxious watch, at all hours and in all weathers. As age and infirmity increased upon him, these trials became the more severe. His constitution must originally have been wonderfully vigorous; but constitutions of this powerful kind, if exposed to severe hardships at an advanced period of life, when the frame has become somewhat rigid and unaccommodating, are apt to be suddenly broken up, and to be a prey to violent aches and maladies. In this last voyage Columbus had been parched and consumed by fever, racked by gout, and his whole system disordered by incessant watchfulness.

* Las Casas, *Hist. Ind.*, lib. i. cap. 148.

He came into port haggard, emaciated, and almost blind. His spirit, however, was as usual superior to all bodily affliction or decay, and he looked forward with magnificent anticipations to the result of his recent discoveries, which he intended should be immediately prosecuted by his hardy and enterprising brother.

The natural phenomena of a great and striking nature presented to the ardent mind of Columbus in the course of this voyage, led to certain sound deductions and imaginative speculations. The immense body of fresh water flowing into the Gulf of Paria, and thence rushing into the ocean, was too vast to be produced by an island or by islands. It must be the congregated streams of a great extent of country pouring forth in one mighty river; and the land necessary to furnish such a river must be a continent. He now supposed that most of the tracts of land which he had seen about the gulf were connected; that the coast of Paria extended westward far beyond a chain of mountains which he had beheld afar off from Margarita; and that the land opposite to Trinidad, instead of being an island, continued to the south, far beyond the equator, into that hemisphere hitherto unknown to civilized man. He considered all this an extension of the Asiatic continent, thus presuming that the greater part of the surface of the globe was firm land. In this last opinion he found himself supported by authors of the highest name, both ancient and modern; among whom he cites Aristotle and Seneca, St Augustine, and Cardinal Pedro de Aliaco. He lays particular stress also on the assertion of the apocryphal Esdras, that of seven parts of the world, six are dry land, and one part only is covered with water.

The land, therefore, surrounding the Gulf of Paria was but the border of an almost boundless continent, stretching far to the west and to the south, including the most precious regions of the earth, lying under the most auspicious stars and benignant skies, but as yet unknown and uncivilized, free to be discovered and appropriated by any Christian nation. 'May it please our Lord,' he exclaims in his letter to the sovereigns, 'to give long life and health to your highnesses, that you may prosecute this noble enterprise, in which, methinks, God will receive great service, Spain vast increase of grandeur, and all Christians much consolation and delight, since the name of our Saviour will be divulged throughout these lands.'

Thus far the deductions of Columbus, though sanguine, admit of little cavil; but he carried them still further, until they ended in what may appear to some mere chimerical reveries. In his letter to the sovereigns, he stated that, on his former voyages, when he steered westward from the Azores, he had observed, after sailing about a hundred leagues, a sudden and great change in the sky and the stars, the temperature of the air, and the calmness of the ocean. It seemed as if a line ran from north to south, beyond which everything became different. The needle, which had previously inclined toward the north-east, now varied a whole point to the north-west. The sea, hitherto clear, was covered with weeds so dense that in his first voyage he had expected to run aground upon shoals. A universal tranquillity reigned throughout the elements, and the climate was mild and genial, whether in summer or winter. On taking his astronomical observations at night, after crossing that imaginary line, the north star appeared to him to describe a diurnal circle in the heavens of five degrees in diameter.

On his present voyage he had varied his route, and had run southward from the Cape de Verde Islands for the equinoctial line. Before reaching it, however, the heat had become insupportable, and a wind springing up from the east, he had been induced to strike westward, when in the parallel of Sierra Leone in Guinea. For several days he had been almost consumed by scorching and stifling heat under a sultry yet clouded sky, and in a drizzling atmosphere, until he arrived at the ideal line already mentioned, extending from north to south. Here suddenly, to his great relief, he had emerged into serene weather, with a clear blue sky and a sweet and temperate atmosphere. The further he had proceeded west, the more pure and genial he had found the climate, the sea tranquil, the breezes soft and balmy. All these phenomena coincided with those he had remarked at the same line, though farther north, in his former voyages, excepting that here there was no herbage in the sea, and the movements of stars were different. The polar star appeared to him here to describe a diurnal circle of ten degrees instead of five; an augmentation which struck him with astonishment, but which he says he ascertained by observations taken in different nights, with his quadrant. Its greatest altitude at the former place, in the parallel of the Azores, he had found to be ten degrees, and in the present place fifteen.

From these and other circumstances, he was inclined to doubt the received theory with respect to the form of the earth. Philosophers had described it as spherical; but they knew nothing of the part of the world which he had discovered. The ancient part, known to them, he had no doubt was spherical, but he now supposed the real form of the earth to be that of a pear, one part much more elevated than the rest, and tapering upward toward the skies. This part he supposed to be in the interior of this newly-found continent, and immediately under the equator. All the phenomena which he had previously noticed appeared to corroborate this theory. The variations which he had observed in passing the imaginary line running from north to south, he concluded to be caused by the ships having arrived at this supposed swelling of the earth, where they began gently to mount towards the skies into a purer and more celestial atmosphere.[*] The variation of the needle he ascribed to the same cause, being affected by the coolness and mildness of the climate, varying to the north-west in proportion as the ships continued onward on their ascent.[†] So also the altitude of the north star, and the circle it described in the heavens, appeared to be greater, in consequence of being regarded from a greater elevation, less obliquely, and through a purer medium of atmosphere; and these phenomena would be found to increase the more the navigator approached the equator, from the still-increasing eminence of this part of the earth.

He noticed also the difference of climate, vegetation, and people of this part of the New World from those under the same parallel in Africa. There the heat was insupportable, the land parched and

[*] Peter Martyr mentions that the admiral told him that, from the climate of great heat and unwholesome air, he had ascended the back of the sea, as it were ascending a high mountain towards heaven. – Decad. i. lib. vi.

[†] Columbus, in his attempts to account for the variation of the needle, supposed that the north star possessed the quality of the four cardinal points, as did likewise the lodestone – that if the needle were touched with one part of the lodestone, it would point east, with another west, and so on. Wherefore, he adds, those who prepare or magnetize the needles cover the lodestone with a cloth, so that the north part only remains out; that is to say, the part which possesses the virtue of causing the needle to point to the north. – *Hist. del Almirante*, cap. 66.

sterile; the inhabitants were black, with crisped wool, ill-shapen in
their forms, and dull and brutal in their natures. Here, on the
contrary, although the sun was in Leo, he found the noontide heat
moderate, the mornings and evenings fresh and cool, the country
green and fruitful, and covered with beautiful forests; the people
fairer even than those in the lands he had discovered farther north,
having long hair, with well-proportioned and graceful forms,
lively minds, and courageous dispositions. All this, in a latitude so
near to the equator, he attributed to the superior altitude of this
part of the world, by which it was raised into a more celestial
region of the air. On turning northward, through the Gulf of
Paria, he had found the circle described by the north star again to
diminish. The current of the sea also increased in velocity, wearing
away, as has already been remarked, the borders of the continent,
and producing by its incessant operation the adjacent islands. This
was a further confirmation of the idea that he ascended in going
southward and descended in returning northward.

Aristotle had imagined that the highest part of the earth, and
nearest to the skies, was under the antarctic pole. Other sages had
maintained that it was under the arctic. Hence it was apparent that
both conceived one part of the earth to be more elevated and
noble, and nearer to the heavens, than the rest. They did not think
of this eminence being under the equinoctial line, observed Columbus, because they had no certain knowledge of this hemisphere,
but only spoke of it theoretically and from conjecture.

As usual, he assisted his theory by Holy Writ. 'The sun, when
God created it,' he observes, 'was in the first point of the Orient,
or the first light was there.' That place, according to his idea, must
be here, in the remotest part of the East, where the ocean and the
extreme part of India meet under the equinoctial line, and where
the highest point of the earth is situated.

He supposed this apex of the world, though of immense height,
to be neither rugged nor precipitous, but that the land rose to it by
gentle and imperceptible degrees. The beautiful and fertile shores
of Paria were situated on its remote borders, abounding of course
with those precious articles which are congenial with the most
favoured and excellent climates. As one penetrated the interior and
gradually ascended, the land would be found to increase in beauty
and luxuriance and in the exquisite nature of its productions, until

one arrived at the summit under the equator. This he imagined
to be the noblest and most perfect place on earth, enjoying, from
its position, an equality of nights and days, and a uniformity of
seasons, and being elevated into a serene and heavenly temperature, above the heats and colds, the clouds and vapours, the
storms and tempests which deform and disturb the lower regions.
In a word, here he supposed to be situated the original abode of
our first parents, the primitive seat of human innocence and bliss,
the Garden of Eden, or terrestrial paradise!

He imagined this place, according to the opinion of the most
eminent fathers of the church, to be still flourishing, possessed of all
its blissful delights, but inaccessible to mortal feet, excepting by
divine permission. From this height he presumed, though of course
from a great distance, proceeded the mighty stream of fresh water
which filled the Gulf of Paria and sweetened the salt ocean in its
vicinity, being supplied by the fountain mentioned in Genesis as
springing from the tree of life in the Garden of Eden.

Such was the singular speculation of Columbus, which he
details at full length in a letter to the Castilian sovereigns,* citing
various authorities for his opinions, among which were St Augustine, St Isidor, and St Ambrosius, and fortifying his theory with
much of that curious and speculative erudition in which he was
deeply versed.† It shows how his ardent mind was heated by the
magnificence of his discoveries. Shrewd men, in the coolness and
quietude of ordinary life, and in these modern days of cautious
and sober fact, may smile at such a reverie; but it was countenanced by the speculations of the most sage and learned of those
times. And if this had not been the case, could we wonder at any
sally of the imagination in a man placed in the situation of
Columbus? He beheld a vast world rising, as it were, into existence before him, its nature and extent unknown and undefined, as
yet a mere region for conjecture. Every day displayed some new

* Navarrete, *Colec. de Viages*, tom. i. p. 242.

† A great part of these speculations appear to have been founded on the treatise of
the Cardinal Pedro de Aliaco, in which Columbus found a compendium of the
opinions of various eminent authors on the subject, though it is very probable he
consulted many of their works likewise. In the volume of Pedro de Aliaco,
existing in the library of the cathedral at Seville, I have traced the germs of these
ideas in various passages of the text, opposite to which marginal notes have been
made in the handwriting of Columbus.

feature of beauty and sublimity – island after island, where the rocks, he was told, were veined with gold, the groves teemed with spices, or the shores abounded with pearls; interminable ranges of coast, promontory beyond promontory, stretching as far as the eye could reach; luxuriant valleys sweeping away into a vast interior, whose distant mountains, he was told, concealed still happier lands and realms of greater opulence. When he looked upon all this region of golden promise, it was with the glorious conviction that his genius had called it into existence; he regarded it with the triumphant eye of a discoverer. Had not Columbus been capable of these enthusiastic soarings of the imagination, he might, with other sages, have reasoned calmly and coldly in his closet about the probability of a continent existing in the west, but he would never have had the daring enterprise to adventure in search of it into the unknown realms of ocean.

Still, in the midst of his fanciful speculations, we find that sagacity which formed the basis of his character. The conclusion which he drew from the great flow of the Orinoco, that it must be the outpouring of a continent, was acute and striking. A learned Spanish historian has also ingeniously excused other parts of his theory. 'He suspected,' observes he, 'a certain elevation of the globe at one part of the equator: philosophers have since determined the world to be a spheroid, slightly elevated in its equatorial circumference. He suspected that the diversity of temperatures influenced the needle, not being able to penetrate the cause of its inconstant variations: the successive series of voyages and experiments have made this inconstancy more manifest, and have shown that extreme cold sometimes divests the needle of all its virtue. Perhaps new observations may justify the surmise of Columbus. Even his error concerning the circle described by the polar star, which he thought augmented by an optical illusion in proportion as the observer approached the equinox, manifests him a philosopher superior to the time in which he lived.' *

* Muñoz, *Hist. N. Mundo*, lib. vi. § 32.

BOOK II

CHAPTER I

1498

Columbus had anticipated repose from his toils on arriving at Hispaniola, but a new scene of trouble and anxiety opened upon him, destined to impede the prosecution of his enterprises, and to affect all his future fortunes. To explain this, it is necessary to relate the occurrences of the island during his long detention in Spain.

When he sailed for Europe in March, 1496, his brother, Don Bartholomew, who remained as Adelantado, took the earliest measures to execute his directions with respect to the mines recently discovered by Miguel Diaz on the south side of the island. Leaving Don Diego Columbus in command at Isabella, he repaired with a large force to the neighbourhood of the mines, and, choosing a favourable situation in a place most abounding in ore, built a fortress, to which he gave the name of San Christoval. The workmen, however, finding grains of gold among the earth and stone employed in its construction, gave it the name of the Golden Tower.*

The Adelantado remained here three months, superintending the building of the fortress, and making the necessary preparations for working the mines and purifying the ore. The progress of the work, however, was greatly impeded by scarcity of provisions, having frequently to detach a part of the men about the country in quest of supplies. The former hospitality of the island was at an end. The Indians no longer gave their provisions freely; they had learnt from the white men to profit by the necessities of the stranger, and to exact a price for bread. Their scanty stores, also, were soon exhausted, for their frugal habits, and their natural

* Peter Martyr, decad. i. lib. iv.

indolence and improvidence, seldom permitted them to have
more provisions on hand than was requisite for present support.*
The Adelantado found it difficult, therefore, to maintain so large
a force in the neighbourhood, until they should have time to
cultivate the earth, and raise livestock, or should receive supplies
from Spain. Leaving ten men to guard the fortress, with a dog to
assist them in catching utias, he marched with the rest of his men,
about four hundred in number, to Fort Conception, in the
abundant country of the Vega. He passed the whole month of
June collecting the quarterly tribute, being supplied with food by
Guarionex and his subordinate caciques. In the following month
(July 1496) the three caravels commanded by Niño arrived from
Spain, bringing a reinforcement of men, and, what was still more
needed, a supply of provisions. The latter was quickly distributed
among the hungry colonists, but unfortunately a great part had
been injured during the voyage. This was a serious misfortune in
a community where the least scarcity produced murmur and
sedition.

By these ships the Adelantado received letters from his brother,
directing him to found a town and sea-port at the mouth of the
Ozema, near to the new mines. He requested him, also, to send
prisoners to Spain such of the caciques and their subjects as had
been concerned in the death of any of the colonists; that being
considered as sufficient ground, by many of the ablest jurists and
theologians of Spain, for selling them as slaves. On the return of
the caravels, the Adelantado despatched three hundred Indian
prisoners, and three caciques. These formed the ill-starred cargoes
about which Niño had made such absurd vaunting, as though the
ships were laden with treasure; and which had caused such mortification, disappointment, and delay to Columbus.

Having obtained by this arrival a supply of provisions, the
Adelantado returned to the fortress of San Christoval, and thence
proceeded to the Ozema, to choose a site for the proposed
seaport. After a careful examination, he chose the eastern bank of
a natural haven at the mouth of the river. It was easy of access, of
sufficient depth, and good anchorage. The river ran through a
beautiful and fertile country; its waters were pure and salubrious,
and well stocked with fish; its banks were covered with trees

* Peter Martyr, decad. i. lib. v.

bearing the fine fruits of the island, so that in sailing along, the fruits and flowers might be plucked with the hand from the branches which overhung the stream.* This delightful vicinity was the dwelling-place of the female cacique who had conceived an affection for the young Spaniard Miguel Diaz, and had induced him to entice his countrymen to that part of the island. The promise she had given of a friendly reception on the part of her tribe was faithfully performed.

On a commanding bank of the harbour, Don Bartholomew erected a fortress, which at first was called Isabella, but afterwards San Domingo, and was the origin of the city which still bears that name. The Adelantado was of an active and indefatigable spirit. No sooner was the fortress completed, than he left in it a garrison of twenty men, and with the rest of his forces set out to visit the dominions of Behechio, one of the principal chieftains of the island. This cacique, as has already been mentioned, reigned over Xaragua, a province comprising almost the whole coast at the west end of the island, including Cape Tiburon, and extending along the south side as far as Point Aguida, or the small island of Beata. It was one of the most populous and fertile districts, with a delightful climate; and its inhabitants were softer and more graceful in their manners than the rest of the islanders. Being so remote from all the fortresses, the cacique, although he had taken a part in the combination of the chieftains, had hitherto remained free from the incursions and exactions of the white men.

With this cacique resided Anacaona, widow of the late formidable Caonabo. She was sister to Behechio, and had taken refuge with her brother after the capture of her husband. She was one of the most beautiful females of the island; her name in the Indian language signified 'the Golden Flower'. She possessed a genius superior to the generality of her race, and was said to excel in composing those little legendary ballads, or areytos, which the natives chanted as they performed their national dances. All the Spanish writers agree in describing her as possessing a natural dignity and grace hardly to be credited in her ignorant and savage condition. Notwithstanding the ruin with which her husband had been overwhelmed by the hostility of the white men, she appears to have entertained no vindictive feeling towards them, knowing

* Peter Martyr, decad. i. lib. v.

that he had provoked their vengeance by his own voluntary warfare. She regarded the Spaniards with admiration as almost superhuman beings, and her intelligent mind perceived the futility and impolicy of any attempt to resist their superiority in arts and arms. Having great influence over her brother Behechio, she counseled him to take warning by the fate of her husband, and to conciliate the friendship of the Spaniards; and it is supposed that a knowledge of the friendly sentiments and powerful influence of this princess in a great measure prompted the Adelantado to his present expedition.*

In passing through those parts of the island which had hitherto been unvisited by Europeans, the Adelantado adopted the same imposing measures which the admiral had used on a former occasion; he put his cavalry in the advance, and entered all the Indian towns in martial array, with standards displayed, and the sound of drum and trumpet.

After proceeding about thirty leagues, he came to the river Neyva, which, issuing from the mountains of Cibao, divides the southern side of the island. Crossing this stream, he despatched two parties of ten men each along the sea-coast in search of brazil-wood. They found great quantities, and felled many trees, which they stored in the Indian cabins, until they could be taken away by sea.

Inclining with his main force to the right, the Adelantado met, not far from the river, the cacique Behechio, with a great army of his subjects, armed with bows and arrows and lances. If he had come forth with the intention of opposing the inroad into his forest domains, he was probably daunted by the formidable appearance of the Spaniards. Laying aside his weapons, he advanced and accosted the Adelantado very amicably, professing that he was thus in arms for the purpose of subjecting certain villages along the river, and inquiring, at the same time, the object of this incursion of the Spaniards. The Adelantado assured him that he came on a peaceful visit to pass a little time in friendly intercourse at Xaragua. He succeeded so well in allaying the apprehensions of the cacique, that the latter dismissed his army, and sent swift messengers to order preparations for the suitable reception of so distinguished a guest. As the Spaniards advanced into the territories of the chieftain, and passed through the districts of his inferior caciques, the latter

* Charlevoix, *Hist. St Domingo*, lib. ii. p. 147; Muñoz, *Hist. N. Mundo*, lib. vi. sec. 6.

Forest scene in the province of Xaragua

brought forth cassava bread, hemp, cotton, and various other productions of the land. At length they drew near to the residence of Behechio, which was a large town situated in a beautiful part of the country near the coast, at the bottom of that deep bay called at present the Bight of Leogan.

The Spaniards had heard many accounts of the soft and delightful region of Xaragua, in one part of which Indian traditions placed their Elysian fields. They had heard much, also, of the beauty and urbanity of the inhabitants: the mode of their reception was calculated to confirm their favourable prepossessions. As they approached the place, thirty females of the cacique's household came forth to meet them, singing their areytos, or traditionary ballads, and dancing and waving palm branches. The married females wore aprons of embroidered cotton, reaching half way to the knee; the young women were entirely naked, with merely a fillet round the forehead, their hair falling upon their shoulders. They were beautifully proportioned; their skin smooth and delicate, and their complexion of a clear agreeable brown. According to old Peter Martyr, the Spaniards, when they beheld them issuing forth from their green woods, almost imagined they beheld the fabled dryads, or native nymphs and fairies of the fountains, sung by the ancient poets.* When they came before Don Bartholomew, they knelt and gracefully presented him the green branches. After these came the female cacique Anacaona, reclining on a kind of light litter borne by six Indians. Like the other females, she had no other covering than an apron of various-coloured cotton. She wore round her head a fragrant garland of red and white flowers, and wreaths of the same round her neck and arms. She received the Adelantado and his followers with that natural grace and courtesy for which she was celebrated; manifesting no hostility towards them for the fate her husband had experienced at their hands.

The Adelantado and his officers were conducted to the house of Behechio, where a banquet was served up of utias, a great variety of sea and river fish, with roots and fruits of excellent quality. Here first the Spaniards conquered their repugnance to the guana, the favourite delicacy of the Indians, but which the former had regarded with disgust, as a species of serpent. The

* Peter Martyr, decad. i. lib. v.

Adelantado, willing to accustom himself to the usages of the
country, was the first to taste this animal, being kindly pressed
thereto by Anacaona. His followers imitated his example; they
found it to be highly palatable and delicate; and from that time
forward, the guana was held in repute among Spanish epicures.*

The banquet being over, Don Bartholomew with six of his
principal cavaliers were lodged in the dwelling of Behechio; the rest
were distributed in the houses of the inferior caciques, where they
slept in hammocks of matted cotton, the usual beds of the natives.

For two days they remained with the hospitable Behechio,
entertained with various Indian games and festivities, among which
the most remarkable was the representation of a battle. Two
squadrons of naked Indians, armed with bows and arrows, sallied
suddenly into the public square and began to skirmish in a manner
similar to the Moorish play of canes, or tilting reeds. By degrees
they became excited, and fought with such earnestness, that four
were slain, and many wounded, which seemed to increase the
interest and pleasure of the spectators. The contest would have
continued longer, and might have been still more bloody, had not
the Adelantado and the other cavaliers interfered and begged that
the game might cease.†

When the festivities were over, and familiar intercourse had promoted mutual confidence, the Adelantado addressed the cacique
and Anacaona on the real object of his visit. He informed him
that his brother, the admiral, had been sent to this island by the
sovereigns of Castile, who were great and mighty potentates, with
many kingdoms under their sway. That the admiral had returned to
apprise his sovereigns how many tributary caciques there were in
the island, leaving him in command, and that he had come to
receive Behechio under the protection of these mighty sovereigns,

---

* 'These serpentes are lyke unto crocodiles, saving in bygness; they call them
guanas. Unto that day none of owre men durste adventure to taste of them, by
reason of theyre horrible deformitie and lothsomnes. Yet the Adelantado being
entysed by the pleasantnes of the king's sister, Anacaona, determined to taste the
serpentes. But when he felte the flesh thereof to be so delycate to his tongue, he
fel to amayne without al feare. The which thyng his companions perceiving,
were not behynde hym in greedynesse: insomuche that they had now none other
talke than of the sweetnesse of these serpentes, which they affirm to be of more
pleasant taste, than eyther our phesantes or partriches.' Peter Martyr, decad. i.
book v, Eden's Eng. trans.

† Las Casas, *Hist. Ind.*, tom. i. cap. 113.

and to arrange a tribute to be paid by him, in such manner as should be most convenient and satisfactory to himself.*

The cacique was greatly embarrassed by this demand, knowing the sufferings inflicted on the other parts of the island by the avidity of the Spaniards for gold. He replied that he had been apprised that gold was the great object for which the white men had come to their island, and that a tribute was paid in it by some of his fellow-caciques; but that in no part of his territories was gold to be found; and his subjects hardly knew what it was. To this the Adelantado replied with great adroitness, that nothing was farther from the intention or wish of his sovereigns than to require a tribute in things not produced in his dominions, but that it might be paid in cotton, hemp, and cassava bread, with which the surrounding country appeared to abound. The countenance of the cacique brightened at this intimation; he promised cheerful compliance, and instantly sent orders to all his subordinate caciques to sow abundance of cotton for the first payment of the stipulated tribute. Having made all the requisite arrangements, the Adelantado took a most friendly leave of Behechio and his sister, and set out for Isabella.

Thus, by amicable and sagacious management, one of the most extensive provinces of the island was brought into cheerful subjection, and had not the wise policy of the Adelantado been defeated by the excesses of worthless and turbulent men, a large revenue might have been collected, without any recourse to violence or oppression. In all instances, these simple people appear to have been extremely tractable, and meekly and even cheerfully to have resigned their rights to the white men, when treated with gentleness and humanity.

* Las Casas, *Hist. Ind.*, tom. i. cap. 114.

On arriving at Isabella, Don Bartholomew found it, as usual, a scene of misery and repining. Many had died during his absence; most were ill. Those who were healthy complained of the scarcity of food, and those who were ill, of the want of medicines. The provisions distributed among them, from the supply brought out a few months before by Pedro Alonzo Niño, had been consumed. Partly from sickness, and partly from a repugnance to labour, they had neglected to cultivate the surrounding country, and the Indians, on whom they chiefly depended, outraged by their oppressions, had abandoned the vicinity, and fled to the mountains; choosing rather to subsist on roots and herbs, in their rugged retreats, than remain in the luxuriant plains, subject to the wrongs and cruelties of the white men. The history of this island presents continual pictures of the miseries, the actual want and poverty, produced by the grasping avidity of gold. It had rendered the Spaniards heedless of all the less obvious, but more certain and salubrious, sources of wealth. All labour seemed lost that was to produce profit by a circuitous process. Instead of cultivating the luxuriant soil around them, and deriving real treasures from its surface, they wasted their time in seeking for mines and golden streams, and were starving in the midst of fertility.

No sooner were the provisions exhausted which had been brought out by Niño, than the colonists began to break forth in their accustomed murmurs. They represented themselves as neglected by Columbus, who, amidst the blandishments and delights of a court, thought little of their sufferings. They considered themselves equally forgotten by government; while, having no vessel in the harbour, they were destitute of all means of sending home intelligence of their disastrous situation, and imploring relief.

To remove this last cause of discontent, and furnish some object for their hopes and thoughts to rally round, the Adelantado ordered that two caravels should be built at Isabella, for the use of the island. To relieve the settlement, also, from all useless and repining individuals, during this time of scarcity, he distributed such as were too ill to labour, or to bear arms, into the interior, where they would have the benefit of a better climate, and more abundant supply of Indian provisions. He at the same time completed and garrisoned the chain of military posts established by his brother in the preceding year, consisting of five fortified houses, each surrounded by its dependent hamlet. The first of these was about nine leagues from Isabella, and was called la Esperanza. Six leagues beyond was Santa Catalina. Four leagues and a half further was Magdalena, where the first town of Santiago was afterwards founded; and five leagues further Fort Conception – which was fortified with great care, being in the vast and populous Vega, and within half a league from the residence of its cacique, Guarionex.[*] Having thus relieved Isabella of all its useless population, and left none but such as were too ill to be removed, or were required for the service and protection of the place, and the construction of the caravels, the Adelantado returned, with a large body of the most effective men, to the fortress of San Domingo.

The military posts, thus established, succeeded for a time in overawing the natives; but fresh hostilities were soon manifested, excited by a different cause from the preceding. Among the missionaries who had accompanied Friar Boyle to the island, were two of far greater zeal than their superior. When he returned to Spain, they remained, earnestly bent upon the fulfillment of their mission. One was called Roman Pane, a poor hermit, as he styled himself, of the order of St Geronimo; the other was Juan Borgoñon, a Franciscan. They resided for some time among the Indians of the Vega, strenuously endeavouring to make converts, and had succeeded with one family, of sixteen persons, the chief of which, on being baptized, took the name of Juan Mateo. The conversion of the cacique Guarionex, however, was their main object. The extent of his possessions made his conversion of great importance to the interests of the colony, and

---

[*] P. Martyr, decad. i. lib. v. Of the residence of Guarionex, which must have been a considerable town, not the least vestige can be discovered at present.

was considered by the zealous fathers a means of bringing his numerous subjects under the dominion of the church. For some time he lent a willing ear; he learnt the Pater Noster, the Ave Maria, and the Creed, and made his whole family repeat them daily. The other caciques of the Vega and of the provinces of Cibao, however, scoffed at him for meanly conforming to the laws and customs of strangers, usurpers of his domains, and oppressors of his nation. The friars complained that, in consequence of these evil communications, their convert suddenly relapsed into infidelity; but another and more grievous cause is assigned for his recantation. His favourite wife was seduced or treated with outrage by a Spaniard of authority; and the cacique renounced all faith in a religion which, as he supposed, admitted of such atrocities. Losing all hope of effecting his conversion, the missionaries removed to the territories of another cacique, taking with them Juan Mateo, their Indian convert. Before their departure, they erected a small chapel, and furnished it with an altar, crucifix, and images, for the use of the family of Mateo.

Scarcely had they departed, when several Indians entered the chapel, broke the images in pieces, trampled them under foot, and buried them in a neighbouring field. This, it was said, was done by order of Guarionex, in contempt of the religion from which he had apostatized. A complaint of this enormity was carried to the Adelantado, who ordered a suit to be immediately instituted, and those who were found culpable, to be punished according to law. It was a period of great rigor in ecclesiastical law, especially among the Spaniards. In Spain, all heresies in religion, all recantations from the faith, and all acts of sacrilege, either by Moor or Jew, were punished with fire and fagot. Such was the fate of the poor ignorant Indians, convicted of this outrage on the church. It is questionable whether Guarionex had any hand in this offence, and it is probable that the whole affair was exaggerated. A proof of the credit due to the evidence brought forward may be judged by one of the facts recorded by Roman Pane, 'the poor hermit'. The field in which the holy images were buried was planted, he says, with certain roots shaped like a turnip, or radish, several of which coming up in the neighbourhood of the images, were found to have grown most miraculously in the form of a cross.[*]

* Escritura de Fr. Roman; *Hist. del Almirante.*

The cruel punishment inflicted on these Indians, instead of
daunting their countrymen, filled them with horror and indignation. Unaccustomed to such stern rule and vindictive justice,
and having no clear ideas nor powerful sentiments with respect to
religion of any kind, they could not comprehend the nature nor
extent of the crime committed. Even Guarionex, a man naturally
moderate and pacific, was highly incensed with the assumption of
power within his territories, and the inhuman death inflicted on
his subjects. The other caciques perceived his irritation, and
endeavoured to induce him to unite in a sudden insurrection,
that by one vigorous and general effort they might break the yoke
of their oppressors. Guarionex wavered for some time. He knew
the martial skill and prowess of the Spaniards; he stood in awe
of their cavalry, and he had before him the disastrous fate of
Caonabo; but he was rendered bold by despair, and he beheld in
the domination of these strangers the assured ruin of his race. The
early writers speak of a tradition current among the inhabitants of
the island, respecting this Guarionex. He was of an ancient line of
hereditary caciques. His father, in times long preceding the
discovery, having fasted for five days, according to their superstitious observances, applied to his zemi, or household deity, for
information of things to come. He received for answer, that
within a few years there should come to the island a nation
covered with clothing, which should destroy all their customs
and ceremonies, and slay their children or reduce them to painful
servitude.* The tradition was probably invented by the Butios, or
priests, after the Spaniards had begun to exercise their severities.
Whether their prediction had an effect in disposing the mind of
Guarionex to hostilities is uncertain. Some have asserted that he
was compelled to take up arms by his subjects, who threatened, in
case of his refusal, to choose some other chieftain; others have
alleged the outrage committed upon his favourite wife, as the
principal cause of his irritation.† It was probably these things
combined, which at length induced him to enter into the conspiracy. A secret consultation was held among the caciques,
wherein it was concerted, that on the day of payment of their
quarterly tribute, when a great number could assemble without

* Peter Martyr, decad. i. lib. ix.
† Las Casas, *Hist. Ind.*, lib. i. cap. 121.

causing suspicion, they should suddenly rise upon the Spaniards and massacre them.[*]

By some means the garrison at Fort Conception received intimation of this conspiracy. Being but a handful of men, and surrounded by hostile tribes, they wrote a letter to the Adelantado, at San Domingo, imploring immediate aid. As this letter might be taken from their Indian messenger, the natives having discovered that these letters had a wonderful power of communicating intelligence, and fancying they could talk, it was inclosed in a reed, to be used as a staff. The messenger was, in fact, intercepted; but, affecting to be dumb and lame, and intimating by signs that he was returning home, was permitted to limp forward on his journey. When out of sight he resumed his speed, and bore the letter safely and expeditiously to San Domingo.[†]

The Adelantado, with his characteristic promptness and activity, set out immediately with a body of troops for the fortress; and though his men were much enfeebled by scanty fare, hard service, and long marches, hurried them rapidly forward. Never did aid arrive more opportunely. The Indians were assembled on the plain, to the amount of many thousands, armed after their manner, and waiting for the appointed time to strike the blow. After consulting with the commander of the fortress and his officers, the Adelantado concerted a mode of proceeding. Ascertaining the places in which the various caciques had distributed their forces, he appointed an officer with a body of men to each cacique, with orders, at an appointed hour of the night, to rush into the villages, surprise them asleep and unarmed, bind the caciques, and bring them off prisoners. As Guarionex was the most important personage, and his capture would probably be attended with most difficulty and danger, the Adelantado took the charge of it upon himself, at the head of one hundred men.

This stratagem, founded upon a knowledge of the attachment of the Indians to their chieftains, and calculated to spare a great effusion of blood, was completely successful. The villages, having no walls nor other defences, were quietly entered at midnight; and the Spaniards, rushing suddenly into the houses where the caciques were quartered, seized and bound them, to the number

---

[*] Herrera, *Hist. Ind.*, decad. i. lib. iii. cap. 65; Peter Martyr, decad. vi. lib.v.

[†] Herrera, *Hist. Ind.*, decad. i. lib. iii. cap. 7.

of fourteen, and hurried them off to the fortress, before any effort
could be made for their defence or rescue. The Indians, struck with
terror, made no resistance, nor any show of hostility; surrounding
the fortress in great multitudes, but without weapons, they filled
the air with doleful howlings and lamentations, imploring the
release of their chieftains. The Adelantado completed his enterprise with the spirit, sagacity, and moderation with which he had
hitherto conducted it. He obtained information of the causes of this
conspiracy, and the individuals most culpable. Two caciques, the
principal movers of the insurrection, and who had most wrought
upon the easy nature of Guarionex, were put to death. As to that
unfortunate cacique, the Adelantado, considering the deep wrongs
he had suffered, and the slowness with which he had been provoked to revenge, magnanimously pardoned him; nay, according
to Las Casas, he proceeded with stern justice against the Spaniard
whose outrage on his wife had sunk so deeply in his heart. He
extended his lenity also to the remaining chieftains of the conspiracy; promising great favours and rewards, if they should continue
firm in their loyalty; but terrible punishments should they again be
found in rebellion. The heart of Guarionex was subdued by this
unexpected clemency. He made a speech to his people, setting
forth the irresistible might and valour of the Spaniards; their great
lenity to offenders, and their generosity to such as were faithful; and
he earnestly exhorted them henceforth to cultivate their friendship.
The Indians listened to him with attention; his praises of the white
men were confirmed by their treatment of himself; when he had
concluded, they took him up on their shoulders, bore him to his
habitation with songs and shouts of joy, and for some time the
tranquillity of the Vega was restored.*

---

* Peter Martyr, decad. i. lib. v; Herrera, *Hist. Ind.*, decad. i. lib. iii. cap. 6.

With all his energy and discretion, the Adelantado found it difficult to manage the proud and turbulent spirit of the colonists.
They could ill brook the sway of a foreigner, who, when they
were restive, curbed them with an iron hand. Don Bartholomew
had not the same legitimate authority in their eyes as his brother.
The admiral was the discoverer of the country, and the authorized
representative of the sovereigns; yet even him they with difficulty
brought themselves to obey. The Adelantado, on the contrary, was
regarded by many as a mere intruder, assuming high command
without authority from the crown, and shouldering himself into
power on the merits and services of his brother. They spoke with
impatience and indignation, also, of the long absence of the
admiral, and his fancied inattention to their wants; little aware of
the incessant anxieties he was suffering on their account, during his
detention in Spain. The sagacious measure of the Adelantado in
building the caravels for some time diverted their attention. They
watched their progress with solicitude, looking upon them as a
means either of obtaining relief, or of abandoning the island.
Aware that repining and discontented men should never be left
in idleness, Don Bartholomew kept them continually in movement; and indeed a state of constant activity was congenial to his
own vigorous spirit. About this time messengers arrived from
Behechio, cacique of Xaragua, informing him that he had large
quantities of cotton, and other articles, in which his tribute was to
be paid, ready for delivery. The Adelantado immediately set forth
with a numerous train, to revisit this fruitful and happy region. He
was again received with songs and dances, and all the national
demonstrations of respect and amity by Behechio and his sister
Anacaona. The latter appeared to be highly popular among the
natives, and to have almost as much sway in Xaragua as her

brother. Her natural ease, and the graceful dignity of her manners, more and more won the admiration of the Spaniards.

The Adelantado found thirty-two inferior caciques assembled in the house of Behechio, awaiting his arrival with their respective tributes. The cotton they had brought was enough to fill one of their houses. Having delivered this, they gratuitously offered the Adelantado as much cassava bread as he desired. The offer was most acceptable in the present necessitous state of the colony; and Don Bartholomew sent to Isabella for one of the caravels, which was nearly finished, to be despatched as soon as possible to Xaragua, to be freighted with bread and cotton.

In the meantime, the natives brought from all quarters large supplies of provisions, and entertained their guests with continual festivity and banqueting. The early Spanish writers, whose imaginations, heated by the accounts of the voyagers, could not form an idea of the simplicity of savage life, especially in these newly-discovered countries, which were supposed to border upon Asia, often speak in terms of oriental magnificence of the entertainments of the natives, the palaces of the caciques, and the lords and ladies of their courts, as if they were describing the abodes of Asiatic potentates. The accounts given of Xaragua, however, have a different character; and give a picture of savage life, in its perfection of idle and ignorant enjoyment. The troubles which distracted the other parts of devoted Hayti had not reached the inhabitants of this pleasant region. Living among beautiful and fruitful groves, on the borders of a sea apparently for ever tranquil and unvexed by storms; having few wants, and those readily supplied, they appeared emancipated from the common lot of labour, and to pass their lives in one uninterrupted holiday. When the Spaniards regarded the fertility and sweetness of this country, the gentleness of its people, and the beauty of its women, they pronounced it a perfect paradise.

At length the caravel arrived which was to be freighted with the articles of tribute. It anchored about six miles from the residence of Behechio, and Anacaona proposed to her brother that they should go together to behold what she called the great canoe of the white men. On their way to the coast, the Adelantado was lodged one night in a village, in a house where Anacaona treasured up those articles which she esteemed most rare and precious. They consisted of various manufactures of cotton, ingeniously wrought; of vessels of clay, moulded into different forms; of chairs, tables, and like articles of furniture, formed of ebony and other kinds of wood, and carved with various devices – all evincing great skill and ingenuity, in a people who had no iron tools to work with. Such were the simple treasures of this Indian princess, of which she made numerous presents to her guest.

Nothing could exceed the wonder and delight of this intelligent woman, when she first beheld the ship. Her brother, who treated her with a fraternal fondness and respectful attention worthy of civilized life, had prepared two canoes, gayly painted and decorated; one to convey her and her attendants, and the other for himself and his chieftains. Anacaona, however, preferred to embark, with her attendants, in the ship's boat with the Adelantado. As they approached the caravel, a salute was fired. At the report of the cannon, and the sight of the smoke, Anacaona, overcome with dismay, fell into the arms of the Adelantado, and her attendants would have leaped overboard, but the laughter and the cheerful words of Don Bartholomew speedily reassured them. As they drew nearer to the vessel, several instruments of martial music struck up, with which they were greatly delighted. Their admiration increased on entering on board. Accustomed only to their simple and slight canoes, everything here appeared wonderfully vast and complicated. But when the anchor was weighed, the sails were spread, and, aided by a gentle breeze, they beheld this vast mass, moving apparently by its own volition, veering from side to side, and playing like a huge monster in the deep, the brother and sister remained gazing at each other in mute astonishment.[*] Nothing seems to have filled the mind of the most stoical savage with more wonder than that sublime and beautiful triumph of genius, a ship under sail.

Having freighted and despatched the caravel, the Adelantado made many presents to Behechio, his sister, and their attendants, and took leave of them, to return by land with his troops to Isabella. Anacaona showed great affliction at their parting, entreating him to remain some time longer with them, and appearing fearful that they had failed in their humble attempt to please him. She even offered to follow him to the settlement, nor would she be consoled until he had promised to return again to Xaragua.[†]

[*] Peter Martyr, decad. i. lib. v; Herrera, decad. i. lib. iii. cap. 6.
[†] Ramusio, vol. iii. p. 9.

We cannot but remark the ability shown by the Adelantado in the course of his transient government of the island. Wonderfully alert and active, he made repeated marches of great extent, from one remote province to another, and was always at the post of danger at the critical moment. By skillful management, with a handful of men, he defeated a formidable insurrection without any effusion of blood. He conciliated the most inveterate enemies among the natives by great moderation, while he deterred all wanton hostilities by the infliction of signal punishments. He had made firm friends of the most important chieftains, brought their dominions under cheerful tribute, opened new sources of supplies for the colony, and procured relief from its immediate wants. Had his judicious measures been seconded by those under his command, the whole country would have been a scene of tranquil prosperity, and would have produced great revenues to the crown, without cruelty to the natives; but, like his brother the admiral, his good intentions and judicious arrangements were constantly thwarted by the vile passions and perverse conduct of others. While he was absent from Isabella, new mischiefs had been fomented there, which were soon to throw the whole island into confusion.

The prime mover of the present mischief was one Francisco Roldan, a man under the deepest obligations to the admiral. Raised by him from poverty and obscurity, he had been employed at first in menial capacities; but, showing strong natural talents, and great assiduity, he had been made ordinary alcalde, equivalent to justice of the peace. The able manner in which he acquitted himself in this situation, and the persuasion of his great fidelity and gratitude, induced Columbus, on departing for Spain, to appoint him alcalde mayor, or chief judge of the island. It is true he was an uneducated man, but, as there were as yet no intricacies of law in the colony, the office required little else than shrewd good sense and upright principles for its discharge.[*]

Roldan was one of those base spirits which grow venomous in the sunshine of prosperity. His benefactor had returned to Spain apparently under a cloud of disgrace; a long interval had elapsed without tidings from him; he considered him a fallen man, and began to devise how he might profit by his downfall. He was intrusted with an office inferior only to that of the Adelantado; the brothers of Columbus were highly unpopular; he imagined it possible to ruin them, both with the colonists and with the government at home, and by dextrous cunning and bustling activity to work his way into the command of the colony. The vigorous and somewhat austere character of the Adelantado for some time kept him in awe; but when he was absent from the settlement, Roldan was able to carry on his machinations with confidence. Don Diego, who then commanded at Isabella, was an upright and worthy man, but deficient in energy. Roldan felt himself his superior in talent and spirit, and his self-conceit was wounded at being inferior to him in authority. He soon made a

[*] Herrera, decad. i. lib. iii. cap. i.

party among the daring and dissolute of the community, and
secretly loosened the ties of order and good government, by
listening to and encouraging the discontents of the common
people, and directing them against the character and conduct of
Columbus and his brothers. He had heretofore been employed as
superintendent of various public works; this brought him into
familiar communication with workmen, sailors, and others of the
lower order. His originally vulgar character enabled him to adapt
himself to their intellects and manners, while his present station
gave him consequence in their eyes. Finding them full of murmurs
about hard treatment, severe toil, and the long absence of the
admiral, he affected to be moved by their distresses. He threw out
suggestions that the admiral might never return, being disgraced
and ruined in consequence of the representations of Aguado. He
sympathized with the hard treatment they experienced from the
Adelantado and his brother Don Diego, who, being foreigners,
could take no interest in their welfare, nor feel a proper respect for
the pride of a Spaniard; but who used them merely as slaves, to
build houses and fortresses for them, or to swell their state and
secure their power, as they marched about the island enriching
themselves with the spoils of the caciques. By these suggestions he
exasperated their feelings to such a height, that they had at one
time formed a conspiracy to take away the life of the Adelantado,
as the only means of delivering themselves from an odious tyrant.
The time and place for the perpetration of the act were concerted.
The Adelantado had condemned to death a Spaniard of the name
of Berahona, a friend of Roldan, and of several of the conspirators.
What was his offence is not positively stated, but from a passage in
Las Casas[*] there is reason to believe that he was the very Spaniard
who had violated the favourite wife of Guarionex, the cacique of
the Vega. The Adelantado would be present at the execution. It
was arranged, therefore, that when the populace had assembled, a
tumult should be made as if by accident, and in the confusion of
the moment, Don Bartholomew should be despatched with a
poniard. Fortunately for the Adelantado, he pardoned the criminal, the assemblage did not take place, and the plan of the
conspirators was disconcerted.[†]

[*] Las Casas, *Hist. Ind.*, lib. i. cap. 118.
[†] *Hist. del Almirante*, cap. 73.

When Don Bartholomew was absent collecting the tribute in Xaragua, Roldan thought it was a favourable time to bring affairs to a crisis. He had sounded the feelings of the colonists, and ascertained that there was a large party disposed for open sedition. His plan was to create a popular tumult, to interpose in his official character of alcalde mayor, to throw the blame upon the oppression and injustice of Don Diego and his brother, and, while he usurped the reins of authority, to appear as if actuated only by zeal for the peace and prosperity of the island, and the interests of the sovereigns.

A pretext soon presented itself for the proposed tumult. When the caravel returned from Xaragua laden with the Indian tributes, and the cargo was discharged, Don Diego had the vessel drawn up on the land, to protect it from accidents, or from any sinister designs of the disaffected colonists. Roldan immediately pointed this circumstance out to his partisans. He secretly inveighed against the hardship of having this vessel drawn on shore, instead of being left afloat for the benefit of the colony, or sent to Spain to make known their distresses. He hinted that the true reason was the fear of the Adelantado and his brother, lest accounts should be carried to Spain of their misconduct, and he affirmed that they wished to remain undisturbed masters of the island, and keep the Spaniards there as subjects, or rather as slaves. The people took fire at these suggestions. They had long looked forward to the completion of the caravels as their only chance for relief; they now insisted that the vessel should be launched and sent to Spain for supplies. Don Diego endeavoured to convince them of the folly of their demand, the vessel not being rigged and equipped for such a voyage; but the more he attempted to pacify them, the more unreasonable and turbulent they became. Roldan, also, became more bold and explicit in his instigations. He advised them to launch and take possession of the caravel, as the only mode of regaining their independence. They might then throw off the tyranny of these upstart strangers, enemies in their hearts to Spaniards, and might lead a life of ease and pleasure; sharing equally all that they might gain by barter in the island, employing the Indians as slaves to work for them, and enjoying unrestrained indulgence with respect to the Indian women.*

* *Hist. del Almirante*, cap. 73.

Don Diego received information of what was fermenting among
the people, yet feared to come to an open rupture with Roldan in
the present mutinous state of the colony. He suddenly detached
him, therefore, with forty men, to the Vega, under pretext of
overawing certain of the natives who had refused to pay their
tribute, and had shown a disposition to revolt. Roldan made use of
this opportunity to strengthen his faction. He made friends and
partisans among the discontented caciques, secretly justifying them
in their resistance to the imposition of tribute, and promising them
redress. He secured the devotion of his own soldiers by great acts
of indulgence, disarming and dismissing such as refused full participation in his plans, and returned with his little band to Isabella,
where he felt secure of a strong party among the common people.

The Adelantado had by this time returned from Xaragua; but
Roldan, feeling himself at the head of a strong faction, and arrogating to himself great authority from his official station, now
openly demanded that the caravel should be launched, or permission given to himself and his followers to launch it. The
Adelantado peremptorily refused, observing that neither he nor his
companions were mariners, nor was the caravel furnished and
equipped for sea, and that neither the safety of the vessel, nor of
the people, should be endangered by their attempt to navigate her.

Roldan perceived that his motives were suspected, and felt that
the Adelantado was too formidable an adversary to contend with
in any open sedition at Isabella. He determined, therefore, to carry
his plans into operation in some more favourable part of the island,
always trusting to excuse any open rebellion against the authority of
Don Bartholomew, by representing it as a patriotic opposition to his
tyranny over Spaniards. He had seventy well-armed and determined
men under his command, and he trusted, on erecting his standard,
to be joined by all the disaffected throughout the island. He set off
suddenly, therefore, for the Vega, intending to surprise the fortress
of Conception, and by getting command of that post and the rich
country adjacent, to set the Adelantado at defiance.

He stopped, on his way, at various Indian villages in which the
Spaniards were distributed, endeavouring to enlist the latter in his
party, by holding out promises of great gain and free living. He
attempted also to seduce the natives from their allegiance, by
promising them freedom from all tribute. Those caciques with

whom he had maintained a previous understanding, received him with open arms; particularly one who had taken the name of Diego Marque, whose village he made his headquarters, being about two leagues from Fort Conception. He was disappointed in his hopes of surprising the fortress. Its commander, Miguel Ballester, was an old and staunch soldier, both resolute and wary. He drew himself into his stronghold on the approach of Roldan, and closed his gates. His garrison was small, but the fortification, situated on the side of a hill, with a river running at its foot, was proof against any assault. Roldan had still some hopes that Ballester might be disaffected to government, and might be gradually brought into his plans, or that the garrison would be disposed to desert, tempted by the licentious life which he permitted among his followers. In the neighbourhood was the town inhabited by Guarionex. Here were quartered thirty soldiers, under the command of Captain Garcia de Barrantes. Roldan repaired thither with his armed force, hoping to enlist Barrantes and his party; but the captain shut himself up with his men in a fortified house, refusing to permit them to hold any communication with Roldan. The latter threatened to set fire to the house; but after a little consideration, contented himself with seizing their store of provisions, and then marched towards Fort Conception, which was not quite half a league distant.[*]

---

[*] Herrera, decad. i. lib. iii. cap. 7; *Hist. del Almirante*, cap. 74.

Extract of a letter from T. S. Heneken, Esq., 1847 – Fort Conception is situated at the foot of a hill now called Santo Cerro. It is constructed of bricks, and is almost as entire at the present day as when just finished. It stands in the gloom of an exuberant forest which has invaded the scene of former bustle and activity; a spot once considered of great importance and surrounded by swarms of intelligent beings.

What has become of the countless multitudes this fortress was intended to awe? Not a trace of them remains excepting in the records of history. The silence of the tomb prevails where their habitations responded to their songs and dances. A few indigent Spaniards, living in miserable hovels, scattered widely apart in the bosom of the forest, are now the sole occupants of this once fruitful and beautiful region.

A Spanish town gradually grew up round the fortress, the ruins of which extend to a considerable distance. It was destroyed by an earthquake, at nine o'clock of the morning of Saturday, 20th April, 1564, during the celebration of mass. Part of the massive walls of a handsome church still remain, as well as those of a very large convent or hospital, supposed to have been constructed in pursuance of the testamentary dispositions of Columbus. The inhabitants who survived the catastrophe retired to a small chapel, on the banks of a river, about a league distant, where the new town of La Vega was afterwards built.

1497

The Adelantado had received intelligence of the flagitious proceedings of Roldan, yet hesitated for a time to set out in pursuit of him. He had lost all confidence in the loyalty of the people around him, and knew not how far the conspiracy extended, nor on whom he could rely. Diego de Escobar, alcayde of the fortress of La Madalena, together with Adrian de Moxica and Pedro de Valdivieso, all principal men, were in league with Roldan. He feared that the commander of Fort Conception might likewise be in the plot, and the whole island in arms against him. He was reassured, however, by tidings from Miguel Ballester. That loyal veteran wrote to him pressing letters for succour; representing the weakness of his garrison, and the increasing forces of the rebels.

Don Bartholomew hastened to his assistance with his accustomed promptness, and threw himself with a reinforcement into the fortress. Being ignorant of the force of the rebels, and doubtful of the loyalty of his own followers, he determined to adopt mild measures. Understanding that Roldan was quartered at a village but half a league distant, he sent a message to him, remonstrating on the flagrant irregularity of his conduct, the injury it was calculated to produce in the island, and the certain ruin it must bring upon himself, and summoning him to appear at the fortress, pledging his word for his personal safety. Roldan repaired accordingly to Fort Conception, where the Adelantado held a parley with him from a window, demanding the reason of his appearing in arms, in opposition to royal authority. Roldan replied boldly, that he was in the service of his sovereigns, defending their subjects from the oppression of men who sought their destruction. The Adelantado ordered him to surrender his staff of office, as alcalde mayor, and to submit peaceably to superior authority. Roldan refused to resign his office, or to put himself in the power of Don Bartholomew,

whom he charged with seeking his life. He refused also to submit
to any trial, unless commanded by the king. Pretending, however,
to make no resistance to the peaceable exercise of authority, he
offered to go with his followers, and reside at any place the
Adelantado might appoint. The latter immediately designated the
village of the cacique Diego Colon, the same native of the Lucayos
Islands who had been baptized in Spain, and had since married a
daughter of Guarionex. Roldan objected, pretending there were
not sufficient provisions to be had there for the subsistence of his
men, and departed, declaring that he would seek a more eligible
residence elsewhere.*

He now proposed to his followers to take possession of the
remote province of Xaragua. The Spaniards who had returned
thence gave enticing accounts of the life they had led there; of the
fertility of the soil, the sweetness of the climate, the hospitality
and gentleness of the people, their feasts, dances, and various
amusements, and, above all, the beauty of the women; for they
had been captivated by the naked charms of the dancing nymphs
of Xaragua. In this delightful region, emancipated from the iron
rule of the Adelantado, and relieved from the necessity of irksome
labour, they might lead a life of perfect freedom and indulgence,
and have a world of beauty at their command. In short, Roldan
drew a picture of loose sensual enjoyment, such as he knew to be
irresistible with men of idle and dissolute habits. His followers
acceded with joy to his proposition. Some preparations, however,
were necessary to carry it into effect. Taking advantage of the
absence of the Adelantado, he suddenly marched with his band to
Isabella, and entering it in a manner by surprise, endeavoured to
launch the caravel, with which they might sail to Xaragua. Don
Diego Columbus, hearing the tumult, issued forth with several
cavaliers; but such was the force of the mutineers, and their
menacing conduct, that he was obliged to withdraw, with his
adherents, into the fortress. Roldan held several parleys with him,
and offered to submit to his command, provided he would set
himself up in opposition to his brother the Adelantado. His
proposition was treated with scorn. The fortress was too strong
to be assailed with success; he found it impossible to launch
the caravel, and feared the Adelantado might return, and he be

* Herrera, decad. i. lib. iii. cap. 7; *Hist. del Almirante*, cap. 74.

inclosed between two forces. He proceeded, therefore, in all haste to make provisions for the proposed expedition to Xaragua. Still pretending to act in his official capacity, and to do everything from loyal motives, for the protection and support of the oppressed subjects of the crown, he broke open the royal warehouse, with shouts of 'Long live the king!' supplied his followers with arms, ammunition, clothing, and whatever they desired from the public stores; proceeded to the inclosure where the cattle and other European animals were kept to breed, took such as he thought necessary for his intended establishment, and permitted his followers to kill such of the remainder as they might want for present supply. Having committed this wasteful ravage, he marched in triumph out of Isabella.[*] Reflecting, however, on the prompt and vigorous character of the Adelantado, he felt that his situation would be but little secure with such an active enemy behind him; who, on extricating himself from present perplexities, would not fail to pursue him to his proposed paradise of Xaragua. He determined, therefore, to march again to the Vega, and endeavour either to get possession of the person of the Adelantado, or to strike some blow, in his present crippled state, that should disable him from offering further molestation. Returning, therefore, to the vicinity of Fort Conception, he endeavoured in every way, by the means of subtle emissaries, to seduce the garrison to desertion, or to excite it to revolt.

The Adelantado dared not take the field with his forces, having no confidence in their fidelity. He knew that they listened wistfully to the emissaries of Roldan, and contrasted the meagre fare and stern discipline of the garrison with the abundant cheer and easy misrule that prevailed among the rebels. To counteract these seductions, he relaxed from his usual strictness, treating his men with great indulgence, and promising them large rewards. By these means he was enabled to maintain some degree of loyalty amongst his forces, his service having the advantage over that of Roldan, of being on the side of government and law.

Finding his attempts to corrupt the garrison unsuccessful, and fearing some sudden sally from the vigorous Adelantado, Roldan drew off to a distance, and sought by insidious means to strengthen his own power, and weaken that of the government. He asserted

[*] *Hist. del Almirante*, cap. 74; Herrera, decad. i. lib. iii. cap. 7.

equal right to manage the affairs of the island with the Adelantado, and pretended to have separated from him on account of his being passionate and vindictive in the exercise of his authority. He represented him as the tyrant of the Spaniards, the oppressor of the Indians. For himself, he assumed the character of a redresser of grievances and champion of the injured. He pretended to feel a patriotic indignation at the affronts heaped upon Spaniards by a family of obscure and arrogant foreigners; and professed to free the natives from tributes wrung from them by these rapacious men for their own enrichment, and contrary to the beneficent intentions of the Spanish monarchs. He connected himself closely with the Carib cacique Manicaotex, brother of the late Caonabo, whose son and nephew were in his possession as hostages for payment of tributes. This warlike chieftain he conciliated by presents and caresses, bestowing on him the appellation of brother.* The unhappy natives, deceived by his professions, and overjoyed at the idea of having a protector in arms for their defence, submitted cheerfully to a thousand impositions, supplying his followers with provisions in abundance, and bringing to Roldan all the gold they could collect; voluntarily yielding him heavier tributes than those from which he pretended to free them.

The affairs of the island were now in a lamentable situation. The Indians, perceiving the dissensions among the white men, and encouraged by the protection of Roldan, began to throw off all allegiance to the government. The caciques at a distance ceased to send in their tributes, and those who were in the vicinity were excused by the Adelantado, that by indulgence he might retain their friendship in this time of danger. Roldan's faction daily gained strength; they ranged insolently and at large in the open country, and were supported by the misguided natives; while the Spaniards who remained loyal, fearing conspiracies among the natives, had to keep under shelter of the fort, or in the strong houses which they had erected in the villages. The commanders were obliged to palliate all kinds of slights and indignities, both from their soldiers and from the Indians, fearful of driving them to sedition by any severity. The clothing and munitions of all kinds, either for maintenance or defence, were rapidly wasting away, and the want of all supplies or tidings from Spain was

* Las Casas, *Hist. Ind.*, lib. i. cap. 118.

sinking the spirits of the well-affected into despondency. The Adelantado was shut up in Fort Conception, in daily expectation of being openly besieged by Roldan, and was secretly informed that means were taken to destroy him, should he issue from the walls of the fortress.[*]

Such was the desperate state to which the colony was reduced, in consequence of the long detention of Columbus in Spain, and the impediments thrown in the way of all his measures for the benefit of the island by the delays of cabinets and the chicanery of Fonseca and his satellites. At this critical juncture, when faction reigned triumphant, and the colony was on the brink of ruin, tidings were brought to the Vega that Pedro Fernandez Coronal had arrived at the port of San Domingo, with two ships, bringing supplies of all kinds, and a strong reinforcement of troops.[†]

---

[*] Las Casas, *Hist. Ind.*, lib. i. cap. 119.
[†] Las Casas; Herrera; *Hist. del Almirante.*

The arrival of Coronal, which took place on the third of February, was the salvation of the colony. The reinforcements of troops, and of supplies of all kinds, strengthened the hands of Don Bartholomew. The royal confirmation of his title and authority as Adelantado at once dispelled all doubts as to the legitimacy of his power; and the tidings that the admiral was in high favour at court, and would soon arrive with a powerful squadron, struck consternation into those who had entered into the rebellion on the presumption of his having fallen into disgrace.

The Adelantado no longer remained mewed up in his fortress, but set out immediately for San Domingo with a part of his troops, although a much superior rebel force was at the village of the cacique Guarionex, at a very short distance. Roldan followed slowly and gloomily with his party, anxious to ascertain the truth of these tidings, to make partisans, if possible, among those who had newly arrived, and to take advantage of every circumstance that might befriend his rash and hazardous projects. The Adelantado left strong guards on the passes of the roads to prevent his near approach to San Domingo, but Roldan paused within a few leagues of the place.

When the Adelantado found himself secure in San Domingo with this augmentation of force, and the prospect of a still greater reinforcement at hand, his magnanimity prevailed over his indignation, and he sought by gentle means to allay the popular seditions, that the island might be restored to tranquillity before his brother's arrival. He considered that the colonists had suffered greatly from the want of supplies; that their discontents had been heightened by the severities he bad been compelled to inflict; and that many had been led to rebellion by doubts of the legitimacy of his authority. While, therefore, he proclaimed the royal act sanctioning his title

and powers, he promised amnesty for all past offences, on condition of immediate return to allegiance. Hearing that Roldan was
within five leagues of San Domingo with his band, he sent Pedro
Fernandez Coronal, who had been appointed by the sovereigns
alguazil mayor of the island, to exhort him to obedience, promising him oblivion of the past. He trusted that the representations
of a discreet and honourable man like Coronal, who had been
witness of the favour in which his brother stood in Spain, would
convince the rebels of the hopelessness of their course.

Roldan, however, conscious of his guilt, and doubtful of the
clemency of Don Bartholomew, feared to venture within his
power; he determined, also, to prevent his followers from communicating with Coronal, lest they should be seduced from him
by the promise of pardon. When that emissary, therefore, approached the encampment of the rebels, he was opposed in a
narrow pass by a body of archers, with their crossbows levelled.
'Halt there! traitor!' cried Roldan, 'had you arrived eight days
later, we should all have been united as one man.' *

In vain Coronal endeavoured by fair reasoning and earnest entreaty to win this perverse and turbulent man from his career.
Roldan answered with hardihood and defiance, professing to oppose
only the tyranny and misrule of the Adelantado, but to be ready to
submit to the admiral on his arrival. He, and several of his principal
confederates, wrote letters to the same effect to their friends in San
Domingo, urging them to plead their cause with the admiral when
he should arrive, and to assure him of their disposition to acknowledge his authority.

When Coronal returned with accounts of Roldan's contumacy,
the Adelantado proclaimed him and his followers traitors. That
shrewd rebel, however, did not suffer his men to remain within
either the seduction of promise or the terror of menace; he
immediately set out on his march for his promised land of Xaragua, trusting to impair every honest principle and virtuous tie of
his misguided followers by a life of indolence and libertinage.

In the meantime the mischievous effects of his intrigues among
the caciques became more and more apparent. No sooner had the
Adelantado left Fort Conception, than a conspiracy was formed
among the natives to surprise it. Guarionex was at the head of this

* Herrera, decad. i. lib. iii. cap. 8.

conspiracy, moved by the instigations of Roldan, who had promised him protection and assistance, and led on by the forlorn hope, in this distracted state of the Spanish forces, of relieving his paternal domains from the intolerable domination of usurping strangers. Holding secret communications with his tributary caciques, it was concerted that they should all rise simultaneously and massacre the soldiery, quartered in small parties in their villages; while he, with a chosen force, should surprise the fortress of Conception. The night of the full moon was fixed upon for the insurrection.

One of the principal caciques, however, not being a correct observer of the heavenly bodies, took up arms before the appointed night, and was repulsed by the soldiers quartered in his village. The alarm was given, and the Spaniards were all put on the alert. The cacique fled to Guarionex for protection, but the chieftain, enraged at his fatal blunder, put him to death upon the spot.

No sooner did the Adelantado hear of this fresh conspiracy, than he put himself on the march for the Vega with a strong body of men. Guarionex did not await his coming. He saw that every attempt was fruitless to shake off these strangers, who had settled like a curse upon his territories. He had found their very friendship withering and destructive, and he now dreaded their vengeance. Abandoning, therefore, his rightful domain, the once happy Vega, he fled with his family and a small band of faithful followers to the mountains of Ciguay. This is a lofty chain, extending along the north side of the island, between the Vega and the sea. The inhabitants were the most robust and hardy tribe of the island, and far more formidable than the mild inhabitants of the plains. It was a part of this tribe which displayed hostility to the Spaniards in the course of the first voyage of Columbus, and in a skirmish with them in the Gulf of Semana the first drop of native blood had been shed in the New World. The reader may remember the frank and confiding conduct of these people the day after the skirmish, and the intrepid faith with which their cacique trusted himself on board of the caravel of the admiral, and in the power of the Spaniards. It was to this same cacique, named Mayobanex, that the fugitive chieftain of the Vega now applied for refuge. He came to his residence at an Indian town near Cape Cabron, about forty leagues east of Isabella, and implored shelter for his wife and children, and his handful of loyal followers. The noble-minded cacique of the mountains received him with open arms. He not only gave an asylum to his family, but engaged to stand by him in his distress, to defend his cause, and share his desperate fortunes.[*] Men in civilized life learn magnanimity from precept, but their most generous actions are often rivaled by the deeds of untutored savages, who act only from natural impulse.

---

[*] Las Casas, *Hist. Ind.*, cap. 121, MS; Peter Martyr, decad. i. cap. 5.

Aided by his mountain ally, and by bands of hardy Ciguayans, Guarionex made several descents into the plain, cutting off straggling parties of the Spaniards, laying waste the villages of the natives which continued in allegiance to them, and destroying the fruits of the earth. The Adelantado put a speedy stop to these molestations; but he determined to root out so formidable an adversary from the neighbourhood. Shrinking from no danger nor fatigue, and leaving nothing to be done by others which he could do himself, he set forth in the spring with a band of ninety men, a few cavalry, and a body of Indians, to penetrate the Ciguay mountains.

After passing a steep defile, rendered almost impracticable for troops by rugged rocks and exuberant vegetation, he descended into a beautiful valley or plain, extending along the coast, and embraced by arms of the mountains which approached the sea. His advance into the country was watched by the keen eyes of Indian scouts who lurked among rocks and thickets. As the Spaniards were seeking the ford of a river at the entrance of the plain, two of these spies darted from among the bushes on its bank. One flung himself headlong into the water, and swimming across the mouth of the river escaped; the other being taken, gave information that six thousand Indians lay in ambush on the opposite shore, waiting to attack them as they crossed.

The Adelantado advanced with caution, and finding a shallow place, entered the river with his troops. They were scarcely midway in the stream when the savages, hideously painted, and looking more like fiends than men, burst from their concealment. The forest rang with their yells and howlings. They discharged a shower of arrows and lances, by which, notwithstanding the protection of their targets, many of the Spaniards were wounded. The Adelantado, however, forced his way across the river, and the

Indians took to flight. Some were killed, but their swiftness of
foot, their knowledge of the forest, and their dexterity in winding
through the most tangled thickets, enabled the greater number to
elude the pursuit of the Spaniards, who were encumbered with
armour, targets, crossbows, and lances.

By the advice of one of his Indian guides, the Adelantado
pressed forward along the valley to reach the residence of Mayobanex, at Cabron. In the way he had several skirmishes with the
natives, who would suddenly rush forth with furious war-cries
from ambuscades among the bushes, discharge their weapons,
and take refuge again in the fastnesses of their rocks and forests,
inaccessible to the Spaniards.

Having taken several prisoners, the Adelantado sent one accompanied by an Indian of a friendly tribe, as a messenger to
Mayobanex, demanding the surrender of Guarionex; promising
friendship and protection in case of compliance, but threatening,
in case of refusal, to lay waste his territory with fire and sword.
The cacique listened attentively to the messenger: 'Tell the
Spaniards,' said he in reply, 'that they are bad men, cruel and
tyrannical; usurpers of the territories of others, and shedders of
innocent blood. I desire not the friendship of such men; Guarionex is a good man, he is my friend, he is my guest, he has fled
to me for refuge, I have promised to protect him, and I will keep
my word.'

This magnanimous reply, or rather defiance, convinced the
Adelantado that nothing was to be gained by friendly overtures.
When severity was required, he could be a stern soldier. He
immediately ordered the village in which he had been quartered,
and several others in the neighbourhood, to be set on fire. He
then sent further messengers to Mayobanex, warning him that,
unless he delivered up the fugitive cacique, his whole dominions
should be laid waste in like manner; and he would see nothing in
every direction but the smoke and flames of burning villages.
Alarmed at this impending destruction, the Ciguayans surrounded
their chieftain with clamorous lamentations, cursing the day that
Guarionex had taken refuge among them, and urging that he
should be given up for the salvation of the country. The generous
cacique was inflexible. He reminded them of the many virtues of
Guarionex, and the sacred claims he had on their hospitality, and

declared he would abide all evils, rather than it should ever be said Mayobanex had betrayed his guest.

The people retired with sorrowful hearts, and the chieftain, summoning Guarionex into his presence, again pledged his word to protect him, though it should cost him his dominions. He sent no reply to the Adelantado, and lest further messages might tempt the fidelity of his subjects, he placed men in ambush, with orders to slay any messenger who might approach. They had not lain in wait long, before they beheld two men advancing through the forest, one of whom was a captive Ciguayan, and the other an Indian ally of the Spaniards. They were both instantly slain. The Adelantado was following at no great distance, with only ten foot-soldiers and four horsemen. When he found his messengers lying dead in the forest path, transfixed with arrows, he was greatly exasperated, and resolved to deal rigorously with this obstinate tribe. He advanced, therefore, with all his force to Cabron, where Mayobanex and his army were quartered. At his approach the inferior caciques and their adherents fled, overcome by terror of the Spaniards. Finding himself thus deserted, Mayobanex took refuge with his family in a secret part of the mountains. Several of the Ciguayans sought for Guarionex, to kill him or deliver him up as a propitiatory offering, but he fled to the heights, where he wandered about alone, in the most savage and desolate places.

The density of the forests and the ruggedness of the mountains rendered this expedition excessively painful and laborious, and protracted it far beyond the time that the Adelantado had contemplated. His men suffered, not merely from fatigue, but hunger. The natives had all fled to the mountains; their villages remained empty and desolate; all the provisions of the Spaniards consisted of cassava bread, and such roots and herbs as their Indian allies could gather for them, with now and then a few utias taken with the assistance of their dogs. They slept almost always on the ground, in the open air, under the trees, exposed to the heavy dew which falls in this climate. For three months they were thus ranging the mountains, until almost worn out with toil and hard fare. Many of them had farms in the neighbourhood of Fort Conception, which required their attention; they, therefore, entreated permission, since the Indians were terrified and dispersed, to return to their abodes in the Vega.

The Adelantado granted many of them passports and an allowance out of the scanty stock of bread which remained. Retaining
only thirty men, he resolved with these to search every den and
cavern of the mountains until he should find the two caciques.
It was difficult, however, to trace them in such a wilderness.
There was no one to give a clue to their retreat, for the whole
country was abandoned. There were the habitations of men,
but not a human being to be seen; or if, by chance, they caught
some wretched Indian stealing forth from the mountains in quest
of food, he always professed utter ignorance of the hiding-place
of the caciques.

It happened one day, however, that several Spaniards, while
hunting utias, captured two of the followers of Mayobanex, who
were on their way to a distant village in search of bread. They were
taken to the Adelantado, who compelled them to betray the place
of concealment of their chieftain, and to act as guides. Twelve
Spaniards volunteered to go in quest of him. Stripping themselves
naked, staining and painting their bodies so as to look like Indians,
and covering their swords with palm-leaves, they were conducted
by the guides to the retreat of the unfortunate Mayobanex. They
came secretly upon him, and found him surrounded by his wife
and children and a few of his household, totally unsuspicious of
danger. Drawing their swords, the Spaniards rushed upon them,
and made them all prisoners. When they were brought to the
Adelantado, he gave up all further search after Guarionex, and
returned to Fort Conception.

Among the prisoners thus taken was the sister of Mayobanex.
She was the wife of another cacique of the mountains, whose
territories had never yet been visited by the Spaniards; and she
was reputed to be one of the most beautiful women of the island.
Tenderly attached to her brother, she had abandoned the security
of her own dominions, and had followed him among rocks and
precipices, participating in all his hardships, and comforting him
with a woman's sympathy and kindness. When her husband
heard of her captivity, he hastened to the Adelantado and offered
to submit himself and all his possessions to his sway, if his wife
might be restored to him. The Adelantado accepted his offer
of allegiance, and released his wife and several of his subjects
who had been captured. The cacique, faithful to his word,

became a firm and valuable ally of the Spaniards, cultivating large tracts of land, and supplying them with great quantities of bread and other provisions.

Kindness appears never to have been lost upon the people of this island. When this act of clemency reached the Ciguayans, they came in multitudes to the fortress, bringing presents of various kinds, promising allegiance, and imploring the release of Mayobanex and his family. The Adelantado granted their prayers in part, releasing the wife and household of the cacique, but still detaining him prisoner to insure the fidelity of his subjects.

In the meantime the unfortunate Guarionex, who had been hiding in the wildest parts of the mountains, was driven by hunger to venture down occasionally into the plain in quest of food. The Ciguayans looking upon him as the cause of their misfortunes, and perhaps hoping by his sacrifice to procure the release of their chieftain, betrayed his haunts to the Adelantado. A party was despatched to secure him. They lay in wait in the path by which he usually returned to the mountains. As the unhappy cacique, after one of his famished excursions, was returning to his den among the cliffs, he was surprised by the lurking Spaniards, and brought in chains to Fort Conception. After his repeated insurrections, and the extraordinary zeal and perseverance displayed in his pursuit, Guarionex expected nothing less than death from the vengeance of the Adelantado. Don Bartholomew, however, though stern in his policy, was neither vindictive nor cruel in his nature. He considered the tranquillity of the Vega sufficiently secured by the captivity of the cacique; and ordered him to be detained a prisoner and hostage in the fortress. The Indian hostilities in this important part of the island being thus brought to a conclusion, and precautions taken to prevent their recurrence, Don Bartholomew returned to the city of San Domingo, where, shortly after his arrival, he had the happiness of receiving his brother, the admiral, after nearly two years and six months' absence.*

Such was the active, intrepid, and sagacious, but turbulent and disastrous administration of the Adelantado, in which we find evidences of the great capacity, the mental and bodily vigour of

* The particulars of this chapter are chiefly from P. Martyr, decad. i. lib. vi.; the manuscript history of Las Casas, lib. i. cap. 121; and Herrera, *Hist. Ind.*, decad. i. lib. iii. cap. 8, 9.

this self-formed and almost self-taught man. He united, in a singular degree, the sailor, the soldier, and the legislator. Like his brother, the admiral, his mind and manners rose immediately to the level of his situation, showing no arrogance nor ostentation, and exercising the sway of sudden and extraordinary power with the sobriety and moderation of one who had been born to rule. He has been accused of severity in his government, but no instance appears of a cruel or wanton abuse of authority. If he was stern towards the factious Spaniards, he was just; the disasters of his administration were not produced by his own rigour, but by the perverse passions of others, which called for its exercise; and the admiral, who had more suavity of manner and benevolence of heart, was not more fortunate in conciliating the good will, and insuring the obedience of the colonists. The merits of Don Bartholomew do not appear to have been sufficiently appreciated by the world. His portrait has been suffered to remain too much in the shade; it is worthy of being brought into the light, as a companion to that of his illustrious brother. Less amiable and engaging, perhaps, in its lineaments, and less characterized by magnanimity, its traits are nevertheless bold, generous, and heroic, and stamped with iron firmness.

BOOK 12

CHAPTER I
August 30, 1498

Columbus arrived at San Domingo wearied by a long and arduous voyage, and worn down by infirmities; both mind and body craved repose, but from the time he first entered into public life, he had been doomed never again to taste the sweets of tranquillity. The island of Hispaniola, the favourite child as it were of his hopes, was destined to involve him in perpetual troubles, to fetter his fortunes, impede his enterprises, and imbitter the conclusion of his life. What a scene of poverty and suffering had this opulent and lovely island been rendered by the bad passions of a few despicable men! The wars with the natives and the seditions among the colonists had put a stop to the labours of the mines, and all hopes of wealth were at an end. The horrors of famine had succeeded to those of war. The cultivation of the earth had been generally neglected; several of the provinces had been desolated during the late troubles; a great part of the Indians had fled to the mountains, and those who remained had lost all heart to labour, seeing the produce of their toils liable to be wrested from them by ruthless strangers. It is true, the Vega was once more tranquil, but it was a desolate tranquillity. That beautiful region, which the Spaniards but four years before had found so populous and happy, seeming to inclose in its luxuriant bosom all the sweets of nature, and to exclude all the cares and sorrows of the world, was now a scene of wretchedness and repining. Many of those Indian towns, where the Spaniards had been detained by genial hospitality, and almost worshiped as beneficent deities, were now silent and deserted. Some of their late inhabitants were lurking among rocks and caverns; some were reduced to slavery; many had perished with hunger, and many had fallen by the sword. It seems almost incredible, that so small a number of men, restrained too by

well-meaning governors, could in so short a space of time have
produced such wide-spreading miseries. But the principles of evil
have a fatal activity. With every exertion, the best of men can do
but a moderate amount of good; but it seems in the power of the
most contemptible individual to do incalculable mischief.

The evil passions of the white men, which had inflicted such
calamities upon this innocent people, had insured likewise a merited
return of suffering to themselves. In no part was this more truly
exemplified than among the inhabitants of Isabella, the most idle,
factious, and dissolute of the island. The public works were un-
finished; the gardens and fields they had begun to cultivate lay
neglected: they had driven the natives from their vicinity by
extortion and cruelty, and had rendered the country around them
a solitary wilderness. Too idle to labour, and destitute of any resources with which to occupy their indolence, they quarrelled
among themselves, mutinied against their rulers, and wasted their
time in alternate riot and despondency. Many of the soldiery
quartered about the island had suffered from ill health during the
late troubles, being shut up in Indian villages where they could take
no exercise, and obliged to subsist on food to which they could not
accustom themselves. Those actively employed had been worn
down by hard service, long marches, and scanty food. Many of
them were broken in constitution, and many had perished by
disease. There was a universal desire to leave the island, and escape
from miseries created by themselves. Yet this was the favoured and
fruitful land to which the eyes of philosophers and poets in Europe
were fondly turned, as realizing the pictures of the golden age. So
true it is, that the fairest Elysium fancy ever devised would be
turned into a purgatory by the passions of bad men!

One of the first measures of Columbus on his arrival was to issue
a proclamation approving of all the measures of the Adelantado,
and denouncing Roldan and his associates. That turbulent man
had taken possession of Xaragua, and been kindly received by the
natives. He had permitted his followers to lead an idle and
licentious life among its beautiful scenes, making the surrounding
country and its inhabitants subservient to their pleasures and their
passions. An event happened previous to their knowledge of the
arrival of Columbus, which threw supplies into their hands, and
strengthened their power. As they were one day loitering on the

sea-shore, they beheld three caravels at a distance, the sight of which, in this unfrequented part of the ocean, filled them with wonder and alarm. The ships approached the land, and came to anchor. The rebels apprehended at first they were vessels despatched in pursuit of them. Roldan, however, who was sagacious as he was bold, surmised them to be ships which had wandered from their course, and been borne to the westward by the currents, and that they must be ignorant of the recent occurrences of the island. Enjoining secrecy on his men, he went on board, pretending to be stationed in that neighbourhood for the purpose of keeping the natives in obedience, and collecting tribute. His conjectures as to the vessels were correct. They were, in fact, the three caravels detached by Columbus from his squadron at the Canary Islands, to bring supplies to the colonies. The captains, ignorant of the strength of the currents, which set through the Caribbean Sea, had been carried west far beyond their reckoning, until they had wandered to the coast of Xaragua.

Roldan kept his secret closely for three days. Being considered a man in important trust and authority, the captains did not hesitate to grant all his requests for supplies. He procured swords, lances, crossbows, and various military stores; while his men, dispersed through the three vessels, were busy among the crews, secretly making partisans, representing the hard life of the colonists at San Domingo, and the ease and revelry in which they passed their time at Xaragua. Many of the crews had been shipped in compliance with the admiral's ill-judged proposition, to commute criminal punishments into transportation to the colony. They were vagabonds, the refuse of Spanish towns, and culprits from Spanish dungeons; the very men, therefore, to be wrought upon by such representations, and they promised to desert on the first opportunity and join the rebels.

It was not until the third day, that Alonzo Sanchez de Carvajal, the most intelligent of the three captains, discovered the real character of the guests he had admitted so freely on board of his vessels. It was then too late; the mischief was effected. He and his fellow captains had many earnest conversations with Roldan, endeavouring to persuade him from his dangerous opposition to the regular authority. The certainty that Columbus was actually on his way to the island, with additional forces, and augmented authority, had operated strongly on his mind. He had, as has already been intimated, prepared his friends at San Domingo to plead his cause with the admiral, assuring him that he had only acted in opposition to the injustice and oppression of the Adelantado, but was ready to submit to Columbus on his arrival. Carvajal perceived that the resolution of Roldan and of several of his principal confederates was shaken, and flattered himself, that, if he were to remain some little time among the rebels, he might succeed in drawing them back to their duty. Contrary winds rendered it impossible for the ships to work up against the currents to San Domingo. It was arranged among the captains, therefore, that a large number of the people on board, artificers and others most important to the service of the colony, should proceed to the settlement by land. They were to be conducted by Juan Antonio Colombo, captain of one of the caravels, a relative of the admiral, and zealously devoted to his interests. Arana was to proceed with the ships, when the wind would permit, and Carvajal volunteered to remain on shore, to endeavour to bring the rebels to their allegiance.

On the following morning, Juan Antonio Colombo landed with forty men well armed with crossbows, swords, and lances, but was astonished to find himself suddenly deserted by all his party excepting eight. The deserters went off to the rebels, who received with exultation this important reinforcement of kindred spirits. Juan Antonio endeavoured in vain by remonstrances and threats to bring them back to their duty. They were most of them convicted culprits, accustomed to detest order, and to set law at defiance. It was equally in vain that he appealed to Roldan, and reminded him of his professions of loyalty to the government. The latter replied that he had no means of enforcing obedience; his was a mere 'Monastery of Observation', where everyone was at liberty to adopt the habit of the order. Such was the first of a long train of evils, which sprang from this most ill-judged expedient of peopling a colony with criminals, and thus mingling vice and villany with the fountain-head of its population.

Juan Antonio, grieved and disconcerted, returned on board with the few who remained faithful. Fearing further desertions, the two captains immediately put to sea, leaving Carvajal on shore, to prosecute his attempt at reforming the rebels. It was not without great difficulty and delay that the vessels reached San Domingo; the ship of Carvajal having struck on a sand-bank, and sustained great injury. By the time of their arrival, the greater part of the provisions with which they had been freighted was either exhausted or damaged. Alonzo Sanchez de Carvajal arrived shortly afterwards by land, having been escorted to within six leagues of the place by several of the insurgents, to protect him from the Indians. He failed in his attempt to persuade the band to immediate submission; but Roldan had promised that the moment he heard of the arrival of Columbus, he would repair to the neighbourhood of San Domingo, to be at hand to state his grievances, and the reasons of his past conduct, and to enter into a negotiation for the adjustment of all differences. Carvajal brought a letter from him to the admiral to the same purport; and expressed a confident opinion, from all that he observed of the rebels, that they might easily be brought back to their allegiance by an assurance of amnesty.*

---

* Las Casas, lib. i. cap. 149, 150; Herrera, decad. i. lib. iii. cap. 12; *Hist. del Almirante*, cap. 77.

Notwithstanding the favourable representations of Carvajal, Columbus was greatly troubled by the late event at Xaragua. He saw that the insolence of the rebels, and their confidence in their strength, must be greatly increased by the accession of such a large number of well-armed and desperate confederates. The proposition of Roldan to approach to the neighbourhood of San Domingo startled him. He doubted the sincerity of his professions, and apprehended great evils and dangers from so artful, daring, and turbulent a leader, with a rash and devoted crew at his command. The example of this lawless horde, roving at large about the island, and living in loose revel and open profligacy, could not but have a dangerous effect upon the colonists newly arrived; and when they were close at hand, to carry on secret intrigues, and to hold out a camp of refuge to all malcontents, the loyalty of the whole colony might be sapped and undermined.

Some measures were immediately necessary to fortify the fidelity of the people against such seductions. He was aware of a vehement desire among many to return to Spain; and of an assertion industriously propagated by the seditious, that he and his brothers wished to detain the colonists on the island through motives of self-interest. On the 12th of September, therefore, he issued a proclamation, offering free passage and provisions for the voyage to all who wished to return to Spain, in five vessels nearly ready to put to sea. He hoped by this means to relieve the colony from the idle and disaffected; to weaken the party of Roldan, and to retain none about him but such as were sound-hearted and well-disposed.

He wrote at the same time to Miguel Ballester, the staunch and well-tried veteran who commanded the fortress of Conception, advising him to be upon his guard, as the rebels were coming into his neighbourhood. He empowered him also to have an interview with Roldan; to offer him pardon and oblivion of the past, on condition of his immediate return to duty; and to invite him to repair to San Domingo to have an interview with the admiral, under a solemn, and, if required, a written assurance from the latter, of personal safety. Columbus was sincere in his intentions. He was of a benevolent and placable disposition, and singularly free from all vindictive feelings towards the many worthless and wicked men who heaped sorrow on his head.

Ballester had scarcely received this letter, when the rebels began to arrive at the village of Bonao. This was situated in a beautiful valley, or Vega, bearing the same name, about ten leagues from Fort Conception, and about twenty from San Domingo, in a well-peopled and abundant country. Here Pedro Riquelme, one of the ringleaders of the sedition, had large possessions, and his residence became the headquarters of the rebels. Adrian de Moxica, a man of turbulent and mischievous character, brought his detachment of dissolute ruffians to this place of rendezvous. Roldan and others of the conspirators drew together there by different routes.

No sooner did the veteran Miguel Ballester hear of the arrival of Roldan, than he set forth to meet him. Ballester was a venerable man, gray-headed, and of a soldier-like demeanor. Loyal, frank, and virtuous, of a serious disposition, and great simplicity of heart, he was well chosen as a mediator with rash and profligate men; being calculated to calm their passions by his sobriety; to disarm their petulance by his age; to win their confidence by his artless probity; and to awe their licentiousness by his spotless virtue.*

Ballester found Roldan in company with Pedro Riquelme, Pedro de Gamez, and Adrian de Moxica, three of his principal confederates. Flushed with a confidence of his present strength, Roldan treated the proffered pardon with contempt, declaring that he did not come there to treat of peace, but to demand the release of certain Indians captured unjustifiably, and about to be shipped to Spain as slaves, notwithstanding that he, in his capacity of alcalde mayor, had pledged his word for their protection. He declared that, until these Indians were given up, he would listen to no terms of compact; throwing out an insolent intimation at the same time, that he held the admiral and his fortunes in his hand, to make and mar them as he pleased.

* Las Casas, *Hist. Ind.*, lib. i. cap. 153.

The Indians he alluded to were certain subjects of Guarionex, who had been incited by Roldan to resist the exaction of tribute, and who, under the sanction of his supposed authority, had engaged in the insurrections of the Vega. Roldan knew that the enslavement of the Indians was an unpopular feature in the government of the island, especially with the queen; and the artful character of this man is evinced in his giving his opposition to Columbus the appearance of a vindication of the rights of the suffering islanders. Other demands were made of a highly insolent nature, and the rebels declared that, in all further negotiations, they would treat with no other intermediate agent than Carvajal, having had proofs of his fairness and impartiality in the course of their late communications with him at Xaragua.

This arrogant reply to his proffer of pardon was totally different from what the admiral had been led to expect, and placed him in an embarrassing situation. He seemed surrounded by treachery and falsehood. He knew that Roldan had friends and secret partisans even among those who professed to remain faithful; and he knew not how far the ramifications of the conspiracy might extend. A circumstance soon occurred to show the justice of his apprehensions. He ordered the men of San Domingo to appear under arms, that he might ascertain the force with which he could take the field in case of necessity. A report was immediately circulated that they were to be led to Bonao, against the rebels. Not above seventy men appeared under arms, and of these not forty were to be relied upon. One affected to be lame, another ill; some had relations, and others had friends among the followers of Roldan: almost all were disaffected to the service.[*]

Columbus saw that a resort to arms would betray his own weakness and the power of the rebels, and completely prostrate the dignity and authority of government. It was necessary to temporize, therefore, however humiliating such conduct might be deemed. He had detained the five ships for eighteen days in port, hoping in some way to have put an end to this rebellion, so as to send home favourable accounts of the island to the sovereigns. The provisions of the ships, however, were wasting. The Indian prisoners on board were suffering and perishing; several of them threw themselves overboard, or were suffocated with heat in the

* Hist. del Almirante, cap. 78.

holds of the vessels. He was anxious, also, that as many of the discontented colonists as possible should make sail for Spain before any commotion should take place.

On the 18th of October, therefore, the ships put to sea.* Columbus wrote to the sovereigns an account of the rebellion, and of his proffered pardon being refused. As Roldan pretended that it was a mere quarrel between him and the Adelantado, of which the admiral was not an impartial judge, the latter entreated that Roldan might be summoned to Spain, where the sovereigns might be his judges; or that an investigation might take place in presence of Alonzo Sanchez de Carvajal, who was friendly to Roldan, and of Miguel Ballester, as witness on the part of the Adelantado. He attributed, in a great measure, the troubles of this island to his own long detention in Spain, and the delays thrown in his way by those appointed to assist him, who had retarded the departure of the ships with supplies, until the colony had been reduced to the greatest scarcity. Hence had arisen discontent, murmuring, and finally rebellion. He entreated the sovereigns, in the most pressing manner, that the affairs of the colony might not be neglected, and those at Seville, who had charge of its concerns, might be instructed at least not to devise impediments instead of assistance. He alluded to his chastisement of the contemptible Ximeno Breviesca, the insolent minion of Fonseca, and entreated that neither that nor any other circumstance might be allowed to prejudice him in the royal favour, through the misrepresentations of designing men. He assured them that the natural resources of the island required nothing but good management to supply all the wants of the colonists; but that the latter were indolent and profligate. He proposed to send home, by every ship, as in the present instance, a number of the discontented and worthless, to be replaced by sober and industrious men. He begged also that ecclesiastics might be sent out for the instruction and conversion of the Indians; and, what was equally necessary, for the reformation of the dissolute Spaniards. He required also a man learned in the law, to officiate as judge over the island, together with several officers of the royal revenue. Nothing could surpass the soundness and policy of these suggestions; but unfortunately one clause marred the moral beauty

---

* In one of these ships sailed the father of the venerable historian Las Casas, from whom he derived many of the facts of his history. Las Casas, lib. i. cap. 153.

of this excellent letter. He requested that for two years longer the
Spaniards might be permitted to employ the Indians as slaves; only
making use of such, however, as were captured in wars and
insurrections. Columbus had the usage of the age in excuse for this
suggestion; but it is at variance with his usual benignity of feeling,
and his paternal conduct towards these unfortunate people.

At the same time he wrote another letter, giving an account of
his recent voyage, accompanied by a chart, and by specimens of
the gold, and particularly of the pearls found in the Gulf of Paria.
He called especial attention to the latter as being the first specimens of pearls found in the New World. It was in this letter that
he described the newly-discovered continent in such enthusiastic
terms, as the most favoured part of the east, the source of inexhaustible treasures, the supposed seat of the terrestrial Paradise;
and he promised to prosecute the discovery of its glorious realms
with the three remaining ships, as soon as the affairs of the island
should permit.

By this opportunity, Roldan and his friends likewise sent letters to
Spain, endeavouring to justify their rebellion by charging Columbus and his brothers with oppression and injustice, and painting
their whole conduct in the blackest colors. It would naturally be
supposed that the representations of such men would have little
weight in the balance against the tried merits and exalted services of
Columbus: but they had numerous friends and relatives in Spain;
they had the popular prejudice on their side, and there were
designing persons in the confidence of the sovereigns ready to
advocate their cause. Columbus, to use his own simple but affecting words, was 'absent, envied, and a stranger'.[*]

---

[*] Las Casas, *Hist. Ind.*, lib. i. cap. 157.

The ships being despatched, Columbus resumed his negotiation with the rebels; determined at any sacrifice to put an end to a sedition which distracted the island and interrupted all his plans of discovery. His three remaining ships lay idle in the harbour, though a region of apparently boundless wealth was to be explored. He had intended to send his brother on the discovery, but the active and military spirit of the Adelantado rendered his presence indispensable, in case the rebels should come to violence. Such were the difficulties encountered at every step of his generous and magnanimous enterprises; impeded at one time by the insidious intrigues of crafty men in place, and checked at another by the insolent turbulence of a handful of ruffians.

In his consultations with the most important persons about him, Columbus found that much of the popular discontent was attributed to the strict rule of his brother, who was accused of dealing out justice with a rigorous hand. Las Casas, however, who saw the whole of the testimony collected from various sources with respect to the conduct of the Adelantado, acquits him of all charges of the kind, and affirms that, with respect to Roldan in particular, he had exerted great forbearance. Be this as it may, Columbus now, by the advice of his counselors, resolved to try the alternative of extreme lenity. He wrote a letter to Roldan, dated the 20th of October, couched in the most conciliating terms, calling to mind past kindnesses, and expressing deep concern for the feud existing between him and the Adelantado. He entreated him, for the common good, and for the sake of his own reputation, which stood well with the sovereigns, not to persist in his present insubordination, and repeated the assurance, that he and his companions might come to him, under the faith of his word for the inviolability of their persons.

There was a difficulty as to who should be the bearer of this letter. The rebels had declared that they would receive no one as mediator but Alonzo Sanchez de Carvajal. Strong doubts, however, existed in the minds of those about Columbus as to the integrity of that officer. They observed that he had suffered Roldan to remain two days on board of his caravel at Xaragua; had furnished him with weapons and stores; had neglected to detain him on board, when he knew him to be a rebel; had not exerted himself to retake the deserters; had been escorted on his way to San Domingo by the rebels, and had sent refreshments to them at Bonao. It was alleged, moreover, that he had given himself out as a colleague of Columbus, appointed by government to have a watch and control over his conduct. It was suggested, that, in advising the rebels to approach San Domingo, he had intended, in case the admiral did not arrive, to unite his pretended authority as colleague, to that of Roldan, as chief judge, and to seize upon the reins of government. Finally, the desire of the rebels to have him sent to them as an agent, was cited as proof that he was to join them as a leader, and that the standard of rebellion was to be hoisted at Bonao.* These circumstances, for some time, perplexed Columbus: but he reflected that Carvajal, as far as he had observed his conduct, had behaved like a man of integrity; most of the circumstances alleged against him admitted of a construction in his favour; the rest were mere rumours, and he had unfortunately experienced, in his own case, how easily the fairest actions, and the fairest characters, may be falsified by rumour. He discarded, therefore, all suspicion, and determined to confide implicitly in Carvajal; nor had he ever any reason to repent of his confidence.

The admiral had scarcely despatched this letter, when he received one from the leaders of the rebels, written several days previously. In this they not merely vindicated themselves from the charge of rebellion, but claimed great merit, as having dissuaded their followers from a resolution to kill the Adelantado, in revenge of his oppressions, prevailing upon them to await patiently for redress from the admiral. A month had elapsed since his arrival, during which they had waited anxiously for his orders, but he had manifested nothing but irritation against them. Considerations of

* *Hist. del Almirante*, cap. 78.

honour and safety, therefore, obliged them to withdraw from his service, and they accordingly demanded their discharge. This letter was dated from Bonao, the 17th of October, and signed by Francisco Roldan, Adrian de Moxica, Pedro de Gamez, and Diego de Escobar.*

In the meantime, Carvajal arrived at Bonao, accompanied by Miguel Ballester. They found the rebels full of arrogance and presumption. The conciliating letter of the admiral, however, enforced by the earnest persuasions of Carvajal, and the admonitions of the veteran Ballester, had a favourable effect on several of the leaders, who had more intellect than their brutal followers. Roldan, Gamez, Escobar, and two or three others, actually mounted their horses to repair to the admiral, but were detained by the clamorous opposition of their men; too infatuated with their idle, licentious mode of life, to relish the idea of a return to labour and discipline. These insisted that it was a matter which concerned them all; whatever arrangement was to be made, therefore, should be made in public, in writing, and subject to their approbation or dissent. A day or two elapsed before this clamour could be appeased. Roldan then wrote to the admiral, that his followers objected to his coming, unless a written assurance, or passport, were sent, protecting the persons of himself and such as should accompany him. Miguel Ballester wrote, at the same time, to the admiral, urging him to agree to whatever terms the rebels might demand. He represented their forces as continually augmenting, the soldiers of his garrison daily deserting to them; unless, therefore, some compromise were speedily effected, and the rebels shipped off to Spain, he feared that not merely the authority, but even the person of the admiral would be in danger; for though the hidalgos and the officers and servants immediately about him would, doubtless, die in his service, the common people were but little to be depended upon.†

Columbus felt the increasing urgency of the case, and sent the required passport. Roldan came to San Domingo; but, from his conduct, it appeared as if his object was to make partisans, and gain deserters, rather than to effect a reconciliation. He had several conversations with the admiral, and several letters passed between

* *Hist. del Almirante*, cap. 79; Herrera, decad. i. lib. iii. cap 13.
† Las Casas, *Hist. Ind.*, lib. i. cap. 153.

them. He made many complaints, and numerous demands; Columbus made large concessions, but some of the pretensions were
too arrogant to be admitted.* Nothing definite was arranged.
Roldan departed under the pretext of conferring with his people,
promising to send his terms in writing. The admiral sent his mayor-
domo, Diego de Salamanca, to treat in his behalf.†

On the 6th of November, Roldan wrote a letter from Bonao,
containing his terms, and requesting that a reply might be sent
to him to Conception, as scarcity of provisions obliged him to
leave Bonao. He added that he should wait for a reply until the
following Monday (the 11th). There was an insolent menace
implied in this note, accompanied as it was by insolent demands.
The admiral found it impossible to comply with the latter; but to
manifest his lenient disposition, and to take from the rebels all plea
of rigor, he had a proclamation affixed for thirty days at the gate of
the fortress, promising full indulgence and complete oblivion of
the past to Roldan and his followers, on condition of their presenting themselves before him and returning to their allegiance to
the crown within a month; together with free conveyance for all
such as wished to return to Spain; but threatening to execute
rigorous justice upon those who should not appear within the
limited time. A copy of this paper he sent to Roldan by Carvajal,
with a letter, stating the impossibility of compliance with his
terms, but offering to agree to any compact drawn up with the
approbation of Carvajal and Salamanca.

When Carvajal arrived, he found the veteran Ballester actually
besieged in his fortress of Conception by Roldan, under pretext of
claiming, in his official character of alcalde mayor, a culprit who
had taken refuge there from justice. He had cut off the supply of
water from the fort, by way of distressing it into a surrender.
When Carvajal posted up the proclamation of the admiral on the
gate of the fortress, the rebels scoffed at the proffered amnesty,
saying that, in a little while, they would oblige the admiral to ask
the same at their hands. The earnest intercessions of Carvajal,
however, brought the leaders at length to reflection, and through
his mediation articles of capitulation were drawn up. By these it
was agreed that Roldan and his followers should embark for Spain

---

* Las Casas, *Hist. Ind.*, lib. i. cap. 158.
† *Hist. del Almirante*, cap. 79.

from the port of Xaragua in two ships, to be fitted out and victualled within fifty days: that they should each receive from the admiral a certificate of good conduct, and an order for the amount of their pay, up to the actual date: that slaves should be given to them, as had been given to others, in consideration of services performed; and as several of their company had wives, natives of the island, who were pregnant, or had lately been delivered, they might take them with them, if willing to go, in place of the slaves: that satisfaction should be made for property of some of the company which had been sequestrated, and for livestock which had belonged to Francisco Roldan. There were other conditions, providing for the security of their persons: and it was stipulated that, if no reply were received to these terms within eight days, the whole should be void.*

This agreement was signed by Roldan and his companions at Fort Conception on the 16th of November, and by the admiral at San Domingo on the 21st. At the same time, he proclaimed a further act of grace, permitting such as chose to remain in the island either to come to San Domingo, and enter into the royal service, or to hold lands in any part of the island. They preferred, however, to follow the fortunes of Roldan, who departed with his band for Xaragua, to await the arrival of the ships, accompanied by Miguel Ballester, sent by the admiral to superintend the preparations for their embarkation.

Columbus was deeply grieved to have his projected enterprise to Terra Firma impeded by such contemptible obstacles, and the ships which should have borne his brother to explore that newly-found continent devoted to the use of this turbulent and worthless rabble. He consoled himself, however, with the reflection, that all the mischief which had so long been lurking in the island, would thus be at once shipped off, and thenceforth everything restored to order and tranquillity. He ordered every exertion to be made, therefore, to get the ships in readiness to be sent round to Xaragua; but the scarcity of sea-stores, and the difficulty of completing the arrangements for such a voyage in the disordered state of the colony, delayed their departure far beyond the stipulated time. Feeling that he had been compelled to a kind of deception towards the sovereigns, in the certificate of good conduct given to Roldan

---

* *Hist. del Almirante*, cap. 80.

and his followers, he wrote a letter to them, stating the circumstances under which that certificate had been in a manner wrung
from him to save the island from utter confusion and ruin. He
represented the real character and conduct of those men; how they
had rebelled against his authority; prevented the Indians from
paying tribute; pillaged the island; possessed themselves of large
quantities of gold, and carried off the daughters of several of the
caciques. He advised, therefore, that they should be seized, and
their slaves and treasure taken from them, until their conduct
could be properly investigated. This letter he intrusted to a confidential person, who was to go in one of the ships.*

The rebels having left the neighbourhood, and the affairs of San
Domingo being in a state of security, Columbus put his brother
Don Diego in temporary command, and departed with the Adelantado on a tour of several months to visit the various stations, and
restore the island to order.

The two caravels destined for the use of the rebels sailed from
San Domingo for Xaragua about the end of February; but, encountering a violent storm, were obliged to put into one of the
harbours of the island, where they were detained until the end of
March. One was so disabled as to be compelled to return to San
Domingo. Another vessel was despatched to supply its place, in
which the indefatigable Carvajal set sail, to expedite the embarkation of the rebels. He was eleven days in making the voyage, and
found the other caravel at Xaragua.

The followers of Roldan had in the meantime changed their
minds, and now refused to embark; as usual, they threw all the
blame on Columbus, affirming that he had purposely delayed the
ships far beyond the stipulated time; that he had sent them in
a state not seaworthy, and short of provisions; with many other
charges, artfully founded on circumstances over which they knew
he could have no control. Carvajal made a formal protest before a
notary who had accompanied him, and finding that the ships were
suffering great injury from the teredo or worm, and their provisions failing, he sent them back to San Domingo, and set out on
his return by land. Roldan accompanied him a little distance on
horseback, evidently disturbed in mind. He feared to return to
Spain, yet was shrewd enough to know the insecurity of his present

* Herrera, *Hist. Ind.*, decad. i. lib. iii. cap. 16.

situation at the head of a band of dissolute men, acting in defiance of authority. What tie had he upon their fidelity stronger than the sacred obligations which they had violated? After riding thoughtfully for some distance, he paused, and requested some private conversation with Carvajal before they parted. They alighted under the shade of a tree. Here Roldan made further professions of the loyalty of his intentions, and finally declared, that if the admiral would once more send him a written security for his person, with the guarantee also of the principal persons about him, he would come to treat with him, and trusted that the whole matter would be arranged on terms satisfactory to both parties. This offer, however, he added, must be kept secret from his followers.

Carvajal, overjoyed at this prospect of a final arrangement, lost no time in conveying the proposition of Roldan to the admiral. The latter immediately forwarded the required passport or security, sealed with the royal seal, accompanied by a letter written in amicable terms, exhorting his quiet obedience to the authority of the sovereigns. Several of the principal persons also, who were with the admiral, wrote, at his request, a letter of security to Roldan, pledging themselves for the safety of himself and his followers during the negotiation; provided they did nothing hostile to the royal authority or its representative.

While Columbus was thus, with unwearied assiduity and loyal zeal, endeavouring to bring the island back to its obedience, he received a reply from Spain, to the earnest representations made by him, in the preceding autumn, of the distracted state of the colony and the outrages of these lawless men, and his prayers for royal countenance and support. The letter was written by his invidious enemy, the Bishop Fonseca, superintendent of Indian affairs. It acknowledged the receipt of his statement of the alleged insurrection of Roldan, but observed that this matter must be suffered to remain in suspense, as the sovereigns would investigate and remedy it presently.[*]

This cold reply had a disheartening effect upon Columbus. He saw that his complaints had little weight with the government; he feared that his enemies were prejudicing him with the sovereigns; and he anticipated redoubled insolence on the part of the rebels, when they should discover how little influence he possessed in

[*] Herrera, decad. i. lib. iii. cap. 16.

Spain. Full of zeal, however, for the success of his undertaking, and of fidelity to the interests of the sovereigns, he resolved to spare no personal sacrifice of comfort or dignity in appeasing the troubles of the island. Eager to expedite the negotiation with Roldan, therefore, he sailed in the latter part of August with two caravels to the port of Azua, west of San Domingo, and much nearer to Xaragua. He was accompanied by several of the most important personages of the colony. Roldan repaired thither likewise, with the turbulent Adrian de Moxica, and a number of his band. The concessions already obtained had increased his presumption; and he had, doubtless, received intelligence of the cold manner in which the complaints of the admiral had been received in Spain. He conducted himself more like a conqueror, exacting triumphant terms, than a delinquent seeking to procure pardon by atonement. He came on board of the caravel, and with his usual effrontery, propounded the preliminaries upon which he and his companions were disposed to negotiate.

First, that he should be permitted to send several of his company, to the number of fifteen, to Spain, in the vessels which were at San Domingo. Secondly, that those who remained should have lands granted them, in place of royal pay. Thirdly, that it should be proclaimed, that everything charged against him and his party had been grounded upon false testimony, and the machinations of persons disaffected to the royal service. Fourthly, that he should be reinstated in his office of alcalde mayor, or chief judge.[*]

These were hard and insolent conditions to commence with, but they were granted. Roldan then went on shore, and communicated them to his companions. At the end of the two days the insurgents sent their capitulations, drawn up in form, and couched in arrogant language, including all the stipulations granted at Fort Conception, with those recently demanded by Roldan, and concluding with one, more insolent than all the rest, namely, that if the admiral should fail in the fulfilment of any of these articles, they should have a right to assemble together, and compel his performance of them by force, or by any other means they might think proper.[†] The conspirators thus sought not merely exculpation of the past, but a pretext for future rebellion.

[*] Herrera, decad. i. lib. iii. cap. 16.
[†] Herrera, decad. i. lib. iii. cap. 16; *Hist. del Almirante*, cap. 83.

The mind grows wearied and impatient with recording, and the heart of the generous reader must burn with indignation at perusing, this protracted and ineffectual struggle of a man of the exalted merits and matchless services of Columbus, in the toils of such miscreants. Surrounded by doubt and danger, a foreigner among a jealous people, an unpopular commander in a mutinous island, distrusted and slighted by the government he was seeking to serve, and creating suspicion by his very services, he knew not where to look for faithful advice, efficient aid, or candid judgment. The very ground on which he stood seemed giving way under him, for he was told of seditious symptoms among his own people. Seeing the impunity with which the rebels rioted in the possession of one of the finest parts of the island, they began to talk among themselves of following their example, of abandoning the standard of the admiral, and seizing upon the province of Higuey, at the eastern extremity of the island, which was said to contain valuable mines of gold.

Thus critically situated, disregarding every consideration of personal pride and dignity, and determined, at any individual sacrifice, to secure the interests of an ungrateful sovereign, Columbus forced himself to sign this most humiliating capitulation. He trusted that afterwards, when he could gain quiet access to the royal ear, he should be able to convince the king and queen that it had been compulsory, and forced from him by the extraordinary difficulties in which he had been placed, and the imminent perils of the colony. Before signing it, however, he inserted a stipulation, that the commands of the sovereigns, of himself, and of the justices appointed by him, should be punctually obeyed.*

---

* Herrera, *Hist. Ind.*, decad. i. lib. iii. cap. 16.

CHAPTER 4

1499

When Roldan resumed his office of alcalde mayor, or chief judge, he displayed all the arrogance to be expected from one who had intruded himself into power by profligate means. At the city of San Domingo, he was always surrounded by his faction; communed only with the dissolute and disaffected; and, having all the turbulent and desperate men of the community at his beck, was enabled to intimidate the quiet and loyal by his frowns. He bore an impudent front against the authority even of Columbus himself, discharging from office one Rodrigo Perez, a lieutenant of the admiral, declaring that none but such as he appointed should bear a staff of office in the island.* Columbus had a difficult and painful task in bearing with the insolence of this man, and of the shameless rabble which had returned, under his auspices, to the settlements. He tacitly permitted many abuses; endeavouring by mildness and indulgence to allay the jealousies and prejudices awakened against him, and by various concessions to lure the factious to the performance of their duty. To such of the colonists generally as preferred to remain in the island, he offered a choice of either royal pay or portions of lands, with a number of Indians, some free, others as slaves, to assist in the cultivation. The latter was generally preferred; and grants were made out, in which he endeavoured, as much as possible, to combine the benefit of the individual with the interests of the colony.

Roldan presented a memorial signed by upwards of one hundred of his late followers, demanding grants of lands and licenses to settle, and choosing Xaragua for their place of abode. The admiral feared to trust such a numerous body of factious partisans in so remote a province; he contrived, therefore, to distribute them in various parts of the island; some at Bonao, where their settlement

* Herrera, *Hist. Ind.*, decad. i. lib. iii cap. 16.

gave origin to the town of that name; others on the bank of the Rio Verde, or Green River, in the Vega; others about six leagues thence, at St Jago. He assigned to them liberal portions of land, and numerous Indian slaves, taken in the wars. He made an arrangement, also, by which the caciques in their vicinity, instead of paying tribute, should furnish parties of their subjects, free Indians, to assist the colonists in the cultivation of their lands: a kind of feudal service, which was the origin of the repartimientos, or distributions of free Indians among the colonists, afterwards generally adopted, and shamefully abused, throughout the Spanish colonies: a source of intolerable hardships and oppressions to the unhappy natives, and which greatly contributed to exterminate them from the island of Hispaniola.* Columbus considered the island in the light of a conquered country, and arrogated to himself all the rights of a conqueror, in the name of the sovereigns for whom he fought. Of course all his companions in the enterprise were entitled to take part in the acquired territory, and to establish themselves there as feudal lords, reducing the natives to the condition of villains or vassals.† This was an arrangement widely different from his original intention of treating the natives with kindness, as peaceful subjects of the crown. But all his plans had been subverted, and his present measures forced upon him by the exigency of the times, and the violence of lawless men. He appointed a captain with an armed band, as a kind of police, with orders to range the provinces, oblige the Indians to pay their tributes, watch over the conduct of the colonists, and check the least appearance of mutiny or insurrection.‡

Having sought and obtained such ample provisions for his followers, Roldan was not more modest in making demands for himself. He claimed certain lands in the vicinity of Isabella, as having belonged to him before his rebellion; also a royal farm, called La Esperanza, situated on the Vega, and devoted to the rearing of poultry. These the admiral granted him, with permission to employ, in the cultivation of the farm, the subjects of the cacique whose ears had been cut off by Alonzo de Ojeda in his first military expedition into the Vega. Roldan received also

* Herrera, decad. i. lib. iii. cap. 16.
† Muñoz, *Hist. N. Mundo*, lib. vi. § 50.
‡ *Hist. del Almirante*, cap. 84.

grants of land in Xaragua, and a variety of livestock from the cattle and other animals belonging to the crown. These grants were made to him provisionally, until the pleasure of the sovereigns should be known; * for Columbus yet trusted, that when they should understand the manner in which these concessions had been extorted from him, the ringleaders of the rebels would not merely be stripped of their ill-gotten possessions, but receive well-merited punishment.

Roldan, having now enriched himself beyond his hopes, requested permission of Columbus to visit his lands. This was granted with great reluctance. He immediately departed for the Vega, and stopping at Bonao, his late headquarters, made Pedro Riquelme, one of his most active confederates, alcalde, or judge of the place, with the power of arresting all delinquents, and sending them prisoners to the fortress of Conception, where he reserved to himself the right of sentencing them. This was an assumption of powers not vested in his office, and gave great offence to Columbus. Other circumstances created apprehensions of further troubles from the late insurgents. Pedro Riquelme, under pretext of erecting farming buildings for his cattle, began to construct a strong edifice on a hill, capable of being converted into a formidable fortress. This, it was whispered, was done in concert with Roldan, by way of securing a stronghold in case of need. Being in the neighbourhood of the Vega, where so many of their late partisans were settled, it would form a dangerous rallying place for any new sedition. The designs of Riquelme were suspected and his proceedings opposed by Pedro de Arana, a loyal and honourable man, who was on the spot. Representations were made by both parties to the admiral, who prohibited Riquelme from proceeding with the construction of his edifice.†

Columbus had prepared to return, with his brother Don Bartholomew, to Spain, where he felt that his presence was of the utmost importance to place the late events of the island in a proper light; having found that his letters of explanation were liable to be counteracted by the misrepresentations of malevolent enemies. The island, however, was still in a feverish state. He was not well assured of the fidelity of the late rebels, though

---

* Herrera, decad. i. lib. iii. cap. 16.
† Ibid.; *Hist. del Almirante*, cap. 83, 84.

so dearly purchased; there was a rumour of a threatened descent into the Vega, by the mountain tribes of Ciguay, to attempt the rescue of their captive cacique Mayobanex, still detained a prisoner in the fortress of Conception. Tidings were brought about the same time from the western parts of the island, that four strange ships had arrived at the coast, under suspicious appearances. These circumstances obliged him to postpone his departure, and held him involved in the affairs of this favourite but fatal island.

The two caravels were despatched for Spain in the beginning of October, taking such of the colonists as chose to return, and among them a number of Roldan's partisans. Some of these took with them slaves, others carried away the daughters of caciques whom they had beguiled from their families and homes. At these iniquities, no less than at many others which equally grieved his spirit, the admiral was obliged to connive. He was conscious, at the same time, that he was sending home a reinforcement of enemies and false witnesses, to defame his character and traduce his conduct, but he had no alternative. To counteract, as much as possible, their misrepresentations, he sent by the same caravel the loyal and upright veteran Miguel Ballester, together with Garcia de Barrantes, empowered to attend to his affairs at court, and furnished with the dispositions taken relative to the conduct of Roldan and his accomplices.

In his letters to the sovereigns, he entreated them to inquire into the truth of the late transactions. He stated his opinion that his capitulations with the rebels were null and void, for various reasons, viz. – they had been extorted from him by violence, and at sea, where he did not exercise the office of viceroy; there had been two trials relative to the insurrection, and the insurgents having been condemned as traitors, it was not in the power of the admiral to absolve them from their criminality; the capitulations treated of matters touching the royal revenue, over which he had no control, without the intervention of the proper officers; lastly, Francisco Roldan and his companions, on leaving Spain, had taken an oath to be faithful to the sovereigns, and to the admiral in their name, which oath they had violated. For these and similar reasons, some just, others rather sophistical, he urged the sovereigns not to consider themselves bound to ratify the compulsory terms ceded to these profligate men, but to inquire into their offences, and treat them accordingly.*

He repeated the request made in a former letter, that a learned judge might be sent out to administer the laws in the island, since he himself had been charged with rigor, although conscious of having always observed a guarded clemency. He requested also that discreet persons should be sent out to form a council, and others for certain fiscal employments, entreating, however, that their powers should be so limited and defined, as not to interfere with his dignity and privileges. He bore strongly on this point; as his prerogatives on former occasions had been grievously invaded. It appeared to him, he said, that princes ought to show much confidence in their governors; for without the royal favour to give them strength and consequence, everything went to ruin under their command; a sound maxim, forced from the admiral by his recent experience, in which much of his own perplexities, and the triumph of the rebels, had been caused by the distrust of the crown, and its inattention to his remonstrances.

Finding age and infirmity creeping upon him, and his health much impaired by his last voyage, he began to think of his son Diego, as an active coadjutor; who, being destined as his successor, might gain experience under his eye, for the future discharge of his high duties. Diego, though still serving as a page at the court, was grown to man's estate, and capable of entering into the important concerns of life. Columbus entreated, therefore, that he might be sent out to assist him, as he felt himself infirm in health and broken in constitution, and less capable of exertion than formerly.†

* Herrera, decad. i. lib. iii. cap. 16.
† Ibid.

1499

Among the causes which induced Columbus to postpone his departure for Spain, has been mentioned the arrival of four ships at the western part of the island. These had anchored on the 5th of September in a harbour a little below Jacquemel, apparently with the design of cutting dye-woods, which abound in that neighbourhood, and of carrying off the natives for slaves. Further reports informed him that they were commanded by Alonzo de Ojeda, the same hot-headed and bold-hearted cavalier who had distinguished himself on various occasions in the previous voyages of discovery, and particularly in the capture of the cacique Caonabo. Knowing the daring and adventurous spirit of this man, Columbus felt much disturbed at his visiting the island in this clandestine manner, on what appeared to be little better than a freebooting expedition. To call him to account, and oppose his aggressions, required an agent of spirit and address. No one seemed better fitted for the purpose than Roldan. He was as daring as Ojeda, and of a more crafty character. An expedition of the kind would occupy the attention of himself and his partisans, and divert them from any schemes of mischief. The large concessions recently made to them would, he trusted, secure their present fidelity, rendering it more profitable for them to be loyal than rebellious.

Roldan readily undertook the enterprise. He had nothing further to gain by sedition, and was anxious to secure his ill-gotten possessions and atone for past offences by public services. He was vain as well as active, and took a pride in acquitting himself well in an expedition which called for both courage and shrewdness. Departing from San Domingo with two caravels, he arrived on the 29th of September within two leagues of the harbour where the ships of Ojeda were anchored. Here he landed with five-and-twenty resolute followers, well armed, and accustomed to range the forests. He sent five scouts to reconnoitre. They brought word that Ojeda was several leagues distant from his ships, with only fifteen men, employed in making cassava bread in an Indian village. Roldan threw himself between them and the ships, thinking to take them by surprise. They were apprised, however, of his approach by the Indians, with whom the very name of Roldan inspired terror, from his late excesses in Xaragua. Ojeda saw his danger; he supposed Roldan had been sent in pursuit of him, and he found himself cut off from his ships. With his usual intrepidity he immediately presented himself before Roldan, attended merely by half a dozen followers. The latter craftily began by conversing on general topics. He then inquired into his motives for landing on the island, particularly on that remote and lonely part, without first reporting his arrival to the admiral. Ojeda replied, that he had been on a voyage of discovery, and had put in there in distress, to repair his ships and procure provisions. Roldan then demanded, in the name of the government, a sight of the license under which he sailed. Ojeda, who knew the resolute character of the man he had to deal with, restrained his natural impetuosity, and replied that his papers were on board of his ship. He declared his intention, on departing thence, to go to San Domingo, and pay his homage to the admiral, having many things to tell him which were for his private ear alone. He intimated to Roldan that the admiral was in complete disgrace at court; that there was a talk of taking from him his command, and that the queen, his patroness, was ill beyond all hopes of recovery. This intimation, it is presumed, was referred to by Roldan in his dispatches to the admiral, wherein he mentioned that certain things had been communicated to him by Ojeda, which he did not think it safe to confide to a letter.

Roldan now repaired to the ships. He found several persons on board with whom he was acquainted, and who had already been in Hispaniola. They confirmed the truth of what Ojeda had said, and showed a license signed by the Bishop of Fonseca, as superintendent of the affairs of the Indias, authorizing him to sail on a voyage of discovery.[*]

It appeared, from the report of Ojeda and his followers, that the glowing accounts sent home by Columbus of his late discoveries on the coast of Paria, his magnificent speculations with respect to

---

[*] Herrera, decad. i. lib. iv. cap. 3.

the riches of the newly-found country, and the specimen of pearls transmitted to the sovereigns, had inflamed the cupidity of various adventurers. Ojeda happened to be at that time in Spain. He was a favourite of the Bishop of Fonseca, and obtained a sight of the letter written by the admiral to the sovereigns, and the charts and maps of his route by which it was accompanied. Ojeda knew Columbus to be embarrassed by the seditions of Hispaniola; he found, by his conversations with Fonseca and other of the admiral's enemies, that strong doubts and jealousies existed in the mind of the king with respect to his conduct, and that his approaching downfall was confidently predicted. The idea of taking advantage of these circumstances struck Ojeda, and, by a private enterprise, he hoped to be the first in gathering the wealth of these newly-discovered regions. He communicated his project to his patron, Fonseca. The latter was but too ready for anything that might defeat the plans and obscure the glory of Columbus; and it may be added that he always showed himself more disposed to patronize mercenary adventurers than upright and high-minded men. He granted Ojeda every facility; furnishing him with copies of the papers and charts of Columbus, by which to direct himself in his course, and a letter of license signed with his own name, though not with that of the sovereigns. In this, it was stipulated that he should not touch at any land belonging to the King of Portugal, nor any that had been discovered by Columbus prior to 1495. The last provision shows the perfidious artifice of Fonseca, as it left Paria and the Pearl Islands free to the visits of Ojeda, they having been discovered by Columbus subsequent to the designated year. The ships were to be fitted out at the charges of the adventurers, and a certain proportion of the products of the voyage were to be rendered to the crown.

Under this license Ojeda fitted out four ships at Seville, assisted by many eager and wealthy speculators. Among the number was the celebrated Amerigo Vespucci, a Florentine merchant, well acquainted with geography and navigation. The principal pilot of the expedition was Juan de la Cosa, a mariner of great repute, a disciple of the admiral, whom he had accompanied in his first voyage of discovery, and in that along the southern coast of Cuba, and round the island of Jamaica. There were several also of the mariners, and Bartholomew Roldan, a distinguished pilot, who

had been with Columbus in his voyage to Paria.* Such was the
expedition which, by a singular train of circumstances, eventually
gave the name of this Florentine merchant, Amerigo Vespucci, to
the whole of the New World.

This expedition had sailed in May 1499. The adventurers had
arrived on the southern continent, and ranged along its coast, from
two hundred leagues east of the Orinoco to the Gulf of Paria.
Guided by the charts of Columbus, they had passed through this
gulf, and through the Boca del Dragon, and had kept along
westward to Cape de la Vela, visiting the island of Margarita and
the adjacent continent, and discovering the Gulf of Venezuela.
They had subsequently touched at the Caribbee Islands, where
they had fought with the fierce natives, and made many captives,
with the intention of selling them in the slave-markets of Spain.
Thence, being in need of supplies, they had sailed to Hispaniola,
having performed the most extensive voyage hitherto made along
the shores of the New World.[†]

Having collected all the information that he could obtain concerning these voyagers, their adventures and designs, and trusting
to the declaration of Ojeda, that he should proceed forthwith to
present himself to the admiral, Roldan returned to San Domingo
to render a report of his mission.

---

* Las Casas.

[†] Herrera, *Hist. Ind.*, decad. i. lib. iv. cap. 4; Muñoz, *Hist. N. Mundo*, part in MS
unpublished.

When intelligence was brought to Columbus of the nature of the expedition of Ojeda, and the license under which he sailed, he considered himself deeply aggrieved, it being a direct infraction of his most important prerogatives, and sanctioned by authority which ought to have held them sacred. He awaited patiently, however, the promised visit of Alonzo de Ojeda to obtain fuller explanations. Nothing was further from the intention of that roving commander than to keep such promise: he had made it merely to elude the vigilance of Roldan. As soon as he had refitted his vessels and obtained a supply of provisions, he sailed round to the coast of Xaragua, where he arrived in February. Here he was well received by the Spaniards resident in that province, who supplied all his wants. Among them were many of the late comrades of Roldan; loose, random characters, impatient of order and restraint, and burning with animosity against the admiral, for having again brought them under the wholesome authority of the laws.

Knowing the rash and fearless character of Ojeda, and finding that there were jealousies between him and the admiral, they hailed him as a new leader, come to redress their fancied grievances, in place of Roldan, whom they considered as having deserted them. They made clamorous complaints to Ojeda of the injustice of the admiral, whom they charged with withholding from them the arrears of their pay.

Ojeda was a hot-headed man, with somewhat of a vaunting spirit, and immediately set himself up for a redresser of grievances. It is said also that he gave himself out as authorized by government, in conjunction with Carvajal, to act as counsellors, or rather supervisors of the admiral; and that one of the first measures they were to take, was to enforce the payment of all salaries due to

the servants of the crown.* It is questionable, however, whether
Ojeda made any pretension of the kind, which could so readily be
disproved, and would have tended to disgrace him with the
government. It is probable that he was encouraged in his inter-
meddling, chiefly by his knowledge of the tottering state of the
admiral's favour at court, and of his own security in the powerful
protection of Fonseca. He may have imbibed also the opinion,
diligently fostered by those with whom he had chiefly communicated in Spain, just before his departure, that these people had
been driven to extremities by the oppression of the admiral and his
brothers. Some feeling of generosity, therefore, may have mingled
with his usual love of action and enterprise, when he proposed to
redress all their wrongs, put himself at their head, march at once to
San Domingo, and oblige the admiral to pay them on the spot, or
expel him from the island.

The proposition of Ojeda was received with acclamations of
transport by some of the rebels; others made objections. Quarrels
arose: a ruffianly scene of violence and brawl ensued, in which
several were killed and wounded on both sides; but the party for
the expedition to San Domingo remained triumphant.

Fortunately for the peace and safety of the admiral, Roldan
arrived in the neighbourhood just at this critical juncture, attended
by a crew of resolute fellows. He had been despatched by Columbus to watch the movements of Ojeda, on hearing of his arrival
on the coast of Xaragua. Apprised of the violent scenes which were
taking place, Roldan, when on the way, sent to his old confederate
Diego de Escobar, to follow him with all the trusty force he could
collect. They reached Xaragua within a day of each other. An
instance of the bad faith usual between bad men was now evinced.
The former partisans of Roldan, finding him earnest in his intention
of serving the government, and that there was no hope of engaging
him in their new sedition, sought to waylay and destroy him on his
march, but his vigilance and celerity prevented them.†

Ojeda, when he heard of the approach of Roldan and Escobar,
retired on board of his ships. Though of a daring spirit, he had no
inclination, in the present instance, to come to blows where there
was a certainty of desperate fighting and no gain; and where he

* *Hist. del Almirante*, cap. 84.
† *Hist. del Almirante*, cap. 84.

must raise his arm against government. Roldan now issued such remonstrances as had often been ineffectually addressed to himself. He wrote to Ojeda, reasoning with him on his conduct, and the confusion he was producing in the island, and inviting him on shore to an amicable arrangement of all alleged grievances. Ojeda, knowing the crafty, violent character of Roldan, disregarded his repeated messages, and refused to venture within his power. He even seized one of his messengers, Diego de Truxillo, and landing suddenly at Xaragua, carried off another of his followers, named Toribio de Lenares; both of whom he detained in irons, on board of his vessel, as hostages for a certain Juan Pintor, a one-armed sailor, who had deserted, threatening to hang them if the deserter was not given up.*

Various manoeuvres took place between these two well-matched opponents; each wary of the address and prowess of the other. Ojeda made sail and stood twelve leagues to the northward, to the province of Cahay, one of the most beautiful and fertile parts of the country, and inhabited by a kind and gentle people. Here he landed with forty men, seizing upon whatever he could find of the provisions of the natives. Roldan and Escobar followed along shore, and were soon at his heels. Roldan then despatched Escobar in a light canoe, paddled swiftly by Indians, who, approaching within hail of the ship, informed Ojeda that, since he would not trust himself on shore, Roldan would come and confer with him on board, if he would send a boat for him.

Ojeda now thought himself secure of his enemy; he immediately despatched a boat within a short distance of the shore, where the crew lay on their oars, requiring Roldan to come to them. 'How many may accompany me?' demanded the latter. 'Only five or six,' was the reply. Upon this Diego de Escobar and four others waded to the boat. The crew refused to admit more. Roldan then ordered one man to carry him to the barge, and another to walk by his side, and assist him. By this stratagem, his party was eight strong. The instant he entered the boat, he ordered the oarsmen to row to shore. On their refusing, he and his companions attacked them sword in hand, wounded several, and made all prisoners, excepting an Indian archer, who, plunging under the water, escaped by swimming.

* Las Casas, *Hist. Ind.*, lib. i. cap. 169, MS.

This was an important triumph for Roldan. Ojeda, anxious for
the recovery of his boat, which was indispensable for the service of
the ship, now made overtures of peace. He approached the shore in
his remaining boat, of small size, taking with him his principal
pilot, an arquebusier, and four oarsmen. Roldan entered the boat he
had just captured, with seven rowers and fifteen fighting men,
causing fifteen others to be ready on shore to embark in a large
canoe, in case of need. A characteristic interview took place
between these doughty antagonists, each keeping warily on his
guard. Their conference was carried on at a distance. Ojeda justified his hostile movements by alleging that Roldan had come with
an armed force to seize him. This the latter positively denied,
promising him the most amicable reception from the admiral, in
case he would repair to San Domingo. An arrangement was at
length effected; the boat was restored, and mutual restitution of the
men took place, with the exception of Juan Pintor, the one-armed
deserter, who had absconded; and on the following day, Ojeda,
according to agreement, set sail to leave the island, threatening
however to return at a future time with more ships and men.[*]

Roldan waited in the neighbourhood, doubting the truth of his
departure. In the course of a few days, word was brought that
Ojeda had landed on a distant part of the coast. He immediately
pursued him with eighty men in canoes, sending scouts by land.
Before he arrived at the place, Ojeda had again made sail, and
Roldan saw and heard no more of him. Las Casas asserts, however,
that Ojeda departed either to some remote district of Hispaniola,
or to the island of Porto Rico, where he made up what he called
his *cavalgada*, or drove of slaves; carrying off numbers of the unhappy natives, whom he sold in the slave-market of Cadiz.[†]

[*] Letter of Columbus to the nurse of Prince Juan.
[†] Las Casas, lib. i. cap. 169.

When men have been accustomed to act falsely, they take great merit to themselves for an exertion of common honesty. The followers of Roldan were loud in trumpeting forth their unwonted loyalty, and the great services they had rendered to government in driving Ojeda from the island. Like all reformed knaves, they expected that their good conduct would be amply rewarded. Looking upon their leader as having everything in his gift, and being well pleased with the delightful province of Cahay, they requested him to share the land among them, that they might settle there. Roldan would have had no hesitation in granting their request, had it been made during his freebooting career; but he was now anxious to establish a character for adherence to the laws. He declined, therefore, acceding to their wishes, until sanctioned by the admiral. Knowing, however, that he had fostered a spirit among these men which it was dangerous to contradict, and that their rapacity, by long indulgence, did not admit of delay, he shared among them certain lands of his own, in the territory of his ancient host Behechio, cacique of Xaragua. He then wrote to the admiral for permission to return to San Domingo, and received a letter in reply, giving him many thanks and commendations for the diligence and address which he had manifested, but requesting him to remain for a time in Xaragua, lest Ojeda should be yet hovering about the coast, and disposed to make another descent in that province.

The troubles of the island were not yet at an end, but were destined again to break forth, and from somewhat of a romantic cause. There arrived about this time at Xaragua a young cavalier of noble family, named Don Hernando de Guevara. He possessed an agreeable person and winning manners, but was headstrong in his passions and dissolute in his principles. He was cousin to Adrian de Moxica, one of the most active ringleaders in the late rebellion of Roldan, and had conducted himself with such licentiousness at San Domingo, that Columbus had banished him from the island. There being no other opportunity of embarking, he had been sent to Xaragua, to return to Spain in one of the ships of Ojeda, but arrived after their departure. Roldan received him favourably, on account of his old comrade, Adrian de Moxica, and permitted him to choose some place of residence until further orders concerning him should arrive from the admiral. He chose the province of Cahay, at the place where Roldan had captured the boat of Ojeda. It was a delightful part of that beautiful coast; but the reason why Guevara chose it, was the vicinity to Xaragua. While at the latter place, in consequence of the indulgence of Roldan, he was favourably received at the house of Anacaona, the widow of Caonabo, and sister of the cacique Behechio. That remarkable woman still retained her partiality to the Spaniards, notwithstanding the disgraceful scenes which had passed before her eyes; and the native dignity of her character had commanded the respect even of the dissolute rabble which infested her province. By her late husband, the cacique Caonabo, she had a daughter named Higuenamota, just grown up, and greatly admired for her beauty. Guevara being often in company with her, a mutual attachment ensued. It was to be near her that he chose Cahay as a residence, at a place where his cousin Adrian de Moxica kept a number of dogs and hawks, to be employed in the chase. Guevara delayed his departure. Roldan discovered the reason, and warned him to desist from his pretensions and leave the province. Las Casas intimates that Roldan was himself attached to the young Indian beauty, and jealous of her preference of his rival. Anacaona, the mother, pleased with the gallant appearance and ingratiating manners of the youthful cavalier, favoured his attachment; especially as he sought her daughter in marriage. Notwithstanding the orders of Roldan, Guevara still lingered in Xaragua, in the house of Anacaona; and sending for a priest, desired him to baptize his intended bride.

Hearing of this, Roldan sent for Guevara, and rebuked him sharply for remaining at Xaragua, and attempting to deceive a person of the importance of Anacaona, by ensnaring the affections of her daughter. Guevara avowed the strength of his passion, and his correct intentions, and entreated permission to remain. Roldan was inflexible. He alleged that some evil construction might be put on his conduct by the admiral; but it is probable his true motive was a desire to send away a rival, who interfered with his own amorous designs. Guevara obeyed; but had scarce been three days at Cahay, when, unable to remain longer absent from the object of his passion, he returned to Xaragua, accompanied by four or five friends, and concealed himself in the dwelling of Anacaona. Roldan, who was at that time confined by a malady in his eyes, being apprised of his return, sent orders for him to depart instantly to Cahay. The young cavalier assumed a tone of defiance. He warned Roldan not to make foes when he had such great need of friends; for, to his certain knowledge, the admiral intended to behead him. Upon this, Roldan commanded him to quit that part of the island, and repair to San Domingo, to present himself before the admiral. The thoughts of being banished entirely from the vicinity of his Indian beauty checked the vehemence of the youth. He changed his tone of haughty defiance into one of humble supplication; and Roldan, appeased by this submission, permitted him to remain for the present in the neighbourhood.

Roldan had instilled wilfulness and violence into the hearts of his late followers, and now was doomed to experience the effects. Guevara, incensed at his opposition to his passion, meditated revenge. He soon made a party among the old comrades of Roldan, who detested as a magistrate the man they had idolized as a leader. It was concerted to rise suddenly upon him, and either to kill him or put out his eyes. Roldan was apprised of the plot, and proceeded with his usual promptness. Guevara was seized in the dwelling of Anacaona, in the presence of his intended bride; seven of his accomplices were likewise arrested. Roldan immediately sent an account of the affair to the admiral, professing, at present, to do nothing without his authority, and declaring himself not competent to judge impartially in the case. Columbus, who was at that time at Fort Conception, in the Vega, ordered the prisoner to be conducted to the fortress of San Domingo.

The vigorous measures of Roldan against his old comrades produced commotions in the island. When Adrian de Moxica heard that his cousin Guevara was a prisoner, and that, too, by command of his former confederate, he was highly exasperated, and resolved on vengeance. Hastening to Bonao, the old haunt of rebellion, he obtained the co-operation of Pedro Riquelme, the recently-appointed alcalde. They went round among their late companions in rebellion, who had received lands and settled in various parts of the Vega, working upon their ready passions, and enlisting their feelings in the cause of an old comrade. These men seem to have had an irresistible propensity to sedition. Guevara was a favourite with them all; the charms of the Indian beauty had probably their influence; and the conduct of Roldan was pronounced a tyrannical interference, to prevent a marriage agreeable to all parties, and beneficial to the colony. There is no being so odious to his former associates as a reformed robber, or a rebel enlisted in the service of justice. The old scenes of faction were renewed; the weapons which had scarce been hung up from the recent rebellions were again snatched down from the walls, and rash preparations were made for action. Moxica soon saw a body of daring and reckless men ready, with horse and weapon, to follow him on any desperate enterprise. Blinded by the impunity which had attended their former outrages, he now threatened acts of greater atrocity, meditating not merely the rescue of his cousin, but the death of Roldan and the admiral.

Columbus was at Fort Conception, with an inconsiderable force, when this dangerous plot was concerted in his very neighbourhood. Not dreaming of any further hostilities from men on whom he had lavished favours, he would doubtless have fallen into their power, had not intelligence been brought him of the plot by a deserter from the conspirators. He saw at a glance the perils by which he was surrounded, and the storm about to burst upon the island. It was no longer a time for lenient measures; he determined to strike a blow which should crush the very head of rebellion.

Taking with him but six or seven trusty servants, and three esquires, all well armed, he set out in the night for the place where the ringleaders were quartered. Confiding probably in the secrecy of their plot, and the late passiveness of the admiral, they appear to have been perfectly unguarded. Columbus came upon them by surprise, seized Moxica and several of his principal confederates, and bore them off to Fort Conception. The moment was critical; the Vega was ripe for a revolt; he had the fomenter of the conspiracy in his power, and an example was called for, that should strike terror into the factious. He ordered Moxica to be hanged on the top of the fortress. The latter entreated to be allowed to confess himself previous to execution. A priest was summoned. The miserable Moxica, who had been so arrogant in rebellion, lost all courage at the near approach of death. He delayed to confess, beginning and pausing, and recommencing, and again hesitating, as if he hoped, by whiling away time, to give a chance for rescue. Instead of confessing his own sins, he accused others of criminality, who were known to be innocent; until Columbus, incensed at this falsehood and treachery, and losing all patience, in his mingled indignation and scorn, ordered the dastard wretch to be swung off from the battlements.*

This sudden act of severity was promptly followed up. Several of the accomplices of Moxica were condemned to death and thrown in irons to await their fate. Before the conspirators had time to recover from their astonishment, Pedro Riquelme was taken, with several of his compeers, in his ruffian den at Bonao, and conveyed to the fortress of San Domingo, where was also confined the original mover of this second rebellion, Hernando de Guevara, the lover of the young Indian princess. These unexpected acts of rigour, proceeding from a quarter which had been long so lenient, had the desired effect. The conspirators fled for the most part to Xaragua, their old and favourite retreat. They were not suffered to congregate there again, and concert new seditions. The Adelantado, seconded by Roldan, pursued them with his characteristic rapidity of movement and vigour of arm. It has been said that he carried a priest with him, in order that, as he arrested delinquents, they might be confessed and hanged upon the spot; but the more probable account is that he transmitted them prisoners to San Domingo. He had seventeen of them at one time confined in one common dungeon, awaiting their trial, while he continued in indefatigable pursuit of the remainder.†

These were prompt and severe measures; but when we consider how long Columbus had borne with these men; how much he had ceded and sacrificed to them; how he had been interrupted in all his great undertakings, and the welfare of the colony destroyed by their contemptible and seditious brawls; how they had abused his lenity, defied his authority, and at length attempted his life, we

---

* Herrera, decad. i. lib. iv. cap. 5.
† Las Casas, *Hist. Ind.*, lib. i. cap. 170, MS; Herrera, decad. i. lib. iv. cap. 7.

cannot wonder that he should at last let fall the sword of justice, which he had hitherto held suspended.

The power of faction was now completely subdued; and the good effects of the various measures taken by Columbus, since his last arrival, for the benefit of the island, began to appear. The Indians, seeing the inefficacy of resistance, submitted to the yoke. Many gave signs of civilization, having, in some instances, adopted clothing and embraced Christianity. Assisted by their labours, the Spaniards now cultivated their lands diligently, and there was every appearance of settled and regular prosperity.

Columbus considered all this happy change as brought about by the especial intervention of heaven. In a letter to Dona Juana de la Torre, a lady of distinction, aya or nurse of Prince Juan, he gives an instance of those visionary fancies to which he was subject in times of illness and anxiety. In the preceding winter, he says, about the festival of Christmas, when menaced by Indian war and domestic rebellion, when distrustful of those around him and apprehensive of disgrace at court, he sank for a time into complete despondency. In this hour of gloom, when abandoned to despair, he heard in the night a voice addressing him in words of comfort, 'Oh man of little faith! why art thou cast down? Fear nothing, I will provide for thee. The seven years of the term of gold are not expired; in that, and in all other things, I will take care of thee.'

The seven years term of gold here mentioned, alludes to a vow made by Columbus on discovering the New World, and recorded by him in a letter to the sovereigns, that within seven years he would furnish, from the profits of his discoveries, fifty thousand foot and five thousand horse, for the deliverance of the holy sepulchre, and an additional force of like amount, within five years afterwards.

The comforting assurance given him by the voice was corroborated, he says, that very day, by intelligence received of the discovery of a large tract of country rich in mines.* This imaginary promise of divine aid thus mysteriously given, appeared to him at present in still greater progress of fulfilment. The troubles and dangers of the island had been succeeded by tranquillity. He now anticipated the prosperous prosecution of his favourite enterprise,

* Letter of Columbus to the nurse of Prince Juan; *Hist. del Almirante*, cap. 84.

so long interrupted – the exploring of the regions of Paria, and the establishment of a fishery in the Gulf of Pearls. How illusive were his hopes! At this moment events were maturing which were to overwhelm him with distress, strip him of his honours, and render him comparatively a wreck for the remainder of his days!

BOOK 13

CHAPTER I

1500

While Columbus was involved in a series of difficulties in the factious island of Hispaniola, his enemies were but too successful in undermining his reputation in the court of Spain. The report brought by Ojeda of his anticipated disgrace was not entirely unfounded; the event was considered near at hand, and every perfidious exertion was made to accelerate it. Every vessel from the New World came freighted with complaints, representing Columbus and his brothers as new men, unaccustomed to command, inflated by their sudden rise from obscurity; arrogant and insulting towards men of birth and lofty spirit; oppressive of the common people, and cruel in their treatment of the natives. The insidious and illiberal insinuation was continually urged, that they were foreigners, who could have no interest in the glory of Spain, or the prosperity of Spaniards; and contemptible as this plea may seem, it had a powerful effect. Columbus was even accused of a design to cast off all allegiance to Spain, and either make himself sovereign of the countries he had discovered, or yield them into the hands of some other power: a slander which, however extravagant, was calculated to startle the jealous mind of Ferdinand.

It is true, that by every ship Columbus likewise sent home statements, written with the frankness and energy of truth, setting forth the real cause and nature of the distractions of the island, and pointing out and imploring remedies, which, if properly applied, might have been efficacious. His letters, however, arriving at distant intervals, made but single and transient impressions on the royal mind, which were speedily effaced by the influence of daily and active misrepresentation. His enemies at court, having continual access to the sovereigns, were enabled to place everything urged against him in the strongest point of view, while they secretly neutralized the force of his vindications. They used a plausible logic to prove either bad management or bad faith on his part. There was an incessant drain upon the mother country for the support of the colony. Was this compatible with the extravagant pictures he had drawn of the wealth of the island, and its golden mountains, in which he had pretended to find the Ophir of ancient days, the source of all the riches of Solomon? They inferred that he had either deceived the sovereigns by designing exaggerations, or grossly wronged them by malpractices, or was totally incapable of the duties of government.

The disappointment of Ferdinand, in finding his newly-discovered possessions a source of expense instead of profit, was known to press sorely on his mind. The wars, dictated by his ambition, had straitened his resources, and involved him in perplexities. He had looked with confidence to the New World for relief, and for ample means to pursue his triumphs; and grew impatient at the repeated demands which it occasioned on his scanty treasury. For the purpose of irritating his feelings and heightening his resentment, every disappointed and repining man who returned from the colony was encouraged, by the hostile faction, to put in claims for pay withheld by Columbus, or losses sustained in his service. This was especially the case with the disorderly ruffians shipped off to free the island from sedition. Finding their way to the court of Granada, they followed the king when he rode out, filling the air with their complaints, and clamouring for their pay. At one time, about fifty of these vagabonds found their way into the inner court of the Alhambra, under the royal apartments, holding up bunches of grapes, as the meagre diet left them by their poverty, and railing aloud at the deceits of Columbus, and the cruel neglect of government. The two sons of Columbus, who were pages to the queen, happening to pass by, they followed them with imprecations, exclaiming, 'There go the sons of the admiral, the whelps of him who discovered the land of vanity and delusion, the grave of Spanish hidalgos.'*

The incessant repetition of falsehood will gradually wear its way into the most candid mind. Isabella herself began to entertain doubts respecting the conduct of Columbus. Where there was

* *Hist. del Almirante*, cap. 85.

such universal and incessant complaint, it seemed reasonable to conclude that there must exist some fault. If Columbus and his brothers were upright, they might be injudicious; and, in government, mischief is oftener produced through error of judgment than iniquity of design. The letters written by Columbus himself presented a lamentable picture of the confusion of the island. Might not this arise from the weakness and incapacity of the rulers? Even granting that the prevalent abuses arose in a great measure from the enmity of the people to the admiral and his brothers, and their prejudices against them as foreigners, was it safe to intrust so important and distant a command to persons so unpopular with the community?

These considerations had much weight in the candid mind of Isabella, but they were all-powerful with the cautious and jealous Ferdinand. He had never regarded Columbus with real cordiality; and ever since he had ascertained the importance of his discoveries, had regretted the extensive powers vested in his hands. The excessive clamours which had arisen during the brief administration of the Adelantado, and the breaking out of the faction of Roldan, at length determined the king to send out some person of consequence and ability, to investigate the affairs of the colony, and, if necessary for its safety, to take upon himself the command. This important and critical measure it appears had been decided upon, and the papers and powers actually drawn out, in the spring of 1499. It was not carried into effect, however, until the following year. Various reasons have been assigned for this delay. The important services rendered by Columbus in the discovery of Paria and the Pearl Islands may have had some effect on the royal mind. The necessity of fitting out an armament just at that moment, to co-operate with the Venetians against the Turks; the menacing movements of the new king of France, Louis XII; the rebellion of the Moors of the Alpuxarra mountains in the lately-conquered kingdom of Granada; all these have been alleged as reasons for postponing a measure which called for much consideration, and might have important effects upon the newly-discovered possessions.[*] The most probable reason, however, was the strong disinclination of Isabella to take so harsh a step against a man for whom she entertained such ardent gratitude and high admiration.

[*] Muñoz, *Hist. N. Mundo*, part unpublished.

At length the arrival of the ships with the late followers of Roldan, according to their capitulation, brought matters to a crisis. It is true that Ballester and Barrantes came in these ships, to place the affairs of the island in a proper light; but they brought out a host of witnesses in favour of Roldan, and letters written by himself and his confederates, attributing all their late conduct to the tyranny of Columbus and his brothers. Unfortunately, the testimony of the rebels had the greatest weight with Ferdinand; and there was a circumstance in the case which suspended for a time the friendship of Isabella, hitherto the greatest dependence of Columbus.

Having a maternal interest in the welfare of the natives, the queen had been repeatedly offended by what appeared to her pertinacity on the part of Columbus, in continuing to make slaves of those taken in warfare, in contradiction to her known wishes. The same ships which brought home the companions of Roldan, brought likewise a great number of slaves. Some, Columbus had been obliged to grant to these men by the articles of capitulation; others they had brought away clandestinely. Among them were several daughters of caciques, seduced away from their families and their native island by these profligates. Some of these were in a state of pregnancy, others had new-born infants. The gifts and transfers of these unhappy beings were all ascribed to the will of Columbus, and represented to Isabella in the darkest colours. Her sensibility as a woman, and her dignity as a queen, were instantly in arms. 'What power,' exclaimed she indignantly, 'has the admiral to give away my vassals?' * Determined, by one decided and peremptory act, to show her abhorrence of these outrages upon humanity, she ordered all the Indians to be restored to their country and friends. Nay more, her measure was retrospective. She commanded that those formerly sent to Spain by the admiral should be sought out, and sent back to Hispaniola. Unfortunately for Columbus, at this very juncture, in one of his letters, he advised the continuance of Indian slavery for some time longer, as a measure important for the welfare of the colony. This contributed to heighten the indignation of Isabella, and induced her no longer to oppose the sending out of a commission to investigate his conduct, and, if necessary, to supersede him in command.

* Las Casas, lib. i.

Ferdinand was exceedingly embarrassed in appointing this commission, between his sense of what was due to the character and services of Columbus, and his anxiety to retract with delicacy the powers vested in him. A pretext at length was furnished by the recent request of the admiral that a person of talents and probity, learned in the law, might be sent out to act as chief judge; and that an impartial umpire might be appointed, to decide in the affair between himself and Roldan. Ferdinand proposed to consult his wishes, but to unite those two officers in one; and as the person he appointed would have to decide in matters touching the highest functions of the admiral and his brothers, he was empowered, should he find them culpable, to supersede them in the government; a singular mode of insuring partiality!

The person chosen for this momentous and delicate office was Don Francisco de Bobadilla, an officer of the royal household, and a commander of the military and religious order of Calatrava. Oviedo pronounces him a very honest and religious man; * but he is represented by others, and his actions corroborate the description, as needy, passionate, and ambitious; three powerful objections to his exercising the rights of judicature in a case requiring the utmost patience, candour, and circumspection, and where the judge was to derive wealth and power from the conviction of one of the parties.

The authority vested in Bobadilla is defined in letters from the sovereigns still extant, and which deserve to be noticed chronologically; for the royal intentions appear to have varied with times and circumstances. The first was dated on the 21st of March, 1499, and mentions the complaint of the admiral that an alcalde, and certain other persons, had risen in rebellion against him. 'Wherefore,' adds the latter, 'we order you to inform yourself of the truth of the foregoing; to ascertain who and what persons they were who rose against the said admiral and our magistracy, and for what cause; and what robberies and other injuries they have committed; and furthermore, to extend your inquiries to all other matters relating to the premises; and the information obtained, and the truth known, whomsoever you find culpable, *arrest their persons, and sequestrate their effects*; and thus taken, proceed against them and the absent, both civilly and criminally, and impose and inflict such

* Oviedo, *Cronica*, lib. iii. cap. 6.

fines and punishments as you may think fit.' To carry this into effect, Bobadilla was authorized, in case of necessity, to call in the assistance of the admiral, and of all other persons in authority.

The powers here given are manifestly directed merely against the rebels, and in consequence of the complaints of Columbus. Another letter, dated on the 21st of May, two months subsequently, is of quite different purport. It makes no mention of Columbus, but is addressed to the various functionaries and men of property of the islands and Terra Firma, informing them of the appointment of Bobadilla to the government, with full civil and criminal jurisdiction. Among the powers specified, is the following: 'It is our will, that if the said commander, Francisco de Bobadilla, should think it necessary for our service, and the purposes of justice, that any cavaliers, or other persons who are at present in those islands, or may arrive there, should leave them, and not return and reside in them, and that they should come and present themselves before us, he may command it in our name, and oblige them to depart; and whomsoever he thus commands, we hereby order that immediately, without waiting to inquire or consult us, or to receive from us any other letter or command, and without interposing appeal or supplication, they obey whatever he shall say and order, under the penalties which he shall impose on our part,' etc. etc.

Another letter, dated likewise on the 21st of May, in which Columbus is styled simply 'admiral of the ocean sea', orders him and his brothers to surrender the fortress, ships, houses, arms, ammunition, cattle, and all other royal property, into the hands of Bobadilla, as governor, under penalty of incurring the punishments to which those subject themselves who refuse to surrender fortresses and other trusts, when commanded by their sovereigns.

A fourth letter, dated on the 26th of May, and addressed to Columbus, simply by the title of admiral, is a mere letter of credence, ordering him to give faith and obedience to whatever Bobadilla should impart.

The second and third of these letters were evidently provisional, and only to be produced if, on examination, there should appear such delinquency on the part of Columbus and his brothers as to warrant their being divested of command.

This heavy blow, as has been shown, remained suspended for a year; yet that it was whispered about, and triumphantly anticipated

by the enemies of Columbus, is evident from the assertions of
Ojeda, who sailed from Spain about the time of the signature of
those letters, and had intimate communications with Bishop Fonseca, who was considered instrumental in producing this measure.
The very license granted by the bishop to Ojeda to sail on a voyage
of discovery, in contravention of the prerogatives of the admiral, has
the air of being given on a presumption of his speedy downfall; and
the same presumption, as has already been observed, must have
encouraged Ojeda in his turbulent conduct at Xaragua.

At length the long-projected measure was carried into effect.
Bobadilla set sail for San Domingo about the middle of July 1500,
with two caravels, in which were twenty-five men, enlisted for a
year, to serve as a kind of guard. There were six friars likewise, who
had charge of a number of Indians sent back to their country.
Besides the letters patent, Bobadilla was authorized, by royal order,
to ascertain and discharge all arrears of pay due to persons in the
service of the crown; and to oblige the admiral to pay what was due
on his part, 'so that those people might receive what was owing to
them, and there might be no more complaints.' In addition to all
these powers, Bobadilla was furnished with many blank letters
signed by the sovereigns, to be filled up by him in such manner and
directed to such persons as he might think advisable, in relation to
the mission with which he was intrusted.*

* Herrera, decad. i. lib. iv. cap. 7.

Columbus was still at Fort Conception, regulating the affairs of
the Vega, after the catastrophe of the sedition of Moxica; his
brother, the Adelantado, accompanied by Roldan, was pursuing
and arresting the fugitive rebels in Xaragua; and Don Diego
Columbus remained in temporary command at San Domingo.
Faction had worn itself out; the insurgents had brought down ruin
upon themselves; and the island appeared delivered from the
domination of violent and lawless men.

Such was the state of public affairs, when, on the morning of the
23d of August, two caravels were descried off the harbour of San
Domingo, about a league at sea. They were standing off and on,
waiting until the sea breeze, which generally prevails about ten
o'clock, should carry them into port. Don Diego Columbus supposed them to be ships sent from Spain with supplies, and hoped to
find on board his nephew Diego, whom the admiral had requested
might be sent out to assist him in his various concerns. A canoe was
immediately despatched to obtain information; which, approaching
the caravels, inquired what news they brought, and whether Diego,
the son of the admiral, was on board. Bobadilla himself replied from
the principal vessel, announcing himself as a commissioner sent out
to investigate the late rebellion. The master of the caravel then
inquired about the news of the island, and was informed of the
recent transactions. Seven of the rebels, he was told, had been
hanged that week, and five more were in the fortress of San
Domingo, condemned to suffer the same fate. Among these were
Pedro Riquelme and Fernando de Guevara, the young cavalier
whose passion for the daughter of Anacaona had been the original
cause of the rebellion. Further, conversation passed, in the course of
which Bobadilla ascertained that the admiral and the Adelantado
were absent, and Don Diego Columbus in command.

When the canoe returned to the city, with the news that a
commissioner had arrived to make inquisition into the late troubles,
there was a great stir and agitation throughout the community.
Knots of whisperers gathered at every corner; those who were
conscious of malpractices were filled with consternation; while
those who had grievances, real or imaginary, to complain of,
especially those whose pay was in arrear, appeared with joyful
countenances.*

As the vessels entered the river, Bobadilla beheld on either bank
a gibbet with the body of a Spaniard hanging on it, apparently but
lately executed. He considered these as conclusive proofs of the
alleged cruelty of Columbus. Many boats came off to the ship,
everyone being anxious to pay early court to this public censor.
Bobadilla remained on board all day, in the course of which he
collected much of the rumours of the place; and as those who
sought to secure his favour were those who had most to fear from
his investigations, it is evident that the nature of the rumours must
generally have been unfavourable to Columbus. In fact, before
Bobadilla landed, if not before he arrived, the culpability of the
admiral was decided in his mind.

The next morning he landed with all his followers, and went to
the church to attend mass, where he found Don Diego Columbus,
Rodrigo Perez, the lieutenant of the admiral, and other persons of
note. Mass being ended, and those persons, with a multitude of the
populace, being assembled at the door of the church, Bobadilla
ordered his letters patent to be read, authorizing him to investigate
the rebellion, seize the persons, and sequestrate the property of
delinquents, and proceed against them with the utmost rigour of the
law; commanding also the admiral, and all others in authority, to
assist him in the discharge of his duties. The letter being read, he
demanded of Don Diego and the alcaldes to surrender to him the
persons of Fernando Guevara, Pedro Riquelme, and the other
prisoners, with the depositions taken concerning them; and ordered
that the parties by whom they were accused, and those by whose
command they had been taken, should appear before him.

Don Diego replied that the proceedings had emanated from the
orders of the admiral, who held superior powers to any Bobadilla
could possess, and without whose authority he could do nothing.

* Las Casas, *Hist. Ind.*, lib i. cap. 169; Herrera, *Hist. Ind.*, decad. i. lib. v. cap. 8.

He requested, at the same time, a copy of the letter patent, that he might send it to his brother, to whom alone the matter appertained. This Bobadilla refused, observing that, if Don Diego had power to do nothing, it was useless to give him a copy. He added, that since the office and authority he had proclaimed appeared to have no weight, he would try what power and consequence there was in the name of governor; and would show them that he had command, not merely over them, but over the admiral himself.

The little community remained in breathless suspense, awaiting the portentous movements of Bobadilla. The next morning he appeared at mass, resolved on assuming those powers which were only to have been produced after full investigation, and ample proof of the malconduct of Columbus. When mass was over, and the eager populace had gathered round the door of the church, Bobadilla, in presence of Don Diego and Rodrigo Perez, ordered his other royal patent to be read, investing him with the government of the islands, and of Terra Firma.

The patent being read, Bobadilla took the customary oath, and then claimed the obedience of Don Diego, Rodrigo Perez, and all present, to this royal instrument; on the authority of which he again demanded the prisoners confined in the fortress. In reply, they professed the utmost deference to the letter of the sovereigns, but again observed that they held the prisoners in obedience to the admiral, to whom the sovereigns had granted letters of a higher nature.

The self-importance of Bobadilla was incensed at this non-compliance, especially as he saw it had some effect upon the populace, who appeared to doubt his authority. He now produced the third mandate of the crown, ordering Columbus and his brothers to deliver up all fortresses, ships, and other royal property. To win the public completely to his side, he read also the additional mandate issued on the 30th of May, of the same year, ordering him to pay the arrears of wages due to all persons in the royal service, and to compel the admiral to pay the arrears of those to whom he was accountable.

This last document was received with shouts by the multitude, many having long arrears due to them in consequence of the poverty of the treasury. Flushed with his growing importance,

Bobadilla again demanded the prisoners; threatening, if refused, to take them by force. Meeting with the same reply, he repaired to the fortress to execute his threats. This post was commanded by Miguel Diaz, the same Aragonian cavalier who had once taken refuge among the Indians on the banks of the Ozema, won the affections of the female cacique Catalina, received from her information of the neighbouring gold mines, and induced his countrymen to remove to those parts.

When Bobadilla came before the fortress, he found the gates closed, and the alcayde, Miguel Diaz, upon the battlements. He ordered his letters patent to be read with a loud voice, the signatures and seals to be held up to view, and then demanded the surrender of the prisoners. Diaz requested a copy of the letters; but this Bobadilla refused, alleging that there was no time for delay, the prisoners being under sentence of death, and liable at any moment to be executed. He threatened, at the same time, that if they were not given up, he would proceed to extremities, and Diaz should be answerable for the consequences. The wary alcayde again required time to reply, and a copy of the letters; saying that he held the fortress for the king, by the command of the admiral, his lord, who had gained these territories and islands, and that when the latter arrived, he should obey his orders.*

The whole spirit of Bobadilla was roused within him at the refusal of the alcayde. Assembling all the people he had brought from Spain, together with the sailors of the ships, and the rabble of the place, he exhorted them to aid him in getting possession of the prisoners, but to harm no one unless in case of resistance. The mob shouted assent, for Bobadilla was already the idol of the multitude. About the hour of vespers he set out, at the head of this motley army, to storm a fortress destitute of a garrison, and formidable only in name, being calculated to withstand only a naked and slightly-armed people. The accounts of this transaction have something in them bordering on the ludicrous, and give it the air of absurd rhodomontade. Bobadilla assailed the portal with great impetuosity, the frail bolts and locks of which gave way at the first shock, and allowed him easy admission. In the meantime, however, his zealous myrmidons applied ladders to the walls, as if about to carry the place by assault, and to experience a desperate

* Las Casas, *Hist. Ind.*, lib. i. cap. 179.

defence. The alcayde, Miguel Diaz, and Don Diego de Alvarado, alone appeared on the battlements; they had drawn swords, but offered no resistance. Bobadilla entered the fortress in triumph, and without molestation. The prisoners were found in a chamber in irons. He ordered that they should be brought up to him to the top of the fortress, where, having put a few questions to them, as a matter of form, he gave them in charge to an alguazil named Juan de Espinosa.[*]

Such was the arrogant and precipitate entrance into office of Francisco de Bobadilla. He had reversed the order of his written instructions; having seized upon the government before he had investigated the conduct of Columbus. He continued his career in the same spirit; acting as if the case had been prejudged in Spain, and he had been sent out merely to degrade the admiral from his employments, not to ascertain the manner in which he had fulfilled them. He took up his residence in the house of Columbus, seized upon his arms, gold, plate, jewels, horses, together with his letters, and various manuscripts, both public and private, even to his most secret papers. He gave no account of the property thus seized, and which he no doubt considered already confiscated to the crown, excepting that he paid out of it the wages of those to whom the admiral was in arrears.[†] To increase his favour with the people, he proclaimed, on the second day of his assumption of power, a general license for the term of twenty years to seek for gold, paying merely one eleventh to government, instead of a third as heretofore. At the same time, he spoke in the most disrespectful and unqualified terms of Columbus, saying that he was empowered to send him home in chains, and that neither he nor any of his lineage would ever again be permitted to govern in the island.[‡]

---

[*] Las Casas, *Hist. Ind.*, lib. i. cap. 179; Herrera, decad. i. lib. v. cap. 8.
[†] *Hist. del Almirante*, cap. 85; Las Casas; Herrera, ubi sup.
[‡] Letter of Columbus to the nurse of Prince Juan.

When the tidings reached Columbus at Fort Conception of the high-handed proceedings of Bobadilla, he considered them the unauthorized acts of some rash adventurer like Ojeda. Since government had apparently thrown open the door to private enterprise, he might expect to have his path continually crossed, and his jurisdiction infringed by bold intermeddlers, feigning or fancying themselves authorized to interfere in the affairs of the colony. Since the departure of Ojeda another squadron had touched upon the coast, and produced a transient alarm, being an expedition under one of the Pinzons, licensed by the sovereigns to make discoveries. There had also been a rumour of another squadron hovering about the island, which proved, however, to be unfounded.*

The conduct of Bobadilla bore all the appearance of a lawless usurpation of some intruder of the kind. He had possessed himself forcibly of the fortress, and consequently of the town. He had issued extravagant licenses injurious to the government, and apparently intended only to make partisans among the people; and had threatened to throw Columbus himself in irons. That this man could really be sanctioned by government in such intemperate measures was repugnant to belief. The admiral's consciousness of his own services, the repeated assurances he had received of high consideration on the part of the sovereigns, and the perpetual prerogatives granted to him under their hand and seal, with all the solemnity that a compact could possess, all forbade him to consider the transactions at San Domingo otherwise than as outrages on his authority by some daring or misguided individual.

To be nearer to San Domingo, and obtain more correct information, he proceeded to Bonao, which was now beginning to

---

* Letter of Columbus to the nurse of Prince Juan.

assume the appearance of a settlement, several Spaniards having erected houses there and cultivated the adjacent country. He had scarcely reached the place, when an alcalde, bearing a staff of office, arrived there from San Domingo, proclaiming the appointment of Bobadilla to the government, and bearing copies of his letters patent. There was no especial letter or message sent to the admiral, nor were any of the common forms of courtesy and ceremony observed in superseding him in the command; all the proceedings of Bobadilla towards him were abrupt and insulting.

Columbus was exceedingly embarrassed how to act. It was evident that Bobadilla was intrusted with extensive powers by the sovereigns, but that they could have exercised such a sudden, unmerited, and apparently capricious act of severity, as that of divesting him of all his commands, he could not believe. He endeavoured to persuade himself that Bobadilla was some person sent out to exercise the functions of chief judge, according to the request he had written home to the sovereigns, and that they had intrusted him likewise with provisional powers to make an inquest into the late troubles of the island. All beyond these powers he tried to believe were mere assumptions and exaggerations of authority, as in the case of Aguado. At all events, he was determined to act upon such presumption, and to endeavour to gain time. If the monarchs had really taken any harsh measures with respect to him, it must have been in consequence of misrepresentations. The least delay might give them an opportunity of ascertaining their error, and making the necessary amends.

He wrote to Bobadilla, therefore, in guarded terms, welcoming him to the island; cautioning him against precipitate measures, especially in granting licenses to collect gold; informing him that he was on the point of going to Spain, and in a little time would leave him in command, with everything fully and clearly explained. He wrote at the same time to the like purport to certain monks who had come out with Bobadilla, though he observes that these letters were only written to gain time.* He received no replies: but while an insulting silence was observed towards him, Bobadilla filled up several of the blank letters, of which he had a number signed by the sovereigns, and sent them to Roldan, and other of the admiral's enemies, the very men whom

* Letter of Columbus to the nurse of Prince Juan.

he had been sent out to judge. These letters were full of civilities and promises of favour.*

To prevent any mischief which might arise from the licenses and indulgences so prodigally granted by Bobadilla, Columbus published by word and letter that the powers assumed by him could not be valid, nor his licenses availing, as he himself held superior powers granted to him in perpetuity by the crown, which could no more be superseded in this instance, than they had been in that of Aguado.

For some time Columbus remained in this anxious and perplexed state of mind, uncertain what line of conduct to pursue in so singular and unlooked-for a conjuncture. He was soon brought to a decision. Francisco Velasquez, deputy treasurer, and Juan de Trasierra, a Franciscan friar, arrived at Bonao, and delivered to him the royal letter of credence, signed by the sovereigns on the 26th of May 1499, commanding him to give implicit faith and obedience to Bobadilla; and they delivered, at the same time, a summons from the latter to appear immediately before him.

This laconic letter from the sovereigns struck at once at the root of all his dignity and power. He no longer made hesitation or demur, but, complying with the peremptory summons of Bobadilla, departed, almost alone and unattended, for San Domingo.†

---

* Ibid.
† Herrera, decad. i. lib. iv. cap. 9; Letter to the nurse of Prince Juan.

The tidings that a new governor had arrived, and that Columbus was in disgrace, and to be sent home in chains, circulated rapidly through the Vega, and the colonists hastened from all parts to San Domingo to make interest with Bobadilla. It was soon perceived that there was no surer way than that of vilifying his predecessor. Bobadilla felt that he had taken a rash step in seizing upon the government, and that his own safety required the conviction of Columbus. He listened eagerly, therefore, to all accusations, public or private; and welcome was he who could bring any charge, however extravagant, against the admiral and his brothers.

Hearing that the admiral was on his way to the city, he made a bustle of preparation, and armed the troops, affecting to believe a rumour that Columbus had called upon the caciques of the Vega to aid him with their subjects in a resistance to the commands of government. No grounds appear for this absurd report, which was probably invented to give a colouring of precaution to subsequent measures of violence and insult. The admiral's brother, Don Diego, was seized, thrown in irons, and confined on board of a caravel, without any reason being assigned for his imprisonment.

In the meantime Columbus pursued his journey to San Domingo, travelling in a lonely manner, without guards or retinue. Most of his people were with the Adelantado, and he had declined being attended by the remainder. He had heard of the rumours of the hostile intentions of Bobadilla; and although he knew that violence was threatened to his person, he came in this unpretending manner, to manifest his pacific feelings, and to remove all suspicion.*

No sooner did Bobadilla hear of his arrival, than he gave orders to put him in irons, and confine him in the fortress. This outrage

* Las Casas, *Hist. Ind.*, lib. i. cap. 180.

to a person of such dignified and venerable appearance, and such eminent merit, seemed, for the time, to shock even his enemies. When the irons were brought, everyone present shrank from the task of putting them on him, either from a sentiment of compassion at so great a reverse of fortune, or out of habitual reverence for his person. To fill the measure of ingratitude meted out to him, it was one of his own domestics, 'a graceless and shameless cook,' says Las Casas, 'who, with unwashed front, riveted the fetters with as much readiness and alacrity, as though he were serving him with choice and savory viands. I knew the fellow,' adds the venerable historian, 'and I think his name was Espinosa.'*

Columbus conducted himself with characteristic magnanimity under the injuries heaped upon him. There is a noble scorn which swells and supports the heart, and silences the tongue of the truly great, when enduring the insults of the unworthy. Columbus could not stoop to deprecate the arrogance of a weak and violent man like Bobadilla. He looked beyond this shallow agent, and all his petty tyranny, to the sovereigns who had employed him. Their injustice or ingratitude alone could wound his spirit; and he felt assured that when the truth came to be known, they would blush to find how greatly they had wronged him. With this proud assurance, he bore all present indignities in silence.

Bobadilla, although he had the admiral and Don Diego in his power, and had secured the venal populace, felt anxious and ill at ease. The Adelantado, with an armed force under his command, was still in the distant province of Xaragua, in pursuit of the rebels. Knowing his soldier-like and determined spirit, he feared he might take some violent measure when he should hear of the ignominious treatment and imprisonment of his brothers. He doubted whether any order from himself would have any effect, except to exasperate the stern Don Bartholomew. He sent a demand, therefore, to Columbus, to write to his brother, requesting him to repair peaceably to San Domingo, and forbidding him to execute the persons he held in confinement: Columbus readily complied. He exhorted his brother to submit quietly to the authority of his sovereigns, and to endure all present wrongs and

---

* Las Casas, *Hist. Ind.*, lib. i. cap. 180.

indignities, under the confidence that when they arrived at Castile, everything would be explained and redressed.*

On receiving this letter, Don Bartholomew immediately complied. Relinquishing his command, he hastened peacefully to San Domingo, and on arriving experienced the same treatment with his brothers, being put in irons and confined on board of a caravel. They were kept separate from each other, and no communication permitted between them. Bobadilla did not see them himself, nor did he allow others to visit them; but kept them in ignorance of the cause of their imprisonment, the crimes with which they were charged, and the process that was going on against them.[†]

It has been questioned whether Bobadilla really had authority for the arrest and imprisonment of the admiral and his brothers;[‡] and whether such violence and indignity was in any case contemplated by the sovereigns. He may have fancied himself empowered by the clause in the letter of instructions, dated March 21st 1499, in which, speaking of the rebellion of Roldan, 'he is authorized to *seize the persons and sequestrate the property* of those who appeared to be culpable, and then to proceed against them and against the absent, with the highest civil and criminal penalties.' This evidently had reference to the persons of Roldan and his followers, who were

---

* Peter Martyr mentions a vulgar rumour of the day, that the admiral, not knowing what might happen, wrote a letter in cipher to the Adelantado, urging him to come with arms in his hands to prevent any violence that might be contrived against him; that the Adelantado advanced, in effect, with his armed force, but having the imprudence to proceed some distance ahead of it, was surprised by the governor, before his men could come to his succour, and that the letter in cipher had been sent to Spain. This must have been one of the groundless rumours of the day, circulated to prejudice the public mind. Nothing of the kind appears among the charges in the inquest made by Bobadilla, and which was seen, and extracts made from it, by Las Casas, for his history. It is, in fact, in total contradiction to the statements of Las Casas, Herrera, and Fernando Columbus.

† Charlevoix, in his *History of San Domingo* (lib. iii. p. 199), states that the suit against Columbus was conducted in writing; that written charges were sent to him, to which he replied in the same way. This is contrary to the statements of Las Casas, Herrera, and Fernando Columbus. The admiral himself, in his letter to the nurse of Prince Juan, after relating the manner in which he and his brothers had been thrown into irons, and confined separately, without being visited by Bobadilla, or permitted to see any other persons, expressly adds, 'I make oath that I do not know for what I am imprisoned.' Again, in a letter written some time afterwards from Jamaica, he says, 'I was taken and thrown with two of my brothers in a ship, loaded with irons, with little clothing and much ill-treatment, without being summoned or convicted by justice.'

‡ Herrera, decad. i. lib. iv. cap. 10; Oviedo, *Cronica*. lib. iii. cap. 6.

then in arms, and against whom Columbus had sent home complaints; and this, by a violent construction, Bobadilla seems to have
wrested into an authority for seizing the person of the admiral
himself. In fact, in the whole course of his proceedings, he reversed
and confounded the order of his instructions. His first step should
have been to proceed against the rebels; this he made the last. His
last step should have been, in case of ample evidence against the
admiral, to have superseded him in office; and this he made the
first, without waiting for evidence. Having predetermined, from
the very outset, that Columbus was in the wrong, by the same rule
he had to presume that all the opposite parties were in the right. It
became indispensable to his own justification to inculpate the
admiral and his brothers; and the rebels he had been sent to judge
became, by this singular perversion of rule, necessary and cherished
evidences, to criminate those against whom they had rebelled.

The intentions of the crown, however, are not to be vindicated
at the expense of its miserable agent. If proper respect had been felt
for the rights and dignities of Columbus, Bobadilla would never
have been intrusted with powers so extensive, undefined, and dis-
cretionary; nor would he have dared to proceed to such lengths,
with such rudeness and precipitation, had he not felt assured that it
would not be displeasing to the jealous-minded Ferdinand.

The old scenes of the time of Aguado were now renewed with
tenfold virulence, and the old charges revived, with others still
more extravagant. From the early and never-to-be-forgotten
outrage upon Castilian pride, of compelling hidalgos, in time of
emergency, to labour in the construction of works necessary to
the public safety, down to the recent charge of levying war against
the government, there was not a hardship, abuse, nor sedition in
the island, that was not imputed to the misdeeds of Columbus and
his brothers. Besides the usual accusations of inflicting oppressive
labour, unnecessary tasks, painful restrictions, short allowances of
food, and cruel punishments upon the Spaniards, and waging
unjust wars against the natives, they were now charged with
preventing the conversion of the latter, that they might send them
slaves to Spain, and profit by their sale. This last charge, so
contrary to the pious feelings of the admiral, was founded on his
having objected to the baptism of certain Indians of mature age,
until they could be instructed in the doctrines of Christianity;

justly considering it an abuse of that holy sacrament to administer it thus blindly.*

Columbus was charged, also, with having secreted pearls, and other precious articles, collected in his voyage along the coast of Paria, and with keeping the sovereigns in ignorance of the nature of his discoveries there, in order to exact new privileges from them; yet it was notorious that he had sent home specimens of the pearls, and journals and charts of his voyage, by which others had been enabled to pursue his track.

Even the late tumults, now that the rebels were admitted as evidence, were all turned into matters of accusation. They were represented as spirited and loyal resistances to tyranny exercised upon the colonists and the natives. The well-merited punishments inflicted upon certain of the ring-leaders were cited as proofs of a cruel and revengeful disposition, and a secret hatred of Spaniards. Bobadilla believed, or affected to believe, all these charges. He had, in a manner, made the rebels his confederates in the ruin of Columbus. It was become a common cause with them. He could no longer, therefore, conduct himself towards them as a judge. Guevara, Riquelme, and their fellow-convicts, were discharged almost without the form of a trial, and it is even said were received into favour and countenance. Roldan, from the very first, had been treated with confidence by Bobadilla, and honoured with his correspondence. All the others, whose conduct had rendered them liable to justice, received either a special acquittal or a general pardon. It was enough to have been opposed in any way to Columbus, to obtain full justification in the eyes of Bobadilla.

The latter had now collected a weight of testimony, and produced a crowd of witnesses, sufficient, as he conceived, to insure the condemnation of the prisoners, and his own continuance in command. He determined, therefore, to send the admiral and his brothers home in chains, in the vessels ready for sea, transmitting at the same time the inquest taken in their case, and writing private letters, enforcing the charges made against them, and advising that Columbus should on no account be restored to the command, which he had so shamefully abused.

San Domingo now swarmed with miscreants just delivered from the dungeon and the gibbet. It was a perfect jubilee of triumphant

* Muñoz, *Hist. N. Mundo*, part unpublished.

villainy and dastard malice. Every base spirit, which had been awed
into obsequiousness by Columbus and his brothers when in power,
now started up to revenge itself upon them when in chains. The
most injurious slanders were loudly proclaimed in the streets; insulting pasquinades and inflammatory libels were posted up at every
corner; and horns were blown in the neighbourhood of their
prisons, to taunt them with the exultings of the rabble.* When these
rejoicings of his enemies reached him in his dungeon, and Columbus reflected on the inconsiderate violence already exhibited by
Bobadilla, he knew not how far his rashness and confidence might
carry him, and began to entertain apprehensions for his life.

The vessels being ready to make sail, Alonzo de Villejo was
appointed to take charge of the prisoners, and carry them to Spain.
This officer had been brought up by an uncle of Fonseca, was in
the employ of that bishop, and had come out with Bobadilla. The
latter instructed him, on arriving at Cadiz, to deliver his prisoners
into the hands of Fonseca, or of his uncle, thinking thereby to give
the malignant prelate a triumphant gratification. This circumstance
gave weight with many to a report that Bobadilla was secretly
instigated and encouraged in his violent measures by Fonseca, and
was promised his protection and influence at court, in case of any
complaints of his conduct.†

Villejo undertook the office assigned him, but he discharged it in
a more generous manner than was intended. 'This Alonzo de
Villejo,' says the worthy Las Casas, 'was a hidalgo of honourable
character, and my particular friend.' He certainly showed himself
superior to the low malignity of his patrons. When he arrived with
a guard to conduct the admiral from the prison to the ship, he
found him in chains in a state of silent despondency. So violently
had he been treated, and so savage were the passions let loose
against him, that he feared he should be sacrificed without an
opportunity of being heard, and his name go down sullied and
dishonoured to posterity. When he beheld the officer enter with
the guard, he thought it was to conduct him to the scaffold.
'Villejo,' said he, mournfully, 'whither are you taking me?' 'To
the ship, your Excellency, to embark,' replied the other. 'To
embark!' repeated the admiral, earnestly; 'Villejo! do you speak

* *Hist. del Almirante*, cap. 86.
† Las Casas, *Hist. Ind.*, lib. i. cap. 180, MS.

the truth?' 'By the life of your Excellency,' replied the honest officer, 'it is true!' With these words the admiral was comforted, and felt as one restored from death to life. Nothing can be more touching and expressive than this little colloquy, recorded by the venerable Las Casas, who doubtless had it from the lips of his friend Villejo.

The caravels set sail early in October, bearing off Columbus shackled like the vilest of culprits, amidst the scoffs and shouts of a miscreant rabble, who took a brutal joy in heaping insults on his venerable head, and sent curses after him from the shores of the island he had so recently added to the civilized world. Fortunately the voyage was favourable, and of but moderate duration, and was rendered less disagreeable by the conduct of those to whom he was given in custody. The worthy Villejo, though in the service of Fonseca, felt deeply moved at the treatment of Columbus. The master of the caravel, Andreas Martin, was equally grieved: they both treated the admiral with profound respect and assiduous attention. They would have taken off his irons, but to this he would not consent. 'No,' said he proudly, 'their majesties commanded me by letter to submit to whatever Bobadilla should order in their name; by their authority he has put upon me these chains; I will wear them until they shall order them to be taken off, and I will preserve them afterwards as relics and memorials of the reward of my services.'*

'He did so,' adds his son Fernando; 'I saw them always hanging in his cabinet, and he requested that when he died they might be buried with him.'†

---

* Las Casas, *Hist. Ind.*, lib. i. cap. 180, MS.
† *Hist. del Almirante*, cap. 86.

BOOK 14

CHAPTER I

1500

The arrival of Columbus at Cadiz, a prisoner and in chains, produced almost as great a sensation as his triumphant return from his first voyage. It was one of those striking and obvious facts, which speak to the feelings of the multitude, and preclude the necessity of reflection. No one stopped to inquire into the case. It was sufficient to be told that Columbus was brought home in irons from the world he had discovered. There was a general burst of indignation in Cadiz, and in the powerful and opulent Seville, which was echoed throughout all Spain. If the ruin of Columbus had been the intention of his enemies, they had defeated their object by their own violence. One of those reactions took place, so frequent in the public mind, when persecution is pushed to an unguarded length. Those of the populace who had recently been loud in their clamour against Columbus, were now as loud in their reprobation of his treatment, and a strong sympathy was expressed, against which it would have been odious for the government to contend.

The tidings of his arrival, and of the ignominious manner in which he had been brought, reached the court at Granada, and filled the halls of the Alhambra with murmurs of astonishment. Columbus, full of his wrongs, but ignorant how far they had been authorized by the sovereigns, had forborne to write to them. In the course of his voyage, however, he had penned a long letter to Dona Juana de la Torre, the aya of Prince Juan, a lady high in favour with Queen Isabella. This letter, on his arrival at Cadiz, Andreas Martin, the captain of the caravel, permitted him to send off privately by express. It arrived, therefore, before the protocol of the proceedings instituted by Bobadilla, and from this document the sovereigns

derived their first intimation of his treatment.* It contained a statement of the late transactions of the island, and of the wrongs he had
suffered, written with his usual artlessness and energy. To specify
the contents would be but to recapitulate circumstances already
recorded. Some expressions, however, which burst from him in the
warmth of his feelings, are worthy of being noted. 'The slanders of
worthless men,' says he, 'have done me more injury than all my
services have profited me.' Speaking of the misrepresentations to
which he was subjected, he observes: 'Such is the evil name which I
have acquired, that if I were to build hospitals and churches, they
would be called dens of robbers.' After relating in indignant terms
the conduct of Bobadilla, in seeking testimony respecting his administration from the very men who had rebelled against him, and
throwing himself and his brothers in irons, without letting them
know the offences with which they were charged, 'I have been
much aggrieved,' he adds, 'in that a person should be sent out to
investigate my conduct, who knew that if the evidence which he
could send home should appear to be of a serious nature, he would
remain in the government.' He complains that, in forming an
opinion of his administration, allowances had not been made for the
extraordinary difficulties with which he had to contend, and the
wild state of the country over which he had to rule. 'I was judged,'
he observes, 'as a governor who had been sent to take charge of a
well-regulated city, under the dominion of well-established laws,
where there was no danger of everything running to disorder and
ruin; but I ought to be judged as a captain, sent to subdue a numerous and hostile people, of manners and religion opposite to ours,
living not in regular towns, but in forests and mountains. It ought to
be considered that I have brought all these under subjection to their
majesties, giving them dominion over another world, by which
Spain, heretofore poor, has suddenly become rich. Whatever errors
I may have fallen into, they were not with an evil intention; and I
believe their majesties will credit what I say. I have known them to
be merciful to those who have willfully done them disservice; I am
convinced that they will have still more indulgence for me, who
have erred innocently, or by compulsion, as they will hereafter be
more fully informed; and I trust they will consider my great services,
the advantages of which are every day more and more apparent.'

* Las Casas, *Hist. Ind.*, lib. i. cap. 182.

When this letter was read to the noble-minded Isabella, and she found how grossly Columbus had been wronged and the royal authority abused, her heart was filled with mingled sympathy and indignation. The tidings were confirmed by a letter from the alcalde or corregidor of Cadiz, into whose hands Columbus and his brothers had been delivered, until the pleasure of the sovereigns should be known; * and by another letter from Alonzo de Villejo, expressed in terms accordant with his humane and honourable conduct towards his illustrious prisoner.

However Ferdinand might have secretly felt disposed against Columbus, the momentary tide of public feeling was not to be resisted. He joined with his generous queen in her reprobation of the treatment of the admiral, and both sovereigns hastened to give evidence to the world, that his imprisonment had been without their authority, and contrary to their wishes. Without waiting to receive any documents that might arrive from Bobadilla, they sent orders to Cadiz that the prisoners should be instantly set at liberty, and treated with all distinction. They wrote a letter to Columbus, couched in terms of gratitude and affection, expressing their grief at all that he had suffered, and inviting him to court. They ordered, at the same time, that two thousand ducats should be advanced to defray his expenses.†

The loyal heart of Columbus was again cheered by this declaration of his sovereigns. He felt conscious of his integrity, and anticipated an immediate restitution of all his rights and dignities. He appeared at court in Granada on the 17th of December, not as a man ruined and disgraced, but richly dressed, and attended by an honourable retinue. He was received by the sovereigns with unqualified favour and distinction. When the queen beheld this venerable man approach, and thought on all he had deserved and all he had suffered, she was moved to tears. Columbus had borne up firmly against the rude conflicts of the world, he had endured with lofty scorn the injuries and insults of ignoble men; but he possessed strong and quick sensibility. When he found himself thus kindly received by his sovereigns, and beheld tears in the benign eyes of Isabella, his long-suppressed feelings burst forth: he threw

---

* Oviedo, *Cronica*, lib. iii. cap. 6.

† Las Casas, lib. i. cap. 182. Two thousand ducats, or two thousand eight hundred and forty-six dollars, equivalent to eight thousand five hundred and thirty-eight dollars of the present day.

himself on his knees, and for some time could not utter a word for the violence of his tears and sobbings.[*]

Ferdinand and Isabella raised him from the ground, and endeavoured to encourage him by the most gracious expressions. As soon as he regained self-possession, he entered into an eloquent and high-minded vindication of his loyalty, and the zeal he had ever felt for the glory and advantage of the Spanish crown, declaring that if at any time he had erred, it had been through inexperience in government, and the extraordinary difficulties by which he had been surrounded.

There needed no vindication on his part. The intemperance of his enemies had been his best advocate. He stood in presence of his sovereigns a deeply-injured man, and it remained for them to vindicate themselves to the world from the charge of ingratitude towards their most deserving subject. They expressed their indignation at the proceedings of Bobadilla, which they disavowed, as contrary to their instructions, and declared that he should be immediately dismissed from his command.

In fact, no public notice was taken of the charges sent home by Bobadilla, nor of the letters written in support of them. The sovereigns took every occasion to treat Columbus with favour and distinction, assuring him that his grievances should be redressed, his property restored, and he reinstated in all his privileges and dignities.

It was on the latter point that Columbus was chiefly solicitous. Mercenary considerations had scarcely any weight in his mind. Glory had been the great object of his ambition, and he felt that, as long as he remained suspended from his employments, a tacit censure rested on his name. He expected, therefore, that the moment the sovereigns should be satisfied of the rectitude of his conduct, they would be eager to make him amends; that a restitution of his viceroyalty would immediately take place, and he should return in triumph to San Domingo. Here, however, he was doomed to experience a disappointment which threw a gloom over the remainder of his days. To account for this flagrant want of justice and gratitude in the crown, it is expedient to notice a variety of events which had materially affected the interests of Columbus in the eyes of the politic Ferdinand.

[*] Herrera, decad. i. lib. iv. cap. 10.

The general license granted by the Spanish sovereigns in 1495, to undertake voyages of discovery, had given rise to various expeditions by enterprising individuals, chiefly persons who had sailed with Columbus in his first voyages. The government, unable to fit out many armaments itself, was pleased to have its territories thus extended, free of cost, and its treasury at the same time benefited by the share of the proceeds of these voyages, reserved as a kind of duty to the crown. These expeditions had chiefly taken place while Columbus was in partial disgrace with the sovereigns. His own charts and journal served as guides to the adventurers; and his magnificent accounts of Paria and the adjacent coasts had chiefly excited their cupidity.

Beside the expedition of Ojeda, already noticed, in the course of which he touched at Xaragua, one had been undertaken at the same time by Pedro Alonzo Niño, native of Moguer, an able pilot, who had been with Columbus in the voyages to Cuba and Paria. Having obtained a license, he interested a rich merchant of Seville in the undertaking, who fitted out a caravel of fifty tons burden, under condition that his brother Christoval Guevra should have the command. They sailed from the bar of Saltes, a few days after Ojeda had sailed from Cadiz, in the spring of 1499, and arriving on the coast of Terra Firma, to the south of Paria, ran along it for some distance, passed through the Gulf, and thence went one hundred and thirty leagues along the shore of the present republic of Colombia, visiting what was afterwards called the Pearl Coast. They landed in various places, disposed of their European trifles to immense profit, and returned with a large store of gold and pearls, having made, in their diminutive bark, one of the most extensive and lucrative voyages yet accomplished.

About the same time, the Pinzons, that family of bold and opulent navigators, fitted out an armament of four caravels at

Palos, manned in a great measure by their own relations and friends. Several experienced pilots embarked in it who had been with Columbus to Paria, and it was commanded by Vicente Yañez Pinzon, who had been captain of a caravel in the squadron of the admiral on his first voyage.

Pinzon was a hardy and experienced seaman, and did not, like the others, follow closely in the track of Columbus. Sailing in December, 1499, he passed the Canary and Cape Verde Islands, standing south-west until he lost sight of the polar star. Here he encountered a terrible storm, and was exceedingly perplexed and confounded by the new aspect of the heavens. Nothing was yet known of the southern hemisphere, nor of the beautiful constellation of the cross, which in those regions has since supplied to mariners the place of the north star. The voyagers had expected to find at the south pole a star correspondent to that of the north. They were dismayed at beholding no guide of the kind, and thought there must be some prominent swelling of the earth, which hid the pole from their view.*

Pinzon continued on, however, with great intrepidity. On the 26th of January 1500, he saw at a distance a great headland, which he called Cape Santa Maria de la Consolacion, but which has since been named Cape St Augustine. He landed and took possession of the country in the name of their Catholic majesties; being a part of the territories since called the Brazils. Standing thence westward, he discovered the Maragnon, since called the River of the Amazons, traversed the Gulf of Paria, and continued across the Caribbean Sea and the Gulf of Mexico, until he found himself among the Bahamas, where he lost two of his vessels on the rocks, near the island of Jumeto. He returned to Palos in September, having added to his former glory that of being the first European who had crossed the equinoctial line in the western ocean, and of having discovered the famous kingdom of Brazil, from its commencement at the River Maragnon to its most eastern point. As a reward for his achievements, power was granted to him to colonize and govern the lands which he had discovered, and which extended southward from a little beyond the River of Maragnon to Cape St Augustine.†

* Peter Martyr, decad. i. lib. ix.
† Herrera, decad. i. lib. iv. cap. 12; Muñoz, *Hist. N. Mundo*, part unpublished.

The little port of Palos, which had been so slow in furnishing the first squadron for Columbus, was now continually agitated by the passion for discovery. Shortly after the sailing of Pinzon, another expedition was fitted out there, by Diego Lepe, a native of the place, and manned by his adventurous townsmen. He sailed in the same direction with Pinzon, but discovered more of the southern continent than any other voyager of the day, or for twelve years afterwards. He doubled Cape St Augustine, and ascertained that the coast beyond ran to the southwest. He landed and performed the usual ceremonies of taking possession in the name of the Spanish sovereigns, and in one place carved their names on a magnificent tree, of such enormous magnitude, that seventeen men with their hands joined could not embrace the trunk. What enhanced the merit of his discoveries was that he had never sailed with Columbus. He had with him, however, several skilful pilots, who had accompanied the admiral in his voyage.[*]

Another expedition of two vessels sailed from Cadiz, in October 1500, under the command of Rodrigo Bastides of Seville. He explored the coast of Terra Firma, passing Cape de la Vela, the western limits of the previous discoveries on the mainland, continuing on to a port since called the Retreat, where afterwards was founded the seaport of Nombre de Dios. His vessels being nearly destroyed by the teredo, or worm which abounds in those seas, he had great difficulty in reaching Xaragua in Hispaniola, where he lost his two caravels, and proceeded with his crew by land to San Domingo. Here he was seized and imprisoned by Bobadilla, under pretext that he had treated for gold with the natives of Xaragua.[†]

Such was the swarm of Spanish expeditions immediately resulting from the enterprises of Columbus; but others were also undertaken by foreign nations. In the year 1497, Sebastian Cabot, son of a Venetian merchant resident in Bristol, sailing in the service of Henry VII of England, navigated to the northern seas of the New World. Adopting the idea of Columbus, he sailed in quest of the shores of Cathay, and hoped to find a north-west passage to India. In this voyage he discovered Newfoundland,

---

[*] Las Casas, *Hist. Ind.*, lib. ii. cap. 2; Muñoz, part unpublished.
[†] Las Casas, *Hist. Ind.*, lib. ii. cap. 2; Muñoz, part unpublished.

coasted Labrador to the fifty-sixth degree of north latitude, and then returning, ran down south-west to the Floridas, when, his provisions beginning to fail, he returned to England.* But vague and scanty accounts of this voyage exist, which was important as including the first discovery of the northern continent of the New World.

The discoveries of rival nations, however, which most excited the attention and jealousy of the Spanish crown, were those of the Portuguese. Vasco de Gama, a man of rank and consummate talent and intrepidity, had at length accomplished the great design of the late Prince Henry of Portugal, and by doubling the Cape of Good Hope, in the year 1497, had opened the long-sought-for route to India.

Immediately after Gama's return, a fleet of thirteen sail was fitted out to visit the magnificent countries of which he brought accounts. This expedition sailed on the 9th of March 1500, for Calicut, under the command of Pedro Alvarez de Cabral. Having passed the Cape de Verde Islands, he sought to avoid the calms prevalent on the coast of Guinea, by stretching far to the west. Suddenly, on the 25th of April, he came in sight of land unknown to anyone in his squadron; for, as yet, they had not heard of the discoveries of Pinzon and Lepe. He at first supposed it to be some great island; but after coasting it for some time, he became persuaded that it must be part of a continent. Having ranged along it somewhat beyond the fifteenth degree of southern latitude, he landed at a harbour which he called Porto Securo, and taking possession of the country for the crown of Portugal, despatched a ship to Lisbon with the important tidings.† In this way did the Brazils come into the possession of Portugal, being to the eastward of the conventional line settled with Spain as the boundaries of their respective territories. Dr Robertson, in recording this voyage of Cabral, concludes with one of his just and elegant remarks.

'Columbus's discovery of the New World was,' he observes, 'the effort of an active genius, guided by experience, and acting upon a regular plan, executed with no less courage than perseverance. But from this adventure of the Portuguese, it appears that

---

* Hakluyt's *Collection of Voyages*, vol. iii. p. 7; vol. ii. p. 9.
† Lafiteau, *Conquêtes des Portugais*, lib. ii.

chance might have accomplished that great design, which it is now the pride of human reason to have formed and perfected. If the sagacity of Columbus had not conducted mankind to America, Cabral, by a fortunate accident, might have led them, a few years later, to the knowledge of that extensive continent.'*

* Robertson, *Hist. America*, book ii.

CHAPTER 3

1501

The numerous discoveries briefly noticed in the preceding chapter had produced a powerful effect upon the mind of Ferdinand. His ambition, his avarice, and his jealousy were equally inflamed. He beheld boundless regions, teeming with all kinds of riches, daily opening before the enterprises of his subjects; but he beheld at the same time other nations launching forth into competition, emulous for a share of the golden world which he was eager to monopolize. The expeditions of the English, and the accidental discovery of the Brazils by the Portuguese, caused him much uneasiness. To secure his possession of the continent, he determined to establish local governments or commands, in the most important places, all to be subject to a general government, established at San Domingo, which was to be the metropolis.

With these considerations, the government, heretofore granted to Columbus, had risen vastly in importance; and while the restitution of it was the more desirable in his eyes, it became more and more a matter of repugnance to the selfish and jealous monarch. He had long repented having vested such great powers and prerogatives in any subject, particularly in a foreigner. At the time of granting them, he had no anticipation of such boundless countries to be placed under his command. He appeared almost to consider himself outwitted by Columbus in the arrangement; and every succeeding discovery, instead of increasing his grateful sense of the obligation, only made him repine the more at the growing magnitude of the reward. At length, however, the affair of Bobadilla had effected a temporary exclusion of Columbus from his high office, and that without any odium to the crown; and the wary monarch secretly determined that the door thus closed between him and his dignities should never again be opened.

Perhaps Ferdinand may really have entertained doubts as to the innocence of Columbus, with respect to the various charges made against him. He may have doubted also the sincerity of his loyalty, being a stranger, when he should find himself strong in his command, at a great distance from the parent country, with immense and opulent regions under his control. Columbus himself, in his letters, alludes to reports circulated by his enemies, that he intended either to set up an independent sovereignty, or to deliver his discoveries into the hands of other potentates; and he appears to fear that these slanders might have made some impression on the mind of Ferdinand. But there was one other consideration which had no less force with the monarch in withholding this great act of justice – Columbus was no longer indispensable to him. He had made his great discovery; he had struck out the route to the New World, and now anyone could follow it. A number of able navigators had sprung up under his auspices, and acquired experience in his voyages. They were daily besieging the throne with offers to fit out expeditions at their own cost, and to yield a share of the profits to the crown. Why should he, therefore, confer princely dignities and prerogatives for that which men were daily offering to perform gratuitously?

Such, from his after conduct, appears to have been the jealous and selfish policy which actuated Ferdinand in forbearing to reinstate Columbus in those dignities and privileges so solemnly granted to him by treaty, and which it was acknowledged he had never forfeited by misconduct.

This deprivation, however, was declared to be but temporary; and plausible reasons were given for the delay in his reappointment. It was observed that the elements of those violent factions, recently in arms against him, yet existed in the island; his immediate return might produce fresh exasperation; his personal safety might be endangered, and the island again thrown into confusion. Though Bobadilla, therefore, was to be immediately dismissed from command, it was deemed advisable to send out some officer of talent and discretion to supersede him, who might dispassionately investigate the recent disorders, remedy the abuses which had arisen, and expel all dissolute and factious persons from the colony. He should hold the government for two years, by which time it was trusted that all angry passions would be allayed, and turbulent individuals removed: Columbus might then resume the command with comfort to himself and advantage to the crown. With these reasons, and the promise which accompanied them, Columbus was obliged to content himself. There can be no doubt that they were sincere on the part of Isabella, and that it was her intention to reinstate him in the full enjoyment of his rights and dignities, after his apparently necessary suspension. Ferdinand, however, by his subsequent conduct, has forfeited all claim to any favourable opinion of the kind.

The person chosen to supersede Bobadilla was Don Nicholas de Ovando, commander of Lares, of the order of Alcantara. He is described as of the middle size, fair complexioned, with a red beard, and a modest look, yet a tone of authority. He was fluent in speech, and gracious and courteous in his manners. A man of great prudence, says Las Casas, and capable of governing many people, but not of governing the Indians, on whom he inflicted incalculable injuries. He possessed great veneration for justice, was an enemy to avarice, sober in his mode of living, and of such humility, that when he rose afterwards to be grand commander of the order of Alcantara, he would never allow himself to be addressed by the title of respect attached to it.[*] Such is the picture drawn of him by historians; but his conduct in several important instances is in direct contradiction to it. He appears to have been plausible and subtle, as well as fluent and courteous; his humility concealed a great love of command, and in his transactions with Columbus he was certainly both ungenerous and unjust.

The various arrangements to be made, according to the new plan of colonial government, delayed for some time the departure of Ovando. In the meantime, every arrival brought intelligence of the disastrous state of the island, under the maladministration of Bobadilla. He had commenced his career by an opposite policy to that of Columbus. Imagining that rigorous rule had been the rock on which his predecessors had split, he sought to conciliate the public by all kinds of indulgence. Having at the very outset relaxed the reins of justice and morality, he lost all command over the community; and such disorder and licentiousness ensued, that many, even of the opponents of Columbus, looked back with regret upon the strict but wholesome rule of himself and the Adelantado.

[*] Las Casas, *Hist. Ind.*, lib. ii. cap. 3.

Bobadilla was not so much a bad as an imprudent and a weak man. He had not considered the dangerous excesses to which his policy would lead. Rash in grasping authority, he was feeble and temporizing in the exercise of it: he could not look beyond the present exigency. One dangerous indulgence granted to the colonists called for another; each was ceded in its turn, and thus he went on from error to error – showing that in government there is as much danger to be apprehended from a weak as from a bad man.

He had sold the farms and estates of the crown at low prices, observing that it was not the wish of the monarchs to enrich themselves by them, but that they should redound to the profit of their subjects. He granted universal permission to work the mines, exacting only an eleventh of the produce for the crown. To prevent any diminution in the revenue, it became necessary, of course, to increase the quantity of gold collected. He obliged the caciques, therefore, to furnish each Spaniard with Indians, to assist him both in the labours of the field and of the mine. To carry this into more complete effect, he made an enumeration of the natives of the island, reduced them into classes, and distributed them, according to his favour or caprice, among the colonists. The latter, at his suggestion, associated themselves in partnerships of two persons each, who were to assist one another with their respective capitals and Indians, one superintending the labours of the field, and the other the search for gold. The only injunction of Bobadilla was to produce large quantities of ore. He had one saying continually in his mouth, which shows the pernicious and temporizing principle upon which he acted: 'Make the most of your time,' he would say, 'there is no knowing how long it will last,' alluding to the possibility of his being speedily recalled. The colonists acted up to his advice, and so hard did they drive the poor natives, that the eleventh yielded more revenue to the crown than had ever been produced by the third under the government of Columbus. In the meantime, the unhappy natives suffered under all kinds of cruelties from their inhuman task-masters. Little used to labour, feeble of constitution, and accustomed in their beautiful and luxuriant island to a life of ease and freedom, they sank under the toils imposed upon them, and the severities by which they were enforced. Las Casas gives an indignant picture of the capricious tyranny exercised over the Indians by worthless Spaniards, many of whom had been transported convicts from the dungeons of Castile. These wretches, who in their own countries had been the vilest among the vile, here assumed the tone of grand cavaliers. They insisted upon being attended by trains of servants. They took the daughters and female relations of caciques for their domestics, or rather for their concubines, nor did they limit themselves in number. When they travelled, instead of using the horses and mules with which they were provided, they obliged the natives to transport them upon their shoulders in litters, or hammocks, with others attending to hold umbrellas of palm-leaves over their heads to keep off the sun, and fans of feathers to cool them; and Las Casas affirms that he has seen the backs and shoulders of the unfortunate Indians who bore these litters raw and bleeding from the task. When these arrogant upstarts arrived at an Indian village, they consumed and lavished away the provisions of the inhabitants, seizing upon whatever pleased their caprice, and obliging the cacique and his subjects to dance before them for their amusement. Their very pleasures were attended with cruelty. They never addressed the natives but in the most degrading terms, and on the least offence, or the least freak of ill-humour, inflicted blows and lashes, and even death itself.[*]

Such is but a faint picture of the evils which sprang up under the feeble rule of Bobadilla, and are sorrowfully described by Las Casas from actual observation, as he visited the island just at the close of his administration. Bobadilla had trusted to the immense amount of gold, wrung from the miseries of the natives, to atone for all errors, and secure favour with the sovereigns; but he had totally mistaken his course. The abuses of his government soon reached the royal ear, and above all, the wrongs of the natives reached the benevolent heart of Isabella. Nothing was more calculated to arouse her indignation, and she urged the speedy departure of Ovando, to put a stop to these enormities.

In conformity to the plan already mentioned, the government of Ovando extended over the islands and Terra Firma, of which Hispaniola was to be the metropolis. He was to enter upon the exercise of his powers immediately upon his arrival, by procuration, sending home Bobadilla by the return of the fleet. He was instructed to inquire diligently into the late abuses, punishing the

[*] Las Casas, *Hist. Ind.*, lib. ii. cap. 1, MS.

delinquents without favour or partiality, and removing all worthless persons from the island. He was to revoke immediately the
license granted by Bobadilla for the general search after gold, it
having been given without royal authority. He was to require, for
the crown, a third of what was already collected, and one half of
all that should be collected in future. He was empowered to build
towns, granting them the privileges enjoyed by municipal corpor-
ations of Spain, and obliging the Spaniards, and particularly the
soldiers, to reside in them, instead of scattering themselves over
the island. Among many sage provisions, there were others
injurious and illiberal, characteristic of an age when the principles
of commerce were but little understood; but which were continued by Spain long after the rest of the world had discarded
them as the errors of dark and unenlightened times. The crown
monopolized the trade of the colonies. No one could carry
merchandises there on his own account. A royal factor was
appointed, through whom alone were to be obtained supplies of
European articles. The crown reserved to itself not only exclusive
property in the mines, but in precious stones, and like objects of
extraordinary value, and also in dye-woods. No strangers, and
above all, no Moors nor Jews, were permitted to establish themselves in the island, nor to go upon voyages of discovery. Such
were some of the restrictions upon trade which Spain imposed
upon her colonies, and which were followed up by others equally
illiberal. Her commercial policy has been the scoff of modern
times; but may not the present restrictions on trade, imposed by
the most intelligent nations, be equally the wonder and the jest
of future ages?

Isabella was particularly careful in providing for the kind treatment of the Indians. Ovando was ordered to assemble the caciques,
and declare to them that the sovereigns took them and their people
under their especial protection. They were merely to pay tribute
like other subjects of the crown, and it was to be collected with the
utmost mildness and gentleness. Great pains were to be taken in
their religious instruction; for which purpose twelve Franciscan
friars were sent out, with a prelate named Antonio de Espinal, a
venerable and pious man. This was the first formal introduction of
the Franciscan order into the New World.[*]

* Las Casas, *Hist. Ind.* lib. ii. cap. 3, MS.

All these precautions with respect to the natives were defeated by one unwary provision. It was permitted that the Indians might be compelled to work in the mines, and in other employments; but this was limited to the royal service. They were to be engaged as hired labourers, and punctually paid. This provision led to great abuses and oppressions, and was ultimately as fatal to the natives as could have been the most absolute slavery.

But, with that inconsistency frequent in human conduct, while the sovereigns were making regulations for the relief of the Indians, they encouraged a gross invasion of the rights and welfare of another race of human beings. Among their various decrees on this occasion, we find the first trace of negro slavery in the New World. It was permitted to carry to the colony negro slaves born among Christians; * that is to say, slaves born in Seville and other parts of Spain, the children and descendants of natives brought from the Atlantic coast of Africa, where such traffic had for some time been carried on by the Spaniards and Portuguese. There are signal events in the course of history, which sometimes bear the appearance of temporal judgments. It is a fact worthy of observation that Hispaniola, the place where this flagrant sin against nature and humanity was first introduced into the New World, has been the first to exhibit an awful retribution.

Amidst the various concerns which claimed the attention of the sovereigns, the interests of Columbus were not forgotten. Ovando was ordered to examine into all his accounts, without undertaking to pay them off. He was to ascertain the damages he had sustained by his imprisonment, the interruption of his privileges, and the confiscation of his effects. All the property confiscated by Bobadilla was to be restored; or if it had been sold, to be made good. If it had been employed in the royal service, Columbus was to be indemnified out of the treasury; if Bobadilla had appropriated it to his own use, he was to account for it out of his private purse. Equal care was to be taken to indemnify the brothers of the admiral for the losses they had wrongfully suffered by their arrest.

Columbus was likewise to receive the arrears of his revenues; and the same were to be punctually paid to him in future. He was permitted to have a factor resident in the island, to be present at the melting and marking of the gold, to collect his dues, and in

* Herrera, *Hist. Ind.*, decad. i. lib. iv. cap. 12.

short to attend to all his affairs. To this office he appointed Alonzo
Sanchez de Carvajal; and the sovereigns commanded that his agent
should be treated with great respect.

The fleet appointed to convey Ovando to his government was
the largest that had yet sailed to the New World. It consisted of
thirty sail, five of them from ninety to one hundred and fifty tons
burden, twenty-four caravels from thirty to ninety, and one bark
of twenty-five tons.* The number of souls embarked in this fleet
was about twenty-five hundred; many of them persons of rank and
distinction, with their families.

That Ovando might appear with dignity in his new office, he
was allowed to use silks, brocades, precious stones, and other
articles of sumptuous attire, prohibited at that time in Spain in
consequence of the ruinous ostentation of the nobility. He was
permitted to have seventy-two esquires as his bodyguard, ten of
whom were horsemen. With this expedition sailed Don Alonzo
Maldonado, appointed as alguazil mayor, or chief justice, in place
of Roldan, who was to be sent to Spain. There were artisans of
various kinds: to these were added a physician, surgeon, and
apothecary; and seventy-three married men† with their families, all
of respectable character, destined to be distributed in four towns,
and to enjoy peculiar privileges, that they might form the basis of a
sound and useful population. They were to displace an equal
number of the idle and dissolute who were to be sent from the
island: this excellent measure had been especially urged and entreated by Columbus. There was also livestock, artillery, arms,
munitions of all kinds; everything, in short, that was required for
the supply of the island.

Such was the style in which Ovando, a favourite of Ferdinand,
and a native subject of rank, was fitted out to enter upon the
government withheld from Columbus. The fleet put to sea on
the 13th of February 1502. In the early part of the voyage it was
encountered by a terrible storm; one of the ships foundered,
with one hundred and twenty passengers; the others were obliged
to throw overboard everything on deck, and were completely
scattered. The shores of Spain were strewed with articles from the

---

* Muñoz, part inedit. Las Casas says the fleet consisted of thirty-two sail. He states
from memory, however; Muñoz from documents.

† Muñoz, H. N. Mundo, part inedit.

fleet, and a rumour spread that all the ships had perished. When this reached the sovereigns, they were so overcome with grief that they shut themselves up for eight days, and admitted no one to their presence. The rumour proved to be incorrect: but one ship was lost. The others assembled again at the island of Gomera in the Canaries, and, pursuing their voyage, arrived at San Domingo on the 15th of April.*

* Las Casas, *Hist. Ind.*, lib. ii. cap. 3, MS.

Columbus remained in the city of Granada upwards of nine months, endeavouring to extricate his affairs from the confusion into which they had been thrown by the rash conduct of Boba-dilla, and soliciting the restoration of his offices and dignities. During this time he constantly experienced the smiles and atten-tions of the sovereigns, and promises were repeatedly made him that he should ultimately be reinstated in all his honours. He had long since, however, ascertained the great interval that may exist between promise and performance in a court. Had he been of a morbid and repining spirit, he had ample food for misanthropy. He beheld the career of glory which he had opened, thronged by favoured adventurers; he witnessed preparations making to convey with unusual pomp a successor to that government from which he had been so wrongfully and rudely ejected; in the meanwhile his own career was interrupted, and as far as public employ is a gauge of royal favour, he remained apparently in disgrace.

His sanguine temperament was not long to be depressed; if checked in one direction it broke forth in another. His visionary imagination was an internal light, which, in the darkest times, repelled all outward gloom, and filled his mind with splendid images and glorious speculations. In this time of evil, his vow to furnish, within seven years from the time of his discovery, fifty thousand foot-soldiers, and five thousand horse, for the recovery of the Holy Sepulchre, recurred to his memory with peculiar force. The time had elapsed, but the vow remained unfulfilled, and the means to perform it had failed him. The New World, with all its treasures, had as yet produced expense instead of profit; and so far from being in a situation to set armies on foot by his own contributions, he found himself without property, without power, and without employ.

Destitute of the means of accomplishing his pious intentions, he considered it his duty to incite the sovereigns to the enterprise; and he felt emboldened to do so, from having originally proposed it as the great object to which the profits of his discoveries should be dedicated. He set to work, therefore, with his accustomed zeal, to prepare arguments for the purpose. During the intervals of business, he sought into the prophecies of the Holy Scriptures, the writings of the fathers, and all kinds of sacred and speculative sources, for mystic portents and revelations which might be construed to bear upon the discovery of the New World, the conversion of the Gentiles, and the recovery of the Holy Sepulchre: three great events which he supposed to be predestined to succeed each other. These passages, with the assistance of a Carthusian friar, he arranged in order, illustrated by poetry, and collected into a manuscript volume, to be delivered to the sovereigns. He prepared, at the same time, a long letter, written with his usual fervour of spirit and simplicity of heart. It is one of those singular compositions which lay open the visionary part of his character, and show the mystic and speculative reading with which he was accustomed to nurture his solemn and soaring imagination.

In this letter he urged the sovereigns to set on foot a crusade for the deliverance of Jerusalem from the power of the unbelievers. He entreated them not to reject his present advice as extravagant and impracticable, nor to heed the discredit that might be cast upon it by others; reminding them that his great scheme of discovery had originally been treated with similar contempt. He avowed in the fullest manner his persuasion that, from his earliest infancy, he had been chosen by Heaven for the accomplishment of those two great designs, the discovery of the New World, and the rescue of the Holy Sepulchre. For this purpose, in his tender years, he had been guided by a divine impulse to embrace the profession of the sea, a mode of life, he observes, which produces an inclination to inquire into the mysteries of nature; and he had been gifted with a curious spirit, to read all kinds of chronicles, geographical treatises, and works of philosophy. In meditating upon these, his understanding had been opened by the Deity, 'as with a palpable hand', so as to discover the navigation to the Indies, and he had been inflamed with ardour to undertake the enterprise. 'Animated as by a heavenly fire,' he adds, 'I came to your highnesses: all who heard of my enterprise mocked at it; all the sciences I had acquired profited me nothing; seven years did I pass in your royal court, disputing the case with persons of great authority and learned in all the arts, and in the end they decided that all was vain. In your highnesses alone remained faith and constancy. Who will doubt that this light was from the Holy Scriptures, illumining you as well as myself with rays of marvellous brightness?'

These ideas, so repeatedly, and solemnly, and artlessly expressed, by a man of the fervent piety of Columbus, show how truly his discovery arose from the working of his own mind, and not from information furnished by others. He considered it a divine intim- ation, a light from Heaven, and the fulfilment of what had been foretold by our Saviour and the prophets. Still he regarded it but as a minor event, preparatory to the great enterprise, the recovery of the Holy Sepulchre. He pronounced it a miracle effected by Heaven, to animate himself and others to that holy undertaking; and he assured the sovereigns that, if they had faith in his present as in his former proposition, they would assuredly be rewarded with equally triumphant success. He conjured them not to heed the sneers of such as might scoff at him as one unlearned, as an ignorant mariner, a worldly man; reminding them that the Holy Spirit works not merely in the learned, but also in the ignorant; nay, that it reveals things to come, not merely by rational beings, but by prodigies in animals, and by mystic signs in the air and in the heavens.

The enterprise here suggested by Columbus, however idle and extravagant it may appear in the present day, was in unison with the temper of the times, and of the court to which it was proposed. The vein of mystic erudition by which it was enforced, likewise, was suited to an age when the reveries of the cloister still con- trolled the operations of the cabinet and the camp. The spirit of the crusades had not yet passed away. In the cause of the church, and at the instigation of its dignitaries, every cavalier was ready to draw his sword; and religion mingled a glowing and devoted enthusiasm with the ordinary excitement of warfare. Ferdinand was a religious bigot; and the devotion of Isabella went as near to bigotry as her liberal mind and magnanimous spirit would permit. Both the sovereigns were under the influence of ecclesiastical politicians, constantly guiding their enterprises in a direction to redound to the temporal power and glory of the church. The recent conquest of Granada had been considered a European crusade, and had gained to the sovereigns the epithet of Catholic. It was natural to think of extending their sacred victories still further, and retaliating upon the infidels their domination of Spain and their long triumphs over the cross. In fact, the Duke of Medina Sidonia had made a recent inroad into Barbary, in the course of which he had taken the city of Melilla, and his expedition had been pronounced a renewal of the holy wars against the infidels in Africa.[*]

There was nothing, therefore, in the proposition of Columbus that could be regarded as preposterous, considering the period and circumstances in which it was made, though it strongly illustrates his own enthusiastic and visionary character. It must be recollected that it was meditated in the courts of the Alhambra, among the splendid remains of Moorish grandeur, where, but a few years before, he had beheld the standard of the faith elevated in triumph above the symbols of infidelity. It appears to have been the offspring of one of those moods of high excitement, when, as has been observed, his soul was elevated by the contemplation of his great and glorious office; when he considered himself under divine inspiration, imparting the will of Heaven, and fulfilling the high and holy purposes for which he had been predestined.[†]

---

[*] Garibay, *Hist. España*, lib. xix. cap. 6. Among the collections existing in the library of the late Prince Sebastian, there is a folio which, among other things, contains a paper or letter in which is a calculation of the probable expenses of an army of twenty thousand men, for the conquest of the Holy Land. It is dated in 1509 or 1510, and the handwriting appears to be of the same time.

[†] Columbus was not singular in his belief; it was entertained by many of his zealous and learned admirers. The erudite lapidary, Jayme Ferrer, in the letter written to Columbus in 1495, at the command of the sovereigns, observes: 'I see in this a great mystery: the divine and infallible Providence sent the great St Thomas from the west into the east, to manifest in India our holy and Catholic faith; and you, Señor, he sent in an opposite direction, from the east into the west, until you have arrived in the Orient, into the extreme part of Upper India, that the people may hear that which their ancestors neglected of the preaching of St Thomas. Thus shall be accomplished what was written, *in omnem terram exibit sonus eorum.*' . . . And again, 'The office which you hold, Señor, places you in the light of an apostle and ambassador of God, sent by his divine judgment, to make known his holy name in unknown lands.' – Letra de Mossen, Jayme Ferrer, Navarrete, *Coleccion*, tom. ii. decad. 68. See also the opinion expressed by Agostino Giustiniani, his contemporary, in his Polyglot Psalter.

The speculation relative to the recovery of the Holy Sepulchre held but a temporary sway over the mind of Columbus. His thoughts soon returned, with renewed ardour, to their wonted channel. He became impatient of inaction, and soon conceived a leading object for another enterprise of discovery. The achievement of Vasco de Gama, of the long-attempted navigation to India by the Cape of Good Hope, was one of the signal events of the day. Pedro Alvarez Cabral, following in his track, had made a most successful voyage, and returned with his vessels laden with the precious commodities of the East. The riches of Calicut were now the theme of every tongue, and the splendid trade now opened in diamonds and precious stones from the mines of Hindostan; in pearls, gold, silver, amber, ivory, and porcelain; in silken stuffs, costly woods, gums, aromatics, and spices of all kinds. The discoveries of the savage regions of the New World, as yet, brought little revenue to Spain; but this route, suddenly opened to the luxurious countries of the East, was pouring immediate wealth into Portugal.

Columbus was roused to emulation by these accounts. He now conceived the idea of a voyage, in which, with his usual enthusiasm, he hoped to surpass not merely the discovery of Vasco de Gama, but even those of his own previous expeditions. According to his own observations in his voyage to Paria, and the reports of other navigators, who had pursued the same route to a greater distance, it appeared that the coast of Terra Firma stretched far to the west. The southern coast of Cuba, which he considered a part of the Asiatic continent, stretched onwards towards the same point. The currents of the Caribbean sea must pass between those lands. He was persuaded, therefore, that there must be a strait existing somewhere thereabout, opening into the Indian sea. The situation in which he placed his conjectural strait, was somewhere about what at present is called the Isthmus of Darien.* Could he but discover such a passage, and thus link the New World he had discovered with the opulent oriental regions of the Old, he felt that he should make a magnificent close to his labours, and consummate this great object of his existence.

When he unfolded his plan to the sovereigns, it was listened to with great attention. Certain of the royal council, it is said, endeavoured to throw difficulties in the way; observing that the various exigencies of the times, and the low state of the royal treasury, rendered any new expedition highly inexpedient. They intimated also that Columbus ought not to be employed, until his good conduct in Hispaniola was satisfactorily established by letters from Ovando. These narrow-minded suggestions failed in their aim: Isabella had implicit confidence in the integrity of Columbus. As to the expense, she felt that while furnishing so powerful a fleet and splendid retinue to Ovando, to take possession of his government, it would be ungenerous and ungrateful to refuse a few ships to the discoverer of the New World, to enable him to prosecute his illustrious enterprises. As to Ferdinand, his cupidity was roused at the idea of being soon put in possession of a more direct and safe route to those countries with which the crown of Portugal was opening so lucrative a trade. The project also would occupy the admiral for a considerable time, and, while it diverted him from claims of an inconvenient nature, would employ his talents in a way most beneficial to the crown. However the king might doubt his abilities as a legislator, he had the highest opinion of his skill and judgment as a navigator. If such a strait as the one supposed were really in existence, Columbus was, of all men in the world, the one to discover it. His proposition, therefore, was promptly acceded to; he was authorized to fit out an armament immediately; and repaired to Seville in the autumn of 1501, to make the necessary preparations.

Though this substantial enterprise diverted his attention from his romantic expedition for the recovery of the Holy Sepulchre, it still continued to haunt his mind. He left his manuscript collection of researches among the prophecies in the hands of a devout friar of the name of Gaspar Gorricio, who assisted to complete it. In

---

* Las Casas, lib. ii. cap. 4. Las Casas specifics the vicinity of Nombre de Dios as the place.

February, also, he wrote a letter to Pope Alexander VII, in which he apologizes, on account of indispensable occupations, for not having repaired to Rome, according to his original intention, to give an account of his grand discoveries. After briefly relating them, he adds that his enterprises had been undertaken with intent of dedicating the gains to the recovery of the Holy Sepulchre. He mentions his vow to furnish, within seven years, fifty thousand foot and five thousand horse for the purpose, and another of like force within five succeeding years. This pious intention, he laments, had been impeded by the arts of the devil, and he feared, without divine aid, would be entirely frustrated, as the government which had been granted to him in perpetuity had been taken from him. He informs his Holiness of his being about to embark on another voyage, and promises solemnly, on his return, to repair to Rome without delay, to relate everything by word of mouth, as well as to present him with an account of his voyages, which he had kept from the commencement to the present time, in the style of the Commentaries of Caesar.*

It was about this time, also, that he sent his letter on the subject of the Sepulchre to the sovereigns, together with the collection of prophecies.† We have no account of the manner in which the proposition was received. Ferdinand, with all his bigotry, was a shrewd and worldly prince. Instead of a chivalrous crusade against

---

* Navarrete, *Colec. Viag.*, tom. ii. p. 145.

† A manuscript volume containing a copy of this letter and of the collection of prophecies is in the Columbian Library in the Cathedral of Seville, where the author of this work has seen and examined it since publishing the first edition. The title and some of the early pages of the work are in the handwriting of Fernando Columbus; the main body of the work is by a strange hand, probably by the Friar Gaspar Gorricio, or some brother of his convent. There are trifling marginal notes or corrections, and one or two trivial additions in the handwriting of Columbus, especially a passage added after his return from his fourth voyage, and shortly before his death, alluding to an eclipse of the moon which took place during his sojourn in the island of Jamaica. The handwriting of this last passage, like most of the manuscript of Columbus which the author has seen, is small and delicate, but wants the firmness and distinctness of his earlier writing, his hand having doubtless become unsteady by age and infirmity.

This document is extremely curious as containing all the passages of Scripture and of the works of the fathers which had so powerful an influence on the enthusiastic mind of Columbus, and were construed by him into mysterious prophecies and revelations. The volume is in good preservation, excepting that a few pages have been cut out. The writing, though of the beginning of the fifteenth century, is very distinct and legible. The library-mark of the book is Estante Z. Tab. 138, No. 25.

Jerusalem, he preferred making a pacific arrangement with the Grand Soldan of Egypt, who had menaced the destruction of the sacred edifice. He despatched, therefore, the learned Peter Martyr, so distinguished for his historical writings, as ambassador to the Soldan, by whom all ancient grievances between the two powers were satisfactorily adjusted, and arrangements made for the conservation of the Holy Sepulchre, and the protection of all Christian pilgrims resorting to it.

In the meantime Columbus went on with the preparations for his contemplated voyage, though but slowly, owing, as Charlevoix intimates, to the artifices and delays of Fonseca and his agents. He craved permission to touch at the island of Hispaniola for supplies on his outward voyage. This, however, the sovereigns forbade, knowing that he had many enemies in the island, and that the place would be in great agitation from the arrival of Ovando, and the removal of Bobadilla. They consented, however, that he should touch there briefly on his return, by which time they hoped the island would be restored to tranquillity. He was permitted to take with him, in this expedition, his brother the Adelantado, and his son Fernando, then in his fourteenth year; also two or three persons learned in Arabic, to serve as interpreters, in case he should arrive at the dominions of the Grand Khan, or of any other Eastern prince where that language might be spoken, or partially known. In reply to letters relative to the ultimate restoration of his rights, and to matters concerning his family, the sovereigns wrote him a letter, dated March 14, 1502, from Valencia de Torre, in which they again solemnly assured him that their capitulations with him should be fulfilled to the letter, and the dignities therein ceded enjoyed by him, and his children after him; and if it should be necessary to confirm them anew, they would do so, and secure them to his son. Beside which, they expressed their disposition to bestow further honours and rewards upon himself, his brothers, and his children. They entreated him, therefore, to depart in peace and confidence, and to leave all his concerns in Spain to the management of his son Diego.*

This was the last letter that Columbus received from the sovereigns, and the assurances it contained were as ample and absolute as he could desire. Recent circumstances, however, had apparently

* Las Casas, *Hist. Ind.*, lib. ii. cap. 4.

rendered him dubious of the future. During the time that he passed in Seville, previous to his departure, he took measures to secure his fame, and preserve the claims of his family, by placing them under the guardianship of his native country. He had copies of all the letters, grants, and privileges from the sovereigns, appointing him admiral, viceroy, and governor of the Indies, copied and authenticated before the alcades of Seville. Two sets of these were transcribed, together with his letter to the nurse of Prince Juan, containing a circumstantial and eloquent vindication of his rights; and two letters to the Bank of St George, at Genoa, assigning to it the tenth of his revenues, to be employed in diminishing the duties on corn and other provisions – a truly benevolent and patriotic donation, intended for the relief of the poor of his native city. These two sets of documents he sent by different individuals to his friend, Doctor Nicolo Oderigo, formerly ambassador from Genoa to the court of Spain, requesting him to preserve them in some safe deposit, and to apprise his son Diego of the same. His dissatisfaction at the conduct of the Spanish court may have been the cause of this precautionary measure, that an appeal to the world, or to posterity, might be in the power of his descendants, in case he should perish in the course of his voyage.*

* These documents lay unknown in the Oderigo family until 1670, when Lorenzo Oderigo presented them to the government of Genoa, and they were deposited in the archives. In the disturbances and revolutions of after times, one of these copies was taken to Paris, and the other disappeared. In 1816 the latter was discovered in the library of the deceased Count Michel Angelo Cambiaso, a senator of Genoa. It was procured by the king of Sardinia, then sovereign of Genoa, and given up by him to the city of Genoa in 1821. A custodia, or monument, was erected in that city for its preservation, consisting of a marble column supporting an urn, surmounted by a bust of Columbus. The documents were deposited in the urn. These papers have been published, together with an historical memoir of Columbus, by D. Gio. Battista Spotorno, Professor of Eloquence, etc. in the University of Genoa.

BOOK 15

CHAPTER I

1502

Age was rapidly making its advances upon Columbus when he undertook his fourth and last voyage of discovery. He had already numbered sixty-six years, and they were years filled with care and trouble, in which age outstrips the march of time. His constitution, originally vigorous in the extreme, had been impaired by hardships and exposures in every clime, and silently preyed upon by the sufferings of the mind. His frame, once powerful and commanding, and retaining a semblance of strength and majesty even in its decay, was yet crazed by infirmities and subject to paroxysms of excruciating pain. His intellectual forces alone retained their wonted health and energy, prompting him, at a period of life when most men seek repose, to sally forth with youthful ardour, on the most toilsome and adventurous of expeditions.

His squadron for the present voyage consisted of four caravels, the smallest of fifty tons burden, the largest not exceeding seventy, and the crews amounting in all to one hundred and fifty men. With this little armament and these slender barks did the venerable discoverer undertake the search after a strait which, if found, must conduct him into the most remote seas, and lead to a complete circumnavigation of the globe.

In this arduous voyage, however, he had a faithful counsellor, and an intrepid and vigorous coadjutor, in his brother Don Bartholomew, while his younger son Fernando cheered him with his affectionate sympathy. He had learnt to appreciate such comforts, from being too often an isolated stranger, surrounded by false friends and perfidious enemies.

The squadron sailed from Cadiz on the 9th of May, and passed over to Ercilla, on the coast of Morocco, where it anchored on the 13th. Understanding that the Portuguese garrison was closely besieged in the fortress by the Moors, and exposed to great peril, Columbus was ordered to touch there, and render all the assistance in his power. Before his arrival the siege had been raised, but the governor lay ill, having been wounded in an assault. Columbus sent his brother, the Adelantado, his son Fernando, and the captains of the caravels on shore, to wait upon the governor, with expressions of friendship and civility, and offers of the services of his squadron. Their visit and message gave high satisfaction, and several cavaliers were sent to wait upon the admiral in return, some of whom were relatives of his deceased wife, Dona Felippa Muñoz. After this exchange of civilities, the admiral made sail on the same day, and continued his voyage.[*] On the 25th of May, he arrived at the Grand Canary, and remained at that and the adjacent islands for a few days, taking in wood and water. On the evening of the 25th, he took his departure for the New World. The trade winds were so favourable, that the little squadron swept gently on its course, without shifting a sail, and arrived on the 15th of June at one of the Caribbee Islands, called by the natives Mantinino.[†] After stopping here for three days, to take in wood and water, and allow the seamen time to wash their clothes, the squadron passed to the west of the island, and sailed to Dominica, about ten leagues distant.[‡] Columbus continued hence along the inside of the Antilles, to Santa Cruz, then along the south side of Porto Rico, and steered for San Domingo. This was contrary to the original plan of the admiral, who had intended to steer to Jamaica,[§] and thence to take a departure for the continent, and explore its coasts in search of the supposed strait. It was contrary to the orders of the sovereigns also, prohibiting him on his outward voyage to touch at Hispaniola. His excuse was, that his principal vessel sailed extremely ill, could not carry any canvas, and continually

[*] *Hist. del Almirante*, cap. 88.

[†] Señor Navarrete supposes this island to be the same at present called Santa Lucia. From the distance between it and Dominica, as stated by Fernando Columbus, it was more probably the present Martinica.

[‡] *Hist. del Almirante*, cap. 88.

[§] Letter of Columbus from Jamaica; Journal of Porras, Navarrete, tom. i.

embarrassed and delayed the rest of the squadron.* He wished, therefore, to exchange it for one of the fleet which had recently conveyed Ovando to his government, or to purchase some other vessel at San Domingo; and he was persuaded that he would not be blamed for departing from his orders, in a case of such importance to the safety and success of his expedition.

It is necessary to state the situation of the island at this moment. Ovando had reached San Domingo on the 15th of April. He had been received with the accustomed ceremony on the shore, by Bobadilla, accompanied by the principal inhabitants of the town. He was escorted to the fortress, where his commission was read in form, in presence of all the authorities. The usual oaths were taken, and ceremonials observed; and the new governor was hailed with great demonstrations of obedience and satisfaction. Ovando entered upon the duties of his office with coolness and prudence; and treated Bobadilla with a courtesy totally opposite to the rudeness with which the latter had superseded Columbus. The emptiness of mere official rank, when unsustained by merit, was shown in the case of Bobadilla. The moment his authority was at an end, all his importance vanished. He found himself a solitary and neglected man, deserted by those whom he had most favoured, and he experienced the worthlessness of the popularity gained by courting the prejudices and passions of the multitude. Still there is no record of any suit having been instituted against him; and Las Casas, who was on the spot, declares that he never heard any harsh thing spoken of him by the colonists.†

The conduct of Roldan and his accomplices, however, underwent a strict investigation, and many were arrested to be sent to Spain for trial. They appeared undismayed, trusting to the influence of their friends in Spain to protect them, and many relying on the well-known disposition of the Bishop of Fonseca to favour all who had been opposed to Columbus.

The fleet which had brought out Ovando was now ready for sea; and was to take out a number of the principal delinquents, and many of the idlers and profligates of the island. Bobadilla was to embark in the principal ship, on board of which he put an immense amount of gold, the revenue collected for the crown

* *Hist. del Almirante*, cap. 88; Las Casas, lib. ii. cap. 5.
† Las Casas, *Hist. Ind.*, lib. ii. cap. 3.

during his government, and which he confidently expected would atone for all his faults. There was one solid mass of virgin gold on board of this ship, which is famous in the old Spanish chronicles. It had been found by a female Indian in a brook, on the estate of Francisco de Garay and Miguel Diaz, and had been taken by Bobadilla to send to the king, making the owners a suitable compensation. It was said to weigh three thousand six hundred castellanos.[*]

Large quantities of gold were likewise shipped in the fleet by the followers of Roldan, and other adventurers; the wealth gained by the sufferings of the unhappy natives. Among the various persons who were to sail in the principal ship was the unfortunate Guarionex, the once powerful cacique of the Vega. He had been confined in Fort Conception ever since his capture after the war of Higuey, and was now to be sent a captive in chains to Spain. In one of the ships Alonzo Sanchez de Carvajal, the agent of Columbus, had put four thousand pieces of gold, to be remitted to him; being part of his property, either recently collected, or recovered from the hands of Bobadilla.[†]

The preparations were all made, and the fleet was ready to put to sea, when, on the 29th of June, the squadron of Columbus arrived at the mouth of the river. He immediately sent Pedro de Terreros, captain of one of the caravels, on shore, to wait on Ovando, and explain to him that the purpose of his coming was to procure a vessel in exchange for one of his caravels, which was extremely defective. He requested permission also to shelter his squadron in the harbour; as he apprehended, from various indications, an approaching storm. This request was refused by Ovando. Las Casas thinks it probable that he had instructions from the sovereigns not to admit Columbus, and that he was further swayed by prudent considerations, as San Domingo was at that moment crowded with the most virulent enemies of the admiral, many of them in a high state of exasperation, from recent proceedings which had taken place against them.[‡]

When the ungracious refusal of Ovando was brought to Columbus, and he found all shelter denied him, he sought at least to

[*] Las Casas, cap. 5.
[†] Las Casas, cap. 5.
[‡] Las Casas lib. ii. cap. 5

avert the danger of the fleet, which was about to sail. He sent back the officer therefore to the governor, entreating him not to permit the fleet to put to sea for several days; assuring him that there were indubitable signs of an impending tempest. This second request was equally fruitless with the first. The weather, to an inexperienced eye, was fair and tranquil; the pilots and seamen were impatient to depart. They scoffed at the prediction of the admiral, ridiculing him as a false prophet, and they persuaded Ovando not to detain the fleet on so unsubstantial a pretext.

It was hard treatment of Columbus, thus to be denied the relief which the state of his ships required, and to be excluded in time of distress from the very harbour he had discovered. He retired from the river full of grief and indignation. His crew murmured loudly at being shut out from a port of their own nation, where even strangers, under similar circumstances, would be admitted. They repined at having embarked with a commander liable to such treatment; and anticipated nothing but evil from a voyage in which they were exposed to the dangers of the sea and repulsed from the protection of the land.

Being confident, from his observations of those natural phenomena in which he was deeply skilled, that the anticipated storm could not be distant, and expecting it from the land side, Columbus kept his feeble squadron close to the shore, and sought for secure anchorage in some wild bay or river of the island.

In the meantime, the fleet of Bobadilla set sail from San Domingo, and stood out confidently to sea. Within two days, the predictions of Columbus were verified. One of those tremendous hurricanes, which sometimes sweep those latitudes, had gradually gathered up. The baleful appearance of the heavens, the wild look of the ocean, the rising murmur of the winds, all gave notice of its approach. The fleet had scarcely reached the eastern point of Hispaniola, when the tempest burst over it with awful fury, involving everything in wreck and ruin. The ship on board of which were Bobadilla, Roldan, and a number of the most inveterate enemies of Columbus, was swallowed up with all its crew, and with the celebrated mass of gold and the principal part of the ill-gotten treasure gained by the miseries of the Indians. Many of the ships were entirely lost, some returned to San Domingo, in shattered condition, and only one was enabled to continue her voyage to Spain. That one, according to Fernando Columbus, was the weakest of the fleet, and had on board the four thousand pieces of gold, the property of the admiral.

During the early part of this storm, the little squadron of Columbus remained tolerably well sheltered by the land. On the second day the tempest increased in violence, and the night coming on with unusual darkness, the ships lost sight of each other and were separated. The admiral still kept close to the shore, and sustained no damage. The others, fearful of the land in such a dark and boisterous night, ran out for sea-room, and encountered the whole fury of the elements. For several days they were driven about at the mercy of wind and wave, fearful each moment of shipwreck, and giving up each other as lost. The Adelantado, who commanded the ship already mentioned as being scarcely seaworthy, ran the most imminent hazard, and nothing but his consummate seamanship enabled him to keep her afloat. At length, after various vicissitudes, they all arrived safe at Port Hermoso, to the west of San Domingo. The Adelantado had lost his long boat; and all the vessels, with the exception of that of the admiral, had sustained more or less injury.

When Columbus learnt the signal destruction that had overwhelmed his enemies, almost before his eyes, he was deeply impressed with awe, and considered his own preservation as little less than miraculous. Both his son Fernando and the venerable historian Las Casas looked upon the event as one of those awful judgments, which seem at times to deal forth temporal retribution. They notice the circumstance, that while the enemies of the admiral were swallowed up by the raging sea, the only ship of the fleet which was enabled to pursue her voyage and reach her port of destination was the frail bark freighted with the property of Columbus. The evil, however, in this, as in most circumstances, overwhelmed the innocent as well as the guilty. In the ship with Bobadilla and Roldan perished the captive Guarionex, the unfortunate cacique of the Vega.*

---

* Las Casas, *Hist. Ind.*, lib. ii. cap. 5; *Hist. del Almirante*, cap. 88.

For several days Columbus remained in Port Hermosa to repair his vessels, and permit his crews to repose and refresh themselves after the late tempest. He had scarcely left this harbour, when he was obliged to take shelter from another storm in Jacquemel, or, as it was called by the Spaniards, Port Brazil. Hence he sailed on the 14th of July, steering for Terra Firma. The weather falling perfectly calm, he was borne away by the currents until he found himself in the vicinity of some little islands near Jamaica,* destitute of springs, but where the seamen obtained a supply of water by digging holes in the sand on the beach.

The calm continuing, he was swept away to the group of small islands, or keys, on the southern coast of Cuba, to which in 1494 he had given the name of the Gardens. He had scarcely touched there, however, when the wind sprang up from a favourable quarter, and he was enabled to make sail on his destined course. He now stood to the south-west, and after a few days discovered, on the 30th of July, a small but elevated island, agreeable to the eye from the variety of trees with which it was covered. Among these was a great number of lofty pines, from which circumstance Columbus named it Isla de Pinos. It has always, however, retained its Indian name of Guanaja,† which has been extended to a number of smaller islands surrounding it. This group is within a few leagues of the coast of Honduras, to the east of the great bay or gulf of that name.

The Adelantado, with two launches full of people, landed on the principal island, which was extremely verdant and fertile. The inhabitants resembled those of other islands, excepting that their foreheads were narrower. While the Adelantado was on shore, he

---

* Supposed to be the Morant Keys.
† Called in some of the English maps Bonacca.

beheld a great canoe arriving, as from a distant and important voyage. He was struck with its magnitude and contents. It was eight feet wide, and as long as a galley, though formed of the trunk of a single tree. In the centre was a kind of awning or cabin of palm-leaves, after the manner of those in the gondolas of Venice, and sufficiently close to exclude both sun and rain. Under this sat a cacique with his wives and children. Twenty-five Indians rowed the canoe, and it was filled with all kinds of articles of the manufacture and natural production of the adjacent countries. It is supposed that this bark had come from the province of Yucatan, which is about forty leagues distant from this island.

The Indians in the canoe appeared to have no fear of the Spaniards, and readily went alongside of the admiral's caravel. Columbus was overjoyed at thus having brought to him at once, without trouble or danger, a collection of specimens of all the important articles of this part of the New World. He examined, with great curiosity and interest, the contents of the canoe. Among various utensils and weapons similar to those already found among the natives, he perceived others of a much superior kind. There were hatchets for cutting wood, formed not of stone but copper; wooden swords, with channels on each side of the blade, in which sharp flints were firmly fixed by cords made of the intestines of fishes; being the same kind of weapon afterwards found among the Mexicans. There were copper bells and other articles of the same metal, together with a rude kind of crucible in which to melt it; various vessels and utensils neatly formed of clay, of marble, and of hard wood; sheets and mantles of cotton, worked and dyed with various colours; great quantities of cacao, a fruit as yet unknown to the Spaniards, but which, as they soon found, the natives held in great estimation, using it both as food and money. There was a beverage also extracted from maize or Indian corn, resembling beer. Their provisions consisted of bread made of maize, and roots of various kinds, similar to those of Hispaniola. From among these articles, Columbus collected such as were important to send as specimens to Spain, giving the natives European trinkets in exchange, with which they were highly satisfied. They appeared to manifest neither astonishment nor alarm when on board of the vessels, and surrounded by people who must have been so strange and wonderful to them. The women wore mantles, with which they wrapped themselves, like the female Moors of Granada, and the men had cloths of cotton round their loins. Both sexes appeared more particular about these coverings, and to have a quicker sense of personal modesty than any Indians Columbus had yet discovered.

These circumstances, together with the superiority of their implements and manufactures, were held by the admiral as indications that he was approaching more civilized nations. He endeavoured to gain particular information from these Indians about the surrounding countries; but as they spoke a different language from that of his interpreters, he could understand them but imperfectly. They informed him that they had just arrived from a country, rich, cultivated, and industrious, situated to the west. They endeavoured to impress him with an idea of the wealth and magnificence of the regions, and the people in that quarter, and urged him to steer in that direction. Well would it have been for Columbus had he followed their advice. Within a day or two he would have arrived at Yucatan; the discovery of Mexico and the other opulent countries of New Spain would have necessarily followed; the Southern Ocean would have been disclosed to him, and a succession of splendid discoveries would have shed fresh glory on his declining age, instead of its sinking amidst gloom, neglect, and disappointment.

The admiral's whole mind, however, was at present intent upon discovering the strait. As the countries described by the Indians lay to the west, he supposed that he could easily visit them at some future time, by running with the trade-winds along the coast of Cuba, which he imagined must continue on, so as to join them. At present he was determined to seek the mainland, the mountains of which were visible to the south, and apparently not many leagues distant:* by keeping along it steadfastly to the east, he must at length arrive to where he supposed it to be severed from the coast of Paria by an intervening strait; and passing through this, he should soon make his way to the Spice Islands and the richest parts of India.†

He was encouraged the more to persist in his eastern course by information from the Indians, that there were many places in

---

* Journal of Porras, Navarrete, tom. i.
† Las Casas, lib. ii. cap. 20; Letter of Columbus from Jamaica.

that direction which abounded with gold. Much of the information which he gathered among these people was derived from
an old man more intelligent than the rest, who appeared to be
an ancient navigator of these seas. Columbus retained him to
serve as a guide along the coast, and dismissed his companions
with many presents.

Leaving the island of Guanaja, he stood southwardly for the
mainland, and after sailing a few leagues, discovered a cape, to
which he gave the name of Caxinas, from its being covered with
fruit trees, so called by the natives. It is at present known as Cape
Honduras. Here, on Sunday the 14th of August, the Adelantado
landed with the captains of the caravels and many of the seamen,
to attend mass, which was performed under the trees on the sea-
shore, according to the pious custom of the admiral, whenever
circumstances would permit. On the 17th, the Adelantado again
landed at a river about fifteen miles from the point, on the bank
of which he displayed the banners of Castile, taking possession of
the country in the name of their Catholic majesties; from which
circumstances he named this the River of Possession.*

At this place they found upwards of a hundred Indians assembled, laden with bread and maize, fish and fowl, vegetables, and
fruits of various kinds. These they laid down as presents before the
Adelantado and his party, and drew back to a distance without
speaking a word. The Adelantado distributed among them various
trinkets, with which they were well pleased, and appeared the next
day in the same place, in greater numbers, with still more abundant
supplies of provisions.

The natives of this neighbourhood, and for a considerable
distance eastward, had higher foreheads than those of the islands.
They were of different languages, and varied from each other in
their decorations. Some were entirely naked; and their bodies
were marked by means of fire with the figures of various animals.
Some wore coverings about the loins; others short cotton jerkins
without sleeves: some wore tresses of hair in front. The chieftains
had caps of white or coloured cotton. When arrayed for any
festival, they painted their faces black, or with stripes of various
colours, or with circles round the eyes. The old Indian guide
assured the admiral that many of them were cannibals. In one part

* Journal of Porras, Navarrete, *Colec.*, tom. i.

of the coast the natives had their ears bored, and hideously distended; which caused the Spaniards to call that region *la Costa de la Oreja*, or 'the Coast of the Ear'.*

From the River of Possession, Columbus proceeded along what is at present called the coast of Honduras, beating against contrary winds, and struggling with currents which swept from the east like the constant stream of a river. He often lost in one tack what he had laboriously gained in two, frequently making but two leagues in a day, and never more than five. At night he anchored under the land, through fear of proceeding along an unknown coast in the dark, but was often forced out to sea by the violence of the currents.† In all this time he experienced the same kind of weather that had prevailed on the coast of Hispaniola, and had attended him more or less for upwards of sixty days. There was, he says, almost an incessant tempest of the heavens, with heavy rains, and such thunder and lightning, that it seemed as if the end of the world was at hand. Those who know anything of the drenching rains and rending thunder of the tropics, will not think his description of the storms exaggerated. His vessels were strained so that their seams opened; the sails and rigging were rent, and the provisions were damaged by the rain and by the leakage. The sailors were exhausted with labour, and harassed with terror. They many times confessed their sins to each other, and prepared for death. 'I have seen many tempests,' says Columbus, 'but none so violent or of such long duration.' He alludes to the whole series of storms for upwards of two months, since he had been refused shelter at San Domingo. During a great part of this time, he had suffered extremely from the gout, aggravated by his watchfulness and anxiety. His illness did not prevent his attending to his duties; he had a small cabin or chamber constructed on the stern, whence, even when confined to his bed, he could keep a look-out and regulate the sailing of the ships. Many times he was so ill that he thought his end approaching. His anxious mind was distressed about his brother the Adelantado, whom he had persuaded against his will to come on this expedition, and who was in the worst vessel of the squadron. He lamented also having brought with him his son Fernando, exposing him at so tender an age to such perils

---

* Las Casas, lib. ii. cap. 21; *Hist. del Almirante*, cap. 90.
† *Hist. del Almirante*, cap. 80.

and hardships, although the youth bore them with the courage and fortitude of a veteran. Often, too, his thoughts reverted to his son Diego, and the cares and perplexities into which his death might plunge him.[*] At length, after struggling for upwards of forty days since leaving the Cape of Honduras, to make a distance of about seventy leagues, they arrived on the 14th of September at a cape where the coast, making an angle, turned directly south, so as to give them an easy wind and free navigation. Doubling the point, they swept off with flowing sails and hearts filled with joy; and the admiral, to commemorate this sudden relief from toil and peril, gave to the Cape the name of *Gracias a Dios*, or Thanks to God.[†]

[*] Letter from Jamaica; Navarrete, *Colec.*, tom. i.
[†] Las Casas, lib ii. cap. 21; *Hist. del Almirante*, cap. 91.

After doubling Cape Gracias a Dios, Columbus sailed directly south, along what is at present called the Mosquito shore. The land was of varied character, sometimes rugged, with craggy promontories and points stretching into the sea, at other places verdant and fertile, and watered by abundant streams. In the rivers grew immense reeds, sometimes of the thickness of a man's thigh: they abounded with fish and tortoises, and alligators basked on the banks. At one place Columbus passed a cluster of twelve small islands, on which grew a fruit resembling the lemon, on which account he called them the Limonares.[*]

After sailing about sixty-two leagues along this coast, being greatly in want of wood and water, the squadron anchored on the 16th of September, near a copious river, up which the boats were sent to procure the requisite supplies. As they were returning to their ships, a sudden swelling of the sea, rushing in and encountering the rapid current of the river, caused a violent commotion, in which one of the boats was swallowed up, and all on board perished. This melancholy event had a gloomy effect upon the crews, already dispirited and careworn from the hardships they had endured, and Columbus, sharing their dejection, gave the stream the sinister name of *El rio del Desastre*, or the River of Disaster.[†]

Leaving this unlucky neighbourhood, they continued for several days along the coast, until, finding both his ships and his people nearly disabled by the buffetings of the tempests, Columbus, on the 25th of September, cast anchor between a small island and the mainland, in what appeared a commodious and delightful situation. The island was covered with groves of palm-trees, coconut-trees,

[*] P. Martyr, decad. iii. lib. iv. These may have been the lime, a small and extremely acid species of the lemon.

[†] Las Casas, lib. ii. cap. 21; *Hist. del Almirante*, cap. 91; Journal of Porras.

bananas, and a delicate and fragrant fruit, which the admiral continually mistook for the mirabolane of the East Indies. The fruits and flowers and odoriferous shrubs of the island sent forth grateful perfumes, so that Columbus gave it the name of La Huerta, or the Garden. It was called by the natives Quiribiri. Immediately opposite, at a short league's distance, was an Indian village, named Cariari, situated on the bank of a beautiful river. The country around was fresh and verdant, finely diversified by noble hills and forests, with trees of such height that Las Casas says they appeared to reach the skies.

When the inhabitants beheld the ships, they gathered together on the coast, armed with bows and arrows, war-clubs, and lances, and prepared to defend their shores. The Spaniards, however, made no attempt to land during that or the succeeding day, but remained quietly on board repairing the ships, airing and drying the damaged provisions, or reposing from the fatigues of the voyage. When the savages perceived that these wonderful beings, who had arrived in this strange manner on their coast, were perfectly pacific, and made no movement to molest them, their hostility ceased, and curiosity predominated. They made various pacific signals, waving their mantles like banners, and inviting the Spaniards to land. Growing still more bold, they swam to the ships, bringing off mantles and tunics of cotton, and ornaments of the inferior sort of gold called guanin, which they wore about their necks. These they offered to the Spaniards. The admiral, however, forbade all traffic, making them presents, but taking nothing in exchange, wishing to impress them with a favourable idea of the liberality and disinterestedness of the white men. The pride of the savages was touched at the refusal of their proffered gifts, and this supposed contempt for their manufactures and productions. They endeavoured to retaliate, by pretending like indifference. On returning to shore, they tied together all the European articles which had been given them, without retaining the least trifle, and left them lying on the strand, where the Spaniards found them on a subsequent day.

Finding the strangers still declined to come on shore, the natives tried in every way to gain their confidence, and dispel the distrust which their hostile demonstrations might have caused. A boat approaching the shore cautiously one day, in quest of some safe place to procure water, an ancient Indian, of venerable demeanour, issued from among the trees, bearing a white banner on the end of a staff, and leading two girls, one about fourteen years of age, the other about eight, having jewels of guanin about their necks. These he brought to the boat and delivered to the Spaniards, making signs that they were to be detained as hostages while the strangers should be on shore. Upon this the Spaniards sallied forth with confidence and filled their water-casks, the Indians remaining at a distance, and observing the strictest care, neither by word nor movement to cause any new distrust. When the boats were about to return to the ships, the old Indian made signs that the young girls should be taken on board, nor would he admit of any denial. On entering the ships the girls showed no signs of grief nor alarm, though surrounded by what to them must have been uncouth and formidable beings. Columbus was careful that the confidence thus placed in him should not be abused. After feasting the young females, and ordering them to be clothed and adorned with various ornaments, he sent them on shore. The night, however, had fallen, and the coast was deserted. They had to return to the ship, where they remained all night under the careful protection of the admiral. The next morning he restored them to their friends. The old Indian received them with joy, and manifested a grateful sense of the kind treatment they had experienced. In the evening, however, when the boats went on shore, the young girls appeared, accompanied by a multitude of their friends, and returned all the presents they had received, nor could they be prevailed upon to retain any of them, although they must have been precious in their eyes; so greatly was the pride of these savages piqued at having their gifts refused.

On the following day, as the Adelantado approached the shore, two of the principal inhabitants, entering the water, took him out of the boat in their arms, and carrying him to land, seated him with great ceremony on a grassy bank. Don Bartholomew endeavoured to collect information from them respecting the country, and ordered the notary of the squadron to write down their replies. The latter immediately prepared pen, ink, and paper, and proceeded to write; but no sooner did the Indians behold this strange and mysterious process, than, mistaking it for some necromantic spell, intended to be wrought upon them, they fled with terror.

After some time they returned, cautiously scattering a fragrant powder in the air, and burning some of it in such a direction that the smoke should be borne towards the Spaniards by the wind. This was apparently intended to counteract any baleful spell, for they regarded the strangers as beings of a mysterious and supernatural order.

The sailors looked upon these counter-charms of the Indians with equal distrust, and apprehended something of magic; nay, Fernando Columbus, who was present, and records the scene, appears to doubt whether these Indiana were not versed in sorcery, and thus led to suspect it in others.*

Indeed, not to conceal a foible which was more characteristic of the superstition of the age than of the man, Columbus himself entertained an idea of the kind, and assures the sovereigns, in his letter from Jamaica, that the people of Cariari and its vicinity are great enchanters, and he intimates that the two Indian girls who had visited his ship had magic powder concealed about their persons. He adds that the sailors attributed all the delays and hardships experienced on that coast to their being under the influence of some evil spell, worked by the witchcraft of the natives, and that they still remained in that belief.†

For several days the squadron remained at this place, during which time the ships were examined and repaired, and the crews enjoyed repose and the recreation of the land. The Adelantado, with a band of armed men, made excursions on shore to collect information. There was no pure gold to be met with here, all their

---

* *Hist. del Almirante*, cap. 91.

† Letter from Jamaica.

Note. We find instances of the same kind of superstition in the work of Marco Polo, and as Columbus considered himself in the vicinity of the countries described by that traveller, he may have been influenced in this respect by his narrations. Speaking of the island of Soccotera (Socotra), Marco Polo observes: 'The inhabitants deal more in sorcery and witchcraft than any other people, although forbidden by their archbishop, who excommunicates and anathematizes them for the sin. Of this, however, they make little account, and if any vessel belonging to a pirate should injure one of theirs, they do not fail to lay him under a spell, so that he cannot proceed on his cruise until he has made satisfaction for the damage; and even although he should have a fair and leading wind, they have the power of causing it to change, and thereby obliging him, in spite of himself, to return to the island. They can, in like manner, cause the sea to become calm, and at their will can raise tempests, occasion shipwrecks, and produce many other extraordinary effects that need not be particularized.' – Marco Polo, Book iii. cap. 35, Eng. translation by W. Marsden.

ornaments were of guanin; but the natives assured the Adelantado that, in proceeding along the coast, the ships would soon arrive at a country where gold was in great abundance.

In examining one of the villages, the Adelantado found, in a large house, several sepulchres. One contained a human body embalmed; in another, there were two bodies wrapped in cotton, and so preserved as to be free from any disagreeable odour. They were adorned with the ornaments most precious to them when living; and the sepulchres were decorated with rude carvings and paintings representing various animals, and sometimes what appeared to be intended for portraits of the deceased.* Throughout most of the savage tribes, there appears to have been great veneration for the dead, and an anxiety to preserve their remains undisturbed.

When about to sail, Columbus seized seven of the people, two of whom, apparently the most intelligent, he selected to serve as guides; the rest he suffered to depart. His late guide he had dismissed with presents at Cape Gracias a Dios. The inhabitants of Cariari manifested unusual sensibility at this seizure of their countrymen. They thronged the shore, and sent off four of their principal men with presents to the ships, imploring the release of the prisoners.

The admiral assured them that he only took their companions as guides, for a short distance along the coast, and would restore them soon in safety to their homes. He ordered various presents to be given to the ambassadors; but neither his promises nor gifts could soothe the grief and apprehension of the natives at beholding their friends carried away by beings of whom they had such mysterious apprehensions.†

* Las Casas, lib. ii. cap. 21; *Hist. del Almirante*, cap. 91.
† Las Casas, lib. ii. cap. 21; *Hist. del Almirante*, cap. 91; Letter of Columbus from Jamaica.

CHAPTER 4

1502

On the 5th of October, the squadron departed from Cariari, and sailed along what is at present called Costa Rica (or the Rich Coast), from the gold and silver mines found in after years among its mountains. After sailing about twenty-two leagues, the ships anchored in a great bay, about six leagues in length and three in breadth, full of islands, with channels opening between them, so as to present three or four entrances. It was called by the natives Caribaro,* and had been pointed out by the natives of Cariari as plentiful in gold.

The islands were beautifully verdant, covered with groves, and sent forth the fragrance of fruits and flowers. The channels between them were so deep and free from rocks that the ships sailed along them as if in canals in the streets of a city, the spars and rigging brushing the overhanging branches of the trees. After anchoring, the boats landed on one of the islands, where they found twenty canoes. The people were on shore among the trees. Being encouraged by the Indians of Cariari who accompanied the Spaniards, they soon advanced with confidence. Here, for the first time on this coast, the Spaniards met with specimens of pure gold, the natives wearing large plates of it suspended round their necks by cotton cords; they had ornaments likewise of guanin, rudely shaped like eagles. One of them exchanged a plate of gold, equal in value to ten ducats, for three hawks'-bells.†

On the following day, the boats proceeded to the mainland at the bottom of the bay. The country around was high and rough, and the villages were generally perched on the heights. They met with ten canoes of Indians, their heads decorated with garlands of

---

* In some English maps this bay is called Almirante, or Carnabaco Bay. The channel by which Columbus entered is still called Boca del Almirante, or the mouth of the Admiral.

† Journal of Porras, Navarrete, tom. i.

flowers, and coronets formed of the claws of beasts and the quills of birds; [*] most of them had plates of gold about their necks, but refused to part with them. The Spaniards brought two of them to the admiral to serve as guides. One had a plate of pure gold worth fourteen ducats, another an eagle worth twenty-two ducats. Seeing the great value which the strangers set upon this metal, they assured them it was to be had in abundance within the distance of two days' journey; and mentioned various places along the coast, whence it was procured, particularly Veragua, which was about twenty-five leagues distant.[†]

The cupidity of the Spaniards was greatly excited, and they would gladly have remained to barter, but the admiral discouraged all disposition of the kind. He barely sought to collect specimens and information of the riches of the country, and then pressed forward in quest of the great object of his enterprise, the imaginary strait.

Sailing on the 17th of October from this bay, or rather gulf, he began to coast this region of reputed wealth, since called the coast of Veragua; and after sailing about twelve leagues, arrived at a large river, which his son Fernando calls the Guaig. Here, on the boats being sent to land, about two hundred Indians appeared on the shore, armed with clubs, lances, and swords of palm-wood. The forests echoed with the sound of wooden drums, and the blasts of conch shells, their usual war signals. They rushed into the sea up to their waists, brandishing their weapons, and splashing the water at the Spaniards in token of defiance; but were soon pacified by gentle signs, and the intervention of the interpreters; and willingly bartered away their ornaments, giving seventeen plates of gold, worth one hundred and fifty ducats, for a few toys and trifles.

When the Spaniards returned the next day to renew their traffic, they found the Indians relapsed into hostility, sounding their drums and shells, and rushing forward to attack the boats. An arrow from a crossbow, which wounded one of them in the arm, checked their fury, and on the discharge of a cannon, they fled with terror. Four of the Spaniards sprang on shore, pursuing and calling after them. They threw down their weapons, and

[*] P. Martyr, decad. iii. lib. v.
[†] Columbus's Letter from Jamaica.

came, awe-struck, and gentle as lambs, bringing three plates of gold, and meekly and thankfully receiving whatever was given in exchange.

Continuing along the coast, the admiral anchored in the mouth of another river, called the Catiba. Here likewise the sound of drums and conchs from among the forests gave notice that the warriors were assembling. A canoe soon came off with two Indians, who, after exchanging a few words with the interpreters, entered the admiral's ship with fearless confidence; and being satisfied of the friendly intentions of the strangers, returned to their cacique with a favourable report. The boats landed, and the Spaniards were kindly received by the cacique. He was naked like his subjects, nor distinguished in any way from them, except by the great deference with which he was treated, and by a trifling attention paid to his personal comfort, being protected from a shower of rain by an immense leaf of a tree. He had a large plate of gold, which he readily gave in exchange, and permitted his people to do the same. Nineteen plates of pure gold were procured at this place. Here, for the first time in the New World, the Spaniards met with signs of solid architecture; finding a great mass of stucco, formed of stone and lime, a piece of which was retained by the admiral as a specimen,* considering it an indication of his approach to countries where the arts were in a higher state of cultivation.

He had intended to visit other rivers along this coast, but the wind coming on to blow freshly, he ran before it, passing in sight of five towns, where his interpreters assured him he might procure great quantities of gold. One they pointed out as Veragua, which has since given its name to the whole province. Here, they said, were the richest mines, and here most of the plates of gold were fabricated. On the following day, they arrived opposite a village called Cubiga, and here Columbus was informed that the country of gold terminated.† He resolved not to return to explore it, considering it as discovered, and its mines secured to the crown, and being anxious to arrive at the supposed strait, which he flattered himself could be at no great distance.

In fact, during his whole voyage along the coast, he had been under the influence of one of his frequent delusions. From the

* *Hist. del Almirante*, cap. 92.
† Idem.

Indians met with at the island of Guanaja, just arrived from Yuc-atan, he had received accounts of some great and, as far as he could understand, civilized nation in the interior. This intimation had been corroborated, as he imagined, by the various tribes with which he had since communicated. In a subsequent letter to the sover-eigns, he informs them that all the Indians of this coast concurred in extolling the magnificence of the country of Ciguare, situated at ten days' journey by land to the west. The people of that region wore crowns, and bracelets, and anklets of gold, and garments embroidered with it. They used it for all their domestic purposes, even to the ornamenting and embossing of their seats and tables. On being shown coral, the Indians declared that the women of Ciguare wore bands of it about their heads and necks. Pepper and other spices being shown them, were equally said to abound there. They described it as a country of commerce, with great fairs and sea-ports, in which ships arrived armed with cannon. The people were warlike also, armed like the Spaniards with swords, bucklers, cuir-asses, and crossbows, and they were mounted on horses. Above all, Columbus understood from them that the sea continued round to Ciguare, and that ten days beyond it was the Ganges.

These may have been vague and wandering rumours concerning the distant kingdoms of Mexico and Peru, and many of the details may have been filled up by the imagination of Columbus. They made, however, a strong impression on his mind. He supposed that Ciguare must be some province belonging to the Grand Khan, or some other Eastern potentate, and as the sea reached it, he concluded it was on the opposite side of a peninsula: bearing the same position with respect to Veragua that Fontarabia does with Tortosa in Spain, or Pisa with Venice in Italy. By proceeding farther eastward, therefore, he must soon arrive at a strait, like that of Gibraltar, through which he could pass into another sea, and visit this country of Ciguare, and, of course, arrive at the banks of the Ganges. He accounted for the circumstance of his having arrived so near to that river, by the idea which he had long entertained, that geographers were mistaken as to the circum-ference of the globe; that it was smaller than was generally imagined, and that a degree of the equinoctial line was but fifty-six miles and two-thirds.*

* Letter of Columbus from Jamaica; Navarrete, *Colec.*, tom. i. vol. ii.—12.

With these ideas Columbus determined to press forward, leaving the rich country of Veragua unexplored. Nothing could evince more clearly his generous ambition than hurrying in this brief manner along a coast where wealth was to be gathered at every step, for the purpose of seeking a strait which, however it might produce vast benefit to mankind, could yield little else to himself than the glory of the discovery.

On the 2nd of November, the squadron anchored in a spacious and commodious harbour, where the vessels could approach close to the shore without danger. It was surrounded by an elevated country; open and cultivated, with houses within bow-shot of each other, surrounded by fruit-trees, groves of palms, and fields producing maize, vegetables, and the delicious pineapple, so that the whole neighbourhood had the mingled appearance of orchard and garden. Columbus was so pleased with the excellence of the harbour, and the sweetness of the surrounding country, that he gave it the name of Puerto Bello.* It is one of the few places along this coast which retain the appellation given by the illustrious discoverer. It is to be regretted that they have so generally been discontinued, as they were so often records of his feelings, and of circumstances attending the discovery.

For seven days they were detained in this port by heavy rain and stormy weather. The natives repaired from all quarters in canoes, bringing fruits and vegetables and balls of cotton, but there was no longer gold offered in traffic. The cacique, and seven of his principal chieftains, had small plates of gold hanging in their noses, but the rest of the natives appear to have been destitute of all ornaments of the kind. They were generally naked and painted red; the cacique alone was painted black.†

Sailing hence on the 9th of November, they proceeded eight leagues to the eastward, to the point since known as Nombre de Dios; but being driven back for some distance, they anchored in a harbour in the vicinity of three small islands. These, with the adjacent country of the mainland, were cultivated with fields of Indian corn, and various fruits and vegetables, whence Columbus

* Las Casas, lib. ii. cap. 23; *Hist. del Almirante.*
† Peter Martyr, decad. iii. lib. iv.

called the harbour Puerto de Bastimentos, or Port of Provisions. Here they remained until the 23rd, endeavouring to repair their vessels, which leaked excessively. They were pierced in all parts by the teredo or worm which abounds in the tropical seas. It is of the size of a man's finger, and bores through the stoutest planks and timbers, so as soon to destroy any vessel that is not well coppered. After leaving this port, they touched at another called Guiga, where above three hundred of the natives appeared on the shore, some with provisions, and some with golden ornaments, which they offered in barter. Without making any stay, however, the admiral urged his way forward; but rough and adverse winds again obliged him to take shelter in a small port, with a narrow entrance, not above twenty paces wide, beset on each side with reefs of rocks, the sharp points of which rose above the surface. Within, there was not room for more than five or six ships; yet the port was so deep, that they had no good anchorage, unless they approached near enough to the land for a man to leap on shore.

From the smallness of the harbour, Columbus gave it the name of *El Retrete*, or The Cabinet. He had been betrayed into this inconvenient and dangerous port by the misrepresentations of the seamen sent to examine it, who were always eager to come to anchor, and have communication with the shore.*

The adjacent country was level and verdant, covered with herbage, but with few trees. The port was infested with alligators, which basked in the sunshine on the beach, filling the air with a powerful and musky odour. They were timorous, and fled on being attacked, but the Indians affirmed that if they found a man sleeping on shore they would seize and drag him into the water. These alligators Columbus pronounced to be the same as the crocodiles of the Nile. For nine days the squadron was detained in this port by tempestuous weather. The natives of this place were tall, well-proportioned, and graceful, of gentle and friendly manners, and brought whatever they possessed to exchange for European trinkets.

As long as the admiral had control over the actions of his people, the Indians were treated with justice and kindness, and everything went on amicably. The vicinity of the ships to land, however, enabled the seamen to get on shore in the night without license.

* Las Casas, lib. ii. cap. 23; *Hist. del Almirante*, cap. 92.

The natives received them in their dwellings with their accustomed hospitality; but the rough adventurers, instigated by avarice and lust, soon committed excesses that roused their generous hosts to revenge. Every night there were brawls and fights on shore, and blood was shed on both sides. The number of the Indians daily augmented by arrivals from the interior. They became more powerful and daring as they became more exasperated; and seeing that the vessels lay close to the shore, approached in a great multitude to attack them.

The admiral thought at first to disperse them by discharging cannon without ball, but they were not intimidated by the sound, regarding it as a kind of harmless thunder. They replied to it by yells and howlings, beating their lances and clubs against the trees and bushes in furious menace. The situation of the ships so close to the shore exposed them to assaults, and made the hostility of the natives unusually formidable. Columbus ordered a shot or two, therefore, to be discharged among them. When they saw the havoc made, they fled in terror, and offered no further hostility.[*]

The continuance of stormy winds from the east and the northeast, in addition to the constant opposition of the currents, disheartened the companions of Columbus, and they began to murmur against any further prosecution of the voyage. The seamen thought that some hostile spell was operating, and the commanders remonstrated against attempting to force their way in spite of the elements, with ships crazed and worm-eaten, and continually in need of repair. Few of his companions could sympathize with Columbus in his zeal for mere discovery. They were actuated by more gainful motives, and looked back with regret on the rich coast they had left behind, to go in search of an imaginary strait. It is probable that Columbus himself began to doubt the object of his enterprise. If he knew the details of the recent voyage of Bastides, he must have been aware that he had arrived from an opposite quarter to about the place where that navigator's exploring voyage from the east had terminated; consequently that there was but little probability of the existence of the strait he had imagined.[†]

[*] Las Casas. lib. ii. cap. 23; *Hist. del Almirante*, cap. 92.

[†] It appears doubtful whether Columbus was acquainted with the exact particulars of that voyage, as they could scarcely have reached Spain previously to his sailing.

At all events, he determined to relinquish the further prosecution of his voyage eastward for the present, and to return to the coast of Veragua, to search for those mines of which he had heard so much, and seen so many indications. Should they prove equal to his hopes, he would have wherewithal to return to Spain in triumph, and silence the reproaches of his enemies, even though he should fail in the leading object of his expedition.

Here, then, ended the lofty anticipations which had elevated Columbus above all mercenary interests; which had made him regardless of hardships and perils, and given an heroic character to the early part of this voyage. It is true, he had been in pursuit of a mere chimera, but it was the chimera of a splendid imagination, and a penetrating judgment. If he was disappointed in his expectation of finding a strait through the Isthmus of Darien, it was because nature herself had been disappointed, for she appears to have attempted to make one, but to have attempted it in vain.

Bastides had been seized in Hispaniola by Bobadilla, and was on board of that very fleet which was wrecked at the time that Columbus arrived off San Domingo. He escaped the fate that attended most of his companions, and returned to Spain, where he was rewarded by the sovereigns for his enterprise. Though some of his seamen had reached Spain previous to the sailing of Columbus, and had given a general idea of the voyage, it is doubtful whether he had transmitted his papers and charts. Porras, in his journal of the voyage of Columbus, states that they arrived at the place where the discoveries of Bastides terminated; but this information he may have obtained subsequently at San Domingo.

On the 5th of December, Columbus sailed from El Retrete, and relinquishing his course to the east, returned westward in search of the gold mines of Veragua. On the same evening he anchored in Puerto Bello, about ten leagues distant; whence departing on the succeeding day, the wind suddenly veered to the west, and began to blow directly adverse to the new course he had adopted. For three months he had been longing in vain for such a wind, and now it came merely to contradict him. Here was a temptation to resume his route to the east, but he did not dare trust to the continuance of the wind, which, in these parts, appeared but seldom to blow from that quarter. He resolved, therefore, to keep on in the present direction, trusting that the breeze would soon change again to the eastward.

In a little while the wind began to blow with dreadful violence, and to shift about in such manner as to baffle all seamanship. Unable to reach Veragua, the ships were obliged to put back to Puerto Bello, and when they would have entered that harbour, a sudden veering of the gale drove them from the land. For nine days they were blown and tossed about, at the mercy of a furious tempest, in an unknown sea, and often exposed to the awful perils of a lee shore. It is wonderful that such open vessels, so crazed and decayed, could outlive such a commotion of the elements. Nowhere is a storm so awful as between the tropics. The sea, according to the description of Columbus, boiled at times like a cauldron; at other times it ran in mountain waves, covered with foam. At night the raging billows resembled great surges of flame, owing to those luminous particles which cover the surface of the water in these seas, and throughout the whole course of the Gulf Stream. For a day and night the heavens glowed as a furnace with the incessant flashes of lightning; while the loud claps of thunder were often mistaken by the affrighted mariners for signal guns of distress from their foundering companions. During the whole time, says Columbus, it poured down from the skies, not rain, but as it were a second deluge. The seamen were almost drowned in their open vessels. Haggard with toil and affright, some gave themselves over for lost; they confessed their sins to each other according to the rites of the Catholic religion, and prepared themselves for death; many, in their desperation, called upon death as a welcome relief from such overwhelming horrors. In the midst of this wild tumult of the elements, they beheld a new object of alarm. The ocean in one place became strangely agitated. The water was whirled up into a kind of pyramid or cone, while a livid cloud, tapering to a point, bent down to meet it. Joining together, they formed a vast column, which rapidly approached the ships, spinning along the surface of the deep, and drawing up the waters with a rushing sound. The affrighted mariners, when they beheld this water-spout advancing towards them, despaired of all human means to avert it, and began to repeat passages from St John the Evangelist. The water-spout passed close by the ships without injuring them, and the trembling mariners attributed their escape to the miraculous efficacy of their quotations from the Scriptures.*

In this same night, they lost sight of one of the caravels, and for three dark and stormy days gave it up for lost. At length, to their great relief, it rejoined the squadron, having lost its boat, and been obliged to cut its cable, in an attempt to anchor on a boisterous coast, and having since been driven to and fro by the storm. For one or two days, there was an interval of calm, and the tempest-tossed mariners had time to breathe. They looked upon this tranquillity, however, as deceitful, and, in their gloomy mood, beheld everything with a doubtful and foreboding eye. Great numbers of sharks, so abundant and ravenous in these latitudes, were seen about the ships. This was construed into an evil omen; for among the superstitions of the seas, it is believed that these voracious fish can smell dead bodies at a distance; that they have a kind of presentiment of their prey; and keep about vessels which have sick persons on board, or which are in danger of being wrecked. Several of these fish they caught, using large hooks

* Las Casas, lib. ii. cap. 24; *Hist. del Almirante*, cap. 90.

fastened to chains, and sometimes baited merely with a piece of coloured cloth. From the maw of one they took out a living tortoise; from that of another the head of a shark, recently thrown from one of the ships; such is the indiscriminate voracity of these terrors of the ocean. Notwithstanding their superstitious fancies, the seamen were glad to use a part of these sharks for food, being very short of provisions. The length of the voyage had consumed the greater part of their sea-stores; the heat and humidity of the climate, and the leakage of the ships, had damaged the remainder, and their biscuit was so filled with worms, that, notwithstanding their hunger, they were obliged to eat it in the dark, lest their stomachs should revolt at its appearance.[*]

At length, on the 17th, they were enabled to enter a port resembling a great canal, where they enjoyed three days of repose. The natives of this vicinity built their cabins in trees, on stakes or poles laid from one branch to another. The Spaniards supposed this to be through the fear of wild beasts, or of surprisals from neighbouring tribes, the different nations of these coasts being extremely hostile to one another. It may have been a precaution against inundations caused by floods from the mountains. After leaving this port, they were driven backwards and forwards, by the changeable and tempestuous winds, until the day after Christmas; when they sheltered themselves in another port, where they remained until the 3rd of January 1503, repairing one of the caravels, and procuring wood, water, and a supply of maize or Indian corn. These measures being completed, they again put to sea, and on the day of Epiphany, to their great joy, anchored at the mouth of a river called by the natives Yebra, within a league or two of the river Veragua, and in the country said to be so rich in mines. To this river, from arriving at it on the day of Epiphany, Columbus gave the name of Belen or Bethlehem.

For nearly a month he had endeavoured to accomplish the voyage from Puerto Bello to Veragua, a distance of about thirty leagues; and had encountered so many troubles and adversities, from changeable winds and currents, and boisterous tempests, that he gave this intermediate line of sea-board the name of *La Costa de los Contrastes*, or the Coast of Contradictions.[†]

[*] *Hist. del Almirante*, cap. 94.
[†] *Hist. del Almirante*, cap. 94.

Columbus immediately ordered the mouths of the Belen, and of its neighbouring river of Veragua, to be sounded. The latter proved too shallow to admit his vessels, but the Belen was somewhat deeper, and it was thought they might enter it with safety. Seeing a village on the banks of the Belen, the admiral sent the boats on shore to procure information. On their approach, the inhabitants issued forth with weapons in hand to oppose their landing, but were readily pacified. They seemed unwilling to give any intelligence about the gold mines; but on being importuned, declared that they lay in the vicinity of the river of Veragua. To that river the boats were despatched on the following day. They met with the reception so frequent along this coast, where many of the tribes were fierce and warlike, and are supposed to have been of Carib origin. As the boats entered the river, the natives sallied forth in their canoes, and others assembled in menacing style on the shores. The Spaniards, however, had brought with them an Indian of that coast, who put an end to this show of hostility by assuring his countrymen that the strangers came only to traffic with them.

The various accounts of the riches of these parts appeared to be confirmed by what the Spaniards saw and heard among these people. They procured in exchange for the veriest trifles twenty plates of gold, with several pipes of the same metal, and crude masses of ore. The Indians informed them that the mines lay among distant mountains; and that when they went in quest of it they were obliged to practice rigorous fasting and continence.[*]

The favourable report brought by the boats determined the admiral to remain in the neighbourhood. The river Belen having the greatest depth, two of the caravels entered it on the 9th of January, and the two others on the following day at high tide, which on that coast does not rise above half a fathom.[†] The natives came to them in the most friendly manner, bringing great quantities of fish, with which that river abounded. They brought also

---

[*] A superstitious notion with respect to gold appears to have been very prevalent among the natives. The Indians of Hispaniola observed the same privations when they sought for it, abstaining from food and from sexual intercourse. Columbus, who seemed to look upon gold as one of the sacred and mystic treasures of the earth, wished to encourage similar observances among the Spaniards; exhorting them to purify themselves for the research of the mines by fasting, prayer, and chastity. It is scarcely necessary to add, that his advice was but little attended to by his rapacious and sensual followers.

[†] *Hist. del Almirante*, cap. 95.

golden ornaments to traffic; but continued to affirm that Veragua was the place whence the ore was procured.

The Adelantado, with his usual activity and enterprise, set off on the third day, with the boats well armed, to ascend the Veragua about a league and a half, to the residence of Quibian, the principal cacique. The chieftain, hearing of his intention, met him near the entrance of the river, attended by his subjects, in several canoes. He was tall, of powerful frame, and warlike demeanour: the interview was extremely amicable. The cacique presented the Adelantado with the golden ornaments which he wore, and received as magnificent presents a few European trinkets. They parted mutually well pleased. On the following day Quibian visited the ships, where he was hospitably entertained by the admiral. They could only communicate by signs, and as the chieftain was of a taciturn and cautious character, the interview was not of long duration. Columbus made him several presents; the followers of the cacique exchanged many jewels of gold for the usual trifles, and Quibian returned, without much ceremony, to his home.

On the 24th of January, there was a sudden swelling of the river. The waters came rushing from the interior like a vast torrent; the ships were forced from their anchors, tossed from side to side, and driven against each other; the foremast of the admiral's vessel was carried away, and the whole squadron was in imminent danger of shipwreck. While exposed to this peril in the river, they were prevented from running out to sea by a violent storm, and by the breakers which beat upon the bar. This sudden rising of the river Columbus attributed to some heavy fall of rain among a range of distant mountains, to which he had given the name of the mountains of San Christoval. The highest of these rose to a peak far above the clouds.*

The weather continued extremely boisterous for several days. At length, on the 6th of February, the sea being tolerably calm, the Adelantado, attended by sixty-eight men well armed, proceeded in the boats to explore the Veragua, and seek its reputed mines. When he ascended the river and drew near to the village of Quibian, situated on the side of a hill, the cacique came down to the bank to meet him, with a great train of his subjects, unarmed, and making signs of peace. Quibian was naked, and painted after

* Las Casas, lib. ii. cap. 25; *Hist. del Almirante*, cap. 95.

the fashion of the country. One of his attendants drew a great stone out of the river, and washed and rubbed it carefully, upon which the chieftain seated himself as upon a throne.* He received the Adelantado with great courtesy; for the lofty, vigorous, and iron form of the latter, and his look of resolution and command, were calculated to inspire awe and respect in an Indian warrior. The cacique, however, was wary and politic. His jealousy was awakened by the intrusion of these strangers into his territories; but he saw the futility of any open attempt to resist them. He acceded to the wishes of the Adelantado, therefore, to visit the interior of his dominions, and furnished him with three guides to conduct him to the mines.

Leaving a number of his men to guard the boats, the Adelantado departed on foot with the remainder. After penetrating into the interior about four leagues and a half, they slept for the first night on the banks of a river, which seemed to water the whole country with its windings, as they had crossed it upwards of forty times. On the second day, they proceeded a league and a half farther, and arrived among thick forests, where their guides informed them the mines were situated. In fact, the whole soil appeared to be impregnated with gold. They gathered it from among the roots of the trees, which were of an immense height, and magnificent foliage. In the space of two hours each man had collected a little quantity of gold, gathered from the surface of the earth. Hence the guides took the Adelantado to the summit of a high hill, and showing him an extent of country as far as the eye could reach, assured him that the whole of it, to the distance of twenty days' journey westward, abounded in gold, naming to him several of the principal places.† The Adelantado gazed with enraptured eye over a vast wilderness of continued forest, where only here and there a bright column of smoke from amidst the trees gave sign of some savage hamlet, or solitary wigwam, and the wild unappropriated aspect of this golden country delighted him more than if he had beheld it covered with towns and cities, and adorned with all the graces of cultivation. He returned with his party, in high spirits, to the ships, and rejoiced the admiral with the favourable report of his expedition. It was soon discovered, however, that the politic

* Peter Martyr, decad. iii. lib. iv.
† Letter of the Admiral from Jamaica.

Quibian had deceived them. His guides, by his instructions, had taken the Spaniards to the mines of a neighbouring cacique with whom he was at war, hoping to divert them into the territories of his enemy. The real mines of Veragua, it was said, were nearer and much more wealthy.

The indefatigable Adelantado set forth again on the 16th of February, with an armed band of fifty-nine men, marching along the coast westward, a boat with fourteen men keeping pace with him. In this excursion he explored an extensive tract of country, and visited the dominions of various caciques, by whom he was hospitably entertained. He met continually with proofs of abundance of gold, the natives generally wearing great plates of it suspended round their necks by cotton cords. There were tracts of land, also, cultivated with Indian corn, one of which continued for the extent of six leagues; and the country abounded with excellent fruits. He again heard of a nation in the interior, advanced in arts and arms, wearing clothing, and being armed like the Spaniards. Either these were vague and exaggerated rumours concerning the great empire of Peru, or the Adelantado had misunderstood the signs of his informants. He returned, after an absence of several days, with a great quantity of gold, and with animating accounts of the country. He had found no port, however, equal to the river of Belen, and was convinced that gold was nowhere to be met with in such abundance as in the district of Veragua.[*]

* Las Casas, lib. ii. cap. 25; *Hist. del Almirante*, cap. 95.

The reports brought to Columbus from every side of the wealth of the neighbourhood; the golden tract of twenty days' journey in extent shown to his brother from the mountain; the rumours of a rich and civilized country at no great distance, all convinced him that he had reached one of the most favoured parts of the Asiatic continent. Again his ardent mind kindled up with glowing anticipations. He fancied himself arrived at a fountain-head of riches, at one of the sources of the unbounded wealth of King Solomon. Josephus, in his work on the antiquities of the Jews, had expressed an opinion that the gold for the building of the temple of Jerusalem had been procured from the mines of the Aurea Chersonesus. Columbus supposed the mines of Veragua to be the same. They lay, as he observed, 'within the same distance from the pole and from the line'; and if the information which he fancied he had received from the Indians was to be depended on, they were situated about the same distance from the Ganges.

Here, then, it appeared to him, was a place at which to found a colony, and establish a mart that should become the emporium of a vast tract of mines. Within the two first days after his arrival in the country, as he wrote to the sovereigns, he had seen more signs of gold than in Hispaniola during four years. That island, so long the object of his pride and hopes, had been taken from him, and was a scene of confusion; the pearl coast of Paria was ravaged by mere adventurers; all his plans concerning both had been defeated; but here was a far more wealthy region than either, and one calculated to console him for all his wrongs and deprivations.

On consulting with his brother, therefore, he resolved immediately to commence an establishment here, for the purpose of securing the possession of the country, and exploring and working

* Letter of Columbus from Jamaica.

the mines. The Adelantado agreed to remain with the greater part of the people, while the admiral should return to Spain for reinforcements and supplies. The greatest dispatch was employed in carrying this plan into immediate operation. Eighty men were selected to remain. They were separated into parties of about ten each, and commenced building houses on a small eminence, situated on the bank of a creek, about a bow-shot within the mouth of the river Belen. The houses were of wood, thatched with the leaves of palm-trees. One larger than the rest was to serve as a magazine, to receive their ammunition, artillery, and a part of their provisions. The principal part was stored, for greater security, on board of one of the caravels, which was to be left for the use of the colony. It was true they had but a scanty supply of European stores remaining, consisting chiefly of biscuit, cheese, pulse, wine, oil, and vinegar; but the country produced bananas, plantains, pineapples, coconuts, and other fruit. There was also maize in abundance, together with various roots, such as were found in Hispaniola. The rivers and sea-coast abounded with fish. The natives, too, made beverages of various kinds. One from the juice of the pineapple, having a vinous flavor; another from maize, resembling beer; and another from the fruit of a species of palm-tree.[*] There appeared to be no danger, therefore, of suffering from famine. Columbus took pains to conciliate the good-will of the Indians, that they might supply the wants of the colony during his absence, and he made many presents to Quibian, by way of reconciling him to this intrusion into his territories.[†]

The necessary arrangements being made for the colony, and a number of the houses being roofed and sufficiently finished for occupation, the admiral prepared for his departure, when an unlooked-for obstacle presented itself. The heavy rains which had so long distressed him during this expedition had recently ceased. The torrents from the mountains were over, and the river which had once put him to such peril by its sudden swelling had now become so shallow that there was not above half a fathom water on the bar. Though his vessels were small, it was impossible to draw them over the sands, which choked the mouth of the river, for there was a swell rolling and tumbling upon them, enough to

[*] *Hist. del Almirante*, cap. 96.
[†] Letter from Jamaica.

dash his worm-eaten barks to pieces. He was obliged, therefore, to wait with patience, and pray for the return of those rains which he had lately deplored.

In the meantime, Quibian beheld, with secret jealousy and indignation, these strangers erecting habitations, and manifesting an intention of establishing themselves in his territories. He was of a bold and warlike spirit, and had a great force of warriors at his command; and being ignorant of the vast superiority of the Europeans in the art of war, thought it easy, by a well-concerted artifice, to overwhelm and destroy them. He sent messengers round, and ordered all his fighting-men to assemble at his residence on the river Veragua, under pretext of making war upon a neighbouring province. Numbers of the warriors, in repairing to his headquarters, passed by the harbour. No suspicions of their real design were entertained by Columbus or his officers; but their movements attracted the attention of the chief notary, Diego Mendez, a man of a shrewd and prying character, and zealously devoted to the admiral. Doubting some treachery, he communicated his surmises to Columbus, and offered to coast along in an armed boat to the river Veragua, and reconnoitre the Indian camp. His offer was accepted, and he sallied from the river accordingly, but had scarcely advanced a league when he descried a large force of Indians on the shore. Landing alone, and ordering that the boat should be kept afloat, he entered among them. There were about a thousand armed and supplied with provisions, as if for an expedition. He offered to accompany them with his armed boat; his offer was declined with evident signs of impatience. Returning to his boat, he kept watch upon them all night, until, seeing they were vigilantly observed, they returned to Veragua.

Mendez hastened back to the admiral, and gave it as his opinion that the Indians had been on their way to surprise the Spaniards. The admiral was loth to believe in such treachery, and was desirous of obtaining clearer information before he took any step that might interrupt the apparently good understanding that existed with the natives. Mendez now undertook, with a single companion, to penetrate by land to the headquarters of Quibian, and endeavour to ascertain his intentions. Accompanied by one Rodrigo de Escobar, he proceeded on foot along the seaboard, to avoid the tangled forests, and arriving at the mouth of the Veragua, found two canoes with Indians, whom he prevailed on, by presents, to convey him and his companion to the village of the cacique. It was on the bank of the river; the houses were detached and interspersed among trees. There was a bustle of warlike preparation in the place, and the arrival of the two Spaniards evidently excited surprise and uneasiness. The residence of the cacique was larger than the others, and situated on a hill which rose from the water's edge. Quibian was confined to the house by indisposition, having been wounded in the leg by an arrow. Mendez gave himself out as a surgeon come to cure the wound: with great difficulty and by force of presents he obtained permission to proceed. On the crest of the hill and in front of the cacique's dwelling was a broad, level, open place, round which, on posts, were the heads of three hundred enemies slain in battle. Undismayed by this dismal array, Mendez and his companion crossed the place towards the den of this grim warrior. A number of women and children about the door fled into the house with piercing cries. A young and powerful Indian, son of the cacique, sallied forth in a violent rage, and struck Mendez a blow which made him recoil several paces. The latter pacified him by presents and assurances that he came to cure his father's wound, in proof of which he produced a box of ointment. It was impossible, however, to gain access to the cacique, and Mendez returned with all haste to the harbour to report to the admiral what he had seen and learnt. It was evident there was a dangerous plot impending over the Spaniards, and as far as Mendez could learn from the Indians who had taken him up the river in their canoe, the body of a thousand warriors which he had seen on his previous reconnoitring expedition had actually been on a hostile enterprise against the harbour, but had given it up on finding themselves observed.

This information was confirmed by an Indian of the neighbour-hood, who had become attached to the Spaniards and acted as interpreter. He revealed to the admiral the designs of his country-men, which he had overheard. Quibian intended to surprise the harbour at night with a great force, burn the ships and houses, and make a general massacre. Thus forewarned, Columbus immed-iately set a double watch upon the harbour. The military spirit of the Adelantado suggested a bolder expedient. The hostile plan of Quibian was doubtless delayed by his wound, and in the meantime he would maintain the semblance of friendship. The Adelantado determined to march at once to his residence, capture him, his family, and principal warriors, send them prisoners to Spain, and take possession of his village.

With the Adelantado, to conceive a plan was to carry it into immediate execution, and, in fact, the impending danger admitted of no delay. Taking with him seventy-four men, well armed, among whom was Diego Mendez, and being accompanied by the Indian interpreter who had revealed the plot, he set off on the 30th of March, in boats, to the mouth of the Veragua, ascended it rapidly, and before the Indians could have notice of his movements, landed at the foot of the hill on which the house of Quibian was situated.

Lest the cacique should take alarm and fly at the sight of a large force, he ascended the hill accompanied by only five men, among whom was Diego Mendez; ordering the rest to come on, with great caution and secrecy, two at a time, and at a distance from each other. On the discharge of an arquebuse, they were to surround the dwelling and suffer no one to escape.

As the Adelantado drew near to the house, Quibian came forth, and seating himself in the portal, desired the Adelantado to approach singly. Don Bartholomew now ordered Diego Mendez and his four companions to remain at a little distance, and when they should see him take the cacique by the arm, to rush immediately to his assistance. He then advanced with his Indian interpreter, through whom a short conversation took place, relative to the surrounding country. The Adelantado then adverted to the wound of the cacique, and pretending to examine it, took him by the arm. At the concerted signal four of the Spaniards rushed forward, the fifth discharged the arquebuse. The cacique attempted to get loose, but was firmly held in the iron grasp of the Adelantado. Being both men of great muscular power, a violent struggle ensued. Don Bartholomew, however, maintained the mastery, and Diego Mendez and his companions coming to his assistance, Quibian was bound hand and foot. At the report of the arquebuse, the main body of the Spaniards surrounded the house, and seized most of those who were within, consisting of fifty persons, old and young. Among these were the wives and children of Quibian, and several of his principal subjects. No one was wounded, for there was no resistance, and the Adelantado never permitted wanton blood-shed. When the poor savages saw their prince a captive, they filled the air with lamentations; imploring his release, and offering for his ransom a great treasure, which they said lay concealed in a neighbouring forest.

The Adelantado was deaf to their supplications and their offers. Quibian was too dangerous a foe to be set at liberty; as a prisoner, he would be a hostage for the security of the settlement. Anxious to secure his prize, he determined to send the cacique and the other prisoners on board of the boats, while he remained on shore with a part of his men to pursue the Indians who had escaped. Juan Sanchez, the principal pilot of the squadron, a powerful and spirited man, volunteered to take charge of the captives. On committing the chieftain to his care, the Adelantado warned him to be on his guard against any attempt at rescue or escape. The sturdy pilot replied that if the cacique got out of his hands, he would give them leave to pluck out his beard, hair by hair; with this vaunt he departed, bearing off Quibian bound hand and foot. On arriving at the boat, he secured him by a strong cord to one of the benches. It was a dark night. As the boat proceeded down the river, the cacique complained piteously of the painfulness of his bonds. The rough heart of the pilot was touched with compassion, and he loosened the cord by which Quibian was tied to the bench, keeping the end of it in his hand. The wily Indian watched his opportunity, and when Sanchez was looking another way, plunged into the water and disappeared. So sudden and violent was his plunge, that the pilot had to let go the cord, lest he should be drawn in after him. The darkness of the night, and the bustle which took place, in preventing the escape of the other prisoners, rendered it impossible to pursue the cacique, or even to ascertain his fate. Juan Sanchez hastened to the ships with the residue of the captives, deeply mortified at being thus outwitted by a savage.

The Adelantado remained all night on shore. The following morning, when he beheld the wild, broken, and mountainous nature of the country, and the scattered situation of the habit-ations, perched on different heights, he gave up the search after the Indians, and returned to the ships with the spoils of the cacique's mansion. These consisted of bracelets, anklets, and massive plates of gold, such as were worn round the neck, together with two golden coronets. The whole amounted to the value of three hundred ducats.[*] One fifth of the booty was set apart for the crown. The residue was shared among those concerned in the enterprise. To the Adelantado one of the coronets was assigned, as a trophy of his exploit.[†]

[*] Equivalent to one thousand two hundred and eighty-one dollars at the present day.

[†] *Hist. del Almirante*, cap. 98; Las Casas, lib. ii. cap. 27. Many of the particulars of this chapter are from a short narrative given by Diego Mendez, and inserted in his last will and testament. It is written in a strain of simple egotism, as he represents himself as the principal and almost the sole actor in every affair. The facts, however, have all the air of veracity, and being given on such a solemn occasion, the document is entitled to high credit. He will be found to distinguish himself on another hazardous and important occasion in the course of this history. – Vide Navarrete, *Colec.*, tom. i.

It was hoped by Columbus that the vigorous measure of the Adelantado would strike terror into the Indians of the neighbourhood, and prevent any further designs upon the settlement. Quibian had probably perished. If he survived, he must be disheartened by the captivity of his family, and several of his principal subjects, and fearful of their being made responsible for any act of violence on his part. The heavy rains, therefore, which fall so frequently among the mountains of this isthmus, having again swelled the river, Columbus made his final arrangements for the management of the colony, and having given much wholesome counsel to the Spaniards who were to remain, and taken an affectionate leave of his brother, got under weigh with three of the caravels, leaving the fourth for the use of the settlement. As the water was still shallow at the bar, the ships were lightened of a great part of their cargoes, and towed out by the boats in calm weather, grounding repeatedly. When fairly released from the river, and their cargoes re-shipped, they anchored within a league of the shore, to await a favourable wind. It was the intention of the admiral to touch at Hispaniola, on his way to Spain, and send thence supplies and reinforcements. The wind continuing adverse, he sent a boat on shore on the 6th of April, under the command of Diego Tristan, captain of one of the caravels, to procure wood and water, and make some communications to the Adelantado. The expedition of this boat proved fatal to its crew, but was providential to the settlement.

The cacique Quibian had not perished as some had supposed. Though both hands and feet were bound, yet in the water he was as in his natural element. Plunging to the bottom, he swam below the surface until sufficiently distant to be out of view in the darkness of the night, and then emerging made his way to shore.

The desolation of his home, and the capture of his wives and children, filled him with anguish; but when he saw the vessels in which they were confined leaving the river, and bearing them off, he was transported with fury and despair. Determined on a signal vengeance, he assembled a great number of his warriors, and came secretly upon the settlement. The thick woods by which it was surrounded enabled the Indians to approach unseen within ten paces. The Spaniards, thinking the enemy completely discomfited and dispersed, were perfectly off their guard. Some had strayed to the sea-shore, to take a farewell look at the ships; some were on board of the caravel in the river; others were scattered about the houses. On a sudden, the Indians rushed from their concealment with yells and howlings, launched their javelins through the roofs of palm-leaves, hurled them in at the windows, or thrust them through the crevices of the logs which composed the walls. As the houses were small, several of the inhabitants were wounded. On the first alarm, the Adelantado seized a lance, and sallied forth with seven or eight of his men. He was joined by Diego Mendez and several of his companions, and they drove the enemy into the forest, killing and wounding several of them. The Indians kept up a brisk fire of darts and arrows from among the trees, and made furious sallies with their war-clubs; but there was no withstanding the keen edge of the Spanish weapons, and a fierce blood-hound being let loose upon them, completed their terror. They fled howling through the forest, leaving a number dead on the field, having killed one Spaniard, and wounded eight. Among the latter was the Adelantado, who received a slight thrust of a javelin in the breast.

Diego Tristan arrived in his boat during the contest, but feared to approach the land, lest the Spaniards should rush on board in such numbers as to sink him. When the Indians had been put to flight, he proceeded up the river in quest of fresh water, disregarding the warnings of those on shore that he might be cut off by the enemy in their canoes.

The river was deep and narrow, shut in by high banks and overhanging trees. The forests on each side were thick and impenetrable, so that there was no landing-place, excepting here and there where a footpath wound down to some fishing-ground, or some place where the natives kept their canoes.

The boat had ascended about a league above the village, to a part of the river where it was completely overshadowed by lofty banks and spreading trees. Suddenly, yells and war-whoops and blasts of conch shells rose on every side. Light canoes darted forth in every direction from dark hollows and overhanging thickets, each dextrously managed by a single savage, while others stood up brandishing and hurling their lances. Missiles were launched also from the banks of the river and the branches of the trees. There were eight sailors in the boat and three soldiers. Galled and wounded by darts and arrows, confounded by the yells and blasts of conchs, and the assaults which thickened from every side, they lost all presence of mind, neglected to use either oars or firearms, and only sought to shelter themselves with their bucklers. Diego Tristan had received several wounds, but still displayed great intrepidity, and was endeavouring to animate his men, when a javelin pierced his right eye and struck him dead. The canoes now closed upon the boat, and a general massacre ensued. But one Spaniard escaped, Juan de Noya, a cooper of Seville. Having fallen overboard in the midst of the action, he dived to the bottom, swam under water, gained the bank of the river unperceived, and made his way down to the settlement, bringing tidings of the massacre of his captain and comrades.

The Spaniards were completely dismayed, were few in number, several of them were wounded, and they were in the midst of tribes of exasperated savages, far more fierce and warlike than those to whom they had been accustomed. The admiral, being ignorant of their misfortunes, would sail away without yielding them assistance, and they would be left to sink beneath the overwhelming force of barbarous foes, or to perish with hunger on this inhospitable coast. In their despair they determined to take the caravel which had been left with them, and abandon the place altogether. The Adelantado remonstrated with them in vain; nothing would content them but to put to sea immediately. Here a new alarm awaited them. The torrents having subsided, the river was again shallow, and it was impossible for the caravel to pass over the bar. They now took the boat of the caravel, to bear tidings of their danger to the admiral, and implore him not to abandon them; but the wind was boisterous, a high sea was rolling, and a heavy surf, tumbling and breaking at the mouth of the river, prevented the boat from getting out. Horrors increased upon them. The mangled bodies of Diego Tristan and his men came floating down the stream, and drifted about the harbour, with flights of crows, and other carrion birds, feeding on them, and hovering, and screaming, and fighting about their prey. The forlorn Spaniards contemplated this scene with shuddering; it appeared ominous of their own fate.

In the meantime the Indians, elated by their triumph over the crew of the boat, renewed their hostilities. Whoops and yells answered each other from various parts of the neighbourhood. The dismal sound of conchs and war-drums in the deep bosom of the woods showed that the number of the enemy was continually augmenting. They would rush forth occasionally upon straggling parties of Spaniards, and make partial attacks upon the houses. It was considered no longer safe to remain in the settlement, the close forest which surrounded it being a covert for the approaches of the enemy. The Adelantado chose, therefore, an open place on the shore at some distance from the wood. Here he caused a kind of bulwark to be made of the boat of the caravel, and of chests, casks, and similar articles. Two places were left open as embrasures, in which were placed a couple of falconets, or small pieces of artillery, in such a manner as to command the neighbourhood. In this little fortress the Spaniards shut themselves up; its walls were sufficient to screen them from the darts and arrows of the Indians, but mostly they depended upon their firearms, the sound of which struck dismay into the savages, especially when they saw the effect of the balls, splintering and rending the trees around them, and carrying havoc to such a distance. The Indians were thus kept in check for the present, and deterred from venturing from the forest; but the Spaniards, exhausted by constant watching and incessant alarms, anticipated all kinds of evil when their ammunition should be exhausted, or they should be driven forth by hunger to seek for food.[*]

---

[*] *Hist. del Almirante*, cap. 98; Las Casas, lib. ii; Letter of Columbus from Jamaica; Relation of Diego Mendez and Journal of Porras, Navarrete, tom. i.

CHAPTER 9

1503

While the Adelantado and his men were exposed to such imminent peril on shore, great anxiety prevailed on board of the ships.
Day after day elapsed without the return of Diego Tristan and his
party, and it was feared some disaster had befallen them. Columbus
would have sent on shore to make inquiries; but there was only
one boat remaining for the service of the squadron, and he dared
not risk it in the rough sea and heavy surf. A dismal circumstance
occurred to increase the gloom and uneasiness of the crews. On
board of one of the caravels were confined the family and household of the cacique Quibian. It was the intention of Columbus to
carry them to Spain, trusting that as long as they remained in the
power of the Spaniards their tribe would be deterred from further
hostilities. They were shut up at night in the forecastle of the
caravel, the hatchway of which was secured by a strong chain and
padlock. As several of the crew slept upon the hatch, and it was so
high as to be considered out of reach of the prisoners, they
neglected to fasten the chain. The Indians discovered their negligence. Collecting a quantity of stones from the ballast of the vessel,
they made a great heap directly under the hatchway. Several of
the most powerful warriors mounted upon the top, and, bending
their backs, by a sudden and simultaneous effort forced up the
hatch, flinging the seamen who slept upon it to the opposite side
of the ship. In an instant the greater part of the Indians sprang
forth, plunged into the sea, and swam for shore. Several, however,
were prevented from sallying forth; others were seized on the
deck, and forced back into the forecastle; the hatchway was
carefully chained down, and a guard was set for the rest of the
night. In the morning, when the Spaniards went to examine the
captives, they were all found dead. Some had hanged themselves
with the ends of ropes, their knees touching the floor; others had

strangled themselves by straining the cords tight with their feet. Such was the fierce, unconquerable spirit of these people, and their horror of the white men.*

The escape of the prisoners occasioned great anxiety to the admiral, fearing they would stimulate their countrymen to some violent act of vengeance; and he trembled for the safety of his brother. Still this painful mystery reigned over the land. The boat of Diego Tristan did not return, and the raging surf prevented all communication. At length, one Pedro Ledesma, a pilot of Seville, a man of about forty-five years of age, and of great strength of body and mind, offered, if the boat would take him to the edge of the surf, to swim to shore and bring off news. He had been piqued by the achievement of the Indian captives in swimming to land at a league's distance, in defiance of sea and surf. 'Surely,' he said, 'if they dare venture so much to procure their individual liberties, I ought to brave at least a part of the danger, to save the lives of so many companions.' His offer was gladly accepted by the admiral, and was boldly accomplished. The boat approached with him as near to the surf as safety would permit, where it was to await his return. Here, stripping himself, he plunged into the sea, and after buffeting for some time with the breakers, sometimes rising upon their surges, sometimes buried beneath them and dashed upon the sand, he succeeded in reaching the shore.

He found his countrymen shut up in their forlorn fortress, beleaguered by savage foes, and learnt the tragical fate of Diego Tristan and his companions. Many of the Spaniards, in their horror and despair, had thrown off all subordination, refused to assist in any measure that had in view a continuance in this place, and thought of nothing but escape. When they beheld Ledesma, a messenger from the ships, they surrounded him with frantic eagerness, urging him to implore the admiral to take them on board, and not abandon them on a coast where their destruction was inevitable. They were preparing canoes to take them to the ships when the weather should moderate, the boat of the caravel being too small; and swore that, if the admiral refused to take them on board, they would embark in the caravel, as soon as it could be extricated from the river, and abandon themselves to the mercy of the seas, rather than remain upon that fatal coast.

* *Hist. del Almirante*, cap. 99.

Having heard all that his forlorn countrymen had to say, and communicated with the Adelantado and his officers, Ledesma set out on his perilous return. He again braved the surf and the breakers, reached the boat which was waiting for him, and was conveyed back to the ships. The disastrous tidings from the land filled the heart of the admiral with grief and alarm. To leave his brother on shore would be to expose him to the mutiny of his own men and the ferocity of the savages. He could spare no reinforcement from his ships, the crews being so much weakened by the loss of Tristan and his companions. Rather than the settlement should be broken up, he would gladly have joined the Adelantado with all his people; but in such case how could intelligence be conveyed to the sovereigns of this important discovery, and how could supplies be obtained from Spain? There appeared no alternative, therefore, but to embark all the people, abandon the settlement for the present, and return at some future day, with a force competent to take secure possession of the country.* The state of the weather rendered the practicability even of this plan doubtful. The wind continued high, the sea rough, and no boat could pass between the squadron and the land. The situation of the ships was itself a matter of extreme solicitude. Feebly manned, crazed by storms, and ready to fall to pieces from the ravages of the teredo, they were anchored on a lee shore, with a boisterous wind and sea, in a climate subject to tempests, and where the least augmentation of the weather might drive them among the breakers. Every hour increased the anxiety of Columbus for his brother, his people, and his ships, and each hour appeared to render the impending dangers more imminent. Days of constant perturbation and nights of sleepless anxiety preyed upon a constitution broken by age, by maladies, and hardships, and produced a fever of the mind, in which he was visited by one of those mental hallucinations deemed by him mysterious and supernatural. In a letter to the sovereigns he gives a solemn account of a kind of vision by which he was comforted in a dismal night, when full of despondency and tossing on a couch of pain –

'Wearied and sighing,' says he, 'I fell into a slumber, when I heard a piteous voice saying to me, "O fool, and slow to believe and serve thy God, who is the God of all! What did he more for Moses, or

---

* Letter of Columbus from Jamaica.

for his servant David, than he has done for thee? From the time of thy birth he has ever had thee under his peculiar care. When he saw thee of a fitting age, he made thy name to resound marvellously throughout the earth, and thou wert obeyed in many lands, and didst acquire honourable fame among Christians. Of the gates of the Ocean Sea, shut up with such mighty chains, he delivered thee the keys; the Indies, those wealthy regions of the world, he gave thee for thine own, and empowered thee to dispose of them to others, according to thy pleasure. What did he more for the great people of Israel when he led them forth from Egypt? Or for David, whom, from being a shepherd, he made a king in Judea? Turn to him, then, and acknowledge thine error; his mercy is infinite. He has many and vast inheritances yet in reserve. Fear not to seek them. Thine age shall be no impediment to any great undertaking. Abraham was above an hundred years when he begat Isaac; and was Sarah youthful? Thou urgest despondingly for succour. Answer! Who hath afflicted thee so much, and so many times? – God, or the world? The privileges and promises which God hath made thee he hath never broken; neither hath he said, after having received thy services, that his meaning was different, and to be understood in a different sense. He performs to the very letter. He fulfils all that he promises, and with increase. Such is his custom. I have shown thee what thy creator hath done for thee, and what he doeth for all. The present is the reward of the toils and perils thou hast endured in serving others." I heard all this,' adds Columbus, 'as one almost dead, and had no power to reply to words so true, excepting to weep for my errors. Whoever it was that spake to me, finished by saying, "Fear not! Confide! All these tribulations are written in marble, and not without cause." '

Such is the singular statement which Columbus gave to the sovereigns of his supposed vision. It has been suggested that this was a mere ingenious fiction, adroitly devised by him to convey a lesson to his prince; but such an idea is inconsistent with his character. He was too deeply imbued with awe of the Deity, and with reverence for his sovereign, to make use of such an artifice. The words here spoken to him by the supposed voice are truths which dwelt upon his mind and grieved his spirit during his waking hours. It is natural that they should recur vividly and coherently in his feverish dreams; and in recalling and relating a dream one is unconsciously apt to give it a little coherency. Besides, Columbus had a solemn belief that he was a peculiar instrument in the hands of Providence, which, together with a deep tinge of superstition, common to the age, made him prone to mistake every striking dream for a revelation. He is not to be measured by the same standard with ordinary men in ordinary circumstances. It is difficult for the mind to realize his situation, and to conceive the exaltations of spirit to which he must have been subjected. The artless manner in which, in his letter to the sovereigns, he mingles up the rhapsodies and dreams of his imagination with simple facts and sound practical observations, pouring them forth with a kind of scriptural solemnity and poetry of language, is one of the most striking illustrations of a character richly compounded of extraordinary and apparently contradictory elements.

Immediately after this supposed vision, and after a duration of nine days, the boisterous weather subsided, the sea became calm, and the communication with the land was restored. It was found impossible to extricate the remaining caravel from the river, but every exertion was made to bring off the people and the property before there should be a return of bad weather. In this, the exertions of the zealous Diego Mendez were eminently efficient. He had been for some days preparing for such an emergency. Cutting up the sails of the caravel, he made great sacks to receive the biscuit. He lashed two Indian canoes together with spars, so that they could not be overturned by the waves, and made a platform on them capable of sustaining a great burden. This kind of raft was laden repeatedly with the stores, arms, and ammunition which had been left on shore, and with the furniture of the caravel, which was entirely dismantled. When well freighted, it was towed by the boat to the ships. In this way, by constant and sleepless exertions, in the space of two days, almost everything of value was transported on board the squadron, and little else left than the hull of the caravel, stranded, decayed, and rotting in the river. Diego Mendez superintended the whole embarkation with unwearied watchfulness and activity. He and five companions were the last to leave the shore, remaining all night at their perilous post, and embarking in the morning with the last cargo of effects.

Nothing could equal the transports of the Spaniards when they found themselves once more on board of the ships, and saw a space of ocean between them and those forests which had lately seemed destined to be their graves. The joy of their comrades seemed little inferior to their own, and the perils and hardships which yet surrounded them were forgotten for a time in mutual congratulations. The admiral was so much impressed with a sense of the high services rendered by Diego Mendez throughout the late time of danger and disaster that he gave him the command of the caravel, vacant by the death of the unfortunate Diego Tristan.*

* *Hist. del Almirante*, cap. 99, 100; Las Casas, lib. ii. cap. 29; Relacion por Diego Mendez; Letter of Columbus from Jamaica; Journal of Porras, Navarrete, *Colec.*, tom. i.

CHAPTER 10

1503

The wind at length becoming favourable, Columbus set sail, towards the end of April, from the disastrous coast of Veragua. The wretched condition of the ships, the enfeebled state of the crews, and the scarcity of provisions, determined him to make the best of his way to Hispaniola, where he might refit his vessels and procure the necessary supplies for the voyage to Europe. To the surprise of his pilot and crews, however, on making sail he stood again along the coast to the eastward, instead of steering north, which they considered the direct route to Hispaniola. They fancied that he intended to proceed immediately for Spain, and murmured loudly at the madness of attempting so long a voyage with ships destitute of stores and consumed by the worms. Columbus and his brother, however, had studied the navigation of those seas with a more observant and experienced eye. They considered it advisable to gain a considerable distance to the east, before standing across for Hispaniola, to avoid being swept away far below their destined port by the strong currents setting constantly to the west.[*] The admiral, however, did not impart his reasons to the pilots, being anxious to keep the knowledge of his routes as much to himself as possible, seeing that there were so many adventurers crowding into the field, and ready to follow on his track. He even took from the mariners their charts,[†] and boasts, in a letter to the sovereigns, that none of his pilots would be able to retrace the route to and from Veragua, nor to describe where it was situated.

Disregarding the murmurs of his men, therefore, he continued along the coast eastward as far as Puerto Bello. Here he was obliged to leave one of the caravels, being so pierced by worms

[*] *Hist. del Almirante*; Letter from Jamaica.
[†] Journal of Porras, Navarrete, *Colec.*, tom. i.

that it was impossible to keep her afloat. All the crews were now crowded into two caravels, and these were little better than mere wrecks. The utmost exertions were necessary to keep them free from water; while the incessant labour of the pumps bore hard on men enfeebled by scanty diet and dejected by various hardships. Continuing onward, they passed Port Retrete, and a number of islands to which the admiral gave the name of Las Barbas, now termed the Mulatas, a little beyond Point Blas. Here he supposed that he had arrived at the province of Mangi in the territories of the Grand Khan, described by Marco Polo as adjoining to Cathay.* He continued on about ten leagues farther, until he approached the entrance of what is at present called the Gulf of Darien. Here he had a consultation with his captains and pilots, who remonst-rated at his persisting in this struggle against contrary winds and currents, representing the lamentable plight of the ships and the infirm state of the crews.† Bidding farewell, therefore, to the mainland, he stood northward on the 1st of May, in quest of Hispaniola. As the wind was easterly, with a strong current setting to the west, he kept as near the wind as possible. So little did his pilots know of their situation that they supposed themselves to the east of the Caribbee Islands, whereas the admiral feared that, with all his exertions, he should fall to the westward of Hispaniola.‡ His apprehensions proved to be well founded; for, on the 10th of the month, he came in sight of two small low islands to the north-west of Hispaniola, to which, from the great quantities of tortoises seen about them, he gave the name of the Tortugas; they are now known as the Caymans. Passing wide of these, and continuing directly north, he found himself, on the 30th of May, among the cluster of islands on the south side of Cuba, to which he had formerly given the name of the Queen's Gardens, having been carried between eight and nine degrees west of his destined port. Here he cast anchor near one of the keys, about ten leagues from the main island. His crews were suffering excessively through scanty provisions and great fatigue; nothing was left of the sea-stores but a little biscuit, oil, and vinegar; and they were obliged to labour incessantly at the pumps to keep the vessels afloat. They

* Letter from Jamaica.
† Testimony of Pedro de Ledesma; Pleito de los Colones.
‡ Letter from Jamaica.

had scarcely anchored at these islands when there came on, at midnight, a sudden tempest of such violence that, according to the strong expression of Columbus, it seemed as if the world would dissolve.[*] They lost three of their anchors almost immediately, and the caravel *Bermuda* was driven with such violence upon the ship of the admiral that the bow of the one and the stern of the other were greatly shattered. The sea running high, and the wind being boisterous, the vessels chafed and injured each other dreadfully, and it was with great difficulty that they were separated. One anchor only remained to the admiral's ship, and this saved him from being driven upon the rocks; but at daylight the cable was found nearly worn asunder. Had the darkness continued an hour longer, he could scarcely have escaped shipwreck.[†]

At the end of six days, the weather having moderated, he resumed his course, standing eastward for Hispaniola: 'his people,' as he says, 'dismayed and down-hearted; almost all his anchors lost, and his vessels bored as full of holes as a honeycomb.' After struggling against contrary winds and the usual currents from the east, he reached Cape Cruz, and anchored at a village in the province of Macaca,[‡] where he had touched in 1494, in his voyage along the southern coast of Cuba. Here he was detained by head winds for several days, during which he was supplied with cassava bread by the natives. Making sail again, he endeavoured to beat up to Hispaniola; but every effort was in vain. The winds and currents continued adverse; the leaks continually gained upon his vessels, though the pumps were kept incessantly going, and the seamen even baled the water out with buckets and kettles. The admiral now stood, in despair, for the island of Jamaica, to seek some secure port; for there was imminent danger of foundering at sea. On the eve of St John, the 23rd of June, they put into Puerto Bueno, now called Dry Harbour, but met with none of the natives from whom they could obtain provisions, nor was there any fresh water to be had in the neighbourhood. Suffering from hunger and thirst, they sailed eastward on the following day to another harbour, to which the admiral on his first visit to the island had given the name of Port Santa Gloria.

[*] Letter from Jamaica.
[†] *Hist. del Almirante*, cap. 100; Letter of Columbus from Jamaica.
[‡] *Hist. del Almirante*; Journal of Porras.

Here, at last, Columbus had to give up his long and arduous struggle against the unremitting persecution of the elements. His ships, reduced to mere wrecks, could no longer keep the sea, and were ready to sink even in port. He ordered them, therefore, to be run aground, within a bow-shot of the shore, and fastened together, side by side. They soon filled with water to the deck. Thatched cabins were then erected at the prow and stern for the accommodation of the crews, and the wreck was placed in the best possible state of defence. Thus castled in the sea, he trusted to be able to repel any sudden attack of the natives, and at the same time to keep his men from roving about the neighbourhood and indulging in their usual excesses. No one was allowed to go on shore without especial license, and the utmost precaution was taken to prevent any offence being given to the Indians. Any exasperation of them might be fatal to the Spaniards in their present forlorn situation. A firebrand thrown into their wooden fortress might wrap it in flames, and leave them defenceless amidst hostile thousands.

BOOK 16

CHAPTER I
1503

The island of Jamaica was extremely populous and fertile; and the harbour soon swarmed with Indians, who brought provisions to barter with the Spaniards. To prevent any disputes in purchasing or sharing these supplies, two persons were appointed to superintend all bargains, and the provisions thus obtained were divided every evening among the people. This arrangement had a happy effect in promoting a peaceful intercourse. The stores thus furnished, however, coming from a limited neighbourhood of improvident beings, were not sufficient for the necessities of the Spaniards, and were so irregular as often to leave them in pinching want. They feared, too, that the neighbourhood might soon be exhausted, in which case they should be reduced to famine. In this emergency, Diego Mendez stepped forward with his accustomed zeal, and volunteered to set off, with three men, on a foraging expedition about the island. His offer being gladly accepted by the admiral, he departed with his comrades well armed. He was everywhere treated with the utmost kindness by the natives. They took him to their houses, set meat and drink before him and his companions, and performed all the rites of savage hospitality. Mendez made an arrangement with the cacique of a numerous tribe that his subjects should hunt and fish, and make cassava bread, and bring a quantity of provisions every day to the harbour. They were to receive, in exchange, knives, combs, beads, fishhooks, hawks' bells, and other articles, from a Spaniard, who was to reside among them for that purpose. The agreement being made, Mendez despatched one of his comrades to apprise the admiral. He then pursued his journey three leagues farther, when he made a similar arrangement, and despatched another of his companions to the admiral. Proceeding onward, about thirteen leagues from the ships, he arrived at the residence of another cacique, called Huarco, where he was generously entertained. The cacique ordered his subjects to bring a large quantity of provisions, for which Mendez paid him on the spot, and made arrangements for a like supply at stated intervals. He despatched his third companion with this supply to the admiral, requesting, as usual, that an agent might be sent to receive and pay for the regular deliveries of provisions.

Mendez was now left alone, but he was fond of any enterprise that gave individual distinction. He requested of the cacique two Indians to accompany him to the end of the island; one to carry his provisions, and the other to bear the hammac or cotton net in which he slept. These being granted, he pushed resolutely forward along the coast until he reached the eastern extremity of Jamaica. Here he found a powerful cacique of the name of Ameyro. Mendez had buoyant spirits, great address, and an ingratiating manner with the savages. He and the cacique became great friends, exchanged names, which is a kind of token of brotherhood, and Mendez engaged him to furnish provisions to the ships. He then bought an excellent canoe of the cacique, for which he gave a splendid brass basin, a short frock or cassock, and one of the two shirts which formed his stock of linen. The cacique furnished him with six Indians to navigate his bark, and they parted mutually well pleased. Diego Mendez coasted his way back, touching at the various places where he had made his arrangements. He found the Spanish agents already arrived at them, loaded his canoe with provisions, and returned in triumph to the harbour, where he was received with acclamations by his comrades, and with open arms by the admiral. The provisions he brought were a most seasonable supply, for the Spaniards were absolutely fasting; and thenceforward Indians arrived daily, well laden, from the marts which he had established.[*]

The immediate wants of his people being thus provided for, Columbus revolved in his anxious mind the means of getting from this island. His ships were beyond the possibility of repair, and there was no hope of any chance sail arriving to his relief, on the shores of a savage island in an unfrequented sea. The most likely

[*] Relacion por Diego Mendez; Navarrete, tom. i.

Coast scene, Jamaica

measure appeared to be to send notice of his situation to Ovando, the governor at San Domingo, entreating him to despatch a vessel to his relief. But how was this message to be conveyed? The distance between Jamaica and Hispaniola was forty leagues, across a gulf swept by contrary currents; there were no means of transporting a messenger except in the light canoes of the savages; and who would undertake so hazardous a voyage in a frail bark of the kind? Suddenly the idea of Diego Mendez, and the canoe he had recently purchased, presented itself to the mind of Columbus. He knew the ardour and intrepidity of Mendez, and his love of distinction by any hazardous exploit. Taking him aside, therefore, he addressed him in a manner calculated both to stimulate his zeal and flatter his self-love. Mendez himself gives an artless account of this interesting conversation, which is full of character.

'Diego Mendez, my son,' said the venerable admiral, 'none of those whom I have here understand the great peril in which we are placed, excepting you and myself. We are few in number, and these savage Indians are many, and of fickle and irritable natures. On the least provocation they may throw firebrands from the shore, and consume us in our straw-thatched cabins. The arrangement which you have made with them for provisions, and which at present they fulfil so cheerfully, tomorrow they may break in their caprice, and may refuse to bring us anything; nor have we the means to compel them by force, but are entirely at their pleasure. I have thought of a remedy, if it meets with your views. In this canoe which you have purchased someone may pass over to Hispaniola, and procure a ship, by which we may all be delivered from this great peril into which we have fallen. Tell me your opinion on the matter.'

'To this,' says Diego Mendez, 'I replied: "Señor, the danger in which we are placed, I well know, is far greater than is easily conceived. As to passing from this island to Hispaniola in so small a vessel as a canoe, I hold it not merely difficult but impossible; since it is necessary to traverse a gulf of forty leagues, and between islands where the sea is extremely impetuous and seldom in repose. I know not who there is would adventure upon so extreme a peril."'

Columbus made no reply, but from his looks and the nature of his silence, Mendez plainly perceived himself to be the person whom the admiral had in view. 'Whereupon,' continues he, 'I added: "Señor, I have many times put my life in peril of death to save you and all those who are here, and God has hitherto preserved me in a miraculous manner. There are, nevertheless, murmurers, who say that your Excellency intrusts to me all affairs wherein honour is to be gained, while there are others in your company who would execute them as well as I do. Therefore I beg that you would summon all the people and propose this enterprise to them, to see if among them there is anyone who will undertake it, which I doubt. If all decline it, I will then come forward and risk my life in your service, as I many times have done."'[*]

The admiral gladly humoured the wishes of the worthy Mendez, for never was simple egotism accompanied by more generous and devoted loyalty. On the following morning the crew was assembled, and the proposition publicly made. Everyone drew back at the thoughts of it, pronouncing it the height of rashness. Upon this, Diego Mendez stepped forward. 'Señor,' said he, 'I have but one life to lose, yet I am willing to venture it for your service and for the good of all here present, and I trust in the protection of God, which I have experienced on so many other occasions.'

Columbus embraced this zealous follower, who immediately set about preparing for his expedition. Drawing his canoe on shore, he put on a false keel, nailed weather-boards along the bow and stern to prevent the sea from breaking over it, payed it with a coat of tar, furnished it with a mast and sail, and put in provisions for himself, a Spanish comrade, and six Indians.

In the meantime, Columbus wrote letters to Ovando, requesting that a ship might be immediately sent to bring him and his men to Hispaniola. He wrote a letter likewise to the sovereigns; for, after fulfilling his mission at San Domingo, Diego Mendez was to proceed to Spain on the admiral's affairs. In the letter to the sovereigns, Columbus depicted his deplorable situation, and entreated that a vessel might be despatched to Hispaniola to convey himself and his crew to Spain. He gave a comprehensive account of his voyage, most particulars of which have already been incorporated in this history, and he insisted greatly on the importance of the discovery of Veragua. He gave it as his opinion that here were the mines of the Aurea Chersonesus, whence Solomon had derived

---

[*] Relacion por Diego Mendez; Navarrete, *Colec*, tom. i.

such wealth for the building of the Temple. He entreated that this
golden coast might not, like other places which he had discovered,
be abandoned to adventurers, or placed under the government of
men who felt no interest in the cause. 'This is not a child,' he adds,
'to be abandoned to a step-mother. I never think of Hispaniola and
Paria without weeping. Their case is desperate and past cure; I
hope their example may cause this region to be treated in a
different manner.' His imagination becomes heated. He magnifies
the supposed importance of Veragua, as transcending all his former
discoveries; and he alludes to his favourite project for the deliverance of the Holy Sepulchre. 'Jerusalem,' he says, 'and Mount Sion,
are to be rebuilt by the hand of a Christian. Who is he to be? God,
by the mouth of the Prophet, in the fourteenth Psalm, declares it.
The abbot Joachim * says that he is to come out of Spain.' His
thoughts then revert to the ancient story of the Grand Khan, who
had requested that sages might be sent to instruct him in the
Christian faith. Columbus, thinking that he had been in the very
vicinity of Cathay, exclaims with sudden zeal, 'Who will offer
himself for this task? If our Lord permit me to return to Spain, I
engage to take him there, God helping, in safety.'

Nothing is more characteristic of Columbus than his earnest,
artless, at times eloquent, and at times almost incoherent letters.
What an instance of soaring enthusiasm and irrepressible enterprise
is here exhibited! At the time that he was indulging in these
visions, and proposing new and romantic enterprises, he was
broken down by age and infirmities, racked by pain, confined to
his bed, and shut up in a wreck on the coast of a remote and savage
island. No stronger picture can be given of his situation, than that
which shortly follows this transient glow of excitement; when,
with one of his sudden transitions of thought, he awakens, as it
were, to his actual condition.

* Joachim, native of the burgh of Celico, near Cozenza, travelled in the Holy
Land. Returning to Calabria, he took the habit of the Cistercians in the
monastery of Corazzo, of which he became prior and abbot, and afterwards rose
to higher monastic importance. He died in 1202, having attained 72 years of
age, leaving a great number of works; among the most known are commentaries
on Isaiah, Jeremiah, and the Apocalypse. There are also prophecies by him,
'which,' (says the *Dictionnaire Historique*) 'during his life, made him to be admired
by fools, and despised by men of sense; at present the latter sentiment prevails.
He was either very weak or very presumptuous, to flatter himself that he had the
keys of things of which God reserves the knowledge to himself.' – *Dict. Hist.*,
tom. v, Caen, 1785.

'Hitherto,' says he, 'I have wept for others; but now, have pity upon me, heaven, and weep for me, O earth! In my temporal concerns, without a farthing to offer for a mass; cast away here in the Indies; surrounded by cruel and hostile savages; isolated, infirm, expecting each day will be my last: in spiritual concerns, separated from the holy sacraments of the church, so that my soul, if parted here from my body, must be for ever lost! Weep for me, whoever has charity, truth, and justice! I came not on this voyage to gain honour or estate, that is most certain, for all hope of the kind was already dead within me. I came to serve your majesties with a sound intention and an honest zeal, and I speak no falsehood. If it should please God to deliver me hence, I humbly supplicate your majesties to permit me to repair to Rome, and perform other pilgrimages.'

The dispatches being ready, and the preparations of the canoe completed, Diego Mendez embarked with his Spanish comrade and his six Indians, and departed along the coast to the eastward. The voyage was toilsome and perilous. They had to make their way against strong currents. Once they were taken by roving canoes of Indians, but made their escape, and at length arrived at the end of the island; a distance of thirty-four leagues from the harbour. Here they remained, waiting for calm weather to venture upon the broad gulf, when they were suddenly surrounded and taken prisoners by a number of hostile Indians, who carried them off a distance of three leagues, where they determined to kill them. Some dispute arose about the division of the spoils taken from the Spaniards, whereupon the savages agreed to settle it by a game of chance. While they were thus engaged, Diego Mendez escaped, found his way to his canoe, embarked in it, and returned alone to the harbour after fifteen days' absence. What became of his companions he does not mention, being seldom apt to speak of any person but himself. This account is taken from the narrative inserted in his last will and testament.

Columbus, though grieved at the failure of his message, was rejoiced at the escape of the faithful Mendez. The latter, nothing daunted by the perils and hardships he had undergone, offered to depart immediately on a second attempt, provided he could have persons to accompany him to the end of the island, and protect him from the natives. This the Adelantado offered to undertake, with a large party well armed. Bartholomew Fiesco, a Genoese, who had been captain of one of the caravels, was associated with Mendez in this second expedition. He was a man of great worth, strongly attached to the admiral, and much esteemed by him. Each had a large canoe under his command, in which were six Spaniards and ten Indians – the latter were to serve as oarsmen. The canoes were to keep in company. On reaching Hispaniola, Fiesco was to return immediately to Jamaica, to relieve the anxiety of the admiral and his crew by tidings of the safe arrival of their messenger. In the meantime, Diego Mendez was to proceed to San Domingo, deliver his letter to Ovando, procure and despatch a ship, and then depart for Spain with a letter to the sovereigns.

All arrangements being made, the Indians placed in the canoes their frugal provisions of cassava bread, and each his calabash of water. The Spaniards, beside their bread, had a supply of the flesh of utias, and each his sword and target. In this way they launched forth upon their long and perilous voyage, followed by the prayers of their countrymen.

The Adelantado, with his armed band, kept pace with them along the coast. There was no attempt of the natives to molest them, and they arrived in safety at the end of the island. Here they remained three days before the sea was sufficiently calm for them to venture forth in their feeble barks. At length, the weather being quite serene, they bade farewell to their comrades, and committed themselves to the broad sea. The Adelantado remained watching them, until they became mere specks on the ocean, and the evening hid them from his view. The next day he set out on his return to the harbour, stopping at various villages on the way, and endeavouring to confirm the good-will of the natives.[*]

---

[*] *Hist. del Almirante*, cap. 101.

It might have been thought that the adverse fortune which had so long persecuted Columbus was now exhausted. The envy which had once sickened at his glory and prosperity could scarcely have devised for him a more forlorn heritage in the world he had discovered. The tenant of a wreck on a savage coast, in an untraversed ocean, at the mercy of barbarous hordes, who, in a moment, from precarious friends might be transformed into ferocious enemies; afflicted, too, by excruciating maladies which confined him to his bed, and by the pains and infirmities which hardship and anxiety had heaped upon his advancing age. But he had not yet exhausted his cup of bitterness. He had yet to experience an evil worse than storm, or shipwreck, or bodily anguish, or the violence of savage hordes – the perfidy of those in whom he confided.

Mendez and Fiesco had not long departed when the Spaniards in the wreck began to grow sickly, partly from the toils and exposures of the recent voyage, partly from being crowded in narrow quarters in a moist and sultry climate, and partly from want of their accustomed food, for they could not habituate themselves to the vegetable diet of the Indians. Their maladies were rendered more insupportable by mental suffering, by that suspense which frets the spirit, and that hope deferred which corrodes the heart. Accustomed to a life of bustle and variety, they had now nothing to do but loiter about the dreary hulk, look out upon the sea, watch for the canoe of Fiesco, wonder at its protracted absence, and doubt its return. A long time elapsed, much more than sufficient for the voyage, but nothing was seen or heard of the canoe. Fears were entertained that their messenger had perished. If so, how long were they to remain here, vainly looking for relief which was never to arrive? Some sank into deep despondency, others became peevish and impatient. Murmurs broke forth, and, as usual with men in distress, murmurs of the most unreasonable kind. Instead of sympathizing with their aged and infirm commander, who was involved in the same calamity, who in suffering transcended them all, and yet who was incessantly studious of their welfare, they began to rail against him as the cause of all their misfortunes.

The factious feeling of an unreasonable multitude would be of little importance if left to itself, and might end in idle clamour; it is the industry of one or two evil spirits which generally directs it to an object and makes it mischievous. Among the officers of Columbus were two brothers, Francisco and Diego de Porras. They were related to the royal treasurer Morales, who had married their sister, and had made interest with the admiral to give them some employment in the expedition.* To gratify the treasurer, he had appointed Francisco de Porras captain of one of the caravels, and had obtained for his brother Diego the situation of notary and accountant-general of the squadron. He had treated them, as he declares, with the kindness of relatives, though both proved incompetent to their situations. They were vain and insolent men, and, like many others whom Columbus had benefited, requited his kindness with black ingratitude.†

These men, finding the common people in a highly impatient and discontented state, wrought upon them with seditious insinuations, assuring them that all hope of relief through the agency of Mendez was idle, it being a mere delusion of the admiral to keep them quiet, and render them subservient to his purposes. He had no desire nor intention to return to Spain, and in fact was banished thence. Hispaniola was equally closed to him, as had been proved by the exclusion of his ships from its harbour in a time of peril. To him, at present, all places were alike, and he was content to remain in Jamaica until his friends could make interest at court, and procure his recall from banishment. As to Mendez and Fiesco, they had been sent to Spain by Columbus on his own private affairs, not to procure a ship for the relief of his followers. If this were not the case, why did not the ships arrive, or why did not Fiesco return, as had been promised? Or if the canoes had really been sent for succour, the long time that had elapsed without tidings of them,

---

* *Hist. del Almirante*, cap. 102.
† Letter of Columbus to his son Diego; Navarrete, *Colec.* tom. ii.

gave reason to believe they had perished by the way. In such case, their only alternative would be to take the canoes of the Indians and endeavour to reach Hispaniola. There was no hope, however, of persuading the admiral to such an undertaking; he was too old, and too helpless from the gout, to expose himself to the hardships of such a voyage. What then? Were they to be sacrificed to his interests or his infirmities? – to give up their only chance for escape, and linger and perish with him in this desolate wreck? If they succeeded in reaching Hispaniola, they would be the better received for having left the admiral behind. Ovando was secretly hostile to him, fearing that he would regain the government of the island; on their arrival in Spain, the bishop Fonseca, from his enmity to Columbus, would be sure to take their part; the brothers Porras had powerful friends and relatives at court, to counteract any representations that might be made by the admiral; and they cited the case of Roldan's rebellion, to show that the prejudices of the public, and of men in power, would always be against him. Nay, they insinuated that the sovereigns, who on that occasion had deprived him of part of his dignities and privileges, would rejoice at a pretext for stripping him of the remainder.*

Columbus was aware that the minds of his people were imbittered against him. He had repeatedly been treated with insolent impatience, and reproached with being the cause of their disasters. Accustomed, however, to the unreasonableness of men in adversity, and exercised, by many trials, in the mastery of his passions, he bore with their petulance, soothed their irritation, and endeavoured to cheer their spirits by the hopes of speedy succour. A little while longer, and he trusted that Fiesco would arrive with good tidings, when the certainty of relief would put an end to all these clamours. The mischief, however, was deeper than he apprehended: a complete mutiny had been organized.

On the 2nd of January 1504, he was in his small cabin on the stern of his vessel, being confined to his bed by the gout, which had now rendered him a complete cripple. While ruminating on his disastrous situation, Francisco de Porras suddenly entered. His abrupt and agitated manner betrayed the evil nature of his visit. He had the flurried impudence of a man about to perpetrate an open crime. Breaking forth into bitter complaints at their being kept

* *Hist. del Almirante*, cap. 102.

week after week, and month after month, to perish piecemeal in
that desolate place, he accused the admiral of having no intention
to return to Spain. Columbus suspected something sinister from
this unusual arrogance; he maintained, however, his calmness, and,
raising himself in his bed, endeavoured to reason with Porras. He
pointed out the impossibility of departing until those who had
gone to Hispaniola should send them vessels. He represented how
much more urgent must be his desire to depart, since he had not
merely his own safety to provide for, but was accountable to God
and his sovereigns for the welfare of all who had been committed
to his charge. He reminded Porras that he had always consulted
with them all as to the measures to be taken for the common
safety, and that what he had done had been with the general
approbation; still, if any other measure appeared advisable, he
recommended that they should assemble together, and consult
upon it, and adopt whatever course appeared most judicious.

The measures of Porras and his comrades, however, were already concerted, and when men are determined on mutiny, they
are deaf to reason. He bluntly replied that there was no time for
further consultations. 'Embark immediately or remain in God's
name, were the only alternatives.' 'For my part,' said he, turning
his back upon the admiral, and elevating his voice so that it
resounded all over the vessel, 'I am for Castile! those who choose
may follow me!' Shouts arose immediately from all sides, 'I will
follow you! and I! and I!' Numbers of the crew sprang upon the
most conspicuous parts of the ship, brandishing weapons, and
uttering mingled threats and cries of rebellion. Some called upon
Porras for orders what to do; others shouted 'To Castile! to
Castile!' while, amidst the general uproar, the voices of some
desperadoes were heard menacing the life of the admiral.

Columbus, hearing the tumult, leaped from his bed, ill and
infirm as he was, and tottered out of the cabin, stumbling and
falling in the exertion, hoping by his presence to pacify the mutineers. Three or four of his faithful adherents, however, fearing some
violence might he offered him, threw themselves between him
and the throng, and taking him in their arms, compelled him to
return to his cabin.

The Adelantado likewise sallied forth, but in a different mood.
He planted himself, with lance in hand, in a situation to take the

whole brunt of the assault. It was with the greatest difficulty that several of the loyal part of the crew could appease his fury, and prevail upon him to relinquish his weapon, and retire to the cabin of his brother. They now entreated Porras and his companions to depart peaceably, since no one sought to oppose them. No advantage could be gained by violence; but should they cause the death of the admiral, they would draw upon themselves the severest punishment from the sovereigns.[*]

These representations moderated the turbulence of the mutineers, and they now proceeded to carry their plans into execution. Taking ten canoes which the admiral had purchased of the Indians, they embarked in them with as much exultation as if certain of immediately landing on the shores of Spain. Others, who had not been concerned in the mutiny, seeing so large a force departing, and fearing to remain behind when so reduced in number, hastily collected their effects and entered likewise into the canoes. In this way forty-eight abandoned the admiral. Many of those who remained were only detained by sickness, for had they been well, most of them would have accompanied the deserters.[†] The few who remained faithful to the admiral, and the sick, who crawled forth from their cabins, saw the departure of the mutineers with tears and lamentations, giving themselves up for lost. Notwithstanding his malady, Columbus left his bed, mingling among those who were loyal, and visiting those who were ill, endeavouring in every way to cheer and comfort them. He entreated them to put their trust in God, who would yet relieve them; and he promised, on his return to Spain, to throw himself at the feet of the queen, represent their loyalty and constancy, and obtain for them rewards that should compensate for all their sufferings.[‡]

In the meantime, Francisco de Porras and his followers, in their squadron of canoes, coasted the island to the eastward, following the route taken by Mendez and Fiesco. Wherever they landed, they committed outrages upon the Indians, robbing them of their provisions and of whatever they coveted of their effects. They endeavoured to make their own crimes redound to the prejudice of Columbus, pretending to act under his authority, and affirming

---

[*] Las Casas, *Hist. Ind.*, lib. ii. cap. 32; *Hist. del Almirante*, cap. 102.

[†] *Hist. del Almirante*, cap. 102.

[‡] Las Casas, lib. ii. cap. 32.

that he would pay for everything they took. If he refused, they told the natives to kill him. They represented him as an implacable foe to the Indians; as one who had tyrannized over other islands, causing the misery and death of the natives, and who only sought to gain a sway here for the purpose of inflicting like calamities.

Having reached the eastern extremity of the island, they waited until the weather should be perfectly calm before they ventured to cross the gulf. Being unskilled in the management of canoes, they procured several Indians to accompany them. The sea being at length quite smooth, they set forth upon their voyage. Scarcely had they proceeded four leagues from land when a contrary wind arose, and the waves began to swell. They turned immediately for shore. The canoes, from their light structure, and being nearly round and without keels, were easily overturned and required to be carefully balanced. They were now deeply freighted by men unaccustomed to them, and as the sea rose they frequently let in the water. The Spaniards were alarmed, and endeavoured to lighten them by throwing overboard everything that could be spared, retaining only their arms and a part of their provisions. The danger augmented with the wind. They now compelled the Indians to leap into the sea, excepting such as were absolutely necessary to navigate the canoes. If they hesitated, they drove them overboard with the edge of the sword. The Indians were skilful swimmers, but the distance to land was too great for their strength. They kept about the canoes, therefore, taking hold of them occasionally to rest themselves and recover breath. As their weight disturbed the balance of the canoes, and endangered their overturning, the Spaniards cut off their hands, and stabbed them with their swords. Some died by the weapons of these cruel men, others were exhausted and sank beneath the waves; thus eighteen perished miserably, and none survived but such as had been retained to manage the canoes.

When the Spaniards got back to land, different opinions arose as to what course they should next pursue. Some were for crossing to Cuba, for which island the wind was favourable. It was thought they might easily cross thence to the end of Hispaniola. Others advised that they should return and make their peace with the admiral, or take from him what remained of arms and stores, having thrown almost everything overboard during their late danger. Others counselled another attempt to cross over to Hispaniola as soon as the sea should become tranquil.

This last advice was adopted. They remained for a month at an Indian village near the eastern point of the island, living on the substance of the natives, and treating them in the most arbitrary and capricious manner. When at length the weather became serene, they made a second attempt, but were again driven back by adverse winds. Losing all patience, therefore, and despairing of the enterprise, they abandoned their canoes and returned westward; wandering from village to village, a dissolute and lawless gang, supporting themselves by fair means or foul, according as they met with kindness or hostility, and passing like a pestilence through the island.*

* *Hist. del Almirante*, cap. 102; Las Casas, lib. ii. cap. 32.

CHAPTER 3

1504

While Porras and his crew were ranging about with that desperate and joyless licentiousness which attends the abandonment of principle, Columbus presented the opposite picture of a man true to others and to himself, and supported, amidst hardships and difficulties, by conscious rectitude. Deserted by the healthful and vigorous portion of his garrison, he exerted himself to soothe and encourage the infirm and desponding remnant which remained. Regardless of his own painful maladies, he was only attentive to relieve their sufferings. The few who were fit for service were required to mount guard on the wreck or attend upon the sick; there were none to forage for provisions. The scrupulous good faith and amicable conduct maintained by Columbus towards the natives had now their effect. Considerable supplies of provisions were brought by them from time to time, which he purchased at a reasonable rate. The most palatable and nourishing of these, together with the small stock of European biscuit that remained, he ordered to be appropriated to the sustenance of the infirm. Knowing how much the body is affected by the operations of the mind, he endeavoured to rouse the spirits and animate the hopes of the drooping sufferers. Concealing his own anxiety, he maintained a serene and even cheerful countenance, encouraging his men by kind words, and holding forth confident anticipations of speedy relief. By his friendly and careful treatment, he soon recruited both the health and spirits of his people, and brought them into a condition to contribute to the common safety. Judicious regulations, calmly but firmly enforced, maintained everything in order. The men became sensible of the advantages of wholesome discipline, and perceived that the restraints imposed upon them by their commander were for their own good, and ultimately productive of their own comfort.

Columbus had thus succeeded in guarding against internal ills, when alarming evils began to menace from without. The Indians, unused to lay up any stock of provisions, and unwilling to subject themselves to extra labour, found it difficult to furnish the quantity of food daily required for so many hungry men. The European trinkets, once so precious, lost their value in proportion as they became common. The importance of the admiral had been greatly diminished by the desertion of so many of his followers; and the malignant instigations of the rebels had awakened jealousy and enmity in several of the villages which had been accustomed to furnish provisions.

By degrees, therefore, the supplies fell off. The arrangements for the daily delivery of certain quantities, made by Diego Mendez, were irregularly attended to, and at length ceased entirely. The Indians no longer thronged to the harbour with provisions, and often refused them when applied for. The Spaniards were obliged to forage about the neighbourhood for their daily food, but found more and more difficulty in procuring it; thus, in addition to their other causes for despondency, they began to entertain horrible apprehensions of famine.

The admiral heard their melancholy forebodings and beheld the growing evil, but was at a loss for a remedy. To resort to force was an alternative full of danger, and of but temporary efficacy. It would require all those who were well enough to bear arms to sally forth, while he and the rest of the infirm would be left defenceless on board of the wreck, exposed to the vengeance of the natives.

In the meantime, the scarcity daily increased. The Indians perceived the wants of the white men, and had learnt from them the art of making bargains. They asked ten times the former quantity of European articles for any amount of provisions, and brought their supplies in scanty quantities, to enhance the eagerness of the hungry Spaniards. At length, even this relief ceased, and there was an absolute distress for food. The jealousy of the natives had been universally roused by Porras and his followers, and they withheld all provisions, in hopes either of starving the admiral and his people, or of driving them from the island.

In this extremity, a fortunate idea presented itself to Columbus. From his knowledge of astronomy, he ascertained that within three days there would be a total eclipse of the moon in the early part of the night. He sent, therefore, an Indian of Hispaniola, who served as his interpreter, to summon the principal caciques to a grand conference, appointing for it the day of the eclipse. When all were assembled, he told them by his interpreter that he and his followers were worshippers of a Deity who dwelt in the skies, who favoured such as did well, but punished all transgressors; that, as they must all have noticed, he had protected Diego Mendez and his companions in their voyage, because they went in obedience to the orders of their commander, but had visited Porras and his companions with all kinds of afflictions, in consequence of their rebellion. This great Deity, he added, was incensed against the Indians who refused to furnish his faithful worshippers with provisions, and intended to chastise them with famine and pestilence. Lest they should disbelieve this warning, a signal would be given that night. They would behold the moon change its colour, and gradually lose its light; a token of the fearful punishment which awaited them.

Many of the Indians were alarmed at the prediction, others treated it with derision – all, however, awaited with solicitude the coming of the night. When they beheld a dark shadow stealing over the moon, they began to tremble; with the progress of the eclipse their fears increased, and when they saw a mysterious darkness covering the whole face of nature, there were no bounds to their terror. Seizing upon whatever provisions were at hand, they hurried to the ships, threw themselves at the feet of Columbus, and implored him to intercede with his God to withhold the threatened calamities, assuring him they would thenceforth bring him whatever he required. Columbus shut himself up in his cabin, as if to commune with the Deity, and remained there during the increase of the eclipse, the forests and shores all the while resounding with the howlings and supplications of the savages. When the eclipse was about to diminish, he came forth and informed the natives that his God had deigned to pardon them, on condition of their fulfilling their promises; in sign of which he would withdraw the darkness from the moon.

When the Indians saw that planet restored to its brightness, and rolling in all its beauty through the firmament, they overwhelmed the admiral with thanks for his intercession, and repaired to their homes, joyful at having escaped such great disasters. Regarding Columbus with awe and reverence, as a man in the peculiar favour and confidence of the Deity, since he knew upon earth what was passing in the heavens, they hastened to propitiate him with gifts; supplies again arrived daily at the harbour, and from that time forward, there was no want of provisions.*

* *Hist. del Almirante,* cap. 103; Las Casas, *Hist. Ind.*, lib. ii. cap. 33.

CHAPTER 4

1504

Eight months had now elapsed since the departure of Mendez and Fiesco, without any tidings of their fate. For a long time the Spaniards had kept a wistful look-out upon the ocean, flattering themselves that every Indian canoe gliding at a distance might be the harbinger of deliverance. The hopes of the most sanguine were now fast sinking into despondency. What thousand perils awaited such frail barks, and so weak a party, on an expedition of the kind! Either the canoes had been swallowed up by boisterous waves and adverse currents, or their crews had perished among the rugged mountains and savage tribes of Hispaniola. To increase their despondency, they were informed that a vessel had been seen, bottom upwards, drifting with the currents along the coasts of Jamaica. This might be the vessel sent to their relief; and if so, all their hopes were shipwrecked with it. This rumour, it is affirmed, was invented and circulated in the island by the rebels, that it might reach the ears of those who remained faithful to the admiral, and reduce them to despair.* It no doubt had its effect. Losing all hope of aid from a distance, and considering themselves abandoned and forgotten by the world, many grew wild and desperate in their plans. Another conspiracy was formed by one Bernardo, an apothecary of Valencia, with two confederates, Alonzo de Zamora and Pedro de Villatoro. They designed to seize upon the remaining canoes, and seek their way to Hispaniola.†

The mutiny was on the very point of breaking out, when one evening towards dusk a sail was seen standing towards the harbour. The transports of the poor Spaniards may be more easily conceived than described. The vessel was of small size; it kept out to sea, but sent its boat to visit the ships. Every eye was eagerly

---

* *Hist. del Almirante*, cap. 104.
† Las Casas, *Hist. Ind.*, lib. ii. cap. 33.

bent to hail the countenances of Christians and deliverers. As the
boat approached, they descried in it Diego de Escobar, a man who
had been one of the most active confederates of Roldan in his
rebellion, who had been condemned to death under the administration of Columbus, and pardoned by his successor Bobadilla.
There was bad omen in such a messenger.

Coming alongside of the ships, Escobar put a letter on board
from Ovando, governor of Hispaniola, together with a barrel of
wine and a side of bacon, sent as presents to the admiral. He then
drew off, and talked with Columbus from a distance. He told him
that he was sent by the governor to express his great concern at his
misfortunes, and his regret at not having in port a vessel of
sufficient size to bring off himself and his people, but that he
would send one as soon as possible. Escobar gave the admiral
assurances likewise, that his concerns in Hispaniola had been
faithfully attended to. He requested him, if he had any letter to
write to the governor in reply, to give it to him as soon as possible,
as he wished to return immediately.

There was something extremely singular in this mission, but
there was no time for comments; Escobar was urgent to depart.
Columbus hastened, therefore, to write a reply to Ovando, depict-
ing the dangers and distresses of his situation, increased as they
were by the rebellion of Porras, but expressing his reliance on his
promise to send him relief, confiding in which he should remain
patiently on board of his wreck. He recommended Diego Mendez
and Bartholomew Fiesco to his favour, assuring him that they were
not sent to San Domingo with any artful design, but simply to
represent his perilous situation, and to apply for succour.* When
Escobar received this letter, he returned immediately on board of
his vessel, which made all sail, and soon disappeared in the gathering gloom of the night.

If the Spaniards had hailed the arrival of this vessel with transport,
its sudden departure and the mysterious conduct of Escobar inspired
no less wonder and consternation. He had kept aloof from all
communication with them, as if he felt no interest in their welfare
or sympathy in their misfortunes. Columbus saw the gloom that
had gathered in their countenances, and feared the consequences.
He eagerly sought, therefore, to dispel their suspicions, professing

* Las Casas, *Hist. Ind.*, lib. ii. cap. 34.

himself satisfied with the communications received from Ovando, and assuring them that vessels would soon arrive to take them all away. In confidence of this, he said, he had declined to depart with Escobar because his vessel was too small to take the whole, preferring to remain with them and share their lot, and had despatched the caravel in such haste that no time might be lost in expediting the necessary ships. These assurances, and the certainty that their situation was known in San Domingo, cheered the hearts of the people. Their hopes again revived, and the conspiracy, which had been on the point of breaking forth, was completely disconcerted.

In secret, however, Columbus was exceedingly indignant at the conduct of Ovando. He had left him for many months in a state of the utmost danger and most distressing uncertainty, exposed to the hostilities of the natives, the seditions of his men, and the suggestions of his own despair. He had, at length, sent a mere tantalizing message, by a man known to be one of his bitterest enemies, with a present of food which, from its scantiness, seemed intended to mock their necessities.

Columbus believed that Ovando had purposely neglected him, hoping that he might perish on the island, being apprehensive that, should he return in safety, he would be reinstated in the government of Hispaniola; and he considered Escobar merely as a spy sent to ascertain the state of himself and his crew, and whether they were yet in existence. Las Casas, who was then at San Domingo, expresses similar suspicions. He says that Escobar was chosen because Ovando was certain that, from ancient enmity, he would have no sympathy for the admiral; that he was ordered not to go on board of the vessels, nor to land, neither was he to hold conversation with any of the crew, nor to receive any letters, except those of the admiral. In a word, that he was a mere scout to collect information.[*]

Others have ascribed the long neglect of Ovando to extreme caution. There was a rumour prevalent that Columbus, irritated at the suspension of his dignities by the court of Spain, intended to transfer his newly-discovered countries into the hands of his native republic Genoa, or of some other power. Such rumours had long been current, and to their recent circulation Columbus himself alludes in his letter sent to the sovereigns by Diego Mendez. The

[*] Las Casas, *Hist. Ind.*, lib. ii. cap. 33; *Hist. del Almirante* cap. 103.

most plausible apology given, is that Ovando was absent for several months in the interior, occupied in wars with the natives, and that there were no ships at San Domingo of sufficient burden to take Columbus and his crew to Spain. He may have feared that, should they come to reside for any length of time on the island, either the admiral would interfere in public affairs, or endeavour to make a party in his favour; or that, in consequence of the number of his old enemies still resident there, former scenes of faction and turbulence might be revived.* In the meantime the situation of Columbus in Jamaica, while it disposed of him quietly until vessels should arrive from Spain, could not, he may have thought, be hazardous. He had sufficient force and arms for defence, and he had made amicable arrangements with the natives for the supply of provisions, as Diego Mendez, who had made those arrangements, had no doubt informed him. Such may have been the reasoning by which Ovando, under the real influence of his interest, may have reconciled his conscience to a measure which excited the strong reprobation of his contemporaries, and has continued to draw upon him the suspicions of mankind.

* Las Casas, ubi sup.; *Hist. del Almirante*, ubi sup.

It is proper to give here some account of the mission of Diego Mendez and Bartholomew Fiesco, and of the circumstances which prevented the latter from returning to Jamaica. Having taken leave of the Adelantado at the east end of the island, they continued all day in a direct course, animating the Indians who navigated their canoes, and who frequently paused at their labour. There was no wind, the sky was without a cloud, and the sea perfectly calm; the heat was intolerable, and the rays of the sun, reflected from the surface of the ocean, seemed to scorch their very eyes. The Indians, exhausted by heat and toil, would often leap into the water to cool and refresh themselves, and, after remaining there a short time, would return with new vigour to their labours. At the going down of the sun they lost sight of land. During the night the Indians took turns, one half to row while the others slept. The Spaniards, in like manner, divided their forces: while one half took repose, the others kept guard with their weapons in hand, ready to defend themselves in case of any perfidy on the part of their savage companions.

Watching and toiling in this way through the night, they were exceedingly fatigued at the return of day. Nothing was to be seen but sea and sky. Their frail canoes, heaving up and down with the swelling and sinking of the ocean, seemed scarcely capable of sustaining the broad undulations of a calm; how would they be able to live amid waves and surges, should the wind arise? The commanders did all they could to keep up the flagging spirits of the men. Sometimes they permitted them a respite; at other times they took the paddles and shared their toils. But labour and fatigue were soon forgotten in a new source of suffering. During the preceding sultry day and night, the Indians, parched and fatigued, had drunk up all the water. They now began to experience the torments of thirst. In proportion as the day advanced, their thirst increased; the calm, which favoured the navigation of the canoes, rendered this misery the more intense. There was not a breeze to fan the air, nor counteract the ardent rays of a tropical sun. Their sufferings were irritated by the prospect around them – nothing but water, while they were perishing with thirst. At midday their strength failed them, and they could work no longer. Fortunately, at this time the commanders of the canoes found, or pretended to find, two small kegs of water, which they had perhaps secretly reserved for such an extremity. Administering the precious contents from time to time, in sparing mouthfuls, to their companions, and particularly to the labouring Indians, they enabled them to resume their toils. They cheered them with the hopes of soon arriving at a small island called Navasa, which lay directly in their way, and was only eight leagues from Hispaniola. Here they would be able to procure water, and might take repose.

For the rest of the day they continued faintly and wearily labouring forward, and keeping an anxious look-out for the island. The day passed away, the sun went down, yet there was no sign of land, not even a cloud on the horizon that might deceive them into a hope. According to their calculations, they had certainly come the distance from Jamaica at which Navasa lay. They began to fear that they had deviated from their course. If so, they should miss the island entirely, and perish with thirst before they could reach Hispaniola.

The night closed upon them without any sight of the island. They now despaired of touching at it, for it was so small and low that, even if they were to pass near, they would scarcely be able to perceive it in the dark. One of the Indians sank and died, under the accumulated sufferings of labour, heat, and raging thirst. His body was thrown into the sea. Others lay panting and gasping at the bottom of the canoes. Their companions, troubled in spirit, and exhausted in strength, feebly continued their toils. Sometimes they endeavoured to cool their parched palates by taking sea-water in their mouths, but its briny acrimony rather increased their thirst. Now and then, but very sparingly, they were allowed a drop of water from the kegs; but this was only in cases of the utmost extremity, and principally to those who were employed in rowing.

The night had far advanced, but those whose turn it was to take repose were unable to sleep, from the intensity of their thirst; or if they slept, it was but to be tantalized with dreams of cool fountains and running brooks, and to awaken in redoubled torment. The last drop of water had been dealt out to the Indian rowers, but it only served to irritate their sufferings. They scarce could move their paddles; one after another gave up, and it seemed impossible they should live to reach Hispaniola.

The commanders, by admirable management, had hitherto kept up this weary struggle with suffering and despair: they now, too, began to despond. Diego Mendez sat watching the horizon, which was gradually lighting up with those faint rays which precede the rising of the moon. As that planet rose, he perceived it to emerge from behind some dark mass elevated above the level of the ocean. He immediately gave the animating cry of 'land!' His almost ex-piring companions were roused by it to new life. It proved to be the island of Navasa, but so small, and low, and distant, that had it not been thus revealed by the rising of the moon, they would never have discovered it. The error in their reckoning with respect to the island had arisen from miscalculating the rate of sailing of the canoes, and from not making sufficient allowance for the fatigue of the rowers and the opposition of the current.

New vigour was now diffused throughout the crews. They exerted themselves with feverish impatience; by the dawn of day they reached the land, and springing on shore, returned thanks to God for such signal deliverance. The island was a mere mass of rocks half a league in circuit. There was neither tree, nor shrub, nor herbage, nor stream, nor fountain. Hurrying about, however, with anxious search, they found to their joy abundance of rain-water in the hollows of the rocks. Eagerly scooping it up with their calabashes, they quenched their burning thirst by immoderate draughts. In vain the more prudent warned the others of their danger. The Spaniards were in some degree restrained; but the poor Indians, whose toils had increased the fever of their thirst, gave way to a kind of frantic indulgence. Several died upon the spot, and others fell dangerously ill.[*]

---

[*] Not far from the island of Navasa there gushes up in the sea a pure fountain of fresh water that sweetens the surface for some distance: this circumstance was of course unknown to the Spaniards at the time. (Oviedo, *Cronica*, lib. vi. cap. 12.)

Having allayed their thirst, they now looked about in search of food. A few shellfish were found along the shore, and Diego Mendez striking a light and gathering driftwood, they were enabled to boil them, and to make a delicious banquet. All day they remained reposing in the shade of the rocks, refreshing themselves after their intolerable sufferings and gazing upon Hispaniola, whose mountains rose above the horizon at eight leagues distance.

In the cool of the evening they once more embarked, invigorated by repose, and arrived safely at Cape Tiburon on the following day, the fourth since their departure from Jamaica. Here they landed on the banks of a beautiful river, where they were kindly received and treated by the natives. Such are the particulars, collected from different sources, of this adventurous and interesting voyage, on the precarious success of which depended the deliverance of Columbus and his crews.* The voyagers remained for two days among the hospitable natives on the banks of the river to refresh themselves. Fiesco would have returned to Jamaica, according to promise, to give assurance to the Admiral and his companions of the safe arrival of their messenger; but both Spaniards and Indians had suffered so much during the voyage, that nothing could induce them to encounter the perils of a return in the canoes.

Parting with his companions, Diego Mendez took six Indians of the island, and set off resolutely to coast in his canoe one hundred and thirty leagues to San Domingo. After proceeding for eighty leagues, with infinite toil, always against the currents, and subject to perils from the native tribes, he was informed that the governor had departed for Xaragua, fifty leagues distant. Still undaunted by fatigues and difficulties, he abandoned his canoe, and proceeded alone and on foot through forests and over mountains, until he arrived at Xaragua, achieving one of the most perilous expeditions ever undertaken by a devoted follower for the safety of his commander.

Ovando received him with great kindness, expressing the utmost concern at the unfortunate situation of Columbus. He made many promises of sending immediate relief, but suffered day after

* *Hist. del Almirante*, cap. 105; Las Casas, lib. ii. cap. 31; Testament of Diego Mendez; Navarrete, tom. i.

day, week after week, and even month after month to elapse
without carrying his promises into effect. He was at that time
completely engrossed by wars with the natives, and had a ready
plea that there were no ships of sufficient burden at San Domingo.
Had he felt a proper zeal, however, for the safety of a man like
Columbus, it would have been easy, within eight months, to have
devised some means, if not of delivering him from his situation, at
least of conveying to him ample reinforcements and supplies.

The faithful Mendez remained for seven months in Xaragua,
detained there under various pretexts by Ovando, who was
unwilling that he should proceed to San Domingo; partly, as is
intimated, from his having some jealousy of his being employed
in secret agency for the admiral, and partly from a desire to throw
impediments in the way of his obtaining the required relief. At
length, by daily importunity, he obtained permission to go to San
Domingo, and await the arrival of certain ships which were
expected, of which he proposed to purchase one on account of
the admiral. He immediately set out on foot a distance of seventy
leagues, part of his toilsome journey lying through forests and
among mountains infested by hostile and exasperated Indians.
It was after his departure that Ovando despatched the caravel
commanded by the pardoned rebel Escobar, on that singular and
equivocal visit which, in the eyes of Columbus, had the air of a
mere scouting expedition to spy into the camp of an enemy.

CHAPTER 6
1503

When Columbus had soothed the disappointment of his men at the brief and unsatisfactory visit and sudden departure of Escobar he endeavoured to turn the event to some advantage with the rebels. He knew them to be disheartened by the inevitable miseries attending a lawless and dissolute life; that many longed to return to the safe and quiet path of duty; and that the most malignant, seeing how he had foiled all their intrigues among the natives to produce a famine, began to fear his ultimate triumph and consequent vengeance. A favourable opportunity, he thought, now presented to take advantage of these feelings, and by gentle means to bring them back to their allegiance. He sent two of his people, therefore, who were most intimate with the rebels, to inform them of the recent arrival of Escobar with letters from the Governor of Hispaniola, promising him a speedy deliverance from the island. He now offered a free pardon, kind treatment, and a passage with him in the expected ships, on condition of their immediate return to obedience. To convince them of the arrival of the vessel, he sent them a part of the bacon which had been brought by Escobar.

On the approach of these ambassadors, Francisco de Porras came forth to meet them, accompanied solely by a few of the ringleaders of his party. He imagined that there might be some propositions from the admiral, and he was fearful of their being heard by the mass of his people, who, in their dissatisfied and repentant mood, would be likely to desert him on the least prospect of pardon. Having listened to the tidings and overtures brought by the messengers, he and his confidential confederates consulted for some time together. Perfidious in their own nature, they suspected the sincerity of the admiral; and conscious of the extent of their offences, doubted his having the magnanimity to pardon them. Determined, therefore, not to confide in his proffered amnesty,

they replied to the messengers that they had no wish to return
to the ships, but preferred living at large about the island. They
offered to engage, however, to conduct themselves peaceably and
amicably, on receiving a solemn promise from the admiral, that
should two vessels arrive, they should have one to depart in;
should but one arrive, that half of it should be granted to them; and
that, moreover, the admiral should share with them the stores and
articles of Indian traffic remaining in the ships, having lost all that
they had in the sea. These demands were pronounced extravagant
and inadmissible, upon which they replied insolently that if they
were not peaceably conceded, they would take them by force; and
with this menace they dismissed the ambassadors.[*]

This conference was not conducted so privately but that the rest
of the rebels learnt the purport of the mission; and the offer of
pardon and deliverance occasioned great tumult and agitation.
Porras, fearful of their desertion, assured them that these offers of
the admiral were all deceitful; that he was naturally cruel and
vindictive, and only sought to get them into his power to wreak on
them his vengeance. He exhorted them to persist in their opposition to his tyranny, reminding them that those who had formerly
done so in Hispaniola had eventually triumphed, and sent him
home in irons; he assured them that they might do the same; and
again made vaunting promises of protection in Spain, through the
influence of his relatives. But the boldest of his assertions was with
respect to the caravel of Escobar. It shows the ignorance of the age,
and the superstitious awe which the common people entertained
with respect to Columbus and his astronomical knowledge. Porras
assured them that no real caravel had arrived, but a mere phantasm
conjured up by the admiral, who was deeply versed in necromancy.
In proof of this, he adverted to its arriving in the dusk of the
evening, its holding communication 'with no one but the admiral',
and its sudden disappearance in the night. Had it been a real caravel,
the crew would have sought to talk with their countrymen; the
admiral, his son and brother, would have eagerly embarked on
board, and it would at any rate have remained a little while in port,
and not have vanished so suddenly and mysteriously.[†]

By these and similar delusions, Porras succeeded in working
upon the feelings and credulity of his followers. Fearful, however,

---

[*] Las Casas, lib. ii. cap. 35; *Hist. del Almirante*, cap. 106.
[†] *Hist. del Almirante*, cap. 106; Las Casas, lib. ii. cap. 35.

that they might yield to after reflection, and to further offers from the admiral, he determined to involve them in some act of violence which would commit them beyond all hopes of forgiveness. He marched them, therefore, to an Indian village called Maima,* about a quarter of a league from the ships, intending to plunder the stores remaining on board the wreck, and to take the admiral prisoner.†

Columbus had notice of the designs of the rebels, and of their approach. Being confined by his infirmities, he sent his brother to endeavour with mild words to persuade them from their purpose and win them to obedience, but with sufficient force to resist any violence. The Adelantado, who was a man rather of deeds than of words, took with him fifty followers, men of tried resolution, and ready to fight in any cause. They were well armed and full of courage, though many were pale and debilitated from recent sickness, and from long confinement to the ships. Arriving on the side of a hill, within a bow-shot of the village, the Adelantado discovered the rebels, and despatched the same two messengers to treat with them who had already carried them the offer of pardon. Porras and his fellow-leaders, however, would not permit them to approach. They confided in the superiority of their numbers, and in their men being, for the most part, hardy sailors, rendered robust and vigorous by the roving life they had been leading in the forests and the open air. They knew that many of those who were with the Adelantado were men brought up in a softer mode of life. They pointed to their pale countenances, and persuaded their followers that they were mere household men, fair-weather troops, who could never stand before them. They did not reflect that, with such men, pride and lofty spirit often more than supply the place of bodily force, and they forgot that their adversaries had the incalculable advantage of justice and law upon their side. Deluded by their words, their followers were excited to a transient glow of courage, and brandishing their weapons, refused to listen to the messengers.

Six of the stoutest rebels made a league to stand by one another and attack the Adelantado; for, he being killed, the rest would be easily defeated. The main body formed themselves into a squadron, drawing their swords and shaking their lances. They did not wait to be assailed, but uttering shouts and menaces, rushed upon the enemy. They were so well received, however, that at the

* At present Mammee Bay.
† *Hist. del Almirante*, ubi sup.

first shock four or five were killed, most of them the confederates
who had leagued to attack the Adelantado. The latter, with his own
hand, killed Juan Sanchez, the same powerful mariner who had
carried off the cacique Quibian; and Juan Barber also, who had first
drawn a sword against the admiral in this rebellion. The Adelantado with his usual vigour and courage was dealing his blows about
him in the thickest of the affray, where several lay killed and
wounded, when he was assailed by Francisco de Porras. The rebel
with a blow of his sword cleft the buckler of Don Bartholomew,
and wounded the hand which grasped it. The sword remained
wedged in the shield, and before Porras could withdraw it, the
Adelantado closed upon him, grappled him, and being assisted by
others, after a severe struggle took him prisoner.*

When the rebels beheld their leader a captive, their transient
courage was at an end, and they fled in confusion. The Adelantado
would have pursued them, but was persuaded to let them escape
with the punishment they had received; especially as it was necessary to guard against the possibility of an attack from the Indians.

The latter had taken arms and drawn up in battle array, gazing
with astonishment at this fight between white men, but without
taking part on either side. When the battle was over, they approached the field, gazing upon the dead bodies of the beings they
had once fancied immortal. They were curious in examining the
wounds made by the Christian weapons. Among the wounded
insurgents was Pedro Ledesma, the same pilot who so bravely
swam ashore at Veragua, to procure tidings of the colony. He was
a man of prodigious muscular force and a hoarse deep voice. As the
Indians, who thought him dead, were inspecting the wounds with
which he was literally covered, he suddenly uttered an ejaculation
in his tremendous voice, at the sound of which the savages fled in
dismay. This man, having fallen into a cleft or ravine, was not
discovered by the white men until the dawning of the following
day, having remained all that time without a drop of water. The
number and severity of the wounds he is said to have received
would seem incredible, but they are mentioned by Fernando
Columbus, who was an eye-witness, and by Las Casas, who had
the account from Ledesma himself. For want of proper remedies,
his wounds were treated in the roughest manner, yet, through the

* *Hist. del Almirante*, cap. 107; Las Casas, *Hist. Ind.*, lib ii. cap. 35.

aid of a vigorous constitution, he completely recovered. Las Casas conversed with him several years afterwards at Seville, when he obtained from him various particulars concerning this voyage of Columbus. Some few days after this conversation, however, he heard that Ledesma had fallen under the knife of an assassin.[*]

The Adelantado returned in triumph to the ships, where he was received by the admiral in the most affectionate manner, thanking him as his deliverer. He brought Porras and several of his followers prisoners. Of his own party only two had been wounded; himself in the hand, and the admiral's steward, who had received an apparently slight wound with a lance, equal to one of the most insignificant of those with which Ledesma was covered; yet, in spite of careful treatment, he died.

On the next day, the 20th of May, the fugitives sent a petition to the admiral, signed with all their names, in which, says Las Casas, they confessed all their misdeeds, and cruelties, and evil intentions, supplicating the admiral to have pity on them and pardon them for their rebellion, for which God had already punished them. They offered to return to their obedience and to serve him faithfully in future, making an oath to that effect upon a cross and a missal, accompanied by an imprecation worthy of being recorded: 'They hoped, should they break their oath, that no priest nor other Christian might ever confess them; that repentance might be of no avail; that they might be deprived of the holy sacraments of the Church; that at their death they might receive no benefit from bulls nor indulgences; that their bodies might be cast out into the fields like those of heretics and renegadoes, instead of being buried in holy ground; and that they might not receive absolution from the Pope, nor from cardinals, nor archbishops, nor bishops, nor any other Christian priests.'[†] Such were the awful imprecations by which these men endeavoured to add validity to an oath. The worthlessness of a man's word may always be known by the extravagant means he uses to enforce it.

The admiral saw, by the abject nature of this petition, how completely the spirit of these misguided men was broken; with his wonted magnanimity, he readily granted their prayer and pardoned their offences; but on one condition, that their ringleader, Francisco Porras, should remain a prisoner.

[*] Las Casas, *Hist. Ind.*, lib. ii. cap. 35.
[†] Las Casas, *Hist. Ind.*, lib. ii. cap. 32.

As it was difficult to maintain so many persons on board of the ships, and as quarrels might take place between persons who had so recently been at blows, Columbus put the late followers of Porras under the command of a discreet and faithful man; and giving in his charge a quantity of European articles for the purpose of purchasing food of the natives, directed him to forage about the island until the expected vessels should arrive.

At length, after a long year of alternate hope and despondency, the doubts of the Spaniards were joyfully dispelled by the sight of two vessels standing into the harbour. One proved to be a ship hired and well victualled, at the expense of the admiral, by the faithful and indefatigable Diego Mendez; the other had been subsequently fitted out by Ovando, and put under the command of Diego de Salcedo, the admiral's agent employed to collect his rents in San Domingo.

The long neglect of Ovando to attend to the relief of Columbus had, it seems, roused the public indignation, insomuch that animadversions had been made upon his conduct even in the pulpits. This is affirmed by Las Casas, who was at San Domingo at the time. If the governor had really entertained hopes that, during the delay of relief, Columbus might perish in the island, the report brought back by Escobar must have completely disappointed him. No time was to be lost if he wished to claim any merit in his deliverance, or to avoid the disgrace of having totally neglected him. He exerted himself, therefore, at the eleventh hour, and despatched a caravel at the same time with the ship sent by Diego Mendez. The latter, having faithfully discharged this part of his mission, and seen the ships depart, proceeded to Spain on the further concerns of the admiral.[*]

---

[*] Some brief notice of the further fortunes of Diego Mendez may be interesting to the reader. When King Ferdinand heard of his faithful services, says Oviedo, he bestowed rewards upon Mendez, and permitted him to bear a canoe in his coat of arms, as a memento of his loyalty. He continued devotedly attached to the admiral, serving him zealously after his return to Spain, and during his last illness. Columbus retained the most grateful and affectionate sense of his fidelity. On his death-bed he promised Mendez that, in reward for his services, he should be appointed principal Alguazil of the island of Hispaniola; an engagement which the admiral's son, Don Diego, who was present, cheerfully undertook to perform. A few years afterwards, when the latter succeeded to the office of his father, Mendez reminded him of the promise, but Don Diego informed him that he had given the office to his uncle Don Bartholomew; he assured him, however, that he should receive something equivalent. Mendez shrewdly replied, that the equivalent had better be given

BOOK 17

CHAPTER I

1503

Before relating the return of Columbus to Hispaniola, it is proper to notice some of the principal occurrences which took place in that island under the government of Ovando. A great crowd of adventurers of various ranks had thronged his fleet – eager

---

to Don Bartholomew, and the office to himself, according to agreement. The promise, however, remained unperformed, and Diego Mendez unrewarded. He was afterwards engaged on voyages of discovery in vessels of his own, but met with many vicissitudes, and appears to have died in impoverished circumstances. His last will, from which these particulars are principally gathered, was dated in Valladolid, the 19th of June 1536, by which it is evident he must have been in the prime of life at the time of his voyage with the admiral. In this will he requested that the reward which had been promised to him should be paid to his children, by making his eldest son principal Alguazil for life of the city of San Domingo, and his other son lieutenant to the admiral for the same city. It does not appear whether this request was complied with under the successors of Don Diego.

In another clause of his will, he desired that a large stone should be placed upon his sepulchre, on which should be engraved, 'Here lies the honourable Cavalier Diego Mendez, who served greatly the royal crown of Spain, in the conquest of the Indies, with the admiral Don Christopher Columbus, of glorious memory, who made the discovery; and afterwards by himself, with ships at his own cost. He died, etc., etc. Bestow in charity a Paternoster, and an Ave Maria.'

He ordered that in the midst of this stone there should be carved an Indian canoe, as given him by the king for armorial bearings in memorial of his voyage from Jamaica to Hispaniola, and above it should be engraved in large letters the word 'CANOA'. He enjoined upon his heirs to be loyal to the Admiral (Don Diego Columbus) and his lady, and gave them much ghostly counsel, mingled with pious benedictions. As an heirloom in his family, he bequeathed his library, consisting of a few volumes, which accompanied him in his wanderings; viz. *The Art of Holy Dying*, by Erasmus; a sermon of the same author, in Spanish; the *Lingua*, and the *Colloquies* of the same; the *History* of Josephus; the *Moral Philosophy* of Aristotle; the *Book of the Holy Land*; a book called *The Contemplation of the Passion of our Saviour*; a tract on the *Vengeance of the Death of Agamemnon*, and several other short treatises. This curious and characteristic testament is in the archives of the Duke of Veragua in Madrid.

speculators, credulous dreamers, and broken-down gentlemen of desperate fortunes; all expecting to enrich themselves suddenly in an island where gold was to be picked up from the surface of the soil, or gathered from the mountain-brooks. They had scarcely landed, says Las Casas, who accompanied the expedition, when they all hurried off to the mines, about eight leagues distant. The roads swarmed like ant-hills, with adventurers of all classes. Everyone had his knapsack stored with biscuit or flour, and his mining implements on his shoulders. Those hidalgos, or gentlemen, who had no servants to carry their burdens, bore them on their own backs, and lucky was he who had a horse for the journey; he would be able to bring back the greater load of treasure. They all set out in high spirits, eager who should first reach the golden land; thinking they had but to arrive at the mines, and collect riches; 'for they fancied,' says Las Casas, 'that gold was to be gathered as easily and readily as fruit from the trees.' When they arrived, however, they discovered, to their dismay, that it was necessary to dig painfully into the bowels of the earth – a labour to which most of them had never been accustomed; that it required experience and sagacity to detect the veins of ore; that, in fact, the whole process of mining was exceedingly toilsome, demanded vast patience and much experience, and, after all, was full of uncertainty. They digged eagerly for a time, but found no ore. They grew hungry, threw by their implements, sat down to eat, and then returned to work. It was all in vain. 'Their labour,' says Las Casas, 'gave them a keen appetite and quick digestion, but no gold.' They soon consumed their provisions, exhausted their patience, cursed their infatuation, and in eight days set off drearily on their return along the roads they had lately trod so exultingly. They arrived at San Domingo without an ounce of gold, half-famished, downcast, and despairing.* Such is too often the case of those who ignorantly engage in mining – of all speculations the most brilliant, promising, and fallacious.

Poverty soon fell upon these misguided men. They exhausted the little property brought from Spain. Many suffered extremely from hunger, and were obliged to exchange even their apparel for bread. Some formed connections with the old settlers of the island; but the greater part were like men lost and bewildered, and just

* Las Casas, *Hist. Ind.*, lib. ii. cap. 6.

awakened from a dream. The miseries of the mind, as usual, heightened the sufferings of the body. Some wasted away and died broken-hearted; others were hurried off by raging fevers, so that there soon perished upwards of a thousand men.

Ovando was reputed a man of great prudence and sagacity, and he certainly took several judicious measures for the regulation of the island, and the relief of the colonists. He made arrangements for distributing the married persons and the families which had come out in his fleet, in four towns in the interior, granting them important privileges. He revived the drooping zeal for mining, by reducing the royal share of the product from one-half to a third, and shortly after to a fifth; but he empowered the Spaniards to avail themselves, in the most oppressive manner, of the labour of the unhappy natives in working the mines. The charge of treating the natives with severity had been one of those chiefly urged against Columbus. It is proper, therefore, to notice, in this respect, the conduct of his successor, a man chosen for his prudence and his supposed capacity to govern.

It will be recollected, that when Columbus was in a manner compelled to assign lands to the rebellious followers of Francisco Roldan, in 1499, he had made an arrangement that the caciques in their vicinity should, in lieu of tribute, furnish a number of their subjects to assist them in cultivating their estates. This, as has been observed, was the commencement of the disastrous system of repartimientos, or distributions of Indians. When Bobadilla administered the government, he constrained the caciques to furnish a certain number of Indians to each Spaniard, for the purpose of working the mines; where they were employed like beasts of burden. He made an enumeration of the natives, to prevent evasion, reduced them into classes, and distributed them among the Spanish inhabitants. The enormous oppressions which ensued have been noticed. They roused the indignation of Isabella, and when Ovando was sent out to supersede Bobadilla, in 1502, the natives were pronounced free; they immediately refused to labour in the mines.

Ovando represented to the Spanish sovereigns, in 1503, that ruinous consequences resulted to the colony from this entire liberty granted to the Indians. He stated that the tribute could not be collected, for the Indians were lazy and improvident; that they could only be kept from vices and irregularities by occupation; that they now kept aloof from the Spaniards, and from all instruction in the Christian faith.

The last representation had an influence with Isabella, and drew a letter from the sovereigns to Ovando, in 1503, in which he was ordered to spare no pains to attach the natives to the Spanish nation and the Catholic religion; to make them labour moderately, if absolutely essential to their own good, but to temper authority with persuasion and kindness; to pay them regularly and fairly for their labour, and to have them instructed in religion on certain days.

Ovando availed himself of the powers given him by this letter to their fullest extent. He assigned to each Castilian a certain number of Indians, according to the quality of the applicant, the nature of the application, or his own pleasure. It was arranged in the form of an order on a cacique for a certain number of Indians, who were to be paid by their employer, and instructed in the Catholic faith. The pay was so small as to be little better than nominal; the instruction was little more than the mere ceremony of baptism; and the term of labour was at first six months, and then eight months in the year. Under cover of this hired labour, intended for the good both of their bodies and their souls, more intolerable toil was exacted from them, and more horrible cruelties were inflicted, than in the worst days of Bobadilla. They were separated often the distance of several days' journey from their wives and children, and doomed to intolerable labour of all kinds, extorted by the cruel infliction of the lash. For food they had the cassava bread, an unsubstantial support for men obliged to labour; sometimes a scanty portion of pork was distributed among a great number of them, scarce a mouthful to each. When the Spaniards who superintended the mines were at their repast, says Las Casas, the famished Indians scrambled under the table, like dogs, for any bone thrown to them. After they had gnawed and sucked it, they pounded it between stones and mixed it with their cassava bread, that nothing of so precious a morsel might be lost. As to those who laboured in the fields, they never tasted either flesh or fish; a little cassava bread and a few roots were their support. While the Spaniards thus withheld the nourishment necessary to sustain their health and strength, they exacted a degree of labour sufficient to break down the most vigorous man. If the

Indians fled from this incessant toil and barbarous coercion, and took refuge in the mountains, they were hunted out like wild beasts, scourged in the most inhuman manner, and laden with chains to prevent a second escape. Many perished long before their term of labour had expired. Those who survived their term of six or eight months were permitted to return to their homes, until the next term commenced. But their homes were often forty, sixty, and eighty leagues distant. They had nothing to sustain them through the journey but a few roots or agi peppers, or a little cassava bread. Worn down by long toil and cruel hardships, which their feeble constitutions were incapable of sustaining, many had not strength to perform the journey, but sank down and died by the way; some by the side of a brook, others under the shade of a tree, where they had crawled for shelter from the sun. 'I have found many dead in the road,' says Las Casas, 'others gasping under the trees, and others in the pangs of death, faintly crying, Hunger! hunger!'* Those who reached their homes most commonly found them desolate. During the eight months they had been absent, their wives and children had either perished or wandered away; the fields on which they depended for food were overrun with weeds, and nothing was left them but to lie down, exhausted and despairing, and die at the threshold of their habitations.†

It is impossible to pursue any further the picture drawn by the venerable Las Casas, not of what he had heard, but of what he had seen; nature and humanity revolt at the details. Suffice it to say that so intolerable were the toils and sufferings inflicted upon this weak and unoffending race, that they sank under them, dissolving, as it were, from the face of the earth. Many killed themselves in despair, and even mothers overcame the powerful instinct of nature, and destroyed the infants at their breasts, to spare them a life of wretchedness. Twelve years had not elapsed since the discovery of the island, and several hundred thousand of its native inhabitants had perished, miserable victims to the grasping avarice of the white men.

---

* Las Casas, *Hist. Ind.*, lib. ii. cap. 14, MS.
† Idem.

The sufferings of the natives under the civil policy of Ovando have been briefly shown; it remains to give a concise view of the military operations of this commander, so lauded by certain of the early historians for his prudence. By this notice a portion of the eventful history of this island will be recounted which is connected with the fortunes of Columbus, and which comprises the thorough subjugation, and, it may also be said, extermination of the native inhabitants. And first, we must treat of the disasters of the beautiful province of Xaragua, the seat of hospitality, the refuge of the suffering Spaniards; and of the fate of the female cacique, Anacaona, once the pride of the island, and the generous friend of white men.

Behechio, the ancient cacique of this province, being dead, Anacaona, his sister, had succeeded to the government. The marked partiality which she once manifested for the Spaniards had been greatly weakened by the general misery they had produced in her country, and by the brutal profligacy exhibited in her immediate dominions by the followers of Roldan. The unhappy story of the loves of her beautiful daughter Higuenamota, with the young Spaniard Hernando de Guevara, had also caused her great affliction; and, finally, the various and enduring hardships inflicted on her once happy subjects by the grinding systems of labour enforced by Bobadilla and Ovando, had at length, it is said, converted her friendship into absolute detestation.

This disgust was kept alive and aggravated by the Spaniards who lived in her immediate neighbourhood, and had obtained grants of land there; a remnant of the rebel faction of Roldan, who retained the gross licentiousness and open profligacy in which they had been indulged under the loose misrule of that commander, and who made themselves odious to the inferior caciques, by exacting services tyrannically and capriciously under the baneful system of repartimientos.

The Indians of this province were uniformly represented as a more intelligent, polite, and generous-spirited race than any others of the islands. They were the more prone to feel and resent the overbearing treatment to which they were subjected. Quarrels sometimes took place between the caciques and their oppressors. These were immediately reported to the governor as dangerous mutinies; and a resistance to any capricious and extortionate exaction was magnified into a rebellious resistance to the authority of government. Complaints of this kind were continually pouring in upon Ovando, until he was persuaded by some alarmist, or some designing mischief-maker, that there was a deep-laid conspiracy among the Indians of this province to rise upon the Spaniards.

Ovando immediately set out for Xaragua at the head of three hundred foot-soldiers, armed with swords, arquebuses, and cross-bows, and seventy horsemen, with cuirasses, bucklers, and lances. He pretended that he was going on a mere visit of friendship to Anacaona, and to make arrangements about the payment of tribute.

When Anacaona heard of the intended visit, she summoned all her tributary caciques, and principal subjects, to assemble at her chief town, that they might receive the commander of the Spaniards with becoming homage and distinction. As Ovando, at the head of his little army, approached, she went forth to meet him, according to the custom of her nation, attended by a great train of her most distinguished subjects, male and female; who, as has been before observed, were noted for superior grace and beauty. They received the Spaniards with their popular areytos, their national songs; the young women waving palm branches and dancing before them, in the way that had so much charmed the followers of the Adelantado, on his first visit to the province.

Anacaona treated the governor with that natural graciousness and dignity for which she was celebrated. She gave him the largest house in the place for his residence, and his people were quartered in the houses adjoining. For several days the Spaniards were entertained with all the natural luxuries that the province afforded. National songs and dances and games were performed for their amusement, and there was every outward demonstration of the same hospitality, the same amity, that Anacaona had uniformly shown to white men.

Notwithstanding all this kindness, and notwithstanding her uniform integrity of conduct, and open generosity of character, Ovando was persuaded that Anacaoua was secretly meditating a massacre of himself and his followers. Historians tell us nothing of the grounds for such a belief. It was too probably produced by the misrepresentations of the unprincipled adventurers who infested the province. Ovando should have paused and reflected before he acted upon it. He should have considered the improbability of such an attempt by naked Indians against so large a force of steel-clad troops, armed with European weapons: and he should have reflected upon the general character and conduct of Anacaona. At any rate, the example set repeatedly by Columbus and his brother the Adelantado should have convinced him that it was a sufficient safeguard against the machinations of the natives to seize upon their caciques and detain them as hostages. The policy of Ovando, however, was of a more rash and sanguinary nature; he acted upon suspicion as upon conviction. He determined to anticipate the alleged plot by a counter-artifice, and to overwhelm this defenceless people in an indiscriminate and bloody vengeance.

As the Indians had entertained their guests with various national games, Ovando invited them in return to witness certain games of his country. Among these was a tilting match or joust with reeds; a chivalrous game which the Spaniards had learnt from the Moors of Granada. The Spanish cavalry, in those days, were as remarkable for the skilful management, as for the ostentatious caparison of their horses. Among the troops brought out from Spain by Ovando, one horseman had disciplined his horse to prance and curvet in time to the music of a viol.[*] The joust was appointed to take place of a Sunday after dinner, in the public square, before the house where Ovando was quartered. The cavalry and foot-soldiers had their secret instructions. The former were to parade, not merely with reeds or blunted tilting lances, but with weapons of a more deadly character. The foot-soldiers were to come apparently as mere spectators, but likewise armed and ready for action at a concerted signal.

At the appointed time the square was crowded with the Indians, waiting to see this military spectacle. The caciques were assembled

* Las Casas, lib. ii. cap. 9.

in the house of Ovando, which looked upon the square. None were armed; an unreserved confidence prevailed among them, totally incompatible with the dark treachery of which they were accused. To prevent all suspicion, and take off all appearance of sinister design, Ovando, after dinner, was playing at quoits with some of his principal officers, when the cavalry having arrived in the square, the caciques begged the governor to order the joust to commence.[*] Anacaona, and her beautiful daughter Higuena-mota, with several of her female attendants, were present and joined in the request.

Ovando left his game and came forward to a conspicuous place. When he saw that everything was disposed according to his orders, he gave the fatal signal. Some say it was by taking hold of a piece of gold which was suspended about his neck,[†] others by laying his hand on the cross of Alcantara, which was embroidered on his habit.[‡] A trumpet was immediately sounded. The house in which Anacaona and all the principal caciques were assembled was surrounded by soldiery, commanded by Diego Velasquez and Rodrigo Mexiatrillo, and no one was permitted to escape. They entered, and seizing upon the caciques, bound them to the posts which supported the roof. Anacaona was led forth a prisoner. The unhappy caciques were then put to horrible tortures, until some of them, in the extremity of anguish, were made to accuse their queen and themselves of the plot with which they were charged. When this cruel mockery of judicial form had been executed, instead of preserving them for after-examination, fire was set to the house, and all the caciques perished miserably in the flames.

While these barbarities were practised upon the chieftains, a horrible massacre took place among the populace. At the signal of Ovando, the horsemen rushed into the midst of the naked and defenceless throng, trampling them under the hoofs of their steeds, cutting them down with their swords, and transfixing them with their spears. No mercy was shown to age or sex; it was a savage and indiscriminate butchery. Now and then a Spanish horseman, either through an emotion of pity or an impulse of avarice, caught up a child to bear it off in safety; but it was

---

[*] Oviedo, *Cronica de las Indias*, lib. iii. cap. 12.

[†] Las Casas, *Hist. Ind.*, lib. ii. cap. 9.

[‡] Charlevoix, *Hist. San Domingo*, lib. xxiv. p. 235.

barbarously pierced by the lances of his companions. Humanity turns with horror from such atrocities, and would fain discredit them; but they are circumstantially and still more minutely recorded by the venerable bishop Las Casas, who was resident in the island at the time, and conversant with the principal actors in this tragedy. He may have coloured the picture strongly, in his usual indignation when the wrongs of the Indians are in question; yet, from all concurring accounts, and from many precise facts which speak for themselves, the scene must have been most sanguinary and atrocious. Oviedo, who is loud in extolling the justice, and devotion, and charity, and meekness of Ovando, and his kind treatment of the Indians, and who visited the province of Xaragua a few years afterwards, records several of the preceding circumstances; especially the cold-blooded game of quoits played by the governor on the verge of such a horrible scene, and the burning of the caciques to the number, he says, of more than forty. Diego Mendez, who was at Xaragua at the time, and doubtless present on such an important occasion, says incidentally, in his last will and testament, that there were eighty-four caciques either burnt or hanged.[*] Las Casas says that there were eighty who entered the house with Anacaona. The slaughter of the multitude must have been great; and this was inflicted on an unarmed and unresisting throng. Several who escaped from the massacre fled in their canoes to an island about eight leagues distant, called Guanabo. They were pursued and taken, and condemned to slavery.

As to the princess Anacaona, she was carried in chains to San Domingo. The mockery of a trial was given her, in which she was found guilty on the confessions wrung by tortures from her subjects, and on the testimony of their butchers; and she was ignominiously hanged in the presence of the people whom she had so long and so signally befriended.[†] Oviedo has sought to throw a stigma on the character of this unfortunate princess, accusing her of great licentiousness; but he was prone to criminate the character of the native princes who fell victims to the ingratitude and injustice of his countrymen. Contemporary writers of greater authority have concurred in representing Anacaona as remarkable for her native propriety and dignity. She was adored by her subjects, so as to hold

---

[*] Relacion hecha por Don Diego Mendez; Navarrete, *Colec.*, tom. i. p. 314.

[†] Oviedo, *Cronica de las Indias*, lib. iii. cap. 12; Las Casas, *Hist. Ind.*, lib. ii. cap. 9.

a kind of dominion over them even during the lifetime of her brother; she is said to have been skilled in composing the areytos, or legendary ballads of her nation, and may have conduced much towards producing that superior degree of refinement remarked among her people. Her grace and beauty had made her renowned throughout the island, and had excited the admiration both of the savage and the Spaniard. Her magnanimous spirit was evinced in her amicable treatment of the white men, although her husband, the brave Caonabo, had perished a prisoner in their hands; and defence-less parties of them had been repeatedly in her power, and lived at large in her dominions. After having, for several years, neglected all safe opportunities of vengeance, she fell a victim to the absurd charge of having conspired against an armed body of nearly four hundred men, seventy of them horsemen; a force sufficient to have subjugated large armies of naked Indians.

After the massacre of Xaragua, the destruction of its inhabitants still continued. The favourite nephew of Anacaona, the cacique Guaora, who had fled to the mountains, was hunted like a wild beast, until he was taken, and likewise hanged. For six months the Spaniards continued ravaging the country with horse and foot, under pretext of quelling insurrections; for wherever the affrighted natives took refuge in their despair, herding in dismal caverns and in the fastnesses of the mountains, they were represented as assembling in arms to make a head of rebellion. Having at length hunted them out of their retreats, destroyed many, and reduced the survivors to the most deplorable misery and abject submission, the whole of that part of the island was considered as restored to good order; and in commemoration of this great triumph, Ovando founded a town near to the lake, which he called Santa Maria de la Verdadera Paz (St Mary of the True Peace).*

Such is the tragical history of the delightful region of Xaragua, and of its amiable and hospitable people – a place which the Europ-eans, by their own account, found a perfect paradise, but which, by their vile passions, they filled with horror and desolation.

---

* Oviedo, *Cronica de las Indias*, lib. iii. cap. 12.

The subjugation of four of the Indian sovereignties of Hispaniola, and the disastrous fate of their caciques, have been already related. Under the administration of Ovando was also accomplished the downfall of Higuey, the last of those independent districts; a fertile province which comprised the eastern extremity of the island.

The people of Higuey were of a more warlike spirit than those of the other provinces, having learned the effectual use of their weapons from frequent contests with their Carib invaders. They were governed by a cacique named Cotabanama. Las Casas describes this chieftain from actual observation, and draws the picture of a native hero. He was, he says, the strongest of his tribe, and more perfectly formed than one man in a thousand of any nation whatever. He was taller in stature than the tallest of his countrymen, a yard in breadth from shoulder to shoulder, and the rest of his body in admirable proportion. His aspect was not handsome, but grave and courageous. His bow was not easily bent by a common man; his arrows were three-pronged, tipped with the bones of fishes, and his weapons appeared to be intended for a giant. In a word, he was so nobly proportioned, as to be the admiration even of the Spaniards.

While Columbus was engaged in his fourth voyage, and shortly after the accession of Ovando to office, there was an insurrection of this cacique and his people. A shallop, with eight Spaniards, was surprised at the small island of Saona, adjacent to Higuey, and all the crew slaughtered. This was in revenge for the death of a cacique, torn to pieces by a dog wantonly set upon him by a Spaniard, and for which the natives had in vain sued for redress.

Ovando immediately despatched Juan de Esquibel, a courageous officer, at the head of four hundred men, to quell the insurrection, and punish the massacre. Cotabanama assembled his warriors, and prepared for vigorous resistance. Distrustful of the mercy of the Spaniards, the chieftain rejected all overtures of peace, and the war was prosecuted with some advantage to the natives. The Indians had now overcome their superstitious awe of the white men as supernatural beings, and though they could ill withstand the superiority of European arms, they manifested a courage and dexterity that rendered them enemies not to be despised. Las Casas and other historians relate a bold and romantic encounter between a single Indian and two mounted cavaliers named Valtenebro and Portevedra, in which the Indian, though pierced through the body by the lances and swords of both his assailants, retained his fierceness, and continued the combat, until he fell dead in the possession of all their weapons.* This gallant action, says Las Casas, was public and notorious.

The Indians were soon defeated and driven to their mountain retreats. The Spaniards pursued them into their recesses, discovered their wives and children, wreaked on them the most indiscriminate slaughter, and committed their chieftains to the flames. An aged female cacique of great distinction, named Higuanama, being taken prisoner, was hanged.

A detachment was sent in a caravel to the island of Saona, to take particular vengeance for the destruction of the shallop and its crew. The natives made a desperate defence and fled. The island was mountainous, and full of caverns, in which the Indians vainly sought for refuge. Six or seven hundred were imprisoned in a dwelling, and all put to the sword or poniarded. Those of the inhabitants who were spared were carried off as slaves; and the island was left desolate and deserted.

The natives of Higuey were driven to despair, seeing that there was no escape for them even in the bowels of the earth:† they sued for peace, which was granted them, and protection promised on condition of their cultivating a large tract of land, and paying a great quantity of bread in tribute. The peace being concluded, Cotabanama visited the Spanish camp, where his gigantic proportions and martial demeanour made him an object of curiosity and admiration. He was received with great distinction by Esquibel, and they exchanged names; an Indian league of fraternity and

* Las Casas, *Hist. Ind.*, lib. ii. cap. 8.
† Idem.

perpetual friendship. The natives thenceforward called the cacique
Juan de Esquibel, and the Spanish commander Cotabanama. Esquibel then built a wooden fortress in an Indian village near the sea,
and left in it nine men, with a captain named Martin de Villaman.
After this, the troops dispersed, every man returning home with
his proportion of slaves gained in this expedition.

The pacification was not of long continuance, About the time
that succours were sent to Columbus, to rescue him from the
wrecks of his vessels at Jamaica, a new revolt broke out in Higuey,
in consequence of the oppressions of the Spaniards and a violation
of the treaty made by Esquibel. Martin de Villaman demanded that
the natives should not only raise the grain stipulated for by the
treaty, but convey it to San Domingo, and he treated them with
the greatest severity on their refusal. He connived also at the
licentious conduct of his men towards the Indian women, the
Spaniards often taking from the natives their daughters and sisters,
and even their wives.* The Indians, roused at last to fury, rose on
their tyrants, slaughtered them, and burnt their wooden fortress to
the ground. Only one of the Spaniards escaped, and bore the
tidings of this catastrophe to the city of San Domingo.

Ovando gave immediate orders to carry fire and sword into the
province of Higuey. The Spanish troops mustered from various
quarters on the confines of that province, when Juan de Esquibel
took the command, and had a great number of Indians with him
as allies. The towns of Higuey were generally built among the
mountains. Those mountains rose in terraces, from ten to fifteeen
leagues in length and breadth; rough and rocky, interspersed with
glens of a red soil, remarkably fertile, where they raised their
cassava bread. The ascent from terrace to terrace was about fifty
feet, steep and precipitous, formed of the living rock, and resembling a wall wrought with tools into rough diamond points. Each
village had four wide streets, a stone's throw in length, forming a
cross, the trees being cleared away from them, and from a public
square in the centre.

When the Spanish troops arrived on the frontiers, alarm-fires
along the mountains and columns of smoke spread the intelligence
by night and day. The old men, the women, and children were
sent off to the forests and caverns, and the warriors prepared for

* Las Casas, *Hist. Ind.*, lib. ii. cap. 8.

battle. The Castilians paused in one of the plains clear of forests, where their horses could be of use. They made prisoners of several of the natives, and tried to learn from them the plans and forces of the enemy. They applied tortures for the purpose, but in vain, so devoted was the loyalty of these people to their caciques. The Spaniards penetrated into the interior. They found the warriors of several towns assembled in one, and drawn up in the streets with their bows and arrows, but perfectly naked, and without defensive armour. They uttered tremendous yells, and discharged a shower of arrows; but from such a distance that they fell short of their foe. The Spaniards replied with their crossbows, and with two or three arquebuses, for at this time they had but few firearms. When the Indians saw several of their comrades fall dead, they took to flight, rarely waiting for the attack with swords: some of the wounded, in whose bodies the arrows from the cross-bows had penetrated to the very feather, drew them out with their hands, broke them with their teeth, and hurling them at the Spaniards with impotent fury, fell dead upon the spot.

The whole force of the Indians was routed and dispersed, each family or band of neighbours fled in its own direction, and concealed itself in the fastness of the mountains. The Spaniards pursued them, but found the chase difficult amidst the close forests, and the broken and stony heights. They took several prisoners as guides, and inflicted incredible torments on them, to compel them to betray their countrymen. They drove them before them, secured by cords fastened round their necks; and some of them, as they passed along the brinks of precipices, suddenly threw themselves headlong down, in hopes of dragging after them the Spaniards. When at length the pursuers came upon the unhappy Indians in their concealments, they spared neither age nor sex; even pregnant women, and mothers with infants in their arms, fell beneath their merciless swords. The cold-blooded acts of cruelty which followed this first slaughter would be shocking to relate.

Hence Esquibel marched to attack the town where Cotabanama resided, and where that cacique had collected a great force to resist him. He proceeded direct for the place along the sea-coast, and came to where two roads led up the mountain to the town. One of the roads was open and inviting, the branches of the trees being lopped, and all the underwood cleared away. Here the Indians had stationed an ambuscade to take the Spaniards in the rear. The other road was almost closed up by trees and bushes cut down and thrown across each other. Esquibel was wary and distrustful; he suspected the stratagem, and chose the encumbered road. The town was about a league and a half from the sea. The Spaniards made their way with great difficulty for the first half league. The rest of the road was free from all embarrassment, which confirmed their suspicion of a stratagem. They now advanced with great rapidity, and, having arrived near the village, suddenly turned into the other road, took the party in ambush by surprise, and made great havoc among them with their crossbows.

The warriors now sallied from their concealment, others rushed out of the houses into the streets, and discharged flights of arrows, but from such a distance as generally to fall harmless. They then approached nearer and hurled stones with their hands, being unacquainted with the use of slings. Instead of being dismayed at seeing their companions fall, it rather increased their fury. An irregular battle, probably little else than wild skirmishing and bush-fighting, was kept up from two o'clock in the afternoon until night. Las Casas was present on the occasion, and, from his account, the Indians must have shown instances of great personal bravery, though the inferiority of their weapons, and the want of all defensive armour, rendered their valour totally ineffectual. As the evening shut in, their hostilities gradually ceased, and they disappeared in the profound gloom and close thickets of the surrounding forest. A deep silence succeeded to their yells and war-whoops, and throughout the night the Spaniards remained in undisturbed possession of the village.

CHAPTER 4

1504

On the morning after the battle, not an Indian was to be seen. Finding that even their great chief, Cotabanama, was incapable of vying with the prowess of the white men, they had given up the contest in despair, and fled to the mountains. The Spaniards, separating into small parties, hunted them with the utmost diligence; their object was to seize the caciques, and, above all, Cotabanama. They explored all the glens and concealed paths leading into the wild recesses where the fugitives had taken refuge. The Indians were cautious and stealthy in their mode of retreating, treading in each other's footprints, so that twenty would make no more track than one, and stepping so lightly as scarce to disturb the herbage; yet there were Spaniards so skilled in hunting Indians that they could trace them even by the turn of a withered leaf, and among the confused tracks of a thousand animals.

They could scent afar off, also, the smoke of the fires which the Indians made whenever they halted, and thus they would come upon them in their most secret haunts. Sometimes they would hunt down a straggling Indian, and compel him by torments to betray the hiding-place of his companions, binding him and driving him before them as a guide. Wherever they discovered one of these places of refuge, filled with the aged and the infirm, with feeble women and helpless children, they massacred them without mercy. They wished to inspire terror throughout the land, and to frighten the whole tribe into submission. They cut off the hands of those whom they took roving at large, and sent them, as they said, to deliver them as letters to their friends, demanding their surrender. Numberless were those, says Las Casas, whose hands were amputated in this manner, and many of them sank down and died by the way, through anguish and loss of blood.

The conquerors delighted in exercising strange and ingenious cruelties. They mingled horrible levity with their blood-thirstiness. They erected gibbets long and low, so that the feet of the sufferers might reach the ground, and their death be lingering. They hanged thirteen together, in reverence, says the indignant Las Casas, of our blessed Saviour and the twelve apostles. While their victims were suspended, and still living, they hacked them with their swords, to prove the strength of their arms and the edge of their weapons. They wrapped them in dry straw, and setting fire to it, terminated their existence by the fiercest agony.

These are horrible details, yet a veil is drawn over others still more detestable. They are related circumstantially by Las Casas, who was an eye-witness. He was young at the time, but records them in his advanced years. 'All these things,' says the venerable Bishop, 'and others revolting to human nature, did my own eyes behold; and now I almost fear to repeat them, scarce believing myself, or whether I have not dreamt them.' *

These details would have been withheld from the present work as disgraceful to human nature, and from an unwillingness to advance anything which might convey a stigma upon a brave and generous nation. But it would be a departure from historical veracity, having the documents before my eyes, to pass silently over transactions so atrocious, and vouched for by witnesses beyond all suspicion of falsehood. Such occurrences show the extremity to which human cruelty may extend when stimulated by avidity of gain, by a thirst of vengeance, or even by a perverted zeal in the holy cause of religion. Every nation has in turn furnished proofs of this disgraceful truth. As in the present instance, they are commonly the crimes of individuals rather than of the nation. Yet it behoves governments to keep a vigilant eye upon those to whom they delegate power in remote and helpless colonies. It is the imperious duty of the historian to place these matters upon record, that they may serve as warning beacons to future generations.

Juan de Esquibel found that, with all his severities, it would be impossible to subjugate the tribe of Higuey, as long as the cacique Cotabanama was at large. That chieftain had retired to the little island of Saona, about two leagues from the coast of Higuey, in the

* Las Casas, lib. ii. cap. 17, MS.

centre of which, amidst a labyrinth of rocks and forests, he had taken shelter with his wife and children in a vast cavern.

A caravel, recently arrived from the city of San Domingo with supplies for the camp, was employed by Esquibel to entrap the cacique. He knew that the latter kept a vigilant look-out, stationing scouts upon the lofty rocks of his island to watch the movements of the caravel. Esquibel departed by night, therefore, in the vessel with fifty followers, and keeping under the deep shadows cast by the land, arrived at Saona unperceived, at the dawn of morning. Here he anchored close in with the shore, hid by its cliffs and forests, and landed forty men before the spies of Cotabanama had taken their station. Two of these were surprised and brought to Esquibel, who, having learnt from them that the cacique was at hand, poniarded one of the spies, and bound the other, making him serve as guide.

A number of Spaniards ran in advance, each anxious to signalize himself by the capture of the cacique. They came to two roads, and the whole party pursued that to the right, excepting one Juan Lopez, a powerful man, skilful in Indian warfare. He proceeded in a footpath to the left, winding among little hills, so thickly wooded that it was impossible to see anyone at the distance of half a bow-shot. Suddenly, in a narrow pass, overshadowed by rocks and trees, he encountered twelve Indian warriors, armed with bows and arrows, and following each other in single file according to their custom. The Indians were confounded at the sight of Lopez, imagining that there must be a party of soldiers behind him. They might readily have transfixed him with their arrows, but they had lost all presence of mind. He demanded their chieftain. They replied that he was behind, and, opening to let him pass, Lopez beheld the cacique in the rear. At sight of the Spaniard, Cotabanama bent his gigantic bow, and was on the point of launching one of his three-pronged arrows, but Lopez rushed upon him and wounded him with his sword. The other Indians, struck with panic, had already fled. Cotabanama, dismayed at the keenness of the sword, cried out that he was Juan de Esquibel, claiming respect as having exchanged names with the Spanish commander. Lopez seized him with one hand by the hair, and with the other aimed a thrust at his body; but the cacique struck down the sword with his hand, and, grappling with his antagonist, threw him with his back

upon the rocks. As they were both men of great power, the
struggle was long and violent. The sword was beneath them, but
Cotabanama, seizing the Spaniard by the throat with his mighty
hand, attempted to strangle him. The sound of the contest brought
the other Spaniards to the spot. They found their companion
writhing and gasping, and almost dead, in the grip of the gigantic
Indian. They seized the cacique, bound him, and carried him
captive to a deserted Indian village in the vicinity. They found the
way to his secret cave, but his wife and children, having received
notice of his capture by the fugitive Indians, had taken refuge in
another part of the island. In the cavern was found the chain with
which a number of Indian captives had been bound, who had risen
upon and slain three Spaniards who had them in charge, and had
made their escape to this island. There were also the swords of the
same Spaniards, which they had brought off as trophies to their
cacique. The chain was now employed to manacle Cotabanama.

The Spaniards prepared to execute the chieftain on the spot,
in the centre of the deserted village. For this purpose a pyre was
built of logs of wood laid crossways, in form of a gridiron, on
which he was to be slowly broiled to death. On further consultation, however, they were induced to forego the pleasure of this
horrible sacrifice. Perhaps they thought the cacique too important a
personage to be executed thus obscurely. Granting him, therefore,
a transient reprieve, they conveyed him to the caravel, and sent
him, bound with heavy chains, to San Domingo. Ovando saw
him in his power, and incapable of doing further harm; but he
had not the magnanimity to forgive a fallen enemy, whose only
crime was the defence of his native soil and lawful territory. He
ordered him to be publicly hanged like a common culprit.* In this
ignominious manner was the cacique Cotabanama executed, the
last of the five sovereign princes of Hayti. His death was followed
by the complete subjugation of his people, and sealed the last
struggle of the natives against their oppressors. The island was
almost unpeopled of its original inhabitants, and meek and mournful submission and mute despair settled upon the scanty remnant
that survived.

Such was the ruthless system which had been pursued, during
the absence of the admiral, by the commander Ovando – this man

---

* Las Casas, *Hist. Ind.*, lib. ii. cap. 18.

of boasted prudence and moderation, who was sent to reform the abuses of the island, and above all, to redress the wrongs of the natives. The system of Columbus may have borne hard upon the Indians, born and brought up in untasked freedom, but it was never cruel nor sanguinary. He inflicted no wanton massacres nor vindictive punishments; his desire was to cherish and civilize the Indians, and to render them useful subjects; not to oppress, and persecute, and destroy them. When he beheld the desolation that had swept them from the land during his suspension from authority, he could not restrain the strong expression of his feelings. In a letter written to the king after his return to Spain, he thus expresses himself on the subject: 'The Indians of Hispaniola were and are the riches of the island; for it is they who cultivate and make the bread and the provisions for the Christians; who dig the gold from the mines, and perform all the offices and labours both of men and beasts. I am informed that, since I left this island, six parts out of seven of the natives are dead, all through ill treatment and inhumanity; some by the sword, others by blows and cruel usage, others through hunger. The greater part have perished in the mountains and glens, whither they had fled from not being able to support the labour imposed upon them.' For his own part, he added, although he had sent many Indians to Spain to be sold, it was always with a view to their being instructed in the Christian faith and in civilized arts and usages, and afterwards sent back to their island to assist in civilizing their countrymen.*

The brief view that has been given of the policy of Ovando, on certain points on which Columbus was censured, may enable the reader to judge more correctly of the conduct of the latter. It is not to be measured by the standard of right and wrong established in the present more enlightened age. We must consider him in connection with the era in which he lived. By comparing his measures with those men of his own times praised for their virtues and abilities, placed in precisely his own situation, and placed there expressly to correct his faults, we shall be the better able to judge how virtuously and wisely, under the peculiar circumstances of the case, he may be considered to have governed.

---

* Las Casas, *Hist. Ind.*, lib. ii. cap. 36.

BOOK 18

The arrival at Jamaica of the two vessels under the command of Salcedo had caused a joyful reverse in the situation of Columbus. He hastened to leave the wreck in which he had been so long immured, and hoisting his flag on board of one of the ships, felt as if the career of enterprise and glory were once more open to him. The late partisans of Porras, when they heard of the arrival of the ships, came wistful and abject to the harbour, doubting how far they might trust to the magnanimity of a man whom they had so greatly injured, and who had now an opportunity of vengeance. The generous mind, however, never harbours revenge in the hour of returning prosperity; but feels noble satisfaction in sharing its happiness even with its enemies. Columbus forgot, in his present felicity, all that he had suffered from these men; he ceased to consider them enemies, now that they had lost the power to injure; and he not only fulfilled all that he had promised them, by taking them on board the ships, but relieved their necessities from his own purse, until their return to Spain, and afterwards took unwearied pains to recommend them to the bounty of the sovereigns. Francisco Porras alone continued a prisoner, to be tried by the tribunals of his country.

Oviedo assures us that the Indians wept when they beheld the departure of the Spaniards; still considering them as beings from the skies. From the admiral, it is true, they had experienced nothing but just and gentle treatment, and continual benefits; and the idea of his immediate influence with the Deity, manifested on the memorable occasion of the eclipse, may have made them consider him as more than human, and his presence as propitious to their island; but it is not easy to believe that a lawless gang like that of

Porras, could have been ranging for months among their villages, without giving cause for the greatest joy at their departure.

On the 28th of June the vessels set sail for San Domingo. The adverse winds and currents which had opposed Columbus throughout this ill-starred expedition still continued to harass him. After a weary struggle of several weeks, he reached, on the 3rd of August, the little island of Beata, on the coast of Hispaniola. Between this place and San Domingo the currents are so violent that vessels are often detained months, waiting for sufficient wind to enable them to stem the stream. Hence Columbus despatched a letter by land to Ovando, to inform him of his approach and to remove certain absurd suspicions of his views, which he had learnt from Salcedo were still entertained by the governor, who feared his arrival in the island might produce factions and disturbances. In this letter he expresses, with his usual warmth and simplicity, the joy he felt at his deliverance, which was so great, he says, that since the arrival of Diego de Salcedo with succour, he had scarcely been able to sleep. The letter had barely time to precede the writer, for a favourable wind springing up, the vessels again made sail, and on the 13th of August anchored in the harbour of San Domingo.

If it is the lot of prosperity to awaken envy and excite detraction, it is certainly the lot of misfortune to atone for a multitude of faults. San Domingo had been the very hot-bed of sedition against Columbus in the day of his power; he had been hurried from it in ignominious chains, amidst the shouts and taunts of the triumphant rabble; he had been excluded from its harbour when, as commander of a squadron, he craved shelter from an impending tempest; but now that he arrived in its waters, a broken-down and shipwrecked man, all past hostility was overpowered by the popular sense of his late disasters. There was a momentary burst of enthusiasm in his favour; what had been denied to his merits was granted to his misfortunes; and even the envious, appeased by his present reverses, seemed to forgive him for having once been so triumphant.

The governor and principal inhabitants came forth to meet him, and received him with signal distinction. He was lodged as a guest in the house of Ovando, who treated him with the utmost courtesy and attention. The governor was a shrewd and discreet man, and much of a courtier; but there were causes of jealousy and distrust between him and Columbus too deep to permit of cordial intercourse. The admiral and his son Fernando always pronounced the civility of Ovando overstrained and hypocritical; intended to obliterate the remembrance of past neglect, and to conceal lurking enmity. While he professed the utmost friendship and sympathy for the admiral, he set at liberty the traitor Porras, who was still a prisoner, to be taken to Spain for trial. He also talked of punishing those of the admiral's people who had taken arms in his defence, and in the affray at Jamaica had killed several of the mutineers. These circumstances were loudly complained of by Columbus; but, in fact, they rose out of a question of jurisdiction between him and the governor. Their powers were so undefined as to clash with each other, and they were both disposed to be extremely punctilious. Ovando assumed a right to take cognizance of all transactions at Jamaica, as happening within the limits of his government, which included all the islands and Terra Firma. Columbus, on the other hand, asserted the absolute command, and the jurisdiction both civil and criminal given to him by the sovereigns, over all persons who sailed in his expedition, from the time of departure until their return to Spain. To prove this, he produced his letter of instructions. The governor heard him with great courtesy and a smiling countenance; but observed, that the letter of instructions gave him no authority within the bounds of his government.* He relinquished the idea, however, of investigating the conduct of the followers of Columbus, and sent Porras to Spain, to be examined by the board which had charge of the affairs of the Indies.

The sojourn of Columbus at San Domingo was but little calculated to yield him satisfaction. He was grieved at the desolation of the island by the oppressive treatment of the natives, and the horrible massacre which had been perpetrated by Ovando and his agents. He had fondly hoped, at one time, to render the natives civilized, industrious, and tributary subjects to the crown, and to derive from their well-regulated labour a great and steady revenue. How different had been the event! The five great tribes which peopled the mountains and the valleys at the time of the discovery, and rendered, by their mingled towns and villages and tracts of cultivation, the rich levels of the Vegas so many 'painted gardens', had almost all

* Letter of Columbus to his son Diego, Seville, Nov. 21, 1504.

passed away, and the native princes had perished chiefly by violent or ignominious deaths. Columbus regarded the affairs of the island with a different eye from Ovando. He had a paternal feeling for its prosperity, and his fortunes were implicated in its judicious management. He complained, in subsequent letters to the sovereigns, that all the public affairs were ill conducted; that the ore collected lay unguarded in large quantities in houses slightly built and thatched, inviting depredation; that Ovando was unpopular, the people were dissolute, and the property of the crown and the security of the island in continual risk from mutiny and sedition.[*] While he saw all this, he had no power to interfere, and any observation or remonstrance on his part was ill received by the governor.

He found his own immediate concerns in great confusion. His rents and dues were either uncollected, or he could not obtain a clear account and a full liquidation of them. Whatever he could collect was appropriated to the fitting out of the vessels which were to convey himself and his crews to Spain. He accuses Ovando, in his subsequent letters, of having neglected, if not sacrificed, his interests during his long absence, and of having impeded those who were appointed to attend to his concerns. That he had some grounds for these complaints would appear from two letters still extant,[†] written by Queen Isabella to Ovando, on the 27th of November 1503, in which she informs him of the complaint of Alonzo Sanchez de Carvajal, that he was impeded in collecting the rents of the admiral; and expressly commands Ovando to observe the capitulations granted to Columbus; to respect his agents, and to facilitate instead of obstructing his concerns. These letters, while they imply ungenerous conduct on the part of the governor towards his illustrious predecessor, evince likewise the personal interest taken by Isabella in the affairs of Columbus during his absence. She had, in fact, signified her displeasure at his being excluded from the port of San Domingo, when he applied there for succour for his squadron, and for shelter from a storm; and had censured Ovando for not taking his advice and detaining the fleet of Bobadilla, by which it would have escaped its disastrous fate.[‡] And here it may be observed, that the sanguinary acts of

[*] Letter of Columbus to his son Diego, dated Seville, 3rd Dec. 1504.
[†] Navarrete, *Colec.*, tom. ii. decad. 151, 152.
[‡] Herrera, *Hist. Ind.*, decad. i. lib. v. cap. 12.

Ovando towards the natives, in particular the massacre at Xaragua, and the execution of the unfortunate Anacaona, awakened equal horror and indignation in Isabella; she was languishing on her death-bed when she received the intelligence, and with her dying breath she exacted a promise from King Ferdinand that Ovando should immediately be recalled from his government. The promise was tardily and reluctantly fulfilled, after an interval of about four years, and not until induced by other circumstances; for Ovando contrived to propitiate the monarch, by forcing a revenue from the island.

The continual misunderstandings between the admiral and the governor, though always qualified on the part of the latter with great complaisance, induced Columbus to hasten as much as possible his departure from the island. The ship in which he had returned from Jamaica was repaired and fitted out, and put under the command of the Adelantado; another vessel was freighted, in which Columbus embarked with his son and his domestics. The greater part of his late crews remained at San Domingo; as they were in great poverty, he relieved their necessities from his own purse, and advanced the funds necessary for the voyage home of those who chose to return. Many thus relieved by his generosity had been among the most violent of the rebels.

On the 12th of September he set sail; but had scarcely left the harbour when, in a sudden squall, the mast of his ship was carried away. He immediately went with his family on board of the vessel commanded by the Adelantado, and sending back the damaged ship to port, continued on his course. Throughout the voyage he experienced the most tempestuous weather. In one storm the mainmast was sprung in four places. He was confined to his bed at the time by the gout; by his advice, however, and the activity of the Adelantado, the damage was skilfully repaired; the mast was shortened; the weak parts were fortified by wood taken from the castles or cabins which the vessels in those days carried on the prow and stern; and the whole was well secured by cords. They were still more damaged in a succeeding tempest, in which the ship sprung her foremast. In this crippled state they had to traverse seven hundred leagues of a stormy ocean. Fortune continued to persecute Columbus to the end of this, his last and most disastrous expedition. For several weeks he was tempest-tossed – suffering at the same time the most excruciating pains from his malady – until, on the seventh day of November, his crazy and shattered bark anchored in the harbour of San Lucar. Hence he had himself conveyed to Seville, where he hoped to enjoy repose of mind and body, and to recruit his health after such a long series of fatigues, anxieties, and hardships.*

* *Hist. del Almirante*, cap. 108; Las Casas, *Hist. Ind.*, lib. ii. cap. 36.

CHAPTER 2

1504

Broken by age and infirmities, and worn down by the toils and hardships of his recent expedition, Columbus had looked forward to Seville as to a haven of rest, where he might repose awhile from his troubles. Care and sorrow, however, followed him by sea and land. In varying the scene he but varied the nature of his distress. 'Wearisome days and nights' were appointed to him for the remainder of his life; and the very margin of his grave was destined to be strewed with thorns.

On arriving at Seville, he found all his affairs in confusion. Ever since he had been sent home in chains from San Domingo, when his house and effects had been taken possession of by Bobadilla, his rents and dues had never been properly collected; and such as had been gathered had been retained in the hands of the governor Ovando. 'I have much vexation from the governor,' says he, in a letter to his son Diego.* 'All tell me that I have there eleven or twelve thousand castellanos; and I have not received a quarto. . . . I know well, that, since my departure, he must have received upwards of five thousand castellanos.' He entreated that a letter might be written by the king, commanding the payment of these arrears without delay; for his agents would not venture even to speak to Ovando on the subject, unless empowered by a letter from the sovereign.

Columbus was not of a mercenary spirit; but his rank and situation required large expenditure. The world thought him in the possession of sources of inexhaustible wealth; but, as yet, those sources had furnished him but precarious and scanty streams. His last voyage had exhausted his finances, and involved him in perplexities. All that he had been able to collect of the money due to him in Hispaniola, to the amount of twelve hundred castellanos,

* Let. Seville, 13 Dec. 1504; Navarrete, v. i. p. 343.

had been expended in bringing home many of his late crew, who were in distress; and for the greater part of the sum the crown remained his debtor. While struggling to obtain his mere pecuniary dues, he was absolutely suffering a degree of penury. He repeatedly urges the necessity of economy to his son Diego, until he can obtain a restitution of his property, and the payment of his arrears. 'I receive nothing of the revenue due to me,' says he, in one letter; 'I live by borrowing.' 'Little have I profited,' he adds, in another, 'by twenty years of service, with such toils and perils; since, at present, I do not own a roof in Spain. If I desire to eat or sleep, I have no resort but an inn; and, for the most times, have not wherewithal to pay my bill.'

Yet in the midst of these personal distresses, he was more solicitous for the payment of his seamen than of himself. He wrote strongly and repeatedly to the sovereigns, entreating the discharge of their arrears, and urged his son Diego, who was at court, to exert himself in their behalf. 'They are poor,' said he, 'and it is now nearly three years since they left their homes. They have endured infinite toils and perils, and they bring invaluable tidings, for which their majesties ought to give thanks to God and rejoice.' Notwithstanding his generous solicitude for these men, he knew several of them to have been his enemies; nay, that some of them were at this very time disposed to do him harm rather than good; such was the magnanimity of his spirit and his forgiving disposition.

The same zeal, also, for the interests of his sovereigns, which had ever actuated his loyal mind, mingled with his other causes of solicitude. He represented in his letter to the king the mismanagement of the royal rents in Hispaniola, under the administration of Ovando. Immense quantities of ore lay unprotected in slightly-built houses, and liable to depredations. It required a person of vigour, and one who had an individual interest in the property of the island, to restore its affairs to order, and draw from it the immense revenues which it was capable of yielding; and Columbus plainly intimated that he was the proper person.

In fact, as to himself, it was not so much pecuniary indemnification that he sought as the restoration of his offices and dignities. He regarded them as the trophies of his illustrious achievements; he had received the royal promise that he should be reinstated in them; and he felt that as long as they were withheld, a tacit censure rested upon his name. Had he not been proudly impatient on this subject, he would have belied the loftiest part of his character; for he who can be indifferent to the wreath of triumph is deficient in the noble ambition which incites to glorious deeds.

The unsatisfactory replies received to his letters disquieted his mind. He knew that he had active enemies at court ready to turn all things to his disadvantage, and felt the importance of being there in person to defeat their machinations: but his infirmities detained him at Seville. He made an attempt to set forth on the journey, but the severity of the winter and the virulence of his malady obliged him to relinquish it in despair. All that he could do was to reiterate his letters to the sovereigns, and to entreat the intervention of his few but faithful friends. He feared the disastrous occurrences of the last voyage might be represented to his prejudice. The great object of the expedition, the discovery of a strait opening from the Caribbean to a southern sea, had failed. The secondary object, the acquisition of gold, had not been completed. He had discovered the gold mines of Veragua, it is true; but he had brought home no treasure; because, as he said in one of his letters, 'I would not rob nor outrage the country; since reason requires that it should be settled, and then the gold may be procured without violence.'

He was especially apprehensive that the violent scenes in the island of Jamaica might, by the perversity of his enemies, and the effrontery of the delinquents, be wrested into matters of accusation against him, as had been the case with the rebellion of Roldan. Porras, the ringleader of the late faction, had been sent home by Ovando to appear before the board of the Indies, but without any written process setting forth the offences charged against him. While at Jamaica, Columbus had ordered an inquest of the affair to be taken; but the notary of the squadron who took it, and the papers which he drew up, were on board of the ship in which the admiral had sailed from Hispaniola, but which had put back dismasted. No cognizance of the case, therefore, was taken by the council of the Indies; and Porras went at large, armed with the power and the disposition to do mischief. Being related to Morales, the royal treasurer, he had access to people in place, and an opportunity of enlisting their opinions and prejudices on his side. Columbus wrote to Morales, enclosing a copy of the petition which the rebels had sent to him when in Jamaica, in which they acknowledged their culpability and implored his forgiveness; and he entreated the treasurer not to be swayed by the representations of his relative, nor to pronounce an opinion unfavourable to him, until he had an opportunity of being heard.

The faithful and indefatigable Diego Mendez was at this time at the court, as well as Alonzo Sanchez de Carvajal, and an active friend of Columbus named Geronimo. They could bear the most important testimony as to his conduct, and he wrote to his son Diego to call upon them for their good offices. 'I trust,' said he, 'that the truth and diligence of Diego Mendez will be of as much avail as the lies of Porras.' Nothing can surpass the affecting earnestness and simplicity of the general declaration of loyalty contained in one of his letters. 'I have served their majesties,' says he, 'with as much zeal and diligence as if it had been to gain Paradise; and if I have failed in anything, it has been because my knowledge and powers went no further.'

While reading these touching appeals, we can scarcely realize the fact that the dejected individual thus wearily and vainly applying for unquestionable rights, and pleading almost like a culprit, in cases wherein he had been flagrantly injured, was the same who but a few years previously had been received at this very court with almost regal honours, and idolized as a national benefactor; that this, in a word, was Columbus, the discoverer of the New World; broken in health, and impoverished in his old days by his very discoveries.

At length the caravel bringing the official proceedings relative to the brothers Porras arrived at the Algarves, in Portugal, and Columbus looked forward with hope that all matters would soon be placed in a proper light. His anxiety to get to court became every day more intense. A litter was provided to convey him thither, and was actually at the door, but the inclemency of the weather and his increasing infirmities obliged him again to abandon the journey. His resource of letter-writing began to fail him: he could only write at night, for in the daytime the severity of his malady deprived him of the use of his hands. The tidings from the court were every day more and more adverse to his hopes; the intrigues of his enemies were prevailing; the cold-hearted Ferdinand treated all his applications with indifference; the generous

Isabella lay dangerously ill. On her justice and magnanimity he still relied for the full restoration of his rights, and the redress of all his grievances. 'May it please the Holy Trinity,' says he, 'to restore our sovereign queen to health; for by her will everything be adjusted which is now in confusion.' Alas! while writing that letter, his noble benefactress was a corpse!

The health of Isabella had long been undermined by the shocks of repeated domestic calamities. The death of her only son, the prince Juan; of her beloved daughter and bosom friend, the princess Isabella; and of her grandson and prospective heir, the prince Miguel, had been three cruel wounds to a heart full of the tenderest sensibility. To these was added the constant grief caused by the evident infirmity of intellect of her daughter Juana, and the domestic unhappiness of that princess with her husband, the archduke Philip. The desolation which walks through palaces admits not the familiar sympathies and sweet consolations which alleviate the sorrows of common life. Isabella pined in state, amidst the obsequious homages of a court, surrounded by the trophies of a glorious and successful reign, and placed at the summit of earthly grandeur. A deep and incurable melancholy settled upon her, which undermined her constitution, and gave a fatal acuteness to her bodily maladies. After four months of illness, she died on the 26th of November 1504, at Medina del Campo, in the fifty-fourth year of her age; but long before her eyes closed upon the world, her heart had closed on all its pomps and vanities. 'Let my body,' said she in her will, 'be interred in the monastery of San Francisco, which is in the Alhambra of the city of Granada, in a low sepulchre, without any monument except a plain stone, with the inscription cut on it. But I desire and command, that if the king, my lord, should choose a sepulchre in any church or monastery in any other part or place of these my kingdoms, my body be transported thither, and buried beside the body of his highness; so that the union we have enjoyed while living, and which, through the mercy of God, we hope our souls will experience in heaven, may be represented by our bodies in the earth.' *

* The dying command of Isabella has been obeyed. The author of this work has seen her tomb in the royal chapel of the Cathedral of Granada, in which her remains are interred with those of Ferdinand. Their effigies, sculptured in white marble, lie side by side on a magnificent sepulchre. The altar of the chapel is adorned with bas reliefs representing the conquest and surrender of Granada.

Such was one of several passages in the will of this admirable woman, which bespoke the chastened humility of her heart; and in which, as has been well observed, the affections of conjugal love were delicately entwined with piety, and with the most tender melancholy. She was one of the purest spirits that ever ruled over the destinies of a nation. Had she been spared, her benignant vigilance would have prevented many a scene of horror in the colonization of the New World, and might have softened the lot of its native inhabitants. As it is, her fair name will ever shine with celestial radiance in the dawning of its history.

The news of the death of Isabella reached Columbus when he was writing a letter to his son Diego. He notices it in a postscript or memorandum, written in the haste and brevity of the moment, but in beautifully touching and mournful terms. 'A memorial,' he writes, 'for thee, my dear son Diego, of what is at present to be done. The principal thing is to commend affectionately, and with great devotion, the soul of the queen our sovereign to God. Her life was always catholic and holy, and prompt to all things in his holy service: for this reason we may rest assured that she is received into his glory, and beyond the cares of this rough and weary world. The next thing is to watch and labour in all matters for the service of our sovereign the king, and to endeavour to alleviate his grief. His majesty is the head of Christendom. Remember the proverb which says, when the head suffers all the members suffer. Therefore all good Christians should pray for his health and long life; and we, who are in his employ, ought more than others to do this with all study and diligence.'*

It is impossible to read this mournful letter without being moved by the simply eloquent yet artless language in which Columbus expresses his tenderness for the memory of his benefactress, his weariness under the gathering cares and ills of life, and his persevering and enduring loyalty towards the sovereign who was so ungratefully neglecting him. It is in these unstudied and confidential letters that we read the heart of Columbus.

* Letter to his son Diego, Dec. 3, 1504.

The death of Isabella was a fatal blow to the fortunes of Columbus. While she lived, he had everything to anticipate from her high sense of justice, her regard for her royal word, her gratitude for his services, and her admiration of his character. With her illness, however, his interests had languished, and when she died, he was left to the justice and generosity of Ferdinand!

During the remainder of the winter and a part of the spring, he continued at Seville, detained by painful illness, and endeavouring to obtain redress from the government by ineffectual letters. His brother the Adelantado, who supported him with his accustomed fondness and devotion through all his trials, proceeded to court to attend to his interests, taking with him the admiral's younger son Fernando, then aged about seventeen. The latter, the affectionate father repeatedly represents to his son Diego as a man in understanding and conduct, though but a stripling in years; and inculcates the strongest fraternal attachment, alluding to his own brethren with one of those simply eloquent and affecting expressions which stamp his heart upon his letters. 'To thy brother conduct thyself as the elder brother should unto the younger. Thou hast no other, and I praise God that this is such a one as thou dost need. Ten brothers would not be too many for thee. Never have I found a better friend to right or left than my brothers.'

Among the persons whom Columbus employed at this time in his missions to the court was Amerigo Vespucci. He describes him as a worthy but unfortunate man, who had not profited as much as he deserved by his undertakings, and who had always been disposed to render him service. His object in employing him appears to have been to prove the value of his last voyage, and that he had been in the most opulent parts of the New World, Vespucci having since touched upon the same coast, in a voyage with Alonzo de Ojeda.

One circumstance occurred at this time which shed a gleam of hope and consolation over his gloomy prospects. Diego de Deza, who had been for some time bishop of Palencia, was expected at court. This was the same worthy friar who had aided him to advocate his theory before the board of learned men at Salamanca, and had assisted him with his purse when making his proposals to the Spanish court. He had just been promoted and made archbishop of Seville, but had not yet been installed in office. Columbus directs his son Diego to intrust his interests to this worthy prelate. 'Two things,' says he, 'require particular attention. Ascertain whether the queen, who is now with God, has said anything concerning me in her testament, and stimulate the bishop of Palencia, he who was the cause that their highnesses obtained possession of the Indies, who induced me to remain in Castile when I was on the road to leave it.'* In another letter he says, 'If the bishop of Palencia has arrived, or should arrive, tell him how much I have been gratified by his prosperity, and that if I come, I shall lodge with his grace, even though he should not invite me, for we must return to our ancient fraternal affection.'

The incessant applications of Columbus, both by letter and by the intervention of friends, appear to have been listened to with cool indifference. No compliance was yielded to his requests, and no deference was paid to his opinions, on various points concerning which he interested himself. New instructions were sent out to Ovando, but not a word of their purport was mentioned to the admiral. It was proposed to send out three bishops, and he entreated in vain to be heard previous to their election. In short, he was not in any way consulted in the affairs of the New World. He felt deeply this neglect, and became every day more impatient of his absence from court. To enable himself to perform the journey with more ease, he applied for permission to use a mule, a royal ordinance having prohibited the employment of those animals under the saddle, in consequence of their universal use having occasioned a decline in the breed of horses. A royal permission was accordingly granted to Columbus, in consideration that his age and infirmities incapacitated

---

* Letter of December 21, 1504; Navarrete, tom. i. p. 346.

him from riding on horseback; but it was a considerable time before the state of his health would permit him to avail himself of that privilege.

The foregoing particulars, gleaned from letters of Columbus recently discovered, show the real state of his affairs, and the mental and bodily affliction sustained by him during his winter's residence at Seville, on his return from his last disastrous voyage. He has generally been represented as reposing there from his toils and troubles. Never was honourable repose more merited, more desired, and less enjoyed.

It was not until the month of May that he was able, in company with his brother the Adelantado, to accomplish his journey to court, at that time held at Segovia. He who but a few years before had entered the city of Barcelona in triumph, attended by the nobility and chivalry of Spain, and hailed with rapture by the multitude, now arrived within the gates of Segovia a wayworn, melancholy, and neglected man; oppressed more by sorrow than even by his years and infirmities. When he presented himself at court, he met with none of that distinguished attention, that cordial kindness, that cherishing sympathy, which his unparalleled services and his recent sufferings had merited.[*]

The selfish Ferdinand had lost sight of his past services, in what appeared to him the inconvenience of his present demands. He received him with many professions of kindness: but with those cold ineffectual smiles, which pass like wintry sunshine over the countenance, and convey no warmth to the heart.

The admiral now gave a particular account of his late voyage, describing the great tract of Terra Firma which he had explored, and the riches of the province of Veragua. He related also the disasters sustained in the island of Jamaica; the insurrection of the Porras and their band; and all the other griefs and troubles of this unfortunate expedition. He had but a cold-hearted auditor in the king; and the benignant Isabella was no more at hand to soothe him with a smile of kindness, or a tear of sympathy. 'I know not,' says the venerable Las Casas, 'what could cause this dislike and this want of princely countenance in the king, towards one who had rendered him such pre-eminent benefits; unless it was that his mind was swayed by the false testimonies which

[*] Las Casas, *Hist. Ind.*, lib. ii. cap. 37; Herrera, *Hist. Ind.*, decad. i. lib. vi. cap. 13.

had been brought against the admiral; of which I have been enabled to learn something from persons much in favour with the sovereigns.' *

After a few days had elapsed, Columbus urged his suit in form; reminding the king of all that he had done, and all that had been promised him under the royal word and seal, and supplicating that the restitutions and indemnifications which had been so frequently solicited might be awarded to him; offering in return to serve his majesty devotedly for the short time he had yet to live; and trusting, from what he felt within him, and from what he thought he knew with certainty, to render services which should surpass all that he had yet performed a hundred-fold. The king, in reply, acknowledged the greatness of his merits, and the importance of his services, but observed that, for the more satisfactory adjustment of his claims, it would be advisable to refer all points in dispute to the decision of some discreet and able person. The admiral immediately proposed as arbiter his friend the archbishop of Seville, Don Diego de Deza, one of the most able and upright men about the court, devotedly loyal, high in the confidence of the king, and one who had always taken great interest in the affairs of the New World. The king consented to the arbitration, but artfully extended it to questions which he knew would never be put at issue by Columbus; among these was his claim to the restoration of his office of viceroy. To this Columbus objected with becoming spirit, as compromising a right which was too clearly defined and solemnly established to be put for a moment in dispute. It was the question of rents and revenues alone, he observed, which he was willing to submit to the decision of a learned man, not that of the government of the Indies. As the monarch persisted, however, in embracing both questions in the arbitration, the proposed measure was never carried into effect.

It was, in fact, on the subject of his dignities alone that Columbus was tenacious; all other matters he considered of minor importance. In a conversation with the king he absolutely disavowed all wish of entering into any suit or pleading as to his pecuniary dues; on the contrary, he offered to put all his privileges and writings into the hands of his sovereign, and to receive out of the dues arising from them whatever his majesty might think

* Las Casas, *Hist. Ind*, lib. ii. cap. 37, MS.

proper to award. All that he claimed without qualification or reserve were his official dignities, assured to him under the royal seal with all the solemnity of a treaty. He entreated, at all events, that these matters might speedily be decided, so that he might be released from a state of miserable suspense, and enabled to retire to some quiet corner, in search of that tranquillity and repose necessary to his fatigues and his infirmities.

To this frank appeal to his justice and generosity, Ferdinand replied with many courteous expressions, and with those general evasive promises which beguile the ear of the court applicant, but convey no comfort to his heart. 'As far as actions went,' observes Las Casas, 'the king not merely showed him no signs of favour, but, on the contrary, discountenanced him as much as possible; yet he was never wanting in complimentary expressions.'

Many months were passed by Columbus in unavailing solicitation, during which he continued to receive outward demonstrations of respect from the king, and due attention from cardinal Ximenes, archbishop of Toledo, and other principal personages; but he had learned to appreciate and distrust the hollow civilities of a court. His claims were referred to a tribunal, called 'The council of the discharges of the conscience of the deceased queen, and of the king.' This is a kind of tribunal, commonly known by the name of the Junta de Descargos, composed of persons nominated by the sovereign, to superintend the accomplishment of the last will of his predecessor, and the discharge of his debts. Two consultations were held by this body, but nothing was determined. The wishes of the king were too well known to be thwarted. 'It was believed,' says Las Casas, 'that if the king could have done so with a safe conscience, and without detriment to his fame, he would have respected few or none of the privileges which he and the queen-had conceded to the admiral, and which had been so justly merited.'

Columbus still flattered himself that, his claims being of such importance, and touching a question of sovereignty, the adjustment of them might be only postponed by the king until he could consult with his daughter Juana, who had succeeded to her mother as queen of Castile, and who was daily expected from Flanders, with her husband, King Philip. He endeavoured, therefore, to bear

* Las Casas, *Hist. Ind*, lib. ii. cap. 37, MS.

his delays with patience; but he had no longer the physical strength and glorious anticipations which once sustained him through his long application at this court. Life itself was drawing to a close.

He was once more confined to his bed by a tormenting attack of the gout, aggravated by the sorrows and disappointments which preyed upon his heart. From this couch of anguish he addressed one more appeal to the justice of the king. He no longer petitioned for himself: it was for his son Diego. Nor did he dwell upon his pecuniary dues; it was the honourable trophies of his services which he wished to secure and perpetuate in his family. He entreated that his son Diego might be appointed, in his place, to the government of which he had been so wrongfully deprived. 'This,' he said, 'is a matter which concerns my honour; as to all the rest, do as your majesty may think proper; give or withhold, as may be most for your interest, and I shall be content. I believe the anxiety caused by the delay of this affair is the principal cause of my ill health.' A petition to the same purpose was presented at the same time by his son Diego, offering to take with him such persons for counsellors as the king should appoint, and to be guided by their advice.

These petitions were treated by Ferdinand with his usual professions and evasions. 'The more applications were made to him,' observes Las Casas, 'the more favourably did he reply; but still he delayed, hoping, by exhausting their patience, to induce them to waive their privileges, and accept in place thereof titles and estates in Castile.' Columbus rejected all propositions of the kind with indignation, as calculated to compromise those titles which were the trophies of his achievements. He saw, however, that all further hope of redress from Ferdinand was vain. From the bed to which he was confined, he addressed a letter to his constant friend Diego de Deza, expressive of his despair. 'It appears that his majesty does not think fit to fulfil that which he, with the queen, who is now in glory, promised me by word and seal. For me to contend for the contrary would be to contend with the wind. I have done all that I could do. I leave the rest to God, whom I have ever found propitious to me in my necessities.'*

The cold and calculating Ferdinand beheld this illustrious man sinking under infirmity of body, heightened by that deferred hope

* Navarrete, *Colec.*, tom. i.

which 'maketh the heart sick'. A little more delay, a little more disappointment, and a little longer infliction of ingratitude, and this loyal and generous heart would cease to beat: he should then be delivered from the just claims of a well-tried servant, who, in ceasing to be useful, was considered by him to have become importunate.

CHAPTER 4

In the midst of illness and despondency, when both life and hope were expiring in the bosom of Columbus, a new gleam was awakened and blazed up for the moment with characteristic fervour. He heard with joy of the landing of King Philip and Queen Juana, who had just arrived from Flanders to take possession of their throne of Castile. In the daughter of Isabella he trusted once more to find a patroness and a friend. King Ferdinand and all the court repaired to Laredo to receive the youthful sovereigns. Columbus would gladly have done the same, but he was confined to his bed by a severe return of his malady; neither in his painful and helpless situation could he dispense with the aid and ministry of his son Diego. His brother, the Adelantado, therefore, his main dependence in all emergencies, was sent to represent him, and to present his homage and congratulations. Columbus wrote by him to the new king and queen, expressing his grief at being prevented by illness from coming in person to manifest his devotion, but begging to be considered among the most faithful of their subjects. He expressed a hope that he should receive at their hands the restitution of his honours and estates, and assured them that, though cruelly tortured at present by disease, he would yet be able to render them services, the like of which had never been witnessed.

Such was the last sally of his sanguine and unconquerable spirit; which, disregarding age and infirmities, and all past sorrows and disappointments, spoke from his dying bed with all the confidence of youthful hope, and talked of still greater enterprises, as if he had a long and vigorous life before him. The Adelantado took leave of his brother, whom he was never to behold again, and set out on his mission to the new sovereigns. He experienced the most gracious reception. The claims of the admiral were treated with great attention by the young king and queen, and flattering hopes were given of a speedy and prosperous termination to his suit.

In the meantime the cares and troubles of Columbus were drawing to a close. The momentary fire which had reanimated him was soon quenched by accumulating infirmities. Immediately after the departure of the Adelantado, his illness increased in violence. His last voyage had shattered beyond repair a frame already worn and wasted by a life of hardship; and continual anxieties robbed him of that sweet repose so necessary to recruit the weariness and debility of age. The cold ingratitude of his sovereign chilled his heart. The continued suspension of his honours, and the enmity and defamation experienced at every turn, seemed to throw a shadow over that glory which had been the great object of his ambition. This shadow, it is true, could be but of transient duration; but it is difficult for the most illustrious man to look beyond the present cloud which may obscure his fame, and anticipate its permanent lustre in the admiration of posterity.

Being admonished by failing strength and increasing sufferings that his end was approaching, he prepared to leave his affairs in order for the benefit of his successors.

It is said that on the 4th of May he wrote an informal testamentary codicil on the blank page of a little breviary, given him by Pope Alexander VI. In this he bequeathed that book to the republic of Genoa, which he also appointed successor to his privileges and dignities on the extinction of his male line. He directed likewise the erection of an hospital in that city with the produce of his possessions in Italy. The authenticity of this document is questioned, and has become a point of warm contest among commentators. It is not, however, of much importance. The paper is such as might readily have been written by a person like Columbus in the paroxysm of disease, when he imagined his end suddenly approaching, and shows the affection with which his thoughts were bent on his native city. It is termed among commentators a military codicil, because testamentary dispositions of this kind are executed by the soldier at the point of death, without the usual formalities required by the civil law. About two weeks afterwards, on the eve of his death, he executed a final and regularly authenticated codicil, in which he bequeathed his dignities and estates with better judgment.

In these last and awful moments, when the soul has but a brief space in which to make up its accounts between heaven and earth, all dissimulation is at an end, and we read unequivocal evidences of character. The last codicil of Columbus, made at the very verge of the grave, is stamped with his ruling passion and his benignant virtues. He repeats and enforces several clauses of his original testament, constituting his son Diego his universal heir. The entailed inheritance, or mayorazgo, in case he died without male issue, was to go to his brother Don Fernando, and from him, in like case, to pass to his uncle Don Bartholomew, descending always to the nearest male heir; in failure of which it was to pass to the female nearest in lineage to the admiral. He enjoined upon whoever should inherit his estate never to alienate or diminish it, but to endeavour by all means to augment its prosperity and importance. He likewise enjoined upon his heirs to be prompt and devoted at all times, with person and estate, to serve their sovereign and promote the Christian faith. He ordered that Don Diego should devote one tenth of the revenues which might arise from his estate, when it came to be productive, to the relief of indigent relatives and of other persons in necessity; that, out of the remainder, he should yield certain yearly proportions to his brother Don Fernando, and his uncles Don Bartholomew and Don Diego; and that the part allotted to Don Fernando should be settled upon him and his male heirs in an entailed and unalienable inheritance. Having thus provided for the maintenance and per-petuity of his family and dignities, he ordered that Don Diego, when his estates should be sufficiently productive, should erect a chapel in the island of Hispaniola, which God had given to him so marvellously, at the town of Conception, in the Vega, where masses should be daily performed for the repose of the souls of himself, his father, his mother, his wife, and of all who died in the faith. Another clause recommends to the care of Don Diego, Beatrix Enriquez, the mother of his natural son Fernando. His connection with her had never been sanctioned by matrimony, and either this circumstance, or some neglect of her, seems to have awakened deep compunction in his dying moments. He orders Don Diego to provide for her respectable maintenance;

'and let this be done,' he adds, 'for the discharge of my conscience, for it weighs heavy on my soul.'* Finally, he noted with his own hand several minute sums, to be paid to persons at different and distant places, without their being told whence they received them. These appear to have been trivial debts of conscience, or rewards for petty services received in times long past. Among them is one of half a mark of silver to a poor Jew, who lived at the gate of the Jewry, in the city of Lisbon. These minute provisions evince the scrupulous attention to justice in all his dealings, and that love of punctuality in the fulfilment of duties, for which he was remarked. In the same spirit, he gave much advice to his son Diego as to the conduct of his affairs, enjoining upon him to take every month an account with his own hand of the expenses of his household, and to sign it with his name; for a want of regularity in this, he observed, lost both property and servants, and turned the last into enemies.[†] His dying bequests were made in presence of a few faithful followers and servants, and among them we find the name of Bartholomew Fiesco, who had accompanied Diego Mendez in the perilous voyage in a canoe from Jamaica to Hispaniola.

Having thus scrupulously attended to all the claims of affection, loyalty, and justice upon earth, Columbus turned his thoughts to heaven; and having received the holy sacrament, and performed all the pious offices of a devout Christian, he expired with great resignation, on the day of ascension, the 20th of May 1506, being about seventy years of age.[‡] His last words were, '*In manus tuas, Domine, commendo spiritum meum*': Into thy hands, O Lord, I commend my spirit.[§]

His body was deposited in the convent of S. Francisco, and his obsequies were celebrated with funereal pomp at Valladolid, in the parochial church of Santa Maria de la Antigua. His remains were

---

* Diego, the son of the admiral, notes in his own testament this bequest of his father, and says that he was charged by him to pay Beatrix Enriquez 10,000 maravedies a year, which for some time he had faithfully performed; but as he believes that for three or four years previous to her death he had neglected to do so, he orders that the deficiency shall be ascertained and paid to her heirs. *Memorial ajustado sobre la propriedad del mayorazgo que fondo D. Christ. Colon*, sec. 245.

[†] *Memorial ajustado*, § 248.

[‡] Cura de los Palacios, cap. 121.

[§] Las Casas, *Hist. Ind.*, lib. ii. cap. 38; *Hist. del Almirante*, cap. 108.

transported afterwards, in 1513, to the Carthusian monastery of Las Cuevas of Seville, to the chapel of St Ann or of Santo Christo, in which chapel were likewise deposited those of his son Don Diego, who died in the village of Montalban, on the 23rd of February 1526. In the year 1536 the bodies of Columbus and his son Diego were removed to Hispaniola, and interred in the principal chapel of the cathedral of the city of San Domingo; but even here they did not rest in quiet, having since been again disinterred and conveyed to the Havannah, in the island of Cuba.

We are told that Ferdinand, after the death of Columbus, showed a sense of his merits by ordering a monument to be erected to his memory, on which was inscribed the motto already cited, which had formerly been granted to him by the sovereigns: *A Castilla y a Leon nuevo mundo dio Colon* (To Castile and Leon Columbus gave a new world). However great an honour a monument may be for a subject to receive, it is certainly but a cheap reward for a sovereign to bestow. As to the motto inscribed upon it, it remains engraved in the memory of mankind, more indelibly than in brass or marble; a record of the great debt of gratitude due to the discoverer, which the monarch had so faithlessly neglected to discharge.

Attempts have been made in recent days, by loyal Spanish writers, to vindicate the conduct of Ferdinand towards Columbus. They were doubtless well intended, but they have been futile, nor is their failure to be regretted. To screen such injustice in so eminent a character from the reprobation of mankind is to deprive history of one of its most important uses. Let the ingratitude of Ferdinand stand recorded in its full extent, and endure throughout all time. The dark shadow which it casts upon his brilliant renown will be a lesson to all rulers, teaching them what is important to their own fame in their treatment of illustrious men.

Havannah

In narrating the story of Columbus, it has been the endeavour of the author to place him in a clear and familiar point of view; for this purpose he has rejected no circumstance, however trivial, which appeared to evolve some point of character; and he has sought all kinds of collateral facts which might throw light upon his views and motives. With this view also he has detailed many facts hitherto passed over in silence, or vaguely noticed by historians, probably because they might be deemed instances of error or misconduct on the part of Columbus; but he who paints a great man merely in great and heroic traits, though he may produce a fine picture, will never present a faithful portrait. Great men are compounds of great and little qualities. Indeed, much of their greatness arises from their mastery over the imperfections of their nature, and their noblest actions are sometimes struck forth by the collision of their merits and their defects.

In Columbus was singularly combined the practical and the poetical. His mind had grasped all kinds of knowledge, whether procured by study or observation, which bore upon his theories; impatient of the scanty aliment of the day, 'his impetuous ardour,' as has well been observed, 'threw him into the study of the fathers of the church, the Arabian Jews, and the ancient geographers'; while his daring but irregular genius, bursting from the limits of imperfect science, bore him to conclusions far beyond the intellectual vision of his contemporaries. If some of his conclusions were erroneous, they were at least ingenious and splendid; and their error resulted from the clouds which still hung over his peculiar path of enterprise. His own discoveries enlightened the ignorance of the age, guided conjecture to certainty, and dispelled that very darkness with which he had been obliged to struggle.

In the progress of his discoveries he has been remarked for the extreme sagacity and the admirable justness with which he seized upon the phenomena of the exterior world. The variations, for instance, of terrestrial magnetism, the direction of currents, the groupings of marine plants, fixing one of the grand climacteric divisions of the ocean, the temperatures changing not solely with the distance to the equator, but also with the difference of meridians: these and similar phenomena, as they broke upon him, were discerned with wonderful quickness of perception, and made to contribute important principles to the stock of general knowledge. This lucidity of spirit, this quick convertibility of facts to principles, distinguish him from the dawn to the close of his sublime enterprise, insomuch that, with all the sallying ardour of his imagination, his ultimate success has been admirably charact-erized as a 'conquest of reflection'.*

It has been said that mercenary views mingled with the ambition of Columbus, and that his stipulations with the Spanish court were selfish and avaricious. The charge is inconsiderate and unjust. He aimed at dignity and wealth in the same lofty spirit in which he sought renown; they were to be part and parcel of his achieve-ment, and palpable evidence of its success; they were to arise from the territories he should discover, and be commensurate in im-portance. No condition could be more just. He asked nothing of the sovereigns but a command of the countries he hoped to give them, and a share of the profits to support the dignity of his command. If there should be no country discovered, his stipulated viceroyalty would be of no avail; and if no revenues should be produced, his labour and peril would produce no gain. If his command and revenues ultimately proved magnificent, it was from the magnificence of the regions he had attached to the Castilian crown. What monarch would not rejoice to gain empire on such conditions? But he did not risk merely a loss of labour, and a disappointment of ambition, in the enterprise; on his motives being questioned, he voluntarily undertook, and with the assist-ance of his coadjutors actually defrayed, one-eighth of the whole charge of the first expedition.

It was, in fact, this rare union already noticed, of the practical man of business with the poetical projector, which enabled him to carry his grand enterprises into effect through so many difficulties; but the pecuniary calculations and cares, which gave feasibility to

* D. Humboldt, *Examen Critique.*

his schemes, were never suffered to chill the glowing aspirations of his soul. The gains that promised to arise from his discoveries, he intended to appropriate in the same princely and pious spirit in which they were demanded. He contemplated works and achievements of benevolence and religion; vast contributions for the relief of the poor of his native city; the foundation of churches, where masses should be said for the souls of the departed; and armies for the recovery of the Holy Sepulchre in Palestine. Thus his ambition was truly noble and lofty, instinct with high thought and prone to generous deed.

In the discharge of his office he maintained the state and ceremonial of a viceroy, and was tenacious of his rank and privileges; not from a mere vulgar love of titles, but because he prized them as testimonials and trophies of his achievements: these he jealously cherished as his great rewards. In his repeated applications to the king, he insisted merely on the restitution of his dignities. As to his pecuniary dues and all questions relative to mere revenue, he offered to leave them to arbitration or even to the absolute disposition of the monarch; but not so his official dignities. 'These things,' said he nobly, 'affect my honour.' In his testament, he enjoined on his son Diego, and whoever after him should inherit his estates, whatever dignities and titles might afterwards be granted by the king, always to sign himself simply 'the Admiral', by way of perpetuating in the family its real source of greatness.

His conduct was characterized by the grandeur of his views and the magnanimity of his spirit. Instead of scouring the newly-found countries, like a grasping adventurer eager only for immediate gain, as was too generally the case with contemporary discoverers, he sought to ascertain their soil and productions, their rivers and harbours: he was desirous of colonizing and cultivating them; of conciliating and civilizing the natives; of building cities; introducing the useful arts; subjecting everything to the control of law, order, and religion; and thus of founding regular and prosperous empires. In this glorious plan he was constantly defeated by the dissolute rabble which it was his misfortune to command, with whom all law was tyranny, and all order restraint. They interrupted all useful works by their seditions, provoked the peaceful Indians to hostility, and after they had thus drawn down misery and warfare upon their own heads, and overwhelmed Columbus

with the ruins of the edifice he was building, they charged him
with being the cause of the confusion.

Well would it have been for Spain had those who followed in
the track of Columbus possessed his sound policy and liberal
views. The New World, in such cases, would have been settled
by pacific colonists, and civilized by enlightened legislators; instead
of being overrun by desperate adventurers, and desolated by avaricious conquerors.

Columbus was a man of quick sensibility, liable to great excitement, to sudden and strong impressions, and powerful impulses. He
was naturally irritable and impetuous, and keenly sensible to injury
and injustice; yet the quickness of his temper was counteracted by
the benevolence and generosity of his heart. The magnanimity of
his nature shone forth through all the troubles of his stormy career.
Though continually outraged in his dignity, and braved in the
exercise of his command; though foiled in his plans, and endangered
in his person by the seditions of turbulent and worthless men, and
that too at times when suffering under anxiety of mind and anguish
of body sufficient to exasperate the most patient, yet he restrained
his valiant and indignant spirit by the strong powers of his mind,
and brought himself to forbear, and reason, and even to supplicate:
nor should we fail to notice how free he was from all feeling of
revenge, how ready to forgive and forget, on the least signs of
repentance and atonement. He has been extolled for his skill in
controlling others; but far greater praise is due to him for his
firmness in governing himself.

His natural benignity made him accessible to all kinds of pleasurable sensations from external objects. In his letters and journals,
instead of detailing circumstances with the technical precision of a
mere navigator, he notices the beauties of nature with the enthusiasm of a poet or a painter. As he coasts the shores of the New
World, the reader participates in the enjoyment with which he
describes, in his imperfect but picturesque Spanish, the varied
objects around him; the blandness of the temperature, the purity of
the atmosphere, the fragrance of the air, 'full of dew and sweetness',
the verdure of the forests, the magnificence of the trees, the grandeur of the mountains, and the limpidity and freshness of the running
streams. New delight springs up for him in every scene. He extols
each new discovery as more beautiful than the last, and each as the

most beautiful in the world; until, with his simple earnestness, he tells the sovereigns, that having spoken so highly of the preceding islands, he fears that they will not credit him when he declares that the one he is actually describing surpasses them all in excellence.

In the same ardent and unstudied way he expresses his emotions on various occasions, readily affected by impulses of joy or grief, of pleasure or indignation. When surrounded and overwhelmed by the ingratitude and violence of worthless men, he often, in the retirement of his cabin, gave way to bursts of sorrow, and relieved his overladen heart by sighs and groans. When he returned in chains to Spain, and came into the presence of Isabella, instead of continuing the lofty pride with which he had hitherto sustained his injuries, he was touched with grief and tenderness at her sympathy, and burst forth into sobs and tears.

He was devoutly pious; religion mingled with the whole course of his thoughts and actions, and shone forth in his most private and unstudied writings. Whenever he made any great discovery, he celebrated it by solemn thanks to God. The voice of prayer and melody of praise rose from his ships when they first beheld the New World, and his first action on landing was to prostrate himself upon the earth and return thanksgivings. Every evening, the *Salve Regina* and other vesper hymns were chanted by his crew and masses were performed in the beautiful groves bordering the wild shores of this heathen land. All his great enterprises were undertaken in the name of the Holy Trinity, and he partook of the communion previous to embarkation. He was a firm believer in the efficacy of vows and penances and pilgrimages, and resorted to them in times of difficulty and danger. The religion thus deeply seated in his soul diffused a sober dignity and benign composure over his whole demeanour. His language was pure and guarded, and free from all imprecations, oaths, and other irreverent expressions.

It cannot be denied, however, that his piety was mingled with superstition, and darkened by the bigotry of the age. He evidently concurred in the opinion that all nations which did not acknowledge the Christian faith were destitute of natural rights; that the sternest measures might be used for their conversion, and the severest punishments inflicted upon their obstinacy in unbelief. In this spirit of bigotry he considered himself justified in making captives of the Indians, and transporting them to Spain to have

them taught the doctrines of Christianity, and in selling them for
slaves if they pretended to resist his invasions. In so doing he
sinned against the natural goodness of his character, and against the
feelings which he had originally entertained and expressed towards
this gentle hospitable people; but he was goaded on by the
mercenary impatience of the crown, and by the sneers of his
enemies at the unprofitable result of his enterprises. It is but justice
to his character to observe that the enslavement of the Indians thus
taken in battle was at first openly countenanced by the crown,
and that when the question of right came to be discussed at the
entreaty of the queen, several of the most distinguished jurists and
theologians advocated the practice; so that the question was finally
settled in favour of the Indians solely by the humanity of Isabella.
As the venerable bishop Las Casas observes, where the most
learned men have doubted, it is not surprising that an unlearned
mariner should err.

These remarks, in palliation of the conduct of Columbus, are
required by candour. It is proper to show him in connection with
the age in which he lived, lest the errors of the times should be
considered as his individual faults. It is not the intention of the
author, however, to justify Columbus on a point where it is
inexcusable to err. Let it remain a blot on his illustrious name, and
let others derive a lesson from it.

We have already hinted at a peculiar trait in his rich and varied
character; that ardent and enthusiastic imagination which threw a
magnificence over his whole course of thought. Herrera intimates
that he had a talent for poetry, and some slight traces of it are on
record in the book of prophecies which he presented to the
Catholic sovereigns. But his poetical temperament is discernible
throughout all his writings and in all his actions. It spread a golden
and glorious world around him, and tinged everything with its
own gorgeous colours. It betrayed him into visionary speculations which subjected him to the sneers and cavillings of men
of cooler and safer but more grovelling minds. Such were the
conjectures formed on the coast of Paria about the form of the
earth, and the situation of the terrestrial paradise; about the mines
of Ophir in Hispaniola, and the Aurea Chersonesus in Veragua;
and such was the heroic scheme of a crusade for the recovery of
the Holy Sepulchre. It mingled with his religion, and filled his

mind with solemn and visionary meditations on mystic passages of the Scriptures, and the shadowy portents of the prophecies. It exalted his office in his eyes, and made him conceive himself an agent sent forth upon a sublime and awful mission, subject to impulses and supernatural intimations from the Deity; such as the voice which he imagined spoke to him in comfort amidst the troubles of Hispaniola, and in the silence of the night on the disastrous coast of Veragua.

He was decidedly a visionary, but a visionary of an uncommon and successful kind. The manner in which his ardent, imaginative, and mercurial nature was controlled by a powerful judgment, and directed by an acute sagacity, is the most extraordinary feature in his character. Thus governed, his imagination, instead of exhausting itself in idle flights, lent aid to his judgment, and enabled him to form conclusions at which common minds could never have arrived, nay, which they could not perceive when pointed out.

To his intellectual vision it was given to read the signs of the times, and to trace, in the conjectures and reveries of past ages, the indications of an unknown world; as soothsayers were said to read predictions in the stars, and to foretell events from the visions of the night. 'His soul,' observes a Spanish writer, 'was superior to the age in which he lived. For him was reserved the great enterprise of traversing that sea which had given rise to so many fables, and of deciphering the mystery of his time.'[*]

With all the visionary fervour of his imagination, its fondest dreams fell short of the reality. He died in ignorance of the real grandeur of his discovery. Until his last breath he entertained the idea that he had merely opened a new way to the old resorts of opulent commerce, and had discovered some of the wild regions of the East. He supposed Hispaniola to be the ancient Ophir which had been visited by the ships of Solomon, and that Cuba and Terra Firma were but remote parts of Asia. What visions of glory would have broken upon his mind could he have known that he had indeed discovered a new continent, equal to the whole of the old world in magnitude, and separated by two vast oceans from all the earth hitherto known by civilized man! And how would his magnanimous spirit have been consoled, amidst the afflictions of age and the cares of penury, the neglect of a fickle

[*] Cladera, *Investigaciones Historias*, p. 43.

public and the injustice of an ungrateful king, could he have anticipated the splendid empires which were to spread over the beautiful world he had discovered; and the nations, and tongues, and languages which were to fill its lands with his renown, and revere and bless his name to the latest posterity!